# *Mandelson*

## and the Making of New Labour

### DONALD MACINTYRE

D1198251

HarperCollins*Publishers*

HarperCollins*Publishers*
77–85 Fulham Palace Road,
Hammersmith, London W6 8JB

www.fireandwater.com
This paperback edition 2000

1 3 5 7 9 8 6 4 2

First published in Great Britain by
HarperCollins*Publishers* 1999

ISBN 0 00 653062 1

Set in Sabon by
Rowland Phototypesetting Ltd,
Bury St Edmunds, Suffolk

Printed and bound in Great Britain by
Omnia Books Ltd, Glasgow

TO JAMES

# Contents

# List of Illustrations

Party conferences, 1987–90:

12 With Neil Kinnock. (Denis Doran/Network)

13 With Tony Blair. (The *Independent*/John Voos)

14 With Julie Hall and Philip Gould. (The *Independent*/John Voos)

15 Writing the *People* column with Alastair Campbell.

16 At Hutton Avenue, Hartlepool. (Frank Reid)

17 At a *Mirror* party with Neil and Glenys Kinnock and Julie Hall.

18 With MP, Huw Edwards, Monmouth by-election, 17 May 1991. (Kayte Brimacombe/Network)

19 At the dedication of a bench to the memory of Tony Mandelson, Hampstead Garden Suburb, 1991. (Nigel Sutton)

20 Constituency summer barbecue and dance, Hartlepool.

21 Campaigning in Hartlepool, general election 1992. (North News & Pictures)

22 With Ben and Rosie Nye Davies.

23 At Leo Gillen's house, Hartlepool.

24 Arthur Scargill speaks, Peter Mandelson listens. Bernard Carr chairs Clause Four meeting, 1995. (North News & Pictures)

25 Peter Mandelson speaks, Princess Diana listens. English National Ballet reception on the day of the royal divorce, summer 1996.

26 Gordon Brown and Peter Mandelson before the launch of the Youth Employment Initiative, ICE, 18 September 1996. (Peter Marlow/Magnum)

27 Gordon Brown, Peter Mandelson and Ed Balls at a press conference pre-briefing by Tony Blair, ICE, 18 September 1996. (Peter Marlow/Magnum)

28 At Millbank Tower, September 1996. (The *Guardian*/Sean Smith)

29 At Hutton Avenue, Hartlepool. (North News & Pictures)

# Acknowledgements

First, a disclaimer. This is not an authorised biography, nor was it ever intended to be one. I have known Peter Mandelson since the mid-1980s. When I approached him towards the end of 1997 to tell him that I intended to write this book, he replied that he did not relish the prospect of a biography but that he would agree to be interviewed in the interests of accuracy. In fact he was more generous with his time, and in allowing me access to many of his papers, than I expected. He was very candid and informative on many, if not all, aspects of his life. He did not discourage me from interviewing his family and he has not exercised any control over the book itself. His former assistant, Benjamin Wegg-Prosser, was unfailingly considerate, and usually very helpful, in responding to a wide range of what must have frequently been tiresome queries.

I have spoken to or interviewed over eighty colleagues, constituents and others. Interviews are normally attributed in footnotes, though some sources preferred to remain anonymous. A small number of people whom I would have have liked to interview, declined to speak. I am extremely grateful to Professor Dennis Kavanagh and Dr David Butler for allowing me to see some of the important material amassed for their indispensable Nuffield General Election Studies. Professor Kavanagh was also kind enough to read an earlier version of the manuscript and make a series of insightful comments; but it is more than the usual truism to say that the mistakes and misjudgements are all mine. I would also like to thank Hugo Young for generously allowing me to see some of his notes.

I am very grateful to Simon Kelner, the Editor of the *Independent* who kindly allowed me time off to complete this book, and to three other *Independent* colleagues, John Rentoul and Andrew Grice, who shared some of their insights on different aspects of the Mandelson story, and to Sean O'Grady who also read the manuscript, did some research and made numerous helpful suggestions. It may be invidious to single out published sources, but three are indispensable for any study of Peter Mandelson: the careful chapter in Andy McSmith's *Faces of Labour*, Philip Gould's *The Unfinished Revolution*, and John Rentoul's biography of Tony Blair. Although some of my conclusions about what happened after John Smith's death vary from his, Rentoul's remains the best account of the period of Labour Party history covered by much of this book. For the section on Peter Mandelson's period in Northern Ireland as Secretary of State, I am particularly grateful for the help and forbearance of Sir Ivor Roberts, the British ambassador in Dublin, Tom Kelly, Director of Information at the Northern Ireland Office, and the *Independent*'s Ireland correspondent David McKittrick, who has patiently shared his unrivalled insight and knowledge with me many times during the past decade. Again, none of them are responsible for errors, omissions and misjudgements in this account.

Miles and Mary Mandelson were very generous with time, photographs, and in Mrs Mandelson's case cuttings. For further invaluable help with research, I owe a particularly large debt to Victoria Manisty. I would also like to thank Bernadine Green, Tom Happold, for research into Peter Mandelson's early life, Steve Howell, for all his help in Hartlepool, Steve Wallace; at HarperCollins, Michael Fishwick and for superb copy-editing under difficult circumstances, Sophie Nelson and Kate Johnson; for picture research, Caroline Hotblack; for her wise advice and support, my agent Felicity Rubinstein. To Sarah Spankie, my love and gratitude.

# Chronology

**1953**

21 October      Peter Benjamin Mandelson born in Hampstead Garden Suburb, the second son of George (Tony) Mandelson and Mary Mandelson, daughter of Herbert Morrison.

**1965–72**      Attends Hendon County Grammar School.

**1972–73**      Spends year off between school and university in Tanzania teaching and working in a hospital.

**1973–76**      Reads Philosophy, Politics and Economics at St Catherine's College, Oxford.

**1977**      Joins British Youth Council (BYC).

7 March      Begins work at the Trades Union Congress in the Economics Department (leaves in September 1978).

March      Publication of *Youth Unemployment: Causes and Cures*. Mandelson had been part of the BYC working party that had written it and visits Downing Street to discuss its contents with Callaghan.

May      Becomes chairman of BYC (until 1980).

**1978**      Member of delegation to World Youth Festival in Havana.

**1979**

6 December      Elected as member of Lambeth Council (until 1982).

**1980**
September        Writes and publishes *Broadcasting and Youth*. Starts work for Albert Booth, Labour's transport spokesman.

**1981**
March              SDP formed.
September        Denis Healey defeats Tony Benn for deputy leadership of Labour Party.

**1982**            Mandelson joins London Weekend Television, first as a researcher on *The London Programme*, and then as producer of *Weekend World*.

**1983**            Labour suffers defeat at general election. Neil Kinnock replaces Michael Foot as leader.

**1984**            Mandelson buys cottage near Ross-on-Wye, Herefordshire.

**1985**
July                 Mandelson acts as minder to Labour candidate at Brecon and Radnor by-election.
24 September    Becomes Director of Campaigns and Communications for the Labour Party.
1 October         Kinnock gives speech at Labour Party Conference attacking Militant.

**1986**
4 April             Fulham by-election. Labour's Nick Raynsford defeats the SDP's Roger Liddle.

**1987**
26 February      Greenwich by-election. The SDP's Rosie Barnes wins.
11 June           Labour defeated at general election.

**1988**
2 March           The Liberals and SDP vote for merger.

| | |
|---|---|
| 2 October | Hattersley defeats Prescott for Labour deputy leadership. |

**1989**
| | |
|---|---|
| 17 December | Mandelson selected as candidate for Hartlepool. |

**1990**
| | |
|---|---|
| | Works for management consultants, SRU (until 1992), Prima, and City and Corporate Council. |
| 1 April | Introduction of poll tax into England. |
| August | Mandelson moves into Doughty Mews with Colin Byrne and Julie Hall. |
| Autumn | Mandelson buys house in Hutton Avenue, Hartlepool and sells cottage in Ross-on-Wye. |
| 8 October | UK joins ERM. Mandelson stands down as Director of Campaigns and Communications and is replaced by John Underwood. |

**1991**
| | |
|---|---|
| 16 May | Mandelson runs Monmouth by-election, Labour wins. |
| 10 December | Maastricht summit. Britain allowed to opt out of EMU and the Social Chapter. |

**1992**
| | |
|---|---|
| 9 April | Labour suffers fourth consecutive general election defeat leading to Kinnock standing down as leader of the Party. Mandelson wins Hartlepool. |
| 18 July | John Smith elected leader of the Labour Party. |

**1993**
| | |
|---|---|
| 6 May | Mandelson acts as minder at Newbury by-election. |

**1994**
| | |
|---|---|
| 12 May | John Smith dies. |
| 21 July | Tony Blair is elected leader of the Labour Party. |
| 26 October | Mandelson becomes Opposition Whip (until 1995). |

## 1995

| | |
|---|---|
| 29 April | Labour members endorse new Clause Four. |
| 27 July | Littleborough and Saddleworth by-election. |
| 20 October | Mandelson becomes Opposition spokesman on Civil Service. |

## 1996

| | |
|---|---|
| January | Outcry over Harriet Harman's choice of school for her son. |
| February | Publication of *The Blair Revolution*, co-written by Mandelson and Roger Liddle. |
| 26 February | Mandelson becomes chairman of Labour's General Election Planning Committee. |
| 11 May | Reports emerge of a rift with Gordon Brown. |

## 1997

| | |
|---|---|
| 20 January | Gordon Brown announces that there will be no income tax increases in a first Labour parliament. |
| 1 May | General election, Labour landslide. Mandelson appointed as Minister without Portfolio at the Cabinet Office; responsibilities include the Millennium Dome. |
| 29 September | Mandelson fails to be elected on to the NEC; Ken Livingstone wins seat. |

## 1998

| | |
|---|---|
| 5 July | Drapergate. |
| 27 July | Mandelson promoted to Secretary of State for Trade and Industry. |
| 7 September | Announcement that BSkyB to make bid for Manchester United. |
| 23 December | Mandelson resigns over secret home loan from Geoffrey Robinson, who had become Paymaster General. Revelation of loan also leads to resignation of Robinson and Charlie Whelan, adviser to Gordon Brown. |

**1999**

| | |
|---|---|
| 11 May | Elizabeth Filkin of the Parliamentary Commission for Standards upholds complaints over Mandelson's Geoffrey Robinson home loan. |
| 8 June | Blair-Schröder paper on economic reform published. |
| 30 June | Select Committee on Standards and Privileges acquits Mandelson of 'dishonest intention' over his home loan and recommends no further action. |
| 11 October | Mandelson reappointed to Cabinet as Secretary of State for Northern Ireland. |
| 29 November | New Northern Ireland power-sharing Executive formed. |

**2000**

| | |
|---|---|
| 11 February | Mandelson suspends Northern Ireland Executive. |
| 6 May | IRA says it will 'initiate process that will completely and verifiably put arms beyond use'. |
| 27 May | Ulster Unionists agree to rejoin Executive. Mandelson signs order restoring devolved institutions. |

# *Prologue*

Clad in the sparkling grey granite from the Wicklow Hills which overlook it, Glencairn has long been one of the more unusual official residences which the Foreign Office keeps for British ambassadors abroad. Set in thirty-six acres of formal gardens and pasture outside Dublin, it was once described by one of its residents as a 'a mediaeval castle built by an American gangster in 1905'. The description is only slightly inaccurate: having been built in the nineteenth century, it was then transformed by its most famous owner, 'Boss' Richard Croker, the colourful racehorse breeder and political fixer from Clonakilty who became the chief of New York's Tammany Hall and bought the house on his return to Ireland in 1904.

Since the government has now sold Glencairn – for an estimated £25 million – to save some money and replace it with something a little more modest, it is unlikely it will ever again see a dinner quite as rich in historical resonance as the one which took place there in honour of Peter Mandelson, the new Secretary of State for Northern Ireland, on the evening of Wednesday, 1 December 1999. Hosted by the British ambassador Ivor Roberts, and his wife Elizabeth, on the very night that power passed from London to the new cross-community Executive and Parliament in Belfast, it seemed to mark the beginning of the end of the seemingly irreconcilable conflict over Northern Ireland, which had lasted since partition in 1921. Mandelson had come South to sign, the following morning with the Irish Foreign Minister David Andrews, documents which would set in train a new era for British-Irish relations.

Several of the guests who gathered by candlelight beneath the extravagantly carved mahogany ceiling in Croker's Edwardian dining-room, would later confess to being awed by the historic timing of the occasion. It was also the night of the Irish budget so most senior members of the Dublin government had been detained in the Dail. But those present included Garrett Fitzgerald, architect and signatory with Margaret Thatcher of the 1985 Anglo-Irish agreement; two members of the coalition government, the Irish Attorney General Michael McDowell and his Progressive Democrat colleague Liz O'Donnell, Minister of State at the Department of Foreign Affairs; Martin Mansergh, the Oxford-educated adviser on Northern Ireland affairs to three successive Fianna Fail taoiseachs; the US ambassador Michael Sullivan; two of Ireland's leading businessmen, Gavin O'Reilly, managing director of Independent Newspapers and Lochlann Quinn, the chairman of the Allied Irish Bank; and a clutch of leading Dublin academics and journalists, together with three Northern Ireland Office officials down from Belfast.

As the guests dined on scallop salad with Parma ham, roast pheasant with apples and Calvados, and vanilla cream terrine – along with a 1997 Chablis and a 1996 Jaffelin Monthelie – the conversation was suitably serious. Mandelson paid warm tribute to Fitzgerald for his historic role in beginning to change attitudes in the Republic towards Northern Ireland, and to Mansergh for his work in coaxing Sinn Fein towards the agreement finally reached in Belfast a fortnight earlier. Mansergh in turn thanked Mandelson, saying that at crucial moments his role had been indispensable, adding 'We couldn't have done it without you.'

Despite the momentousness of the occasion there were, however, some darker portents, among this exceptionally well-informed gathering, of crises ahead. There was a courteous, but quite sharp, disagreement between the commentator Eoghan Harris, who argued that a very tough line would be needed in ensuring that the Provisional IRA delivered on decommissioning of arms, and the Anglo-Irish expert Ronan Fanning, Professor of History at University College Dublin, who argued that the great distance already travelled by the republicans should not be underestimated. More sharply still, there was a stark contrast between the euphoric attitude of the Irish ministers who were present and that of the journalists. One of the guests recalled that 'Geraldine Kennedy and Dick Walsh [both of the *Irish Times*] were worried about the lack of movement by the IRA in the light of David Trimble's looming threat of resignation [if the IRA had not begun decommissioning its arms by the beginning of February] ... The PD people were dismissive. "Leave it to de Chastelain," Liz O' Donnell had said with an airy wave of the hand.' If Ms O'Donnell was being somewhat cavalier in assuming that the Canadian general entrusted with overseeing disarmament would somehow find a soothing form of words which would eliminate the problem, Michael McDowell was, apparently, 'even more macho'. 'He said that "we were all being too nice to Trimble. He had no choice. Let him call the bluff of the backwoodsmen."'[1] But it would be the Irish journalists' more sober assessment, in little more than two months time, which would prove to be a good deal more accurate than that of the Dublin ministers.

There was some discussion, finally, of Mandelson's own future and whether his job would be diminished by the devolution of many of his responsibilities to the new Assembly. Mandelson reminded his fellow guests that he would still be responsible for matters of security, policing and justice, and that he would certainly want to carry the political process through the many no-doubt difficult months ahead. Then glancing at his watch at around 11.45 he stood up and made to leave, saying good-humouredly, but with a touch of theatre, 'As someone who will see many of his powers reduced at midnight, I think I should be alone.'[2]

It had all been so different almost exactly a year earlier, when Mandelson had been the chief guest at another party, less formal but also to celebrate a milestone in his career as a cabinet minister. On that occasion it had been a far less imposing, windowless basement room under the Department of Trade and Industry which had hummed with euphoric chatter as civil servants gathered to celebrate the Competitiveness White Paper, unveiled in the Commons two hours earlier, and the crowning achievement of Mandelson's six months at the Department.

The euphoria had not lasted long. Mandelson had already left when his young adviser Benjamin Wegg-Prosser, came to the door, looked urgently round the room and beckoned the principal private secretary Anthony Phillipson, glass of white wine in hand, to step outside for a private chat. When Phillipson, unnoticed amid the pleasant hubbub, walked out into the corridor, the twenty-four-year-old Wegg-Prosser, his voice slightly trembling, told him the secret which he himself had harboured since late 1996, but of which none of the officials gathered at the celebration had any inkling. Perhaps because he was feeling so nervous, perhaps because of the significance of the revelation, Wegg-Prosser slipped into the official-ese with which the tall, bespectacled Phillipson would feel most comfortable: 'Before the election, the Paymaster-General lent the Secretary of State a large amount of money to buy his house,' he said. 'And it's going to come out.'

Only a few moments earlier, Wegg-Prosser had broken the news to Mandelson that a forthcoming book, by a writer who had boasted almost a year earlier that he was going to 'kill' Mandelson, would shortly be revealing the existence of the loan. In the event, the same disclosure would be making newspaper headlines within less than a week. But for the moment that was academic. The question was what to do next.

If Mandelson had been terrified by the prospect, he had not shown it. He reflected briefly and told Wegg-Prosser to inform Phillipson, before going on to do a *Channel Four News* interview on his White Paper. The following morning, however, in his large, modernist seventh-floor office, its huge picture window looking down over Westminster Abbey, he convened a meeting with Sir Michael Scholar and other officials. He took this remarkable meeting in what one of those present would later observe was a very 'Peterish' way. He asked Sir Michael to refresh his memory on his role, or lack of it, in the DTI investigation into complaints over the Paymaster-General Geoffrey Robinson's business and financial affairs, including the letters he had written to Conservative MPs on the subject. It would shortly become a matter of public knowledge that, back in September, when Scholar had told Mandelson about the investigation into Robinson, a treasury minister, he had accepted the permanent secretary's recommendation that he and other DTI ministers should not be 'involved in the process'. When Scholar had finished his résumé, Mandelson said quietly: 'Well, even if I had not had a loan to buy my house from Geoffrey, I would have still stood aside from the investigation.' There was a long, ominous pause. 'I didn't know you had a loan to buy your house,' Scholar replied, just as quietly. 'We'll have to look into it.' It was a conversation which should have taken place almost exactly six months earlier, when Mandelson, thrilled to be in the Cabinet at last, and with a department of his own, first arrived to replace Margaret Beckett at the DTI on the day of the reshuffle. Now, although he did not yet realise it, it was too late.

How had it happened? How was it that a politician so famous for being Tony Blair's human radar, so skilled at spotting the treacherous shallows and reefs that lie in wait for any government, could fail to see the jagged rock on which his own boat would founder? Why was the great 'Minister for Looking Ahead' (as he described himself shortly after the 1997 election), so blind to the disaster waiting to happen in his own life? Even on that hot afternoon in 1996 when he first went house-hunting, driving round the streets of Notting Hill with the charming, attentive Geoffrey Robinson in the back of his chauffeur-driven red Daimler/Jaguar – let alone when he borrowed £373,000 to finance his new home – he had exposed himself, as he must, at some subconscious level, have realised, to danger. One of the Labour Party's most uncompromising chieftains puts himself under an enormous obligation, however generously and innocently conferred, to one of his greatest adversaries' closest allies. Then he fails either to consult or inform his own best friend in politics, apparently for no better reason than that his benefactor has exhorted him not to. When he arrives in government, a bloodied veteran of campaigns against Tory violations of ministerial standards, he does not tell the Cabinet Secretary of his plainly embarrassing financial obligations. When, in November 1997, while a minister, Robinson is revealed to be the beneficiary of an offshore trust, he does nothing. In February 1998, when it appears that Robinson's affairs were entangled with those of that notable crook Robert Maxwell, he remains silent even though it is likely that the statements of Geoffrey Robinson's bank account, on which his loan to Mandelson was drawn, will be subpoenaed. Finally, when he arrives at the DTI in July to find that he is presiding over a department charged with investigating complaints against Robinson, he still neglects to tell his permanent secretary, the Prime Minister, or even one of his several close and doggedly loyal friends outside politics. The arch adviser, in other words, turns to no one for advice. At any point he could probably have prevented the coming catastrophe. If a colleague had been in the same position he would have convened crisis meetings, organised swat teams, devised a media strategy, enlisted accountants, told him to sell his house – virtually anything to defuse the ticking explosive under the seat of government. Instead, even when every three months or so Wegg-Prosser mentioned the loan, usually when they were sitting in the very house it had funded, he merely shuddered briefly and changed the subject. This had been a very secret secret.

It would never be easy to explain the behaviour of a man who his own brother had acknowledged to be a 'bit of an enigma'. But the first and main responsibility for his downfall was his own. He chose to spend more – much, much more – on a house that he could afford. It was true that, as culpable misjudgements go, Mandelson's was victimless. There was no evidence that a single executive act carried out by a popular government was influenced one way or another by this transaction. No doubt, too, as the columnist Hugo Young acutely observed the day after he had resigned, 'there was an honourable streak in all this secrecy'.[3] If Blair had known about the loan, Robinson reasoned, he might have felt under an obligation that was even greater than the one he had incurred by holidaying that same summer, and later after he became Prime Minister, in Robinson's house in Tuscany. It was true, too, that Mandelson was not helped in his own party by the enemies he had made in his single-minded ten-year pursuit, with Tony Blair and Gordon Brown, of the relentless project to return Labour to office.

There was also a historical context which had been left to that wise elder statesman and historian, Lord Jenkins, to expound. In an article in the London *Evening Standard*, Jenkins said that Mandelson should 'clearly' have declared the loan when he went to the DTI. But in relation to loan itself he went on to point out that 'the three most admired Prime Ministers of the past 150 years', Disraeli, Gladstone, and Churchill, had all incurred obligations, or made acquisitions arguably much more compromising than Mandelson's. Lord Camrose had raised (at today's values) around £2 million, mainly from himself, and a series of City businessmen, so that Churchill could keep Chartwell Manor, which had long been at the 'edge of his means'. Nor had the Labour Party's most revered figures been immune to such obligations. Had not 'even the sea-green incorruptible Michael Foot' accepted a cottage from Lord Beaverbrook on his Cherkley estate? 'Without doubt', Jenkins mused, 'the present climate would have made it impossible for Disraeli, Gladstone and Churchill and many others of note and talent to have functioned on politics? Do we want an age of party apparatchiks, pygmies and eunuchs?'[4]

In bringing Mandelson back ten months after the loan debacle, Blair had shown that he did not. For whatever else can be said about Mandelson, in some ways the most vivid figure of the Blair government until his fall, he is not a eunuch. He is not, for a start, a timid politician. The Robinson loan was a personal risk; but he had also taken political risks throughout his career. Whether he was leading a revolt against an authoritarian headmaster in the 1960s, leaving his first job at the TUC without another one to go to in the 1970s, backing Roy Hattersley's leadership campaign to the limit and then later pushing the boundaries of his own remit from Neil Kinnock in the 1980s, or grasping the opportunity to run the deeply controversial Millennium Dome and standing for election to the Labour Party National Executive in the 1990s, Mandelson has not lacked courage.

One reason why his failure to declare the Robinson loan was surprising is that Mandelson has also rarely shrunk from difficult face-to-face confrontations. He has many flaws, and has been criticised for many things, but not, in the main, for the vice of tailoring his message to please different audiences – a quality which would stand him in good stead in Northern Ireland. For a man with an easy reputation of being a devious Machiavel, he is, at least in his own party, the least consensual of politicians, with a marked distaste for making the compromise too far.

All this is of a piece with an even more striking aspect of his career – his consistency as a believer in Labour as a party of government. His formation in the 1960s coincided with Harold Wilson's assumption of power after thirteen years of Tory government. His coming of age as a young activist in the British Youth Council brought him into direct contact with the Callaghan regime. And his work for the party throughout the 1980s and the 1990s was devoted without distraction to the task of making it electable once again.

This had all made his fall in December 1998 much more difficult for him to bear. But then, in opposition Labour had set high, perhaps even impossibly high, standards for government. Several of those around Mandelson believed that he had simply been consumed by the media monster, a press whose appetite for scandal had become insatiable. But if that there was true, then in opposition Peter Mandelson and his party had helped to create that monster. There was a justice, however rough, in his departure. It was all too easy to imagine how effectively it would have used the press to campaign against a Conservative Secretary of State caught in the identical position. That, as much as anything, was why the Prime Minister and Mandelson, his most single-mindedly loyal ministerial ally, were right to agree that it was in the interests not only of the government but of Mandelson's own career for him to resign. And so, Mandelson might reflect twelve long months later, it had been.

The morning after the dinner party at Glencairn, Mandelson and David Andrews signed, at the Irish Department of Foreign Affairs at Iveagh House, Dublin, the formal letters which opened a new and epochal chapter in the bloodstained history of Northern Ireland. The signing enacted the momentous changes made by both governments, the amendments of Articles 2 and 3 of the Irish Constitution, which asserted Eire's rights over Northern Ireland, and to the British legislation – including the 1949 Act forced through the Commons with the help of Mandelson's own grandfather Herbert Morrison – which asserted the permanence of British rule over it. Instead, the agreement sealed at Iveagh House enshrined the principle that Northern Ireland's constitutional status would in future be a matter to be decided solely by a majority of its own citizens. Back in the Belfast to which Mandelson would return later that day, the new devolved Assembly – its members including former paramilitaries from both sides of the sectarian divide – was enjoying its first few hours of real power. 'The word is too often used,' Mandelson said in a short speech, 'and I have thought hard before using it now. But this is an historic day.' For almost a decade, many politicians in Ireland and in Britain, including three taoiseachs and two prime ministers, had worked for this moment. There were also, as

Mandelson knew, grave difficulties ahead. There was no guarantee that the IRA would fulfil the hopes that they would start decommissioning arms or that the new dispensation would last beyond February.

But for Mandelson personally, there could hardly be a more spectacular way of marking an extraordinary year. A year which had seen him fall, disgraced, from office; be consigned to exile as a backbencher, and then return as Northern Ireland Secretary at one of the most crucial moments in the province's history. The irony of his fall had been all the greater because he had finally been given the chance to fulfil himself as a politician. It was not simply that, having sat, awestruck, at the cabinet table on a visit to Downing Street at the age of eleven, he had at last been able to sit at it as of right. It was also that having served for thirteen years as the loyal staff officer, Jeeves, *consigliere*, messenger and outrider, first to Neil Kinnock, then to Gordon Brown and Tony Blair, and finally to Blair as leader, he had come out of the shadows, ready to be tested at last as a minister on his own account – only to be dispatched back into those same shadows six months later. Now, thanks to Blair, he had been given his second chance. He was restored, as a cabinet minister, to a role to which he had been ordained not only by his own ambition, but also by heritage, upbringing and birth.

# CHAPTER ONE

## Osmold Smish, the Italian Mind-Your-Own-Businessman

Tony Blair chose the Labour Party; Peter Mandelson was born into it. In the 1950s a particular corner of north-west London came to symbolise the metropolitan Labour establishment, rather as Islington does today. Of the four Labour leaders after Attlee, three – Hugh Gaitskell, Harold Wilson and Michael Foot – all lived within walking distance of Hampstead Heath, in houses that just spanned a single page of a London *A–Z*. But while Gaitskell lived and Foot lives on the fashionable southern fringes of the Heath, Wilson lived on the north side in Hampstead Garden Suburb, a spacious, tree-lined estate which is a classic example of progressive Edwardian town planning. Sir Edwin Lutyens designed some of the early houses, with their silver-grey bricks and white woodwork, along with the Free Church and the Anglican St Jude's. But the real creator of the Garden Suburb was Henrietta Barnett, a canon's wife who was convinced by her husband's thirty years of ministry in the East End slums that the ideal urban neighbourhood was socially mixed, like a village or a small market town – but without pubs, which she abominated. Forming a trust to acquire eighty acres of Hampstead Heath, she laid down clear principles for the construction and operation of the estate: there would be no more than eight houses per acre; gardens would be divided by hedges and trellises rather than walls; the roads would be forty feet wide. Her vision of a socially and economically mixed community, thanks to the growth of owner-occupation and the post-war explosion of house prices, no longer holds good. Hampstead Garden Suburb is overwhelmingly

1

inhabited by the prosperous middle class. But there is still no pub. And physically it is much what the plain-living and high-thinking Henrietta Barnett had always intended it to be: clean, green and safe.

Tony and Mary Mandelson were living in Eastholm, at the North Circular Road end of the Suburb, when their second son Peter was born on 21 October 1953. Mary had wanted to live in the Suburb since she had stayed there with family friends during the war. She almost certainly inherited her liking for it from her mother, who had been brought up in Letchworth, one of the first garden cities, and had been deeply upset by her move to London after her marriage. Several Labour politicians lived in the area, including Patrick Gordon Walker who had been Foreign Secretary under Wilson, and Manny Shinwell, who had sat in the Attlee Cabinet. While Tony and Mary Mandelson were both Labour Party members, neither was a politician – Mary in particular would have recoiled in horror at the idea. But, whether she liked it or not, as Herbert Morrison's only child she could hardly ignore her close connection to the Labour hierarchy. That year had been clouded with sadness for her: exactly four months before Peter's birth her own mother, Margaret, had died. Her father had received condolences from the Queen, and the funeral was attended in force by the Labour great and good: the Attlees and Gaitskells, along with Krishna Menon, were among the hundreds of mourners at Honor Oak crematorium.

Morrison showed little, if any, interest in the birth of his second grandson. He was in the middle of a turbulent, headline-making period. Just over a fortnight earlier he had finally decided not to risk defeat at the hands of the left by challenging the ageing Arthur Greenwood for treasurership of the party at the Margate conference. Ten days later he would comfortably beat Aneurin Bevan in the annual vote for the deputy leadership of the parliamentary party. But mixed fortunes or not, he remained a real force in parliament: according to his biographers, he was 'the real leader of the Opposition to the Tories, while Attlee was ineffective'.[1]

Mary Mandelson's attitude to all this, if not hostile, was at least deeply ambivalent. Her own childhood had given her a strong aversion to the world which had robbed her of her father. Mary, born in 1921, while Morrison was Mayor of Hackney, matured into an

2

intelligent and perceptive woman who was charming, extremely pretty, unaffected, a devoted wife and mother and, as they grew up, infinitely hospitable to her children's friends. And though quiet and much more relaxed at home than outside it, she possessed a sharp sense of humour and strong views, including political views, of her own. But her parents' marriage had not been happy: Morrison's biographers suggest that he 'probably never had sexual relations with his wife from the early 20s' and would frequently leave their house at Eltham early, returning at midnight, too tired or too uninterested to talk to her. In his autobiography he never mentions her, though they were married for thirty-four years.

Beatrice Webb, who met the Morrisons including the eleven-year-old Mary in 1932, wrote in her diary that Morrison's 'little wife is unaffected and dutiful and busies herself with household affairs and her child's education – she stammers badly and is insignificant in looks. They live in a small suburban house without a servant and are wholly untouched by London Society or any kind of servile snobbishness.'[2] This observation says much less about Margaret Morrison, who like her daughter was strikingly attractive but shy, than about Webb's own consuming 'snobbishness' – though not, of course, of the servile kind. Margaret designed and made her own clothes, and loved dancing, ballet and the theatre, though she was seldom able to go in later years. While Morrison was obsessed by politics, she did not enjoy being a political wife. When it was suggested to her in the thirties that Herbert might become Prime Minister, Margaret replied grimly: 'I hope I never live to see the day.'[3]

Mary Morrison inherited much of her mother's revulsion for national politics. At the age of eight she rebuked her father when, in an early example of the now common habit of dragging families into political campaigns, he called on the electors of Hackney to vote for him 'as an eighth birthday present for Mary'. She did not want her name brought into his 'beastly politics', she told him.[4] Being teased or singled out at school because of her famous father made her more shy and withdrawn than she might otherwise have been. If Morrison had been a more attentive parent, she might not have minded so much. But although he was not, so far as one can tell, a cold man, he had warmer relationships with the families (including the children) of his friends than he did with his own. By contrast, thanks to her marriage to Tony as well as to her own maternal instincts, Mary ensured for her own sons the secure and happy home life which she had been denied. Both she and Tony had been only children; both had been briefly and much less happily married before – Mary in 1941 to the accountant son of her father's colleague Tom Williams, then a junior Agriculture minister.

While Mary stuffed envelopes at election time she did not attend party meetings. Tony, on the other hand, was more active, veered towards the left, and was much more enthusiastic about their neighbour Harold Wilson, who succeeded Gaitskell as Labour leader when Peter was nine. He would frequently visit Labour Party conferences on an observer's ticket to mingle with party cronies and those in the wider Wilson circle.

Mandelson has described his mother as 'more intellectually influential within the family', but his father – who preferred to be called Tony than by his real name, George – as more 'socially influential'. And certainly Tony Mandelson's gregariousness and showmanship were inherited by his younger – though not by his elder – son. Friends and colleagues invariably recollect him as a 'lovely man'. Photographs reveal him as exceptionally handsome. Like his son, at least in later life, he took great care of the way he dressed (except at weekends, when he preferred shabby old clothes), sometimes wearing a cravat, and often sporting a carnation in his buttonhole. The adolescent Peter, sometimes embarrassed by his expansive and jokey manner, could be quite sharp with him, but Peter's school friends appear to have universally warmed to him during pleasurable visits to the Mandelson home – one was strongly reminded of the actor Donald Sinden. There would invariably be a bottle of wine on the dinner table – part of the 'sophisticated' atmosphere which impressed the young visitors – and Tony saw nothing wrong with Peter and his friends sharing it. After Mandelson broke down in tears* describing his father's death in 1988, the *Jewish Chronicle*, where 'Mandy' (as he was universally known to his colleagues) had been the 'flamboyant' advertising director for thirty years, compiled a retrospective profile of him. Neither Mary nor Peter's elder brother

---

* In a 1997 BBC2 interview.

Miles liked the article, which dwelt at length on Tony's waggishness and sales technique. Alan Rubinstein, a long-standing colleague and subsequently Tony's successor as advertising director, told the paper: 'He was a formidable operator. But for years he played the eccentric – until finally he was no longer playing at it – he became that part totally.'[5]

No City annual meeting, reported the *JC*, 'was complete without the dapper figure of Mandy Mandelson, glass in hand, spraying "dear boy" around like confetti'. As president of the Press Advertising Managers' Association, instead of uttering the usual welcoming banalities at the Christmas lunch, he had the lights dimmed and then emerged in a single spotlight, dressed as Father Christmas and roaring: 'Shalom, everyone, Merry Christmas from the *Jewish Chronicle*.' He was a little larger than life, a popular raconteur – sometimes, it was said, capable of embellishing the truth to make a better story. Family folklore divided his anecdotes into 'A' stories and 'B' stories – ones which were true and told in deadly earnest, and ones which he expected to be taken with a pinch of salt.[6]

By his own account, Tony Mandelson had had a 'damned good war' as a major in the 1st Royal Dragoons and claimed to have been the first Allied soldier to enter Denmark in 1945. As a cavalry officer, he was proud to share the distinction with the Tory MP Sir Henry d'Avigdor-Goldsmid of being one of the relatively few Jewish members of the Cavalry Club. He was not devout, though he would make a point of visiting the Norrice Lea synagogue in the Suburb during Yom Kippur. He was a highly successful, and sometimes unorthodox, advertising salesman. Mary Mandelson was particularly dismayed to read in the *Jewish Chronicle* an account of how he had ambushed the celebrated advertising agency chairman Peter Marsh by jumping into his olive-green Rolls-Royce to solicit a Midland Bank advertisement. Dick Wrathall, who worked at the celebrated advertising company Masius Wynne Williams – the first to install a media planning computer in the 1970s – remembers Tony Mandelson as a 'much loved', 'delightful' and 'humorous' man built like a 'wiry gentleman jockey'. At a convivial annual launch given by the marketing department of W. D. & H. O. Wills in the seventies, Wrathall recalled him saying, 'I hate Masius', 'Why?' asked Wrathall, 'You feed all the facts about the *Jewish Chronicle* into your computer and then you come up with the *Hampstead and Highgate Express*'.[7] Miles Mandelson, visiting the *Jewish Chronicle* offices with his father as a child, found it a revelation to find him 'in authority over a department. The kind of relationship my parents had meant that my father never really was able to assert his authority at home. The moral authority came from my mother; she taught us manners. My father taught us how to break the rules.'

Both brothers are agreed that it was Mary Mandelson who wielded this 'moral authority' over them. Peter remembered her as 'quiet, elegant, gracious, softly spoken but with tremendous steel'. There was 'no shouting, no histrionics' but 'if you incurred my mother's disapproval you would be aware of it.' She was also a stickler for the post-war concept of U and non-U made famous by Nancy Mitford, preferring 'wireless' to 'radio' and making sure her sons said 'what' and not 'pardon', 'lavatory' and not 'toilet'.

One of the characteristics which Peter inherited from his father was what Miles called a 'great sense of humour, in the off the cuff remark, or observation about someone. He'd be cruelly accurate in talking about people, not always to their face.' Or he would ask a 'very cheeky question' and get away with it because of his charm: 'He didn't mind what he said.' When Tony was invited to leave the *Jewish Chronicle* for the *Observer*, the teenage Peter tried in vain to persuade him to take up the offer. But Mary strongly urged him to stay put rather than risk the notorious insecurity of Fleet Street. 'He was more ambitious for Tony than Tony was himself. I can't think why Peter wanted him to. He was absolutely secure where he was. I know it seemed boring, but it wasn't boring when he was around. Tony was tempted but I said, "Stay where you are. You can never get the sack at the *Jewish Chronicle*."' After his retirement Tony became passionate about local conservation, determinedly preventing *nouveau riche* arrivals in the Suburb from trying to alter the frontages of their homes; he became chairman of the local Residents' Association's Conservation Committee.

While Mandelson was born into the Labour Party he was also born into metropolitan middle-class comfort. As he would explain thirty years later to his friend, the actor Stephen Fry: 'All the things I had I want others to have. I had caring parents, a strong start, discipline instilled, a nice roof over my head. I didn't want for books or encouragement or somewhere to do my homework, friends, leisure time or travel. I want others to have this.'[8] It was a prosperous and lively household to grow up in. The family took holidays abroad; probably Mandelson's first foreign travel was to Majorca. Tony Mandelson chose his cars with discernment: the family owned successively a Sunbeam Talbot, a Sunbeam Rapier coupé, followed by an Alfa Romeo Giulia. He was unwilling to insure his sons to drive the family vehicle – a prohibition which Peter resented. On the other hand he was well off enough to buy Miles a Citroën 2CV and Peter a five-year-old yellow Morris 1100. This at least demonstrated that though he could be very careful (and, indeed, secretive) with money – disliking, for example, expenditure on house repairs – he could be, as Miles put it, 'generous enough ... He supported me at times when I needed financial support and he supported Peter, but it wasn't easily come by. You had to jump through hoops before you could get that support.'[9]

Herbert Morrison's fame as a Labour politician – and Mandelson's own fostering of the Morrison legend – has tended to overshadow the heritage on his father's side of the family. In most ways, however, the family benefited much more from Mandelson's paternal grandfather Norman than it did from Morrison. While Morrison made no secret of the fact that he disapproved of his daughter's divorce, Norman, an extrovert and loving father like his son, supported him – morally and financially – when he divorced his first wife and married Mary Williams. Norman Mandelson, as Jenni Frazer's full account in the *Jewish Chronicle* pointed out, had also worked on the paper. He had also dealt in stocks and shares. On the basis of the money he inherited from his father Tony Mandelson bought the house at Bigwood Road where Peter was brought up and invested the rest. Miles Mandelson recalled that when his father died 'he had hundreds of thousands of pounds in stocks and shares. And actually when you added together his shareholdings, his stock-holding and the value of the house and all the little bits and pieces that were in the bank, he had a small fortune and nobody ever knew it, and we'd never felt like that, he kept it very secret. He didn't talk about things like that at all.' Or not at home, at least. On the City annual meetings circuit he would occasionally boast of being Marks and Spencer's biggest private shareholder; but his colleagues may not have known whether this was an 'A' or a 'B' story.

Tony's younger son did not share his canniness about money: through some of his adult life he lived well above his means. But he has since said that in other ways he is 'so like my father I can feel it'. He was closer to his mother. By contrast Miles, much shyer and more introverted than Peter, was much more like his mother but correspondingly closer to his father. Having been the focus of attention for four and a half years, Miles was less than thrilled by the arrival of his new brother – though on at least one occasion he begged his mother to go upstairs to Peter when he was crying. As is so often the case with second children, Mary was more relaxed with the infant Peter than she had been with Miles; perhaps as a result Peter was 'cuddly' and physically demonstrative towards his mother in a way that Miles was not. Miles always considered Peter to be Mary Mandelson's

favourite son. Still is. I don't say this out of any feelings of jealousy. She's very even handed about these things, and I think she would hate to think she had a favourite. But they are more in tune with one another at an emotional level, as well as an intellectual level, that she and I aren't. And he may seem to have been cosseted, but he cosseted her as much as she cosseted him. I am sure she responded to that, whereas being perhaps a slightly colder fish I have never had the same relationship with my mother as Peter has . . .

According to his mother, Peter 'could lose his temper. He could be a bit emotional if something happened to upset him – friendship or something like that went wrong. He's a very loyal person, Peter. If I made a remark about one of his friends that might be a bit negative, there was a very fierce defence. He was very loyal to people until they let him down.'

While Miles was the quiet, practical male in the family, loading up the car and making sure it had oil and water before family holidays, Peter was much more frequently the centre of attention. Even as a child, according to Miles, his brother was a 'great stylist'.

He was also 'the opposite of a shrinking violet . . . He never seemed to be fazed by anything and he always seemed to predominate in a situation.' He was like a 'miniature adult', comfortable in the company of adults. At the age of thirteen he was cast in the Hampstead Garden Suburb Dramatic Society production of Terence Rattigan's *The Winslow Boy* as the eponymous hero, a cadet accused of stealing money. Despite having done nothing similar before, he showed no sign of stage fright. The *Hendon Times* was enthusiastic: 'Considering his age . . . Peter Mandelson gave an excellent performance . . . Reduced to tears after being expelled, he switched convincingly into a sort of a nonchalant attitude as his case drags on . . .' Whatever anxieties he may have had, according to his elder brother, they were overcome by 'the lure of the limelight'.

He was also adept at getting his way. Much later in life Miles told his mother that Peter 'always knew what he wanted and he got it. It was as simple as that.' When Miles left home, what had been 'the study' on the ground floor became 'Peter's study', commandeered as the room where he did his homework – under a Chris Orr engraving of the youthful Ruskin lying on his bed, bought by his father – and entertained his friends. According to Miles, he was 'very focused and in control' from quite early childhood; his mother, uncharacteristically letting her guard slip when telephoned by a writer from *Punch* in early 1998, described him as a boy who 'organised his friends' and who she 'always knew would be successful. He was in control all the time. He knew what he wanted to do and did it.'

Family recollections are of a humorous, self-confident and sometimes rather mischievous little boy. If Peter was more extrovert than Miles, he could also be an 'infernal nuisance', particularly as a comic stereotype of the annoying younger brother. Walking home with Miles one afternoon shortly after he started at Hendon County grammar school, he saw some girls from Henrietta Barnett on the other side of the road. To Miles's horror, Peter shouted across to the girls, 'What do you think of my brother?' Peter thought it a great joke; to the adolescent Miles it was mortifying enough for him to complain vigorously to his mother about it. When Miles first started going out with his first wife Ann – a Hendon County pupil like himself – 'every so often Peter would pop up out of nowhere, usually on his bike . . . just having a look to see what was going on . . . and occasionally he would say something to Ann about me designed to get her going.' On a family holiday to Spain Miles had only to pass the time of day with a 'Spanish lass' for Peter to dance maddeningly round him, chanting, 'Milo's in love, Milo's in love.'

But although Miles was shyer and less gregarious than his younger brother, he was also able to get the measure of him. Even when the family was alone, mealtime conversation bubbled with banter, stimulated by Tony but watched in quiet amusement by Mary. On one occasion Miles, in a flight of teenage inspiration, conferred a new alias on his brother: 'Osmold Smish, the Italian mind-your-own-businessman.' It conveyed 'the kind of character you could imagine my brother becoming,' explained Miles: 'someone with probably an overinflated sense of his own importance but also some-body who is a wheeler and a dealer or a fixer.' The name may have been suggested by one of Kenneth Horne's radio comedy shows – ritual Saturday morning listening for the Mandelsons: the Home Service, the Third Programme (for talks and, on occasions, music), and the Light Programme were all staple entertainment at Bigwood Road. Peter, by all accounts, revelled in his new celebrity as 'Smish' – the name by which he is still known to his family, to some of his closest friends outside politics, and to their children.

Unlike his brother, Peter made friends easily. He attended the Free Church Hall nursery every morning from the age of two and half. When, at five, he went to Hampstead Garden Suburb primary school, Mary Mandelson was rebuked for allowing her son to stay for school dinners; children in their first term were supposed to go home for lunch. But Peter was quite unperturbed by spending the whole day at school. Miles recalled that 'he was very independent, very self-sufficient. He didn't need his big brother to do anything for him.' He was good at making an impression on all the teachers – a talent of which he was well aware, remarking on it once to his mother. The exception was Mrs Jones, who taught him maths, and seems to have alienated him from mental arithmetic for life. Peter told his mother that he was sure she was a staunch Tory.

Miles, drawing on more than a quarter of a century's experience as a clinical psychologist, thinks that Peter, being closer to his mother, may also have subconsciously competed with his father for her affection, and that this may help to explain the friction in his relationship with 'Papa'. But their political differences did not help. In adult life Peter would disagree so sharply with Tony about the direction of the Labour Party that they had to stop talking about it. Since shaking off a brief and rebellious teenage flirtation with communism, Mary had long shared her father's anti-Bevanite views and, in Mandelson's own words, 'was chiefly responsible for making me into a fairly moderate, mainstream, middle of the road Labour Party member'.[10] But Tony was a romantic – or what Morrison would have called a 'woolly-minded' – socialist. Much later, when Peter, as a young councillor, was engaged in almost daily combat with the Lambeth Trotskyites and their allies on the Bennite left of the party, Tony Mandelson almost certainly supported Tony Benn rather than Denis Healey in the 1981 deputy leadership contest. Miles Mandelson thought his father much less politically 'serious' than his brother. But there were terrible rows between father and son, with Peter furiously stomping off to his mother in the kitchen to complain about his father's 'immature' and 'self-indulgent' views. Mandelson later told Oliver James that his father's views on the Militant Tendency were that 'these young people have got to be given their head, there's got to be tolerance and live and let live in our party'; his own view was that 'these people and their actions stopped Labour from being in power for a generation. My father contributed a wee bit to that.' Their disagreements made Tony's death, when Peter was thirty-five, and Director of Communications at the Labour Party, all the harder to bear. Colleagues at the time agree that he was devastated by it, and Miles thinks that his younger brother found it more difficult to come to terms with than he did because of the sense of 'unfinished business' between them.

Both the Mandelson parents contributed to Peter's childhood initiation into the Labour tribe. His first political memory, he told two old ladies at a party meeting in Wellingborough in 1996, was of watching canvass returns come in during the 1959 election. But while Peter has implied that Miles was much less political as a boy, both brothers canvassed from time to time. On one occasion Miles was reluctant to knock on Manny Shinwell's door, and when his wife answered 'she sort of looked at me as if to say to say "Well of course I shall be voting Labour, you silly idiot. Don't you know who we are?" '* Certainly, according to his mother Peter 'was political from about five', and keenly aware of politics and politicians – in particular his famous grandfather. This interest does not seem to have been reciprocated. In 1997 Mandelson described how Morrison would 'come once a month, steaming up in his little Morris car, bow tie, grey hair . . . to lunch . . . always tucked his napkin into his collar'.[11] But this is almost certainly romanticised: neither Miles nor his mother remembers Morrison as a frequent visitor to Bigwood Road – though Miles recalls that on more than one visit Morrison urged him to go to university, which he himself had never had the opportunity to do. Miles and Peter had gleaned almost as much information about their grandfather from the family's well-thumbed copy of the Labour MP Maurice Edelman's little pictorial biography of Morrison as they had from seeing him in the flesh.

After Morrison remarried in early 1955 he saw much less of his family, with the exception of his sister Edie, who had never been close to his first wife. He had disapproved when Mary left her first husband for Tony, and may have harboured anti-semitic feelings towards Tony. The Jewish Labour MP Leo Abse (whose niece Keren would coincidentally become one of Peter Mandelson's closest friends at Hendon County) claimed that Morrison had once in a 'xenophobic tirade, endeavoured to smear left-wing MPs by pointing out that they were a bunch who, from A to Z, from Abse to Zilliacus, with Mikardo in the middle, had doubtful origins. Given his prejudices, or perhaps because of them, it was ironic that his daughter married the well-liked advertising manager of the *Jewish Chronicle*.'[12] On the other hand, Morrison showed no signs of anti-semitism in his public life. He was pro-Zionist and an early enthusiast for the state of Israel. It may have been rather more significant that Morrison's second wife, Edith, wanted to break off all contact with her husband's earlier life.

---

* Miles did not join the party until his forties, having told Peter he would only do so when One Member One Vote democracy was introduced – a promise of which his younger brother duly reminded him after the conference vote in favour of OMOV in 1993.

When Morrison did call in at Bigwood Road on the way back from some function in North London in the sixties, Mary asked him – in vain – to stay until Peter got back from school. When Peter returned Mary told him of the visit, adding the observation, which she bitterly regretted afterwards, that 'I don't expect we shall ever see him again.' Peter burst into tears, apparently as much because Morrison was a famous politician as because he was his grandfather. Mary Mandelson's prophecy proved to be correct: Morrison died in March 1965, when his younger grandson was just eleven. The Mandelsons always resented first hearing the news on ITN.

In contrast to Tony Blair, the son of a Conservative, Mandelson was ordained by both birth and environment to be Labour. Mary's distaste for 'beastly politics' as a career did not mean that it was a taboo subject in the family. Indeed, it was endlessly discussed in the Mandelson household. The newspaper of choice at Bigwood Road was the liberal *News Chronicle* until it folded in 1960, to be replaced by the *Guardian*. Both children ran errands during local and national elections, taking piles of polling cards back to party headquarters on their bikes. The family knew the Wilsons quite well – much to the disgust of Morrison who had had no time for Harold since his resignation (with Bevan and John Freeman) from the Attlee government in 1951. Mary Mandelson shared some of her father's distrust and thought him 'a bit of a charlatan', but Mary Wilson was quite a frequent visitor to Bigwood Road, and on at least one occasion the Mandelsons joined the Wilsons to see *HMS Pinafore* at the Golders Green Hippodrome, indulging Harold's love of Gilbert and Sullivan.

Later, when Peter insisted, in the face of his parents' freely expressed disapproval, on joining the Cubs, the families were close enough for him to inherit an 'itchy' uniform from the Wilsons' son Giles, a good friend of Miles's. (Mary and Tony, who shared the view of many of their generation on the left that the Cubs and Scouts had neo-imperialist and even fascist overtones, were reluctant to buy him one of his own – and no doubt thought – wrongly – that he would soon grow out of his interest.)

With his father and brother, Peter watched Harold and Mary

Wilson leave Hampstead Garden Suburb on their triumphal drive to Downing Street the morning after Labour's epic election victory in 1964. As an adult Mandelson would even claim that this 'mesmerising' sight of Wilson's departure for Westminster gave him, at the age of ten, his first revelation about the symbiosis between television and politics; among those gathered outside Wilson's house in Southway to see him off, he would recall, was the celebrated US anchorman Walter Cronkite.

In June 1965, when Peter was eleven and Miles sixteen, the family were invited, by individual typewritten letters from Wilson's political secretary Marcia Williams, to Number Ten to watch Trooping the Colour as the Prime Minister's guests. Discussing the visit with Oliver James, Mandelson had no recollection of his brother being there, but Miles still has the letter of invitation announcing that 'Morning Dress will be worn by the Prime Minister and other official guests from overseas governments, but it will be quite in order if you would prefer to wear lounge suits.' Miles was offered cider by Wilson – who himself drank a 'large glass of brandy' – and was delighted to find that the Downing Street lavatory paper had 'government property' printed on it. Peter's main recollection was of smoked salmon and asparagus rolled up in brown bread and butter, and of Marcia's kindly exhortation to fill his plate with cakes – though he would much later recall that 'I was aware I was close to power. I was excited that I was taken into the cabinet room and sat down.'

Mary Mandelson, who as a child had trailed along with her father on a similar visit to Ramsay MacDonald, stayed at home. She disapproved of what Peter Mandelson would, more than thirty years later, call his father's 'social networking': he could not resist maintaining contact – mainly through Mary – with the Wilsons after they had moved to Downing Street. But then, as now, she hated going anywhere near Westminster. Devoted mother though she is, she has never been to see her son at the House of Commons, even to watch his maiden speech. Having kept out of politics for many years, she happened to meet Tony Blair, who dropped into Mandelson's Hartlepool house, where she was staying after her son's selection as candidate. When Blair harmlessly complimented her on the homemade cake she had brought with her, the normally gentle and mild-mannered Mrs Mandelson had to stop herself from saying something cutting just because he was a politician.

Mandelson appears to have been something of an instant success at Hendon County. He was already beginning to show some of the academic ability and leadership potential which marked him down as Maynard Potts's 'absolute pin-up boy, destined for great things'. The reports from his first year at Hendon County were highly impressive. George Renwick, his form master, noted at the end of the second term that the twelve-year-old Mandelson had 'initiative and sense of responsibility; he had made an excellent form captain . . .' Academically he did well in most subjects throughout his school career, with 'excellent' and 'superlative' cropping up regularly in his English and history reports; he was also busy in the school's extracurricular life: in the third form (at the age of fifteen) he was the 'deputy headmaster's monitor' in the choir; he took part in the school production of *The Beggar's Opera*; discovered a lifelong passion by joining the dancing club; when he was sixteen he was committee member of the senior debating society. By the end of the fourth year the formidable Maynard Potts was cautiously marking him out for higher things: 'Can he gain the really high grades which would warrant an application to Oxford and Cambridge?' he asked. He was not exactly sporty, though at fourteen he was in the school rugby team and, the following year, the athletics team as a 'very efficient' manager. One fourth-form PE report on the boy who would later become something of a fitness fanatic, working out and swimming regularly, put it laconically: 'Lazy, but improves with the weather.'

Outside school, the Cubs and then the Scouts – both of which he had joined with his best friend at the time, David Shields (who had a hole in the heart and died tragically young in 1972) – rather than politics, seem to have been his main interest. He also acquired a distinctly bourgeois enthusiasm for horse-riding, to which he was introduced by Katie Oates, the next-door neighbour at Bigwood Road (a Tory, but nevertheless on very friendly terms with the Mandelsons). He was an enthusiastic performer in a 'Gang Show' at the local Free Church hall. By the age of fifteen he was a troop leader in the Scouts, a role often reserved for adults.

15

More than a quarter of a century later the journalist David Aaronovitch, who knew Mandelson from the time he left university, wrote that 'more than anyone I know he has the knack of making you want to belong to his gang. In an instant you are returned to the jungle anxieties of the playground, desperately wanting to be picked, to be confided in, to be joked with, to join in the exchange of snide witticisms . . . His bosses have all tended to become personal friends.'[13] He appears to have shown, however embryonically, at least some of these characteristics, when in 1969, during his fourth year, he made one of the most formative friendships of his teenage years, with his Hendon County fellow-pupil and soon-to-be political comrade Steve Howell.

# CHAPTER TWO

## *An Incredible Anorak*

On a Friday morning in July 1998 Mandelson travelled by train to Newport. It was a low point for him. He was trying to shake off a bad cold, and the media frenzy over claims made by his former researcher, the lobbyist Derek Draper, was at its height. The Welsh press was intrigued. According to the *Western Mail*, local journalists were surprised to find him addressing a business lunch at Citypages, a small local website design company. Alan Clarke, the managing director, would say only that the Minister without Portfolio was 'a friend of a friend'. They would have been more interested still if they had known that the 'friend' involved was one of Mandelson's oldest – Steve Howell, a former BBC journalist who had settled with Welsh wife and three children in Newport, where he runs his own public relations company. Both Citypages and the big Celtic Manor Hotel and Country Club which Mandelson also visited, are clients, and the minister was doing his old school friend a favour.

But then Steve Howell and he had grown up together politically. Howell, who also attended Hendon County, had had little to do with Mandelson until they found themselves in the same set for several O-level subjects. He was struck at the time by two aspects of Mandelson's standing in the school. One was that 'He was much more mature than other people in the year. I remember he used to spend time chatting with the teachers on almost equal terms, which most people in the year wouldn't do.'[1] The other was the expectations about his future among his peers. After Mandelson's resignation in December 1998 one school contemporary, John Harding, was quoted in the *Sun*

17

as saying that 'at school Peter told us over and over again he was going to be Prime Minister'. Howell has no recollection of Mandelson making any such claim when they became friends in September 1969. But he remembers chatting to some girls about Peter during a break 'and some joke was made that, oh well Peter will be Prime Minister'.

Howell, who was to socialise regularly in Mandelson's company over the next four years, also remembers another Mandelson trait that was emerging in his teens: 'Peter's very funny when he's talking about other people. He likes a good gossip. He likes characterising other people.' Mandelson apparently shunned big teenage parties, preferring to meet people 'in smaller circles where he could be the kind of focus of the thing and entertain eyeryone . . . and have a laugh.' Howell's friendship came as Mandelson's enthusiasm with the Scouts – of which Howell was emphatically not a part – was finally waning. His departure appears to be unrelated to an earlier incident involving a local Scoutmaster, who was accused of sexually abusing boys in his charge.

Howell came from an even more identifiably left-wing background than Mandelson. His father was an American town-planner who had joined the Communist Party while working in Puerto Rico and had been chairman of the LSE's Marxist-inclined Socialist Society in the same year, in the late forties, that Bernard Levin was chairman of the Labour Club. His mother Cynthia was an active Labour Party member. Howell used to go up and meet Mandelson occasionally in the Load of Hay pub between Golders Green and Hampstead, where the older members of Mandelson's troop repaired after Scout evenings. Mandelson, quite mature-looking for his sixteen years, had no trouble in ordering his lager and lime, though he would make one or two last for much of the evening. Both boys organised meetings of the school Discussion and Debating Society. According to Howell, Mandelson was already 'an incredible anorak' about the House of Commons, inviting friends, especially on long car journeys, to test him with the names of parliamentary constituencies so that he could answer with the name of the sitting MP.

This is also a vivid memory of Keren Abse,* who was already a

* The daughter of doctor, poet and playwright Dannie Abse; niece of Leo Abse, MP.

close friend. 'He'd be laughing at himself while he was doing this, but actually he could name every single Labour MP.'[2] Steve Howell recalled that Mandelson knew some of the MPs personally: 'That was the difference between his family and mine. His family was very integrated into the Labour hierarchy. He was into history but in a very different way to the way I was. I was into the sweep of things and he was into the details of British political history. He knew every Prime Minister and the dates and the details of the legislation and all that sort of thing.' But Mandelson also followed current affairs very closely. He was impressed by a 'huge argument' with his geography teacher in which he had mounted a stalwart defence of the Wilson government after it had abandoned *In Place of Strife*, Barbara Castle's proposed legislation on union reform, in 1969. But the teacher had been 'very, very hostile' to the climbdown – which was indeed a pivotal moment for Wilson's first administration, and Mandelson would say years later that as he left the geography room he had a sudden sense that the government had 'blown it'. He read – twice – Peter Jenkins's account of the conflict over *In Place of Strife* published the following year: *The Battle of Downing Street*.

But the boys' common interest in party politics did not blossom into activism until one autumn afternoon in 1969, when they were talking to Howell's grandmother Winnie, a local Labour stalwart, in the front room of her house in Egerton Gardens, Hendon. Winnie Fisher suggested the boys re-form the then dormant branch of Young Socialists in the constituency.

They appear to have set about this task with some energy. Howell's diary records that the first meeting of the nascent Hendon YS executive took place on 25 January 1970. Without, apparently, any dissent, Mandelson became chairman, Howell secretary, and Keren Abse, the third Hendon County member of what soon became a politically inseparable trio, social secretary. It is no doubt too fanciful to see Mandelson's relationship with Abse and Howell as a forerunner of that with Blair and Brown; but it is certainly not the only time that he was to operate in a close-knit political threesome. On 6 March, three months before a general election in which Harold Wilson was widely expected to be given a second full term of office, the *Hendon Times* recorded that twenty-seven Young Socialists had attended their inaugural meeting at George Richardson House in Sunningfield Road. Bernard Le Mare, the constituency party president, was so delighted by the attendance that he told the meeting, in the newspaper's sensitively bowdlerised account, that it was a 'b— miracle'. Chairman Mandelson, in his first ever Labour Party speech, was reported as saying that the YS members intended to educate themselves and increase their social awareness by inviting 'knowledgeable speakers to their meetings and by discussing topics with each other'.

But this was to be no mere talking-shop. The chairman added sternly, if a little vaguely: 'We must be a group of action, action in that having discussed, we must make our feelings heard and felt.' The success of the first meeting was partly down to sheer organisation by Howell and Mandelson. It may also have been down to the perception that politics was 'cool'. Maybe there was already a tendency among Mandelson's acquaintances to gravitate, as Aaronovitch put it, to his 'gang'. But both Howell, at once a natural athlete and a natural rebel, and Abse, engaging and free spirited, had a pull and charisma of their own, reinforced by their family backgrounds.

If Mary Mandelson harboured growing qualms that Peter was showing every sign of embarking on a political career, she kept them to herself. 'Duchess' (all Mandelson's school friends knew her by the nickname he had given her) could hardly have been more supportive, providing endless fried egg sandwiches and hot chocolate when Peter and his friends turned up after school. As a teenager, Miles had chosen to withdraw to his room and listen to jazz or write poetry; but Peter did indeed prefer 'organising his friends'. Nevertheless when Peter was revising for his A-levels, Mary would put record after record on the stereogram, which had a speaker in his ground-floor study, to ensure a steady, soothing background of Vivaldi's *Four Seasons*, as well as Bach and Telemann, for him to work to.

But she also laboriously typed out the often indecipherable adolescent outpourings in issue after issue of the YS magazine – receiving from Steve Howell a special message of public thanks in the last issue, dedicated to all-out opposition to the Heath government's 1971 Industrial Relations Bill. She joined her son on the 'Kill the

Bill' demonstration, marching – to her dismay – behind a Communist Party banner. (Mandelson said in 1997 that she had already taken him on a demonstration in protest at Enoch Powell's racist 'Rivers of Blood' speech in April 1968.)

The stencilled YS magazine regularly gave details of social evenings or meetings with guest speakers such as Danny Abse or the Luton Labour MP Will Howie. But a Mandelson editorial in March 1970 was already sternly warning against participation for the wrong reasons. The branch was not a 'Friday night little social club'; it was not enough for members to turn up 'because they had nothing better to do or because they are particularly interested in Atomic Energy [not an obviously frivolous motive] or because they wouldn't mind having a look at Danny Abse or Will Howie . . .' YS members should focus on 'creating interest in social problems, interest in people, and interest in politics – and not just politics from Labour Party propaganda leaflets'. They urgently needed to examine big questions like 'Are we getting the right people along to our branch meetings? Are we really doing anything worthwhile at all?' Mandelson's editorial concluded with a passing, if portentous, endorsement of the party constitution which he would finally help Tony Blair to replace twenty-five years later: 'Our principal aim is to follow Clause Four, but if we are functioning with no purpose, to no aim, then it is hardly worth functioning at all. We might as well pack up and go home. Think on it.'

When Mandelson arrived at Hendon County in 1965, the first storm clouds were already just beginning to gather over it. Tony Crosland, who had famously vowed to his wife Susan that he was 'going to destroy every fucking grammar school in the country',[3] had already, as Secretary of State for Education and Science, issued his first circular, the famous DES 10/65, urging local authorities to abolish selection at eleven-plus. But Hendon was not going to go without a fight. Barnet, the presiding education authority, was a Tory-controlled council ideologically committed to selection. And Maynard Potts, a traditionalist who always wore a gown in school, had no wish to teach pupils who had failed the eleven-plus. To Potts's dismay, Mandelson joined some of his YS colleagues in a vigorous campaign to end selection. A ballot was run by the school in the hope of securing a decisive vote against comprehensivisation;

however, 'Plan C' (proposing a merger with St David's secondary modern school, about a mile away), for which Mandelson campaigned, was eventually implemented, prompting the departure of the deeply disappointed Potts in 1971.

This was not the only respect in which the Hendon YS were 'heard and felt'. During the 1970 election campaign Abse, Howell and Mandelson were evicted from Hendon town hall for over-enthusiastic heckling of Peter Thomas, the Tory candidate for Hendon South – with the result that Tony Mandelson had to plead with Dennis Signy, the editor of the *Hendon Times*, not to publish pictures of the incident, which might have given Maynard Potts an excuse to expel the miscreants. Signy, who knew Keren Abse slightly, followed the trio out of the hall 'to tell us off for being stupid bloody prats'. And she also recalled 'Peter getting terribly pompous [and saying], "Don't you know who my grandfather was?"'

Nor was the branch able to escape the attentions of Militant, then embarking on its slow but ultimately successful national takeover of the YS. The Hendon branch proved to be infertile ground. At one meeting a leading Militant figure harangued a handful of bemused teenagers at George Richardson House on the imminent overthrow of world capitalism in tones more appropriate to a rally of several thousand, reducing Abse and Mandelson to helpless giggles in the process. The speaker may have been the London organiser Bob Labi, who certainly addressed the Hendon YS at least once; but it may have been the legendary Trotskyite ideologue Ted Grant. When Howell and Mandelson travelled to Morecambe on an eye-opening trip to the YS national conference, they were bemused to find that there appeared to be no middle ground between the ranting Militant delegates and their hard-right opponents, 'who thought that poverty was the fault of the working class because they spent all their money on cigarettes'.

While politics did not wholly dominate life in 1970, he did not exactly desert it – even on a summer camping holiday with friends in Scandinavia. In a letter to his parents from Sweden he complained that, 'At the moment we are living on English packets because everything in Sweden is so dreadfully expensive' before going on to ask: 'PS. What is Maurice Edelman's parliamentary history? Which Jews have been leader of the Labour Party?' He reported that, 'the conversation does tend solely to be about school, although we did touch on drugs and euthanasia this evening, and South Africa, the Commonwealth and pornography yesterday'. From Norway he announced that, 'I am sitting on an inflated Lilo in a crowded Nordic campsite, which has just been invaded by a noisy coach load of French . . . The French are now putting up a huge white and blue striped tent and being thoroughly exhibitionist . . . The campsites have now fortunately become consistently good, although I'm getting a little bored with some of the present company.'

When he returned to school in September there was a struggle which, though it may seem trivial in retrospect, sheds a significant and early light on Mandelson's temperament and political – albeit with a small 'p' – perspective. By this time he and Howell had been appointed lower-sixth prefects, entitled to use the prefects' common room. The prefects voted in favour of a radical proposal, which had originated in the upper sixth, to open up this common room to any sixth-former who wanted to use it. Jack Driver, the well-liked deputy head, responded by saying that if that happened, use of the room would be withdrawn. A majority of prefects then voted to back down – but Howell was incensed enough to march into Driver's office with the intention of handing in his prefect's badge.

Driver spent ninety minutes persuading Howell to reconsider; but word quickly reached Howell that some of the prefects who had been outvoted were now threatening to follow his example and resign. The outvoted minority – including Mandelson – then convened in a classroom to decide what to do. 'Peter was very reluctant at that stage,' Howell said. 'He wasn't keen on resigning at all.' But the majority – the majority of the minority – clearly *did* favour resignation and Mandelson resigned with them. Howell then collected up the prefects' badges and presented the 'gobsmacked' Jack Driver with a list of demands signed by the rebels, including Mandelson: he sought the abolition of the school uniform for all sixth formers, the ending of the prefect system and the creation of a new school council. 'I was a little bit headstrong. I tended to react more emotionally whereas Peter was more rational and less inclined to get carried away by the emotion of the moment. But once it got going Peter was very much part of it. He and I were considered the ringleaders.'

Among those considering them the ringleaders was Maynard Potts, who complained that they were behaving like 'industrial militants' after they had organised a petition of support throughout the school. This was an era of agitation among school pupils elsewhere – the Little Red Book was out and the Schools Action Union had already been formed – but the revolt at Hendon County appears to have been largely home grown. Potts appointed substitutes as prefects – instantly identified as 'scabs' – and took two other steps. He made an angry telephone call to Mary Mandelson, reducing her to tears, in a counterproductive attempt to bring pressure to bear on her son. And during assembly he also issued a threat of expulsion, disguised as a call on the pupils not to push the two boys 'too far' and thus provoke reprisals. But although the turmoil died down after a few weeks, the revolt was at least partially successful. The prefect system was eventually abolished, replaced by a rota of duties among the entire sixth form. Given his strong initial reservations, Mandelson could probably have advanced his own position in the school – and restored himself to Potts's good books – by deserting his friends. But outvoted, or at least outargued, by a majority of the rebels, he had instead abided by their decision and joined Howell in leading the protest.

The Hendon YS also fostered more conventional Labour Party activity – including an attack on a local freesheet's coverage of politics. Adopting a tone identical to the one he would use countless times in his later dealings with press, the YS chairman wrote to the paper in April 1970 complaining about a front-page picture of Tory candidates which was a 'quite blatant free advertisement for the Conservative Party'. Mandelson continued with all the menace he could muster: 'It would be regrettable if the *Post* were to start lending itself to political bias and I would be very interested to learn if this photograph does mark the beginning of a change in your editorial policy to remain neutral in politics.'

The following month the rival *Hendon Times* was reporting that the YS branch wanted an October general election because of its fears that 'O- and A-level exams will prevent [members] from canvassing and restrict their earnest work for the return of the Labour government'. (Whether the branch subsequently attributed the surprise Labour defeat in a June election to Wilson's failure to take its advice is not recorded.) Mandelson also, in contrast to his friends, took a close interest in the progress of the then unfashionable campaign on disability rights being promoted by the Labour MP Alf Morris.

Did this and other aspects of Mandelson's YS activity suggest a teenager consciously taking the first step on a politically careerist path? Keren Abse thinks it is not so simple.

> Peter was always very ambitious, that was always clear, which was different from Steve and me. He definitely wanted to go to Oxford, and the fact that he'd been a prefect, his whole persona in the school was like a good person, and the problem was that all the politics got in the way ... What I don't think is that he had some Machiavellian path planned out and [thought] 'I will do this and I won't join that, it will somehow affect a future career.' I don't think he ever thought like that.

At the end of his first term in the sixth form 'E. W. Maynard Potts MA MSC Hon. FRIBA' as he imposingly styled himself, commented: 'Eventually he will wish to undertake some great task on behalf of humanity.' But in a comment which carried a subtext of Mandelson's increasingly firm political convictions, the headmaster added: 'He will need to be receptive to ideas and information of all kinds and from all sources. The solution will emerge. It ought not to be predetermined.' The report was written a matter of weeks before Mandelson joined the Young Communist League.

Abse (who had not been a prefect), Mandelson and Howell, all started to become disenchanted with the YS. As early as September 1970 Mandelson, then still sixteen, was sternly expressing doubts in a long letter to Howell (in the US with his parents) about the commitment of some of his executive committee – the vagueness and practical disinterest of Tim, the frivolity and complete disinterest of Peter Fordham [who nevertheless contributed the only light relief in the Hendon YS magazine – record reviews, featuring, in a typical issue, Neil Young, the Band and James Taylor] and the interest but complete non-contribution of Allan'. Two of these renegades, Pete and Allan, an irritated Mandelson reported, had actually gone to

25

the pub rather than attend the regular Friday meeting, but 'I'm certainly not going to trouble over them. We can get on with the programme, Plan C and election work without them . . .' All this he had discussed with Keren Abse at a party to which he had gone in preference to a meeting of Militant – 'not all that bad not many people there, just dim Upper Sixth . . .' In contrast to those who failed to meet his exacting standards, Keren, 'so natural and unaffected, honest, usually straightforward to the extent of bluntness', was 'an asset and a consolation amid the general rabble of the EC [the Hendon YS executive]'. As so often in the future, people were as important as policies in Mandelson's political firmament.

The letter was also peppered with more mundane complaints. That morning he had gone shopping 'for a bloody pair of school trousers . . . Could the great shops of Golders Green and Hampstead – Cecil Gee, Harry Fenton, smart Weston – satisfy my need? Oh no, not on your life or my life.' Meanwhile, as he wrote, the trusted family cleaner and baby-sitter Mrs Tomlinson 'was now looking at some ghastly programme called *Opportunity Knocks* with Hughie Green, who is the biggest creep I've ever seen – similar to Ralph Reader'. He had on the last day of the holidays helped to finish tidying up the prefects' room and spoken to 'that old bag Mrs East . . . and some new English git who all the girls are going to swoon over. Peggy nearly 'ad 'im in the Stock room behind the elementary Mathematics Book One, before you could bat an eyelid or anything else!'

The first of the three to defect to the Young Communist League was Keren Abse. She had in fact been a member before – then for the self-confessedly frivolous reason of finding the boys more attractive. According to Howell, 'Keren was lukewarm about the Labour Party all along . . . a bit semi-detached. There are some types of people who are not party people. Well, Keren was not really a party person whereas Peter and I were in rather different ways. We were into the organisation of it. I think we were budding little party hacks really.' Abse appears to have persuaded the other two to 'come and have a look' at the nearest YCL branch, in the brick outbuilding of a large West Hampstead house, the bedsit of Anne Champion, the local YCL secretary and the daughter of two prominent local communists. 'It was almost like window-shopping,' said Howell. But they happened to go on the day of the annual general meeting and Barry Van Den Bergh, the district full-time organiser, insisted they would have to join on the spot if they wanted to come in – which they did.

This left the little problem of the YS branch. Showing a commendable, if naive, desire to leave it in good order, Howell and Mandelson remained for several weeks, not resigning their leadership until just before the AGM in February 1971. As one of their last, perhaps slightly mischievous, acts, they secured agreement for half the funds they had raised for the branch – a respectable £10 – to be given to the striking postal workers.

They then wrote – in unusual terms for activists severing their connections with a political party – a polite, but surely rather baffling letter to the constituency secretary, Mrs Miller. Summing up their year as pillars of the YS, they explained that 'we now feel that it would not be wise to tie ourselves down for a further year in this one field of political activity and that it would be far more beneficial, considering our age, to broaden our interest and experience in the political field'. This meant devoting time 'to other political organisations' and abandoning responsibilities in the constituency – including their office in YS, membership of the constituency General Management Committee, and of the Greater London Labour Party conference delegation – which would be 'restricting'. The letter ended: 'We hope that we have contributed as much to the constituency as we have benefited from it, Yours Fraternally . . .'

Some of their disenchantment may well have stemmed from a certain boredom with running the YS branch. They had become a little less interested in political activity and a little more interested in social life at around this time. Keren Abse, who had been a close friend of Mandelson's for longer than Howell – ever since vomiting over him during a school cruise to Gibraltar – recalled that 'we used to go drinking together, and there seemed to be endless parties. I remember Peter dancing . . . I remember smoking quite a lot of dope, but I don't think Peter did. Steve did. I did a bit.' In later years she would find Mandelson's menacing image baffling: 'At the time I remember taking the piss out of him all the time, and also him just laughing, which is why I find it so difficult not knowing him now. Why didn't we take him seriously? The figure of fear . . .

I find it so difficult to understand.' One lifelong trait, however, was already evident: Mandelson frequently complained of tiredness and would take naps, 'whereas most teenagers didn't. I remember we used to take the piss out of him for being middle aged.'

While Mandelson's relationship with Abse was entirely asexual, he did have 'these sort of flirtatious relationships with a number of girls at a time'. One was Caroline Wetzler, who like Keren went on to Sussex University. Another was Rebecca Thomas, with whom Mandelson went out comparatively regularly for a while. During their schooldays Keren Abse certainly had no intimation that Mandelson was gay. 'I don't think I knew what gay was really.' It was only when she visited him at Oxford that she realised: 'looking back, the sort of relationship he had with a couple of these women, it was really quite a camp relationship . . . Peter had these girlfriends, Rebecca and then Caroline, but because I then became very good friends with Caroline I found out from her what hadn't happened, as it were.' In Mandelson's long letter to Steve Howell of September 1970 he reported – somewhat tentatively – on an evening out with Rebecca Thomas (who, he said, sent her love): 'We had a nice evening on Saturday, in a way. He thinks. Yes, it was nice. If you had been at home I would have rung you up when I got home on Saturday. I felt like talking to you. Either for your advice or your blessing . . .' It appears that Mandelson was struggling, like many teenagers, with the question of his own sexual identity at this time.

In joining the YCL Mandelson was almost certainly influenced by his close friendship with Howell, who was rather keener on the idea than he was. At different times Maynard Potts apparently accused each of leading the other astray. In interviews Mandelson has tended to play down his YCL membership – for example, telling the *Independent on Sunday* in 1996: 'I went to the meetings. I really can't remember what led me to the YCL. It was short lived. I felt no identification. I spent far more time setting up a tremendous youth club at the Winchester Arms at Swiss Cottage. Tearing it apart with my bare hands, then rebuilding it to make it structurally sound.'[4]

This is not quite accurate. In the summer of 1972 he did indeed go to work on the Winchester project, after responding to an appeal for help which its organiser Graham Good sent round to all local parties, including the YCL. He not only 'laboured day and night', along with youngsters from the local council tower blocks, to refurbish the pub, but also joined a lobbying campaign to persuade a resistant Camden Council to allow it to be used as a youth club. And certainly Howell, who, in stark contrast to Mandelson, became an active Communist Party member at university, remembers the mixture of horror and amusement with which both of them regarded some of their fellow YCL members at 'dreadful' social evenings: 'You may have the same political attitudes as people but being in the same room as them on a Saturday night at some low budget disco is something different. We did laugh at some of the people – some of them were a bit eccentric, people who were like trainspotters with their Soviet badges down their lapels. We weren't into anything like that.' Howell's diary, peppered with entries like 'Barnet 100 metre trials' or 'Pack for Cottage' as well as those for the regular Tuesday evening YCL meetings, also illustrates how politics was combined with the more normal activities of North London teenagers.

But the Howell diary for the period also suggests that, notwithstanding his later dismissiveness, Mandelson was active for much of the period between February 1971 and September 1972 when he was a YCL member – though less so in the run up to A-levels in the second summer. His energetic participation in the Winchester project did not begin until he had finished his exams. Before that, Howell would routinely go round to Bigwood Road on Friday evenings and – once Mandelson had passed his test in the autumn of 1971 – they would drive over to Kilburn in his Morris 1100 to sell the first edition of the *Morning Star* to people coming out of the pubs. Among those who wanted the following day's paper – especially punters interested in the racing tips – it did a brisk trade.

But they also sold *Challenge*, the YCL newspaper and a less saleable proposition, in Kilburn shopping precinct, on Saturday afternoons, and, on occasions – when Keren Abse refused, on ideological grounds, to join them – *Soviet Weekly*. In April they were dedicated enough to go to the YCL Congress in Scarborough, where the executive – in the face of opposition from the Hampstead branch, which had a hard-line, broadly pro-Soviet local leadership – promoted a long Euro-communist resolution criticising, among other things, the invasion of Czechoslovakia three years earlier. Keren Abse was a delegate and enraged her Hampstead comrades by voting for the anti-Soviet national leadership line – for which she was instantly denounced as a 'bourgeois revisionist'. Howell and Mandelson were mere stewards, charged with scrutinising the credentials of those entering the hall. On one occasion – Howell would later tease Mandelson by claiming that this was his 'first real contact with the working class' – Peter attempted to stop a stocky building worker, unaware that he was Phil Green, a prominent member of the YCL executive, from entering the hall because he didn't have proper identification: '[Green] got really outraged and pinned Peter up against the wall . . . Peter was really quite shaken up by this and someone came to the rescue and explained that this guy could come in.'

According to Howell, Mandelson was visibly less comfortable with some aspects of West Hampstead communism than he was. Both were opposed to the US presence in Vietnam and at one public meeting Mandelson had asked Michael Stewart, Wilson's Foreign Secretary, a critical question about the Labour government's failure to oppose it. But whereas Howell took it as read that opposition to the war meant support for the Vietnamese National Liberation Front, Mandelson, during their surprisingly sophisticated discussions on the subject, expressed a preference for 'some form of compromise'. With the Cold War still the central reference point for left-wing politics, Howell and his elder brother Mark read from cover to cover Alexander Werth's book *Russia Hopes and Fears* and endlessly tried to 'evaluate' the Soviet Union. Mandelson read 'some of it' too, apparently, but was certainly more critical and less 'positive' about the Soviet Union than his friend.

What did Mandelson get from his time as a Young Communist? Looking back, Keren Abse, who is now a teacher, reflected that Mandelson was as discontented a communist as she was but that it may nevertheless have subconsciously influenced his later political style: 'The thing about the YCL is that it is incredibly disciplined, with its committee structure . . . you learn how to manipulate and be Machiavellian . . . I used to do a lot of union negotiations and I always used to think "God almighty, people are bloody naive in this room." So I think that discipline . . . was also attractive.'

However, this does not answer the remaining mystery of Mandelson's teenage politics. In August 1997 the former Security Service agent David Shayler told the *Mail on Sunday* that he had seen photographic evidence from Mandelson's MI5 file which showed that he had held an adult Communist Party membership card. Mandelson himself has been undogmatic on the subject, though he has said that he has no recollection of joining the CP, and that he would probably remember it if he had. According to Keren Abse, who discussed the question of joining at some length with Mandelson, they had both decided against membership; Mandelson was 'pretty fed up with the Stalinism . . . and the lack of being able to take a critical line'.

By contrast, Steve Howell – who certainly did join – thinks it likely that Mandelson did too. As the summer of 1972 drew to a close the Abse-Howell-Mandelson trio were preparing to separate – Howell for a year in the US, Keren Abse to Sussex University, and Mandelson for a gap year in Tanzania. Jim McDonald and Anne Champion, the two leading officers of their local YCL, were certainly keen to sign up all three of them before they went their own ways.

During the summer of 1972, when Mandelson was already 'showing more interest in the Winchester than the YCL', Howell remembers going with McDonald to visit him at the club after a YCL meeting from which Mandelson was probably absent. 'I have a vague feeling that it was something to do with his party membership. I don't know that we weren't trying to deliver him his party card.'

It is possible that the local party had made out a card for him, returning a counterfoil to the district office without ever delivering the original to Mandelson himself – something which would square Shayler's claim with Mandelson's own recollection. This was not unusual: they could bump up their notional membership figures without actually having to persuade the relevant individuals to join. Stephen Lander, Director-General of MI5, in a conversation with Mandelson following the Shayler revelations, appears to have indicated that he was on a CP list seen by the service – adding that the party commonly added names to the membership roll. Shayler, interviewed for this book, said he recalled seeing a card for 1973 in Mandelson's name, which would have been made out after he left for Tanzania on his gap year. It is possible that Mandelson has forgotten or that Shayler is wrong. But even if he held a full CP card it can only have been for a few weeks at most. When Mary Mandelson drove her son to the airport for his flight to Dar es Salaam, he left her with strict instructions to tear up a membership card and then make a telephone call saying she had done so. She did as he asked but, twenty-five years later, was understandably unable to remember exactly what it was or whom she had to ring. Whether it was a YCL or a CP card she destroyed, Mandelson appears to have decided that his flirtation with British communism was over.

# CHAPTER THREE

# *A Bourgeois at Heart*

It seemed to Steve Howell when he first met Mandelson that he had already mapped out his future: head boy (he became instead chairman of the school council which had replaced the prefect system), Philosophy, Politics and Economics at Oxford, and then the long climb up the 'greasy pole', as Disraeli described it. Mandelson's membership of the YCL, he thought, was more than an aberration or a mere 'radical fling which gave him some street cred'. But once he left Hendon County, 'he went back onto some prearranged path'. Oxford, suggested by an economics teacher, had never occurred to him. Neither of his parents appear to have encouraged him, partly because they feared his disappointment if he failed. His father 'was very proud when I went to Oxford University though he never showed any encouragement or pressure to do so', was how he would put it much later. Howell, in sharp contrast to his friend, became a committed communist and remained one throughout his university life. But it would be perverse to assume that Mandelson's intensive three months of social action at the 'Winch', let alone his year in Africa, did not also betray a certain commitment, though of a different kind – possibly even some of the same idealism which had by then prompted his brother Miles to resolve on a career in the NHS treating the mentally ill after seeing a television programme on the subject.

Mandelson was energetic in arranging his post-school year. Having been accepted at St Catherine's College to do PPE, he then set about persuading the college that he needed a gap year; he also wrote some fifty letters in the hope of securing voluntary work in Africa. His mother suggested Tanzania, 'to see how Nyerere is getting on'; 'the conscience of black Africa' was then still regarded by the British left as a model of uncorrupt socialist leadership. One of his letters went to the anti-apartheid priest Trevor Huddleston, then Bishop of Stepney, whom he had heard on the radio talking about Tanzania. He went to see the bishop in his office in Commercial Road and impressed him enough with his determination for Huddleston to write to Maxwell Wiggins, the Bishop of Victoria and Nyanza, asking him if he could put him to work with some of the diocesan missions in rural Tanzania. What Mandelson did not discover until nearly a year later, when he could not resist rifling through his own file while working briefly in the diocesan office in Mwanza, was that, in an act of heroic generosity, Huddleston had secretly promised his fellow-bishop that he would pay Peter's board and lodging for the year out of his own pocket.

'It is hard to imagine the suave and sometimes cynical Member for Hartlepool,' wrote Roy Hattersley in a 1995 profile, 'planting gum trees, teaching in a village school and helping in a primitive hospital "working the anaesthetic machine and holding open Love's *Book of Surgery* so that the doctor could read what to do next". But he speaks of his year in the bush as if it was the best time of his life.'[1] It did not seem like that at first. His arrival within a couple of days of his eighteenth birthday, at his first posting, the rural aid centre at Buhemba, must have been a shock. He spoke no Swahili and none of the Europeans initially had any idea what this rather metropolitan young man was doing there. Nor was he entranced with his fellow-Europeans:

> I'm happy when I think of all the things around me . . . to learn about and discuss [he reported in a letter to Steve Howell days after his arrival]. I just wish that there was someone other than egocentric, sports-fanatical, Canadian engineers and apolitical VSO agro-mechanics from Enfield and Oxford Tech to share it all with. I'm dying for a good bloody argument, a nice laugh and a glass of whisky. And I do wish they wouldn't keep saying 'grace' before they eat. All this religion is positively unhealthy . . .

Almost from the first, his long, fluent letters to family and friends mixed sharp, detailed and sometimes funny observation with – at times dauntingly comprehensive – meditations on the theory and practice of Nyererean socialism.

They also gave a rather surprising picture of an introspective and slightly self-conscious young man trying earnestly to work through the big questions in politics – and even, however 'unhealthy' it may have seemed at first, in religion. He wondered – and he was hardly the first expatriate volunteer to do so – whether 'underdevelopment' did not entail 'a value judgement which I am not sure I have the right to make. It implies worse-off, requiring progress and improvement; yet why, if those who live under these conditions of "underdevelopment" are accustomed to and happier in their present conditions.' A couple of weeks later he was telling Steve Howell that

> the people I am living with are more tolerable now and through one of them I have discovered in myself a new appreciation of nature ... The policies for planned progress and the socialistic framework that is being built ... create a refreshing atmosphere in this country; and one that has filled me with a new sense of idealism and dedication that is easy to lose in the harshness and complexity of life in London.

The work at Buhemba planting gum trees, sorting invoices and building chicken coops, was not too hard: he began at 8.30, with a break for lunch, and finished around 3 p.m because of the heat, though it sometimes resumed in the evening. As he reported to another friend, he had 'a great deal of time – social life is non-existent here – to supplement what I see by reading, mostly Nyerere's writings, TANU reports and newspapers.' But Christmas with the missionary Merry Hart, and his wife, Beatrice, at Musoma was great fun by comparison. 'An inward feeling swept through my body ... of the humorous informality, not to say eccentricity, and the refreshing flow of mangoes, avocados and wholewheat that are the Hart household ...' He went to sleep on Friday night to the sounds 'of a hundred voices and sundry radios', and woke to 'the calls of the local cockerel population and the drumming of tin by the local watoto . . .' Beatrice Hart taught him to make date ginger-bread and cakes; Merry took him to the local hospital, where the patients were 'resigned to their pain in a way that we could not be at home'. On Christmas Eve there was a nativity play with an 'Angel Gabriel with his huge bunny ear wings' and 'as the Three Wise Men followed a torch beam over the roof, the message shone through. It was a message that I had not noticed before, and it portrayed an event that marks the beginning of a life that represents such love and hope to so many people.' During the Harts' 'lavish' Christmas dinner

> I sat next to Mr Method, Merry's appropriately named Swahili teacher, who having been told my full name persistently rather disconcertingly addressed me as 'Mandelson'. Mr Method's English was quite funny on occasions. On being asked if he wanted a cup of tea he boldly replied 'obviously' and when he was offered some more to eat firmly stated that he was 'quite fed up' and couldn't possibly . . .

If anything, Mandelson got on better with the Africans working at the Rural Aid Centre than with his fellow volunteers who were from New Zealand: charged with the 'somewhat uninspiring task of replacing broken window handles . . . enlist the help of Zebron who works in the Centre's kitchen and John Matajiri who is being trained here as an omni-mechanic . . . with laughter and joking we complete our task in a short time and sit down in one of the dormitories to chat.' By January he was writing to two other friends that the season

> is now becoming hotter and hotter, making the snakes more active and the flies more irritating . . . but we are quite high and surrounded by rolling green hills, open bushland and sweeping valleys and a nice breeze keeps everything bearable . . . to the limits of my Swahili and practical capabilities (non existent) I am doing my bit for rural aid and development: mainly driving but also painting houses and constructing chicken cages and spare parts stores.

Mandelson's lifelong and notably natural rapport with children was already evident in Tanzania. After a trip to the economically more advanced Kenya, in which he had had the only glimpse of metropolitan social life during his year in Africa, he wrote home: 'Perhaps the good life of Nairobi house guesting and Mombasa beach partying was too much of a good thing for me! But I have immediately settled down again, especially after a tumultuous welcome from the children: and how Uncle Peter loves it too!' To his patron Trevor Huddleston, he wrote that 'I have returned home an even more confirmed Tanzanophile than when I started out ... I do believe that Kenya is a somewhat morally and politically bankrupt nation whose way of life revolves around making money and virtual economic crime.' Nor did he shrink from sharing with the bishop his latest thoughts from Buhemba on Christianity.

I am not convinced that economic revolution would naturally effect a revolution in human nature. If this is so, alternative revolutionary means have been suggested to me in the person of Jesus Christ. I have talked, read and considered but – with respect – as I look round me and see the established church, Christianity as practised by the morally lazy but self-righteous, and dependence on faith used as an excuse for personal inaction and conformity, I remain unconvinced.

By the spring of 1973 Mandelson appears to have become even more preoccupied by his own beliefs, and what he was himself capable of putting into practice. By now he was at the remote Murgwanza Hospital in Ngara. He labelled specimens in the pathology lab, and for two hours a day helped to look after children in the local orphanage – two of whom, both girls, were so inconsolable each time he left that he asked the nurse whether it would not be less upsetting if he didn't come at all. She assured him that it would not. He also worked from time to time in the operating theatre. It was here that he helped the local missionary-surgeon, the extremely amiable Arthur Adeney, 'a man with a large body, a loud Australian wife and some very unruly children' in the hair-raising circumstances alluded to by Hattersley. If a patient was in urgent need of attention, perhaps because he had been knocked down by a tractor or had 'fallen into a combine harvester', he would be laid out on a concrete slab. According to Mandelson, there was a large cylinder of ether which, on occasion, he was asked to oversee, pumping every fifteen seconds or so to keep the anaesthetic topped up; sometimes he would even read out sections of Love's *Anatomy* to the surgeon (something of a medical generalist) as he operated.

But he also had other things on his mind. In a four-page, single-space typewritten letter to Steve Howell, he wrote that

> sometimes . . . I feel that I . . . am retaining the force and commit-ment of my YCL-bred attitudes and beliefs but am just not having the opportunity to expound on them. And other times I feel that my revolutionary ardour is fading because I am a bourgeois at heart, that the people I enjoy most are from a strictly bourgeois and intellectual background and that the life I enjoy most does not exactly revolve around the class struggle.

Advising Steve to read the 'good persuasive bible-thumping stuff' in Michael Green's book *Man Alive*, he explained that the 'deeply committed Christians' with whom he was working at the Ngara mission '. . . are all genuinely much happier than anyone we know, having an incredible zest for life and are actually very moral and "good" people – not just any church going bod . . .' In a postscript dated 'Sunday evening, in bed with a cup of coffee and banana at my side, and outside my window hordes of brightly arrayed Tanzanian toddlers drifting back from Sunday school singing and shrieking', he added: 'One thing . . . that I have learnt is that no situation or political theory is as black and white as it might appear in print. Perhaps believing this is the first stage to cynicism. Certainly that is the worst possible disease.'

After a long disquisition on the rival claims of revolutionary socialism and Christianity he admitted that

> being a sinful old non-conformist it's more than a little hard to think of oneself as a Christian . . . at times I have felt that I am losing a socialist grip of myself . . . Sometimes I reason that Tanzanian socialism is tremendous and is the only hope for devel-opment, but that socialism in England would be wholly impracti-

cable and that we are living in an ideological cloud-cuckoo land in which England no more has a socialist future than fly in the air. Then I get to thinking that perhaps England does not need socialism at all, and that the processes of revolution would entail far more misery . . . than they are worth. And then I think there is a lot wrong; much injustice and unnecessary poverty and human suffering and that something must be done about it . . . But how? Through the Labour Party in Parliament, through the NCCL, through the CPAG, through pressure . . . and yet more words and demonstrations? and then I wonder whether in fact I am just trying to close my eyes to a too harsh and apparently insoluble reality and merely fall back into my cosy bourgeois existence and assured future . . . Don't let this frankness go beyond your eyes.

Even allowing for the pretensions of youth and the fact that Mandelson was probably trying to announce and justify his disengagement from the YCL to Howell, his letters home from Tanzania call into question assumptions that his political drive was merely careerist in origin. He read, in April, two books which exerted a strong leftwards influence: *Germinal*, Zola's epic novel about a miners' struggle, and William Morris's *News from Nowhere*. His letters from Tanzania convey a sense of a young man wrestling – quite precociously – with the choice between social democracy and its revolutionary alternatives. And by confronting the dilemma earlier than many of those who became his fellow-ministers, he may also have been helped to resolve it earlier as well, so that by the time he first became embroiled in party politics five years later he was in no doubt that he stood on the social democratic right of the Labour Party.

Keren Abse, meeting Mandelson a couple of days after his return from Tanzania, was 'absolutely gobsmacked' to find that he had been 'flirting' with Christianity. 'I remember going for a walk on [Hampstead] Heath with him and his saying that he thought he was a Christian and me being amazed . . . I don't know whether my reaction meant that he never talked to me about it ever again.' Abse's impression was that this 'disappeared within a month of him actually being back in England'. She remembers him as 'down' and 'depressed' during this period, but 'that was probably just in the way that one would be . . . I think that coming back from anywhere after a year is a sort of culture shock.' He went up to Oxford in October 1973 still somewhat preoccupied with religion. He considered joining the Christian Society and even confirmation. His failure to do so appears to have been influenced more by his distinctly irreligious friends at St Catherine's than with Abse's shock at the revelation.

Mandelson was fortunate to get to St Catherine's at all; not only did he later admit that he had not expected to be accepted, but he had also applied to St Edmund Hall by mistake, only to arrive for his interview and find to his horror that, 'it wasn't a modern college, it was a sort of thirteenth-century rowing, rugby college'. He had also been interviewed at Hertford – which he found equally distasteful: 'It was ghastly, it stank of cabbage and was really gloomy and depressing'. He eventually arrived at the far more modern St Catherine's, a little anxious about the impression he would make and eager to shine socially as well as academically. But almost within days he had become more confident, even feeling a little superior to, or at least more adult than, his fellow freshmen. His first impression was that they were dull, more interested in table football than serious discussion; the conversation had been more stimulating in the sixth form at Hendon County. While he felt a slight tinge of regret that he had not gone to – say – Balliol, he nevertheless comforted himself with the thought that the dullness could simply be the result of shyness; his new contemporaries had not yet opened up. Yet nobody 'appeared to be a thinker, or particularly interested in anything beyond their subject at the college', with the possible exception of Giles Keating, 'who will go far if only in drama'. In fact Keating became chief economist at the Crédit Suisse. Mandelson quite liked his tutorial partner Kenneth Enaharo – while noting that he 'does have a rather confident and I'm all right jack air of the specially well educated Nigerian bolstered up by his Marlborough friends. He could be quite good fun if only he wasn't elusive.' But he was relieved to find that most people in his year were not 'cool' or standoffish but quite friendly. By the end of his first week he had drunk port for the first time – and decided he wanted to work on *Cherwell*, the student newspaper.

Though he was certainly ambitious when he arrived at Oxford – 'a climber who likes to be where the action is', as he put it at the time – he did not follow the traditional Oxford path of a budding politician. For example, like Blair and Wilson, he played no part in the Union, which he found 'hurrayish' and 'deeply offputting'; he decided quite early on that he had 'neither the money, friends nor inclination' for it. This decision may have had something to do with the slightly older friends he made almost as soon as he arrived. Dick Newby, now a Liberal Democrat peer, Mike Attwell, who was gay and the son of two South African liberals who had both committed suicide, and David Cockroft, now an international trade union official, were 'very sensible, grown-up, pro-Labour, non-metropolitan grammar school people' with whom he felt instantly comfortable. All second-year PPE students, they were also rather more high-minded than the run of Oxford politicos. To Mandelson the Oxford University Labour Club was peopled by 'hacks, obsessed with running slates and stuffing ballot papers'; by contrast the Cats PPE second years seemed much more grown-up and serious. They were internationalists, active in the UN Students' Association, and a group called Young European Left. According to Newby, 'we were very anti-careerist, quite serious and after our first year not very interested in the Union, which could have influenced Peter a bit in his own hostility to it.'[2]

Mandelson's distaste for Union-centred Oxford politics did not diminish when he later met the future President of Pakistan, Benazir Bhutto, who besides being something of a *femme fatale* in Oxford's social world, was passionate about succeeding in the Union, 'shamelessly vote buying', according to one contemporary, 'taking people out to restaurants and so on', including Mandelson, who enjoyed her company, finding her 'quick and sharp'. But though he agreed to press her case with a few Cats students active in the Union, he found her tea parties to discuss Union affairs 'boring'.

To Newby, the freshly arrived Peter Mandelson appeared 'actually quite glamorous. He'd been in Tanzania and African socialism was still considered pretty exciting at the time.' The impression was reinforced when his friends learned – as they soon did – that he was Morrison's grandson, lived in 'Hampstead' and had a father who 'was a big deal on the *Jewish Chronicle*'. What's more, the new arrival was 'likeable and amusing'. For a while, rather like his father, Mandelson grew sick of his first name – there were a lot of Peters in his year at Cats – and substituted the second; most of his Oxford contemporaries knew him as 'Benj'.

By February Mandelson was running his own rather serious, half-page section in *Cherwell* entitled 'Inside Out'. But having thrown himself into the UN Students' Association, travelling frequently between Oxford and London for meetings, he failed his Politics prelims. 'I was still mentally living in Africa, when I went to Oxford,' he has subsequently said. He was busy campaigning for African causes, including one to raise £12,000 for SWAPO guerrillas in Namibia. A typical 'Inside Out' feature in February 1974 was an interview with Colin Winter, the recently deported Bishop of Damaraland in Namibia. But now, realising he could be sent down if he failed resits in the summer of 1974, Mandelson came up early and worked solidly for several weeks before term.

He had also been distracted by agitation closer to home. When, in his second month at Oxford – November 1973 – students occupied the Examination Schools in support of the campaign for a Students' Union, he covered it for *Cherwell*, contributing a breathless instant 'colour piece': 'Tension has ebbed away with the adrenalin here. The great yell of victory that accompanied the initial invasion at 2.30 this afternoon had developed into a general hubbub of voices and laughter, bottles and crockery, guitars and mouth organs.'[3] A week later he was reflecting more soberly in *Cherwell* on the implications: 'At no time must the actions of the students go beyond the political consciousness and sympathy of those on whom support is dependent,' he wrote, with a hint of Labour Party struggles to come; 'disillusion will become widespread if the supporters are led up blind alleys of militant action which, though they have great emotional and adventurist appeal, cannot lead to any reconciliation of opposing views.'[4]

Mandelson's ability to sympathise with the cause while urging moderate means to achieve it, helped to cement relations with Alan Bullock (historian and biographer of Ernest Bevin), who now returned to his mastership of St Catherine's after a spell as Oxford's Vice-Chancellor, made all the more testing by widespread student turmoil. Just as he had been on more equal terms with the teachers at Hendon County than most of his contemporaries, Mandelson now made it his business to get on with the Master. His election as JCR president clearly enhanced his own prestige in the college; but it was also, if to a lesser extent, useful to Bullock, because Mandelson was prepared to negotiate rather than merely agitate. 'Bullock was rather nervous of the undergraduate body at the college,' Mandelson said later. 'I found reassuring him as big a task as negotiating on behalf of my members.' Not all his internationalist friends approved. 'We rather looked down on his JCR activities,' said Newby. 'There was a feeling that this was just Peter cosying up to Alan Bullock.' After a student sit-in in the Senior Common Room, however, Mandelson negotiated a settlement which gave undergraduates more influence in the running of St Catherine's – and put the JCR president himself onto a new college-wide representative committee.

But in any case, Mandelson did not neglect the interests of which Newby more readily approved: 'He arrived at Cats pretty Zionist and pretty anti-European. We changed that.' He was enthusiastic about Young European Left – an organisation whose politics, according to Newby, was neither leftist nor 'Jenkinsite': 'We were sort of old fashioned social democratic mixed economy types and our position paper on Europe contained proposals for state ownership of some strategic industries.' Through YEL Mandelson also formed a close and lasting friendship with Jenny Jeger, then a student at Hull University; several of his Cats friends – including Newby – who did not know he was gay, assumed she was his girlfriend. Indeed, some contemporaries believe that Jenny herself – who died of cancer in her early forties – thought marriage to Mandelson a serious possibility.

Through the UN Students' Association Mandelson met yet another patron – Lord Caradon, Michael Foot's elder brother and a distinguished diplomat. Partly through an Arab League introduction made by Caradon, he was invited on a trip to the Middle East, financed by a Cadbury grant, during the summer vacation of 1974. Compared with Tanzania, this was travel in style. In Cairo he met Philip Adams, the ambassador, whose daughter Lucy was a contemporary.

The journey dissipated what was left of the youthful Zionism identified by Dick Newby. As from Tanzania, his letters back home show a mature and open-minded, if highly politicised, interest in what he saw and the people he met. He wrote home: 'I was particularly disappointed not to see the President's spokesman/adviser who would have been fascinating to talk to about Kissinger's pending shuttle ... It is very strange to think that Israel does not accept the entity of the Palestinians and recognize the PLO. They are so obviously an entity and "national personality" and the PLO acts in such a responsible and authoritative manner here.' 'It is such a shame that Philip Adams is returning very soon. He is a very energetic ambassador: the only FO man about whom George Brown had anything good to say about in his memoirs apparently ... I shall tell you more about this when I get home, but what is striking and very worrying is what the Arabs really think is so distorted and really not communicated at all by the British media.' From Beirut he grumbled amiably that:

> Of course, no one was at the airport to meet me and after pursuing the Ministry of Information I was finally deposited in this kind of youth hostel. It is good and cheap and despite my initial horrified reaction, I think it is preferable to a hotel. My first couple of days have been characteristically depressing: alone, not being able to contact anyone, finding Beirut rich, showy and altogether unappealing ... Much love from your ever-loving-all-English boy in this outpost of US imperialism!

Later, however, he had better news to report from Amman to 'Mama and Papa' about the Beirut leg of his trip: for one thing he had met David Gilmour (the son of Sir Ian Gilmour, later a prominent and liberal Tory cabinet minister) who was also passing through Beirut. Identifiably a young man in the Labour mainstream in this period, he recorded that in a long discussion

> we talked mainly about Oxford and British politics. He is a moderate coalitionist Jenkinsite and I was very pleased by the way I stood my ground and argued him [onto] it. He is bound to be a Tory minister one day, no doubt of the most insidious, moderate, iron fist in velvet glove kind ...

44

He met the Popular Front for the Liberation of Palestine [PFLP] chief spokesman Bassam Abu Sharif

> in his shuttered, simply lit office, surrounded by souvenirs of past deeds . . . He is himself a rather chilling person to look at because one side of his face was badly damaged by a letter bomb (no comment on the possible source.) He has rather a lot of fingers missing, but he was very civil and quietly spoken . . .

He also visited the Palestinian refugee camps in the Lebanon:

> The conditions in these camps (and I went to a good one) are as gruesome as reported. Thousands of people living in unbearably cramped conditions, although things have improved in the last five years. Of course they will not leave the camps until they are given the opportunity to return to Palestine. It is the middle-aged and younger ones who seem most committed to return to Palestine. They are good humoured, patient and with a will of steel. It is a desperate situation . . .

He lunched with the *Guardian*'s distinguished Middle East correspondent David Hirst, who was 'relaxed and forthcoming' and the most conscientious, objective, un-journalist journalist that I should think I'll ever meet.' In Amman he was granted an hour's audience with Crown Prince Hassan who, he noted, was very 'fluent and informal in his excellent Harrow and Oxford English' and 'works very hard and is the force and guiding light behind Jordan's economic development. Hassan had talked of the "corrupting influence of development, economic sharks and robber barons", which was very brave of him considering Jordan's much protected private sector'. Mandelson was very impressed by the 'very practical' and 'applied' Scientific Society, where he mentioned in passing to the economic research director the 'closeness' of the private and public sector. 'He straight away asked me whether I was a socialist and I said "Yes", and he confided that he was as well'.

Noting from his travels that 'if you are polite and friendly to everyone they will respond the whole world over, although I cannot imagine the average Londoner having much time for a wandering

Jordanian or Syrian student' – he concluded his long filial letter from Amman with a few cheerful requests:

> Don't forget to keep Tuesday 16th free to meet me at Heathrow. And I do hope you are saving all the newspapers. You might also telephone Mr Wahby of the Arab League (under M [for Middle East] in my green book) and tell him how successfully everything has been going. Presents for people are not going to be easy financially. I hope you'll understand . . . Pity you can't sight-see with me when I'm not politicking. I thought of summoning you both to Damascus by cable. It would be nice to have you here,
>
> Love, Smish.

After his tour of Israel, Egypt, Syria and Jordan, he contributed a 'Viewpoint' to the *Jewish Chronicle* which, while falling short of Attwell and Newby's emphatically pro-Arafat views at the time, argued for an independent Palestinian state on the West Bank and Gaza.

But Mandelson also had a busy social life. According to Venetia Porter who, like Keren Abse and Jenny Jeger, became a very close friend, he was 'incredibly fun-loving' for much of the time. Porter, a dark, pretty, Arabic student in the year below Mandelson's, one of the privately educated minority at Cats and uninterested in politics, was brought up in Beirut. Fresh from the French Lycée, she was in the first intake of girls to the college. Mandelson was already a dominant figure there when they met early in her first year. 'I think that was so attractive about him,' she said. 'You definitely had the sense that he was somebody quite powerful. You know what it's like at university – you gravitate towards those people who seem to be somebody, who are interesting, who you want to be with.'[5] They frequently went to parties together, but Mandelson 'hated' a May Ball at Brasenose because it was 'not our scene'. They took rock 'n' roll classes at a dancing school in Broad Street; he was a 'very good dancer. I think he got a tremendous release out of it.' In 1975, at the beginning of Mandelson's third year, they moved, along with Andrew Quartermain, an Arabic friend of Venetia's, into a house in Princes Street, east Oxford, a 'ghastly hovel'.

Mandelson was drawn into the two rather different worlds of each Porter parent (the couple had long been separated). He spent many happy weekends with Venetia's father's family at their house outside Oxford at Marcham. Robert Porter, the chief economist at the Ministry of Overseas Development, helped him to struggle through the economics revision which he found especially difficult – perhaps as a result of being put off maths at primary school. Venetia's mother was the dress designer Thea Porter. Meeting the exacting standards set by Mrs Porter for her daughter's friends, Mandelson was allowed to see something of her bohemian circle from the inside. He was invited to Venetia's dazzling twenty-first birthday party – at which all the guests had to dress as a bride or groom – at the Jardin des Gourmets, and accompanied her to the Colony, the louche drinking club of which Francis Bacon, Daniel Farson and Thea Porter were all members. It was like nothing he had seen before. And he was predictably captivated by the Colony's more outrageous habitués – including the famously rude proprietor Ian Board, and even occasionally the now ageing homosexual Labour left-winger Tom Driberg. About all this Mandelson was endlessly curious. According to Porter, 'he was always interested in knowing what was behind something ... so when, for instance, he'd be introduced to somebody, afterwards he would always want to know more about that person.' The world of Thea Porter may have given him a taste for what in another era might have been called 'Café Society'. He clearly found the Colony set, 'as we all did, I think, strangely fascinating and repellent at the same time'.

Mandelson has never romanticised his time at Oxford; rather the reverse. Indeed, he has suggested that he was not particularly happy or fulfilled there: 'you can either be a success socially, in the Union Society or academically and I fell between three stools.' Venetia Porter remembers that he was

> quite depressed for a time when we were in that house and I don't know why, but there were periods when he was quite low ... one of the things that attracted me about him was that he was terribly grown up, he was much more grown up than a lot of students, he seemed to have done a lot before he came, he was much more worldly and it may have been that this was the

problem, that he was just sort of out of step with people who were his age . . . so he wasn't really into student life particularly.

Although her relationship with Mandelson was purely platonic, she started to see him progressively less when she started going out with a graduate student, Julian Raby. 'Benj didn't like him. I don't know why. It wasn't a violent thing at all, it was just that they didn't get on very well.' This may have reflected a slight possessiveness on Mandelson's part; by Venetia's own account they had been 'very very close'.

Much later Mandelson's main regret was that he had not been more studious at Oxford. Alan Bullock thought he could have got a first instead of a perfectly respectable second – but, as Venetia put it, 'he never struck me as someone who was really, really working hard'. 'I got into a routine, a rhythm,' he said. 'I wouldn't say I revelled in it. I would have done if I had concentrated on my academic work.' What was becoming clear, however, was the extent of his political ambition. On a walk round the park at the bottom of Headington Hill one afternoon he confided in Venetia his desire for a political career. More specifically, he suggested to his friend and flatmate that he would like one day to be Foreign Secretary.

The first time Keren Abse realised how serious Mandelson was about mainstream Labour politics was when he arrived in Brighton in October 1977 in the first flush of his long-lasting – and perhaps never quite extinguished – political crush on Shirley Williams, then Secretary of State for Education and Science. It is strange that Mandelson, whose life has been intertwined with the Labour Party for so long, did not speak at a party conference until 1998. By the standards of William Hague, who first addressed a party conference at the age of sixteen, Mandelson was ancient when he first went to the rostrum. He made his first conference speech as a cabinet minister, nineteen years after he became a councillor at twenty-six and twenty-eight years after he became chairman of the Hendon Young Socialists. He had no intention of speaking at the Brighton conference. He had come on an observer's ticket – as his father had often done – and though he had many friends and acquaintances in the party, he was very much what his credential implied – on the fringe.

After the high drama at Blackpool the year before, when Denis Healey had faced a hostile, jeering audience to explain why the government had called in the IMF, Brighton was a calm, almost cordial affair.

Mandelson stayed with Keren Abse, who was living in the town after graduating from Sussex, still very much the irreverent, uncowable friend she had always been at school. Abse was again struck by a change in her old YCL comrade. This time he had caught the bug not of religion but of politics, with Labour as a party of government. And Shirley Williams – not unnaturally since among the leading cabinet ministers on the right of the party, she had, as the most crusading, passionate and, perhaps, romantic among them, the most appeal to the young – appeared to him to represent all that was good in Labour politics. He was not alone in being charmed; indeed, as Mandelson has noted, Herbert Morrison had earlier taken the young Williams under his wing – 'took her out to lunch, that sort of thing. She was in a category of her own, we all loved her'. Another British Youth Council figure of the period remembers: 'Shirley was a wonderful politician ... She used to transfix you with those eyes, she was the Secretary of State and made you feel that you were the only person in the room.'[6] Keren Abse, still well to the left of the Callaghan government, and much less impressed, argued strongly with him, but to Mandelson it was as if Shirley Williams 'walked on water ... absolutely the bee's knees'.

Abse was also struck by how seriously Mandelson took his visit – a judgement tested by a childish trick played on him by their mutual school friend Naomi Seligman, then sharing the flat.

We sort of said, 'Oh come on, you've got to take us out for a drink. Come on, take us to the Grand or something.' He was sort of hanging round the edges. So me and Naomi got dressed up to meet Peter in the Grand and Peter was obviously completely embarrassed because he really wanted to schmooze and there was us. And Naomi had put some tampons in his pocket because she thought this would be the best way to deflate his pomposity. He was so cross ... in the bar when he put his hand in his pocket.

Mandelson's seriousness was not all that surprising. He was by now in his first full-time job, working in the Economic Department of the TUC, alongside one friend from Oxford, David Cockroft, and another from Hendon County, Paul Marginson. For a young graduate already devoted to Labour it was a highly desirable job; he had been urged to apply by Alan Bullock, who was then chairing the government-established committee on industrial democracy, one of whose members was David Lea, then chairman of the TUC Economic Department. Bullock was also one of his referees, and was certainly influential in Mandelson's appointment. But he had met Shirley Williams through the British Youth Council, a mainly government funded umbrella organisation of youth groups, of which, as the representative of Young European Left on the executive, he had become vice-chairman before leaving Oxford in the summer of 1976 and, since May 1977, national chairman. He had met Mrs Williams to press the case for an expansion of further and higher education as part of a BYC delegation. The DES and the Foreign Office were the principal state sponsors of the BYC which represented organisations right across the political and social spectrum, from the Young Conservatives, Girl Guides and National Baptist Youth Assembly to the National Union of Students and the (now firmly anti-Stalinist) Young Communist League.

The BYC brought Mandelson into contact for the first time with those who, unlike him, had been active in the National Union of Students' leadership, including Charles Clarke, who became president in 1975. The NUS executive regarded themselves as the aristocrats of youth politics and Clarke thought Mandelson 'slightly envious' of them.[7] Both he and David Aaronovitch, a (then) Communist Party member whom Clarke introduced to Mandelson as the NUS's designated representative on the BYC, were contemptuous of YEL, the small body which had sent Mandelson to the BYC, and which Aaronovitch thought anyway misnamed. 'I had loads of Young European Left people at college and they were mostly on the Labour right and called themselves Left in order to distinguish themselves from the Tories who were for Europe.' To Clarke it was a 'completely fake organisation'. But Aaronovitch was struck by Mandelson's skill in the bizarre hotchpotch of organisations which made up the BYC.

[He was] a really very strange figure, in his neat V-neck jumpers. With swept over hair and his beard and moustache, and this particular look, this vulpine grin that used to come across his face whenever there was anything kind of remotely amusing . . . [but] incredibly sort of aged in political terms . . . this very neat and precise person . . . he wasn't the sort of chaotic romantic shambles that a lot of youth politicians would like to think of themselves as . . . an utterly unromantic figure, a powerbroker who understands almost viscerally, in an almost feminine way . . . what people need out of a situation.[8]

Working closely with Mandelson at the time, driving to meetings in his 'little Renault', Aaronovitch was exposed to the 'force of his charm . . . which is the single most remarkable aspect of his character. You have this man who seems to be quite an old man in organisational terms . . . who at the same time is immensely funny, attentive, malicious, witty, always has a funny story to tell everyone, and is always slightly disconcerting because there is a kind of probing.'

By the autumn of 1977 Mandelson had already more than pulled his weight in the BYC. He was a founder member of the governing body of Youthaid – a newly formed pressure group sceptical about the Labour government's job-creation programme, and with the express aim of helping those 'rough and tumble' – as Mandelson put it – young people most likely to escape the safety net of the Manpower Services Commission: those without GCSEs or CSEs. Finally he was research secretary on a BYC team and did most of the work on a report entitled 'Youth Unemployment: Causes and Cures', which attracted considerable media and public attention, and which Mandelson would often say in adult life was 'the best thing I ever did'.

Part of its flavour was Keynesian and even moderately protectionist – recommending measures to expand the manufacturing, extractive and construction industries, and making industrial planning agreements conditional on a guaranteed level of job creation per unit of investment – while stimulating the use of home-produced raw materials rather than imports. However, it also placed an emphasis on training and skills which would survive the election of a New Labour government twenty years later, albeit in a different form. It called for an independent training inspectorate to compel firms to provide training at all skill levels, fining those that did not, along with grants for all school leavers up to eighteen and an ambitious guarantee of vocational training and/or further education for the first two years of employment. Clarke was impressed by Mandelson's 'very good' work on the youth unemployment report, which was also seeking expansion of the job creation programmes being run by Geoffrey Holland, the charismatic director of the MSC. Aaronovitch recalled the 'buzz' around Holland, 'who was something of a hero to a lot of us. You could argue it was the first New Deal programme . . . public–private partnerships which will provide opportunities. And this was '77.' It was this report which would sow the seeds of Mandelson's ultimately terminal row with his employers at the TUC.

The TUC Economic Committee, which Mandelson's department serviced, had long been the most powerful. Moreover, Mandelson arrived at Congress House at a high watermark of the Committee's influence on a Labour government. Increasingly unable to rely on a parliamentary majority and desperately dependent on trade union acquiescence in its counter-inflation strategy, the 1974–9 administration was negotiating large sections of its social and economic policy with the TUC Economic Committee – or more precisely, the union leaders who sat on the National Economic Development Council, the so-called 'Gold Plated Six'. The papers produced by the Economic Department, headed by Mandelson's departmental heads, first David Lea and then Bill Callaghan, were of considerably more importance than anything similar produced either by the party or, it seemed at times, the Treasury.

Twenty years later Mandelson would tell a Unions 21 fringe meeting at the Labour Party conference that he would 'always be grateful to the TUC for the introduction they gave me to the world of trade unionism, practical politics and values of systematic filing.' And he claimed that his most formative experience at the TUC had been taking the notes of meetings, a skill which has never left him – and that his abiding memory was 'of a relationship [between government and unions] that was too close and incestuous. That ultimately did no good either to the Labour government or the trade unions and . . . because of the public perceptions that that relationship generated contributed to our loss of office for the next decade and a half.' Too many ministers, he said, were governing 'with trade union leaders perched on their shoulders telling them what to do'.

A seminal moment came when he was instructed to arrange an urgent meeting between members of the TUC General Council and Bill Rodgers, the Secretary of State for Transport, over some road haulage issue. He rang Rodgers's private secretary who explained politely that it might be difficult for Rodgers to meet the TUC that week. David Lea, overhearing the conversation grabbed the telephone from Mandelson and shouted down it, 'Can't you get it fucking clear? We need to see Bill Rodgers this week.'

Such lessons in how unions could dictate to government were learnt from the lowest possible rung of the ladder. Congress House, undeniably efficient and staffed with officials of high intellectual calibre – considerably higher than those at the Labour Party HQ at Transport House in this period, for example – was nevertheless bureaucratic and hierarchical in the extreme, its structure more or less unchanged since Walter Citrine became general secretary after the 1926 general strike. While he frequently took notes, Mandelson was much too junior to write the minutes himself. He was menial enough to be given the job of fetching visitors from reception (and fastidious enough to be horrified when, as he accompanied the Duke of Kent up in the lift, the portly and, for a future TUC general secretary, untypically informal Norman Willis wedged his foot in the closing doors, exclaimed breezily 'room for a little one' and scrambled aboard, shirt tails flying and brandishing a half-eaten meat pie). It was unheard of for any TUC official – as opposed to a union leader – other than the general secretary actually to speak at a meeting of a TUC committee as august as the Economic. And the various departmental baronies jealously guarded their own territories from each other.

Against this background, a young and recently recruited member of staff would hardly endear himself to his superiors by acquiring a public profile of his own, by using the telephones on BYC rather than TUC business, and least of all by planning to meet the Prime Minister, accompanied by TUC colleagues almost as junior as himself. Through Tom McNally, the Prime Minister's political secretary and Mandelson's principal contact at Number Ten, Callaghan had expressed an interest in discussing the BYC report on youth unemployment with its authors – an opportunity which Mandelson had every intention of grasping. In a formal internal memo his colleague David Cockroft sought the permission of general secretary Len Murray for Mandelson and himself and possibly Paul Marginson, as representatives of the BYC Working Party on Youth Unemployment, to go to Number Ten, which would require them to be temporarily absent from their desks 'during working hours' on 27 April 1977.

It is hard to think of another British institution in which permission to visit the Prime Minister at his own invitation would be anything but a formality. But the TUC, thirty-two years older than the Labour Party it had spawned, had seen prime ministers come and go; and there were other considerations, including Congress House's complex relationship with the TUC-affiliated unions. Murray scrawled a finely calibrated note of reply on the bottom of Cockroft's memo:

1. I discourage involvement of staff in public activities on subjects which are at the centre of TUC policies. If we are to participate in the activities of, and influence, outside bodies it should be through the General Council, or me acting on their behalf, deciding that there should be a formal association. If a member of the TUC staff – or I – promulgate views on matters where the TUC has laid-down policy views which are contrary to that policy, we are heading for trouble of the sort which should and can be avoided. Beekeeping is one thing; industrial relations is another.

2. It is incidental that your report, which I have read, is not only in my view good in substance but in line with TUC policy. The next one might not be

3. Having said that, but taking into account in this situation (2) and being anxious that the Prime Minister should be seen publicly as concerned about youth unemployment, I am prepared to agree – as an exception – in this case. But two people are enough; you decide which two. Please show this to Mr [David] Lea [head of the Economic Department, then abroad] on his return. LM.

Given the strict protocol of Congress House, Murray's terse reply was in fact kind and liberal. But it contained a warning note, which Mandelson (who duly went with Cockroft to see Jim Callaghan) would ignore at his peril. A week later Roy Jackson, head of the Education Department, entered the fray with a memorandum to David Lea. 'I am', he wrote, 'very disturbed that Peter Mandelson (in his capacity as vice-chairman of the BYC) is now publicly involved through "Youthaid" in "research" that aims to challenge the government's industrial strategy (that puts, in their view, too much emphasis on capital intensive projects) and also the approach of the MSC to youth unemployment.' The disparaging quotation marks spoke volumes; Jackson, now backed by Ken Graham, the TUC's assistant general secretary and representative on the MSC, was on the warpath. Lea raised the issue with Mandelson, who wrote back – in terms only slightly conflicting with Clarke's recollection of the BYC reform agenda – that his election as chairman 'marked a significant shift in the politics of the BYC, it having in the past been dominated either by Tories or the boy Scouts or other "non-political" bodies . . . being within the BYC, a political influence can be exerted which supplements the wider role and work of the Labour Party and the trade union movement.' This would no doubt have come as news to Lady Patience Baden-Powell, long a pillar of the BYC, not to mention the Young Conservatives, who were also represented on the council. Nevertheless Mandelson was correct in suggesting that he strengthened the BYC's connections to Labour. In relation to Youthaid, he insisted, 'my employment connection with the TUC has never once come into play: I would be amazed if it did.' He admitted that Murray had spoken to him 'two or three times' about the BYC but then added robustly that the General Secretary had not demanded resignation or prior knowledge of every initiative he was involved in. 'He did say, however, that if my actions embarrassed the TUC or got the TUC into trouble, my head would be on the chopping block . . . I took his response to be firm but not hostile.'

However, any notion that Mandelson might curtail his BYC activities was forlorn. In February he reported to Tom McNally that he had had a meeting with Margaret Jackson (later Beckett), a parliamentary under-secretary at the DES – whom twenty years later he would replace as Trade and Industry Secretary – about the £47,000 of government grants to the BYC, and that he had written directly to the Prime Minister criticising the education service for not doing more for non-academic sixteen- to nineteen-year-olds. Three months later a self-assured Mandelson sent McNally a letter marked 'confidential', suggesting that Callaghan should make a statement on youth policy. He might almost have been advising Neil Kinnock a decade later. The Prime Minister 'will want to be seen caring about vandalism and hooliganism,' he wrote, going on to propose a committee of enquiry into youth issues – this at least was in line with TUC policy – and a community service scheme for young people. Especially excited by this last proposal, he went on to urge that the enquiry must not be headed by an 'ageing or uninspiring minister' and, in tones which would have horrified Roy Jackson, concluded: 'You should know that the BYC is – or rather I am – playing with the idea of asking the PM to receive a young people's delegation at No. Ten.'

By now, however, the conflict of roles was becoming too much even for the tolerant Murray, who had decided that Mandelson would have to choose between the TUC and his BYC work. In early June Mandelson wrote to his immediate boss, Bill Callaghan, announcing that he intended to leave the TUC, acknowledging that both Murray and Callaghan felt that he would have to withdraw from the BYC if he was to remain at Congress House. Instead he had decided to seek another year as BYC chairman because 'there is a great need at present for political continuity in the leadership of the BYC and I am personally identified with and committed to the developments we are pushing forward in the BYC.' He had, moreover, been invited to serve on a three-year study by a Commission on Family and Social Policy, to be chaired by Sir Campbell Adamson and including among its members Frank Field, Barbara Wootton and the senior Conservative Robert Carr. Although he still believed the two jobs were compatible, he had decided 'not to make demands on your sympathy' but to look around for 'a job that will allow me to continue as BYC chairman' – adding hastily that 'I would not want to – and could not – leave until I have an alternative means of support.'

Finally, in August, he gave his notice to Murray, remarking that it had been agreed he would go on being paid until the end of September and adding that 'I do very much regret having to leave the TUC. I had intended staying here for a number of years. I have enjoyed the work and regarded it as a privilege to work for the TUC.' However, he did not yet have a full-time job to go to; indeed he had hardly had time to look. He had been fully preoccupied with the British youth movement's great adventure of the year: the trip to the World Youth Festival in Havana.

Controversy over whether the BYC should go to the festival had dogged it for several months. On the one hand it seemed to be a clear communist front, with all the delegations, including those from western countries, likely to be dominated by their (normally pro-Moscow) CPs. On the other, it might offer a spectacular opportunity for those who sought to take a stand for more liberal democratic values – particularly for the NUS leaders, who were anxious to expunge their previous huge embarrassment: in 1975, an NUS delegation, including Charles Clarke, Trevor Phillips, the NUS president, and the now distinguished television presenter Alastair Stewart, had attended a student conference in Romania; here – more by accident than by design – they had signed up to what Phillips would subsequently describe as an 'extraordinary communiqué which banged on – as these things used to – about the victory of socialism and all this bollocks, and peace solidarity and socialism, and we came back to find that David Hencke [of the *Guardian*] had written this piece saying that British students had gone and agreed to this. Major scandal.'[9] Indeed, Charles Clarke had gone to Havana with the tacit blessing of the Foreign Secretary David Owen, to work on the advance organising committee to try and stop it being a monolithic front organisation.

Mandelson was also attracted to the idea of making a pro-western stand. Having taken no part in previous NUS international delegations, he had no past mistakes to exorcise – although in 1976, when he was still at Oxford, he had gone as BYC vice-chairman to an international youth conference in Warsaw. The twenty-three-year-old British delegate launched a defence of NATO to an audience largely less than entranced to hear it. While supporting détente, he strongly attacked the cliché that it was the product of a 'world-wide peace movement'. At a time when some of the union barons on the TUC Economic Committee (soon to be his bosses) had scarcely begun to detach themselves from their embarrassingly cosy fraternal links with state union organisations in eastern Europe, Mandelson defended western criticisms of the Soviet Union against charges of 'warmongering'. He insisted that 'Détente and peace do not make us any more tolerant of anti-democratic practices and the suppression of individual freedom'; and, in a firmly multilateralist exhortation to 'the representatives here of GDR youth', he proposed they go back and tell the East German leader Erich Honecker that 'unless disarmament is mutual and balanced it will not take place'. Unsurprisingly he later rejected a suggestion that YCND should be invited to join the BYC.

Nevertheless the question of whether the BYC should send a delegation to Havana had been a highly sensitive one for many months. Indeed, it had confronted Mandelson with a personal dilemma the previous year, when his closest school friend Steve Howell, by now a full member of the Communist Party, applied for the year-long job of full-time BYC organiser for the trip. Preliminary interviews narrowed the field down to a shortlist of two – Howell and Rex Osborn, a member of the Labour Party. Between the first and second round of interviews Mandelson, never one to shirk a difficult exchange, sought his friend out and, although by common consent Howell had done the best interview, and although Mandelson himself admitted that Howell was the best person for the job, he 'made it clear in so many words that he wasn't going to back me'. Looking back, Howell said: 'To be honest I think it's fair enough. He had a political position and he stuck to it. There was not a question of sentiment in it. He was quite prepared to stick to his political position.'

In April the Young Conservatives on the BYC decided to pull out of the event on the grounds that the authorities in Havana would give no assurances on freedom of speech and that human rights were not on the agenda. The Foreign Office then withdrew its £5,000 grant and Mandelson, as BYC chairman, was obliged to defend the BYC from an attack by Bernard Levin in *The Times* for its association with 'this unsavoury enterprise'.[10] In a letter to *The Times* he made the point that it was necessary to attend precisely because the festival would otherwise be dominated by the pro-

Moscow line.[11] In June the BYC finally decided to go, approving a 'cautious and complicated resolution reiterating the militantly liberal role' to be adopted by the British delegation. *The Times Higher Education Supplement*, taking a close interest in the trip, found the decision to go ahead 'surprising' and noted that it owed much to Mandelson's 'own efforts of persuasion and it is he who stands to lose most if the Britons are prevented from stemming the tide of Marxist rhetoric that has dominated previous festivals'; he would have his 'work cut out'.[12] This last assessment was correct. The shortage of funds meant that spare places were rapidly filled up by pro-Soviet communists, or their sympathisers. While the YCL leadership was on the liberal Euro-communist wing of the party, many of the individual delegates, including Arthur Scargill's daughter Margaret, now a Yorkshire doctor, were anything but. It was clear that the delegation, which was to be chaired by Phillips, with Mandelson as his deputy, was going to be deeply split on ideological lines.

If nothing else, the ten-day visit was unforgettable – and sleepless. According to one British participant,

> Lots of people including ourselves wanted to have rather a lot of fun in Cuba and it was absolutely fantastic . . . the place was wrecked but you could go to one of those huge abandoned villas on the marina and swim off the jetty. It was like Ibiza with ideological underpinning. Sex, drugs, rock and roll and Marxism. It was great. In a way it did what it was supposed to do because a lot of us made friends, who we've still got.[13]

The British delegation slept in dormitories of fifty in a teacher training college six or seven miles outside Havana. Mandelson and Phillips were the only delegates privileged enough to share a room of their own. Meals were rudimentary and one delegate remembered obligingly going round the tables finding Mandelson some chicken bones to gnaw on. However, they were allowed to give a party amid the vast, fading, splendour of the Havana Yacht Club.

Mandelson, however, appears to have carried himself throughout with a distinctly British stiff upper lip: just before the opening ceremony the British delegation had its first ideological row over what emblem they should carry – 'we were marching out in our rather weedy T-shirts, with rings and semi-Olympic symbols'. Mandelson was adamant that it should be a Union Jack; the hard-line communists were equally strongly opposed. In the end Mandelson prevailed but then found that he was required to stand for some three hours holding it aloft while the rest of the delegation retreated to the covered spectator seats. As Phillips watched the opening ceremony in the shaded VIP area of the main sports stadium, and was introduced to Castro, Mandelson, with only a khaki sun hat for protection, sweltered in pitiless heat for most of the ceremony holding up the Union Jack 'in a very Peterish way'. He cut a memorable figure among the other highly disciplined national delegations, brandishing banners emblazoned with revolutionary or anti-imperialist slogans; the huge East German contingent, for example, held aloft giant photographs of Honecker and Castro. At one point he was greeted by a Rastafarian, who announced that he was from St Lucia; with a hint of self-parody, he turned to Tom Bell, national secretary of YCL, and asked him: 'Is that one of ours?'

The British delegation, sponsored neither by a government nor a Communist Party, had given little thought to the conference carnival. 'We had to give a sort of British performance in front of millions of people. We weren't the best performers and the delegation was totally divided in two, so the idea of pulling together and doing something jovial and artistic was pretty remote.' Mandelson helped to organise a performance of 'Yesterday', which was surprisingly so successful that 'the float was stopped in the middle of this square and we all had to come off and dance'.[14]

In any case, the pleasures of Havana were continually interrupted by an endless round of frequently heated delegation meetings – sometimes in the middle of the night – at the student hostel on the edge of the city, where the British were staying, to agree a line on the various more or less pro-Soviet bloc resolutions. Mostly Phillips and Mandelson narrowly managed to muster a liberal, counter-Stalinist majority, and one of Mandelson's jobs was then to tour the various sessions and ensure that the delegation was sticking to the line. He gave himself plenty of time for more civilised company, however: Sue Robertson, the education officer of the BYC, found herself beleaguered in the so-called 'Political Commission' – a lone voice arguing for the freedom of the Russian dissidents Orlov and Sharansky. Mandelson and Phillips swept in grandly to hear her twenty-minute speech, but then left her to withstand the angry denunciation by a queue of East European communists on her own while they went off to a cocktail party at the British embassy. Mandelson also took it upon himself to brief the journalists gathered in comfort in the bar of the Havana Hilton.

Nevertheless the pro-western stance was successful enough for Nina Temple, of the British YCL, to be denounced to her face by a Soviet Komsomol member as an 'agent of American imperialism'. Mandelson and Phillips had, moreover, managed to prevent the delegation from actually splitting in two. In Cuba, and even more at BYC meetings in London, Phillips noted presciently that Mandelson had a talent

for finding a way that everyone can stay aboard the ship. And I think that's part of the resentment that people have towards him actually. People who know him quite well know that if he does want to embrace everybody he can do. But sometimes he takes the view that the church shouldn't be that broad . . . so he says: 'I know that if I was to widen the compass a little bit further I know that I could include you, but I don't want to do that. What I want is to go faster down this road and either you get on the bus or you're with the enemy.'

Mandelson's briefing of the – mainly – British press was also effective; even Bernard Levin was prepared to admit that the delegation had more or less held its ground against the tyrannies of eastern Europe. The members of the delegation became sufficiently *personae gratae* with the Foreign Office to be invited to a reception at the British embassy at the end of the festival. The endeavour had been risky; but the risk had paid off.

# CHAPTER FOUR

## A Very Grown-Up Young Man

In the period after the Cuba trip Mandelson seemed to Nina Temple, one of the friends he made there, at once 'a very grown-up young man' and, at least in practical matters, somewhat unworldly. When he moved from temporary lodgings in Hackney into a 'bijou flat, everything totally clean', as one friend put it, at Vanbrugh Court, in Lambeth, at the beginning of 1979, with a bed in the living room which folded back into the wall, and a tiny kitchen and bathroom, she arranged for a carpenter to go over and put up some shelves 'because he really didn't know about things like that'.[1] However, he took an 'avuncular' interest in her welfare, and she was struck by the distinctly adult, almost middle-aged atmosphere at a birthday party he gave at Bigwood Road. Nina Temple had arrived, armed with bottle of plonk and pot plant, to find a 'posh dinner' for ten guests, including the ex-ambassador to Laos, a local Labour Party member. 'The dinner conversation was: "Oh do you remember Nye saying this, and so and so saying that?" It really gave me the feeling that Peter had been brought up to rule the country really which I think he fairly clearly wanted to do already by that stage.' The chosen venue also illustrated a point noted by another friend at the time: that Mandelson in his mid-twenties did not have 'the antagonistic relationship with his parents that most of us had, particularly not with his mother'.

It was nevertheless an uncertain period, as it was for some of Mandelson's other contemporaries, including Charles Clarke. The problem was not filling his time: he was an efficient, high-profile

BYC chairman. He and Phillips, who as president of the NUS worked closely with him, 'enjoyed the plotting, it was good fun. It was great to be able to say: "OK, we have a meeting of the council next week and we have to persuade the Guides to do this or that. OK, it's your turn to ring up Patience Baden-Powell and tell her that the Guides really ought to come out in favour of a new allowance to battle against youth unemployment." '[2] He was energetic about following through initiatives, whether it was lobbying MPs on the council's proposal for mandatory grants for sixteen- to eighteen-year-olds staying in education – anticipating, as it happened, Gordon Brown's thinking nearly twenty years later – or attacking an eleventh-hour decision by the Home Secretary William Whitelaw not to open a BYC exhibition at the House of Commons on 'Young People Working for Racial Harmony' and claiming his withdrawal was because of an advance press release critical of the government's immigration policy. For all the criticisms made by those on the left of Mandelson's political stance, he has never been accused of being anything but strongly anti-racist.

More difficult was finding a tangible means of support. He applied for a BBC general traineeship, but failed at the final board. He secured the funding to carry out two impressively solid pieces of research work. One, financed by the Calouste Gulbenkian Foundation, was on 'Young People and Broadcasting'. The other, returning to one of Mandelson's favourite themes, was a comparative study of youth unemployment in Britain, Germany, France and Sweden, for the Aspen Institute for Humanistic Studies, which concluded that 'make good and mend' policies could not deal with the problem, that education and training systems would need a radical overhaul and that ways should be found of funding young people's enterprises, possibly in the form of small entrepreneurial cooperatives.[3]

None of this, however, was enough to satisfy his political appetite. His move to Lambeth from Hackney in early 1979 appears to have marked a turning point. It is hard not to see this as some kind of semi-conscious homage to his grandfather's roots: Lord Morrison of Lambeth had been born in the borough, at Ferndale Road, Brixton, and had attended the Stockwell Board School. It even seems to have represented some belated acceptance that Morrison was indeed his grandfather. Charles Clarke felt that he had 'suppressed' his blood relationship with Herbert Morrison and urged him to 'tell the truth' about it. He remembered going to a party at the flat not long after he had moved in. Tom Ponsonby, then general secretary of the Fabian Society, and a close neighbour, was one of the guests. Finding that photographs and cartoons of Morrison were indeed now decorating the walls. Clarke speculated that 'Herbert Morrison no doubt treated his mother very, very badly . . . I mean he loves his mother . . . deeply and there's something about Herbert Morrison's relationship with his mother which in a sense he will never . . . forgive [while he] admires him immensely.' In fact his mother, who had been teased at school because of her famous father, had urged Peter to keep quiet about him; moreover she strongly disapproved of the idea of 'trading' on his name.

Certainly, he began in Labour politics, just as Morrison had done, by seeking a seat as a borough councillor, in the local authority which had already forged the career paths of at least two other, very different politicians who were to rise to national prominence in the 1980s: John Major and Ken Livingstone. Both had by now left the council, which after the elections of 1978 had seen a takeover by the far left when Ted Knight replaced David Stimpson, a moderate, Croslandite figure, whom Livingstone had admired for his professional competence, as leader of the ruling Labour Group. Despite his fearsome reputation 'Red Ted' Knight was also a competent politician – and in some ways a surprisingly amiable man – but ideologically a conscious vanguardist, backed by an alliance of Bennites and Trotskyites, who supported his consistent policy of raising both spending and council tax rates, and helped to propel him to national notoriety as leader of the most left-wing council in Britain. A particularly virulent Trotskyite sect, with links to the International Marxist Group, was in control of Princes, the ward in which Mandelson lived, when he moved into the borough. This was not untypical of the Vauxhall parliamentary constituency which included Princes, which until 1979 had been represented for half a century by the same MP, George Strauss, and which in the words of one activist at the time was 'full of fairly deranged people'.

But in late 1979 there was a vacancy in the relatively isolated Stockwell ward; here the party was much more mainstream and the two remaining councillors, Paul Ormerod and Patrick Mitchell, were on the centre right of the Labour Party. By now Mandelson was already attending meetings of the beleaguered mainstream Labour moderates in the constituency party; they met in a local pub to discuss the urgent question of who might run in the by-election. 'We were desperate to find some sensible person to stand and Peter Mandelson volunteered to do it.'[4] The candidate's election address was unexceptional, given that by now Lambeth's conflict with the new Tory government over service cuts had already begun: 'living in Vauxhall,' he said, 'I am aware of the many problems which the area faces – poor housing, lack of employment and inadequate amenities'; 'to solve the problems in this area, in common with those throughout the area we need more resources not less'; he would 'join the Labour council in fighting for more money for the Borough to meet our needs'. The local MP Stuart Holland gallantly appeared with the candidate on polling day to help ensure a reasonable turnout.

Mandelson's interventions in full council meetings – at least initially – were relatively sporadic and unexciting by the standards of a council in which it was possible without irony to applaud the choice of Queen Boadicea as the theme of the 1980 Notting Hill Carnival as 'a laudable celebration of the struggle of an indigenous population against colonisation and imperialism'.[5] His rebellions against the whip were reasonably rare: the council minutes record that he voted against the imposition of an unpopular compulsory purchase order in February 1982 and abstained on only a handful of occasions – though at least twice on key issues: in early 1981 on the council's imposition of a supplementary rate after a protest meeting which, the Tories claimed, had been attended by 3,500 angry residents (Knight put the figure at just 200); and on an opposition proposal to make some expenditure reductions to stave off the looming crisis over rates. But to revolt at all was quite dramatic; most frequently he, like all his colleagues across the left–right spectrum, voted loyally with the Labour Group – even when it switched its bank account to the more expensive Co-op in protest at Barclay's links with South Africa, and when in March 1981 it amended a resolution congratulating Prince Charles and Princess Diana on their engagement. A sentence wishing the couple 'every future happiness' was substituted by one hoping 'that the common problems of newly weds – unemployment, housing waiting lists, high mortgage rates and soaring inflation – do not detract from their future happiness'.

Indeed, Mandelson joined about 100 other Labour researchers, activists and staff in avoiding the Royal Wedding celebrations by taking a ferry trip to Boulogne on the public holiday which marked them. The man who would become famous as the only Cabinet member to be invited to Prince Charles's fiftieth birthday party seventeen years later, posed exuberantly in a NUPE T-shirt for a group photograph aboard the ferry. Frank Johnson, who travelled with the party as a journalist, captured the festive mood of the occasion in *The Times*: 'Sympathetic officials of the town's socialist mayor set up a reception centre to receive the refugees. Those Britons who succeeded in getting across the Channel – which is policed by the notorious Royal Navy, itself a tool of the Windsors – were given beefsteak, fries and plonk on the mayor's budget.' Mandelson was in good company: he had been joined not only by his friend Sue Nye, who worked successively for Neil Kinnock and Gordon Brown, and the future trade union moderniser, Jack Dromey, but also by an old friend of Blair's, Alan Haworth, a future secretary of the Parliamentary Labour Party, who cheerfully proclaimed himself to Johnson to be part of the 'bed-sit brigade' which had ousted the ultra right-wing Labour MP Reg Prentice from the Newham North-East constituency.

Even had Mandelson wanted to rebel more frequently against the more left-wing resolutions of the council, it would have been high risk to do so and would have been to invite almost certain expulsion from the Labour Group. The climate in Lambeth at the time was such that when the left-wing local MP Stuart Holland went to the Vauxhall General Management Committee, seeking, in the manner prescribed by the left-wing Campaign for Labour Party Democracy, a 'mandate' on how to vote in the 1980 leadership contest, it would have been unthinkable to propose Denis Healey. The Labour centre-right, including Mandelson, opted for Foot. According to Paul Ormerod, their stance at the time was anyway slightly more main-stream than the most overtly centrist and élitist elements of the party: 'We didn't have much time for metropolitan Jenkinsite think-ing.' This was only partly true. Suspicions of Jenkins at this time fitted with Mandelson's Morrisonian heritage. Morrison, while determinedly on the anti-Bevanite right of the party, was working class in origin, and did not have much time for Hugh Gaitskell, whose mantle Jenkins could be said to have inherited, and who had eclipsed him in the battle for the Labour leadership in 1955. On the other hand, Mandelson was enthusiastic about both Shirley Williams and Bill Rodgers, the other two leading social democrats in the Labour Party.

In the Labour Group Mandelson nevertheless became well known for his willingness to slug it out with the right's Trotskyist opponents in the 'surreal world' of inner London Labour at the time, reminiscent, says Ormerod, of 'the CPSU in the thirties – ordinary branch meetings at which members were denounced as enemies of the people'. This was not a time when it was fashionable to be young, on the right, and provocatively pressing, as Ormerod and Mandelson were, for One Member One Vote democracy in the party – a prescription also denounced as 'anti-socialist'. Indeed, it was a period when many party members unsympathetic to the hard left nevertheless held their tongues. But in meetings, which were often abusive on both sides, 'Peter didn't give a damn what he said. He stood his ground very strongly. He was firm, he argued his case well, and Knight respected him. He was a proper politician, not a backroom operator.'[6]

Oddly relaxed about fraternisation with his councillors, Knight graciously invited both men to a party at his house; here they noted with pleasurable surprise that one entire room had been laid out and decorated as in a pub, with low tables, bar and bar stools. But as his twenty-nine-month tenure on the council wore on, Mandelson increasingly attacked Knight in the press. After the Brixton riots in April 1981, the Lambeth leader called for the police, using the 'same apparatus of surveillance that one sees in concentration camps', to withdraw from Brixton. Mandelson, while also criticising heavy-handed policing, remarked that 'given the choice between having the Labour Party and Ted Knight in the borough or the police, 99 per cent of the population would vote for the police'. He accused Knight of 'screaming and raging and saying the most bizarre things', threatening Labour's vote in the imminent GLC elections, and shouting at the new divisional police commander – a charge subsequently denied by Knight. He added: 'Basically I'm a supporter of much that Ted stands for – after all he's given me an important position within the council. But he's a Jekyll and Hyde figure.'

His disloyalty did not go unpunished. He lost his 'important position' – vice-chairman of the planning committee – when its chairman, Liz du Parcq, was ousted from the post for voting against Knight as Labour leader. If anything this stiffened Mandelson's resolve. By August the 'Stockwell Three', Mitchell, Mandelson and Ormerod, were anyway in open revolt, having written to *Labour Weekly* warning that the local party 'has conspicuously failed to convince its electorate that maintaining its high level of expenditure is desirable or practical. The publicity-seeking statements of the council's leader have come to symbolise the waywardness and irrelevance of the Labour Party for working class people.' In November 1981, when Knight dismissed the Scarman report on the Brixton riots, Mandelson put a motion to the Labour Group urging that the 'radical and useful' Scarman findings at least be discussed in forthcoming meetings with central government on Lambeth race relations. It was defeated, but by only ten votes to nine. He also led the revolt against Knight's 'suicidal' refusal to draw up a budget within the terms of the new Local Authority Bill.

Mandelson was considered an important enough local figure to be invited by *Streatham Forward*, the Labour Party newsletter in the neighbouring constituency, to explain his arguments in November 1981, which he did in robust terms, arguing that 'our Labour Party faces unprecedented danger' from Michael Heseltine's new bill 'as the opportunity approaches for the electorate to catch up on Ted Knight's administration'. Instead of risking bankruptcy, the surcharging of councillors, and the dismissal of large sections of the workforce, the council should sanction no new expenditure, cut waste and seek the 'vital' cooperation of trade unions in the non-replacement of non-essential staff. Those who wanted all-out confrontation with Heseltine were 'kamikaze pilots'.

Two events of crucial importance to Mandelson's career had already taken place. In the early autumn of 1980 he had finally got a job, working for the Shadow Transport Secretary Albert Booth. To Mandelson's evident satisfaction, after trying to secure a post with Neil Kinnock, which went to his friend Charles Clarke, he had

arrived, in however humble a capacity, at Westminster. His appointment had been approved by John Prescott, Booth's deputy. Booth,
a kindly and self-effacing man, on the Tribunite left of the party,
who had been Employment Secretary in the Callaghan government,
always intended that the post should be partly financed out of union
money. Two Labour front benchers, both of whom were to become
important in Mandelson's life – though in strikingly different ways
– used their good offices to persuade the National Union of Rail-
waymen and the Transport and General Workers' Union (then
locked in various conflicts with each other) not to make Mandelson's salary a casualty of their in-fighting: one was Prescott; the
other was Geoffrey Robinson.

Mandelson liked Robinson from the start; he was an 'ideas man',
relatively dynamic as a Transport whip, and would quite often go
out for a drink or a meal with the junior members and staff of the
Shadow Transport team, including Rosie Winterton and the front
bench MP Roger Stott. Mandelson saw much less of him after
Robinson withdrew from front-line politics – while remaining an
MP – to build up his business TransTec. Mandelson remembered
Robinson telling him he had to 'go and make some money'.

The new job also brought him into close contact with David Hill
and, through him, with Hill's boss Roy Hattersley. Hill was the
doyen of the researchers on the shadow cabinet corridor, having
worked for Hattersley in government, and both he and Hattersley
took an avuncular interest in the new young recruit. Hattersley
recalls that Mandelson initially found it difficult to work with John
Prescott: 'We used to laugh about it because we thought they were
temperamentally rather dissimilar. And Peter then was a rather retir-
ing youth in a sweater – he never wore a suit – sweater, little
moustache, and always seemed to be in a state of daze and unhappiness.'[7] Friends of John Prescott also remember them as anything
but soul mates – though they point out that Prescott's office was
some way away from Booth's on the shadow cabinet corridor and
that contact between them was fairly limited. According to Hill,
Mandelson was 'obsessive about politics, of the Labour Party first
and last'. While 'he never made any pretence of being anything
other than on the right', and although he sometimes found Prescott
exhausting, 'I think he had this view that John was more significant

than people then realised. They somehow managed to charm one another.'[8] Indeed, Mandelson may have had a higher regard for Prescott than Prescott had for him. He invited this undoubtedly rising star of Labour's front bench to a party at his Lambeth flat, and when he left to work for LWT he used to write to Prescott from time to time with unsolicited advice on how the party might improve its image. Prescott 'noted' the letters, according to one of his colleagues at the time. Charles Clarke, an ally of Booth's and fellow Foot-supporter, also remembers Mandelson's relations with Prescott as being warmer than might have been expected; when they fell out much later, particularly towards the end of the eighties, 'Prescott felt betrayed because he got on with Peter earlier in life'.

It was through Hattersley, however, that Mandelson joined the Solidarity Group, a right-wing counterweight to the Bennite left; he secured his mentor as star speaker at a Solidarity meeting in Brixton town hall, at which the former cabinet minister graciously said that it was an 'honour to speak in the presence of Herbert Morrison's grandson'. Hattersley recognised Mandelson – by then well over his period of Morrisonian denial – as a 'bright young lad on his side'.[9] Mandelson would later reciprocate by working on his leadership campaign in 1983.

Mandelson's membership of Solidarity also helped him to resist the temptations offered by the Social Democratic Party, formed by the 'Gang of Four' in March 1981. That his idol Shirley Williams should be one of the gang was a blow, but it was not enough to persuade Mandelson to follow the spring exodus into her new party. Writing cheerfully to Tom Shebbeare in March, apologising for his handwritten letter to 'you people in the electric typewriter set', he grumbled about the unions' failure to stump up his funding – particularly the white-collar TSSA, who were 'now playing games saying their political fund is a little dicey which is strange considering that they are not continuing to bear the burden of Tom Bradley's sponsorship money' (Bradley had defected to the SDP). Otherwise he seemed to be the model Labour shadow minister's researcher. He was excited by his work on the Transport Bill, which had been guillotined the previous week, and boasted that 'having read through the countless guillotine precedents I wrote a marvellous outline for Albert, full of inflamed passion, sound argument and political bitching, a fraction of which you can read in Hansard'.

His letter also gives a flavour of the febrile mood at Westminster at the time: 'Otherwise I am spending my time having endless social democratic arguments and post mortems. I have joined Roy Hattersley's Solidarity Campaign to fight, fight and fight again for the Party we love, although I am sure the Party will never be the same again (and perhaps shouldn't be).' He and his friend Sue Robertson had talked to Shirley Williams at the house of another mutual friend:

> I must say I still adore Shirley but I emerged quite confident and confirmed in my Party loyalty. However she was kind enough to say she would keep a place warm for me . . . Charles Clarke has been intolerably self-righteous about Sue Slipman's move* and wrote a thoroughly disloyal letter to the *Guardian* which was not published. I was furious but we're best friends again. He's working part-time for Neil Kinnock, the Education spokesman, which is nice.

But defections by those nearer to home than Shirley Williams, Sue Slipman or, for that matter, Sue Robertson had to be considered, too. One of his close friends in the Vauxhall Labour Party, Roger Liddle, a neighbour at Vanbrugh Court, also joined. In July the Liberals and the SDP each took a seat in by-elections, provoking Mandelson himself to comment that 'Labour has got to learn the lesson that what we say and do needs to be responsive to the people who vote for us . . . The writing is on the wall for the Labour Party. These results cannot be put down to the media, or famous candidates, or razzamatazz.'[10]

Around September three further members of the group, David Stimpson, Malcolm Noble and, perhaps most significant, his fellow Stockwell ward councillor Patrick Mitchell, defected. Mandelson and Ormerod, doing almost nightly battle with the Lambeth Trots, understandably began to feel isolated, and discussed in deepest privacy whether they too should join. Mandelson had also talked to

---

* Sue Slipman had once been a Communist Party member and had subsequently joined the SDP.

two other friends, Elinor Goodman, then a lobby correspondent on the *Financial Times*, and her husband Derek Scott, who did subsequently join and is now an economic adviser to Tony Blair. Both Scott and Mandelson seriously discussed the matter with John Lyttle, Shirley Williams's popular and respected adviser. Scott was temporarily talked out of joining by Denis Healey, for whom he had worked, and the moment passed. By this time Tony Benn had decided to challenge Healey for the deputy leadership. The outcome of the contest, to be decided at the Brighton conference at the end of September, would be a decisive turning point in the history of the party. Ormerod and Mandelson agreed to do nothing until then.

From here on, recollections differ somewhat. Mandelson claims that, once Healey had emerged the victor – albeit by the tiny margin of 50.426 per cent to 49.547 – he abandoned any idea he might have had of joining the SDP – apart from, at one point, mulling over with David Hill the fantastical idea that a majority of the Labour Party might somehow defect and 'take over' the new party. At the conference he remembered standing at the back of the conference hall with key figures on the Labour right, including George Robertson and Mary Goudie (whom he would recommend for a peerage sixteen years later when Labour next came to power again); when the result came through, tangible relief flowed through the company. Certainly, it was decisive in preventing a large-scale haemorrhage of MPs and activists out of the party. Most informed estimates at the time indicated that perhaps eighty, rather than only thirty, MPs would have defected, and Terry Duffy, president of the Amalgamated Union of Engineering Workers, the country's second biggest union, had hinted to Shirley Williams that it would disaffiliate from Labour. Beyond that the domino effect was utterly unpredictable. For the moment that slender 0.879 of the conference vote had secured, if not the Labour Party's continued survival, at least a chance to fight another day.

According to Ormerod, however, while in the event of a Healey defeat 'we would have all [including Mandelson] have gone [to the SDP] . . . we hadn't really decided that if Healey won, especially if he won by a very narrow margin, we would stay'. He recalls speaking to Mandelson about joining the SDP *after* the party conference;

one Sunday later in the year he had a further significant conversation with John Lyttle. Roger Liddle, he remembers, was planning a party (the Lambeth political scene was nothing if not highly socialised), to which he had invited both Ormerod and Mandelson: their attendance would mark their defection, and their joining of the SDP would immediately be announced through a local press release.

This scenario would not have been totally unlikely. There were strongly Pyrrhic elements to Healey's victory, best summed up by Tony Benn himself in his diary entry for 27 September: 'It was the best possible result, because if I had won by 0.8 per cent people would have shouted cheat. It only requires four or six Labour MPs to join the SDP for Healey's majority to disappear, and then he will hold the post but not have the authority.'[11] In fact, in the months after the 1981 conference nine Healey supporters from the PLP joined the SDP, including Mandelson's former contact in Jim Callaghan's office, Tom McNally. A few days before the Liddle party, however, the two councillors got 'cold feet', according to Ormerod, never went to the party, and remained Labour members.

According to a third version, Roger Liddle's, Ormerod and Mandelson had different agendas, in that Ormerod planned to remain on Lambeth Council and was therefore thinking about re-election. Liddle had been applying pressure on him to decide because they needed to draw up a list of SDP candidates by soon after Christmas – 'which is the significance of the New Year party'.[12] Ormerod filled in a membership form, gave it to Liddle and, when he changed his mind, went back to Liddle and said: 'Look I've decided I can't go through with it, will you tear it up and not tell anybody.' Mandelson, by contrast, did not fill in a form, although Liddle had several conversations with him about the SDP:

I don't think it's an outrageous thing to say if Benn had won Peter would have ended up in the SDP but ... his first instinct was that you should do your best and try to save the Labour Party ... Peter had pretty well decided he was going to get out of Lambeth, that it was an absolute nightmare and I never discussed with Peter in the way that I discussed with Paul the possibility of him becoming an SDP candidate because I never thought that Peter wanted that ... I always thought his first instincts were to see how things worked out. I personally think Peter was very pessimistic about the Labour Party and didn't think much could be done about it. I think he was loyal but pessimistic . . . and that he never bore any ill will to people who did join the SDP.

Never, that is, until after the 1983 election, when he began to think of a return to politics. Indeed he did little to discourage his friend Sue Robertson from joining – and had no qualms about buying a house with her in Clapham after she had joined.

In 1989 there was a coda to Liddle's New Year party. Liddle was on holiday with his wife Caroline, then at Channel Four, and their young son, visiting Perugia for the Prix Italia. He was woken up by a telephone call from the journalist Peter Lennon compiling a *Guardian* profile of Mandelson in the run-up to the Hartlepool selection:[13] was it true, he was asked, that Mandelson had nearly joined the SDP? Liddle emphatically denied the story, which would have been much more damaging then than it is now.

It is anyway questionable how far the details matter, given that joining a party is, in political terms, a supremely existential act, and that Mandelson neither left the Labour Party nor joined the SDP. Liddle's guess at Mandelson's pessimism, however, was certainly correct. In a series of musings over the next few months he reflected at length on the party's weaknesses and uncertain future. In a note to Albert Booth, he sought to awaken the old-fashioned Tribunites to the threat posed by Tony Benn and his followers. The so-called 'Alternative Economic Strategy' pursued by Benn – and his own MP Stuart Holland – was 'collectivist bunkum', he said. The support of young people who were not right-wingers was at risk; 'if Benn holds sway' and the Tribunites fail to stand up to the 'kamikaze left' they would have to find a new party: 'This is the politics of realignment and I could not say what will be the outcome of these shifting sands.' Drawing on his vivid experiences at Lambeth he warned that councils which put themselves above the law would lead to the disintegration of services and the loss of public service jobs, and make things difficult for Tribunite councillors. Mandelson's pitch was not anti-union. Indeed, he was worried that the SDP would exploit the unions' reduced dependence on Labour, and remarked – somewhat in contrast to his retrospective memories of his time at the TUC – that the 1976–8 period of the Social Contract was 'the strongest period of Labour government and strategic success for the trade union movement yet'. The pay policy of that period contained inflation and saved the Labour government.

This line does not seem to have been purely for the benefit of the Tribunite Booth. In more private correspondence a month or two later Mandelson said that 'social democrats [with a consciously lower case 's' and 'd'] in the Labour Party [among whom he clearly counted himself] remain committed to a strong trade union movement because this movement is a pillar of any democratic and free society and because in a capitalist society the collective organisation of workers remains essential.' Nevertheless Michael Foot, while brave in trying to stand up to Tony Benn, had been 'like a cork, tossed around on choppy seas . . . the leader who came too late, to the wrong job, and stayed too long'.

Although he privately acknowledged that the SDP might in the long run turn out to be a 'Labour Party Mark II' – something that Roy Jenkins strongly denied – Mandelson did indeed seem settled in his decision not to join when so many of his friends had done so. For the time being, however, he had had his fill of active Labour politics. Right at the end of 1981, indulging a habit of New Year political introspection which would stay with him for many years, he wrote – but did not send – a letter of resignation, not from the party, but from Vauxhall's GMC, lamenting the growing and unrepresentative influence of IMG, Militant, etc. on the GMC, and describing the policy of bankrupting the council as 'crazy and totally hostile to the interests of working people in Lambeth'; he added that, sad as he was to say it, 'being in my family's third generation of active Labour Party membership', he simply did 'not want to associate myself with these policies or their authors any more'.

But while he did not send the letter, he was clearly ready at least to put his ambitions on hold. One day at Westminster, when parliament was out of session, he walked into the empty Commons Chamber with Ormerod. 'It's a great pity neither of us will be able to sit on these benches,' he said, turning to his friend, who inferred that he was saying the social democrats in the Labour Party – like him – were finished. As he would recall in 1985, with his 'profound doubts' about the party he had had two choices: to join the SDP or to escape temporarily from politics. Having discarded the first option, he now looked round for a means of achieving the second.

# CHAPTER FIVE

# *The New Mood*

Mandelson's chosen escape was through what Charles Clarke would always afterwards refer to a little dismissively as the 'media route'. In January 1982 he wrote to Barry Cox, head of News and Current Affairs at London Weekend Television, asking for a job. The coincidence that Cox was already one of Tony Blair's closest friends could not have been less relevant. Mandelson and Blair had not even met in 1982. Rather more relevant was the fact that the department which Cox headed, one of the most innovative in British television at the time, was expanding. Not only that, but it was unusually willing to recruit its staff from outside journalism. In his letter of application Mandelson emphasised his work of 'political liaison research, media and administrative activity' for Albert Booth, his experience at the TUC and his continuing links 'specifically with trade unions'. The defeat of the miners was still two years away; that of the print workers at Wapping would not happen for another four. Knowledge of the trade unions was therefore at a high premium with editors ready to exploit it. Also topically, he made the point that he had been 'involved in local government and inner city issues as a member of Lambeth Council', adding, 'I believe that this background in political affairs could make me suitable for LWT.'

Of course, Mandelson had hoped to go to *Weekend World*, the upmarket flagship programme presented by Brian Walden. He and David Aaronovitch had both written independently seeking jobs and both went before a stiff interview panel – 'LWT boards were like going to a viva at Oxford,'[1] one LWT man would later recall

– of senior executives, including Hugh Pile, the editor of *Weekend World*, and Jeremy Bugler, the editor of the *London Programme*. With some help in preparation the night before from Samir Shah, his old Oxford friend who now worked on *Weekend World*, and Trevor Phillips, who was working on LWT's *Black on Black*, he performed creditably enough to be hired. But it was Aaronovitch who got the one job at *Weekend World*, and Mandelson was sent to the *London Programme* as a researcher. It was still a privileged apprenticeship for someone wholly unversed in television. He was part of a smaller staff than he would have been on *Weekend World*, and Bugler was a first-class editor. Mandelson was part of a team of researchers working for seven weeks on a network LWT documentary series on modern politics, and was given some 'off screen interviewing and script writing' to do. He had an 'encouraging' mid-year management review. By the spring of 1983 his full researcher credits had included an investigation into Metropolitan Police attempts to shake off its reputation for not taking burglary seriously enough. He also, improbably, undertook some old-fashioned, foot-in-the-door journalism: his LWT colleague Trevor Phillips remembers 'this great moment of Peter doorstepping this bunch of corrupt landlords, and the guy is driving out of his driveway in his car and Peter is rushing after him saying: "What about these slum flats?" '[2] Come the 1983 election, however, he was put full time on the team covering the three-way fight between the Tories, the Alliance and Labour in the 'vital killing grounds' – as the *TV Times* blurb put it – of London and the South-East. This gave him a bird's-eye view, at least in one region, of a Labour campaign which would be acknowledged as easily the worst organised of any, before or since.

Within a year, however, he was restless. He applied for a job as a Westminster political correspondent for Granada Television; while he was enjoying his present job, he wrote, 'I would like the pressure of more reactive factual reporting. I am especially keen to report from Westminster because it is the hub of politics and where most political excitement is generated.' With a nice sense of party political balance he cited as referees Peter Shore, Shirley Williams and David Hunt, the left of centre Tory whom he had met through the BYC. It is interesting to speculate that if he had got the job he might have had a career as a lobby correspondent, rising to become a political editor subjected to daily harangues from some alternative 1980s Peter Mandelson. Instead he was offered a job at *Weekend World*.

*Weekend World*, where Mandelson worked first as a researcher and then as a producer, was unlike anything else in broadcast journalism. Although Hugh Pile was now the editor, and David Cox the head of Current Affairs, it had been the brainchild of John Birt, later Director-General of the BBC, a salesman's son from Bootle who had read engineering also at St Catherine's, Oxford and co-edited *World in Action* before he came to LWT, where he was Director of Programmes when Mandelson made his application. Birt's mission to explain, which became one of the prevailing creeds of the programme, flowed at least in part from a candid self-assessment unusual among senior broadcasters. At *World in Action* 'We'd made vivid programmes about Northern Ireland but I knew I didn't understand it; and I knew I understood nothing about foreign affairs, and I became mildly obsessed by the fact that I didn't understand what was going on in the economy.'[3] If a highly intelligent, well-educated current affairs broadcaster found himself in this position, was there not an audience for a programme which sought to deconstruct the issues which dominated the news? As an ex-engineer Birt had been especially intrigued by an edition of *World in Action* made by a journalist called Stephen Clark which tackled the question of why British Rail had had a run of accidents with the 'short wheel-based wagon'. 'It was the first programme that I had been involved with or had seen which took a knotty and complicated problem that normally we would not have tackled ... and told it in a very clear way, using models and graphics. He managed to get the story over and that gave me a lot of pause for thought.' Some of the same analytic energy, Birt thought, might be applied to politics.

The programme had some irritating characteristics. A contemporary account described the rather arch way in which members of the team would converse: 'Good morning, how is one?' and after a read-through: 'Thank you, Brian, that was a thing of beauty and a joy for ever.'[4] The production team took themselves very seriously. Walden was a famously skilful interviewer, adept at extracting a news story for the Monday newspapers, often hungry for a political lead. But as television it was often less than riveting. It was heavily scripted, and invariably consisted of an interview with a leading politician, preceded by a section, as the presenter himself put it, 'preparing the viewer for the interview by providing him with the understanding of where a particular politician is at on a given subject within a rigorously logical framework'.[5] The programme tended to favour a binary approach to political decision-making, summed up by a programme-maker describing an interview with Neil Kinnock in the early 1980s: 'The *Weekend World* proposition is that the Labour leader is always trapped between the public and the party, competing demands, trying to please the trade union activists, the party machine, the voter.'[6] This was true, but 'competing demands' were also *Weekend World*'s stock-in-trade: programmes began with an exegesis of how, if a politician did A, then B (positive) and C (negative) would follow. But if he did X, then Y and Z. And If Z happened . . . All this was in line with Birt's dictum that television should show a 'bias against misunderstanding'. That did not stop one LWT wit nicknaming the programme 'Game for a Dilemma'.

The first half was usually compiled with the help of outside commentators and specialist journalists, first to give an opinion to the programme-makers and then, in theory, to repeat it for the viewer in short interviews. But because the programme was tightly scripted to lay out the rival consequences of alternative political decisions, the journalists, while flattered to be asked to appear, were often disconcerted to arrive at some luxurious hotel room for their interview and find that their contribution had already been written for them. Peter Mandelson or one of his other young colleagues would be there, clipboard in hand, using all his skill and charm to persuade the contributor to say something as close as possible to what was already ordained in the script. Sometimes the contributors found themselves saying things which fitted in with the remorseless internal logic of the programme but not with the messy world of real facts. Thus an industrial correspondent might, during the miners' strike, find himself predicting that the government would use troops to beat the strike when he knew that such an option was highly unlikely. The columnist Peter Jenkins was only one of a number of pundits and journalists, who decided to stop appearing. 'I found myself resisting the storyline,' he said at the time; 'unless I said what they wanted me to, I ended up on the cutting room floor.' Part of the problem was that 'one is led into saying what one doesn't quite believe'.[7] As early as 1980 a Labour MP, Mike Thomas, had also refused to take part in the programme again and told *The Listener*, 'they keep on doing the interview again and again until I have said what they want me to say'.[8] Under the article was a cartoon showing a menacing-looking researcher; his clapperboard said WEEKEND WORLD. TAKE FIVE and he was leaning over a scared-looking interviewee saying, 'We have ways and means of making you say what we want.'

Nevertheless journalists had the advantage of being much more accommodating than politicians. Robin Paxton, the deputy editor of the programme, of whom Mandelson became first a protégé and then a close friend, would tell a good story about going to interview the PLO leader Yasser Arafat for *Weekend World*. If the Americans did such and such, Arafat was asked, what would the PLO then do? But the Americans aren't going to do that, Arafat replied. Yes, but *if* they did. But they're not, are they? Was there something, Arafat asked impatiently, that the producers knew and he didn't? He was failing to play the *Weekend World* game.

It is tempting to see this as an early opportunity for Mandelson to discover his formidably persuasive powers with the press. But he was by no means the most zealous researcher or producer in sticking to the script. Michael Wills, the LWT producer who became an MP in the 1997 election, had a reputation for being especially tenacious. It was certainly an object lesson in the extent – and limits – of journalistic malleability. However, there were other, possibly more fundamental, lessons to be learned from *Weekend World*. It was easy to mock its pretensions, but it was trying to do something genuinely new in television journalism, and brought to it what one LWT researcher at the time called 'an almost Marxist intellectual rigour'.[9] This did not necessarily lead it to Marxist conclusions. Earlier than many of its competitors, it was prepared to test Thatcherite analysis seriously – for example, on privatisation or trade union reform – and sometimes even to accept that on certain issues it might just be right. According to the programme's historian, Michael Tracey, 'Birt had come through the radical movements of the 1960s with a sentimental attachment to the arguments of the left, but with none of the ideological certainties . . . which have characterised 1960s and 1970s radicalism . . . like most engineers he simply wanted to know how things worked.'[10] Samir Shah recalled that

> Birt [as a previous editor and now LWT's Director of Programmes] had this idea that if the BBC was making, say, a programme about nurses' pay, it would show you lots of film about what a wonderful job nurses did, how hard they worked and in what difficult conditions, and then end up saying: 'Give them more money' . . . his approach was to say, well what are the real consequences a politician has to think through? If I pay the nurses more, then I may have to concede other wage claims, and the consequences for public spending are such and such. The question is, do I cut other spending or put taxes up? And so on. We were about saying that no choices are cost free and they are all tough.[11]

Was this emphasis on 'tough choices' proto-Blairism? Certainly Mandelson cannot have escaped its influence. Samir Shah, who later became head of BBC Current Affairs, arrived at the programme – in stark contrast to Mandelson – a self-confessed Bennite and the author of a doctoral thesis on the Marxist thinker Louis Althusser. He was much more agnostic when he left. 'We all grew up at *Weekend World*,' he said. 'We had to think straight.'

As a producer, Mandelson was much more interested in the analytic side of the programme than in the technicalities of film-making. Colleagues remember him as 'very organised' but not particularly 'creative'. At this stage in his life he was 'diligent, rather than workaholic'.[12] However, David Jordan, who was recruited by Mandelson from the Research Department of the General and Municipal Workers' Union, remembers working on a programme with Mandelson in the small hours, both of them wearing gloves, coats and scarves because the office heating was habitually turned off at night. He did not share his colleagues' enthusiasm for going on a directors' training course. Seeing Aaronovitch – who was genuinely interested in film-making – come into view he would say, 'Oh, here comes Mr Zeffirelli.'[13] On the other hand, Michael Maclay, a left-wing Tory who had come from the Foreign Office and would return much later as a political adviser to Douglas Hurd, remembers working for him as a researcher on a programme on the German economy: as the producer, Mandelson 'showed enormous determination to make it work. He was extremely tenacious and talked the story out of me again and again. He did it very competently.' Maclay was also struck that when he arrived on his first day and was on his way to pick up his security pass, 'it was Peter who bothered to come over and say "welcome to the team" '.

Mandelson had a reputation for being an adept office politician, partly because of the close friendship he formed with Robin Paxton – one of a long line of bosses and mentors towards whom Mandelson gravitated during his career. He remained a friend long after leaving *Weekend World*; one Paxton child is among Mandelson's many godchildren, and the family adopted him as a lodger for a period when he was between homes in the late eighties. According to one *Weekend World* producer,

> When you were made a producer the editor told you not to be too friendly with the researchers, to keep some distance, and so likewise the editors were supposed to keep some distance from themselves and the producers. And then all of a sudden you have this editor, deputy editor, Robin, and this new producer who are absolutely best friends, completely inseparable. Now, given that promotion for all of us depended on what Paxton and Hugh Pile [then programme editor] would say, this was kind of an upsetting thing.

When Paxton left *Weekend World* in order to edit the religious programme *Credo*, he was replaced by Paul Neuburg, a Hungarian, whose posting was not popular. 'He was a logical terrorist,' one producer recalls, 'a man who thought "implacable" was a compliment.' Neuburg took the programme's intellectual rigour to extremes, and was such a workaholic that he held a production team meeting in the middle of the night rather than go to the hospital when his wife was having a baby. He was also, even by the standards of the programme, especially determined that interviewees should stick to the script. The senior producer, John Wakefield, circulated a petition protesting about the appointment which, it was feared, would lead to Neuburg becoming editor, and it was signed by all the producers – except Mandelson. According to Aaronovitch, this was partly because Paxton would have been 'cross' with him for signing, since if Neuburg's appointment had been rescinded Paxton might not have been able to take his promotion. 'But I also think Peter understood it was a pathetic, useless gesture, and whilst it was entirely justified, it wasn't going to do any good.' Equally, Maclay remembers Mandelson staying aloof from various desultory and ill-organised plots to press for the replacement of Pile as *Weekend World* editor by Paxton, precisely because as a close friend of Paxton's, he had an all too obvious personal interest in the change.

Northern Ireland was one of the programme's favourite subjects and Mandelson frequently covered the Troubles, often working with the distinguished journalist Mary Holland, and becoming something of an expert. Until he had direct responsibility for the issue as a minister in 1999, he continued to take an interest from a distance, discussing it occasionally with Tony Blair. After Mandelson resigned as Trade and Industry Secretary, Holland wrote a letter of sympathy to him, and in the *Irish Times* recalled him at LWT as having 'brightened the Belfast sky, being gossipy, resourceful and endlessly considerate about any problems one might have had about child care and so on'. Although critical of his home loan from Geoffrey Robinson, she said that Mandelson's 'formidable political skills' had helped to 'put Tony Blair and New Labour into power' and hasten the Northern Ireland peace process.[14]

But Mandelson also had plenty of opportunity to cover mainstream domestic politics. In 1984 he produced 'Franklin Delano Kinnock', which asked whether the Labour leader would in office be able to usher in a job creation New Deal along Rooseveltian lines – an idea which he would revisit after he went to work for the Labour Party more than a year later. But his last programme, shown in September 1985, was one called 'The New Mood'. It was heavily dependent on polling, and much of it, viewed thirteen years later, is quite boring, especially since it did not even include a Walden interview. Its interest lies more in what it reflects of the growing preoccupations of its thirty-two-year-old producer. First, it used a simple version of the focus group, an on-screen panel of 'floating voters' selected by the market research company Qualitative Consulting, explaining their doubts about all three of the main parties. Secondly, in keeping with its title, it was markedly and, in hindsight, over-optimistically upbeat about the Tories' vulnerability to recent electoral trends. It made a lot of David Owen's election as SDP leader and the subsequent haemorrhaging of support from the Tories, which had dropped from 43 per cent to 31 per cent since October 1984, to the Alliance, which had risen from 21 per cent to 31 per cent in the same period. Given that Labour only needed to go from its present rating of 36 per cent to 38 per cent to be within sight of an overall majority, a further erosion of Tory support by the Alliance might help to propel it to power. The pro-gramme also reflected growing concern about unemployment and argued that while the miners' strike did 'not find favour' with the public, there was growing unrest among voters at the sense of 'unfairness' and of a 'divided country' generated by the govern-ment's handling of it. Finally, in one of the more visually arresting sequences, it used film of the two opposition leaders since 1980 to contrast the weak and chaotic state of Labour under Michael Foot and the steps his successor Neil Kinnock had taken to present a 'more vigorous, less extreme and less divided' party. The title was as revealing as the content. At least one producer at *Weekend World* had begun to find his faith in a Labour heritage restored.

# CHAPTER SIX

## *Bonkers About Kinnock*

Mandelson's re-entry into work for the Labour Party began, as did so much in 1980s politics, with a lunch. Charles Clarke, Kinnock's chief of staff – a big, bearded bear of a man – had grown up in Hampstead Garden Suburb a hundred yards away from Bigwood Road, but had never met Mandelson until his BYC days, when Clarke had been NUS president. Although it was brutally ruptured at the end of 1989, in the preceding three years they formed the closest of professional bonds. But on the surface the two men could hardly have been more different, and one might not necessarily have guessed that it was the gruff-mannered Clarke who had been to public school (Highgate), and was the son of Otto Clarke, a high-flying Treasury civil servant. Otto Clarke was once described by one of his bosses as 'ruthless in the demolition of soft advice, soft decisions, soft colleagues and soft ministers'. His son, who has inherited some of these qualities, and was the closest model for the fiercely loyal but abrasive Oliver Dix in David Hare's *Absence of War*, had a low public profile. He could sometimes be spotted 'late at night in the party conference headquarters hotel in jeans and an open necked shirt, relaxing and drinking beer out of a straight glass';[1] but he was careful to keep journalists at arm's length. He and Mandelson had been on warm terms when they worked in neighbouring offices on the shadow cabinet corridor for Neil Kinnock and Albert Booth respectively. But Clarke had stayed with Neil Kinnock throughout Labour's most catastrophic period, from 1981 to 1983, and was slightly wary of Mandelson who, like a number of his contemporaries, had gone down the 'media route' once the party went into free fall in the run-up to the 1983 election.

Although the two met occasionally for lunch – and when Neil Kinnock went to LWT for a rare interview with Brian Walden – their contact during that time was sporadic. Clarke had been appalled on one visit to be introduced by Mandelson to his clever but frequently boorish Conservative colleague Bruce Anderson – with whom Mandelson appeared to be on convivial terms, but who subsequently became, at least in public, one of his journalistic tormentors. 'I've never liked Bruce ... from that moment on,' he said. 'But I laugh at the fact that Bruce had now turned on Peter in the way he has.'[2]

But according to Clarke, it was in the early summer of 1985, at one of their six-monthly lunches in a Pimlico restaurant, that Mandelson revealed that he was 'fed up with all these journalists' and wanted to 'get back involved in politics'. Another old colleague from the shadow cabinet corridor, David Hill, had also lunched with Mandelson a few weeks earlier at RSJ, a South Bank restaurant much favoured by television executives. Hill, now enjoying himself as Roy Hattersley's closest lieutenant and adviser, confided in Mandelson that he was growing a little weary of his pursuit of a safe Labour seat. Mandelson seemed surprised. Hill came away from his lunch reflecting that, just when he was beginning to lose interest in a parliamentary career, Mandelson was rediscovering his enthusiasm.

However, it was Clarke who was immediately in a position to help. Preoccupied by the forthcoming Brecon and Radnor by-election, he realised that, by a happy coincidence, the cottage recently bought by the now relatively high-earning Mandelson at Foy, near Ross-on-Wye, was within driving distance of the constituency, and suggested that he might like to help on the campaign; he was sure the party would try to use him in some full-time capacity, but the best way of demonstrating his commitment was to offer his services in what proved to be a crucially important by-election. Mandelson made the most of his opportunity, characteristically taking a risk to do so. Although *Weekend World* was off the air, and though it prided itself on plucking bright young programme-makers out of politics, overt political activity was frowned on. John Pardoe, the former Liberal MP who worked for LWT, was told he could not be a presenter unless he severed all links with his party.

The campaign was organised by Jean Corston, now an MP and then a senior party official. Mandelson, on summer leave, became 'minder' to the Labour candidate Richard Willey and was, according to Clarke, 'basically looking after him . . . and advising him and helping him to handle himself and so on . . . And doing brilliantly. I mean he was a brilliant person and he came to love Richard. He felt very close and warm to him . . . He did it well . . . He influenced the campaign, it was a good campaign.'

But while it may have been a good campaign, it was spectacularly undermined by Arthur Scargill, who used his presidential address to the National Union of Mineworkers' conference four days before polling day to issue a series of impossible demands to a future Labour government to release all miners imprisoned during the strike (which had ended four months earlier) and to reimburse the union for all the fines and losses it had incurred. The television pictures of Scargill, unbowed by the miners' momentous defeat, proclaiming that the NUM had succeeded in challenging the very heart of the British capitalist system, reverberated through the rural mid-Wales constituency. A late swing to the Liberals in what was essentially a four-cornered contest snuffed out Labour hopes of a victory. Neil Kinnock was in no doubt that Scargill, and Tony Benn, in backing the amnesty campaign, were to blame for the defeat at Brecon and Radnor. This, along with the increasingly grotesque antics of the Militant-dominated Liverpool City Council, stiffened his determination not to compromise with Bennite elements in the party, and triggered a dramatic change in his tactics.

If the Brecon and Radnor by-election became in Kinnock's mind a potent symbol of how urgently the party needed to change, it also opened up Mandelson's way into the Walworth Road headquarters. Nick Grant, the Publicity Director, had just left. He had been an efficient organiser of the party's publicity machine – within the old-fashioned constraints set by a party which still saw campaigns as a matter of leafletting and doorknocking – but failed to establish a sufficiently high profile with journalists to ensure that he was their first point of contact. In one of several conversations during this period, which took place in Mandelson's car in Brecon market place,

Clarke told Mandelson that the party was shortly to advertise the new job of Director of Campaigns and Communications. This followed a surgical restructuring of Walworth Road by the able new general secretary Larry Whitty, which had reduced the number of departments from ten to just four. When Mandelson expressed interest Clarke told him, a little stiffly, that his name would no doubt 'be considered along with all the rest'. But with Kinnock, Clarke was a stronger advocate than this gruff promise suggested.

However, Kinnock had had no 'game plan' to replace Nick Grant with Mandelson when he volunteered for Brecon and Radnor, although it was clear to those working in the party press office at the time that the new director would be an outsider. The preferred candidate of Patricia Hewitt, Kinnock's press secretary, was David Gow, the *Scotsman*'s shrewd, solid labour editor, who had been one of a clandestine group of journalists advising the Labour leader on press relations. But though shortlisted, Gow pulled out – partly on the entirely reasonable grounds that it would sabotage his family life if Labour won the election, and partly because he was not sure he wanted to leave journalism. But behind the scenes support was already being mobilised for Mandelson.

This was largely thanks to the good offices of Roy Hattersley. Hattersley had warm reasons for supporting Mandelson. In particular, when he was at LWT, he worked enthusiastically on Hattersley's leadership campaign in 1983. According to Hattersley, Mandelson 'never backslid, never prevaricated'. On the Saturday before the party conference, when it was obvious that Kinnock was going to win, the General and Municipal Workers proposed to Hattersley that he stand down and release the union from their pledge to vote for him in order to guarantee Kinnock a landslide victory. 'Peter was the most vociferous advocate of not withdrawing. So I started off with a benevolent feeling towards him.' Much later, in 1995, the two men attended a conference together in Paris, and Hattersley recalls Mandelson saying, ' "I've always supported Roy Hattersley because I thought he could make a crusade out of revisionism", I was very pleased at him saying this.'[3] Alarm bells about the new appointment had already rung with Andy McSmith, then one of the party's ablest press officers. He pointed out to Roy Hattersley that the party was really trying to create two jobs in one. The new post required a 'Harvey Thomas' – an equivalent to Conservative Central Office's tireless campaign stage manager, responsible for everything from buying advertising to arranging the sets at party conferences. But it also needed a 'Bernard Ingham' who could represent the leadership in off-the-record briefings to the press as assiduously as Margaret Thatcher's formidably loyal and powerful press secretary. McSmith's worry was that the leadership didn't realise how different the functions were: 'Nick [Grant] hadn't been able to deal with journalists. The worry was they might get someone else who couldn't. Roy said they were in no doubt they needed someone who would be able to deal with journalists. Walworth Road was full of people who completely disliked journalists, which drove me to despair. So this was quite a relief. Roy was quite sure he and Kinnock wanted a briefer.'[4]

McSmith's use of Ingham as a comparison was interestingly apt. Almost throughout the period that Mandelson was at Walworth Road, Ingham, a superbly effective operator, would be at least as famous as Mandelson – and for the first two or three years much more so – for hectoring journalists, complaining to broadcasters, and denouncing enemies in his leader's own ranks. Indeed, three years before Mandelson had arrived in his job, Ingham had already famously put the black spot on Francis Pym's career – after a pessimistic speech about the economy – by comparing him at a lobby briefing to Mona Lott, the lugubrious ITMA character whose catchphrase was: 'It's being so cheerful that keeps me going'. Ingham was not, as Mandelson would be, a smooth spinner, but he was a spinner none the less. If Mandelson could start to match him, he would be well worth his salary.

Mandelson himself, of course, had also lost no time in contacting the deputy leader, on whose leadership campaign he had worked two years earlier, and who, along with David Hill, thought him 'ideal for the job'; he was, after all, an unabashed revisionist. 'Partly it was a matter of you help your old mates,' said David Hill. 'But we also thought he would be the most lively and interesting of the candidates.'[5] In his memoirs Hattersley writes of how 'Neil reacted to my lobbying in classic Kinnock fashion – he read out the list of other possible contenders.' Kinnock, said Hattersley, explained he preferred two of them to Mandelson – Dennis MacShane, now MP for Rotherham, but then working for the International Metal-workers' Federation in Geneva, and Nita Clarke, the press officer of the ILEA, who in 1988 married Tony Benn's son Stephen. Then a week later Hattersley took a call from Kinnock's office; he was informed 'that the leader wanted Peter Mandelson and that he hoped that despite my reservations I would give him my support. I do not know if Neil had forgotten that I had suggested Mandelson to him seven days earlier or if, having been convinced of Peter's merits, he wanted the successful candidate to be his nominee.'[6]

In fact, one of Kinnock's initial worries about Mandelson was precisely that Hattersley was supporting him. He had considerable doubts about his deputy's judgement of people and, more import-antly, says Charles Clarke, 'Neil thought that Hattersley was pro-moting Peter as one of the old right-wing group of the party and he didn't want that.' On the other hand 'he definitely did want somebody who was telly-savvy and knew his stuff and we were short of people on the shortlist'. Kinnock's preoccupation with tele-vision had grown in parallel with his disillusionment with the news-papers, which he had by the autumn of 1985, according to one colleague, already 'written off'. But it was still only after 'really looking on the shortlist, looking at the CV', that Kinnock eventually decided in favour of Mandelson, telling him so on the Sunday before all the candidates were due to appear before the NEC on Tuesday 24 September. But while he refrained from instructing Clarke to 'go out and deliver the votes' for Mandelson, Hattersley and David Hill had already been active. Gwyneth Dunwoody, the right-of-centre MP and member of the NEC women's section, had already been canvassing on Mandelson's behalf – an operation made easier, particularly among trade union members, by Mandelson's back-ground in transport as Albert Booth's researcher. Even at this late stage Kinnock made it clear to Clarke that his support on the day would depend on Mandelson acquitting himself well before the NEC.

Which he did, despite being deeply anxious about his chances on the eve of the crucial NEC meeting. 'I met him the day before his interview,' said Alastair Campbell, then working as news editor for the Sunday edition of *Today*. 'He was very nervous and he desper-ately wanted the job. I have never known anybody quite so desperate for a job.'[7] Of course, the stakes were high: if he failed, *Weekend World* would take a dim view of keeping on someone so overtly political. But Campbell could see he had set his heart on it. His presentation was prepared with characteristic thoroughness – and some help from Robin Paxton. The omens for a Labour recovery were good, he insisted; the polling evidence suggested that voters strongly preferred the 'Swedish' model of social democracy to the 'American' free market of Reagan and Thatcher. In an echo of his *Weekend World* theme he said that the nation's 'mood' had changed – against the government. But too much Labour support was soft; the party's message had to be 'simply encapsulated in memorable phrases and policies, explained in terms people can understand'. (The term 'soundbite' was not yet current.) Its 'press and broadcasting contacts must be dramatically extended' beyond the lobby correspondents – for example, to specialist journalists – and 'we must project our leadership, all of them, as an able and united team'.

After the NEC Kinnock told Charles Clarke that Mandelson had performed 'outstandingly well'; when the NUPE representative on the National Executive, Tom Sawyer, passed him a note asking who he favoured, Kinnock scrawled Mandelson's name on it and passed it back. Hattersley went even further, telling an acquaintance that the new director had been 'stupendous'. He had certainly done his homework, interrogating friends and contacts – among them Bob Worcester of MORI, whom he had met at *Weekend World* – about the view of each member of the National Executive. When Mandelson accepted an invitation from the broadcasting officer Andrew Fox to have a drink with members of the press office staff in a pub near Walworth Road, McSmith was struck by how well informed he appeared to be. McSmith himself had earlier led a delegation from the press office seeking the dismissal of Nick Grant; Mandelson knew about the incident but was able to reassure McSmith that none 'of the four or five people' he had talked to about the press office 'told me you were a troublemaker'. Hattersley was his principal referee, but John Prescott was also persuaded by Rosie Winterton (now the MP for Doncaster Central), who had worked for him when Mandelson was Albert Booth's researcher, to telephone Larry Whitty and testify to his competence. There had been times since, Prescott told the *Guardian* in 1995, when he had 'wondered' about having given Mandelson an important reference for 'his first job in this spin doctor world'; nevertheless 'I can't doubt his skills.'[8]

But there were some sticky moments during the NEC meeting which temporarily shook Kinnock's faith. One was when Joan Maynard, the hard-left MP from North Yorkshire, asked Mandelson how he would have dealt with the miners' strike. It was a very tough question: with the executive deeply divided, he risked alienating one half of it whatever he said. But he gave a skilfully neutral answer, again borrowing from his last *Weekend World* programme: he would have tried to use it, he said, as an illustration of Britain as a divided society; there was still much to be done in the way of achieving justice. This impressed almost the entire executive, with the paradoxical exception of Kinnock, who appeared to twitch uneasily at this point, having by now finally come out against the strike. But his deepest anxieties were sartorial rather than ideological. During a break in the meeting, Kinnock told Hattersley: 'I'm still going to vote for Mandelson.' His deputy murmured: 'I guess you didn't like his answer on the miners.' To which, to Hattersley's surprise, Kinnock replied: 'It wasn't that. Did you notice his socks? He was wearing pale blue socks. You don't come to fucking interviews wearing pale blue socks.' Blue socks or not, he got the job, by a perilously narrow margin: 14–10. Had Tom Sawyer and Eddie Haigh, the Transport and General Workers' Union member of the executive (both of whom normally voted with the left) not switched to Mandelson, his hopes of a Labour Party career might have been stillborn.

Mandelson's appointment was the one which interested political journalists covering the day's NEC proceedings – not surprisingly since the other two made on the same day, that of Joyce Gould (organisation) and Geoff Bish (research) were both promotions of insiders. But reporters, not unreasonably, failed to attribute any massive long-term significance to Mandelson's arrival. 'Herbert Morrison's grandson was yesterday given the job of brushing up the image of the Labour Party for the next election,' wrote James Naughtie in the *Guardian*.[9] And a few weeks later Alan Watkins, the *Observer*'s distinguished political commentator, noted that Kinnock had got 'his boy' Peter Mandelson into 'the recently vacant job of press officer': 'Mr Mandelson is certainly affable,' he added, 'and seems competent, but should the leader concern himself so closely with these appointments?'

One of the best Hollywood films about politics, *The Candidate*, ends with Robert Redford's newly elected senator asking his campaign manager plaintively, 'What do I do now?' Having been appointed by the NEC as one of its three new directors, at a salary of £21,000 (£10,000 less than he had been earning at LWT), Mandelson was similarly nonplussed. 'I was thirty-one,' he would say many years later; 'I'd just been appointed to a job about which I had absolutely no idea whatsoever and I had absolutely no capacity or ability or experience to do.' He betrayed little sign of this insecurity. Indeed, when after his appointment McSmith repeated to him the worries he had expressed to Hattersley – that the post really comprised two jobs, and that he would have to make up his mind which to do – Mandelson made it clear that he had every intention of doing both. 'I thought it would be more than he could take on,' said McSmith. 'I didn't realise what a workaholic he was.'

There is a tendency among Labour modernisers to assume that his arrival was the beginning of a 'Year Zero' in the party's development. In fact, he had been prompted to return precisely because it was already changing, as he had implicitly acknowledged in his presentation to the executive. The Bennites, even at the high point of their success, had begun to sow the seeds of their own slow demise. Even before Kinnock became leader, his decision not to support Benn's deputy leadership attempt in 1981 and a concerted effort by the right wing on the National Executive, led by the combative John Golding of the Post Office Engineering Union, had helped to reassert the influence of the right, so that in November 1982 Tony Benn was removed in a 12–4 vote from the chairmanship of the NEC's Home Policy Committee. It was true that the year-long miners' strike had temporarily halted the painfully slow process of change. The NUM, revelling in their role as labour movement heroes, had helped narrowly to defeat Kinnock's attempt to introduce One Member One Vote democracy at the 1984 conference, in the middle of the strike. It was also true that, while the convinced Bennites were in a minority, Kinnock could still not yet rely on a majority of loyalists on the executive. When Tom Sawyer, who had arrived on the executive as a Bennite, voted for Mandelson, he was later castigated by Eric Clarke, the NUM representative, for not voting for the left-wing candidate Nita Clarke.[10] Indeed, Kinnock himself saw the vote for Mandelson as a welcome 'bit of evidence that things were starting to shift. But I realised at that stage that what I was witnessing was not an avalanche but a glacier.'[11] There was, in other words, much, much more to do.

Kinnock made a dramatic start at the October 1985 Bournemouth Labour Party conference, for which he had been preparing for almost a month, and which Mandelson witnessed as a mere spectator (he had not yet started his new job). Kinnock denounced Militant for a campaign against rate-capping in Liverpool which had ended with the 'grotesque chaos of a . . . Labour council hiring taxis to travel around a city handing out redundancy notices to its own workers'. Mandelson was thrilled by the speech which, thanks to television, stamped Kinnock on the public mind as a courageous national leader. Walking out of the auditorium immediately after the speech, flushed with pleasure, Mandelson bumped into John Birt, who had been a relatively remote figure at LWT. 'That was just wonderful,' he told Birt. 'Wasn't Neil fantastic? That was the most brilliant speech. I'm so excited . . .' At the top of the International Conference Centre escalators he saw Patricia Hewitt; they hugged emotionally and Mandelson repeated that it had been 'the most moving, most exciting speech I've ever heard'.

Bournemouth had electrified Mandelson, strengthening his determination to work single-mindedly for his leader. But he had a lot to learn – and not much time to learn it. His knowledge of television was not as comprehensive as Kinnock had imagined; working on a prestigious, but distinctly minority audience programme was not the same as working on news. Moreover, he knew next to nothing about modern advertising techniques – but he knew a man who did. As he would on many other occasions in the future, Mandelson turned to someone at hand who might just be able to help.

He had first met Philip Gould in 1984 at a dinner party at the flat of Gail Rebuck, who would later marry Gould. Gould was impressed by two incidents: one was that Mandelson had 'blanked out' Don Atyeo, then the editor of Time Out, who had made what he construed as a homophobic remark; the other was that when someone else suggested that he was on the point of joining the SDP, Mandelson, with what Gould called 'threatening charm' – and without any reference to his own vacillations three years earlier – had replied: 'Oh, I don't think that would be a very good idea, would it? The SDP is having its moment in the sun, but it will be Labour that wins in the end. In politics it is best not to follow fashion'. Now, a year later, Gould, after a period in advertising and then at the London Business School, had formed a consultancy, and had persuaded Robin Paxton, a university contemporary, to bring him together with the newly appointed Director of Communications. At the dinner, Gould – thirty-four, rather shy and with untidy, shoulder-length hair – was so nervous that he could only look down throughout his long conversation with Mandelson, who nevertheless listened attentively. Gould's message was relatively simple: Labour's electoral ambitions would only be realised if it started to use some of the modern marketing methods which the Tories had deployed with such success since 1979. In two letters – the first, handed to Mandelson at the Paxton dinner, eleven pages long – Gould urged Mandelson to think about what, given Labour's current policies, the Tories would have in store for their next campaign and how important it was for Labour to retaliate. In a note headlined the fear factor and what to do about it Gould pointed out that in the government's recent drink-driving campaigns the most successful advertisements had been not those which appealed to the motorist's better nature but those which inspired fear of detection. Fear was not the only 'motivator of behavioural change', but it was a 'very powerful' communications tool and 'at the moment the Tories own it'. His note was less impressive on the question of how Labour might actually be able to use the fear weapon – suggesting only that 'we have to associate the government with anxiety; about pensions, health, collapse of the inner cities, etc.' But he warned that 'any reasonably intelligent advertising man' could predict the Tory advertisements in two years' time:

> there will be one showing a picture of [the now reluctantly unilateralist Shadow Foreign Secretary] Denis Healey (probably naked at a conference table) . . . another citing the various 'extremist'

motions passed under Kinnock's leadership, another regurgitating [the left-wing Labour MP Bernie] Grant's Broadwater Farm comments; another using left-wing Labour councils as a parallel to a future Labour government.

As a first step Gould suggested that he should urgently carry out 'an exhaustive review of all relevant aspects of your communications operation'.

It was an offer Mandelson had no intention of refusing. What he found when he arrived at Walworth Road in October had fully justified his foreboding. On the day he arrived an employee in the post room had tried to feed a colleague rat poison.[12] Mandelson would recall later that during his first months 'the atmosphere was not great, and I found myself constantly knocking my head against what seemed to be a brick wall, a sort of total incomprehension of what I was saying, that things that were accepted in the outside world as completely natural, normal, axiomatic, were seen in the culture of the Labour Party at that time as ... really very odd, slightly threatening.'[13] His own 'tiny' office consisted of an unstable chair, a table with three legs, a dying spider plant and a 'World War Two style telephone'. But these privations were negligible compared with the political and presentational tasks that lay ahead – some of them underlined in the confidential reports on Labour's electoral prospects which made up Mandelson's preliminary reading. The previous month, in a detailed paper setting out the need to concentrate resources on target seats, Patricia Hewitt explained that the new Director of Communications needed 'as a priority' to decide on an advertising agency and 'other professional resources'.

This was more than a mere technicality. Organisationally, as well as politically, the 1983 campaign had been a legendary disaster, most eloquently described in a memorandum drawn up by Denis Healey for the private consumption of the National Executive when it held a post-mortem in September 1983. Healey had been scathing about deficiencies which no amount of professional electioneering would have been able to cover up – the party's image, fostered over three years, of 'disunity, extremism, crankiness and unfitness to govern'. But he also had a horror story about the chaotic approach to the campaign itself: radio and TV had been consistently ignored in favour of traditional but now obsolete public meetings. While the Tories had carefully paced the tours of their leading politicians, Labour's had spent most of their time in 'trains, cars or aeroplanes'. Party briefings for constituency visits had been non-existent – to the extent that Healey had suddenly found himself, in the middle of the 'Falklands election', in a factory recently reviled for making spare parts for Argentinian warships. And that wasn't all. While the Tories had the benefit of a 'superb campaign handbook', Labour had toiled to produce a last-minute, 'verbose, over-detailed, and badly argued' document of more use to its enemies than its candidates. Finally Healey lambasted the party's advertising. John Wright, the party's advertising agent, he pointed out, had not once met the party's pollster, Bob Worcester, during the campaign. (Nowadays it would be inconceivable for such meetings not to take place daily.) And, witheringly, he added: 'Did we really advertise in the *Economist*? Did we place an advertisement with the slogan: "Are you going to vote for a Destroyer or a Hospital?" And who approved the copy?' It was hardly surprising that Hewitt would recall over a decade later that Kinnock 'started from the assumption that just about everything that had been done in the 1983 election was a disaster, a shambles, unprofessional, ghastly . . . I mean we just took it for granted we weren't going to do any of that.'[14]

Despite a sober private assessment of the obstacles he would confront in putting this decision of Kinnock's into practice, Mandelson presented a confident image to the outside world. 'Of course we want to use the media,' he told the advertising industry weekly *Campaign*, 'but the media will be our tools, our servants; we are no longer content to let them be our persecutors.' The *Campaign* diarist wondered with leaden irony at the surreal prospect of a '*Sun* writer calling the Party HQ' to see what the Labour leader wanted in the Monday edition (surreal, that is, until under Tony Blair's leadership a decade later it became all too easy to imagine), but noted that at least Mandelson had a clear message.[15]

On 3 October the *Guardian* had also noted that Labour's 'new publicity chief', in Bournemouth for the party conference, had 'struck his first blow for the party' before he had even officially started work. It was a trivial but highly symbolic detail. Mandelson had been appalled to see that Dennis Skinner and his redoubtable fellow left-winger Joan Maynard had been sitting behind Kinnock during the leader's epic denunciation of Militant. As a result, they had both been visible on television screens throughout the speech, wearing thunderous expressions on their faces and ostentatiously refusing to applaud. 'Mr Mandelson, a sharp-eyed young television fellow,' wrote the paper's political editor Ian Aitken, 'concluded that this was not helpful, imagewise. So telephones rang, orders were issued and lo! When yesterday dawned the backdrop to the leader had changed radically. The cameras picked up two stolid trade union members of the executive, both of whom clapped enthusiastically in all the right places.' And, in a subsequent interview with the paper's media page writer Kathy Myers, to whom he looked more 'like a prep school English master' than Labour's communications supremo, Mandelson bluntly summed up the approach that would plunge him into continual controversy over the next five years: 'Communications means throwing your net much wider than publicity. It means deciding what we say, how we say it, and which spokesmen and women we choose to say it'.[16]

Healey's indictment of the 1983 fiasco had underlined the urgency of Hewitt's exhortation to start putting a campaigning machine in place. Most worrying was the threat of a continued squeeze by the Alliance. The Brecon and Radnor by-election had shown only too graphically how Labour did not necessarily benefit from a collapse in Tory support. As Hewitt pointed out, Labour support had yet to break through the 40 per cent barrier. If Liberal or Social Democrat support surged in seats where Labour was already a poor third it would mean a drop in the party's national opinion poll ratings, sending it into a vicious spiral of decline. The unspoken implication was that Labour's worst nightmare, the prospect of coming third in the next general election, could not be discounted. Mandelson commissioned Philip Gould, without further delay, to produce his 'exhaustive review'. The sixty-four-page report, which appeared in December, was seminal in the transformation of Labour Party policy and presentation over the next twelve years. It took about six weeks to produce and cost the party £600. To compile it, Gould set about interviewing some thirty people inside and outside the Labour Party.

Gould's preliminary investigation was not exactly open-ended. For example, its central recommendation – the creation of a Shadow

Communications Agency, with access to modern marketing techniques including, for the first time in Labour's history, qualitative polling through focus groups – had been discussed by Mandelson and Gould before the enquiry even began. Gould had also already taken advice from Chris Powell, the pro-Labour chairman of Boase Massimi Pollitt (which had run the GLC's anti-abolition campaign), who would end up chairing the SCA. This agency was a perfect substitute for the full-time advertising agency which, Mandelson had warned Gould, the party would not be able to afford. It was partly modelled on the Tuesday Group, known to Gould, used by US Republicans – a group of bright advertising and media professionals who worked out of political sympathy rather than for money. In a letter to Mandelson dated 3 November, a full seven weeks before he delivered his report, Gould said that such an agency – a loose, largely voluntary group of advertising and market research professionals – would be 'an organisational mechanism that can act both as a catalyst and a continuing force for change'. Stripped of jargon, this meant an agency which would do more than merely present as attractively as possible whatever policies its client, the party, might decide on. It would also help, in time, to shape those policies by giving objective advice – which of course the party was free to reject if it wished – on which policies would be acceptable and marketable to the electorate and which would not. Gould made another point about the agency which was particularly important, given the Byzantine, crisscrossing structure of campaign planning in the party – that Mandelson himself would be able to control it.

Among Gould's thirty interviews, the one he conducted with Mandelson himself is most revealing of Mandelson's attitudes at the time – and shows how little, in the main, they have changed since. Mandelson certainly knew very little about mass communication, but he knew – and knew he knew – a great deal about the Labour Party. Andy McSmith had already been struck by this – along with the 'extraordinary' extent of his preparations for his appearance before the NEC – at his pub meeting with Mandelson. 'The thing that surprised me most was that I expected him to talk about Neil in the sort of unsophisticated way that non-politicians talk about him. But he had a very sophisticated understanding of the party.' He was also 'a born again Neil Kinnockite'. McSmith, who was later to have a number of sharp differences with Mandelson, added: 'It surprised me. But I didn't think he was putting it on.' This sophistication, not to mention self-confidence, is apparent in his interview with Gould. The conversation was entirely private and off the record; had it been made public some of it would have outraged members of the Shadow Cabinet – especially those who thought they had merely appointed a media technocrat. But it gives an entirely authentic flavour of Mandelson's approach. He spoke very warmly of Kinnock – saying at one point, 'I'm bonkers about Kinnock, I really am' – and also of Patricia Hewitt and Charles Clarke. He was obviously respectful of – though far from awed by – Robin Cook, then chairing the Campaign Strategy Committee. This was sensible: Cook's role is easily overlooked, but he had already demonstrated his support for modernising the party's advertising techniques, working closely with Hewitt and Clarke.

But when it came to the archaic party structures the newly appointed thirty-two-year-old Communications Director was much warier. 'I'm not into committees. Once you set up committees, it generates membership, minutes, interests, scrutiny, jealousy.' Instead, he proposed, there should be a 'Director's Group', with the advertising professionals reporting to him. 'Do not forget this is a political party. All the time in the Labour Party you are boxing with those people in the NEC – to whom at the end of the day we are all ultimately accountable below God – who do not know what we are doing, who if they did would oppose it, who are thoroughly indisposed to all these methods, and with whom you have to play it very carefully.'

But however 'carefully' it had to be played, Mandelson was in little doubt about the need to start reconnecting the party with the voting public:

health, social services, housing benefits, law and order, making people secure in their homes and on the streets. All these are very important issues for Labour which we've got to address . . . have something relevant to say . . . which is attractive and not off putting . . . which is very hard when it comes to law and order and Bernie Grant in one sentence eclipses everything we have to say . . . And we have to say it loudly and repetitively.

The emphasis on law and order is striking: this was not successfully turned into an identifiably Labour issue until Tony Blair's period as Shadow Home Secretary seven years – and two general elections – later. Mandelson then warmed to his deeply revisionist theme:

We have to present an image of the party . . . that chimes in with what people want to think. And that's what I think we've found very difficult to do. You take an issue like disarmament. We are very open to one simple line, 'One-sided disarmament' [which the Tories had exploited to devastating effect during the 1983 election]. It's an inventive phrase which very accurately sums up what Labour is about actually, because Labour isn't about spending more on defence, it isn't about increasing conventional forces, it's not about cooperating with, and therefore making concessions to, our allies. It's not about patriotism and putting the nation's security first. It is about, and was seen quite accurately to be about, unilateral nuclear disarmament. Now that doesn't chime in with the nation's feelings and we'd better take note. And you could say the same about the economy. Where's the money going to come from? The sky's the limit. Don't we care about inflation? Trade union power? Trade union blackmail? These are the big issues and they are the macro-themes that we've got to address ourselves to. We've got to acknowledge our vulnerabilities. It's not just a question of having a neat little formulation extracted from some document placed before the Home Policy Committee of the NEC, or some neat way of saying: 'You're number one with Labour.' People are not idiots.

However routine a description this may now seem, in hindsight, of Labour's weaknesses in the early 1980s, it was, in a paid party official in late 1985, high heresy, even when uttered in deepest privacy. On defence, for example, Labour would go into the next election still committed to 'one-sided disarmament'. Even Tony Blair was listed as a parliamentary supporter in a CND advertisement in May 1986. But the interview makes clear how much 'ideological baggage' Mandelson thought would have to be dumped – some of it, at least, before the next election:

There's going to be a lot of biting on bullets. There's going to be a lot of arm-twisting up the back as we come nearer to a general election. Let me give you an example and that is reflating the economy in order to bring about an expansion in production, growth of manufacturing, and the creation of jobs. The problems are (a) Where's the money going to come from? (b) Won't it cause inflation? Answer: incomes policy and borrowing. Have we got either of those on the block yet? Well yes. We've got prudent borrowing. The Shadow Chancellor has accepted that. He has said we will reflate to the extent that we can control inflation and the extent to which we can do that depends on moderating wage demands . . . Do we have an incomes policy? Well, nudge and wink. Formally we're not in favour of an incomes policy . . . But some rabbit will be pulled out of the hat shortly before the election. But don't rock the boat now; don't talk about it. That would piss off the trade unions. It will come later.

Labour did indeed go into the next election committed to a 'National Economic Assessment' on appropriate income levels agreed with the unions.

Mandelson was candid, to say the least, about some members of the Shadow Cabinet. When Gould suggested that Michael Meacher was 'a disaster', Mandelson said, 'he's not a politician, he's a social administrator, academic . . .' Even friends on the right wing of the Shadow Cabinet do not escape scot-free:

Take Gerald Kaufman as an example. Ex-*That Was the Week That Was*, *Daily Mirror*, *New Statesman* journalist. Great pedigree and calibre. He's the Shadow Home Secretary and therefore has great status . . . Certainly clinical and antiseptic looking and sounding, but by and large a good communicator. Problems: (a) soon to be deeply involved in fighting the Public Order Bill in the House of Commons . . . (b) He won't be drilled, thinks everything he says and does is OK, doesn't need to take orders from anyone else. (c) Has a deep distrust of everyone at Walworth Road.

Some of this last observation might equally, in time, have been applied to Mandelson. But he had a point when he complained about the failure of senior politicians to distinguish between what might obsessively interest them and what might interest the electorate. 'The idea of image making comes hard to the Labour Party.' Hugh Burkitt, an advertising man, had warned him that very day that

> the problem with clients is that they think they know best what element of their product to market, so that when the Branston Pickle man says: 'Look, our vegetables are crunchy and there's lots of brown goo attached to them,' he actually thinks and insists upon the crunchy vegetables being the centrepiece of the advertising because that's what he's into – he's very proud of goo and crunchiness. Just as Michael Meacher is very proud of his formulation of the merging of housing benefit and mortgage interest tax relief. Just as Roy Hattersley is very very proud of his tax benefit scheme for repatriating pension funds to this country without imposing exchange controls.[17]

Finally, Mandelson had well-formed views on the proper role of proactive press officers – one which was finally realised in its purest form under his leadership in the 1997 election, when key officials at Millbank were charged with continually coming up with 'stories' designed to present the party in a positive light and retain the initiative in news bulletins:

> It's argued that you cannot be an effective press officer on a campaign and also man a first line of enquiry press desk. I'm very sympathetic to that. If you sit at a desk with a bank of telephones into which all and sundry ring in and say, 'Can you give me the terms of the resolution on Militant in 1983? Who's been selected as the candidate in Spellthorpe ... Is the leader going to Liverpool next week?' ad nauseam all day ... So there is an argument that being a press officer on a campaign is not compatible with an enquiry desk press officer job and you should physically separate them. If you do that, you're turning your press officers into campaigning journalists. I like that. If you mean by a campaigning press officer not just pumping out infor-

mation to the CLPs but actually taking positive practical action to put helpful stories and publicity into the mass media as part of your campaign, I like that.

Most of these ideas were reflected, in necessarily less blunt terms, in Gould's December report, which recommended setting up the SCA and also proposed that Mandelson's own influence on the press should be exercised – as it would be to great effect over the next four years – 'through the press gallery': in other words, via the lobby correspondents.

There was nothing new in the use of sophisticated media techniques by the Labour Party. Indeed Mandelson himself later commented of Labour's 1959 campaign broadcast presented by Tony Benn, that 'I think it's one of the most effective broadcasts in the history of televised politics' adding 'it shows incidentally what a brilliant performer Tony Benn was in his day as well'.[18] In the 1974 election the actor Stanley Baker and the film producer Michael Dealey, later responsible for *The Deerhunter* and *Blade Runner*, had been among the stage-managers of Wilson's campaign, down to details like the TV camera angles, professional make-up and nightly changes of freshly laundered suits, and a portable backdrop built at Pinewood Studios. But by 1983 all this professionalism had been thrown over and there was still deep suspicion at senior levels of the party of anything that smacked of slickness. Nye Bevan's passing remark that advertising 'took the poetry out of politics' had become an inflexible doctrine. The previous Labour Party general secretary Jim Mortimer, decrying the role played in the Tories' 1983 campaign by the Saatchis and by 'the Man from Mars', the former chocolate marketing man Christopher Lawson, had promised that Labour would never stoop to 'presenting [politicians] as if they were breakfast food or baked beans'. This was still the widespread view in the upper reaches of the party. In their excellent account of the SCA's development, Hughes and Wintour point out that it was a delicate task to maintain party support for the SCA, once it had been approved.

Throughout, [Gould] regarded Mandelson as his client. They spoke to each other every day, and so fused their operations that they often found it hard to distinguish who proposed what. But their division of responsibility was clear: Gould diagnosed and evaluated, Mandelson carried out the surgery. The analysis produced by Gould was delivered with *force majeure* by Mandelson. Sometimes Mandelson openly stated that proposals were coming from 'outside experts' in the belief that the politicians were more likely to swallow their advice than his own. On other occasions he felt obliged to conceal the source of his material, for fear that politicians would shy away from marketing and media manipulators ... it was Mandelson who implemented [the findings], often taking enormous political risks with his own position in order to do so. It follows therefore that few of those present at the February 1986 meeting [of the NEC to approve the establishment of the SCA] knew what they were agreeing to; they only understood that its cost would be minimal compared to its anticipated benefits.

The gravity of the problem was underlined in seminal research presented to Robin Cook, Mandelson, Patricia Hewitt and Gould by Leslie Butterfield of the embryonic SCA on a Saturday early in November 1985. They suggested that the party was still alienating all but its most diehard supporters on every count. Among every group of uncommitted voters – and most markedly among twenty- to twenty-five-year-olds, aptly described in the research as 'Thatcher's children' – the negatives of Labour outweighed the positives. Asked what words summed up the Tories, respondents said: 'Surrey', 'mortgages', 'private pools' and 'private hospitals'; that plutocratic caricature might have provided a glimmer of hope were it not for the fact that, asked to sum up Labour, the same people repeatedly cited 'reds', 'commies', 'you will do what you are told', 'strikes', 'Scargill' and 'Militant'. The findings uncovered fear about social breakdown under the Tories – and also demonstrated that law and order, health, education and taxation were high on the list of voter priorities. But they also exposed a strong core of individualism, at odds with Labour's collectivist ideology. 'I'm not going to vote Labour to get a job for someone in Newcastle,' ran one response. 'I don't suppose he'd think about me.' 'If everyone votes for themselves, the party that gets in will be best for the majority won't it?' Asked to draw pictures to convey Labour and the Conservatives, the respondents invariably drew big houses and big cars for the Tories, small houses and cars for Labour. Gould summed up the findings thus:

> Whilst Labour was still talking the language of nationalisation, unilateralism, and high taxes, the British public was buying council houses and shares in the newly privatised British Telecom and British Petroleum, and revelling in the success of Britain's born again military might ... The minority agenda of the emerging metropolitan left, of militant rights in welfare, race and gender, was completely divorced from what the British middle-classes wanted from a government.

And not only the middle classes, it seemed; the research report emphasised that social groups D1 and D2 were little different – 'everyone wants to be middle-class these days'.

The findings were a sobering antidote to Kinnock's triumph at the Bournemouth conference. They also confirmed the new Director of Campaigns and Communications in his view that the task ahead would require more than mere packaging. When John Prescott telephoned Whitty with his endorsement, he had told him: 'He'll be fine as long as he keeps out of the politics.' Some hope.

# CHAPTER SEVEN

## *Roses and Thorns*

When Mandelson started work at Walworth Road, he had been sharing a house in Clapham Manor Street with Pete Ashby and Sue Robertson for more than three years. His relationship with Ashby, a gentle, outgoing man who worked in the TUC Education Department and, like many of Mandelson's friends, had been active in student politics, was the most important of his adult life – certainly until he met his current partner Reinaldo Avila da Silva. Lean, handsome, and with hardly an enemy in the world, Ashby had been to Latymer Upper School, where he was head boy, and Warwick University. He was bisexual and had been sharing a house in Ormley Road, Balham, with two of Mandelson's BYC friends, David Aaronovitch and Rex Osborn, when they first started seeing each other. When they met, Mandelson was working at the TUC while Ashby was Deputy President of the National Union of Students. They had overlapped briefly at the TUC when Ashby joined the Education Department at Congress House.

How secretive had Mandelson been about his sexuality? The answer appears to be that, in an age notably less liberated on homosexuality than the present one, he neither flaunted it nor deceived in order to conceal it. During the seventies, and even into the eighties, when he first started a relationship with Ashby, some of his heterosexual friends – even those who were quite close to him – took several years to discover that he was gay; others cottoned on much more quickly. Although Mandelson had made no secret of his sexuality at Oxford, Dick Newby, his fellow student at

St Catherine's, claimed to have gone through Oxford without knowing. Trevor Phillips had regarded himself as a good friend for three or four years (he had shared a room with him in Cuba) when, planning a small party, he suggested to David Aaronovitch that he should ask 'Peter if he'd want to bring somebody. And he said: "What are you talking about." And I said, "It's interesting, you know, I've known Peter all this time, we're close friends and he's never talked about anybody." And David said: "You don't know, do you?" and I said, "No, what am I supposed to know?" and David said: "He's gay, you fool." And I went, "What?"[1] Similarly the businessman Dennis Stevenson, who had become a close friend of Mandelson through the BYC, remembered pointing out to him, 'when he was about thirty' – which would put the conversation at around 1983 – that, if he was really serious about a political career, he should get married. Mandelson had given him 'a very Irish, odd, pained look' and Stevenson had realised 'very quickly it wasn't simple for him, getting married'.[2]

The uncertainty among his friends was compounded by Mandelson's lifelong, sometimes flirtatious enjoyment of the company of women. Jenny Jeger, whose family knew the Mandelsons well – her aunt was the Labour MP Lena Jeger – and whom Peter had known since he was in YEL at Oxford, was not the only woman to fall for him, though some of her friends thought that she had done so harder than most. They often went out together. The BBC journalist Michael Crick noted how, when he was courting the Fabians for a nomination as BYC chairman, he would invariably sit next to Jeger at the Society's meetings. She also cooked for him occasionally when he gave parties at Vanburgh Court. As a result many of Mandelson's friends and acquaintances assumed that Jeger was his girlfriend. At a dinner during the late seventies in the Spaghetti House in Sicilian Avenue, close to the BYC, where the party included Ashby, Mandelson, Rex Osborn, Sue Robertson, Jenny Jeger and Charles Clarke, there was a *frisson* when Clarke, whose social outlook was somewhat conventional for a man of the left, bluntly asked Jeger and Mandelson, 'When are you two going to get married?' Clarke was probably the only one present who did not yet know that Mandelson was gay.

Some of Jeger's friends, worried about the strength of her attachment to Mandelson, felt that he had used her, particularly as his political career started to advance in the second half of the eighties, when he saw her much less. She was, however, a guest at his fortieth birthday party, attended by Tony Blair, in 1993, and he became more attentive when he was told she was seriously ill. At a party at Downing Street after the 1997 election Trevor Phillips recalled that when he and his wife were talking to Jeger, Mandelson 'came and sat down for maybe fifteen to twenty minutes, with people desperate to get his ear, he just created a kind of circle around him and Jenny and me and my wife which nobody could enter, because he was focused and intent on her, and being her friend at the moment. It was really rather touching, especially in the midst of this rather glamorous thing.' Jenny Jeger died soon afterwards, at the end of August 1997. Shortly before her death, as a lifelong Fabian, she had bravely walked from her Westminster flat to hear Mandelson's Fabian lecture on Social Exclusion, grumbling cheerfully that he had not paid sufficient tribute to the work of earlier Fabians on poverty. In a warm *Guardian* obituary Mandelson wrote that 'the grief her friends all feel at her death is exacerbated by the fact that it is only comparatively recently that Jenny enjoyed what she described as "happiest years of my life" with her long time friend and loving partner David Bean'.[3]

Against this background, setting up home with Ashby in the three-bedroom house they bought with Sue Robertson in July 1982 for £36,000 was a decisive step. Each of them took out a mortgage for £10,000 and provided deposits of £2,000, though on this occasion Mandelson – in a modest way – did the lending rather than the borrowing to ensure that the purchase could go ahead. The most affluent of the three, since he was working at LWT, he lent £1,000, interest free, to Robertson, who was the worst off, so that she could make up her deposit. Even at this point there was initially a slight confusion about the set-up, though not among their close friends. Some, including Shirley Williams, briefly assumed that Robertson, who had come to know Mandelson well through the BYC, where she had worked as Education Officer between 1978 and 1982, and Mandelson were a couple. Robertson was obliged to resort to the formula that she shared 'a roof but not a ceiling' with Mandelson, and indeed the arrangement, if required, could simply look like three young professional thirty-somethings sharing a house. But most of their close friends – and gradually those who were not so close, including a number of Mandelson's colleagues at LWT – knew by now that Mandelson and Ashby were in a steady and serious sexual relationship.

For most of this period life in the house in Clapham – where Sue Robertson now lives with her husband Graham Paterson – was harmonious and happily domestic – particularly for the first three years. Ashby was the more houseproud, doing much of the cleaning and cooking. Each of them had their own room; but while Robertson had the biggest bedroom, Mandelson, rather as he had in Bigwood Road, commandeered the study he supposedly shared with Ashby. As Miles Mandelson had noted at Bigwood Road some twenty years earlier, life had a habit of revolving round 'Smish'. Mandelson was the only car owner, and Robertson stipulated that she would iron one of his Turnbull and Asser shirts – Mandelson's main clothing extravagance at the time – only if he gave her a lift (to work or to a party) in return. However, Mandelson would sometimes irritate Ashby and Robertson by breaking certain house rules: if he returned home early to find Jackie, the weekly cleaner, still at work he would divert her from her other duties to do his ironing. Ashby and Mandelson were fans of *Brideshead Revisited* when it was first shown on television, but Mandelson and Robertson shared a weakness for 'soaps', when they were not too busy to enjoy them. All three enjoyed each other's company, and remain on warm terms today. Mandelson and Robertson quite often went shopping together; they entertained frequently: John Prescott, with whom Mandelson tried to maintain contact during his time at LWT, attended a party in Clapham Manor Street; so did an increasingly wide circle of people in politics and the media, including Samir Shah, Trevor Phillips and with increasingly regularity, Robin Paxton, sometimes with his girlfriend Linda, from LWT. Mike Attwell and Illtyd Harrington, the deputy leader of the GLC, whom Mandelson had known well since leaving Oxford, and his partner Chris Downes, were also frequent guests at Ashby–Mandelson dinner parties. Mandelson's parents also visited him, and Mandelson, if he was not in Foy at weekends, would often go up to Bigwood Road – occasionally with his laundry – for Sunday lunch, sometimes accompanied by Ashby or Robertson or both.

Of the three Clapham Manor Street residents, Mandelson seemed the most ambitious and upwardly mobile in his career. Robertson and Ashby, though both intelligent and with acute political antennae, would sometimes be expected to withdraw to the kitchen if he was in the middle of some intense conversation about world politics, or the future of *Weekend World*, or both, with Robin Paxton, by now a close friend of Mandelson, and frequently counselled by him on his (at that time) tangled emotional life. Although fond of Mandelson, Sue Robertson's cousin Lindsey christened Ashby 'Nice Peter' and Mandelson 'Nasty Peter', largely because while Ashby always had time to chat on the phone, Mandelson sometimes sounded busy to the point of brusqueness.

The most dramatic event of Mandelson's first year in Clapham Manor Street was the birth of Peter Ashby's child. Ashby had had an affair with Kay Carberry, a female colleague at the TUC; they had gone on holiday together and Kay had unexpectedly become pregnant. Ashby was determined to take his full share of responsibility as a parent, and remained in close contact with her throughout the pregnancy. Mandelson reacted with utter calm; the pregnancy did nothing to damage his relationship with Ashby. One Sunday evening in the summer of 1983, about a month before the baby was due, as Ashby was sharing supper with Mandelson and Robertson, Carberry came to the house for supper anxious that she was about to give birth. Though her three friends were sceptical, they packed the strawberries and a few cans of lager into Mandelson's car, and drove off to University College Hospital, where it rapidly became clear that the mother-to-be had been right. Having persuaded a nurse that Carberry was indeed in labour, within an hour or so the trio found themselves inspecting the infant who was to play an important part in Mandelson's as well as Ashby's life for many years to come, and to whom Mandelson became wholly devoted – to the extent that he played almost as great a part in the boy's life as his parents.

Mandelson and Ashby have never spoken about their relationship, or the reasons they split up at the end of the decade. But, according to friends, one factor was the time and effort spent by Mandelson on his political career. Ashby felt that his own work was overshadowed, and sometimes inhibited, by Mandelson's Labour Party role. More crucial, however, were Ashby's anxieties about his son growing up with his father in a permanent relationship with a man. Ashby is now married.

Politically, at least, the most sensitive aspect of the *ménage* at Clapham Manor Street would prove to be not Mandelson's relationship with Ashby, but the fact that he was sharing a house with Robertson, who was by now not only a member but, as parliamentary secretary, an employee of the SDP. It testified to Mandelson's understanding of friends who left the Labour Party after the formation of the SDP, at least up until the 1983 election, that Robertson had already taken her job with David Owen when they bought the house. A number of Robertson's close friends had fallen out with her over her decision to join the SDP in the late spring of 1981, but Mandelson had gone so far as to help her with the application for her SDP job, digging out lists of weekly parliamentary business and other useful paperwork from his desk in Albert Booth's office to give her an idea of how Westminster worked. Following the 1983 election and Mandelson's work on Roy Hattersley's leadership campaign in the summer and autumn, however, his irritation with the Alliance as an electoral force began to harden, and there were more frequent arguments about politics between him and Robertson – usually with Ashby, though still in the Labour Party, gallantly defending Robertson.

Mandelson's political cohabitation did not become a real issue until September 1985, when he was applying to work at Walworth Road. On the eve of his interview by the National Executive *The Times* diary got hold of the story that the would-be Director of Communications at the Labour Party was sharing a house with the woman by now doing the equivalent job for the SDP.[4] Given the febrile sense of betrayal prevailing in the mid-1980s Labour Party, the story threatened to damage Mandelson's chances of getting the job, possibly even fatally. Out of loyalty to her friend, Robertson tried very hard to persuade Julian Haviland, political editor of *The Times*, to get the story taken out. He did his best, even though he was on holiday, but the story duly appeared on the morning of Mandelson's interview; fortunately few of the NEC members present had read it when they voted to approve his appointment. That night there was a dinner party at Clapham Manor Street, with Samir Shah and Robin Paxton among the guests, to celebrate his triumph.

But the arrangement was now doomed. At first newspapermen like the late Gordon Greig, political editor of the *Daily Mail*, were delighted to be able to ring a single telephone number and ask cheerfully 'for an Owen quote and a Kinnock quote' on some issue of the day. Moreover Greig, an honourable man, would not have dreamt of writing a story about the house which would have embarrassed either Robertson or Mandelson. But for Mandelson, already losing sleep from worry about the difficulties of his new job in its first few months, such calls added unbearably to his anxiety. He soon insisted on a separate telephone line. Shortly afterwards he and Ashby told Robertson that the arrangement would have to end. Initially Mandelson implied it might be better if Robertson herself departed, but she was firm: the clear agreement reached when they took the house in 1982 was that if any one of them wanted to end the arrangement the other(s) would have the right to buy the share out. The house had appreciated in value to £90,000, meaning a clear profit of £8,000 each for Mandelson and Ashby after the mortgages were paid off. And Robertson had found a buyer able to take half the house.

In December Mandelson and Ashby moved out together to a new home in Prince George Road, Stoke Newington, which had the added advantage of being close to where Carberry and her child were now living. Before they left, but after Mandelson had been appointed to the job at Walworth Road, Robertson ventured to give him a tip, based on her short experience of handling press relations for the SDP, as he drove her to work one morning. Keep yourself out of the news, she said. Don't become part of the story yourself. This was easier said than done.

Mandelson's first act after the New Year break in 1986 was to compose a 'Strictly Confidential' memorandum for Kinnock, Charles Clarke and Patricia Hewitt. It was, he argued, time for Kinnock to 'embody the message and tone' of the party's campaign as Harold Wilson had done in 1964 and Margaret Thatcher had done in 1979. He quoted Wilson's famous 'White Heat of the Technological Revolution' speech at the 1963 Labour conference –

hastily adding, 'Never mind about the subsequent record. We're only concerned about the campaign at this stage.' This was tactful, given the leader's very dim view of Wilson. Mandelson's own view of Wilson was more ambivalent. No doubt he inherited some of his mother's – and grandfather's – notion of him as a 'bit of a charlatan'. But he could not fail to admire the skills of a Labour leader who had won not one but four general elections. 'In the sixties I thought he was a visionary', as he put it, 'In the seventies I thought he was a magician.' By contrast Kinnock, as a backbench rebel after coming into Parliament in 1970, had consistently criticised Wilson; in an unguarded interview with the *Mail on Sunday* shortly before becoming leader in 1983 Kinnock had denounced him as a 'petty-bourgeois'.

Mandelson suggested in his memorandum that Kinnock's high scores on his 'understanding of ordinary people', and his image as 'the compassionate, wholesome, nice to be with, family man' were not signs of weakness. 'They are an asset as the country tires of the hectoring, ruthless, inflexible Thatcher and we need to play up these characteristics.' This, too, may have been more tactful than truthful. Thatcher's 'inflexibility' probably attracted at least as many electors as it repelled. Indeed, Mandelson went on to urge Kinnock to exploit his toughness. Recognising a lesson of Bournemouth – that punch-ups with the left in his own party could be turned to Kinnock's advantage – Mandelson added more pointedly: 'his authority over the unacceptable left must continue to be exercised at every stage, up to the election, whatever the carping of certain fainthearts ... the Leader's campaign must have the inner strength and self-confidence to withstand massive attacks from our opponents as well as our bilious internal doubters.'

It is hard to overestimate Mandelson's enthusiasm for Kinnock during this period. 'You've no idea what a difference he made,' he would say much later. 'The whole thing seemed hopeful again. It was both hopeful and desperate. It was like a huge mountain that was before you. You looked at the bottom of it and you saw this great sheer cliff rising up in front of you. But for the first time you felt that you had somebody who was going to scale it and whom you could follow up.' The first nine months of 1986 appeared to vindicate the upbeat tone of Mandelson's New Year memorandum.

If Brecon and Radnor had given an ominous warning of the SDP–Liberal Alliance's strength, Labour's victory at the Fulham by-election in April, seeing off a vigorous SDP challenge, went a long way to avenging it, especially since the campaign had to overcome a number of difficulties at the outset.

The first was the dispute between the print unions and the Murdoch newspapers at Wapping. Rupert Murdoch's imposition of new technology, long resisted by the unions, and the creation of a new plant at Wapping resulted in an uncomfortable stand-off between the unions and the Labour Party. The National Executive swiftly approved a boycott of journalists from *The Times*, the *Sunday Times*, the *Sun*, and the *News of the World*, who were daily crossing picket lines to get to their new place of work. Mandelson was privately appalled at the boycott, which he thought was wholly counter-productive for a party seeking to maximise its appeal among uncommitted supporters. (He also had grave doubts about the minority of journalists who had refused to go into Wapping, as he confided to two Times Newspapers journalists – one a 'refusenik' and one not – over a drink at the then fashionable Zanzibar Club. Personally, he ignored the boycott, regularly speaking to journalists like Philip Webster and Michael Jones after the papers moved to Wapping.) But he knew better than to make a protest which had no chance of carrying the day, and asked *The Times* and *Sun* reporters to leave the Walworth Road briefing at which he announced the boycott on 29 January.

The boycott posed especially grave problems for the party at Fulham, and its personable and 'housetrained' candidate Nick Raynsford. The press office's nightmare was the prospect of a confrontation each morning, with dozens of journalists moving from party to party for the early morning press conferences. The reporters from the News International papers would have to be ejected; other reporters might then walk out in sympathy. The print unions refused point blank a request to lift the ban for the duration of the by-election. But eventually, at Mandelson's and Patricia Hewitt's instigation, the party's NEC agreed that the boycott should not be applied during by-elections.

A peculiarity – if not exactly a problem – of the Fulham campaign was that Raynsford's SDP opponent was Mandelson's old friend from Lambeth days, Roger Liddle. Indeed, of the two candidates, Raynsford in many ways most resembled the middle-class, middle-of-the-road Liberal, while Liddle was instinctively a more typically Gaitskellite Labour man. In any event, on polling night, 4 April, there was a tense moment at the town hall count when Mandelson met Liddle's wife, Caroline Thomson. Daughter of George Thomson, the cabinet minister in Wilson's 1964–70 government, she had been in YEL with Mandelson, and was therefore also an old friend in her own right; she was enraged to see Mandelson in overall charge of a campaign whose main object was to eliminate her husband – someone whose beliefs were, to all intents and purposes, identical to his own. She also decried Mandelson's clinical decision to leave Clapham Manor Street, breaking up a happy household for no better reason than that Sue Robertson was working for David Owen. Mandelson had continued to be on very friendly terms with Liddle while he was at LWT; now there was a separation. Liddle's diary shows that during the period between 1986 and 1992 Mandelson did not once visit their house for dinner – as he had previously done regularly ever since the late 1970s. Indeed, that April night at Fulham town hall, it was hard to imagine that they could ever be friends again, let alone the closest of collaborators.

Much later Mandelson would tell Liddle that he had had relatively little to do with the day-to-day campaign in Fulham and that Patricia Hewitt deserved more of the credit. Nevertheless Fulham was a tryout for some of the new professionalism which Mandelson was determined to inject into the party's campaigning. The leafleting was of high quality, and qualitative research was used to develop a stunningly simple campaign theme – 'Nick Raynsford lives here' – with its implicit suggestion that Liddle, coming from Lambeth, some three miles away, was a carpetbagger descending on the constituency from a distant planet. Indeed David Owen himself conceded that, 'For the first time we saw lavish colour literature from Labour. It was now capable of effective campaigning.'[5] According to Gould, it was 'the first time that professional marketing techniques on this scale had been used in a by-election'; he added, with some justice, that it was an 'important victory, which had helped counter the growing impression that the entire Labour Party in London was in the grip of the "loony left"'.[6] It was also a setback for the Alliance. By all accounts Owen was not alone in being worried by the defeat of Liddle, a clearly credible candidate; if the SDP was to make a breakthrough it needed to show it could take a marginal seat like Fulham from third place.

This was not the only advance made by Labour in 1986. The struggle to purge Militant was now engaged in earnest. It sapped a great deal of the Labour leader's time and emotional energy throughout the year; and before the process was completed in December 1986, fifteen months after it had begun, Militant, and therefore the divisions in the Labour Party, was accorded a great deal of publicity. But Kinnock – rightly – never seems to have doubted that the purge was a necessary condition for the party's electoral progress. A majority of the NEC team which had carried out an investigation into the suspended Liverpool Labour Party in February proposed that sixteen people should be charged with breaking party rules. A left-wing minority report – signed by Audrey Wise and Margaret Beckett – insisted there should be no expulsions, but was eventually defeated by 19 votes to 10 at an all-day meeting of the NEC. Mandelson telephoned the BBC in a vain attempt to persuade the producers of *Question Time* to withdraw their invitation to one of the ten, Tony Benn, to appear on the Thursday. This intervention, to which Benn was alerted by an item in the *Guardian*, was a minor but significant illustration of the fact that Mandelson interpreted his first duty as being to Kinnock, rather than to the National Executive as a whole, or to his immediate boss, Larry Whitty.

Nevertheless, still in his first year, he was reluctant to admit, at least in writing, that this was the case. When, in July, Benn complained formally to Whitty about what he claimed had been a misleading briefing, during which Mandelson had told the BBC that he and Eric Heffer were against pre-strike union ballots, Mandelson denied the charge even though the issue itself was finely balanced: while Benn was not against ballots, he was not in favour of them being imposed by law. More interesting, however, was Mandelson's twin-track defence. To Larry Whitty he accepted, as Benn had demanded, that he worked for the party and not for any 'faction' of the NEC, as Benn had described the leadership loyalists. He had merely been conscientiously giving accounts of 'both the majority and minority positions'. But Benn, he told Whitty, seemed to be conducting a 'vendetta' against him: 'Until the terms of my job in briefing journalists about NEC meetings is changed, I expect full backing in what is a difficult task under great pressure,' he said. To Benn himself he was much more emollient, writing that he 'genuinely believed' Benn had been 'misled' about his position and adding, in terms calculated to appeal to the admired front man of the 1959 election, 'I appreciate the interest you show in my other . . . bits of my work. Your comments and advice are amongst those I value most. I hope the difficulties between us can be kept separate.'

Militant resorted to a series of legal and procedural devices to delay the disciplinary process; and it was not until May that the first five defendants, including Tony Mulhearn and Derek Hatton, Militant's two most prominent figures in Liverpool, were finally brought to Walworth Road for their hearings, greeted by a noisy band of supporters singing the Internationale and booing and jostling all but the hard-left members of the NEC as they arrived. To Mandelson's dismay someone had arranged for the Militant defendants to wait their turn in Whitty's office at the front of the building, overlooking the crowd. Hatton, to the delight of the camera crews, was able to lift the sash window and lean outside to joke with supporters and journalists. 'I was totally horrified,' Mandelson said. 'They had been given open access to an open window and seemed to be holding a public sort of press conference, broadcasting to the entirety of South London . . . that was the sort of guerrilla tactics they were engaged in.' He swiftly arranged for the defendants to wait in a back room.[7]

By the time the Militant leaders were arraigned, Mandelson had made real progress as an image-maker on several less defensive fronts. Although the word 'relaunch' was never used about the 'Freedom and Fairness' campaign, unveiled on 22 April 1986, it could well have been. A campaign on 'social policy' had already been planned when Mandelson arrived at Walworth Road; Kinnock was especially anxious to recover the concept of 'freedom', which Thatcherite economic liberals had made a Conservative totem. Mandelson and Philip Gould now asked the Shadow Communications Agency, in its first important piece of work for the party, to seize the campaign as an opportunity for what Gould rather portentously called 'a political communications revolution'. The main campaign document would contain bread-and-butter pledges on better crime prevention (from vandal-proof glass to secure fencing on council estates), a more patient-driven NHS, with better cervical cancer screening, a ban on lead in petrol and the control of food additives. These would be at least as important, and as noticeable, as the more expensive promise of increases in child benefit and educational grants for all sixteen-year-olds. And they would be 'sold' with all the marketing aggressiveness attached to a new commercial product. The designer commissioned by the party was Trevor Beattie, who went on to create the stunningly successful Wonderbra advertisements. As Mandelson told Larry Whitty in a memo at the beginning of April, the 'sharper, up to date look of the publicity material' was 'vital to reinforce the impression of an innovative party shedding old associations and image'.

'Freedom and Fairness' was a notable *succès d'estime*. True, the *Guardian*, in an otherwise mainly sympathetic editorial, lamented the fact that the document reflected a 'posture of self denial compelled upon British socialism by the ideological promiscuity of its recent past'.[8] But the *Economist* described the campaign – with its 'revolutionary' party political broadcast 'extolling the virtues of bobbies on the beat' and its launch amid 'the thick pile carpets of the International Press Centre' – as the 'brainchild of Mr Peter Mandelson . . . who understands about public images and is determined that Labour shall never again look dowdy and old fashioned'. Following the crackdown on Militant and the Fulham victory, it meant that Neil Kinnock 'has had his best three weeks since 1983'. And, the *Economist* continued, when both Militant and the Tory chairman Norman Tebbit 'denounced its slickness with equal vehemence', it 'made Mr Mandelson's day'.[9]

By modern standards, or those already being applied by the Conservative Party in the mid-1980s, there was nothing special about the Freedom and Fairness campaign. But the contrast to the self-indulgent amateurishness of 1983 could hardly have been more marked, as those on the Bennite left were well aware. Eric Heffer, who had staged a dramatic televised walkout from the Bournemouth conference during Kinnock's attack on Militant, stood at the back of the Press Centre sighing loudly and moaning that 'This is not the party I joined.' Even before the launch Heffer had complained about one highly symbolic element of the campaign. The *Mail on Sunday* correspondent Jill Hartley, arriving at the leader's office for Mandelson's pre-launch briefing of lobby correspondents the previous weekend, had spotted a letter from Kinnock to constituency parties about the campaign: its new graphics were black and white and there was no traditional red flag. Her report – that 'Labour is running down the red flag this week with a massive pre-election facelift'[10] – was shocking enough to Heffer for him to raise it formally with Larry Whitty. Mandelson's letter of explanation to Whitty was a model of the soothingly bureaucratic. He was still taking his own advice, relayed to Philip Gould, to 'play the national executive very carefully'. On the lack of red in the literature, Mandelson pointed out that the graphics had been approved by all the relevant committees; 'obviously', he went on, 'no decision has been taken to change the red colour of the Party. I do not intend making any proposals ... that the Party should be sent into the next General Election wearing black and white rosettes!' Whitty could tell Heffer 'that no decision has been taken to drop the Red Flag permanently from Party publications'.

This sentence was the truth, but not the whole truth, as both Whitty and Mandelson knew. For work was already under way to find the party a distinctive new logo, as proposed by Gould's December report. In later years Peter Mandelson would become inseparably associated with the red rose which replaced the flag – so much so that Prince Charles would greet him with the words: 'Ah, the red rose man.' In fact it was not originally his idea at all but Kinnock's: the leader liked the rose used by the Nordic socialist parties, which he greatly admired, and had been desperate to find a symbol to replace what he called 'the banner with a strange device' – the unfurled banner intertwined with the words 'Labour Party'. An ambitious proposal to have a rose specially bred for the Labour Party was reluctantly dropped. Instead, Mandelson sat down with the consultant Michael Wolff and the designer Philip Sutton to draw up a selection of 'hundreds of different roses, and I said at one stage, because I used to grow a couple of roses in those days, and I'd seen a rose catalogue, "That's the rose we want." My father-in-law was sent one of those catalogues you get in the post because he was the secretary of the gardening club.' Eventually they found a design that matched, 'and I said, "that's the one we need but we want the stalk to be a bit shorter"; that was the one bit of my instructions that was ignored. I said, "The stalk's too bloody long." '[11]

Kinnock was by no means alone in having doubts about the design of a symbol which some thought more suited to a pack of sanitary towels than a political party. Nevertheless, he eventually approved the rose, even though he had been looking for something more graphically representational – something easier to draw in a few simple strokes. But when Patricia Hewitt reminded him that the rose was due for its first exposure at the forthcoming party conference, the leader abruptly demurred. At this point, according to Gould, 'Peter came in; he looked Neil directly in the eye, and said calmly but with enormous authority, "Are you sure, Neil? Are you sure we shouldn't have the rose at the conference?" And gradually won him over.' Even as late as September Mandelson was careful not to suggest to the NEC Press and Publicity Committee, which had to approve the new logo, that the rose heralded a change in the party's entire 'corporate identity'. Instead he relied on the tact and discretion of the committee chairman, Gwyneth Dunwoody, a stalwart of the Labour right, one of his backers for the job the previous year, and an ally since they had worked on transport policy together. 'They didn't know what a logo was or anything . . . Gwyneth Dunwoody, who was really brilliant, protected me and us throughout.'[12] *Elle* magazine reported the apocryphal story that when asked by a young woman journalist at the party conference why the rose had no thorns, 'the new and very sharp' Director of Communications was more caustic: 'We have enough pricks in this party as it is.'[13]

Later Mandelson would also overcome his leader's shocked objections to the apricot-coloured or, as Mandelson preferred it, 'salmon' conference pack, with which delegates were to be issued at the party conference; 'with dainty rosebuds decorating its lid', Kinnock 'thought that it might have originally been designed to market teen-age toilet soap'.[14] The forsaking of the party's traditional red was too much even for Glenys Kinnock, who told him: 'Oh, Peter . . .

you'll never persuade the NUM delegation to walk around with these under their arms.' Mandelson simply told Kinnock: 'I'm sorry, it's too late. They've been printed and we're going to have to use them.'[15] Fortunately the delegates were in the main enthusiastic.

Few of these changes were achieved painlessly, or without opposition. When, in early May 1986, David Blunkett, a prominent NEC member, complained in a letter to Mandelson, copied by Kinnock, that the Freedom and Fairness campaign had hit a new nadir of 'value-free campaigning' and had submerged 'strong and clear socialist policies' in favour of 'saying things which people like', Kinnock was robust. He wrote back that he found Blunkett's comments 'astonishing' and lucidly summed up the rationale behind the initiative:

You suggest that we may 'fall into the trap of merely presenting isolated and unconnected policies'. In fact the campaign deliberately selects symbolic policies ... to illustrate our commitment to general values. The reason for this approach is very simple. The extensive research we did before the Campaign launch showed that in the abstract people found it difficult to see how our values related to their daily lives. Linked to particular policies those values came alive ... This campaign is one of the most successful we have run so far which explicitly presents strong and clear socialist policies in a way which the vast majority of people find very attractive. You have consistently – and rightly – argued for such an approach and I hope that – on reflection – you will realise that your remarks simply do not do justice to the campaign.

But according to one seasoned Labour Party official, Roy Hattersley's lieutenant David Hill, the most striking signs of the new approach were to be seen in the 'Red Rose' rally organised by Mandelson in Northampton. In every way – not least in its sensitivity to television – its style was markedly different from that of the dreadful 1983 campaign. Kinnock, Hattersley and Bryan Gould were all speakers. 'You had a sense that something was happening which went beyond what had happened before,' said Hill. 'Michael Foot had always addressed the audience in the hall and not the people outside. At Northampton Peter had realised how to balance the need to make the event intrinsically successful and to make sure the event was reaching out to an audience beyond.'[16]

After the 1997 election, at a Politics and Media Seminar at Nuffield College, Oxford, Peter Mandelson looked back over the previous three general elections and identified, with the benefit of hindsight, three phases in the changing history of the Labour Party since he had gone to work for it in 1985. The first, in the run-up to the 1987 election, had been the advent of the 'Red Rose', when the party had started to change the way it appeared, in what Mandelson frankly admitted had been a 'triumph of image over substance'. By the autumn of 1986 the image had indeed begun to change; the question, as the next general election approached, was whether it had changed enough to disguise this lack of substance.

# CHAPTER EIGHT

## *Deirdre, Defence and Disarray*

In an implicit tribute to Mandelson, Margaret Thatcher recalled that the 1986 Labour conference 'had been marked by highly professional relations, was undoubtedly effective. Their device of substituting a red rose for the red flag . . . impudent as it was, marked a shrewd understanding that whatever else the electorate might vote for, it was not socialism.'[1] It was a summary with which Mandelson would not have disagreed. But the Conservative Party conference had been even more successful. While the Labour Party had reaffirmed most of the policies which had lost it the 1983 election, the Tories used their conference to gather the government's past reforms – like privatisation and the popular sale of council houses – and planned ones – like greater financial autonomy for schools and the right of tenants' cooperatives to take over poor estates – under the single banner of returning 'power to the people'.

The Tory conference arrested Labour's recovery. A week later 'Investing in People', Labour's second glossily packaged domestic policy launch of the year, failed to make the impact of Freedom and Fairness. On the Friday evening before the launch Mandelson arrived at the house of Alastair Campbell, then working on the *Daily Mirror*, and begged him to help translate the document into accessible English. The funds which could have been used for a full-scale campaign had by now been plundered in an attempt to justify Labour's defence policy – something Mandelson had long resisted: the less said about defence, he felt, the better. By now, too the mood of the press was much less pro-Labour. Norman Tebbit's campaign against Labour's 'loony left' was beginning to bite in earnest, and the Tories were making fresh headway in questioning the tax implications of Labour's menu of spending proposals. All these attacks focused on genuine weaknesses in Labour's armoury.

In December 1986 Mandelson responded. At a meeting in the Commons he urged Labour front benchers to retaliate – like him – against unfavourable coverage by challenging reporters who wrote stories they thought unfair. He told the MPs that the press assaults were part of a plot 'orchestrated' by Downing Street and Conservative Central Office; he singled out Rupert Murdoch's *Sunday Times*, now edited by Andrew Neil, as the 'flagship' of the anti-Labour campaign. One course was simply to give up on the press and concentrate on television and radio, which were at least statutorily required to give impartial coverage. Indeed, this was probably the strategy to which Kinnock himself instinctively – if not intellectually – inclined, but Mandelson did not, of course, say that; instead he pointed out that the press frequently set the agenda for the broadcasters and could not therefore be ignored. As if to prove his point, he then leaked details of his speech to Nick Wood of *The Times*.[2]

But even a more proactive engagement with the press could not prevent the party's poll ratings from slipping as its weaknesses were relentlessly exposed. Having been consistently ahead of the Tories throughout the year (though never passing the 40 per cent barrier), Labour ended October neck and neck with them; the poll lead began to seesaw alarmingly between the two parties. By mid-February Labour's rating had slipped to 34.5 per cent compared with the Tories' 36. At a joint meeting of the NEC and the Shadow Cabinet on 16 February Kinnock was frank about the Tory strengths and the Labour weaknesses. The Tories promised 'higher standards of living, tax cuts, and a successful tackling of inflation'. They would attack Labour for threatening higher taxation, weaker defence, and policies which would lead to higher inflation and national debt. Labour's task must be to turn anxiety about unemployment 'into support for us'.

Following a forthright briefing by the SCA on the party's position, introduced by Mandelson, Tony Benn noted in his diary: 'I find Mandelson a threatening figure for the future of the Party. He came in from the media eighteen months ago and has taken over, and he and Kinnock now work closely together. Whitty is just a figurehead, and Geoff Bish [research director] has been pushed into the background.'[3] The SCA researchers, according to Benn, indicated 'that people were afraid of the loony left, afraid of the future, afraid of inexperience. It was totally defensive. But on the positive side we had a "Leader in control", and so on.' Nevertheless Kinnock emphasised that the party was geared up for an election victory. According to Benn, he said that Margaret Thatcher had won 'because we ran away from the idea of enlightened self-interest'.[4] She was the Tories' biggest weakness and the best slogan for the campaign was 'Get her out'. It was, in other words, still possible despite the poll slippage to believe that Labour was in the race – and would have continued to be had the Greenwich MP Guy Barnet not died the previous Christmas Eve.

Candidates are much more important in by-elections than they are in general elections. And at Greenwich the local party's choice could hardly have been more catastrophic. The selection of Deirdre Wood was scrupulously carried out according to the rules; she had a perfectly acceptable doorstep manner, and in a general election she would have been a more than adequate candidate. But it was exactly the wrong moment for a local politician who, as a GLC member, was associated with Ken Livingstone and could be portrayed as part of Labour's 'loony London' problem, to stand against Rosie Barnes, a market researcher, and the SDP's copybook middle-class candidate, a rival so innocuous that she appeared with a fluffy rabbit in an SDP party political broadcast. When Kinnock was warned by officials in the public sector union NUPE that her selection was unavoidable, he simply told Mandelson forlornly, 'It's Wood. Do what you can.' Mandelson and Hewitt made a valiant effort to focus on Wood's qualities as a local 'Earth Mother' figure, but it was a hopeless cause: on 26 February Labour lost the seat to the SDP by 6,611 votes. Its share of the poll fell to 34 per cent, only 4 per cent more than the figure for 1983.

The gloom and disarray into which the Greenwich defeat plunged the party was greater than at any time since 1983. It is worth considering the period between Greenwich and the general election in some detail, partly because it shows how Mandelson operated, but also because it sheds some new light on the huge pressures bearing down on Kinnock in the run-up to his first general election as leader. After Labour's election victory, twelve years later, it was all too easy to forget the divisions, indiscipline and chaotic policy-making structure with which he was obliged to deal.

Mandelson realised on the morning of polling day that the party was going to lose the seat. The night before, he had been told by journalists that the Tories had conceded defeat, and the morning papers were reporting a late swing to the SDP. He arranged with Charles Clarke for Kinnock to see the shadow cabinet members who had to explain away this body-blow on television that night. He arrived at the meeting in Kinnock's Commons office at 4 p.m. with a clear, defiant 'line to take': Labour's result was good in the circumstances; the real losers had been the Tories; and there had been unprecedented media vilification of the Labour candidate. But Mandelson was sufficiently shaken by the result to wonder aloud 'whether the Labour Party can ever win again with the press we have'.[5]

Roy Hattersley, however, had other ideas. He had already seen Kinnock a few moments before the meeting to argue that the party leadership should now publicly repudiate the hard left, disown the Greenwich campaign, and blame Deirdre Wood. John Smith, Gerald Kaufman and Bryan Gould all dissented strongly from this proposition. Understandably so, since the robust Hattersley line foundered on the inevitable question which would be asked by every TV presenter and political reporter: if the problem in Greenwich had been the hard-left candidate, what was the party going to do about all the others who had been selected for the general election? As Mandelson had realised when constructing his own 'line to take', the question would be a show-stopper, emphasising the dilemma which had long confronted Kinnock in London. The MP Bernie Grant, for example, had become a hate figure for the press ever since he had provoked outrage by appearing to take the side of the rioters when PC Keith Blakelock was murdered on the Broadwater Farm estate. Grant, along with Ken Livingstone and those left-wing London Labour councils who insisted on setting up ratepayer-financed departments for promoting gay and lesbian rights, continued to epitomise 'the London effect'. If Kinnock launched a direct attack, let alone took disciplinary action against them, would he not simply provoke even greater defiance – and look even weaker in the process?

Nevertheless, at first Kinnock appeared to back Hattersley's approach; he retreated only when he saw he was in a minority. When the other politicians left, Hattersley stayed and perched on the windowsill as he, Mandelson and Kinnock shared a consolatory bottle of wine. The mood was like a wake; Hattersley and Kinnock, in a rare moment of genuine personal camaraderie, discussed in light-hearted fashion what they would like to do to the hard left. As the meeting broke up, Kinnock left for North Wales and Mandelson went up to the press gallery. He toured the cramped Commons newspaper offices, making what face-saving remarks he could to reporters. But he knew it was hopeless. He went home to Prince George Road, watched the exit polls and went to bed.

On the Friday morning Mandelson woke up with a growing feeling that Hattersley had been right after all. He telephoned Patricia Hewitt and proposed a new, more confrontational 'line to take' for the Saturday and Sunday papers. This had not, after all, been a defeat for Kinnock's Labour Party. Neither the candidate nor the campaign she had fought had been his. Hewitt was impressed – but reminded Mandelson that the fatal question remained: what was Kinnock going to do about it? In the end she telephoned Kinnock and agreed a compromise: the party would stick to the original line but would add – for 'background' (in other words not for public quotation) – that the party had fallen victim to a 'London effect' (for which there was polling evidence) and that the London Labour Party would be told it was time to take remedial action. Hewitt herself would put a 'bomb' under senior London Labour figures to summon a summit meeting – and Frank Dobson was identified as the politician most capable of chairing it. Mandelson left for a staff general election planning meeting – at Walworth Road – an ordeal which he would describe contemptuously as a 'mixture of funny farm and black comedy' at the best of times. And these were not the best of times. It left him tired and depressed. He drove over to Kinnock's office in the Commons to find Hewitt, fingers flying over her electric typewriter, composing a memorandum to Larry Whitty, Jack Cunningham and Dobson on what needed to be done in London. Mandelson stuffed it, unread, into his jacket pocket and went swimming at the YMCA baths in Bloomsbury.

The following morning Mandelson surveyed the almost uniformly hostile Saturday press. As the day wore on he also noted an unaccustomed silence from the Sunday newspaper journalists who usually rang him on Saturdays. That could only mean bad news; the Sundays had their (no doubt deeply negative) stories sewn up and had little need of him. He spoke on the telephone to Bryan Gould, who had by now replaced Robin Cook as the chairman of the all-important Campaign Management Team; he now agreed with Mandelson that it was up to Kinnock to rally the party's and, for that matter, his own spirits. In the evening he took a train to Brighton for a dinner party to find a message waiting for him from a tired-sounding Kinnock. Did Mandelson have any idea why the *Sunday Times* had been trying to reach him? Mandelson did not, but he quickly found out.

The ex-chief whip Michael Cocks, a close contact of the paper's political editor Michael Jones, was proclaiming all over the front page that 'moderates' in the Labour Party were now in revolt against Kinnock. Worse still, a devastating editorial in the *Observer* attacked Kinnock and called for his replacement. Mandelson telephoned Charles Clarke and told him firmly that Kinnock now needed to take urgent and dramatic action if he was to avoid a full-scale leadership crisis, albeit one manufactured by the press, before the end of the week. Clarke did not demur but confided that Kinnock was almost paralysed by depression, compounded by a lack of self-belief; in January he had even contemplated giving up altogether. Clarke agreed to speak to him along the lines Mandelson had suggested, but he was pessimistic about the outcome. By Monday Kinnock had spoken to Bryan Gould, who subsequently told Mandelson that the leader had expressed 'almost childlike pleasure' at Gould's efforts to rally shadow cabinet members on the right of the party – or the 'moderates', as Cocks called them – like John Smith and Jack Cunningham, to speak up for him. A feature of Kinnock's leadership already evident in this period was his isolation: the left felt he had betrayed them; the essentially Croslandite right, led by Roy Hattersley and Smith, did not embrace him as one of their own (not least because Kinnock had been a disruptive force during the Callaghan government), and this was one of the reasons why Kinnock came increasingly to regard Bryan Gould as his most trustworthy shadow cabinet colleague.

The following morning Mandelson rushed through a series of job interviews at Walworth Road before hastening to Westminster and joining Kinnock and his parliamentary private secretary Kevin Barron for the procession up to the PLP meeting in the Commons committee room corridor. Mandelson had no idea what Kinnock was going to say, but it was a forceful and warmly received speech. Kinnock did not directly blame Wood who, he said generously, had carried herself 'with great dignity'. But he told the MPs: 'The right of Constituency Labour Parties to select candidates carries great responsibilities – to heed the people they are seeking to represent, to listen to the people, to comprehend their feelings and values . . . and to remain in step with them. We operate with the people, not in spite of them. When this is not apparent, or we allow our activities and statements to be distorted by the press, we will pay the penalty.'

The words seem relatively mild in cold print, but Kinnock's audience were in no doubt about whom he was referring to. In his detailed, delicately spun briefing to journalists afterwards, constructed, as usual, from his own full notes, Mandelson declared that the leader had 'torpedoed' the hard left and steadied the nerves of his MPs. However, the most enthusiastic response to the speech came from the man who had made it: suddenly more confident, Kinnock was delighted by its success. Mandelson noticed afterwards that he had a 'new spring in his walk'.

But the crisis was not over. That evening, on the way to a meeting at Boase Massimi Pollitt with the agency volunteers, Mandelson gently pressed Kinnock on the need to reach some conclusions on the message of the forthcoming general election campaign. Kinnock seemed reluctant to confront the question, and when the BMP executives started to show him the advertising they were planning, Mandelson realised that he was still very uncertain. At first Kinnock appeared blank and unresponsive; then he suddenly blurted out his worries. The visual images were too negative; the party would be attacked for them. The slogan 'The time has come for a change of heart' was too soft, and he would be attacked for that, too. 'Everyone thinks we're all heart,' he complained; the policies would not stand up to scrutiny. The only answer was to ram home to everyone who would listen that now was the time for change and choice, and that if you wanted change you had to vote for it. The problem was that everyone believed he 'couldn't knock the skin off a rice pudding' – a favourite Kinnock phrase, which he had already undiplomatically used in a newspaper interview about Michael Meacher. He himself was the problem, he said, warming to his theme. According to Philip Gould, also present at the volunteers' meeting, he declared at one point: 'It's hopeless, it's absolutely hopeless and it's because of me – I'm going to lose the election. Your work's great but you can't change me, I'm the liability.'⁶

Mandelson saw the alarm on the faces of the BMP account and creative executives. They hardly knew whether to be more horrified by the leader's own crisis of confidence or by his rejection of their own brilliant concepts. Tactfully, Mandelson defended the slogan: Kinnock's alternative notion didn't offer a reason for choosing Labour. People needed to be motivated: it was emotion that would sway them. But Kinnock, gripped by self-doubt, remained unconvinced. However, he had a good press the following morning for his PLP speech; and when Mandelson talked to him in the afternoon he appeared to be in better spirits. Just before he left for his son Stephen's school parents' day, he asked Mandelson how he thought his remarks had gone down at the previous evening's meeting at BMP. Mandelson hesitated, and then said that Kinnock should perhaps remember that they were volunteers, there to help the party. Kinnock gracefully agreed; he had been so frank, he explained, only because he trusted the agency volunteers so fully. Mandelson promised to pass on this reassuring message, and the two men parted on relatively cheerful terms – blissfully unaware that the party was about to be plunged into another unforeseen emergency.

Mandelson returned home that Thursday evening to a deluge of messages and telephone calls. The letter from Patricia Hewitt, which he had pocketed unread the previous week, was all over the front page of the following morning's *Sun*. Thanks to the robustness of the language, and the fact that the BBC made it the lead item on its morning bulletins, it was quite a story. It acknowledged that one reason why Tebbit's caricature of the loony left was 'taking its toll' was because there was some truth in it: 'The gays and lesbians issue is costing us dear among the pensioners, and fear of extremism and higher taxes is particularly prominent in the GLC area.'[7] The letter had not been leaked directly to the *Sun* but – a fact totally unknown at the time – to Sue Robertson, Mandelson's former flatmate and now David Owen's right-hand woman at the SDP. The man who had handed it over was a Labour Party researcher, working at the time for a shadow minister, who was angry at the antics of the far left and thought it might make a paragraph or two in the *Guardian* diary; but Robertson saw its importance and – correctly – judged that it would make the biggest impact if it were passed to a tabloid political editor. It did not take her long to find Trevor Kavanagh of the *Sun*. (Labour's embarrassment was compounded by Hewitt's own previous links with the left and her association with a campaign for gay rights – a point gleefully passed on to the *Guardian* diary by Tony Benn.)

However, Roy Hattersley, for one, felt vindicated. As Mandelson arrived at the Commons after exhorting Andrew Fox and his colleagues at the Walworth Road press office to do what they could to limit the damage of the leak, he bumped straight into the deputy leader. Wasn't Hewitt's letter, Hattersley demanded, saying just what he had urged Kinnock to say publicly the day after Greenwich? It was now imperative for Kinnock to seize the opportunity to 'put an oar straight into the London left'. Mandelson was inclined to agree; he promised to pass on Hattersley's views to Clarke and Hewitt. However, he doubted whether even that would be enough to rescue the party from the disarray created by the leak. Arriving at a long-planned all-day meeting of the Campaign Management Team, he was struck by how strained Patricia Hewitt looked, compared with photographs of the youthful, vibrantly attractive woman which had appeared in most of the later editions of the morning newspapers. She was not, of course, remotely to blame for the leak. But, angry and frustrated, she had written the letter on her own initiative. During a break in the meeting Mandelson overheard her making a heartfelt apology to Kinnock, who was on a tour of Yorkshire. Kinnock made a brave face of it on television: the leaked letter, he said, demonstrated that 'when it is obvious that there is an identifiable problem for the party I get on with practical steps to deal with it'. Plans for the London Labour summit referred to in the leaked letter were one such step. But Mandelson could guess how far Kinnock's spirits had sunk. It seemed as if his luck had run out; events were now beyond his control.

And the events were not yet over. As he sat with Kinnock at the breakfast briefing for American correspondents the following Monday, Mandelson became fired with renewed enthusiasm for an idea he had already put to Clarke and Hewitt: that instead of the conventional party political broadcast planned for Wednesday, Kinnock should deliver a direct 'Ronald Reagan-style' address to the British people, unfiltered by a largely hostile media. He had even made some notes for a script. It would be pegged, as planned, to the rather creaky programme for creating one million jobs drawn up by Bryan Gould, due to be launched on the same day. But it would contain a more powerful theme which Mandelson had summed up as: 'I know what you're thinking, but I'm tough. I've sorted out the party now. I can sort out the nation. You can trust me.' Mandelson had tested the idea on Alastair Campbell, on Roy Hattersley, and on David Hill. All had been enthusiastic, but Kinnock flatly rejected it. Worse, he could not make time to hear the case made for the broadcast. Mandelson could not even get in to see him, relying instead on Patricia Hewitt to make a vain effort to persuade him. Clarke appeared equally powerless.

Mandelson was frustrated. On the one hand he was depressed by Kinnock's reluctance to make time for thought and discussion, and his resistance to disinterested outside advice. On the other he had nothing but admiration for the way in which the leader continued to drive himself and the party. That very afternoon Kinnock fought and overcame left-wing opposition to a series of lengthy policy statements on training, industry, Northern Ireland and the NHS. There was certainly no doubt in Mandelson's mind, as he watched Kinnock coax and bludgeon his way through the NEC meeting, that the party would fall apart if he lost his grip on it.

But his grip was about to be tested yet again. At around 6 p.m. news started to filter through to Mandelson that James Callaghan had made a highly controversial speech on defence, supporting the Trident programme – which Labour was now committed to ditching. He left the NEC meeting and arrived at a buzzing Commons members' lobby just as the former Prime Minister was leaving the

Chamber, hotly pursued by a furious John Prescott, who was loudly protesting at Callaghan's disloyalty. Like a discreet nightclub manager ushering out an obstreperous guest, Mandelson quickly led Prescott away from a highly diverted collection of journalists and MPs, and urged him to see that argument of this sort would only fan the flames and ensure an even direr press than was already in store as a result of Callaghan's speech. Unsure whether he had made any impression on Prescott, he went upstairs to tour the press gallery and persuade political reporters that the leadership was 'relaxed' about Callaghan's pro-nuclear views; he was entitled to express them, and it was better that he should do so now than on the eve of polling day. This went some way to quelling the frenzy – for about twelve hours.

The following morning *The Times* carried an article, also roundly attacking Labour defence policy, by Richard Heller, researcher to the senior shadow cabinet member Gerald Kaufman. Heller was one of the more colourful and talented characters to play a walk-on part in Labour's travails; he went on to become a columnist on the *Mail on Sunday*, displaying a sharp and quirky wit. But he was also patently sincere, unusually willing to sacrifice his job for his beliefs. The BBC, to Mandelson's annoyance, treated his apostasy as a major story. That was bad enough, but then in the evening Prescott confronted Callaghan again – this time in front of a gaggle of MPs (including Tories) in the Commons tearoom. In a lethal reference to Callaghan's 1983 attack on Labour for seeking to scrap Polaris, Trident's predecessor, Prescott proclaimed loudly: 'You've lost us two elections in a row ... You are leading us like lambs to the bloody slaughter.' Colin Brown, Prescott's biographer, says, perhaps a shade generously, that Prescott considered the exchange 'no more than jovial banter'.[8] But in any case the news was soon with lobby journalists and it became obvious that the story would be front-page news. Mandelson went home seething about Prescott, whom no one had been able to find. At around 11 p.m. a defensive but unapologetic Prescott telephoned Mandelson, who reminded him of his advice the previous evening. Prescott denied having heard it and Mandelson, infuriated, shouted down the phone that he did not even seem to understand the seriousness of what had happened. It was a bad end to a bad day.

The next day, Wednesday 11 March, Mandelson arrived at Walworth Road early to prepare for the launch of Labour's jobs programme at the International Press Centre. As he surveyed the damage in the morning papers, he pondered that it could hardly have been a more inauspicious time to unveil a programme which was being presented as the centrepiece of the forthcoming election manifesto. Even if Prescott had not been embroiled in a full-scale row on defence, it might not have been easy for him, as the Shadow Employment Secretary, to appear on a press conference platform. Responsibility for realising Kinnock's April 1985 promise to create a million jobs within two years of taking office had been wrested from Prescott and handed to Bryan Gould after Prescott's own proposals for a national job creation programme, based on a local one devised by Southwark council, had been brutally shredded at a shadow cabinet meeting in January. Jack Cunningham, the Environment spokesman, had denounced the plan as 'jobs on the rates'; Kinnock charged Gould with the task of producing something more credible within just three weeks.

Prescott was by no means wholly to blame. London Labour local authorities had become a highly unfashionable model since he began his work; and arguably the promise was itself impossibly rash. Gould would write in his memoirs that the original pledge had been 'ridiculous'; his own alternative package, worked out with the help of Roy Hattersley and Charles Clarke, 'was, I think, as good an attempt as it could have been'. Nevertheless the episode had been a setback for Prescott. Now Patricia Hewitt, with Mandelson's support, tried to persuade him to stay away from the press conference; however, understandably believing that his absence would provoke widespread and humiliating comment, Prescott insisted on going. In the end he maintained a dignified silence and the launch itself passed off uneventfully – which was about all that did that day.

Mandelson watched despairingly as the BBC and ITN interviews with Kinnock, who had arrived grey-faced at the launch, were dominated – at the expense of the jobs programme – by questions on defence and internal squabbling. Kinnock, utterly dejected by the squabble, then proceeded to a meeting of the Parliamentary Labour Party, where he told MPs that unless they could exercise some self-discipline, they could not count on him continuing to lead the

Labour Party. His state of mind was wholly forgivable; it served, however, to aggravate rather than defuse the mood of crisis. That evening Neil and Glenys Kinnock passed Mandelson in a Commons corridor as he was on the telephone to Brendan Barber, the TUC's head of press and information. As Mandelson and Barber exchanged views on the passage dealing with wage restraint in an imminent TUC–Labour document, Kinnock asked Mandelson if anything was wrong. With a confidence he did not feel, Mandelson said: 'No.' He did not have the heart to tell his leader that coverage of the jobs programme would be buried in the columns on the party's internal strife. As he habitually did, Kinnock said quietly but warmly: 'Thanks for all you've done today, kid.'

The next afternoon Mandelson was chairing a meeting in the shadow cabinet room to finalise the text of yet another pre-election document, *New Skills for Britain*. Unexpectedly John Prescott came and sat down beside him. Despite their row the previous night, Prescott was amicable and joshingly good humoured. He relented gracefully when Mandelson told him firmly that Kinnock had now decided that there should be no mention of his cherished training 'levy' in the document. But as the meeting continued Mandelson noticed that Prescott was muttering to himself something about 'Ken Hind'. It took only an hour or so for Mandelson to discover what he was referring to – Prescott's 'second tearoom tiff'. Prescott had confronted Ken Hind, the Tory MP whom Prescott – rightly – suspected of having leaked a colourful version of his conversation with Callaghan three days earlier. Prescott had called the Tory MP a 'bastard', and of course Hind and his colleagues ensured that reporters knew about the fresh incident within minutes.

For the second time that week Mandelson returned to the members' lobby to test the atmosphere. He noticed four members of the BBC's political staff stationed in the lobby or rushing up and down the corridors, as if, as he put it sarcastically later, 'the government had fallen'. When he went upstairs to the press gallery he saw Hind's vivid account of his latest encounter with Prescott being passed from one journalist to another as quickly as shorthand could take it. Mandelson lost his patience – this time not so much with Prescott as with, as he put it, 'the media pack in full yell'.

When he heard that the BBC's *Nine O'Clock News* was producing a special filmed package on the tearoom tiffs he acted as he would on many, many occasions in the future. He telephoned the BBC – specifically the widely and deservedly respected political editor John Cole – and caustically put it to him that 'the BBC's rubbishing of the Labour Party has gone too far'. Cole was a former deputy editor of the *Observer* – in private undoubtedly a Labour sympathiser – and one of the handful of journalists whom Mandelson would take care to brief personally and regularly during the coming election campaign. But that evening Cole robustly defended the package, accusing Mandelson of trying to suppress the truth.

The quarrel between Mandelson and Cole served to illustrate the complexities of the Labour Party's relations with the media during the 1980s, and perhaps even those of political reporting in general. On the one hand the second 'tearoom tiff' was a farcically trivial event, scarcely worthy of coverage, let alone prominent billing on the main evening television news. On the other, editorially Cole was right: he could hardly be expected to suppress a story which would run famously in the newspapers the following morning. More importantly, for all Mandelson's bluster, there was a wider political truth to report about the past week: that the Labour Party had proved itself incapable of maintaining even the rudimentary self-discipline required to convince the electorate it was serious about winning. If senior party figures behaved like this in opposition, what would they be like in government?

Mandelson left the press gallery and went down to Kinnock's Commons office. Through the door he could hear Kinnock, sounding worn and tired, in the tortuous process of dictating a speech. Thinking with admiration that Kinnock never seemed to let up, he crept away, disconsolate. Despite prodigious efforts, Kinnock had failed to master either 'events' or the fever now gripping political reporters. It seemed to Mandelson, as he drove home, that all the work of the previous year lay in ruins.

There was, however, little time to brood. On Sunday night Mandelson was alarmed to read the full draft of the joint TUC–Labour economic statement, which he had told Kinnock he thought misconceived, rambling and potentially damaging. Before the final drafting session at Congress House Mandelson visited Kinnock and outlined his misgivings. Kinnock was energetically shining his shoes, as he often did – he always felt naked without properly polished shoes and a diagonally striped tie – and seemed disinclined to change the document. What did Mandelson want to add? It was more, Mandelson explained, a matter of what he wanted to subtract. At which point Kinnock, still polishing away, admitted his true feelings: 'Kid, you don't think I believe in this shit?' he asked. Mandelson muttered something about having felt doubtful about 'certain aspects' of the document. 'Peter, it's crap, it's crap,' Kinnock replied. It was clear that he was talking less about a single document than about the party's whole range of tax and spending commitments. Indeed, conscious of the Tories' powerful appeal as the party that was fostering individual prosperity, he had already warned the NEC that Labour would be vulnerable to the charge that it would raise taxes to an unacceptable level. But now he was much blunter. The party, he asserted, was in a 'timewarp': 'After the election, we are going to have to draw a lot of teeth,' he went on. What did he mean? Mandelson asked – Go on, er, 'modifying our policies?' 'We've got so much to do,' Kinnock replied. 'But the time is not now; the time will be after the election.' Unclear quite what Kinnock meant, Mandelson said he 'looked forward to being around' when that happened. Kinnock's delphic remark appeared to carry two implications. The first was that he had already abandoned hope of winning the 1987 election; the second was that substantial changes to Labour's economic outlook, including its commitments to nation-alisation, would be a priority after another defeat.

For now the party could hardly be further from such an outcome. Since Hattersley was already committed to reversing any income tax cuts made by Nigel Lawson, Mandelson had been alarmed to read speculation in the Sunday papers that the standard rate might be reduced by 3p or even 4p in the budget the following Tuesday. He and Patricia Hewitt had discussed a possible revision of its pledge – by which the party would promise to hit the rich, help the low paid with a new tax band, and leave open what it would do for the large bulk of middle-income earners. Their hopes were forlorn, however. The party was too strongly committed, and Kinnock, much as he might ideally have liked to take up the suggestion, reacted with hostility to Hewitt when she dared to suggest it to him. In the end, while the budget had a good press – with the broadsheets congratulating the Chancellor for his prudence, the tabloids for his generosity – Kinnock performed more than adequately in his Commons reply. Mandelson joined him and his office staff for a celebratory glass of champagne after the speech, relieved that the budget hadn't left the Opposition reeling: after all, Lawson had cut income tax by 'only' 2p to 27p.

Mandelson also had a more personal reason for modest celebration. During the deliberations at the TUC the previous day Prescott had slipped out of the meeting to talk to him. Magnanimously, Prescott made it clear that he was repentant about the events of the previous week. He told Mandelson frankly that he realised he needed to behave according to his senior status and make less of the 'bull in a china shop' image which he had almost consciously cultivated for several years. Mandelson suggested that he needed to temper his passion and his talent for blunt speaking with a little more 'humour and commonsense'. Prescott agreed and the two men returned to the meeting on positively warm terms.

Welcome as this was, it was not going to change the party's fortunes. Driving down to his cottage on the evening of Friday 20 March, Mandelson wondered how Labour could somehow strengthen its profile and gain the initiative as the election loomed. In two long conversations that evening and the following morning, he and David Hill agreed that somehow the party needed not only to recover some self-discipline but also to shake itself out of what Mandelson called its 'immobilism'. The solution lay chiefly with Kinnock himself, who needed to be 'jump-started'. At present it seemed that he had a taste for battle only when the government was in trouble. If only, the two colleagues concluded, the government could have some of the bad luck it deserved.

Trouble was not what lay in store for the government, however. At the end of the month Margaret Thatcher made her famous first trip to Moscow. Even discounting the natural hype of a now largely fawning press, it was a stunning success. She had lengthy and amazingly warm and wide-ranging talks with Mikhail Gorbachev; she revealed for the first time to a huge Soviet television audience the existence of the Russian Star Wars programme; she strengthened the position of prominent dissidents like Andrei Sakharov by insisting on meeting them; and she drew a large and enthusiastic crowd when she went for a walkabout in a bleak suburban housing estate on the edge of Moscow. The trip almost certainly played a historic role in strengthening Gorbachev's hand against the opponents of reform; and it provided the leader of the British Conservative Party, less than three months away from a general election, with the kind of television pictures no money could ever buy.

It also provided the starkest possible contrast with Neil Kinnock's ill-starred journey to Washington. From 1985 until the late summer of 1986 the Labour hierarchy had been split – not so much on what Labour's defence should be, but how, if at all, to put it across. The unilateralists had consistently argued that the problem in 1983 had been that MPs and activists had not been equipped with the arguments to justify the policy to a suspicious and incredulous electorate, and that it was important to pre-empt Tory attacks by mounting a campaign on defence well in advance of the election. By the autumn of 1986, however, defence had become a dangerously high-profile issue in its own right. To David Owen's disgust, the Liberal Assembly in September had voted down the robustly pro-nuclear Alliance defence policy he had agreed with David Steel. Then, following confusion over whether Labour did or did not intend to ban US nuclear missiles from British territory (it did), the party's defence policy had been described by the US Assistant Defense Secretary Richard Perle as 'wildly irresponsible'.

Mandelson was finally persuaded by these events that a short justificatory defence campaign would be necessary. The argument, long proposed by the more electorally minded unilateralists like Cook, would be that the huge expenditure on nuclear weapons meant less money to spend on 'real defence' – Britain's conventional forces. Mandelson backed a daring idea from BMP for a party political broadcast featuring a straggling line of weary, ragged soldiers staggering across Salisbury Plain and dragging a huge weight behind them. This would gradually come into shot and be revealed as a huge trailer laden with nuclear missiles. The towing cable would be cut – and suddenly the soldiers would be transformed into fearsome warriors with shining boots, gleaming weapons, and a spring in their step. It was a bold image, and the commercial was scripted and ready to shoot; but Kinnock, probably wisely, vetoed the plan on the grounds that Labour would appear to be undermining British forces.

Undaunted, Mandelson set about producing yet another glossy policy document: *The Power to Defend our Country*. Elegantly drafted by Michael Wills, under Mandelson's supervision, the document bravely took the battle to the enemy camp, accusing Margaret Thatcher of a 'nuclear fixation': 'Her delusions of grandeur directly threaten the defence policy for Britain that is possible and is vitally needed . . .' The sticking point was the leader's introduction. Even on the eve of the launch Kinnock – who was certainly already entertaining doubts about the policy – seemed unable to get the words right. Mandelson arrived at his office at around 1 a.m. to find that even the forbearing Clarke had gone home, leaving only a distraught Patricia Hewitt helping Kinnock to wrestle with the text. Mandelson did what he could, and Kinnock began to find the words, but he was at a low ebb, perhaps the lowest of the run-up to the election. 'It's not just what I've got to say,' he told Mandelson; 'I haven't even got a clean shirt for the launch.' The feminist Glenys, he explained to Mandelson, was not in the shirt-ironing business. However, he declined Mandelson's offer to iron his shirt for him and appeared the following morning not only with a serviceable text but also with a freshly laundered – and presumably self-ironed – shirt.

The BBC's political editor John Cole described the campaign as the 'best presentation of a vote-losing policy Labour could wish for'. But the high hopes invested in the launch did not survive scrutiny. Within ten days of its launch Gallup found the Tories 8.5 points ahead. Moreover there was still one more daunting hurdle to negotiate. Although Kinnock faced sharp criticism from US commentators, this first trip to Washington was not a disaster. But faced with the obvious question of why he had not met Ronald Reagan, he left a hostage to fortune: he would return nearer the election and do just that.

Mandelson – not to mention Patricia Hewitt and Charles Clarke – had been dreading Kinnock's second US visit for months. He prayed that Reagan would fall ill – or brusquely decide at the last minute against seeing Kinnock at all. He was prepared to invent virtually any excuse for Kinnock not to go. But the Labour leader bravely insisted, saying that he would be repeatedly attacked during the election campaign if he hadn't presented his policies to the head of Britain's most important ally. Mandelson would have been more than happy for Kinnock to take that risk. In the event, he insisted that Denis Healey accompany Kinnock. When he wished Charles Clarke good luck as the party set off, Clarke replied gloomily that he should not expect the visit to go well: the observation was more prophetic than he realised.

On the evening of 26 March, while Kinnock was still over the Atlantic in Concorde, Walworth Road was absorbing the latest shock – a Gallup poll revealing that Labour was now trailing the Alliance in third place. Mandelson and David Hill toured the press gallery offices declaring that the poll, following as it did unbridled denunciation of the Alliance by Norman Tebbit the previous weekend, showed that the best thing which could happen to any party was to be attacked by the Tory chairman. It was an inventive, if threadbare, line. The Tebbit attack may indeed have had some influence. Privately, however, Mandelson guessed that the press build-up to Kinnock's Washington visit had also played a big part in the new findings. The following day, however, he telephoned Chris Moncrieff, the Press Association's Stakhanovite chief political correspondent. With not much more to go on than a planned advertising poster campaign and a few fighting remarks from an airborne Kinnock interview with Alastair Campbell in that morning's *Daily Mirror*, Mandelson confected an April 'fightback' as the party's response to the poll; obligingly Moncrieff duly filed the fightback story, which put the most positive gloss possible on what was dire news for Labour. As it happened, the poster 'fightback' had indeed assumed a greater than planned urgency because of Labour's dire poll ratings, thanks to what Mandelson would describe, post-election, as the 'three D's: Deirdre, Defence and Disarray'.

Events in Washington, however, were rapidly overtaking this attempt at damage limitation. The White House carefully contrived to make the very worst of the visit: the President gave Kinnock less than the allotted half hour and the White House briefing was calculated to present Kinnock as utterly irrelevant to world events. The travelling press had a first-rate story, made even better when, on the journey home, Healey let slip that Reagan had not recognised him and had addressed the man who had been Chancellor of the Exchequer through the 1974–9 Labour administration as 'Mr Ambassador'. On the aeroplane back Clarke – unusually – opened up his notes on the meeting for the benefit of accompanying journalists. But the damage had been done. Not even a combative – and largely accurate – piece by Campbell for Saturday's *Mirror* on 'The Great White House Stitch-Up' could undo it.

The Kinnock party returned, unsurprisingly, in low spirits. That Monday afternoon, 30 March, Kinnock called Clarke, Patricia Hewitt, Philip Gould and Mandelson into his office for a full discussion on election planning. This was a rare, if not unique, event. In marked contrast to Blair seven years later, Kinnock was almost pathologically inclined to carry his burdens on his own rather than canvass advice. It was a pattern which fits Roy Hattersley's description of him as a 'gregarious loner who wanted to take solitary decisions and then enjoy himself in company'.[9] On this occasion, however, he listened as Mandelson outlined the programme he had drawn up for April – a detailed version of the 'fightback' announced, largely unformed, to Moncrieff at the end of the previous week. Kinnock then gave another glimpse of his despair. The voters did not really think anything was wrong, he said. The electorate was essentially Thatcherite, and only interested in how spending was going to be paid for. That Kinnock was able, beset by such doubts, not only to maintain a largely ebullient public image but to maintain control of a party still chronically prone to acts of self-destruction, is a testament to his will power.

Like his leader, Mandelson had few illusions about the coming struggle. In a private note written in late April he dared to ask whether history would judge that Labour deserved to win the imminent election:

> The first answer must be yes, because of Neil's herculean efforts in transforming the party from a mixed bunch of starry-eyed, ill-disciplined, incredible and warring factions into something approaching a fighting force. He decisively tipped the balance of power in the party and brought style and purpose to the leadership. No leader since Clem Attlee has exercised such control over the party.

Yet, the party retained a unique capacity for self-inflicted wounds. How could you trust the country in the hands of a party which was capable of doing so much damage to itself ... ? I think some on the left really want us to lose because they think they will benefit from discrediting the leadership, the rose, and all our 'travesties'. And in this aim they will certainly be helped by the newspapers and broadcasters. Anything to assist the process of Labour falling apart.

In any case, 'winning', as several Labour figures – including Roy Hattersley – have subsequently admitted, was no longer the job in hand. Stopping the party from 'falling apart' was. To take just one of many alarming statistics, the proportion of voters regarding Labour as 'too extreme' had risen between January and April from 65 to 67 per cent. On the third weekend in April, after responding to a series of calls from journalists about Labour's various left–right splits, Mandelson doggedly telephoned round newspaper offices with a statement on the economy from Bryan Gould. The ever-courteous Nick Comfort, political correspondent of the *Daily Telegraph*, took the Gould words down and told Mandelson: 'I admire your stamina and determination to keep pushing the positive things despite everything.' It was obvious that, like most others in the Westminster village, he thought Labour had already lost. It was a kindly, but hardly cheering message. It would be only three weeks before Margaret Thatcher called the election.

# CHAPTER NINE

## *What to Say on the Night*

Not long after the 1987 campaign *Private Eye* described Bryan Gould and Peter Mandelson as the two men who had 'masterminded Labour's brilliantly successful election defeat'.[1] The phrase sardonically – and perfectly – summed up the paradox of Neil Kinnock's first general election as leader. A Tory Prime Minister who, only a year earlier, had been forced to the brink of resignation by the Westland affair won an overall majority of 102 seats – the second largest of any party since 1945 – and Labour took less than 31 per cent of the national vote.

Both men had had to rise above personal calamities. Gould's much-loved father died in New Zealand in the middle of the campaign, while Mandelson saw the lowest point in his career yet when his relationship with Peter Ashby was splashed all over the *News of the World* early in the campaign.[2] There were also a number of avoidable setbacks in the Labour strategy, particularly on defence and tax. Yet both Gould and Mandelson, who had run the campaign from London, not to mention Kinnock himself, emerged with their standing substantially strengthened, and with their efforts a cause for widespread congratulation within the party and beyond. There is no single reason for this, and some of the explanation is still controversial. But one factor was undoubtedly Labour's success in banishing once and for all the nightmare memories of the shambling amateurism so graphically described by Denis Healey in 1983.

It had been the party's prospects of doing just that which attracted Colin Byrne to take a job in the press office for the general election.

While working at the National Union of Students he had read Mandelson's 1985 interview in the *Guardian*, which had prompted him to write in with an enthusiastic letter: 'Basically he was saying, why is it that the Tories and the private sector should be the only ones with professional communications ... and I thought "My God, this man is saying exactly what I believe ..."' Byrne arrived immediately after the Greenwich disaster, supposedly on a temporary basis, at a time

when it was quite clear Labour didn't have a hope in hell of winning the 1987 election ... But we really hit it off and I was plonked into the press office, which was not exactly state of the art, and I remember noticing in my first meeting with him that he still wrote with an old-fashioned ink fountain pen. Still does ... He didn't use his desk; he sat in a great big executive reclining chair at a meeting table ... It was all terrible, the Pat Hewitt letter about lesbians and gays had leaked but Peter managed to give the impression every day to the troops that everything was going fine ... and it was all terribly exciting. He was this very strange, glamorous character in the middle of this doom – you know, the moustache, very neat smartly pressed suit. He was absolutely the antithesis of everybody else in Walworth Road ... [which] was a bit like a rather old-fashioned trade union headquarters. And the only place that had any buzz about it was Mandelson's little empire on the third floor and all these smart types from the Shadow Agency who were running in and out all the time ... And we felt like his shock troops – the shock troops of what became New Labour and it was all terribly exciting.[3]

Some found this ambience rather more tiresome. Joy Johnson, then working as a political producer at ITN, and later to fall out badly with Mandelson during her year working for the party, also remembers him sitting at the long table in the 'down at heel' Walworth Road office, writing with his fountain pen, when she went to see him to discuss election coverage. 'He knew that I was standing there, he had to continue writing for what seemed quite a time but probably wasn't. Fantastically irritating. And I stood there, and then of course he put down his pen and looked up. "Hello, Joy." That was his way of saying, "OK, I know I need you because we need the media but I'm going to put the parameters of the power relationship here." [4]

He was certainly determined to put his own stamp on the press office. Byrne would eventually – long after the general election – take the job of chief press officer, a post which at the time he arrived was already fast becoming a battleground between Mandelson and Whitty, because of Mandelson's resistance to McSmith's appointment. McSmith, subsequently the author of two substantial books about the Labour Party, was obviously capable and intelligent, as Mandelson knew. But he had several disadvantages, from his boss's point of view. One was that Mandelson wanted to gather his own 'shock troops' around him; and McSmith, well liked by Whitty and the other directors, was more of a Walworth Road man than Mandelson, who, it was increasingly clear, saw his first loyalty as being to the leader rather than to the National Executive and the general secretary. Secondly, there was a political difference of opinion. By coincidence McSmith had found himself at a London party meeting where they were discussing the refusal of Stockwell councillors, of whom Ormerod was still one, to vote in accordance with the Lambeth Labour Group whip. McSmith was among those who questioned this behaviour and Ormerod had mentioned to Mandelson, then still at LWT, his consternation that someone working in the Labour Party press office should be 'defending Ted Knight'. Characteristically, Mandelson had stored this item of intelligence, as he later told McSmith. McSmith had freshly arrived in London from Newcastle and was not yet conversant with the exotically internecine politics of the inner London Labour boroughs. Nevertheless, like most people at Walworth Road, he was certainly – though the term was not yet in vogue – more 'old Labour' than Mandelson.

McSmith felt that Mandelson had cunningly manoeuvred him out of the running for the chief press officer's job when John Booth left it. The NEC panel interviewing the two shortlisted candidates – Andrew Fox, Mandelson's preferred choice, and himself – had opted for Fox, apparently on the grounds that he seemed, mysteriously, to have more ideas about how to run a Key Campaigns Unit – a new mini-department devised by Mandelson for the election and charged with maintaining contact with travelling shadow cabinet stars, other than Kinnock himself. McSmith, unlike Fox, had not been told anything about the unit, or the chief press officer's role. He was therefore taken aback by such detailed questions as: 'How would you keep in touch with Denis Healey during the campaign?' McSmith complained forcefully to a sympathetic Whitty, before setting off for the thankless task of running the press side of the Greenwich by-election campaign. When he returned, it was to find that Whitty had reached an uneasy compromise with Mandelson. There would be two chief press officers – Fox, running the Key Campaigns Unit, and McSmith running the press office.

This may seem like a ridiculously trivial dispute. But the attention devoted to it by senior figures in the party hierarchy illustrates an important point: that the media operation would be crucial to the 1987 campaign in a way it had not been in 1983. Where the earlier campaign had depended on rallies and door-knocking, in 1987 the battle would be fought proactively on television and in the press – which to a large extent set the agenda for the broadcasters, as both main parties recognised. In the nineteenth century it was not unknown for tens of thousands to turn up to political meetings – for example, during Gladstone's Midlothian campaign. That age had long gone, a fact seemingly ignored by Labour's eccentrically media-unfriendly 1983 campaign. The war would now be on the airwaves, and in what Tony Blair would much later, as Labour leader, describe as 'hand to hand fighting for the day's headlines'.

Which was one reason why Byrne, at only twenty-eight, felt that, working for Mandelson, he was very much at the centre. 'He had this office at one end of the press office and he'd be in there and you'd forget he was in there half the time and then all of a sudden he'd appear in the doorway, very tall, and he'd be looking round and he'd point at you and beckon you with his finger and you'd be [thinking] "Jesus".' On one such occasion, two weeks after Byrne arrived, he was summoned to the Mandelson office door at around 8 p.m.

and he said to me. 'You know something about young people and education, don't you?' And I said, 'Yes.' And he said: 'I've got this press conference which Neil Kinnock and Giles Radice [then the education spokesman] are doing. I want you to take it over, I want you to do something interesting.' And then he'd go back into his office and you're thinking, 'My God.' Either Peter was desperate or he thought, if I inspire these people they will deliver for me . . . He always had this ability to inspire the people who worked for him, while all around you other people were mumbling and groaning about 'Oh, it's all terrible.' As far as we were concerned there was Neil Kinnock and Peter Mandelson and we were going to work our socks off for these two people.[5]

The aura of self-confidence which Mandelson managed to generate did not, of course, come without a degree of election preparation which, by the standards of 1983 at least, was intensive. On 24 March Mandelson, Gould and Hewitt agreed with Peter Herd and Chris Powell of the SCA two slogans to run through the campaign, reworked in the light of Kinnock's alarming evening meeting with the BMP volunteers a month earlier. This time Mandelson was firm in his advice, which he crisply noted down for Kinnock the following day:

We have taken back, researched and reconsidered the campaign slogan. I do not think you are going to do better than 'The Country's Crying Out for Change. Vote Labour.' It researches very well, is plausible and works very well in the advertising. I propose we use it. However, I think we need additional lines. Many will come into currency via the newspaper ads, e.g. 'If the Tories had a soul they'd sell it.' But I think we need a particular slogan for rallies, backdrops etc. BMP have thought of 'Restoring the National Health.' It works in a number of ways. Bryan and I like it. OK with you?

If this finalisation of the party's election message seemed almost casual, it was in fact the culmination of months of detailed work on the form of the campaign. Much of this had been to the credit of Patricia Hewitt, who as early as September 1985, before the arrival on the scene of Mandelson and Gould, had warned in a detailed memo that the broadcasting demands of the next election would be unprecedented, not least because of the possibilities offered by the emergent technology of Electronic News Gathering (ENG), which allowed television reporters much more freedom to film interviews at times and places of their own choosing:

> We will be working to four outlets, breakfast, lunchtime news, early evening news, later evening news and *Newsnight*, as well as the morning and afternoon newspapers ... In 1983 although ITV was using ENG in many parts of the country, they weren't geared up to exploit the speed and flexibility that offered. 1987 will be an ENG election, with news editors demanding – and getting – virtually instant responses to every key speech and statement.

Among the many proposals she made for a daily response to this was that there should be 'one terrific photo-opp with the Leader or key campaigner plus a location visit preferably linked to the day's policy statement'. This technique became central to the planning of the '87 campaign which, though it might seem small-scale and amateurish compared to the one which ushered Tony Blair into power ten years later, shared many common features with it.

Exactly five years later Mandelson, in exile in Hartlepool, wrote a friendly and revealing letter to David Hill, then in charge of preparations for the media handling of Kinnock's 1992 general election campaign. He wanted to pass on some practical tips – it was especially important, he wrote, to maintain absolute command of the campaign and to have a direct line to the leader as he travelled the country. This two-page letter helps to explain how Mandelson skilfully strengthened his authority in the party during the election, and is something of a teach-yourself text in political campaigning. Finally, it gives an illuminating account of Mandelson's routine during the 1987 campaign – beginning with his life-long preoccupation with sleep.

> I found this the most difficult aspect to cope with because it affected my energy and judgement ... You should try and arrange meetings so that you can get home at a reasonable time and even try and snooze if you can during the day [something which came more easily to Mandelson than to Hill]. It might

seem OK at first but it will wear you down and the end of the campaign is as important as the beginning.

He then went on to list 'in no particular order' various other points for Hill:

A daily rhythm and management of your team is important. Simultaneously you are directing that day's campaign but you are also preparing the next day's and planning the day after . . . Progress chasing, detailed scrutiny and early warning of problems are important on a daily basis . . . The first steering meeting I had every morning was at 7 a.m. with the agency representatives and Bryan [Gould] in my room. Absolutely no one else. We approved and commissioned all ads at this meeting and took strategic advice on the campaign . . . Bryan and I then attended the [Campaign Management Team] meeting with Larry [Whitty and other Walworth Road directors]. This was the only meeting of its sort I attended during the day. Receiving the various monitoring reports was useful. The ensuing discussion was not. You cannot conduct the campaign through democratic debate and consensus. The judgements are too fine and too quick. It is important for you and Jack [Cunningham, 1992 campaign coordinator] to establish your prime responsibility for the media direction of the campaign from the outset. I remained in constant contact with Neil's travelling circus via a telephone dedicated for that purpose. I spoke to Patricia throughout the day. That cohesion was absolutely essential. The central purpose of the journos is to trip us up in some way and that means all parts of our campaign have to stick together like glue . . . [Kinnock's] home-based representatives had no veto power whatsoever. Any second guessing and countermanding of decisions would have been disastrous.

Mandelson then turned specifically to the handling of journalists. He had, he explained to Hill, maintained a 'range of informal press contacts' to whom he spoke on most days – including the BBC's John Cole. Relations with journalists had depended on 'advance information to them . . . and regular hyping and paving the way for our stories and initiatives . . . We had special and constant contact with the *Mirror*.' He also alluded to a point which, much later, some of his critics would claim went a long way towards explaining the Labour campaign's *succès d'estime* – that the stories fed to the media were 'about the campaign – strategy, broadcasts, ads, polling, as much as political stories'. Certainly these stories helped to instil the image of professionalism which Mandelson was seeking to foster – for the party and, by extension, for himself. But they also helped to improve relations with individual journalists by giving them the impression they were being granted important inside information.

The Sunday [papers] were a particular target. [Mandelson continued]; they sum up the week and set the agenda for the next. They need to know they can depend on a crunchy reportable briefing on Friday evening and a speech or a press conference on Saturday. The story has to be good. A couple of times, we didn't have strong enough material to go with against the Tories. Another problem was that we sometimes didn't have a sharp enough cutting political message . . . at our morning press conference . . . You need to influence this in good time if you think the script is not doing the business. Orchestration is crucial. Your lead politicians are your mouthpiece and they need to know the line to take on a daily/hourly basis . . . Remember, an interview on BBC local radio can be out on Radio Four before you can blink . . . on ticklish matters Bryan and I would talk to politicians directly by phone.

Mandelson's final piece of advice was that 'the old maxim is best. Announce what you are going to say. Say it simply and clearly. And then repeat it again and again. The message has to be absolutely driven and single-minded to get through.'

The letter to Hill describes fairly accurately Mandelson's *modus operandi* during the 1987 election. He spent more time talking to Michael Brunson of ITN and the BBC's Cole than to any other individual journalists. He usually got back to Walworth Road after Gould's briefing and started planning the next day. Then, of course, he saw the first editions before he went to bed, while the final editions were sent to Prince George Road before he left for the 7 a.m. meeting at Walworth Road. The campaign was launched with a slickness unknown in previous elections – even though the *Guardian*'s Michael White memorably described Kinnock and Roy Hattersley walking down the aisle dressed in identical blue suits, with red roses in their buttonholes, as if for a 'gay wedding', before taking up their stations at separate lecterns on the platform. The Labour campaign, and Mandelson's role in it, impressed even hostile newspapers, not least because it was the first to be organised on a minute-by-minute basis by means of the mobile telephone, which made it possible to implement decisions very quickly. Certainly the best day, 4 June, identified two months earlier in the campaign grid as one for a 'health shock' was, for better or worse, a model of modern campaigning, closely followed in the 1997 election. Mandelson and Hewitt described it – proudly but not inaccurately – in their paper for the Essex University election post-mortem:

> The case of Mark Burgess, who had been waiting so long for a heart operation, was drawn to our attention ... we were able to take a quick central decision to accept the Burgesses' offer of featuring Mark's case. That morning Neil Kinnock visited nurses coming off duty at St Thomas's Hospital, creating news pictures for bulletins throughout the day. We then linked Mark's case to the hospital waiting list crisis at the morning news conference. The rest of the story we left to Mrs Thatcher and her memorably insensitive quote, contrasting Mark's experience with her own insistence on seeing the doctor of her choice, when she wanted, on the day of her choosing ... We immediately signalled this quote to our candidates via Telecom Gold to use on every door-step throughout the country ... in the event the campaign day crowned a favourable Gallup poll (rogue, as it turned out) and Conservative Central Office spent a very wobbly Thursday.

Unfortunately for Labour, however, health was not the only issue. However professional the packaging – for the most part – the problem (as Mandelson incautiously put it to the Labour MP Peter Snape after the election) was that 'the product kept seeping through'. There were periods when it seemed that Bryan Gould and Mandelson spent all their time stuffing Polyfilla into the cracks in Labour's programme, occasionally relieving the tension with gallows humour.

The writer Sebastian Faulks, following Bryan Gould for a day for the *Independent*, noted that in the car on the way to the morning press conference 'Mandelson and Gould ... jocularly agree a defence on questions on tax: Gould will talk at such length and with such complexity that "any self-respecting journalist will find his eyes glaze over".'[6]

Some time earlier Mandelson had moved to defuse another potential flashpoint for Labour. The previous October the *Observer* had accused him – possibly for the first of what would certainly be countless times – of being 'Machiavellian', for putting a favourable gloss on a trade union policy document which fell well short of what Kinnock (in many ways much more critical of unions than either his predecessor or his successor) had wanted. He had laid heavy emphasis on the document's acceptance of secret ballots and none on the fact that nothing else had been conceded to the Thatcher union reforms. But the strategy had been largely successful and the issue did not feature in the campaign as it probably deserved to. It was by no means the only time he would 'reinterpret' the work of the Walworth Road policy drafters whom – as he made clear in the privacy of an interview with David Butler and Dennis Kavanagh* after the campaign – he regarded as 'a total disgrace ... ropy and incompetent. They had not worked things out properly on tax or the unions.'

Research also helped to smooth some of Labour's most jagged edges. The big change wrought by Mandelson and Philip Gould – which would reach its absolute zenith a decade later – was the use of focus group research to 'refine' and 'hone' (two favourite Mandelson words) Kinnock's message into something approximating the one electors wanted to hear. Thus for several months Kinnock's economic speeches had come to describe the state as a 'servant' of the people, and Labour as a party of production and investment rather than merely of redistribution. Joe Napolitan, a consultant to the US president hopeful Walter Mondale, brought in by Philip Gould and Patricia Hewitt as a (deeply secret) adviser, wrote a paper in March starkly entitled *Crisis: A Hard Look at the*

---

* Authors of the authoritative accounts of British general elections.

*Labour Party and the General Election.* He pointed out that one respondent had complained: 'Labour wants to make people equal to me that I don't want to be equal with.' It was precisely this sort of highly suggestive answer, he argued, that was exposed by qualitative research, rather than the conventional quantitative private polling undertaken by MORI's Bob Worcester. Napolitan added waspishly: 'Bob Worcester is a very good pollster but I fear he is more interested in being right than he is in being helpful. It doesn't do Labour any good for Bob to be able to say after Labour loses that he predicted its defeat within a fraction of a point; what we need from research is the information that will allow Labour to design and modify a campaign in progress.'[7] Mandelson was more wary of Napolitan than were Hewitt or Philip Gould, and he knew that Kinnock, who had refused to see him, would be furious if he thought the American was influencing the campaign. But Mandelson shared Napolitan's views on focus group research and quantitative private polling; he also objected to Worcester's habit of disseminating research on the Labour's Party election broadcasts, whether they were successful or not. After the election he would eventually freeze Worcester out, first by denying him access to the leader, then by insisting he worked to Mandelson's friend and lieutenant Rex Osborn rather than to him; and then by severing the contract altogether.

Not even the most assiduous use of focus groups, however, could help to smooth away the most rebarbative aspects of Labour's programme. Of these, defence was the most obvious. In his March paper Napolitan had proposed a compromise that the party could effect 'without losing face': a Labour government would not itself spend money on nuclear arms, but 'would permit the United States to maintain a nuclear deterrent force in Great Britain'. That, in effect, was what Healey had hinted at in an October 1986 *Panorama* interview – and subsequently retracted in the face of a left-wing outcry. It is now clear that Kinnock had personally lost faith in the unilateralist policy before the 1987 election, and contemplated trying to ditch it after the Reagan–Gorbachev talks in Reykjavik in 1985. At one point, after returning from Washington, he hinted as much to Bryan Gould, asking him (in the words of Henry of Navarre), 'Is Paris worth a mass?'[8] But even for Kinnock the party management problems were too daunting. 'I would have liked to change it earlier [than after the 1987 election]. I would have liked to have changed it much earlier, but the sentiments and allegiances in the Labour Party were very, very deeply rooted, and obviously that was going to require a big turnaround . . . it would have brought everything tumbling down.'[9]

On defence, the worst moment came on 25 May after Kinnock was interviewed on television by David Frost, who lured the Labour leader into suggesting that a non-nuclear Britain would have to use 'all the resources you have to make occupation wholly untenable' in the event of a Soviet invasion. Over the next forty-eight hours the press – or, as Mandelson would put it after the election, 'a cabal of political reporters in cooperation with [Conservative] Central Office' – freely interpreted this as meaning that Kinnock was ready to leave repulsion of a Soviet threat to 'guerrilla bands' or a 'Dad's Army'. Shortly after the election Mandelson frankly admitted to Butler and Kavanagh that the campaign team should probably have moved more decisively to kill off the 'guerrilla warfare' issue. Although Kinnock, who was out of town for the next three days, and Gould steadily rebutted the changes, Kinnock was not brought back to do a London press conference until the following Thursday, inflaming press accusations that he was 'running away'. However, there was no escape from the fundamental line of attack – to which the Tories devoted an entire election broadcast – that Labour had a hugely unpopular defence policy.

The second issue on which Labour was vulnerable was, inevitably, tax. Its specific manifesto commitments were limited to a £6 billion jobs programme and a £3.6 billion plan to attack poverty. Hattersley had persuaded all his colleagues, including Kinnock, that they should not make the party open to instant treasury scrutiny by giving all the details. Instead they should repeatedly make it clear that no one earning less than £500 per week, or roughly £25,000 a year, would pay more in tax. The refusal to disclose any more would be put down to the need to 'prevent tax evasion' in advance of a Labour budget. Broadly, this formula held until the last week of the campaign, when Kinnock had the honesty to admit that a further decision to lift the ceiling on national insurance might mean that people earning more than £15,000 a year would have to pay 'a few pence more'. On the Saturday before polling day the *Daily Express*, with the help of some efficient Tory research, argued persuasively that Labour's tax promises were based on deceit.[10] This fatally undermined Labour's last-week strategy of appealing to middle-class Alliance voters to 'come home to Labour'. This would have been bad enough, but in a BBC television interview that afternoon Hattersley was trapped into sticking firmly to the agreed formula – in blissful ignorance of the fact that Kinnock had again confirmed that those earning less than £25,000 a year might have to pay more. When he telephoned John Smith after his punch-up with Martyn Lewis to ask him: 'Was it as bad as I think?' Smith replied succinctly: 'Worse.'[11]

After the election Mandelson told Kavanagh and Butler that the tax issue 'was very hard to come back from' for two reasons. One was that the policy had never been (another favourite Mandelson word) 'baked'. The other was that 'Neil and Roy did not see eye to eye on it' – in other words, Kinnock was much less keen on increasing taxes for middle-earners than Hattersley was. Indeed, this argument over tax and spending would only be resolved by Gordon Brown after the 1992 election. However, it looks in retrospect as if the Labour campaign also lost some of its initiative during that last weekend – as witnessed by Mandelson's advice to David Hill five years later to save energy for the last week. Bryan Gould recalled that 'by this time we were all very tired.'[12] Partly as a consequence of this, he said, the party held no press conference on the Saturday, which 'left the field open for the Tories'. Charles Clarke went further: 'We were unable to be flexible and in my opinion we completely collapsed ... I argued very strongly in '92 we should not fall into the error of '87 of having a lot of people going like the clappers. Peter himself actually collapsed ... in the last four or five days because he'd been working so fully, so comprehensively, and so effectively.'[13]

Arguably, the third weakness of the Labour campaign was offensive rather than defensive. A number of MPs in Scotland, where the poll tax was introduced in the winter of 1986–7, tried to persuade Walworth Road that it would cause deep controversy when it was introduced in England (though they cannot have guessed quite how much), and should therefore be more of an election issue. A highly confidential appraisal of the campaign produced by Philip Gould for the SCA drew attention to the fact that the poll tax barely featured in any attacks on the Tories during the election – even though it became a huge campaigning issue for Labour shortly afterwards. Much later Mandelson was prepared to concede that he may have been at fault in not making more of an issue of it – though he claimed that it was difficult to interest the English press in the subject. Kinnock himself remains doubtful that Labour could have campaigned effectively on the issue before its impact had been fully felt. Moreover, he argues, it would have exposed Labour to more criticism over 'loony left councils', and the Tories could have defended the policy on the 'basis of the excesses, as they represented them, of a couple of manic councils'.

Neither this failure to make more of the poll tax, nor the income tax and the defence episodes came anywhere near losing Labour the election; the scale of the Tory victory was far too big for that. But they were more damaging electorally than two attempts by the *News of the World*, edited at the time by David Montgomery, now chairman of Mirror Group Newspapers, to destabilise the Labour campaign by smearing first Mandelson and then Hattersley – which prompted Ted Heath to remark that of the twelve election campaigns he had fought in, this was the 'dirtiest'.

On 16 May the *News of the World* carried a front-page story about Mandelson's relationship with Peter Ashby and about Ashby's child, to whom both men were devoted. The previous afternoon Andy McSmith had accompanied Mandelson to Denis Healey's speech at St James's Church, Piccadilly, and then, having worked the late shift the previous night, gone home to get some sleep. The Healey speech, and the ecclesiastical setting, had been part of Mandelson's masterplan to give Labour's defence policy as much credibility as possible; he had watched over every detail. But it was now that he took a call at the church on his mobile phone from an agitated Ashby, confessing that he had unthinkingly allowed the men from the *News of the World* into their house and spoken to them. According to McSmith: 'In the early afternoon I got a call from Anna Healy [in the press office] telling me to come back as fast as possible.' McSmith returned to find an 'awful atmosphere', with a *News of the World* reporter, John Chapman, ringing up every five minutes. Peter didn't want to answer the phone. It was like the evil empire taking over your home territory. Peter Ashby had rung up very upset. He had spoken to [Chapman] and he was very worried about what he might have said. Peter handled Peter Ashby very calmly. He said: 'Don't worry about what you said, they're only trying to hurt us. Don't speak to anyone again.' But he couldn't handle speaking to the *News of the World*.

The press office secretary Sally Russell, by now distraught, pleaded with McSmith to deal with Chapman's next call. When it came, McSmith deliberately took it in the main 'newsroom' so that everyone could hear – partly, he would say later, to demonstrate that journalists were 'not all-powerful'. Then, without consulting Mandelson, who remained out of sight in his office, he embarked on a strategy which seemed risky but was, in the short term, highly effective. When Chapman

started to say something like 'if Mr Mandelson would have the courtesy to speak to me' I saw red. I knew who he was because he had doorstepped Deirdre Wood's fourteen-year-old son at Greenwich. I said something about him being in the sewer, at the scum end of Fleet Street, and then when he came back at me I said, 'OK, I'll let you interview Peter Mandelson but I'll also call the BBC and ITN so that they can come and see Fleet Street's finest at work.' Whereupon he just rang off.[14]

There was widespread sympathy for Mandelson, not only among his own staff but among other senior party figures. His long-standing relationship with Ashby was well known to his colleagues. Indeed, given that he was not then a high-profile public figure, much less an elected politician, he had to all intents and purposes 'come out' among those he knew. He certainly never pretended to be heterosexual. The Peters had often socialised together. Only three weeks earlier he had visited Bryan and Gill Gould *en famille* with Ashby and his child at their house in Oxfordshire. In his memoirs Gould records that Mandelson was 'terribly upset, not so much on his own account' but on that of his partner and his child; and that when he was subsequently asked at a press conference whether he still had confidence in the party's Director of Communications, he treated the question 'with contempt'.

Nevertheless, although Mandelson forced himself to recover in order to carry on with the campaign, it was a grim experience. As Ashby escaped from Prince George Road to avoid further reporters, Mandelson telephoned his friend Alastair Campbell who, still working, invited him over to the *Sunday Mirror*, where its editor, Mike Molloy went out of his way to be comforting. Molloy pointed out (correctly in this case) that 'these things are one day wonders' and that he should not worry. Nevertheless, on the Saturday night he took refuge at the home of Campbell and his partner Fiona Millar, who in more than fifteen years of friendship would never see him more shattered. Mandelson was extremely anxious not to see the story dredged up again. David Butler and Dennis Kavanagh briefly mentioned the incident in a draft of their book on the 1987 election, which they sent to Mandelson for comment; he wrote – in a series of other detailed remarks about political and campaigning issues – 'You may think mentioning my treatment is necessary for your account but I hope you will reconsider this. It caused enough hurt and dismay at the time without immortalising it in your book – and I think in terms of the campaign I was small fry indeed compared to David Steel* and Roy Hattersley. I hope you find it unnecessary.' The two scholars acceded to his wishes.

This was the first but very far from the last attempt by Mandelson to prevent further references to a story about his sexuality which had been put in the public domain by the country's largest-selling Sunday newspaper. The impact of the story on the election, in stark contrast to that on the individuals involved, was negligible. It was not followed up in other newspapers, though that Saturday night there was a heated debate in at least one office – that of the *Sunday Telegraph* – over whether it should be. Despite his partisan desire to inflict the maximum damage on the Labour Party, the paper's political commentator Bruce Anderson, Mandelson's old LWT

---

* The Liberal leader successfully sued a number of newspapers for airing false allegations about his private life.

colleague, was among those against doing a follow-up. And Philip Gould's regular research report the following morning showed that only one respondent had even mentioned it.

One of those who had been quick to express his strong support for Mandelson was Roy Hattersley – who did not know that the following weekend he, too, would be smeared by the *News of the World*. When on the evening of Saturday 23 May, the *Sunday Mirror* found out that its principal rival Sunday tabloid was reporting that the Labour deputy leader had had an extra-marital affair, the news desk urged its political editor, Alastair Campbell, to find Hattersley. Campbell telephoned Mandelson, by now a close friend, and was more annoyed than surprised to find him clear about where his obligations lay: 'We had a very difficult conversation because we knew that the *News of the World* were doing Roy over his affair and I rang Peter and asked him where Roy was. He was the complete party loyalist and he wouldn't tell me. I said, I do all this work turning your useless documents into something and when I ask you for a bit of help you don't give it. He said, "Look, you're a journalist". And he wouldn't help me.'[15]

From the first, Mandelson had been determined to make the projection of Kinnock as potential Prime Minister the central task of the campaign. Easily the most powerful party election broadcast in the election was the Hugh Hudson film that came to be known as *Kinnock the Movie*. Interviewed by Ruth Wishart of the *Scotsman* in October 1986, Mandelson had told her that he had been shocked when he had arrived at Walworth Road to find that talented Labour sympathisers who telephoned with offers of help had failed to receive a reply. 'I made it a personal priority to return their call and ask how they could help.' One such 'cold caller' was Hudson, the director of *Chariots of Fire*, who contacted Mandelson in August 1986 and was immediately asked to make a take-away video of the party conference. Thrilled with the results, Mandelson and Hewitt asked him to start work on a biographical election broadcast. Hudson included footage of Kinnock's 1985 attack on Militant, preceded by Michael Kamen's throbbing music, reminiscent of *Jaws* ('Just when you thought it was safe to be in the Labour Party . . .' the journalist David Bradshaw wisecracked at the press showing).

But on 15 May, at the beginning of the campaign, Hudson also went to Llandudno; here Kinnock made a speech which seemed to vindicate those who assert that he was, in his day, the best platform orator since Aneurin Bevan. With this speech – 'Why am I the first Kinnock in a thousand generations to go to University?' – the Labour leader seemed to shake off all the depression and self-doubt which had dogged him since Greenwich. According to Kinnock himself, he had spent most of the night writing the speech – a bad habit which, by his own reckoning, 'probably cost us a couple of seats in the 1992 election' –

> and the speech was about freedom and it was about how people had freedom but didn't feel free . . . And I could feel the audience understanding it but not really being moved by it because I couldn't get them into my surgery to show them real people who had the same number of votes as Mrs Thatcher . . . but nonetheless had none of the characteristics of free people, and I thought I've got to get the heat under this. I've got to make them understand. So then I launched into the off-the-cuff stuff, and it went down rather well, and then Hugh turned it into the broadcast and all of a sudden the campaign had a spine to it.

As much as anything, the Hudson film worked because Llandudno had. On the evening of 18 May – three days before its scheduled transmission – Hudson brought the film in to Mandelson. Nothing like it had ever been made before: when the lights went up there was total silence. Hudson nervously started stammering that it was obviously not right, there was time to re-edit, until he was rescued by Mandelson saying, a touch theatrically: 'Hugh. We are knocked out.'[16]

Not everyone was so 'knocked out'. David Blunkett, for one, found it stomach-turning. Nevertheless this commercial – unlike Hudson's second for the campaign, which was much less effective – received such acclaim that it was retransmitted (against Kinnock's own advice) nearer polling day, which meant that a PEB on the NHS had to be withdrawn. According to David Hill, 'Almost everybody in the party was saying, "I didn't join the Labour Party to initiate the cult of personality." But I don't think many people understood why it was needed – to stop us coming third. I believe it was necessary to stop us coming third.'[17] Certainly it entirely fulfilled Mandelson's stipulation that 'because the Murdoch press had spent the year before trying to assassinate Neil's character it was vital that we give a more complete picture of the man.'

But was it quite as successful as Mandelson, among others, made out? It quickly became common knowledge that 'Neil Kinnock's personal ratings went up by sixteen points' as a result of the broadcast. This was not quite accurate. Kinnock's approval ratings as a potential Prime Minister *among those already intending to vote Labour* went up from 66 per cent to 82 per cent. His personal ratings among voters as a whole did indeed go up during the campaign – no doubt with the help of the Hudson PEB. They did so, moreover, while Margaret Thatcher's declined by one point, David Steel's by two, and David Owen's remained static. But the rise was much more modest, with 27 per cent in MORI polls thinking by polling day that he would 'make the most capable Prime Minister', compared with 21 per cent when the election was called. The '16 per cent' claim may have been forgivable hyperbole among a leadership cadre wanting to change policy after the election – and therefore determined that policies, rather than the campaign, should be blamed for the coming defeat. But it was hyperbole none the less.

Only for a brief moment on 'Wobbly Thursday', when three polls showed Labour ahead, did Mandelson, like Hattersley and, deep down, Kinnock, really believe that Labour could win. Mandelson had even prepared, well in advance, a cyclostyled 'What to Say on the Night' briefing paper for party spokesmen, written on the assumption of defeat. Its main message was bullish: 'The only question is not whether but when Neil Kinnock becomes Prime Minister.' Not surprisingly, perhaps, the first item, before 'Liberal and SDP Collapse', 'Tories – Complacent and Arrogant', and 'Neil Kinnock, Stronger than Ever', was 'Labour Wins Campaign'. Introducing the paper presented to the Essex seminar in October, he would sum up his thoughts about the four-and-a-half-week campaign: 'I believe the people of Britain made up their minds about the party of government in the four years of the last parliament. But I believe they made up their minds about the opposition parties in the four weeks of the campaign.' He pointed out that while Kinnock's rating had risen overall by 6 per cent, Thatcher's had fallen by 4; Labour's 'competence to govern' rating had risen by 8 per cent and its 'disunity' rating had fallen by 6 per cent. 'Passion and professionalism lay behind this success. Passion was important because the Alliance was running a reflective, thoughtful campaign, which was simply swamped once Kinnock and Thatcher got into their strides ... Labour's campaign was effective in the battle for Opposition but less so in the battle for government.'

Was this just a story concocted to explain away Labour's third successive election defeat in a way that would not damage those responsible for the campaign? Kinnock's own view was that while there was 'frenetically hard work' – by Mandelson, among others – 'If there was any brilliance in the management of that campaign, it escaped me at the time. There was high morale ... there were people digging for victory ... And given where we started from I have to say they did brilliantly. But the idea that there was a master plan, a strategy, a benign and sagacious corporate leadership, I think you'd have difficulty proving that.'[18]

Charles Clarke, who was to fall out with his colleague over his decision to seek the Hartlepool seat in 1989, would strongly contest the view that 1987 was the Mandelson triumph it was widely assumed to be. He accepted that the Alliance could have won if 'we had done badly' in the campaign. But he also believed both that the campaign could have been better than it was *and* that the glory for the success it was should not be monopolised by Mandelson. After the election he went to Portugal for a fortnight's holiday with his wife and six-month-old son, sat by the pool and analysed the results with his ITN guide to the election. He came to the conclusion that there were more than twenty-five seats 'which we should have won if we had won the best swing of the region'. This suggests that in the 'key seats' the party had not done as well as it might have done.

After the election Clarke also complained to Kinnock that it was 'not right that Peter's immediately taking credit for all of this'. He explained:

I said we beat the SDP but we lost the election and the last week we collapsed and we had a disaster on the Saturday on money

and the Treasury and all the rest of it . . . And [Neil] said – and
it was an important and correct point – 'Look, Charles, don't
ever, ever say this to anybody because our big cred going into
the next period is we ran a good campaign. We don't need anybody raising questions about it inside . . .' The story of the '87
election was flair, which was Peter, organisation until the last
week, and we did a lot of things very well . . . He had no relationship with people in the office – in Walworth Road – he wouldn't
be a team player [at party HQ] at all. But he was brilliant – and
I still think this is his brilliant quality ahead of all other qualities
– he was a brilliant media handler. I mean an outstanding media
handler; and it was a great weakness in '92 – we had no one
who was even half as good as Peter had been in '87. But in terms
of planning the election campaign, the strategy, I don't think he
was that good. I will say to you very strongly that Peter does
not deserve the credit he's had for the '87 election. He did good
things, he was fine but it was not his campaign.[19]

Instead, said Clarke, 'we drove the campaign – the leader's office,
and Neil himself'. Finally, in answer to the question of why, in
view of his assessment of Mandelson's role, he had been angry
about his departure to Hartlepool before the '92 election, Clarke
repeated that it was his 'brilliant media handling' that was missed
when he went.

Kinnock was right to stress the importance of *saying* that the
campaign was a success; if the campaign had been blamed for the
result, it would have made the job of 'drawing the teeth' of Labour's
most unpopular policies all the harder. Yet the claims made for the
campaign are more than a *post hoc* defence of an election defeat.
Thanks to the calamities of April and May, as Kavanagh and Butler
put it in *The British General Election of 1987*, 'in some respects
Labour approached the election in an even worse position than in
1983'. In a perceptive *New Statesman* article in March a 'candid
friend' of Labour, the commentator Peter Kellner, had summed up
the nightmare scenario for Labour after its post-Greenwich slump.
In an echo of Patricia Hewitt's internal warning eighteen months
earlier, Kellner outlined what might happen if 'Labour makes one
or two campaign mistakes':

It is not inconceivable that the Alliance could overtake Labour by mid-campaign. At that point a whole new set of dynamics would come into play. At the moment some voters are frightened into supporting the Tories because of the danger that a vote for the Alliance would let Labour in. They would be released from their fears. Weak Labour supporters wanting not to waste their anti-Thatcher vote would also switch to the Alliance. Each successive poll would show the Alliance's lead over Labour widening . . . It would be like a by-election on a national scale, ending up as a two-party contest with Labour as the third party.

Kellner's scenario had accurately reflected Labour fears as polling day approached. In April and May Gallup recorded Labour hovering at the dangerously low level of 28 per cent. But once the election was over, it would never, through all the vicissitudes ahead under three leaders, fall below 30 per cent again.

Of course, the credit for this – very partial – recovery was not all Mandelson's. Primarily, Kinnock himself came back from the edge of despair to fight a passionate, and at times electrifying campaign. After the election Mandelson himself paid handsome tribute to Bryan Gould who, he told Butler and Kavanagh as they analysed the events for posterity, had not put a 'foot wrong'. The importance of Clarke, and especially Hewitt, to what Kinnock would tell the NEC was the 'most successful campaign in the history of the party' can hardly be overstated. Moreover, Labour's success in winning the battle to come second was greatly helped because of the failures of the Alliance campaign. The Owen-Steel leadership was an unworkable duality, underlined by David Steel's incautious complaint that the two men were like 'Tweedledum and Tweedledee'. The Alliance never wholly recovered from its split on defence in the autumn of 1986, and this failure was accentuated by David Owen's determination to differentiate the SDP from the Liberals with an eye towards the post-election future. It may be going much too far to say – as Tony Blair believes – that Mandelson 'saved the Labour Party' from disintegration in 1987. But Roy Hattersley, who lived through all the traumas of the campaign as deputy leader and Shadow Chancellor, would write that 'the brilliance of Peter's performance during the 1987 election campaign is established beyond dispute. So is (or should be) his success in forcing Labour's publicity machine to face the realities of political life . . . The 1987 election was, in terms of policy and personalities, a total failure. But it was a public relations triumph.'[20] But perhaps the most handsome – through private – tribute came from Mandelson's immediate boss at Walworth Road. Relations between Mandelson and Larry Whitty – now Lord Whitty – were seldom better than frictional, especially during the election. Which made it all the more generous of Whitty to write: 'Peter. Just in case it may on occasion have seemed I felt differently, can I record that I believe your efforts, political judgement and imagination have made this the most effective campaign the Party has ever waged. Well done – and thanks, Larry.'

For now, however, prolonged euphoria or mutual congratulation would have been singularly out of place. The breezy admission in Mandelson's 'What to Say on the Night' briefing that '. . . we failed to achieve absolutely everything we wanted' was understatement on a cosmic scale. Labour had had its second worst result since 1931. It was left needing a swing of over 8 per cent and an extra 97 seats to win next time. The Campaign Management Team had always planned to amend the main advertising slogan in the last week to 'The Country's Crying Out for Labour' if there were any signs of the party breaking through in the polls. Despite the absence of any such breakthrough the change was made, in a rather desperate effort to inject new life into the final days of the Labour campaign. But the new slogan was more hopeful than accurate. Whatever the country was 'crying out for', it was not Labour.

# CHAPTER TEN

## *Neil Feels . . .*

Almost two years after the 1987 general election Peter Mandelson joined Neil Kinnock and his team for what had become an annual drink in his office after the budget speech. After another bout of deep depression, Kinnock seemed a new man, bouncy, outgoing, determined – so much so that Mandelson asked him: 'What's happened to you?' A funny play he had seen at the National Theatre, the Labour leader explained; the therapy of painting his daughter Rachel's bedroom; and 'last but not least, the letter that a true friend sent to me'. He leapt over to his briefcase and extracted a creased note which had been written to him after an especially difficult television interview with Brian Walden. At first Mandelson was baffled, but then it came back to him: he had written the letter himself and its bluntness had verged on the brutal. The future was in Kinnock's hands, it had said; he *could* turn his party's fortunes around, but if he carried on like this, resolutely refusing to take advice – like the extensive briefing Mandelson had given him before the Walden interview – there was little point in carrying on to the election. Mandelson remembered how well Kinnock had received the admonition; at the time the 'two most important words' in the letter, he had said, were the last ('Love Peter'), whereupon he gave Mandelson one of his famous bear hugs.

The exchange said a lot about the relationship which dominated Mandelson's professional life in the three turbulent years after the 1987 election. His loyal service to Kinnock – often executed at the expense of other members of the Shadow Cabinet as well as of his own colleagues at Walworth Road – was founded on more than *Führerprinzip*. A common assumption was that Mandelson was driven purely by what Roy Hattersley would call many years later his 'maniacally ruthless loyalty to his chosen champion',[1] whoever it happened to be at the time: Kinnock, Brown and Blair, and finally Blair. Thus Mandelson would be accused of putting leader above party. But for Mandelson in this period loyalty to the leader *was* loyalty to the party. Kinnock had to be wholeheartedly supported – and this was sometimes a relatively lonely task at Walworth Road – precisely because he represented the party's best interests, and saw that it had to change. Tim Allan, the young BBC producer who would eventually go to work for Blair permanently after John Smith's death in 1994, saw Mandelson's attitude to the party as being like that of a fanatical football supporter: if his team was doing well then he was happy; if it wasn't he was despondent. For the four years after Mandelson arrived at Walworth Road, he had little doubt that Neil Kinnock, the proto-revisionist and moderniser, with all his faults, and all his descents into depression, remained the best hope for driving through the changes that would guarantee Labour's return to electability.

It was an emotional attachment, as well as a clinically professional one, but it was also complex. Mandelson felt frustrated that he did not see more of Kinnock, and sometimes entertained doubts about his ability to lead Labour into the next election; he was often exasperated by Kinnock's 'bunker' mentality and his reluctance to discuss and plan strategy – though Mandelson never betrayed the slightest hint of this concern, even to the journalists he most trusted.

Such doubts were sometimes reciprocated. When, in 1989, the *Independent* ran the first full profile of Mandelson, written (anonymously) by Colin Hughes and headlined LABOUR'S EVIL GENIUS,[2] Kinnock commented: 'Trust the *Independent* to get it half right.' The party augurs dissected this gnomic remark for months, years even: Which half? In fact it was simply too good a joke to resist. Kinnock's views were perhaps better summed up in another observation, made to their close mutual friend Alastair Campbell: 'He's not as good as he thinks he is or as bad as everyone else does.' Mandelson, based in Walworth Road, was not quite as much a part of the inner circle as he would have liked to be. Moreover, Kinnock had grown up on the left of the party, Mandelson on the right, though Kinnock had already, by the 1987 election, travelled far since the time he told Mandelson he 'hated' the Labour right. Nevertheless he knew that Mandelson's advice was disinterested. For all the trials of the next three years, there was a bond between them founded on mutual affection, illustrated by the remarkable exchange after the 1989 budget, and a common realisation of how far the party still had to change if it were to be electable. And, while Mandelson might use his organisational and briefing skills against colleagues in his own party, Kinnock knew that he would not use them against his leader.

Immediately after polling day in 1987, however, any form of recovery seemed a distant prospect. When he was working for *Weekend World*, Mandelson had noticed that he always felt deflated for a couple of days after making a programme. Recovering after election defeats, he would discover, took much longer. Colin Byrne remembered that

after the general election defeat, he literally sat in his office with his door shut for a week and Peter never used to have his door shut unless he was firing somebody or he was having some secret confab. He sat there for a week and those of us who hadn't buggered off on holiday sat there not really knowing what was happening and the buzz was, and I have to say [Andy] McSmith was the one who promoted the idea, that Mandelson was going to quit and go back to television. I remember sort of creeping in there one day with a cup of coffee and saying to him: 'You're not going to resign, are you?'[3]

Mandelson used this period to clarify his thoughts about the party's future as well as his own. He had received an outstanding, even hyperbolic, press from the election: 'Player of the Match' (Peter Jenkins); 'Star of the Campaign' (*New Statesman*). This was highly gratifying – and might have been very useful if he had wanted to bale out. But he was too much of a politician not to understand the enormity of the defeat. Nor had he accepted, as he told Kavanagh and Butler the week after polling day, the fashionable view that so-called 'demographic factors' – like the flight of aspirant working families from the inner cities – could account for more than a small proportion of Labour's decline since the seventies. But this posed acute political problems:

> No serious thought has [yet] taken place [he wrote bleakly on the second weekend after the election], although the balance of analysis is that we cannot make it next time. Part of the reason is the sheer scale of the mountain still to climb . . . But additionally and damagingly is the belief that the climate of me-ism, self-enterprise and greed (laced with North Sea oil and privatisation proceeds) is too entrenched for the Labour Party to overcome.

Perhaps presciently, he added: 'There is not a great distance left for us to travel in embracing this climate without eating into the heart of what we stand for as a party. How Thatcherite must Labour become in order to appeal to the new working class?'

This remained a problem for both Labour and the Alliance – 'planning . . . revenue-raising, collectivist parties like us'. Mandelson went on to denounce David Owen's SDP – 'weak, small, pathetic', but still a 'great disabling force for Labour' – which had demonstrated how far left the party had gone in the early 1980s and had 'stolen that portion – vital portion – of modern, moderate, professional middle ground . . . What right do the Alliance have to exist when there is such serious work to be done?' This broadly reflected his view of Owen – politically rather than personally. The two had chatted amiably from time to time at the house of the columnist Peter Jenkins and his wife Polly Toynbee, and Mandelson had at one point entertained hopes that he might endorse Neil Kinnock in the next general election. In a chance encounter in the late eighties with the Conservative political adviser Patrick Rock, however, he remarked that Owen was a 'fireship' and that he was going to 'send him your way'.

Then Mandelson considered Kinnock's own dilemma. While he had fought to make party members realise that they had to appeal to the 'haves' if they were to be elected, Kinnock's 'values and rhetoric are still tied strongly to the "have-nots". He cares too much. He's too much of a socialist and hates the idea of being seen as anything different. That's where he gets the power and passion of his performance, but is this to the voters' taste? They want a rational . . . almost clinical approach, they don't want to be inspired so much as led.' But unless Kinnock could provide that, the party was in deep trouble. 'Perhaps the national mood will change,' Mandelson concluded. 'Perhaps the Tories will be plunged into terrible scandal. Perhaps pigs will fly. When they do, I want to be part of the action.'

Being part of the action was still not a foregone conclusion, however. Daunted by the exhausting thought – albeit a distant one – of running an election campaign all over again, he seriously considered leaving. He could probably have picked up a job in advertising if he had wanted to; years later Charles Saatchi confided to a mutual friend that he had been 'on the point' of picking up the telephone to invite him to join the company, which since 1979 had been responsible for the Tories' advertising – but could not quite bring himself to do so. Instead, Mandelson applied for a job as Corporate Affairs Director for the BBC. In the event the job went to Howell James who, as a former adviser to the Tory Cabinet minister Lord Young, was better qualified to defend the BBC's licence fee from the depredations of the Thatcher government. Mandelson would certainly have taken the job if it had been offered to him, and might now be a high-ranking BBC bureaucrat. The decision was taken by the Director-General Michael Checkland; but Mandelson had several long telephone conversations with his old boss John Birt, now Checkland's deputy, about Birt's plans for a radical transformation of the corporation. They discussed, for example, whether Birt should force through a 'big bang' or move more gradually, steadily putting his own people into key jobs. These conversations whetted Mandelson's appetite for the job: it seemed to provide the opportunity to be at the cutting edge of change, in an organisation that was perhaps more susceptible to it than the Labour Party. It was in this period, rather than during his time at LWT, that Mandelson's friendship with Birt was formed.

Politics – including that of a newly crushed opposition – has an organic life of its own, however; and even as he was deciding whether to stay or go, Mandelson was sucked back into the collective task of reshaping Labour. As it happened, one of the clouds which had darkened his mood had already begun to disperse. The

Alliance was in trouble. The split within the SDP between supporters of Dr David Owen and supporters of Roy Jenkins, which had been suppressed during the election, now broke out with a rancour that could scarcely be believed of such a 'nice' party. The day after polling day the SDP's electoral fixer Alec McGivan – an Oxford contemporary of Mandelson's and an ardent advocate of merger with the Liberal Party – had told a journalist that there 'is only one game in town now: smash the Doctor'. In the event the doctor did much of his own smashing, rejecting out of hand David Steel's proposal for merger talks on 14 June.

Mandelson was too absorbed with his own party's future to pay much attention to these – from Labour's point of view, welcome – developments when he went to share his still wholly off-the-record thoughts with the XYZ Club the next day. He was, however, much concerned with retaking the portion of the electorate which Dr Owen's party had 'stolen'. XYZ was a venerable and semi-secret dining group, principally of economists and journalists sympathetic to Labour, which had been founded in 1932 by – among others – Nicholas Davenport, the financial journalist and friend of the post-war Labour Chancellor Hugh Dalton, mainly as a means of channelling City advice to the party. Hugh Gaitskell had frequently attended; it was an appropriate venue to transmit what was, by any standards, a highly revisionist message.

Mandelson had no detailed prescriptions to offer, but he was emphatic that, to be electable, 'Labour cannot offer more of the same even better packaged – however good the presentation is'. He called for an 'intellectually driven process of a change without a Bad Godesberg'.* Defence policy and 'extremism', he said, were two factors which had disastrously hobbled Labour's progress among the 'average, unpolitical, non-aligned voters', but far from being Labour's fundamental problem, these may have simply provided a 'justification' for voters struggling to choose between Labour's more attractive social policies and the 'fairly strong sense of economic and financial well being' generated by the Tories. Next time Labour would have to offer policies – especially economic

---

* The Congress of the West German SDP, which renounced Marxism in 1959.

policies – which were 'more original, more exciting, yet more thoroughly worked through than the dull, ropy, threadbare offerings of Walworth Road at the moment'. The party had to be 'conspicuous by our newness next time and not only in the glitter and professionalism of our presentation'. The lessons were clear: the party would have to be reformed so that it was 'not dominated by unrepresentative groups of activists'; not only would defence policy have to be changed, but also, perhaps even more important, economic policy. By implication, though Mandelson did not spell it out to the XYZ diners, that meant such thorny issues as tax and public ownership.

Two weeks later he was (slightly) more tactful about Walworth Road but also more specific in a paper for Charles Clarke entitled 'Moving Ahead' – a phrase which he put forward as a slogan for the party conference. The paper was one of the first to use the eventually famous 'M' word: 'Modernising policy is key to our next election image, particularly in economics, wealth creation, taxation, work. We should make a virtue of change, be as forthright and open as (internally) possible.' Instead of simply using the party's cumbersome policy committee structure, serviced by the Research Director, Geoff Bish – Mandelson's principal *bête noire* at Walworth Road – the party should spread its net wider, which would mean using 'public survey work'. 'Neil's role in implementation is crucial,' he added; 'it's his means of further enhancement. He needs to instigate, participate, guide and finally present to the nation. The last building blocks of the New Model Party.'

But who in the Shadow Cabinet was going to help the leader in this task? At this point the obvious proto-moderniser, apart from Kinnock himself, was Bryan Gould, the clever, charming and articulate New Zealander who had been the hugely successful front man, and easily Mandelson's closest colleague during the election campaign. Following his performance during this campaign, which had made him (after Kinnock) the best-known Labour face on television, Gould topped the shadow cabinet elections. He badly wanted to replace Roy Hattersley as Shadow Chancellor and claimed that Kinnock told him he would have done, had Hattersley not insisted on John Smith as his replacement. Appointed instead as Shadow Trade and Industry spokesman, Gould was quick to offer, if not a blueprint, at least a signpost for the future direction of the party. The day before Mandelson presented his 'Moving Ahead' paper, Gould had said much the same thing: too often the party had brought in a 'group of experts', agreed a policy, and 'then we think, almost as an afterthought, of how it has to be sold to the electorate'. Instead, 'what we ought to be doing is looking at where policies come from, what the demand is ... In that way we can make sure that policy includes its popular appeal from the outset.' Though Gould did not once use the term 'focus group', it was the most striking endorsement yet of their use in policy-making.

Mandelson's political infatuation with Bryan Gould in the latter half of 1987 was pronounced, and much commented on. Gould recalls that they were 'on very friendly terms', which was, if anything, an understatement.[4] Late in 1987 Mandelson was invited by the pro-Labour lobbyist Richard Faulkner to a congenial dinner at a Shropshire restaurant for a discussion with Bryan and Gill Gould; he had assumed that it was to talk about the party's future. Instead they discussed Gould's own future as a Labour star and, in the long term, as a possible leader. Mandelson later claimed that he largely kept his own counsel at the dinner, maintaining a kind of studied neutrality. But, characteristically, he kept quiet about the discussion, and did not mention it to Neil Kinnock, for example.

The promotion of Gould had caused inevitable tensions with senior right-wingers on the Shadow Cabinet. At the end of August those tensions became quite dramatically evident during a long and alarming late-night conversation between Mandelson and Hattersley, John Smith and Donald Dewar at the Smiths' house in Edinburgh.

Mandelson was in the city for the Edinburgh Television Festival and John and Elizabeth Smith, hearing of his visit, had invited him to stay. They were warm and hospitable hosts and to Mandelson's surprise, in view of recent events, Hattersley was also friendly. The deputy leader was, however, infuriated by what he regarded as Gould's weightless electoralism and there was robust discussion among the four men concerning Gould and the Shadow Chancellorship. Smith, who had finally won the position, thought that Patricia Hewitt had been doing him down in press briefings; Mandelson thought that Hattersley and David Hill had been equally active against Gould's candidacy, although Hattersley later told Hill that when Mandelson complained about Hill's briefings, Smith had told him abrasively to 'shut up or fuck off'. But Mandelson himself was not entirely blameless in these proceedings: he had tried to defend Gould to journalists incurring in the process the charge that he was promoting the New Zealander. But what was more apparent, as the three old shadow cabinet friends unwound with Mandelson over whiskies in the Smith living room, was their frustration with the leader himself. Smith began with characteristic bluntness: you never knew where you stood with Kinnock, he said. You never got to see him, and when you did he agreed with everything you said – but then ignored it or did something different. Smith conceded freely that Kinnock was a superb party manager and infighter – but he had to be much more than that. His rhetorical performances during the election had indeed been brilliant, but performances were exactly what they had been: 'froth, pure froth'; where was the real content and authority?[5] Finally, why was he surrounded by such inexperienced staff – top-drawer Cambridge graduates no doubt, but hardly substantial political advisers?

This criticism from Kinnock's supposed allies in the Shadow Cabinet was awkward for Mandelson, to say the least. As it happened, Dewar, Hattersley and Smith were sprawled on sofas and easy chairs in a horseshoe formation; Mandelson was sitting at the open end on a raised seat – as if in the dock, for which the three elected politicians were duly and good-humouredly apologetic. But that was trivial; what was much more worrying was that Smith was patently sincere; his concerns were real rather than merely vindictive. Moreover, Hattersley and his friends belonged to Mandelson's own faction of the party: had he not joined Solidarity, and campaigned in 1983 not for Kinnock but for Hattersley? Mandelson had had his own problems of access to Kinnock: his 'Moving Ahead' memo to Clarke had carried at the bottom a plaintive little handwritten addendum – 'Can we discuss this with Neil?' The discussion had never taken place. In the event the proposal had been approved without any discussion of what it meant in practice. And Mandelson was a mere official, not in the same league as the new Shadow Chancellor. If Mandelson now roundly rebutted these criticisms, he knew he would appear naive at best. Yet agreeing with them meant showing disloyalty to Kinnock. In the event he defended the staff; but this, as he quickly realised, only made matters worse. If the staff were so good, their briefing so excellent, the diary so well kept, why was the leader not able to perform better? The fact was that Kinnock himself – or, rather, his lack of self-assurance – was at least part of the problem; he felt defensive and beleaguered, unable to deal with his colleagues as friends or at least as equal partners.

The following morning Mandelson raised with Hattersley – who, along with his wife Molly, was also staying with the Smiths – one aspect of the previous night's frequently heated discussion. If Smith and Gould could not smooth out the friction between them, what hope was there for cohesion within the Shadow Cabinet? Mandelson did not need to add that this was a crucial question given the battles which would have to be joined against the left. Hattersley's answer was not encouraging. Although he had nothing personally against Bryan Gould, he thought he had been 'precipitate' and 'tactless' in his post-election comments about taxation and public ownership and had 'succeeded in treading on all sorts of corns'. Hattersley also announced that he was going to write an article for the magazine *New Socialist* challenging a number of Gould's pronouncements – including 'all this nonsense about developing policies for the 1990s'. Mandelson felt that the deputy leader was being reactionary about new thinking, new people, new forms of presentation, but he merely expressed his concern that such an article might make Labour look even more divided. He did not want to fall out with Hattersley and, given his position at this stage, could not have afforded to do so. Hattersley and Smith were formidable figures in the Labour Party – some would say the two most formidable. Mandelson did not dare admit to the deputy leader that he himself had been partly responsible for putting 'all this nonsense' into Gould's head.

There was a final coda to the conversation. Hattersley asked Mandelson if he thought Labour would win the next election. Mandelson, by his own account, merely said that he could not be sure. Hattersley also asked him what he thought Kinnock would do if he lost the next election. Mandelson replied that he would have to go; Hattersley replied that that would be 'awful' for him and added – quite wrongly, as it turned out – that there would be no alternative occupation for him to turn to. All this was unexceptional; but each man also inferred – or chose to infer – that the other now expected Kinnock to lose the 1992 election. In a letter 'written in a wholly friendly spirit' to Mandelson a few days later Hattersley said, 'I know from our conversations in Edinburgh that you regard victory at the next election as virtually impossible . . . I am not ready yet to write off 1992 – though I admit that it may be something to do with my age.' But for his part Mandelson, in a letter replying to Hattersley was unequivocal: 'You say I believe victory is virtually impossible next time: in fact I believe this is unlikely if you four [Kinnock, Smith, Hattersley and Gould] do not stand together. As I said, I think Neil would simply resign with the disappointment. I desperately want the opposite outcome – that's why I am prepared for a few risks too.' Mandelson felt aggrieved that Hattersley, having led him into a conversation about what might happen *if* Labour lost, was now attributing to him the view that Labour *would* lose. So much so that he went straight to Kinnock and told him about the correspondence, sensibly covering himself against the letter, or Hattersley's version of the conversation in Edinburgh, being brought to the notice of the leader. Kinnock, to his credit utterly unfazed, told him to take no notice of the Hattersley letter. 'I've got a drawerful of them, kid,' he told Mandelson.

Viewed in retrospect, the episode was probably more significant as an omen of future trouble between Smith and Kinnock than for what it exposed about the conflict with Bryan Gould. The old right's hostility to Gould, warmly reciprocated, hardly produced an epic confrontation – though it might have done so during the next few months if Gould had done more than toy with the idea of standing as deputy leader. In any case, Gould was not in the end the main motor of the sweeping review of policy which he and Mandelson had been pressing for, though he took charge of one part of it. The fraught task of negotiating the idea of such a review through the party machinery, and then coordinating its implementation, was assumed by a publicly much less well-known figure, the trade unionist Tom Sawyer, deputy general secretary of NUPE and chairman of the then pivotal Home Policy Committee of the NEC.

First there was the Brighton 1987 conference to get through. Mandelson was in his element, patrolling the vast Ramada Hotel foyer and ensuring that journalists had properly interpreted events at the nearby Conference Centre. This was no mean feat. The idea of a policy review, robustly advocated by Sawyer, was approved by a largely sullen conference, and the favourable press the following morning – noted by, among others, Tony Benn – owed a lot to the Mandelson mantra, repeated again and again to journalists, that 'nothing will be excluded' from the review. The difficulties ahead were underlined by the issue of defence. In his leader's speech on the Tuesday, Kinnock said that the party's defence policy would be 'capable of dealing with the changed conditions of the 1990s'. But Mandelson's heavily spun line – put out, on this occasion at least, with Kinnock's approval – that this implied an eventual abandonment of unilateralism, was fatally undermined when Ken Livingstone decided to make an issue of the party's non-nuclear defence policy, saying at a Tribune rally that to change it would mean civil war in the party. Joy Johnson of ITN lay in wait at the Ramada with a camera crew for Kinnock's reaction to the Livingstone speech,

> and I just said, 'Mr Kinnock, yesterday you called for unity, and today one of your NEC members is going to say . . .' and you could see Neil getting redder and redder and angrier. So as he was walking away I was saying, 'So you are not going to abandon unilateralism then?' And he turned round: 'We are maintaining a non-nuclear policy and you know it.' And I rushed back and it led Channel Four News . . . and Peter came up to me afterwards and put his arm round me as he is wont to do [and said], 'That was a very interesting intervention that you made there, wasn't it.' And then he didn't speak to me for a year . . . I was on the list of people not to be talked to. He was livid.[6]

Mandelson was indeed furious. His whole carefully woven strategy of dumping unilateralism was, if not unravelled, at least dangerously delayed.

But it was not just a matter of defence. The conference's approval of the policy review had been somewhat reluctant. A gloomy *Guardian* leader mirrored Mandelson's true thoughts much more closely than all his upbeat sloganising to journalists about 'change' and 'dynamism': 'The delegates don't really like what [Kinnock] and

Mr Bryan Gould and Mr Peter Mandelson are doing to them . . . the leader's keynote speech, though admirably frank in many respects, did not move the party far enough towards the real problems it must address.'[7]

Mandelson withdrew to Foy with distinctly mixed feelings about his decision to stay in his job. Several of his friends, including Robin Paxton at LWT, were urging him to leave; and would he ever again get so much credit for an election campaign? However, over dinner one night at the conference Anthony Howard, the deputy editor of the *Observer*, had insisted that he had a 'duty', just like Howard's old friend Roy Hattersley, to remain in his post and see the fight through to the next general election. But the conference itself had suggested that this would be, at best, an uphill struggle. Gould, repeating his remarks about share ownership, had been booed and hissed from the conference floor; so had Sawyer, when he wound up the policy review debate. True, the conference had rejected a move to include a reaffirmation of Clause Four in one resolution – prompting Mandelson to ask himself for the first time why Hugh Gaitskell had run into so much trouble when he tried to change it. But Ken Livingstone had been ruthless in his manipulation of the defence debate and now appeared to Mandelson an even more potent threat to Labour progress than Tony Benn had been. 'Where will we be this time next year?' he wrote at the time. 'No wonder the Tories and our own hard left are smiling. They both think we will have short term victories within the party but that they will prevail in the end. In their own respective spheres they have too much reason for confidence.'

A similar gloom appeared to pervade the Shadow Cabinet the following week, when it met for an 'away-day' at the Rottingdean rest home of the print union SOGAT. Jack Straw, then, as now, a moderniser, made the point that during the election Labour had been seen too much as a party 'taking away things from people'. It needed to be seen in the opposite light: not bribing the electors, but finding ways to improve people's lives. And John Smith, for all his later reputation as a consolidator rather than a radical moderniser, was blunt in saying that the party would have to 'abandon a lot of areas which have been privatised'. He questioned the wisdom, for example, of committing the party to the repurchase of British Telecom shares; they had taken a risk with the public rather than with the party, and had lost out as a result. The sharpest note of dissent – an omen of trouble to come – was sounded by John Prescott. There was, he said, confusion about what the party now stood for. The policy review was a risky undertaking; if it came up with the same programme electors would feel that they had been 'double crossed'. Surely there were two fundamental principles which needed to be restated: full employment and redistribution. Finally, however, Kinnock, candid, sombre and frankly depressing, said that the party would review policy because it had 'nowhere else to go, nothing better to do'. Labour needed 'unhooking' from the electors' prejudices – for example, on ownership. He recognised some 'irreversibles', but not many.

In this bleak political landscape Mandelson also hesitated about staying at Walworth Road for more personal reasons – not least his difficult relations with colleagues (other than those in the press office itself). According to Colin Byrne, 'Peter used to come out of these meetings either depressed or fuming and it was like some sort of awful Monday morning ritual that he had to go through . . . but he also knew he had to work within the confines of the system and push things through.' Mandelson also told Charles Clarke of his disdain for Geoff Bish. His tensions with Whitty were more complicated: Whitty is in many respects a milder, more consensual, and less ruthless man than Mandelson. Moreover, he felt that the Walworth directors were there to serve the whole NEC and the party rather than just the leader. To Mandelson this was a tiresome technicality, to be ignored whenever possible. Consequently tensions persisted between Mandelson and other senior Walworth Road officials, who, Philip Gould noted in his diary, were trying to 'cut out' Mandelson.

Yet serving Kinnock was not always that easy. Mandelson's authority, at least with journalists, depended on the assumption that he spoke directly for the leader. According to Nick Jones, BBC correspondent and enthusiastic spin-watcher, 'His close working relationship with Kinnock made him an authoritative source; journalists would not be satisfied with a story or the accuracy of the party's response until they had spoken to him personally.'[8] Mandelson told Jones that for the first two years in the job he never went out on Saturday evenings because he was rung up continuously by reporters following some 'appalling story in the Sunday news-papers'. On such occasions he would invariably begin his response, 'Neil feels . . .', often continuing with a point-by-point rebuttal, or plan of action, mapped out in advance in his neat handwriting. Yet frequently he had only the haziest knowledge of what Kinnock *did* feel. Sometimes, of course, he would seek direct authority before briefing the press – on occasions with an ostentation which greatly irritated senior figures in the party, especially on the left. Tom Saw-yer remembered that 'He would be visibly at the NEC meeting, sending notes to Neil during the meeting, when a furious debate might be going on, and clearly going outside and telling the *One O'Clock News* while Tony Benn was in the middle of a debate with Neil. And Tony could see this. So it wasn't hard for people to see what was happening.'[9] Frequently, however, he freelanced, acting on his own initiative as a kind of deniable agent of the leader. When Sawyer produced his seminal policy review paper in the late summer, Mandelson, taking a routine call from the quietly persistent George Jones of the *Daily Telegraph*, divulged enough of the document's flavour for the paper to lead the following day with a story sug-gesting that the party was, at long last, abandoning socialism.

Since the Home Policy Committee was meeting that very day, the story could hardly have been more provocative to those resisting change. Kinnock was furious and Mandelson, half-fearing that he might have gone too far this time, did not confess that he was the source. (This happened not infrequently; indeed, sometimes Hewitt and he would cover each other: if asked, each could say that the other had not been responsible.) Instead, he coolly argued that, since the story had now appeared and the press were therefore taking an unhealthily strong interest in the committee – with a dozen journalists camped out in the Commons committee room corridor – Kinnock should say something publicly about the review.

This was a high-risk strategy. For his part, Mandelson thought that Kinnock tended to underestimate the role of the press in gener-ating momentum in the process of change. Conversely, although Kinnock himself was consistently courageous in overcoming resist-ance in the party, he and Charles Clarke sometimes believed that Mandelson was too impatient and cavalier about the dangers posed by such internal resistance. Moreover, journalists on the receiving end of a confident and authoritative 'Neil feels . . .' briefing would have been amazed if they had known that Mandelson's role in the leader's inner court was not always as much of a Kinnock confidant as he would have liked to be.

The relationship between Patricia Hewitt, Mandelson and Charles Clarke – all of whom became ministers in the Blair government – was pivotal at this period. Of the three, Clarke was the closest to Kinnock, the shock-absorber for all his moods, and most frequently the person with whom access to Kinnock had to be negotiated. On strategies like 'Moving Ahead' Mandelson worked closely with Clarke, who was enough of a plenipotentiary to take quite important decisions without discussing the details with his leader. However irritated Clarke may have been by the praise heaped on Mandelson over the election, he had no doubt where his loyalties lay:

> He saw the leader as crucial and the relationship between myself and Peter was very very close. Peter would always check things with me if it was necessary. And if necessary I'd then check them with Neil. And frank, completely frank. We were a combination. I thought Peter got too much on the media's side and didn't understand the party weights and so on. But fundamentally he was absolutely 'Neil's First' in all this. And that was right, he should have been. That's what his job was.[10]

Nevertheless Mandelson frequently felt not only that his talents were under-used but also that insufficient thought and discussion were put into the product he was supposed to sell. This was generally not a matter of rivalry with Patricia Hewitt. Indeed, given the overlap of their two jobs, it is surprising that they got on as well as they did. Their abilities were in many ways complementary. A short item in the *New Statesman* before the 1987 general election had vividly compared their public images. 'Two youngish people who have downwardly mobilised themselves out of the Porsche class to which their birth or talents or both had fitted them . . . she is Australian mandarin class, he has an impeccable Labour pedigree. She is intense, quick to smile and to flare, both impulsively diplomatic at once; He is hugely cool, seeming to inhabit a space comfortably removed from the fray while being in the thick of it.' And not always as cool as he seemed, the piece might have added.

Mandelson's own poor relations with Walworth Road, and the fact that Kinnock trusted Hewitt as the professional press officer she undoubtedly was, contributed somewhat to a sense of isolation of which the journalists with whom Mandelson regularly dealt had no inkling. Yet after the election Mandelson discovered that Hewitt frequently felt as isolated from the rest of the office – and as frustrated by Kinnock's hostility to the press – as he did. On the one hand Kinnock was deeply suspicious of anything that smacked of news management; on the other he had a tendency to study every line in newspapers as if his life depended on it. Moreover, Hewitt went out of her way to keep Mandelson informed about what was happening in the leader's office. Mandelson had a deep respect for Hewitt's undoubted strategic talents; indeed, a decade later, when he was musing about who might replace him when he was finally released from his coordination job at the Cabinet, Hewitt, then a mere backbencher in the 1997 intake, was the one candidate who sprang to his mind (in the event the job went to Blair's old friend, the lawyer Charles Falconer).

When Hewitt was eased out of her job as press officer in 1988 it was widely assumed – for example, in the *Mail on Sunday* – that Mandelson had been the assassin. In fact it was Clarke, who had had mixed feelings, to say the least, about Hewitt ever since she had stayed with the Clarkes in Hampstead Garden Suburb on her first visit to London from Australia (her civil servant father knew Otto Clarke). Everyone was interested in the vivacious, intelligent and sociable teenager, a contemporary recalled; 'she powerfully irritated Charles, always giving parties and going to them and Charles thought she was like Lady Muck.' In the mid-1980s, however, the dynamic was different. According to Clarke himself, Kinnock, having finally decided that she was right for the job, had left a message on Clarke's answering machine saying: 'I'm going to do this unless you *really* object.' Clarke did not fully trust Hewitt; she, in turn, was nervous of him. In the end he told Kinnock that either she went as press officer, or he would. He then hit on the ingenious solution of creating a new job of policy coordinator, modelled on a similar post in the office of the leader of the Israeli Labour Party; this would take her out of the front line without total loss of face. Mandelson maintained a studied neutrality in the affair. He did not, greatly to his later regret, move to try and save Hewitt, rationalising that he was a Walworth Road official and that this was an internal matter within Kinnock's own office. The move was made; but Kinnock paid a heavy price for it. To his great dismay, three months later Hewitt left for a job at the Institute of Public Policy Research.

Mandelson was not helped by the tensions between Clarke and Hewitt. But his real frustrations went much wider than that. Where was the party really going, and would he have a role in the decision-making? After the party conference he summarised his angst to Charles Clarke in a letter which went through more than one draft – written with the help of Alastair Campbell – but which in the end he never sent. Instead he showed it to Patricia Hewitt, who agreed that Clarke would see it as a criticism and react with either anger or, worse, despair. These drafts afford some insight into the problems encountered by the supposedly omnipotent spin doctor. In one, signed affectionately, 'I remain your best friend', he complained that he felt 'neither comfortable nor stretched by the responsibility I'm given . . . I do my job energetically most days, nights and week-ends. I usually gather from Patricia what's going on and I faithfully put out the line. More often I speak to journalists on the basis of a mixture of telepathy, guesswork and invention.' In another version he said that while

I still believe . . . that my institutional entrapment at Walworth Road does put me in a relegated category and obviously I am sorry I cannot exercise much influence . . . the situation is more serious than any personal isolation . . . Unless we all hang together and devote more energy and time and intellectual con-centration to working out where we are going in the policy review and our party's rebirth we will fail and Neil will fail too. The experience of the period between June and October has been telling. I write a memo . . . Moving Ahead. Without any dis-cussion it is agreed. We barely communicate while it is being implemented, we arrive in Brighton with the barest of media strategies and get through the week pinning our reputations to a badly written stream of consciousness emanating from Geoff

Bish. Neil does his damnedest to lift things up and does a good job. But he is still not using the talent and energy of those around him . . . Haven't we got to organise ourselves better?

This version ended even more chattily, 'As ever, Jolly Pierre.'

None of these inner thoughts, needless to say, ever surfaced from behind the suave exterior of the man still widely credited with Labour's 'brilliant election defeat'. His image, at least among journalists, as the modern face of a party climbing steadily back to electability was, if anything, growing. *The Times* saw fit to splash across its front page selected extracts from an unexceptionally revisionist paper – leaked by Mandelson, of course – in which he had stressed that while 'good presentation' was a condition for success 'the policies will ultimately determine success or failure.'[11] Nick Jones's depiction of a man 'always in demand' because 'of his grasp of Labour's inner politics and his ready availability' was widely accepted among lobby journalists. In December 1987, with cheeky confidence Mandelson used a 'My Week' column to confide in readers of the *Independent* that at NEC meetings he liked to sit with the left-wingers – or, as he put it, 'the members who vote in a minority' – partly so that he could pick up the 'aroma of freshly shelled boiled eggs being prepared for the midday sandwiches' and partly so that he could spread out papers (NEC meetings being a 'good opportunity to sign those dozens of invoices which it is my privilege to countersign').[12]

Nor, in the end, did he share all his doubts with Clarke himself. Shortly before Christmas 1987 they lunched together, but the conversation was dominated by what Mandelson called the 'virtual insanity' of trying to work with his colleagues at Walworth Road: he was deeply impatient with Whitty for not attempting to remove the old-stager, as he saw him, Geoff Bish. The two parted on warm, mutually congratulatory terms, but they did not really confront the much wider issues preoccupying Mandelson. Surveying the Shadow Cabinet, he felt that several of its most senior members were now contemptuous of their leader. And one of the party's bright new hopes, Gordon Brown, a fellow Kinnock loyalist and a man to whom Mandelson was now talking with increasing frequency, was impatient at the party's lack of overall strategy and its refusal to find the 'right answers' to the 'right problems'. At the same time Margaret Thatcher seemed to cast as long a shadow as ever over the political landscape. Mandelson was beginning to sense that his present role might be drawing to a close: 1988 might after all be the year to move on. He would have little time to develop the thought in the New Year, however. John Prescott was on the march.

# CHAPTER ELEVEN

## *Aiming for the Stars,*
## *Fighting in the Gutter*

In 1989 Mandelson gave Alastair Campbell a detailed description of his weekend routine in Herefordshire: 'leave London at 7 p.m. on Friday, arrive at Ross-on-Wye before ten, leave a note at the newsagent ordering all the papers, watch the news, go next door for a whisky with the neighbours [Pearl and Graham Bevis] before going to bed.' Then 'Saturday morning is spent mainly on the phone to the Sunday papers, then I go for lunch at Meader's Hungarian Restaurant in Ross. I *always* go there and I always have the same dish, layered cabbage.' Then (inevitably) 'I come back for a sleep and after that I'm really beginning to feel refreshed. Then I tackle the garden. Through the evening I'm back on the phone again, dealing with calls arising out of the early editions.' Sunday, he explained, was the same 'mix of work and leisure'.

The three-bedroom semi-detached farmworker's cottage in a loop of the river Wye in the tiny hamlet of Foy, was the first house Mandelson had owned. He had spotted it while on holiday in Monmouthshire in 1984 and bought it two months later for £31,000. It had a small garden – symbolically complete with a bed of red roses. As Campbell reported, 'there are no carpets, just a collection of variously sized . . . rugs. The three-piece suite is second hand. Paintings vary from originals done by friends to fine Vermeer prints ripped from an art book and framed. Taking pride of place is an original cartoon of Mandelson's grandfather . . . Herbert Morrison.' Foy played a key part in Mandelson's life for five years; it was probably the place where he was happiest during his adult life. He had lent it as a refuge (for a holiday and two weekend breaks) to an appreciative David Hill and Hilary Coffman after their relationship was – fatuously – 'exposed' in the *News of the World*, but spent much of the post-election summer of 1987 there. He went down most weekends – often with Peter Ashby, Kay Carberry and their child – for the 'mix' of leisure and weekend work needed 'to make sure the party is firing on all cylinders and to try see that we're properly reported'.

On the New Year weekend of 1988, however, the party was certainly *not* firing on all cylinders. On the morning of Saturday 2 January the *Guardian* reported that John Prescott was now 'telling journalists' that he intended to stand against Roy Hattersley for the deputy leadership – a move which could not fail to infuriate Kinnock, who was trying to show that the party was now united. What followed gives some insight into what a weekend 'trying to make sure the party is firing on all cylinders' could be like during the 1987–92 parliament. It also illustrates the Keystone Cops nature of the Shadow Cabinet over which Neil Kinnock was obliged to preside in the late eighties, not to mention the extent – and limitations – of Mandelson's delicate role as confidant to its leading members. Having gloomily digested the *Guardian*, Mandelson began his round of telephone conversations with Jill Hartley of the *Sunday Times*, who confirmed that Prescott had indeed talked about his deputy leadership ambitions. On impulse, Mandelson then telephoned Prescott himself; reaching him in Hull as his shivering constituents waited for attention at one of his weekly surgeries, he found him in candid mood. He had made up his mind; it was just a case of finding the best date to announce his plan. He was only speaking to Mandelson (among those in Kinnock's confidence) about it, he explained. He would not discuss the issue with Kinnock himself. He had no wish to undermine Kinnock, but if Kinnock attacked him he would fight back. There was already television film of him in the can and ready for use when he made his announcement. 'I'm going to do it,' he repeated firmly; 'I'm going to do it.' Prescott promised to call back when he had discussed his candidacy with his constituency officers.

At this point Kinnock himself telephoned Mandelson – not, as Mandelson initially assumed, about Prescott, but to find out what disparaging remarks John Edmonds, then general secretary of the GMB, had made about him at a dinner of the 'Shadow Journalists Group', which Mandelson had formed to give media advice to the party. The question was an embarrassing one. By all accounts Edmonds had cast generalised aspersions on Kinnock's leadership. Mandelson managed to sidestep it by warning Kinnock about Prescott's intentions. When Glenys Kinnock phoned her husband on his other line with a homely request to be picked up from Marks and Spencer with the Saturday shopping, Kinnock promised to ring back later. By the time he did, Mandelson had taken a call from David Hill, fulminating on Roy Hattersley's behalf about the latest atrocity committed by Bryan Gould. Gould, asked by Jill Hartley for his view on Prescott's plan, had said that he would also 'consider' standing for the deputy leadership if there was a contest. This, too, was a little awkward; Mandelson was still close to Gould; he knew that Gould was increasingly keen to see Hattersley off, having been subjected to his unrestrained attacks in the wake of last year's general election. Mandelson nevertheless calmed Hill down before taking the call from Kinnock, to whom he now recounted the full details of his morning calls.

Kinnock's response was striking. He roundly denounced Prescott, declaring that he had had enough. He was not going through another four years of fighting battles, 'hand-holding, and nappy-changing', simply to lose all over again. He expressed concern about Gould's remarks. And then he began to muse on how Prescott's ambitions could be undermined through his constituency in Hull and the National Union of Seaman, which sponsored him. A little later Kinnock called Mandelson for a third time, now in a more cheerful mood. He had been told by Hattersley that before Christmas Prescott's own constituency executive had voted against him standing for the deputy leadership. And he had also spoken to Sam McCluskie, deputy general secretary of the NUS, a senior member of the party NEC and a close friend of Prescott's, who confirmed not only that he was personally strongly opposed to the idea but that he had his union's executive 'in his pocket' on the issue. A few minutes later Hattersley telephoned, putting Mandelson directly on the spot. He had sought and got assurances from Kinnock, who had suggested he telephone Mandelson for confirmation: he, Mandelson, wasn't privately supporting Gould as a candidate for the deputy leadership, was he? Once again Mandelson's motivation is interesting; had Kinnock showed any sign of wanting Gould to stand, he would no doubt have been ready to champion his candidacy. But Kinnock had done nothing of the kind; indeed, he had made it clear he did not want a contest. Mandelson now gave Hattersley the reassurance he was seeking. Hattersley was grateful but still worried – what was Gould up to?

Mandelson now realised he had to confront his friend: he telephoned him at home and, while not ruling out the possibility that circumstances might change, told him firmly that he must not now be 'seen to be exacerbating the situation'. Gould, possibly already in two minds about whether he really wanted the deputy leadership, readily agreed. Mandelson then telephoned Jill Hartley and calmly told her that, whatever she might have heard, Gould was not intending to stand for the deputy leadership. Not for the first – or last – time he was acting in accordance with the famous dictum of Richard Nixon's spokesman Ron Ziegler, that 'all previous statements are inoperative'. Hartley, understandably reluctant to see the amputation of an important leg of her story, insisted on hearing this unwelcome news from Gould himself; Mandelson immediately warned him of her call and Gould agreed to confirm what Mandelson had said. Thus, in somewhat haphazard fashion, was a Gould challenge that might have hugely boosted his influence in the party – and perhaps even changed the course of its history – killed off. Mandelson rang Hattersley to tell him the news; Hattersley, as he audibly relaxed, told Mandelson that 'we might save the party after all' and that he might not need to go 'off and make millions in television'. Mandelson was not entirely convinced, but he did not say so either to Hattersley or to Kinnock, whom he now telephoned with a full report. The following morning's *Sunday Times* duly carried a story under the headline: GOULD: I WON'T RUN FOR DEPUTY LEADERSHIP.

Next came a call from John Smith, who wanted to ask Mandelson whether he should accept an invitation from the BBC to appear on the following day's *World This Weekend*. His instincts, he said, were to have nothing to do with it. On the other hand it might be a good moment to show support for his close friend Hattersley and, as he put it, 'put a boot on Prescott's throat'. Mandelson was not so sure: an open attack on Prescott from the pro-Hattersley right wing of the party would make a lot of headlines but would not influence Prescott's attitude; it might be positively counter-productive. Mandelson was already seen as someone who was never lost for an opinion, especially when it came to manipulating his colleagues or rubbishing opponents. But now he suggested rather prosaically that, given the sensitivity of the issue, Smith should telephone Kinnock for advice.

Later that evening Charles Clarke returned the call that Mandelson had made to him much earlier in the day. This time Mandelson was clear: he strongly urged Clarke to persuade Kinnock to make a 'clear, immediate, public request' to Prescott not to stand. This would give Prescott a first-class pretext to withdraw in the interests of party unity. But even Mandelson's confidence was shaken when Prescott, true to his earlier promise, telephoned him back. He had consulted his constituency officers; he would guaran-tee that local branches in Hull would submit resolutions urging him to stand. He would withstand any pressure that was brought to bear upon him; if Kinnock wanted to tough it out, then he was ready – and everybody would be surprised by the support he got. There was, as Mandelson well knew, considerable force in Prescott's arguments – especially his complaint that Hattersley did not put in the effort or really do the job of deputy leader, as Prescott not unreasonably judged it should be done, by touring the country and rallying the party. Such arguments would be attractive in a number of quarters in the party. Reflecting after yet another call, this time to apprise Clarke of Prescott's unflinching determination, Mandelson reached two conclusions: firstly that Hattersley would probably remain as deputy leader; and secondly that there would indeed be a contest, which would mean a long, hard slog ahead.

He proved to be right on both counts. True, there nearly wasn't a contest. In a deal brokered by McCluskie and Rodney Bickerstaffe, the NUPE general secretary, it was agreed in late January that Pre-scott would stand down in return for the promise of a full debate on the role of the deputy leader at the party conference in the autumn. Kinnock even had a hand in the drafting of an NUS motion on the subject. But when Prescott announced that he was standing down as a result of the deal, hostilities broke out again almost immediately. Kinnock, having listened, in the presence of Hattersley, to a tape of the Prescott press conference, reacted angrily to the implication that his present deputy would be stripped of his (home affairs) portfolio in return for remaining in office.

A counter-operation was then mounted by Kinnock's lieutenants – for which Prescott squarely blamed Mandelson, 'souring their relationship for years', as Prescott's biographer Colin Brown put it.[1] Mandelson was certainly involved, though he would later insist that he had intended a more carefully calibrated response than the one given by the understandably partisan Hill. Fierce as the briefing was, however, it was nevertheless partially backed up by a press release directly approved by Kinnock and issued in his name, which asserted that he was 'completely hostile' to the idea of 'excluding a Deputy Leader of the Labour Party from a major parliamentary portfolio'. The Kinnockites' rebuttal certainly went over the top; it even insisted that Prescott had only pulled out of the contest to avoid an overwhelming defeat; Prescott was enraged to see big front-page stories like that in *The Times* trumpeting his 'public humiliation' by Kinnock.[2] The episode provided Prescott with an excuse for retracting his decision not to stand for the deputy leadership. Two months later a decision by the Campaign Group to promote a doomed leadership bid by Tony Benn and Eric Heffer furnished him with the opportunity. If there was going to be a contest anyway, all bets were off.

Formally, Mandelson intervened in the deputy leadership contest only once, in April, when he sent Prescott a 'Dear John' letter marked 'Strictly Personal' and protesting about the (widely held) claim he had made in a *New Statesman* interview that 'it was Walworth Road which kept me off television during the election because of my image'. Mandelson wrote with characteristic precision:

The new Butler/Kavanagh book on the election reveals that out of 56 politicians on the Labour side, you ranked 8 in quotes, appearances, etc. on radio and television. There was not a single occasion when I or the central campaign unit intervened to keep you off television. However much you joked with Andrew [Fox] and Tony [Beeton, both in the press office] about your 'face not fitting' you were continuously put up for programmes.

The accusation was an 'unnecessary slur on my staff'. He concluded: 'I think it would be better if Walworth Road were kept out of the propaganda war.'

Informally, however, he actively worked to limit the damage of Prescott's challenge – not least by 'killing' a sensational story given to the *Observer* by Roy Hattersley, by the simple stratagem of saying, probably falsely, that it was untrue. Hattersley had revealed that Kinnock had told Rodney Bickerstaffe that he would resign as leader if Prescott won the deputy leadership. Hattersley's tactics were questionable: such a threat might encourage some unions, and perhaps even some MPs, to vote for Prescott in order to make it clear that they were not going to be pushed around. Hattersley – and David Hill – were both convinced that Kinnock really would have resigned; according to Hattersley, he said that it would have shown that the party was 'not serious'.[3] Nevertheless Mandelson's quashing of the Hattersley story also protected Kinnock's position. By raising the stakes, such a story might have meant that, in the unlikely event of a Prescott victory, Kinnock would have come under immediate pressure to resign. In the event, Prescott avoided humiliation with a respectable 23.7 per cent of the electoral college vote; but the TGWU's support for Hattersley and the growth of individual balloting in constituency parties ensured a decisive victory for the incumbent, with 66.8 per cent. It was hard to see just what all the fuss had been about.

In May Tony Mandelson had died. This inflicted a deep trauma on all his family, but perhaps especially on his younger son. Despite their sometimes harsh disagreements, usually over politics, Tony Mandelson had, on impulse, visited his son in Foy the previous summer for what turned out to be an entirely reconciliatory and enjoyable day. He had come up on the train, bringing with him a little gift of a ceramic ashtray with a red rose on it. The weather was glorious, and they went for a walk. There were no rows. Mandelson cooked him lunch, and then they had a snooze. Mandelson took him back to Hereford station to catch his train; he would remember the day with pleasure for years afterwards.

Mandelson was stricken with grief by his death. In 1997, asked by Oliver James on *The Chair* where he was when he heard about his father's death, he was unable to answer, saying tearfully, 'I can't talk about that.' It had been so swift; in a letter of condolence written five months later to Steve Howell after *his* father's death he said:

> You may know that my father died in May. It was a terrible surprise. He got a bad chest, then they found cancer and then he had a heart attack in the space of two weeks. My mother is very quiet about it and very alone because she was never one to have many friends. The people she liked in the house were our friends . . . rather than her generation. She misses all that a lot . . . I try to see her and phone her during the week. She'll come to stay with me in Ross at Christmas.

Mandelson had already been very shocked to learn of his father's illness; Neil Kinnock, an emotional and naturally sympathetic man, had affectionately cradled his head in his arms when Mandelson told him that his father had cancer. Andy McSmith remembered him shut in his office, with only the press office secretary Phyllis going in and out, on the morning he heard that he was ill, before emerging to discuss the 'line to take' on that day's meeting of the NEC, tears still streaming down his face.

But the reason why he found the question of where he had been so painful was that when he went to visit his father in the Royal Free Hospital at the end of the previous week, he had found him in relatively good spirits. He had shown Tony Mandelson his new watch, a gold-plated Tissot which his father had cheerfully derided as a 'bit flash'. Exhausted by a difficult week at Walworth Road, he had retired to Ross for the weekend and had been telephoned by his mother at 5 a.m. on the May bank holiday Monday with the news of his father's death, subsequently regretting bitterly that he had not been in London.

In his interview Mandelson, looking back on his father's death, told James that 'He would have had so much amusement and enjoyment from seeing me in the House of Commons. He would have thought it was a great deal of fun.' He was not, of course, an MP when his father died, though he had already begun to contemplate finding a seat. Miles Mandelson was almost certainly right in his assessment that 'the unfinished business' between Mandelson and his father – including the unresolved political differences between them – made his death more painful. Alastair Campbell remembers talking to Mandelson shortly afterwards. 'I thought I was being very banal but he said much later that he never forgot it. He said he thought he would never get over it but I said something like, you get over things like that by being the sort of thing your father would want you to be. The other thing I said was that in our sort of world there are not many people you can count on totally and you have got to be able to count on yourself.'[4]

Peter Mandelson, cleared by customs and proudly sporting his black Russian fur hat, stopped momentarily and peered round the corner into the arrivals hall of Heathrow's Terminal Two. There, waiting, was his lieutenant Colin Byrne, whom he greeted with a conspiratorial stage wink. There, too, was the TV crew from Brenards airport news agency, alerted earlier in the day by Byrne. Everything appeared to be in order. He vanished for a moment, to be replaced by the two unmistakable figures of Gerald Kaufman and Ron Todd, general secretary of the TGWU, the country's biggest union, striding purposefully towards the barrier. Up went the cameras and 150 screaming teenage girls instantly rushed forward to mob the distinctly startled new arrivals.

For a second Mandelson wondered wildly whether he had underestimated the popular impact of Kaufman's subtle alteration of Labour's defence policy on his trip to Moscow with Todd. But the girls had been waiting for the teen band Bros to return from a European tour and, seeing the television lights, had simply assumed that their idols had finally landed. It hardly mattered. The three-day visit to Moscow at the end of January 1989 had been a copybook success in terms of public relations and political management. It was arguably the high point of the policy review and marked the moment at which the post-1979 Labour Party grew up.

The decision to take Todd, a long-standing unilateralist and the man who commanded easily the biggest block vote at the Labour Party conference, turned out to have been a masterstroke. The message to which he and the rest of the Labour team were exposed in Moscow in their talks with Vladimir Petrovsky, the deputy Foreign Secretary, and Alexander Yakovlev, head of the Soviet Communist Party's International Department, had been entirely counter-intuitive for many on the left of the British Labour Party: the Kremlin regarded the prospect of unilateral nuclear disarmament by a future Labour government as a tiresome distraction which would hinder rather than help the next phase of multilateral disarmament talks. Hardly less striking was their attitude to the option being canvassed by several 'soft left' members of the party executive, such as David Blunkett and Robin Cook: that Britain could somehow bargain away its nuclear weapons in 'bilateral' negotiations between London and Moscow.

In a long note to Charles Clarke the previous August Mandelson had explicitly warned against Kinnock adopting such a compromise. 'Solving the defence issue', he said, was a 'necessary condition of success'; he even floated the idea of pledging a national referendum on Trident – which he knew would result in a decisive defeat for unilateralism. Now, he and Kaufman had the support of the Russians, who told their visitors – and the *Guardian*'s Patrick Wintour, in a briefing opportunistically arranged by Mandelson – that bilateral negotiations would 'present technical problems and might complicate other arms reduction talks'.[5] Instead, the Soviets wanted to see Britain involved in multilateral negotiations with the other four big nuclear powers.

Todd behaved impeccably. His presence on the delegation was enough to lure both *The Times* and the *Sun*, owned by Murdoch, plus the *Daily Telegraph* and the *Daily Mail*, onto the Aeroflot flight to Moscow. After all, had he not overshadowed Kinnock's party conference speech the previous year with an attack – made with Mandelson very much in mind – on 'sharp-suited filofax socialists with cordless telephones'? Might he not repudiate Kaufman at the very heart of the evil empire? In fact Todd graciously accepted a news management regime so tight that only Kaufman was allowed to discuss the visit with journalists – Mandelson's *pièce de résistance* being to locate in Red Square, in the shadow of the Kremlin, a press conference at which Kaufman repudiated 'bilateralism' and hinted strongly that the Russians would prefer a Labour government to adopt a multilateral approach to disarmament. When the travelling press pack chanced upon Todd in an alcohol-free jazz dive he would talk only about the genius of Charlie Parker as an alto saxophonist.[6] Although his presence on the delegation did not secure the TGWU vote against unilateralism (at the 1989 conference Kinnock won the conference's backing for the historic switch without the help of the TGWU), it did mean that the left could not claim the visit had been a mere publicity stunt.

Kaufman's handling of the switch in defence policy was superb, given the disasters of the previous year. On defence, as on so much else, 1988 had been an *annus horribilis* for Kinnock, punctuated by a series of almost manically contradictory interviews. It was an odd coincidence that Mandelson should have digested the two most momentous of these in hotel rooms out of London when he was travelling in search of a parliamentary seat. The first, given to Vivian White of *This Week, Next Week* on 5 June, contained the remarkable sentence (coming as it did from the avowedly unilateralist leader of a unilateralist party): 'there is no need now for a something for nothing unilateralism'. Patricia Hewitt, told by Kinnock as they left the studio that the interview had 'put to sleep' a sacred cow, informed several newspapers that his remarks were indeed intended to convey a shift in defence policy. Mandelson read the following day's ample headlines in Bournemouth where, now hoping for the Hartlepool selection, he was attending the conference of his union, the GMB, in the hope that they might support him. He had known since the 1987 conference that Kinnock was serious about changing the defence policy; Mandelson himself had passionately advocated such a change. But he now wondered whether Kinnock was ready for the backlash. It was usually Mandelson, after all, who was chided by the Kinnock office for being too cavalier about opposition within the party.

He rang the Kinnock office nervously, to be told that the leader was happy with the coverage. But within a fortnight it had started to unravel: Kinnock was in the middle of a messy leadership contest; the mighty TGWU, to which unilateralism remained a totem, was meeting to discuss its stance on Hattersley; and Robin Cook and David Blunkett were among those who trooped into Kinnock's office to express their dismay. Then Denzil Davies, the intellectually brilliant but (at that time) emotionally erratic Defence spokesman, resigned in a spectacular 1 a.m. telephone call to the Press Association's chief political correspondent Chris Moncrieff – not because he disagreed with the shift but because he had been kept completely in the dark about it. Mandelson, alerted by Moncrieff to this sensational news, and knowing that Davies was then suffering from marital problems (earlier in the day he had seen him drinking on the House of Commons terrace), pleaded with Moncrieff to hold off with the story. Moncrieff rightly refused to do so but agreed to let Mandelson telephone Davies first. Mandelson found Davies determined – and stone-cold sober. Recognising, for once, that he was beaten, he rang Moncrieff back and told him to go ahead.

Mandelson's advice to Kinnock, endorsed by Hewitt and Clarke, was still to stand firm. It had not, in party management terms, been a good time to announce the shift. But to retract now would dangerously undermine his credibility. And, at least in public, that position held – for the next week or so. So early on 21 June, when Mandelson picked up the papers which had thudded onto the carpet outside his Newcastle hotel room and clambered back into bed, he was dumbfounded to see the front page of the *Independent*. So much so that he sat bolt upright, hitting his head with a fearsome crack on the overhead light above his bed. Kinnock had apparently gone back to square one, repudiating, in a rambling and incoherent interview mercilessly recorded by the paper's political columnist Peter Jenkins, the very shift he had so boldly announced less than three weeks earlier. According to Philip Gould, Kinnock was painfully depressed and exhausted at the time. Citing his own contemporary diary note of a conversation with 'two of those closest' to Kinnock, Gould records that the leader left the *Independent* saying, 'I don't know what I've said in there. It's all words to me, just words.'[7]

The defence review was finally saved principally by a combination of Kaufman's political skill, Kinnock's recovery of nerve in early 1989, and Mandelson's robustly expressed advice to Kinnock, subsequently repeated by Patricia Hewitt, to stop talking about defence in the meantime and 'leave it to Gerald'. In a strongly worded note written in August 1988 Mandelson had told Clarke: 'Neil must not be bounced into what look like new policy pronouncements or pushed into reaffirmations of old policy pronouncements. We should try as far as possible to keep the slate clean and look to 1989.' When, as Mandelson predicted it would, the 1988 conference passed another clutch of unilateralist resolutions, 'we point to the policy review ... and say it's not unreasonable or unexpected for conference to re-state policy because nobody is asking conference to do any different. No alternative policy is being put forward this year.' This characteristically Mandelsonian damage-limitation strategy was followed almost to the letter at the conference. When Kaufman submitted his report, firmly in favour of keeping Trident, to Kinnock after the Moscow visit he was delighted to find the leader accepting it in its entirety. At the crucial meeting of the National Executive on 9 May 1989 Kinnock stunned the left opposition with a devastating repudiation of unilateralism. Opponents of the report, who included two future cabinet ministers, Margaret Beckett and David Blunkett, were vanquished by seventeen votes to eight. Kinnock, Mandelson reported to the journalists waiting outside Transport House, had told the NEC,

Many in this room have protested, demonstrated and marched in favour of unilateral disarmament. I've done something else – I've gone to the White House, the Kremlin and the Elysée and argued down the line for unilateral nuclear disarmament. I followed the line of Labour policy. I knew they would disagree with it. But above that they were totally uncomprehending that we should want to get rid of a nuclear missile without getting elimination of nuclear weapons on other sides too, without getting anything for it in return.

It was natural that Mandelson should play the defence decision for all it was worth. From the 1987 conference onwards, often in the face of strong evidence to the contrary, he had continued to bully and cajole journalists into thinking – and reporting – that the policy would eventually change. That was the point of stressing the importance of the review after the anti-nuclear votes at the 1987 and 1988 conferences, and of stimulating press coverage for the Moscow trip. For journalists who might have written, 'Kinnock rebuffed again', the story became in effect: 'Labour leadership has cunning plan.' This did not apply only to defence. Mandelson was perpetually engaged, as he put it delicately to the BBC journalist Nick Jones, in 'the complex task of managing and then presenting change'. Sheltering behind the anonymity of 'senior Labour sources' or 'a senior Labour figure', he was frequently able to give a clearer impression of the leader's determination to change policy than Kinnock himself was prepared to offer. This had both internal and external ramifications: the fainter hearts among Kinnock's party opponents would be convinced that he was determined to overrule them, and that to try and take him on would mean a damaging public row; and the voters would be assured that Kinnock was hell-bent on turning Labour into a party which could govern. Kinnock became a reluctant convert to the process:

> I started off being very sceptical about that, saying, 'We won't convince the newspapers ... and there's nothing more boring than politicians coming along and announcing a new initiative all the time. I have to say that my view on that changed. Peter could make a few select journalists accept there was something new on the wind; they had an inside track, they had a leak, they had something to write about on Sunday night, that kind of thing, and I always thought it was a very patronising approach to politics, but it worked.[8]

But there was no point whatever in Labour changing unless it was also *seen* to be changing. Colin Byrne recalled that at one point in the May 1989 two-day NEC meeting to consider the seven policy review reports,

> Peter and I went downstairs wondering how we could manage Neil's doorstep on the results of the meeting. And Ken Livingstone went past and winked at me and Peter, and he said, 'Oh well, I'd better go out and talk to the troops, hadn't I?' And he went out there and suddenly produced this tear-stained doorstep interview about how the soul of Labour had been sacrificed that afternoon and all the rest of it, and it was a total act. He'd been smirking at us a few minutes earlier about what he was going

to say, and there he appears with tears in his eyes, and that taught me rather a lot about Ken Livingstone.[9]

On balance, however, the Livingstone approach was probably helpful to Mandelson. The message of change needed enemies to conquer. In presenting each stage of the policy review, according to Colin Byrne, 'Peter's theory was absolutely right: there's no point in going through all these changes unless you tell people. So our job was actually to build things like the change in the unilateral defence policy up as cliffhangers. We always knew it was going to go through. But build it up ... get the journalists writing: "It's a cliffhanger."' Even on defence, where victory was genuinely not guaranteed from the start because of the Cook-Blunkett-Short faction, there was 'still a comfortable margin of error ... but we just had to build it up to a position where everybody in Britain knew that Labour had done something earth-shattering.' It was not surprising that, when the policy review was finally completed in May 1989, Larry Whitty wrote, in another generous tribute, 'Many congratulations – your management of the press comment on the Policy Review Group reports, given the inadequacies and pitfalls, leaves me speechless with admiration. Brilliant. Well done to all.'

Mandelson had also become a master of rebuttal. Much later, when he became a minister, his habit of complaining to editors bordered on the self-destructive. For now, however, this tactic worked almost entirely in his party's interests. A fortnight after the NEC policy review meetings there was an incident which, like many others, illustrated his single-minded pursuit of the art. On a Thursday evening, 25 May, he was sitting in Neil Kinnock's office watching *The Nine o'Clock News*; the BBC carried a story by John Sergeant claiming that the eleven Soviet diplomats recently expelled by the Thatcher government had tried to blackmail Labour MPs. The story hinted at a close relationship between some of the party's MPs and the Soviet embassy. Mandelson, furious that he had not been called to comment on the story, realised he had to act. But Kinnock was in Wales; and Mandelson was not sure whether there was anything in it. So he set about, as he put it, '*carefully*' rubbishing it. In his usual manner he took up pen and paper and composed a 'line to take': 'This is an incredible story for which no evidence has been provided whatsoever and which, at face value, has no credence at all' – as flat a denial as it was possible to construct, given that the story might turn out to be true. Late that night, however, he reached Kinnock, who told him that it was indeed untrue; Mandelson now, by his own account, 'really went to town' with the BBC, ensuring that the story was kept out of two consecutive bulletins – though not the one at midnight. At this point Kinnock spoke directly to Geoffrey Howe, the Foreign Secretary, and two things happened in quick succession. Howe confirmed in writing that the story was not true, and the Foreign Office Minister of State, William Waldegrave, confessed to having lunched with Sergeant on the day in question but insisted that the BBC correspondent had got it wrong. Mandelson first wrote a letter of complaint to Tony Hall, head of News and Current Affairs, which he insisted on making public – on the grounds that 'your report on the 9 o'clock news was not confidential'. Then he proposed a meeting between Kinnock, himself and his old boss John Birt, at which Birt gave what Mandelson told the *Guardian* in October was 'a wholly unsatisfactory explanation'.[10]

Complaining to the reporter himself, or to a senior editor above him, depending on the gravity of the crime, became part of what Nick Jones called Mandelson's 'sheer artistry'. On one occasion, when Jones bridled at his chastisement for being too 'soft' in an interview with the Downing Street press secretary Sir Bernard Ingham, Mandelson scoffed at him: 'Don't give me that. I know all about the come-on, come-on technique. I used to write the questions for Brian Walden.'[11]

Despite his best efforts, however, the policy review had started slowly. 'Labour Listens', the programme of public meetings for ministers to hear the views and complaints of electors – a process repeated by William Hague after the Tories' defeat a decade later – had had a bad press. Colin Byrne recalled that Mandelson

brought me into his office and he said, 'Colin, you know this is a big challenge, this. I want you to lead this . . .' And I thought, 'Am I being flattered or am I being set up?' but anyway I would have done anything the guy said in those circumstances. So we got involved in this odd thing, which was basically about taking shadow ministers to town halls the length and breadth of the country to be shouted at by complete lunatics often. There was one meeting in Manchester . . . and about five people turned up. I remember one meeting some woman turned up who was literally wearing a Tesco's carrier bag on her head. Peter . . . came to a few meetings and then he sort of strategically withdrew. At the time we thought, 'Why are we doing this?' But it was quite clear afterwards that it was a strategy so he could report back to the NEC: 'People hate our policies: we've listened. People hate our policies.'

The Shadow Cabinet members involved, however, were less keen to discern a cunning strategy behind 'Labour Listens'. For Roy Hattersley, the tone was set by the first meeting in Brighton:

The sea was so high and the wind so fierce that the waves broke over the promenade and lashed against the windows of the lounge in which the politicians met the people. It was risibly reminiscent of the climax to *Key Largo* when the typhoon symbolised the destruction of the criminal conspiracy. The room was packed – but not with what we patronisingly called 'ordinary people'. By necessity our guests were representatives of special interests . . . And of course they hated each other far more than they hated us. The ex-servicemen's organisations called for higher defence expenditure whilst the Campaign for Nuclear Disarmament demanded less military spending.[12]

A still more potent means of jolting the Shadow Cabinet lay in opinion research. Mandelson and Philip Gould had attempted, as early as 1987, to dynamite the party's ideological rockface with some genuinely explosive findings, compiled by the SCA, showing the desperate plight the party was in. To extend its influence beyond its immediate audience of the NEC and Shadow Cabinet, Mandelson leaked a judiciously expurgated version to the *Observer*; a starker account obtained by the *Sunday Telegraph* (not through him) spelled out the grim truth more clearly: only 7 per cent of those voting Tory did so out of habit, compared with 27 per cent of those voting Labour, who did so because they 'always' had – a group that could only shrink with time. The report's implications were that unless the party was transformed beyond recognition – and could win back the former Labour voters to whom the Thatcherite ideal of economic self-improvement now had an irresistible appeal – it would be all over between Britain and Labour by the 1990s.

By April 1988 that transformation was not yet happening. Mandelson wrote a personal letter to Tom Sawyer which closely echoed the very warning that Prescott had given at the previous October's shadow cabinet meeting: 'The risk is that when the whole review is published we will be accused of saying nothing. That is even more dangerous than the other undesirable accusation of being revisionist. A lot can be done with good subbing presentation, briefing, etc. But a great deal of the raw material . . . is too insubstantial. It's got to be stronger.' What was needed was not a policy menu – that could wait for next year – but a genuine review of how the world had changed since Labour was last in power, of what account should be taken of 'changing public attitudes', and of the policies which needed to be adapted to those changes. Mandelson proposed that outside 'sympathetic, manageable expertise' should be sought as urgently as possible – meaning, though he did not say so explicitly, Gould and the SCA. By describing as 'undesirable' the charge of revisionism, Mandelson was being diplomatic rather than candid. The whole message of the Gould research was the 'r' word writ large – larger than the elected politicians were prepared to contemplate. As a result, this research played rather less part in the shaping of the review than was thought at the time.

Sawyer, who had already taken considerable political risks to advance the policy review, was not the problem. Kinnock, Mandelson complained, was largely staying aloof from the detail. Mandelson felt frustrated by a paradox: on the one hand Kinnock was a courageous and utterly effective party manager, railroading decisions through left wing opposition – as he did, to Tony Benn's annoyance, at the May 1988 NEC. He was a first-rate instinctive politician, with a feel for public opinion and a strong belief in change. On the other he played little part in the detailed development of policy, content to leave it to others, with the result that modernisation went neither as fast nor as far as Mandelson – not to mention Gould and Hewitt – would have liked. It was also a matter of confidence: Kinnock internalised all too easily the snobbish and unjustified criticisms of his intellect. As Mandelson reflected prophetically after the May 1988 NEC: 'The awful thing is that [Neil] would make a determined and courageous Prime Minister and he would fill out once in office. It's getting there that's such a problem. The hero as fall guy of history ... the likelihood at the moment is that he will be the leader who restored and changed the Labour Party but who could not clinch victory for himself in the process.'

Mandelson set about trying to solve this problem. In his ten-page letter to Charles Clarke of 16 August 1988 he rather typically used the excuse of continual unfavourable press coverage to make a series of much larger points. After complaining that the leadership campaign against Benn had not been exploited, as originally planned, as a means of projecting the leader and the new direction he now proposed for his party, he went on to specify the agenda which Kinnock should now visibly promote: 'turning back on high taxation, industrial relations law, renationalisation and uncontrolled spending ... but also the greater need now to move forward *on those new policies where we can outmanoeuvre the Tories in their free market ideology approach* and make them vulnerable by the next election because of their vested interests.' He also emphasised the importance of advancing One Member One Vote democracy and 'the protection of the party's constitution and rules from the ultra left', adding: 'During the next year Neil's identity in the public's mind needs to be associated not just with changing the party but more directly with the country's future, the emerging social and economic and environmental issues of the 90s and touching more politically on the "me, my family and my hopes" concerns of the public.' To achieve this a heavyweight 'political manager' from the Shadow Cabinet could help Kinnock to drive changes through the party, and, to make up for the 'policy failure' of Walworth Road, 'an intelligent sophisticated fast worker' could pull together the policy review. Kinnock himself should be 'more involved in the research, presentation of ideas, argument and shaping of the review's reports'. Finally, Mandelson proposed that Kinnock 'urgently' repair his press relations, particularly with 'the newspaper commentators who are now widely disaffected ... [who] want to feel better informed and flattered through personal contact'. This would not lead to 'flattering stories', but would mean 'more balanced articles'. He dropped from an earlier draft a suggestion that Kinnock should also 'chat up', in circumstances 'sociable and at their expense', hostile editors like David English (*Daily Mail*), Nick Lloyd (*Daily Express*) and David Montgomery (*Today*) – 'the man who crucified me in the *News of the World*' – because he calculated that no spoon would be long enough for Kinnock to sup with these devils.

Philip Gould complains that the memo was 'largely ignored' and goes on to imply this was one of several reasons why the whole policy review was, ultimately, a failure. Certainly most of the specific suggestions – with the exception of OMOV, which was advanced under John Smith's leadership – were not fully implemented until Tony Blair's leadership (including the zealous 'chatting up' of Tory editors).[13] But Gould's bleak analysis fails to do justice to the courage with which Kinnock took the review process forward. Starting from a much lower base than Blair, it was he who had the political will, usually acting in near-isolation, to force through at NEC meetings in May 1988 and 1989, ratcheted changes from which the party would not slide back. They may not have been enough to bring electoral success; but they were certainly necessary. It is possible to put the failure of Kinnock's project down to the fact that he did not go far enough; in particular he never 'drew the teeth' of Labour's historic commitment to higher tax and spending as he had hoped; but it may be fairer to see it as a heroic achievement within what appear from the retrospective vantage point of New Labour, as the extraordinary constraints of the time.

One of these constraints may have been the relative detachment from policy review details that Mandelson and Gould lamented. But another was the marked resistance of some of Kinnock's most senior colleagues to travel where he wanted them to go. No one was more acutely aware of this, nor more able, through his access to the media, to do something about it, than Mandelson, with serious consequences for his relationship with several members of the Shadow Cabinet. The Labour-supporting journalist David Bradshaw, who now works at Number Ten, compared Mandelson around this time to a willing pantomime villain. 'He's the only

Tony and Mary
Mandelson with
paternal grandfather,
Norman Mandelson.

Herbert Morrison,
Lord President and
acting Prime Minister,
July 1948.

Left: Miles and Peter Mandelson, Eastholm, Hampstead Garden Suburb.

Below: At Hendon County School.

Below: As manager of Hendon County Athletics Team (back row, far right), 1971. Steve Howell (seated to right of teachers, holding cup) and Paul Marginson (front row, second from left).

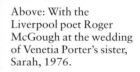

Left: Introducing the British Youth Council report on youth unemployment, 28 March 1977: *left to right* – Sue Ferguson, Peter Bennett, Tom Shebbeare, Peter Mandelson, David Cockroft.

Right: The *Weekend World* team: *left to right* – Charles Leadbeater, Brian Walden, Hugh Pile, Robin Paxton, Mary Beale, Sarah Powell, Peter Mandelson.

Party conferences, 1987–90:

Left: With Neil Kinnock.

Above: With Tony Blair.

Right: With Julie Hall and Philip Gould.

Above: Writing the *People* column with Alastair Campbell.

Left: At Hutton Avenue, Hartlepool.

Above: At a *Mirror* party with Neil and Glenys Kinnock and Julie Hall.

Below: With newly elected MP, Huw Edwards, Monmouth by-election, 17 May 1991.

Above: At the dedication of a bench to the memory of Tony Mandelson, Hampstead Garden Suburb, 1991: *left to right* – Miles Mandelson and his wife, Valerie, Mary Mandelson, Peter Mandelson.

Left: Constituency summer barbecue and dance, Hartlepool.

person whose name always gets a hiss at any party conference: Conservative, Liberal Democrat – or Labour.'[14] His talents, continually exploited in defending Kinnock against attack from the Tories, or from the press, were widely admired within the party and widely feared among its opponents. But they created more dangerous enmities when they were employed against those *within the party* who resisted the changes Kinnock was trying to make.

According to Mandelson, Tom Sawyer, with whom he worked closely in the eighties, understood him better than almost anyone else in the Labour Party. Sawyer saw his role as threefold: firstly, he was a 'brilliant, brilliant, operator' in taming and using a press largely hostile to the Labour Party; secondly he was a strategic political thinker – matched perhaps only by Gordon Brown ('Give him a scenario about where the party is today and where it wants to be tomorrow, and Peter will think through what you need to get there better than anyone else'); and thirdly he was

> a hit man for the leadership . . . He would do things that nobody else would do. He would go out and hit people when other people wouldn't do it. And I think it caused him a lot of personal problems, it was instrumental in building up the reputation that he's got of being untrustworthy, devious, Machiavellian, and of course partly he plays this. He kind of likes it. But then he doesn't like it. He was licensed to kill. He has been licensed to go out and do whatever he thinks is appropriate . . . That demands a certain kind of person, it demands a certain amount of ego, but it also demands a certain amount of courage and a certain amount of risk with your own career.[15]

Nothing would eventually bring Mandelson into more direct conflict with selected members of the Shadow Cabinet than his capacity, as a 'hit man', to 'do things' during the policy review that 'nobody else would do'.

The case of Michael Meacher and the review of industrial relations policy is instructive. Unlike Meacher, his Shadow Employment Secretary, Kinnock was neither sentimental nor naive about the trade unions, belonging to the strand of centre-left opinion exemplified by Barbara Castle's heroic and – for Labour – tragically abortive attempt to legislate on her White Paper *In Place of Strife* in 1969. Kinnock realised faster than many of his party that much of Margaret Thatcher's legislation on the unions, not least curbs on secondary picketing and the democratising of union elections, was popular with the voters. He was helped in his aim of keeping some of the legislation intact by a TUC paper drawn up by the far-sighted head of the TUC's Organisation Department, John Monks. This did not call for full repeal of the Tories' trade union legislation but instead proposed that Labour should focus on expanding individual employee rights to protection from unfair dismissal, to health and safety, and to consultation. Meacher was nevertheless determined to promote a more far-reaching agenda, including full repeal of the main Tory legislation, and the introduction of statutory rights to union recognition – even though, at a meeting between senior members of the Shadow Cabinet and a group of senior union leaders, the SOGAT general secretary Brenda Dean told him: 'You are in a minority of one.'

Mandelson sought to thwart Meacher at every turn. When Meacher ignored his explicit advice not to discuss his proposals, still in draft form, on BBC TV's *On the Record*, Colin Byrne, Mandelson's loyal lieutenant at Walworth Road, 'had to get on the telephone and diss what he was saying to journalists for the Monday papers' – a course, on this occasion, specifically agreed with Clarke. The result was a series of prominent stories portraying Meacher at odds with Kinnock on union legislation. Meacher's bitterness about this was exacerbated when Mandelson then leaked a section of the industrial relations policy draft to the *Sunday Telegraph*. The paper got a story on a hot issue of the day; but Mandelson got an airing for his distinctly revisionist version of the policy.[16] The paper, briefed by Mandelson, said that Labour was going to be tough on the unions, that there would be restrictions on secondary picketing under Labour, and that union funds would be liable in the case of unlawful strikes. Correctly seeing this as an attempt by Mandelson to 'bounce' his colleagues into a more restrictive policy than he himself wanted, Meacher retaliated by seeking to harden up the draft on the freedoms that would be restored to the unions. He was initially successful – though by the 1989 conference, after the Kinnock office had engaged the services of Lord Irvine, then an eminent Labour lawyer, the policy had been pulled back to something akin to that originally proposed by the TUC. Meacher, moreover, paid a heavy price: one of Mandelson's best media contacts, Andrew Grice, reported in May 1989, at the height of the row, that Meacher would be sacked for his obduracy. The story immediately reduced Meacher's clout within the Shadow Cabinet.[17] It was also correct. Six months later Kinnock moved him to Social Security, and replaced him, as Mandelson had expected all along, with Tony Blair.

The more poignant example, given the closeness of their relationship during and well after the 1987 election, was that of Bryan Gould. Right up to the summer of 1989 he and Mandelson remained on cordial terms. Mandelson promoted him heavily – and successfully – as the ideal coordinator and figurehead for the 1989 European elections. According to Colin Byrne,

> Peter's reasoning was twofold. One because Bryan was a good telegenic front man, to which Neil said: 'I agree.' Two, Labour had its own divisions on Europe then but we were out to exploit Tory divisions – the Diet of Brussels and all that stuff. And therefore strategically Peter saw the value of having somebody who was not a Europhile, fronting the election ... it was the first set of national elections Labour had won for a decade. Incidentally that was the election which also brought Mo Mowlam to the public eye ... Peter had spotted her as one of his friends, as it were, and Peter and I lobbied Neil to make her Bryan's deputy. Neil said, 'Why, what's the point of this?' And we came up with the line that women's votes would be very important so we had to have a woman as the deputy co-ordinator.

What finally turned the friendship with Bryan Gould sour, however, was the task of finding a replacement for the poll tax. Gould's own plan for a return to the rates, cushioned by a system of income-related rebates, was opposed by John Smith, Kinnock and Mandelson on the grounds that its complexity – replacing one tax with two – would undermine Labour's offensive against the by now hugely unpopular poll tax. In July 1990 Mandelson executed his most spectacular 'bounce' to date. He dreamt up, in a conversation with Grice, the concept of 'Fair Rates' – a neat phrase to describe a policy much closer to the return to the rates favoured by Smith. Grice reported, again accurately, that the policy would be approved the following day at a meeting of the Economic Subcommittee. How, indeed, could it not be? Potential allies would be deeply reluctant to back Gould against a policy which, they had now read, Kinnock supported. Byrne, for one, was unrepentant:

> [Gould] screwed up. He was manipulated by two people – Nigel Stanley and Mike Lee – who wrote the most appalling bollocks of a policy I'd even seen in my life. 'Labour's two-tax alternative' was how it became known internally. Peter tried to persuade Bryan, but he wouldn't change it . . . Bryan, like Robin [Cook], fancied himself as the left-wing alternative to Kinnock . . . but unlike Robin, Bryan had absolutely zero political judgement.

Some five years later Gould would take his revenge by recalling in his memoirs the painful *News of the World* 'outing' of Mandelson vividly enough for the *Sun* to revive the story.

So how far was Mandelson carrying out orders, and how far was he acting, like Henry's II's knights, against the 'troublesome priests' of the Shadow Cabinet on his own initiative, possibly even to further his own ends? This is a central question, since the answer might explain why Mandelson made so many lasting enemies in the party in this period. According to Byrne

> We consistently briefed in favour of Neil and yes, sometimes that meant taking people to task . . . For example there were . . . people who are now members of the Cabinet who were sitting on the fence as to whether we should expel Trotskyite extremists. What could we do other than attack people who were being criminally irresponsible in terms of the Labour future for their own short-term votes at the Labour Party conference? But it's also the case . . . that Peter, although he became renowned for attacking these people, was also a moderating influence because people like me were like the dogs of war, we wanted to get these people and grind them into the ground. I mean it was terrible, you know, it was like tomorrow belongs to me. There were a

number of us, you know the sort of young turks ... It's a bit like the Young Fabians these days.

Byrne certainly learned many of his skills from Mandelson. But he insisted that the one occasion 'on which I screwed up in a really major league way' was after Mandelson had left:

> I briefed Nick Wapshott of the *Observer* that John Prescott ... was actually risking his place in a future Labour Cabinet if he didn't stop pushing himself personally at the expense of the collective body of the Labour leadership. And Wapshott wrote this big the next day and you know that's not the sort of thing I would ever have done if Peter had been around. Peter would have counselled against such a thing: 'You can't do that, Colin, don't be silly, Colin.' He was actually a moderating influence on people like me whose instincts were to go for these people's jugular.

Moderating influence or not, there is no doubt that Mandelson, albeit more subtly, briefed against those who were, in his opinion, obstructing change in the party: indeed, he used to the full his ability to promote or demote Labour politicians in terms of their television profiles. Not for nothing was the Broadcasting and Key Campaigns Unit known as 'Central Casting'. In the press office this was hardly a matter of formal policy. Byrne recalled that:

> I was intelligent enough to know that when Michael Meacher was making an appalling cods of the employment policy review this was not a man I was going to stick on TV but I didn't need a written instruction from Mandelson to say: 'You will not put these people on television. You will put these people on television.' He was never like that and indeed Peter and I agreed that people like John Prescott were excellent on television, in certain circumstances. There were a lot of people who were very, very good on TV.

Mandelson himself would insist:

I never thought of people, be it Bryan Gould or Gordon Brown or Tony Blair, 'Ah, these people are future leaders, I'm going to groom them at the expense of everyone else.' You know, I'm like an impresario, I'm looking for talent the whole time. I need someone to strut on television on *Newsnight*, *The Nine o'Clock News*, *This Week, Next Week*, who's a safe pair of hands, who's going to be able to master a brief, who's going to be able to put on a really good show for the party and come away winning votes for Labour, that's all I'm interested in. I'm not interested in so and so doing better than so and so . . . you go with people who are prepared to work for you.

However, the discontent of the Shadow Cabinet dissidents stemmed from a belief – accurately reflecting the formalities of his job – that Mandelson had abandoned his constitutional role, which was to serve not the leader but the National Executive and the Shadow Cabinet as a whole. Indeed, this had been central to the complaint that Tony Benn had made about Mandelson early in his appointment. And this was why John Prescott, in particular, resented Mandelson's role. 'John always thought that it was the job of party officers to serve the party,' said one of Prescott's closest friends. As Tom Sawyer put it:

You had the first party officer, the first very able party officer in the history of the party, who saw his line of accountability to the leader rather than to the general secretary. For those members on the left who always wanted to reinforce and underscore the importance of the NEC then Peter was bad news. And I think they probably figured that before he got his job. So Peter was pivotal in the power struggle between those NEC members who wanted to control Kinnock and those who wanted Neil to have a bit more freedom, and to be able to perhaps be a bit more of a presidential leader. So that was the big picture with Peter, he was clearly out to serve Neil and not serve the NEC and that was the first time that had happened.

In fact, this was not unprecedented. Before Larry Whitty's predecessors, Jim Mortimer and Ron Hayward, Labour Party general secretaries had seen their task as delivering for the Leader. Nevertheless Mandelson had crossed members of the NEC and the Shadow Cabinet during this period: he was, he said, 'fulfilling my role as Neil Kinnock's mouthpiece'.[18] A decade later Kinnock was ambivalent. On the one hand he insisted that he neither knew nor approved the extent of hostile briefing – saying that it 'complicated his life' (for example, in the confrontation with Prescott over the deputy leadership, 'because by this time John Prescott and the political classes had been convinced that I didn't think much of him, which wasn't true'.) On the other hand Mandelson 'was doing his job according to modern rules, if you like'. And indeed Kinnock himself used a memorable image to describe his own stance: he had a 'gutters and stars view of politics': 'The stars is where you should be aiming at, the gutter is where you have to do the fighting.'

Moreover, while Mandelson frequently acted without 'cover' from Kinnock it's hard to believe that the leader, on whose authority journalists automatically assumed Mandelson was speaking, could not have stopped him if he had wished to. That was certainly the view of Bryan Gould, who complained to Kinnock about it. 'Neil appeared to be concerned and promised to take the matter up with Peter Mandelson. I heard no more about it.'[19] According to Gould, the belief that 'Mandelson acted with Neil's authority in planting stories, even those which were unfavourable to Neil's Shadow Cabinet colleagues' was

> almost certainly justified in most cases, if Neil's occasional scathing comments to me about our colleagues were anything to go by . . . The relationship between Neil and Peter served them both well. Neil was convinced of Peter's personal loyalty and would often say to critics that anything Peter did was in the best interests of the party (for which read Neil); Peter's power was immensely inflated by Neil's protection. Neil in turn benefited from the services of a lieutenant with no constituency or party colleagues to please

Gould went on to suggest that Mandelson may have become 'jealous' of the praise heaped on him for his part in the 1987 election. If that was true it was odd that it only became evident three years after the election and at a time when it was already a distant, and rather less than glorious memory. Not only that, but Mandelson had ensured that Gould's role was honoured for posterity by lavishly praising him to Kavanagh and Butler after the 1987 election.

Gould accepted that 'Peter was undoubtedly loyal to Neil' but went on to raise a further and, to Gould, darker dimension. Writing in 1995, after John Smith's death, he suggested that Kinnock did not realise that 'he was merely a player in the Mandelson strategy', specifically to ensure that Mandelson's own 'protégés – Gordon Brown as the prime contender but with Tony Blair as a fall-back' should succeed to the leadership. It is true that Mandelson's relationship with Brown and Blair was already central to him by the summer of 1990. Blair's admiration for Mandelson began shortly after he took over as Director of Communications; John Burton, Blair's agent in Sedgefield remembers being introduced to Mandelson by the MP in the House of Lords' bar at the Commons around 1985–6. Blair proudly told Burton that Mandelson had said of Burton: 'I like him, I'm impressed by him.' The relationship had been cemented in the 1987 election when, as Colin Byrne recalled,

a week after I joined the Walworth Road staff . . . Peter took me along to a meeting in the House of Commons and he said: 'Colin, this is Gerald Kaufman; he's a very important man, he's one of our best brains and he's going to run basically a black propaganda operation in this election campaign and you are going to work with him as a smart young press officer.' And he introduced me to two other people, Gordon Brown and Tony Blair, and these two were going to be working with us. Philip Gould was there as well, and they came up with – basically as a scam on the campaign – the 'Real Tory Manifesto' and it was basically what Labour does [now] in every election. It was quite clear . . . that this was a significant threesome. I mean I remember actually describing them to a girlfriend of the time as the 'Three Musketeers' and it was all very much like that . . . They thought alike, they had a relationship which was quite clearly mutually admiring but without being sycophantic.

For Blair, the campaign was not an unalloyed success. As one of what Mandelson had termed the 'grenade lobbers', Blair made his first appearance at a campaign press conference on housing policy. In answer to a question Blair suggested that Margaret Thatcher was 'unhinged'. Seeing that this was the kind of accusation that might ignite the campaign, ITN's Michael Brunson reacted quickly: 'Are you really saying that Mrs Thatcher is mad?' he asked. Gerald Kaufman swiftly jumped in to explain that Blair had merely been using a figure of speech. At this point, 'Blair, blushing slightly and sounding nervous, felt the ground falling away beneath him. He dissembled and retreated. Mandelson meanwhile made straight for Brunson to play down ... what Blair had said. Blair's first sortie had not been wreathed in glory but Mandelson saw in Blair someone who was anxious to learn and to please.'[20]

Mandelson had certainly spotted Tony Blair's potential even before the 1987 election, when Blair was the junior member of Roy Hattersley's treasury team. Blair had earlier attracted some mildly favourable publicity through his attack on the secrecy with which the Bank of England had baled out the stricken bankers Johnson Matthey.[21] Mandelson 'put' him on BBC *Breakfast News*, thinking, as he described it later, that it would be a 'good idea to try him out; he could do with a bit of a push'. One of Blair's colleagues in the team, Oonagh McDonald, meeting Mandelson in the Commons corridor behind the Speaker's chair, seemed almost distraught. 'Why didn't you put me on?' she asked. 'Why did you put Tony Blair on?' Mandelson replied that 'everyone has their turn, everyone has their chance'. McDonald was not consoled, replying: 'I don't think it's fair. I don't know what he's got.' This was an important moment for Mandelson. He realised, first, that Blair had something which other politicians, however reluctantly, could see was special; secondly, and even more vividly, that politicians feel it very keenly when one of their rivals is given media opportunities which they are denied. By contrast, Gordon Brown was much more of a media self-starter, bombarding the newspapers and broadcasters with press releases, leaks, challenges, surveys. He was, as Mandelson would put it much later, 'a non-stop media machine, and therefore tremendous for the press office, absolutely tremendous'. Mandelson started working them both harder, identifying them by the time of the 1987 election as a 'hard-nosed, slightly disownable hit-squad who could hurl grenades at the government'. Their first meetings as a trio –

though much less frequent than they would become – therefore took place before the '87 election.

By the end of the decade Oonagh McDonald's objections were writ large, at a much more senior level, and not only because of Brown's and Blair's increasing access to the media. Shadow cabinet colleagues noted increasingly that the trio, with Brown as the dominant figure, formed, as one rival shadow minister put it, an 'Absalom's Cave', driving forward their common version of where the party ought to be heading. Robin Cook, having already flown down from Edinburgh for the Rottingdean Shadow Cabinet in November 1988, noted with a certain mischievous humour the displeasure on their faces as the three of them drove up to the gates of the print union recreation centre in the Director of Communications' car, to find the future Foreign Secretary giving a doorstep interview to a television crew. For once he had beaten the 'three musketeers' at their own game.

According to one of Blair's closest aides, Mandelson 'trained up' the future Prime Minister and the future Chancellor, in media management. The Barlow Clowes affair, in which Blair shone in the summer of 1988 as the champion of pensioners who had lost their life savings because of a failure of government regulation, was a case in point. 'I remember the first advice I gave to him was: "Do not go over the top. Be measured. Don't become hysterical. Be factual, precise and lethal." I remember managing that with him and I could see him looking slightly nervous, slightly startled but knowing he could do it, and as a barrister he came to the fore. I remember him just looking: "I am going to learn from him. I am going to sort of lock into this person."'

Mandelson had by now identified Brown and Blair as the stars of the future, with Brown the leading figure of the two. Not only had Brown been on the Shadow Cabinet since the autumn of 1987 but, when Smith had his first heart attack in 1988, the increasingly charismatic Shadow Chief Secretary had shone in his place. Listing some of the strengths of the Opposition as early as December 1988, Mandelson had put at the top 'Gordon Brown scoring over Lawson' and 'Tony Blair taking the initiative on electricity [privatisation]'. Blair had only been on the Shadow Cabinet since November 1988. Mandelson privately saw his own role as 'increasingly . . . revolving round the strong future leaders of Gordon Brown and Tony Blair [in that order] and the political nourishment and companionship I get from this group'. He had committed to paper his determination 'to be part of the successor generation in the government. All my political ambition has returned to me with the challenge they hold out.' He admired their 'political gifts'; he also shared the Brown-Blair view that unless the party changed far more than it had so far, it might find itself languishing out of office 'for a generation'.

The weakness of the Gould analysis was that it underestimated the political, rather than personal, nature of the struggles within the Shadow Cabinet, and of Mandelson's hostility to the dissidents, who now included Gould. Gould, for example, had been among those who had voted on the NEC against Kinnock and in favour of cuts in defence spending. He had argued (successfully) against Brown and Smith's promotion in June 1988 of ERM membership – tacitly endorsed by Kinnock – as a means of providing Labour with a credible counter-inflation policy, and he had been annoyed to be confronted, towards the end of the policy review, by demands from Brown and Blair for the elimination of the last vestiges of Labour's commitment to renationalisation.

To assume, as Gould purported to, that Mandelson's switch of loyalty from himself to Brown and Blair was rooted in capriciousness or mere personal ambition, was to underestimate Mandelson's political drive. They became close, and emotionally intense, friendships, but the roots of the relationship were not simply personal. Brown and Blair attracted Mandelson partly because they were the nearest there was to true 'Kinnockites' in the Shadow Cabinet, and partly because of the strength of their belief – and the intellectual weaponry at their disposal to articulate it – that the party's future would be guaranteed only if it confronted some of the truths laid bare by three successive election defeats: that the British people had serially failed to vote not only for unilateralist defence policy, but for public ownership, resistance to trade union reform, or, in the main, higher taxes. While brilliant at opposing the Thatcher government, Brown and Blair were both also viscerally uninterested in permanent opposition. To the Director of Communications, whose political formation had been by Labour as a party of a government, this could not fail to appeal.

That Mandelson's primary agenda was political before it was personal has always been better understood on the left than on the right. In an interesting critique of Mandelson published in 1997 Nyta Mann and Paul Anderson argue that 'he has in fact always been a political operator. "Some people say that Peter is simply Machiavellian because he likes being like that," according to a former colleague. "Not true. Doing what he does is only part of the means to a political end, and to understand him you need to understand that he's a very, very right-wing member of the Labour Party. That's what he fights for and with vigour." '[22] This is a more convincing explanation of his behaviour between 1987 and 1989 than Gould's suggestion that Mandelson's disenchantment with him was motivated by a mixture of malice, vanity and jealousy. His relationship with Brown and Blair grew into close friendship. But it was founded on a common view of what the party needed. Their abilities appealed to the 'impresario' in him; their politics to the 'revisionist'.

The 'political ambition' to which Mandelson had admitted required a parliamentary seat. This would mean a short-term sacrifice; in his capacity as Director of Communications he was gradually becoming famous in his own right. Long profiles in the *Independent*, the *Guardian* and the *Sunday Mirror* during 1989 were evidence of that. In June of that year the *Sunday Express*'s Crossbencher column went into overdrive; after suggesting that the 'real credit' for Labour's revival belonged to Mandelson – who had made sure that the front benchers' 'shirts are ironed, their suits are pressed. He has scraped the soup stains off their ties and taught them all how to look and sound trustworthy on the telly' – it even asked: 'Who can doubt that [Mandelson] would be far more confident of victory if the image builder himself were leading Labour into the next election – instead of just the image?'[23]

Nevertheless this would not be much to sacrifice if Labour failed to win the next election. His new celebrity would not be enhanced by – and indeed might not even survive – a second general election defeat. So had he given up on Labour's prospects in the next election? Certainly, as 1988 drew to a close, he was increasingly worried about Kinnock's lack of self-confidence. He also told one prominent member of the NEC to whom he confided his parliamentary ambitions that he didn't think he could 'package Neil a second time'. Although this could have meant that he thought it was time for someone fresh to present the Labour leader to a still sceptical voting public, the senior trade union figure to whom he made this remark assumed it meant that Mandelson doubted the outcome of the '92 election. The real answer is banal: his mood swung like – and with – Kinnock's. For example, when the Labour leader's spirits later lifted dramatically in the spring of 1989, victory suddenly seemed possible again. Moreover, if he were serious about becoming an MP, this was almost certainly, from his own point of view, the right moment to make the move. Whether the party won or lost, he would probably not be able to attain the first rung of a conventional political career for another five years, by which time he would be forty-four. In this still relatively unenlightened period he might well have had difficulties in a by-election, with opponents raising the *News of the World* outing in an attempt to damage him.

The desire to become an MP had never altogether left him. His experience in Lambeth had suppressed it for a time. After the 1987 election he had again flirted seriously with the prospect of a career outside politics. Being Director of Communications, while it had raised his profile, was not the best preparation for parliamentary life. Even supposing he could get a safe seat, it would mean starting life as an MP with plenty of ready-made enemies. But his parliamentary ambitions were kindled and rekindled during 1988, not least by an enjoyable stay in November with Tony Blair in his Sedgefield constituency. Mentally, by the end of 1988 he had already begun the long march to parliament and the ladder to ministerial office.

# CHAPTER TWELVE

## *I Have This Friend Who Needs a Seat*

The so-called royal box at Earls Court – a rather perilous piece of scaffolding erected for Harvey Goldsmith's spectacular production of *Aida* in early 1988 – was an improbable setting for a turning point in Mandelson's career, especially as he was not even there. But one of his oldest and closest friends, Dennis Stevenson, was. So were two other guests of Goldsmith's, Neil and Glenys Kinnock. The evening was notable, Stevenson recalled, for the embarrassingly rude behaviour – 'sniggering about the Kinnocks and being perfectly foul, I mean really childish' – of two other couples there as Goldsmith's guests: Paul Channon, the Conservative cabinet minister, and his wife, and the British Airways chairman Lord King and Lady King. As if that wasn't enough, it was also the first meeting between Kinnock and another guest, Jim Naughtie, the opera-loving *Today* programme presenter, since their famous clash on air when Kinnock had enriched the English language by telling Naughtie that he was not going to be 'kebabbed' by the BBC.

Not even these tensions, however, could eclipse the significance of the 'extremely civilised' conversation which took place between Stevenson and Kinnock in the interval. The businessman asked Kinnock what he thought Mandelson should do next; Kinnock replied that 'he'll stay in his job, thanks very much'. Stevenson

suddenly realised that, in the nicest possible way, Kinnock was manipulating him. He couldn't care a toss about Peter's long-term career and I said, 'Well, you know it's all very well but you

222

can't go doing the same job for ever' ... And Kinnock said, 'Well, he could go and do some similar job in Europe' ... And I said, 'Well, fine, he does that for five years and then what does he do?' And Kinnock said, 'Well, he can go off and work for the Tories.' Joke. Throwaway line. The next day I rang Peter up and he came and had a drink ... and I said, 'I think you're completely nuts, but it's clear that you wish to become an MP and you'd better go for it.' I said I liked Kinnock but I thought Kinnock was exploiting him and so on, and that he should jerk himself out of it and get a seat.[1]

This was powerful confirmation of what Mandelson was already thinking about his own future. Stevenson had been among those who, ten years earlier, had argued persuasively that it was pointless to become an MP; Mandelson could wield much more power in business or the media. Now he had changed his mind. The charge of exploitation by Kinnock hardly stood up: Mandelson had prospered mightily under Kinnock's leadership. But Stevenson's basic message, that Mandelson was in a dead end, was bound to strike a chord. If he wanted a long-term political future he would have to find a seat. Fortified by his conversation with Stevenson, Mandelson broached the idea with Colin Byrne on a car journey back from the party's local government conference in February 1988. Byrne replied enthusiastically: 'Think of yourself, think of your own career. You're perfectly capable of it.'

However, it would be at least a year before the idea showed any sign of bearing fruit. In the interim Mandelson took advice from Gordon Brown and Tony Blair. At a lunch at the Braganza in Soho he told Philip Gould that he was thinking of a conventional political career. He deliberately put himself about in the country, speaking at more meetings in the regions, particularly in the North-East, the stamping ground of MP friends like Tony Blair, Mo Mowlam and Nick Brown. He confided his ambitions to John Edmonds, general secretary of the GMB, early in 1988 and took the trouble to burnish his credentials as a member of the GMB trade union – especially strong in the North-East – by attending its annual conference. (He had automatically become a member when it took over the white collar union APEX which he had joined when he started at Walworth Road.) He consulted Jack Ashley, the outgoing MP for Stoke, about the possibilities of replacing him. But it was not until the turn of the year that the most concrete opportunity yet came to light – in the neighbouring constituency to Tony Blair's. Though he had given no official notice, even to his own constituency party, Ted Leadbitter, MP for Hartlepool for a quarter of a century, had discreetly let it be known to a few friends that he was contemplating retirement.

For a metropolitan outsider like Mandelson, Hartlepool could not have been, on the face of it, a more unlikely prospect. Twenty-seven years earlier, the young Roy Hattersley had failed to secure the nomination, and he had only come from Sheffield. It had a deep-seated, though not wholly justified, reputation for insularity, compared with the rest of Teesside. When a cargo ship ran aground there during the Napoleonic Wars, so the story goes, a live monkey was washed ashore, only to be hanged from a barber's pole by townsfolk who assumed the creature was a Frenchman. Once a thriving centre of coastal industry, in the past two decades the town had seen more than its fair share of misery resulting from the restructuring of the economy. First the steelworks, then the shipyard and then the docks had closed; unemployment in 1989 was 11 per cent, but it had been much higher before (19 per cent in 1987) and would be higher again (14 per cent in 1992). But as Labour seats went it was undeniably safe. Only in 1959, when the people of Hartlepool agreed with Harold Macmillan that they 'had never had it so good', had the seat been won by the Conservatives. In 1987, not a good year for Labour, Leadbitter had secured 48.5 per cent of the vote and a majority of over 7,000. Whether they would select an outsider, and a relatively controversial one at that, was far from a foregone conclusion – particularly as the long-standing incumbent would be bound to exercise some influence and at least two local candidates were already attracting some support.

It is an irony that the two Labour politicians most closely associated with moves to reduce the level of union influence in the party, Tony Blair and Peter Mandelson, should both have been critically dependent on trade union support to get their seats. Mandelson now took a crucial step in disclosing his intentions, in a conversation outside the St Stephen's entrance to the House of Commons, to Tom

Burlison, the soft-spoken and highly influential northern regional secretary of the GMB.

It is impossible to understand Labour Party politics in the North-East without recognising the importance of the GMB. Until long after the war the miners' union had been a power in the region, its delegates dominating many of the constituency parties, at least in Northumberland and Durham, along with the regional structures of the party. The right-wing Labour Durham miners' leader Sam Watson was a leading figure on the National Executive, a redoubtable hammer of the left throughout the Attlee and Gaitskell periods. But in the sixties, as mine after mine shut down under the rationalisation carried out by Lord Robens, a dynamic General and Municipal Workers' Union official named Andy Cunningham (Jack Cunningham's father) began to assume Watson's role. This was partly because, as a fast-growing general union with strong bases in power supply, shipbuilding, manufacturing industry and, in Newcastle, Sunderland and Hartlepool (though nowhere else in the country), the docks, it rapidly began to outnumber the NUM. But it was also because Cunningham encouraged union branches to play a highly political role. Thus in Houghton le Spring, for example, it had 75 delegates to the party General Management Committee when Roland Boyes was selected before the 1983 election, and in Chester-le-Street the irredeemably southern old Wykehamist GMB researcher Giles Radice had been selected in 1973 through sheer force of the union's numbers on the GMC – 84, or over half the seats. Burlison, Cunningham's successor but one, was not a ruthless, flamboyant, larger than life union boss in the Cunningham mould;* but he attached a similar importance to the union's political role, that the best thing he could do for his members was to secure a Labour government. He had two other great assets as far as Mandelson was concerned. One was that he knew him well, having worked with him closely at Walworth Road since 1987 in his role as the union's member of the National Executive, latterly chairing the Communications Subcommittee, to which Mandelson was directly answerable, and coming to admire him 'because he was

---

* Cunningham was convicted for offences arising out of the Poulson scandal.

225

always on top of the job and he always stood his corner'. The other was that, though he came from Chester-le-Street, Burlison knew and loved Leadbitter's constituency, having played professionally for Hartlepool FC for seven seasons.[2] He liked the town's famous dry humour – remembering fondly how, as a young union negotiator selling a difficult compromise settlement to a mass meeting of striking health workers, he had been heckled by one man who shouted from the back of the hall, 'Yes, and you weren't much good at football either.' The first advice Burlison gave the thirty-five-year-old parliamentary aspirant was to seek an audience with Leadbitter.

Mandelson worked with characteristic energy and thoroughness to secure the nomination, but he also had several strokes of luck, in addition to the signal one of having Burlison as an ally. The initial catalyst for Mandelson's first foray into the town as a potential candidate – though he had already visited the town for a GMB-sponsored football match in December 1988 – was the future Prime Minister, then a recently elected member of the Shadow Cabinet. On a Saturday late in February 1989 Blair took Mandelson, a guest in his house at Trimdon, over to Hartlepool to see Leadbitter. The meeting was inconclusive; Leadbitter was courteous but maintained a studied neutrality. Typically, Mandelson wrote to him as soon as he returned to London thanking him for a 'good honest' talk and adding: 'I hope I can earn people's confidence. But I am not rushing any fences and I understand the local situation.' Since Leadbitter had made it clear that he did not intend to announce his retirement for several months, Mandelson added, a touch conspiratorially: 'For all concerned we need to keep things to ourselves for the moment. But it will mean a lot to me to be put in the correct direction by you (without assuming support) when the time comes.'

Neither Mandelson nor Leadbitter had shown all their cards at the first meeting. Mandelson did not mention that he was already in touch with the GMB about the prospects for securing the union's support in the selection contest, while Leadbitter did not disclose his interest in moves to attract another possible outside candidate – and a rather glamorous one at that. Two local councillors, Bill Isley and Bill Middleton, had already made an approach in January to the actress Glenda Jackson, then known to be seeking a safe seat. A Liberal Democrat supporter, overhearing a conversation between the two Bills in a pub, had leaked the story to Tyne Tees Television and the approach had received some local publicity. It had been firmly and sincerely denied by Ms Jackson; she had not even received the letter from the councillors when the story broke. However, unbeknown to Mandelson, Messrs Isley and Middleton were still energetically wooing her. By the time he met Leadbitter, the two councillors had written to her saying that the publicity about the approach to her – embarrassingly premature as it was, given the secrecy surrounding Leadbitter's intention to retire – had attracted a lot of favourable comment, and adding: 'Ted Leadbitter's private opinion (which perhaps I should not quote) is that once you are officially nominated you should soon emerge as the front runner.'

Mandelson would not learn about his famous rival until early June – and then only by accident. First, he benefited from the selflessness of Tony Blair's agent John Burton, who had already sacrificed his own parliamentary ambitions to Blair's candidacy in Sedgefield. Burton, a thoughtful and far-sighted man, who has been a continual source of down-to-earth advice to Blair, first discussed the Hartlepool seat with the Sedgefield MP in the late spring:

[Tony] said: 'I have this friend who needs a seat and I was wondering about him going for Hartlepool,' and I said, 'Oh well, I was wondering about going for Hartlepool.' 'Oh,' he said, 'if you want to go, there's no problem. We'll support you.' And I said, 'Well, who are you talking about?' And he said: 'Peter Mandelson.' And I said, 'Oh no,' because I knew what Peter had done for the party. I said, 'No, I'm getting on anyway. I'll support Peter if you want Peter in there.' He said, 'I think it's important.' He had a vision for the future, you know, with Peter, Tony had. He realised that this would be a great help to him, if Peter was in the House.[3]

On Saturday 2 June Burton drove Mandelson to the Grand Hotel in Hartlepool for a meeting with someone who was virtually his only contact in the constituency; this just happened to be Bill Isley, a frequent visitor to the Friday night folkclub Burton ran in Sedge-field. Isley had already warned him of Glenda Jackson's interest: 'I think I said, "Oh, I was thinking of Peter Mandelson and Tony was talking about Peter." Of course, at this time Tony didn't have any clout in the party. It wasn't like the leader of the party or the PM asking you to do it. It was just the next door MP. But I think people were aware of the fact that he was doing very well.' Burton was right to mention Blair's relative lack of 'clout'. In the meeting in the cavernous lounge bar of the Grand Isley said frankly that he was not the only local Labour activist who had set his heart on Ms Jackson. Several of the younger members were attracted by the idea. Mandelson, showing no sign of being fazed, then said: 'Well, look, I think Glenda would prefer a London seat and I think I can get her to change her mind.' He then telephoned her that day from Hartlepool.

When Glenda Jackson phoned Bill Isley four days later it was, according to the careful note he took at the time, to report that Mandelson had declared his interest to her but had said that 'he had met people in Hartlepool who were adamant in supporting her if she was still interested but would campaign for him if she didn't go for Hartlepool.' At which point Ms Jackson became the second strong aspirant to make a graceful retreat in the face of Mandelson's interest. She told Isley politely that 'Mandelson would be an excellent candidate because of his close connections with Kinnock' but that she 'wouldn't want to let us down if we were still sure we wanted her'. In the event her candidacy faded almost by default. She herself was not fully committed to Hartlepool, though Isley thought she 'could have been persuaded'. Isley failed, through no fault of his own, to meet up again with the younger Jackson supporters and, a little embarrassed, did not contact her as arranged the weekend after her phone call. And Mandelson was right in thinking that her first preference was for a London seat (she eventually got Hampstead and Highgate); more pertinently, from August until December she was going to be away touring the US in *Mother Courage*, which would have meant altering the expected selection timetable. And while Leadbitter might have cooperated in helping to arrange that, in the interim the Mandelson candidacy had begun to motor.

But even with the two most plausible candidates from outside the constituency painlessly eliminated, the outcome could not be guaranteed. The two local runners, Ray Waller, a former (and future) leader of the town council, and Steve Jones, son of the party's

Welsh spokesman Barry Jones, both had local support. One Member One Vote selections were still four years away; instead, parliamentary selections were by a hybrid system, with 60 per cent in the hands of individual members, and 40 per cent with the affiliated trade unions. This meant that trade union support could prove critical; while Jones had the official backing of the TGWU, the GMB, with five branches in the town, had more influence in the Hartlepool party. But Ray Waller, the most likely alternative candidate, was also a GMB member. The support of local GMB stalwarts, at least locally, was therefore crucial – none more so than that of one of the local party's most redoubtable figures, Olga Mean, a GMB branch secretary in Hartlepool, who also happened to be the union's National President at the time. Burlison was favourably disposed towards Mandelson's candidacy, but sensibly had no intention of wasting the trump card of a formal regional committee endorsement on a candidate who did not meet with the approval of Mrs Mean.

The first requirement was to arrange an introduction. In London for a meeting of the union's Finance Committee, Olga Mean was 'casually' invited by Alan Donnelly, the union's national finance officer and now an MEP, to join him for a drink in the Strangers' Bar at the House of Commons before going on to a Chinese restaurant. Mrs Mean recalled: 'Alan got a drink for me and he said, "I won't be a minute, Olga." And he went, and he came straight back. And I was sat talking to Hilary Armstrong [MP for Durham West], and then the door opened and in came a young man.' Mandelson did not exactly waste time:

He said, 'Move along, Hilary, I just want to have a chat with Olga,' and he asked me all sorts of questions about Hartlepool. Now, when I went to the regional secretaries' meeting the next morning I said to [Tom Burlison], 'Do you know, Alan took me to the House last night.' He said, 'That's a miserable place to go.' But I said, 'There was a young man there, and he was ever so interested in Hartlepool.' And he said: 'What do they call him?' And Alan came in then and says: 'Peter Mandelson.' And Tommy looked at me and said: 'I should have told you, Olga. I didn't know that you were going to meet him last night, but I intended to say something to you, that he's looking for the seat of Hartlepool when Ted goes.' 'Oh,' I said, 'is he? He hung on my every word as if it was pearls of wisdom' ... I've got to say I really was impressed with him the first time I met him. I really thought – he might be weighed down with ministerial problems now – he was a nice, pleasant, happy sort of young man. 'Well,' Tom said, 'what do you think?' 'Well,' I said, 'I see no reason, if he's as nice as I think he is, if he spends the next couple of years getting to know Hartlepool and getting to know various people, I think he might just do it.'[4]

The famous Mandelson charm had worked; Mrs Mean was hooked – not least because she had been less than keen on either Mr Jones or Mr Waller as Ted Leadbitter's successor.

The next time Olga Mean came to London, Mandelson invited her to lunch at the Commons, and

he said What did I think? I said, 'Well, I don't really know. There's funny people in Hartlepool and I think the best thing for you to do is to come to Hartlepool and have a look around and meet people ... I'll give a little buffet for you and I'll invite certain people' ... Because I'd made up my own mind then that I would like to have him as my MP. I mean, Ted was a good MP, solid, and in my opinion we needed someone younger and brighter after the years of Ted. He was a very kind man, Ted, but you know, we've got to think of the future and I felt that we should have somebody younger.

True to her word, Mrs Mean invited a cluster of about forty movers and shakers in Hartlepool Labour, including her husband Jimmy's friend Bill Tindall who 'held the engineers' vote and different things', to a buffet in her conservatory. Bill Tindall told Jimmy Mean: 'One day, Jimmy, that man's going to be a minister.' By March Mandelson was writing to Mrs Mean 'before heading off to Washington with Gerald Kaufman, Ron Todd and all!' announcing that he was due to speak at a trade union forum in Middlesbrough in April and asking, 'Is there anything I could do or anyone I could meet that weekend?'

Needless to say, there was. Olga Mean lubricated contact with two other key figures in the selection process. The first was Jack Doyle, the burly GMB regional officer, who had already met Mandelson with John Burton and Tony Blair at the Dun Cow at Sedgefield to discuss the Hartlepool seat. Through the coming months Doyle, a veteran of constituency selections in the North-East, would, with Burlison's encouragement, use his influence with a trade union branch here and a ward secretary there, frequently driving Mandelson to meetings or lending him his car, and occasionally having him to stay. 'He'd charm the socks off 'em, he'd get chocolate biscuits wherever he went,' he recalled.[5] Burlison agreed that Mandelson was not that hard a candidate to sell. He had had much more trouble persuading hardbitten Geordies that Radice was the right man to represent Chester-le-Street – especially as Radice would absent-mindedly forget to bring any money to buy his round when he and Burlison visited the local workingmen's club. Mandelson, by contrast, seemed less of a toff; more importantly, Burlison recalled, his association with Kinnock and party head-quarters lent him a worldly political glamour – and knowledge of current party policy – which went down well with local activists.

Nevertheless the selection was not all plain sailing. The second figure to whom Mrs Mean sent the would-be candidate was Bernard Carr. Carr proved to be Mandelson's Mandelson in Hartlepool. Highly intelligent, an ex-councillor and a long-time Labour activist, Carr had, like Mandelson, joined Young European Left, though they had never met. Like Mandelson, Carr could be prickly as well as charming. More importantly, he was also a moderniser, essentially on Labour's right wing. With his persistently erratic personal life, and several prominent local enemies, Carr sometimes appeared to court trouble. He would later face a lengthy police investigation into alleged expenses irregularities – arising from a free trip made to London to receive third prize in a *Daily Telegraph* 'Worst Cook' competition at the Atrium restaurant in Westminster. The prize was well deserved: according to the paper, Carr's entry of turnip and fish soup with fishfinger croûtons gave off 'what looked and smelt like some sort of nerve gas'.[6] But he was charged with claiming expenses for the trip – paid for by the *Telegraph* – from the council. Carr claimed that his attendance at a meeting in London organised by a housing trust justified the expenses claim. The council disagreed and Carr repaid the money.

Mandelson has nevertheless remained steadfastly loyal to Carr, publicly criticising the police investigation when, in 1998, the Crown Prosecution Service found that they did not have sufficient evidence to bring a case against him. A central factor appears to have been his respect for Carr's tactical political brain, which soon proved effective during the selection. A Labour Party member since the age of sixteen, brought up in Hartlepool, but only recently returned to the constituency after a spell in Newcastle, Carr was himself deemed a possible successor to Leadbitter. By his own account, however, his ambitions lay more in 'regional and local government', both of which he considered potentially more important than Westminster. Alerted by Mrs Mean, he and his partner at this time, Lindsay, who was also politically active, invited Mandelson to what she described as a 'classic Provençal Sunday lunch with cod and new potatoes and all fresh vegetables, and gallons of garlic mayonnaise. I was impressed with him on the first meeting. I obviously knew about him. I knew what he was doing to the party and that had my admiration and I also had a sense of his politics which wasn't too dissimilar to mine.' Carr believed that Stephen Jones, whom he had 'totally written off', and Ray Waller had both failed to 'read the constituency properly': 'I think Hartlepool is a very ambitious town and the people in it might seem dog in the manger but they actually have very strong ambitions for themselves and their families. I think politically a lot of my colleagues missed that.'[7]

Although Carr did not make up his mind to support Mandelson at this first meeting, he was impressed by the firmness with which Mandelson stood by his revisionist views: 'What I liked, which is what I find strange, is how honest and firm he is in his opinions. He doesn't shift them, you know; if they're inconvenient he holds to them. Both Lindsay and I were very straightforward and honest with him and we tackled some of the issues that others were skirting about, trying to blacken him within the constituency but not having the courage to ask him or raise it.' One of these 'issues' was the fact that Mandelson was gay: the three of them had a 'very frank and very straightforward conversation' about it, interrupted only by the endless routine pager and mobile messages from Walworth Road and Kinnock's office about national Labour Party business.

He asked my opinion, after I broached it and I said, 'Don't read Hartlepool as the metropolitans might describe it. Your first responsibility is to get selected and after that you've 300 ambassadors. If they see you, you can weather anything.' I didn't think it was an issue but I thought it was important to raise . . . because it had to be confronted one way or the other, both in the selection campaign and then obviously in the campaign itself. And I think I was proved right. I genuinely didn't believe it was an issue.

Carr did indeed prove to be right. In the end the selection campaign survived both the anonymous circulation – to the entire Labour Group of the council – of the 1987 *News of the World* story, and a campaign about Mandelson's sexuality launched by Stephen Jones's wife Kay. Mrs Jones's mistake, in any case, was to go well beyond the bounds of credibility: she claimed to union officials – at least one of whom repeated the allegations – that she had been told by journalists that Mandelson had 'skeletons in his cupboard'. Mandelson personally checked her claims – that she had been called first by a reporter from the *Sun* and then by someone from the *News of the World* – with the newspaper concerned and was told firmly that no such enquiries had been made. But when he heard from Alan Doyle, the secretary of the TGWU branch at the Cerebos salt factory (which defied an official TGWU recommendation by voting for Mandelson), that the union's district secretary, Frank Ramsay, had also referred at a branch meeting to 'skeletons in the cupboard', he complained directly to Joe Mills, the TGWU regional secretary in Newcastle. Mills, who had had his own differences with Ramsay over internal union matters, promised that it would be 'something of a pleasure' to 'draw the man's teeth'. On the defensive, Ramsay admitted – in a 'Dear Brother Mills' letter to the union's regional headquarters written on 15 November – discussing the rumours 'with a Labour Party activist' but then promptly came to heel: 'Please accept that at all times I will protect the good name of the TGWU which includes not becoming involved in circulating this kind of malicious rumour.'

In mid-November Ms Jones was equally unsuccessful with a series of complaints to the Labour Party's Northern Regional Office: Mandelson, she claimed, had breached rules against canvassing, had been provided with a list of Hartlepool party members by Walworth Road – which, though denied by Mandelson, was quite common practice in the case of would-be candidates well acquainted with party HQ – and had even offered to 'supply one rather gullible young member with a copy of the transcript of Neil Kinnock's meeting with Mikhail Gorbachev'. She also complained that nominations were delayed until the end of October in order to allow Mandelson time off to go to the Labour Party conference. Mandelson dismissed this charge: the delay, he said, had been solely due to Ted Leadbitter's choice of date to announce his retirement – an argument corroborated by Leadbitter's closest lieutenant in the party, Elsie Reed. Indeed, despite the formal backing for Jones's candidacy by what was then the country's biggest union, Andrew Sharp, the party's regional organiser, unequivocally accepted Mandelson's comprehensive three-page typewritten refutation of each one of the allegations, concluding, 'There is no case to answer.' Worse, from Mrs Jones's point of view, on 27 November an increasingly disillusioned Joe Mills publicly disassociated the union from her complaint. But the final blow to Jones's rapidly faltering campaign came when Mills issued a statement saying that he 'would be well advised to withdraw from the contest because our union would have great difficulty in now supporting him as a candidate'. Jones limped on as a candidate to the end, as he was entitled to do; but his hopes of winning, such as they had been, were extinguished – he came fifth and last with a miserable 2.9 per cent of the vote.

The man to beat had always been Ray Waller, and Mandelson set about this task as if it were a military operation. He had quickly seen that Carr would be hugely valuable. As usual after important meetings, he had written to him in July thanking him for the lunch and explicitly asking for his help and support, undertaking to buy a house in the constituency before the election, and promising 'I will not always agree with comrades in the party and I will openly and vigorously argue my position. But I am not sectarian in my attitudes. I will debate and listen to all and be honest with people.' He added: 'I know you are worried about my "ambitions". I will not disguise from you that I want our party to be successful and I want to play my part in implementing our policies. I don't want to be a mere backbench spectator or critic.' But Hartlepool, he promised, would not be a mere 'stepping stone' but somewhere 'I care for and represent as best as I possibly can regionally, and nationally and even internationally when it comes to getting business and jobs into the town'. Carr, he said pointedly, could take a 'back seat and wait to see how I get on'. But then it might be too late: 'The risk is you are faced in the autumn with a worse choice.' He believed he could win with support 'from right to left and from the older and younger members of the party. But I can't do it without organisation.'

Already favourably inclined, Carr was now won over. 'Peter's instructions to me were very clear: "Overwhelming victory in all elements of the electoral college" and he's actually a dream to work for as a candidate, because if he decides that you can deliver, he does what you tell him to and he's not temperamental.'

Neil Kinnock had warned Mandelson in February against being too hopeful. 'Kid,' he had said, 'I wish you well because I want you to have what you've set your heart on. But Hartlepool won't have you. I know what sort of party it is. You won't be selected.' When, ten months later, he heard with distinctly mixed feelings of the news of Mandelson's selection he said ruefully: 'I should have guessed you would knock on every door and get round every single member of the party.'

Not quite every one. According to Carr, 'I think three or four got away, but they were probably gravely ill ... we approached it professionally like the Labour Party approaches its election campaign.' In July Mandelson wrote formally to Tom Burlison to ask for the endorsement of the GMB regional committee, which he got. But Carr's efforts concentrated mainly on the party's 300 or so individual members, not least because they carried weight in other sections of the electoral college. Carr's value to Mandelson now became apparent. They were able to stick within the letter, if not necessarily the split, of the rules against canvassing because 'I don't need to justify visiting colleagues and friends that I've known since I was sixteen ... my reach with people would come from the fact that I went to school with their children, that we went to the same church, that I'd been a member of Shelter. I could still go to about

90 per cent of the membership of the party today and know them personally through a history, not just through the party ... I'm a very social being so I know most of the pubs as well.' Even with some of Ray Waller's supporters there were tolerably friendly relations; late one night, on a visit to Gladys Worthy, a stalwart who had helped to 'stitch up' two wards for Waller, Bernard Carr, Lindsay and Mandelson ended up singing 'Hey Big Spender'. Few outsiders in a parliamentary selection have the benefit of a campaign manager with this degree of local expertise.

But if Mandelson was not 'temperamental', he certainly suffered from mood swings. A key meeting was that of Carr's own ward, which included the Joneses and a number of Waller supporters. All five candidates were interviewed in the hope of securing the nomination. Carr remembered returning to his house on the headland, overlooking the North Sea, to see Mandelson, who had by then pretty well moved in, 'at the bottom of the stairs almost weeping with frustration and anger at his performance and feeling that he'd fluffed it and let both Lindsay and me down ... He must have slunk back, you know, before the vote was known.' In fact he secured the nomination, despite what he felt was an indifferent interview. The 'diehards' – what would now be called the defiantly old Labour vote – split between Waller and Jones, and Mandelson picked up the rest. 'The raw material was good to work with and in the ward I turned out the votes and Peter got the nomination because it's winner takes all.'

A potentially serious blow came in November, when Leadbitter was quoted in the *Daily Express* complaining that parliament was already too full of 'polished office boys'.[8] He wrote to Mandelson, by now the front runner, assuring him that 'I am personally standing well aside'. Nevertheless Leadbitter was almost certainly in private a Waller supporter; as late as 1998 Elsie Reed, a captivating, if formidable widow with steadfastly old Labour views, refused to disclose how she herself had voted. But Mrs Reed, who had become party secretary even before Leadbitter was selected in 1962 and had, as agent, been his staunchest ally in the constituency for twenty-seven years, was brutally honest when she danced with Mandelson at the party's fund-raising ball before the selection: 'Peter asked what she thought his chances were, and Elsie said, "Oh, I think you've got quite a good chance, but of course I won't be voting for you." And Peter became unconscionably depressed at this news."[9]

As it turned out, Elsie Reed's instincts about the outcome were right. Mandelson nevertheless left little to chance. As late as 4 December, less than a fortnight before the selection meeting, he was writing to Carr on the way back to London with his 'railway thoughts (very warm and comfortable in the weekend supplement first class carriage, save for the hooray henrys behind me)'. These were a series of impressively detailed 'priorities', ranging from names of individual members still to be won over, to a 'return and conquer' strategy for branches still proving resistant, and transport for stated supporters to the selection meeting on the day. Most of the advice on his speech to the selection conference came from Gordon Brown. With characteristic generosity, Brown single-mindedly hammered out a (distinctively Brownite) draft peroration on his own typewriter:

> When I see pensioners, many of whom here in Hartlepool have to choose between heating and eating, when I see children who because of cuts in child benefit are ill clad and undernourished, when I see teenagers in this great town with no jobs, no training place, no cash and no hope . . . when I see all those unmet needs on the one hand and unused resources on the other then that is the socialist challenge – to meet those unmet needs by using those wasted, inefficiently used resources . . .

Mandelson left no button unpushed: he paid tribute to Leadbitter's 'fine record of service'; he mentioned that both his 'grandpa's' experience as an MP and his own as a councillor had prepared him for the task ahead; he littered his speech with references to 'Hartlepool' and 'this town' – although he was not yet presumptuous enough to use Thornton Wilder's phrase 'our town', as he habitually refers to Hartlepool in constituency speeches today. He promised that he would live in the town. And he used the word 'socialist' at least five times. In the event he triumphed: the results were Peter Mandelson 63.2985 per cent; Ray Waller 21.5 per cent; Barbara Hawkins took 3.809 per cent; Russell Hart, another local man, 3.315 per cent; and Stephen Jones 2.9 per cent. Barring a disaster, Mandelson had a seat for life – and one in the north-east heartlands of the modernising tendency of the parliamentary party. Appropriately, his selection took place just as, a few miles away, Blair was delivering his critically important speech pledging that the trade union closed shop would not be restored by a future Labour government.

His euphoria was short-lived. Neil Kinnock's public reaction was generous: 'Peter, as ever, will be a great asset to the Labour Party, and most certainly he will be a fine representative for the people of Hartlepool.' But this belied serious mounting tension between Mandelson and the Kinnock office – particularly Charles Clarke – over his selection.

Early in 1989 Clarke had conceived the notion, on a flight back from Belfast with Kinnock, that Mandelson should be brought into the leader's office as his personal press officer. The snag, as Clarke well knew, was that Mandelson had already indicated his desire for a parliamentary seat. Would he be prepared to give up this ambition, at least until the next election, for a job at Kinnock's side? No, he would not. According to Clarke, 'Neil offered him that job three times, and it's not just that he offered it to him, he *asked* him to come and do that job. Glenys asked him to come and do that job, but the condition on each occasion was that he had to give up a parliamentary seat for this time around and he wouldn't do it.' Mandelson therefore remained in his post at Walworth Road. The first indication that this job might also not be secure in the long term came one night when he and Clarke were walking back to Westminster from a function in the Mall: 'I said: "You can't do this and be Director of Communication" ... and he said, "Don't ever" ... and, you know, he pulled all the loyalty, and I felt loyalty to him – "don't ever put me on the spot about this."'

By Clarke's own account, Kinnock was less upset about Mandelson's search for a seat than he was – even when Tom Burlison checked with Kinnock's office on the leader's feelings about Mandelson's candidacy before deciding whether or not to offer support. 'I don't think [Mandelson] would have said he was Neil's candidate. But he would have said: "Neil's fine about it and Neil will be very happy with me as a candidate."' In fact Mandelson had worded his formal letter to Burlison guardedly: 'I have naturally talked to Neil about my future course and he knows of my decision to seek a parliamentary nomination and stand for the party at the next general election.' But in any case the Kinnock office nodded it through when Burlison called. Clarke 'checked it with Neil and we said: "We're not going to stop him. We could have done. A word would have done it. Everything would have been pulled and he wouldn't have got Hartlepool."'[10] But Kinnock was certainly less than happy with Mandelson's decision. Unwinding in a Paris hotel over a late-night drink with members of his office staff after a trying meeting of the Socialist International, he suddenly let rip to Clarke and Jan Royall (who now works for Kinnock in his Brussels *cabinet*), accusing the absent Mandelson of betrayal; he would be irreplaceable, he thundered, and Walworth Road would collapse. Kinnock had talked to Mandelson 'to voice my disagreement, because we had put together a small grouping of people who utterly trusted each other and who had in mind a realistic objective of fighting to win'. Mandelson was

> candid enough to say he was in with a chance, so I did say to him, 'Don't get yourself hurt and it would be much better if you did not leave us' . . . But I couldn't say to anybody, having fought and won a selection myself, and been a member of parliament by then for nineteen years, 'No, this is for other people, not for you.' And so while I regret his departure very much and would have much preferred him to stay, I couldn't say being an MP is something reserved for Neil Kinnock.[11]

Nevertheless the storm clouds were gathering. Mandelson's later recollection was that, on the Monday evening before the selection, Clarke asked him to step into one of the little offices in the Leader of the Opposition's Commons suite. ' "I gather you're likely to get [Hartlepool]," ' he said. ' "You'll have to decide immediately when to leave your job." ' Mandelson hesitated and replied: 'Let's wait and see.' But Clarke replied: 'Neil is so angry he cannot bring himself to talk about it. I have never known him so furious about anything. We'll want you to go straightaway.' Mandelson, dumbstruck, replied that to leave without a successor and no prospect of continuity would be 'the greatest folly and irresponsibility'. Clarke was equally emphatic, however: it would be irresponsible to delay; if it was up to him Mandelson would clear his desk the day after his selection. Clarke's recollection is of a conversation the day *after* Mandelson's selection: 'I told him I thought he couldn't stay on as Director of Communications. He said: 'You can't win the election without me.' But I said: "Go and talk to Neil, don't necessarily rely on me." But he had to accept that's what Neil thought too.'

Mandelson was adamant that he had made no such suggestion about his own indispensability. But he did immediately seek out two of the women in Kinnock's office to try and establish Kinnock's true feelings. Sue Nye and Julie Hall (recently appointed as Kinnock's press officer) both strongly agreed with him that precipitate departure would be 'madness'. Sue Nye then consulted Jan Royall, who told her about the Paris episode; it was clear that this was the basis for Clarke's view of Kinnock's attitude. Moreover, Clarke may have been suffering from a certain understandable jealousy: after all, Mandelson was doing what he did not feel he could do and, by seeking a seat, moving ahead of Clarke on the political ladder in the process – as he rapidly did.

But Kinnock was perhaps better than Clarke at separating his personal feelings from his own and the party's interests: he let it be known that he thought it would be better for Mandelson to stay until a successor could be found and until the 1990 conference was over. Clarke, however, proved irreconcilable; the bond, which according to both men had been extremely close, had been severed – with what would prove to be deeply destructive consequences.

# CHAPTER THIRTEEN

## Why Don't You Have Peter Back?

True to his word, Mandelson moved into his new constituency. He bought his four-bedroom house in Hutton Avenue for £84,000 almost immediately after his selection – with the help of a £270-a-month Abbey National mortgage and a bridging loan from his mother until he could sell his beloved cottage on the Wye. It was his preferred home, at least until 1996, when, thanks to the famous loan from Geoffrey Robinson, he bought his house in Notting Hill in place of the flat in Wilmington Square, Clerkenwell. His London flat was noisy – he played a vigorous part in a local residents' campaign to stop rush-hour traffic using the square as a rat run – and it never gave him the pleasure he would derive from his famous home in Notting Hill. The house in quiet Hutton Avenue has a large, homely, unmodernised kitchen; the study overlooks the front garden (just as his study at Bigwood Road had done) and the sitting room, comfortably but unremarkably furnished, is festooned with family photographs. This is where the Labourist in Mandelson is still most at home; here he keeps a framed copy of the *Hartlepool Mail* front page from the day of his selection; of his Commons maiden speech; of the mocked-up *Guardian* front page presented to him on his fortieth birthday; of the issue of *Pravda* for the day in 1989 when Gerald Kaufman ditched unilateralism in Red Square; of the Vicky cartoon and of the family snapshot of Herbert Morrison; here also are most of his books – mainly twentieth-century political history: not only the Crossman diaries but also Harold Nicolson's; Middlemass and Barnes's *Life of Stanley*

*Baldwin* as well as Philip Williams's *Gaitskell*; Lewis Minkin's grindingly detailed standard work on the Labour Party conference alongside Roy Jenkins's memoirs.

After the New Year, 1990, he started to spend more time here. Indeed, during Charles Clarke's second confrontation with Mandelson in March that year one of his complaints was precisely that he was spending too many Fridays in Hartlepool. Even by the standards of the previous discussion, it was a brutal exchange, albeit one which took place in the shorthand of two men who knew each other extremely well and had worked closely together for nearly five years. Clarke told Mandelson bluntly that his attempt to be both a parliamentary candidate and the party's Director of Communications was 'untenable' and that he no longer trusted him. Because he no longer trusted him, moreover, 'it was not possible to have a working relationship'. Mandelson, Clarke said, warming to his theme, had 'behaved outrageously over Hartlepool from the very beginning'; this was Kinnock's view as well as his own. The only reason that Kinnock had asked Mandelson to remain until October was 'because he knew he couldn't find someone else to take your job immediately, no other reason'.[1] Mandelson retorted that Clarke should think again about what he had said; Clarke countered by saying he would not withdraw a word. 'In which case', Mandelson replied, a little enigmatically, these statements would have to 'remain on the record'. He then accused Clarke of 'behaving just as you complain Roy Hattersley behaves', and the conversation ended as coldly as it had begun. Mandelson was in effect facing the sack.

The accusation that Mandelson was spending too much time in Hartlepool was not wholly fair. As he had done on his trips to Foy since before the 1987 election, he continued to use what Byrne called his 'suitcase-sized' mobile telephone – not yet as fashionable or as compact a piece of apparatus as it would become – and spent as much time speaking to journalists from Hartlepool in the run-up to Sunday newspaper deadlines as he ever had in London. Nevertheless Clarke insisted that the two roles were incompatible:

> I think it was a question of choosing between serving the party and serving himself, and he chose to serve himself first of all.

Second his key quality, his brilliant quality, was and is managing the media. I still believe he could not have done that, critically in the general election campaign, as the Labour candidate for Hartlepool. Remembering he was a new candidate, you know. Now you can say '97 [in which Mandelson ran the campaign] proves the difference, but actually that's five years on.

After Mandelson's selection the press – and many in the party – remained mesmerised by his supposedly all-pervading influence on the leadership. As late as June Ian Aitken, the *Guardian*'s political editor, was quoting 'a senior Labour front bencher with a major economic portfolio' who said, in a deliberate echo of Herbert Morrison's notorious remark, that 'from now on socialism is what Mr Mandelson says it is'.[2] In fact, thanks – at least partly – to the irretrievable breakdown of relations with Clarke, much of that influence was being steadily eroded. The choice of his own successor was a case in point. Mandelson's original view was clear: he should be replaced by David Hill, still Hattersley's loyal lieutenant and Mandelson's old friend. Hill would indeed have been the ideal choice: a veteran pillar of the right in Labour's internal struggles, with a sharp brain, and the moustache and general demeanour of an amiable Mexican bandit, Hill was as uniformly popular within the parliamentary party as he was respected by journalists. Hattersley, despite his reluctance to lose Hill, accepted the idea, and pressed his case with Kinnock: 'Roy went to see Neil and said: "Well, David's going to put in for this, as you know. Peter thinks he should do it and everybody else has said he should do it." And Neil sort of wouldn't say, and I felt shocked. Neil wouldn't say anything.' As the NEC (at which the appointment was to be made) drew nearer, Mandelson appeared

to become slightly more lukewarm, about which I feel slightly pissed off because I had had to work quite hard to get him his job ... I think Peter was seriously embarrassed by what happened. I think he came with genuine confidence, he believed that the world and his mother recognised that it would be obvious ... and then when he suddenly found it wasn't working very well what Peter did was, he withdrew. I believe that Peter had discussions with

Neil. I believe that Peter realised this was a much more complicated . . . proposition than he'd ever envisaged. But he couldn't
say to me withdraw because Kinnock and Clarke wouldn't say
withdraw.[3]

Hill was struck by the ominous fact that Mandelson did not, as
friends would normally do in such circumstances, make any mention
of how hard he had argued his case.

In fact Mandelson *had* pressed Hill's claim to the job with Kinnock, at least initially, but had been shocked to find, not that the
leader had anything personal against Hill, but that, precisely as Hill
had himself guessed,

> we were now into seven years of Kinnock–Hattersley and in the
> end Neil still couldn't bring himself to deliver someone who
> worked for Roy. What was amazing was that Roy went to the
> meeting believing it was all going to be settled. But meanwhile
> Larry Whitty, realising it was all going to be complete chaos,
> had phoned round the NEC and said: 'You've got to go for
> a couple of our candidates,' so [the television reporter John]
> Underwood got it, thanks to Larry phoning round.

Hill's suspicions were right: having realised that Kinnock would
prefer Byrne to Hill, Mandelson smartly threw his support behind
his deputy. Byrne had always been an unlikely winner, as Mandelson
himself recognised from the start, partly because he threatened to
be 'another Mandelson', but partly because he had if anything made
even more enemies on the NEC than his boss. On the other hand,
if Hill was going to be opposed not only by Hattersley's opponents
on the left of the NEC but also by Kinnock, Byrne might just have
a chance. According to Byrne, by the time it came to the NEC

> I wanted to take over from Peter, Peter wanted me to take over
> from Peter and Neil wanted me to take over from Peter. And I
> lost at the NEC. And I remember thinking, 'If I go in there and
> portray myself as a continuation of the Peter Mandelson regime
> I'm dead' . . . so I went in there and I used the line, 'Peter
> Mandelson's grandfather may have been a cabinet minister, but

my father was a bricklayer. I am not Peter Mandelson.' And I remember Neil winking at me and thinking: 'Well, you've got a tough job, son, but you've started all right.' As far as they were concerned I was Peter and Neil's choice, therefore I couldn't have it.[4]

With the modernising right wing of the party split, Underwood won comfortably, a victory which would swiftly lead to ructions at the highest level in the party.

First, however, there was Mandelson's last party conference to get through. Appropriately it started – and continued – with accusations of excessive stage management. On the Sunday before it formally opened an ITN crew slipped into the Winter Gardens and filmed workmen putting up the final elements of the set – with its slogan, 'Looking to the future'. Mandelson was enraged. As far as he was concerned, the set was 'embargoed' – perhaps the only case of a physical structure being put under the same restriction as a press release. He told ITN's political editor Michael Brunson that he had no right to film without permission. The BBC reporter Nick Jones recorded the following, typically Mandelsonian wind-up, staged, as usual, in front of several witnesses.

> BRUNSON: You are trying to dictate the picture we use. There are no rules at all; all you want is adulatory pictures. But if Labour wants to stage manage the conference, so be it.
> MANDELSON: That is a very interesting point, Michael. The only adulatory pictures I have seen from you are all your flag-waving stuff from the Thatcher tour of Czechoslovakia and Hungary.
> BRUNSON: Don't you impugn my integrity.

At this point, according to Jones, 'ITN's political editor grabbed Mandelson's lapels. Brunson acknowledged afterwards that he lost his cool, but felt he had been unfairly provoked.'[5] It was not the first time that Mandelson had used his rights over the conference set to influence coverage. Joy Johnson, an ITN producer at the time, remembered an incident which demonstrates media manipulation at its most effective. Following Kinnock and Hattersley's straightforward defeat of the leadership challenges on the eve of the 1988 conference, she had been planning a story on the forthcoming battle over the block vote, complete with interviews with truculent union leaders – instead of the 'Kinnock and Hattersley re-elected by acclaim' report that Mandelson was seeking. On the Saturday before the conference she called Mandelson and asked his permission to use the conference set.

> And he said: 'Absolutely fine. By the way, what are you saying?' And I said, 'Well, we're saying Kinnock and Hattersley were elected to acclaim but that you're going to have to come to terms with how you tackle the block vote.' And he said: 'Get off my set. Get off my set.' And I said: 'Come on, Peter, people are talking about it.' He said: 'At dinner parties, at dinner parties.' And I said: 'Peter, I don't go to dinner parties.' 'Give me the editor, give me the editor.'
>
> [Johnson passed the phone to the editor.] And of course the editor said: 'All right, Peter, yes, you're right' . . . The thing that you've got to think of all the time when you work for television, if you don't have contact, you lose the relationship with this guy.[6]

No editor seeking to produce the best possible conference coverage would want to fall out instantly with the person who could give him access or favour rival networks at his expense if he chose; he would be ignoring Mandelson at his peril.

This brutal little episode, in which Mandelson effectively killed a story about Labour splits in favour of a triumphalist portrayal of the leadership election, was typical of what one senior BBC executive would later call the party's 'world class news management'. Mandelson realised quicker than most the potential for control, and had the perseverance to exercise it. Nor was it only the broadcasters who complained about Mandelson's stage management of party conferences. The outgoing Communications Director was held responsible for the new system of allotting key members of the Shadow Cabinet ten minutes – instead of the much-loved one under which they had to 'catch the eye' of the conference chairman like any other delegate (even – absurdly – Chancellor Denis Healey in the middle of the 1976 IMF crisis). Left-wing critics of the new system were briefly consoled at Blackpool in 1990 when one of its beneficiaries, the rapidly rising young Employment spokesman Tony Blair, lost a page in his speech. As he momentarily looked at the audience in mute embarrassment, he saw Mandelson standing at the back of the hall, his face a mask of horror. Despite this discouraging sight, the future leader eventually managed to recover.

However, all this manipulation of the conference and its coverage would be sorely missed by the Kinnock office. Single-mindedly, and sometimes single-handedly, he had changed the image of the party to one much more resembling a cohesive fighting force. Mandelson's passing was nevertheless marked in a fairly low-key fashion. On the Friday of the conference, at a leaving party for Mandelson, Kinnock confessed to having first given currency, during the Brecon and Radnor by-election, to the famous – and famously apocryphal – 'mushy peas' story. He did so after retelling the joke in a Geordie accent – in deference to Mandelson's new political base in the North-East – and presenting him with a screwed-up copy of the *People* containing cod, chips and peas. According to Bryan Appleyard's 1995 profile of Mandelson, it was an American woman party researcher at the Knowsley by-election who first mistook mushy peas for guacamole in a chip shop.[7] But Kinnock insisted that it was a 'very, very, old joke', long pre-dating this. 'He used to quite enjoy a joke. Peter's never effete . . . but he was metropolitan and so I [had] made this joke about a nice metropolitan, cosmopolitan whatever, mediapolitan. I'd always done it and not just with Peter.'[8]

For Mandelson the leaving party was an emotional occasion; the *Guardian* reported that 'this tough exponent of the black arts of political PR actually blubbed'.[9] But it had been arranged at the last minute by Byrne, Julie Hall and a handful of staff members like Anna Healy. Neither the heavyweights of the NEC and Shadow Cabinet, nor his senior colleagues at Walworth Road had felt it necessary to mark his passing. As Byrne and Julie Hall drove with him to Foy through heavy rain, there seemed a certain bathos about the end to Mandelson's career as an employee of the party. They heard about the government's decision to join the European Exchange Rate Mechanism in a Granada service station on the M6.

Some of the Shadow Cabinet's big hitters were hardly in mourning. Robin Cook, who felt with some justice that his access to television and radio had been severely curtailed by Mandelson, summoned Byrne to his office a few days later and made it clear that 'under the new regime' he would be expecting better treatment. However, Mandelson's relationship with the 'new regime' – because it involved his by now mythical powers, manipulation of the media (a topic of obsessive interest to the media itself), a strikingly photogenic blonde (Julie Hall) and accusations of backstabbing at Labour HQ – became the press's favourite political soap opera during the first half of 1991.

One of the main problems concerned Mandelson's new London base. Colin Byrne and Julie Hall – then still a friend of Byrne's rather than, as she later became, his girlfriend – had moved into an interior designed and fully furnished house in Doughty Mews, complete with roof garden, rented from two architects for around £500 per week. Mandelson had by now split up with Peter Ashby and left Prince George Road. Initially he had been without a London home of his own, and lodged with Sue Nye and her husband, the Goldman Sachs economist Gavyn Davies, at their house in Lloyd Square, Islington. However, he now had a job. He had been engaged – at a salary of £28,000 a year – by his old friend Dennis Stevenson at the management consultants SRU, one of whose partners was the style guru Peter York; he needed a London base. Mandelson and Byrne had discussed sharing a home during 1989. But according to Byrne, Mandelson, fielding at the time a barrage of innuendo from Kay Jones during the selection contest, had said, 'We can't do it while I'm still going for Hartlepool because they're looking for all sorts of dirt to throw at me.'

But once Mandelson was selected, he and Byrne suggested to Julie Hall that she join them, to spread the cost. Almost immediately the arrangement led to suspicions of quite another kind. About three weeks after taking over, Underwood summoned Byrne into his office and accused him, along with Mandelson, of briefing the press without consulting him, which Byrne strenuously denied. According to Byrne, the accusation had been made to Underwood by the shadow minister David Clark – who after the 1997 election would be

Mandelson's titular boss at the Cabinet Office. But Clark was not alone. Several of Mandelson's old sparring partners, including, Byrne insisted, Robin Cook, John Prescott, Michael Meacher and Clare Short, had suggested to Underwood that Mandelson was undermining him behind the scenes. This took its toll. Byrne claimed that 'within two months of starting John's health clearly deteriorated. I mean he got bad skin, bags under his eyes.' To Mandelson's enemies, it was as if the Prince of Darkness had cast a spell on Underwood from his exile in Doughty Mews. Charles Clarke was also convinced that Mandelson was operating 'an alternative power base' at Doughty Mews and that 'he couldn't accept that he wasn't close to the leader and so he sought to portray himself as being close to the leader' – trading in his dealings with journalists, Clarke claimed, on conversations that he had had with Kinnock several months before. Clarke was furious – so much so that he tried, as Julie Hall's line manager, to order her not to live with Byrne and Mandelson.

It was not an easy time for Underwood, made all the more difficult by factors utterly out of his control. Margaret Thatcher's removal in November 1990, little more than a month after he took over, changed the political landscape. Philip Gould's view that Major's election as leader made it 'almost impossible for us to win'[10] was not shared at the time by Tony Blair, who told a journalist the day after Thatcher's fall that he thought the Tories had made a serious mistake. But it did result in an immediate 9.5 per cent swing in their favour.

Mandelson certainly continued to advise Byrne. Indeed on one occasion he even advised Underwood, albeit indirectly and without the latter's knowledge. Deeply uncertain about how to brief Sunday political journalists on a Trade and Industry document of Gordon Brown's, Underwood turned to Byrne for help. He telephoned Mandelson, who wrote a four-paragraph briefing note which Understood, in blissful ignorance of its origin, read out verbatim. A very rare row between Byrne and Mandelson during this febrile period arose – after Underwood's eventual resignation in June 1991 – precisely because Byrne had acted without consulting him in recommending the appointment of a separate press officer to the Parliamentary Labour Party at the same seniority to himself.

Peter said: 'Don't ever do things without consulting me, Colin, because you don't think these things through.' He was absolutely right; I'm not as strategic a thinker as he is . . . I think that taught me a lesson, which is that it's not that he's a control freak, it's just that he does actually spend more time thinking these things through in cool, calm terms than a lot of people who are close around him.

Underwood was not so charitable; and his suspicions that Mandelson was still exercising influence were solidly based.

But then the two men saw the job in quite different ways. Underwood's view of his job, by no means dishonourable, was almost diametrically opposed to that of his predecessor, as – accurately – defined by Tom Sawyer. Where Mandelson had seen his role as serving the leader and those who supported him, and confounding the leader's opponents, Underwood aimed (more usually for a Labour Party official) to serve the whole NEC and, by extension, the whole Shadow Cabinet. This meant that he was working for a much broader spectrum of the party's opinion than the leadership alone. As a result he fell foul not only of Mandelson's vicarious influence but of Charles Clarke. When he threatened to go if Kinnock did not sanction the sacking of Byrne, Kinnock let him go rather than Byrne. Mandelson, writing in the *People* a few days afterwards, denied that he had been responsible for Underwood's departure; in the various reports of the affair, he said, 'I found myself engaged to be married, living in a fashionable £200,000 pad, surrounded by Porsche cars and enjoying the kind of power I never knew existed let alone possessed.'[11] By Clarke's own account, even in the midst of the row with the Doughty Mews trio, when he was telling Julie Hall that he would not pay for a fax in a house inhabited by Peter Mandelson, he was independently coming to the conclusion that 'Underwood was a disaster and I sacked Underwood. Well, when I say I sacked him, I told him he had to go, because it was a disaster.'

Indeed, one of the factors that had caused problems for Underwood had been Kinnock's decision – approved by Clarke – that Mandelson should be brought back to run the Monmouth by-election in May. There were parallels with Brecon and Radnor:

Mandelson had still not sold his beloved cottage at Foy, and so had a base within reach of the constituency. And the main worry was that, as at Ribble Valley earlier in the year, a LibDem resurgence might snatch victory from Labour. Mandelson now tried out for the first time a new departure in tactical voting, distributing stickers saying I'M A LIBDEM BUT I'M VOTING LABOUR. A combination of some – to put it mildly – not too fastidious campaigning on the NHS, his own uncanny ability to attract personal publicity, and a signal victory on a 12.6 per cent swing, helped to thrust him into the media spotlight once again. He enraged John Major by claiming that hospitals seeking Trust status, as the Monmouth hospital was considering doing, were preparing to 'opt out of the NHS'. The NHS claim, for which the Monmouth by-election became famous, may have been less important than the Tories claimed afterwards. The *Daily Mirror*, tracking Tory voters who had switched to Labour, failed to mention the hospital.[12] But it certainly contributed to Mandelson's celebrity as a practitioner of the blacker arts.

Nick Wapshott was one of Mandelson's most trusted journalistic contacts (so much so that when he discovered that his tape recorder had not been functioning during an interview with Neil Kinnock, Mandelson, who had been present, patiently reconstructed it from memory for his benefit, joking afterwards that it read better than the original). So it was not all that surprising that, after Monmouth, he wrote in the *Observer* about 'one Labour name which on Friday could be heard with a nervous laugh on the lips of Chris Patten [Tory chairman] and Gus O'Donnell [the Prime Minister's press secretary]: that of Peter Mandelson. Mention of Mandelson appears to cast respectful terror in the hearts of Tory strategists, much as the name Rommel gained a mythical status among Allied generals.'[13] But even the *Sunday Times*'s Bryan Appleyard, a journalist less susceptible to the Mandelson wiles because he was not in the parliamentary lobby, was highly impressed: 'I have seen the future and it smirks. It is mildly prognathous and has a small lightly grizzled moustache. Its hair aspires to a quiff. The eyes are brown and in conversation they lock into an astonishingly immobile stare that challenges you to speculate what is really going on there. Its name is Peter Mandelson.' Appleyard quoted Mandelson as being on a mission to avenge the Greenwich by-election defeat and vividly described his appeal to the political reporters holed up in Monmouth.

> He created a viable opposition by turning a crazed gang of fissiparous ideologues into a seldom army marching behind a designer rose ... He is an operator of genius. He plays the press like a musical instrument, manipulating them with risky chatter, pseudo-confidences and the manly, world-weary style they always fall for. He is fun, edgy and exciting. He is impossible to dislike and he will put Kinnock in Downing Street.[14]

The Appleyard piece authentically captured the Mandelson magnetism of the time. But the last sentence was doubly wrong. Plenty of people found it all too easy to dislike Mandelson, and that in turn helped to ensure that he would not even have the chance to try and 'put Kinnock into Downing Street'. When the NEC discussed the Monmouth victory Dennis Skinner remarked that it had been the collective work of around seventy party workers and that he had been disappointed to read that it had all been achieved by one 'John Wayne' figure.[15] Nothing he had said for many years at an NEC, Skinner commented afterwards, had been so well received, especially – if unsurprisingly – by Underwood. Mandelson, meanwhile, used some diplomacy in trying to consolidate his success. First he wrote to Clarke, thanking him for the chance to work in Monmouth, and saying, 'I think I can contribute more in the same way' – being careful to add, 'in a quite tactful, reasonable way ... I know you don't share this view.'[16] On this last point, at least, Mandelson was right.

Nevertheless, contact with Kinnock himself was not broken off. Unbeknown to Clarke, Kinnock had, the week before Christmas 1990, asked Mandelson down to his constituency in Wales to discuss how he could continue to help. Kinnock was in what Mandelson would describe as 'middling spirits, worried about his staff, performances and speeches'. But with the important exception of Monmouth, Mandelson was not re-engaged. According to Clarke, even he thought that it might be possible to use Mandelson for fund-raising, which he deemed more compatible with his parliamentary candidacy than working on the campaign itself; but 'Jack

Cunningham [the campaign coordinator] was very opposed to involving Peter'. Mandelson had apparently rejected an alternative proposal he made to him – that he should spend the period advising individual backbench candidates on their campaigns. There was also a scheme to 'involve him in various meetings' drawing up campaign plans, but 'a lot of people – Jack, Hattersley, Cook, Prescott, Smith – wouldn't touch Peter with a bargepole. Right or wrong, they wouldn't, so Neil would have had to fight a battle to get some of them to accept.'

Then, on 15 September, before John Major had ruled out the possibility of a November election, Mandelson wrote to Kinnock directly: it was an affectionate, handwritten letter: 'I thought of you today because it reminded me of when the pressure started piling on at the beginning of 1987 – ruthless Tories, vile tabloids, craven broadcasters and flaky colleagues. The difference is that we're stronger, and healthier now and the Tories are older, tireder and above all discredited.' It would be better if the election was delayed, he thought, because we 'could do with more time. There are things – people, methods and message – that need sorting out. But they can be, even if the election is soon, as long as everyone concentrates and pulls together.' He concluded: 'I know you will be anxious about the campaign. But remember May '87 and you had the extraordinary lease of life and burst of energy – you'll find all the words necessary again. Rely on your friends and if there is *anything* I can do please ask. Love to you and Glenys, as always, Peter.'

In October Mandelson visited the Kinnocks in Ealing. By now Kinnock was much more recognisably in that mood of quiet despair poignantly depicted in David Hare's play about Labour in this period, *Absence of War*. He seemed terrified of the coming election and could not find words to fill his speeches. His deep anxiety was compounded by the running battle being waged between Julie Hall and Charles Clarke, and the seeming impossibility of reversing his own poor image and John Major's favourable press. He had already turned down Robert Maxwell's offer to second Alastair Campbell, by now the *Daily Mirror*'s political editor, to his office as press officer, on the grounds that it would suggest he was beholden to Maxwell. Glenys Kinnock asked him, 'Why don't you have Peter back to organise things and get a better press?' Miserably, Kinnock replied: 'Because of the Mandelson myth and what everyone will say about him pulling the strings and controlling me.'

Following the visit Mandelson wrote Kinnock a long note on his laptop: lamenting the fact that the Shadow Communications Agency seemed to be falling apart, he proposed that he and Patricia Hewitt should be included in the agency 'on the grounds of continuity' and that he, Hewitt and Alastair Campbell should form a 'discreet group ... taking a brief from you on speeches and lines of attack and presentation, commissioning and screening work from a range of sources and building this up in preparation for the election campaign'. Kinnock should immediately start to foster 'high-level media contacts ... including newspaper editors and commentators and senior broadcast management and editors', and should resume his weekly briefings to the Westminster lobby. He concluded: 'Last but not least I think we should meet once a month as you suggested, preferably in Ealing with Glenys and I'll do the washing up.'

Mandelson's letter was not, in the end, taken up. He played an important, and for once not particularly high profile, role in the Langbaurgh by-election in November 1991 where the Indian-born British Steel manager Ashok Kumar faced a daunting task as the first black candidate to fight a by-election since David Pitt failed to win Clapham in 1970. The Teeside seat, moreover, was overwhelmingly white, with ethnic minorities making up only 0.6 per cent of the population. As a result of his help through the campaign, Kumar would retain a career-long loyalty to Mandelson, inviting him to a fund-raising dinner in the constituency in 1999 after he had resigned from the Cabinet and being one of the few Labour MPs publicly to call on Tony Blair to bring him back into the Cabinet after the Euro-elections in that year. Kumar recalled that Mandelson gave him a stark pep talk four weeks before polling day in Langbaurgh, pointing out that the Tories had not won a by-election since April 1989. 'He said "the responsibility is on your shoulders. If you lose, your political career will be finished." What impressed me was that he didn't tell you what to say during the campaign. If you had a case he would listen. He asked me what I thought and then he'd say, "OK, but why don't say you it like this?".'

Mandelson was persuaded by Kumar that it would be foolish for the candidate opportunistically to renounce his support for CND.

Instead Kumar was frank about his views on nuclear disarmament, while saying that he would loyally abide by the leadership line if elected. Faced with not particularly subtle racism from his Tory opponents, Kumar began to think he would lose in the week before polling day. Mandelson, who was, according to Kumar, steadfast in encouraging him and lending moral support, arranged for Neil Kinnock to speak to him. Kinnock told the candidate to 'hang on in there for another forty-eight hours and then we'll settle some scores'. Kumar won the by-election.

But apart from a brief face-to-face discussion when Kinnock visited the seat, Mandelson's proposal for regular meetings on election strategy with the leader was not taken up. And meanwhile Kinnock's worries continued to mount. At the heart of the crisis were two closely related issues: the party's economic policy and the man in charge of it, the dominant, and – to both the media and the electorate – weighty and attractive figure of John Smith. Saddled with commitments worth £3 billion to raise child benefit and old age pensions, Smith had pinned himself to a tax increase for those earning more than £16,000 a year and steeper rises in National Insurance contributions for those earning more than £21,500. Philip Gould had consistently come up with research showing that tax was the number-one issue switching voters off Labour. Kinnock was personally convinced that the research was right. At the heart of his worries about Smith's policy as Shadow Chancellor were the differences which would surface between Blair and Brown on the one hand, and Smith (after he became leader) on the other; between a Croslandite, more egalitarian view of political economy, and the modernisers' yen for low taxes. In this respect, as in many others, Kinnock was a moderniser.

But the tensions between Smith and Kinnock meant that the two men either couldn't or wouldn't discuss the matter. Smith took an increasingly dim view of Kinnock's leadership, though he made no move even when, after Margaret Thatcher's fall, there was fresh chatter within the party about replacing him. But, convinced that he could not make a U-turn on tax, he at one point allegedly remarked to a colleague that 'just because we're working for a lunatic it doesn't mean we all have to behave like lunatics'. The conflict culminated in the famous episode later that month at Luigi's restaurant: Kinnock, having written to Smith urging that he phase in the introduction of National Insurance contributions to blunt the Tory attack on tax, indiscreetly mentioned the option at a dinner with journalists. This time Clarke decided that the conflict had gone far enough. With Smith in a rage, he overruled Julie Hall's advice, heavily influenced by the modernisers, which was to admit that the phasing-in option was being considered. Hall argued in vain that phasing-in was right, that it would look weak to retreat; if Kinnock did so he would be saddled with the unpalatable task of defending a policy he did not believe in. But she had virtually no support from the rest of Kinnock's office. The Smith line held. As a result Philip Gould's attempts to confront Smith with the inescapable research findings were fruitless. Mandelson always believed that things might have been different had he been at the centre:

> I think it would have strengthened Neil's hand if I had been there. Patricia and Philip saw the reality and I put it on paper. Philip had always worked through me and if I bought the analysis I would go in and bat. He was the analyst and I was the steel. In a sense Philip was feeding into a vacuum and Charles Clarke was the only strong person around Kinnock. Smith had slammed his fist on the table and said no, no no, these policies are settled. Charles became cross about the fact that Smith would neither change his policies nor would he sell them.

Instead his only role was to discuss – on a daily basis – the problems with Gordon Brown and Tony Blair. All three were convinced that Gould and Kinnock were right and that Smith was wrong. Brown told Gould that Smith 'was making a mistake', while immediately after the election Blair wrote an article in the *Guardian* claiming that tax had been a turn-off not only to those directly affected but to those who *hoped* to earn enough to be affected. The reason for Labour's defeat had been simple: 'it had been the same since 1979; Labour has not been trusted to fulfil the aspirations of a majority of people.'[17] But although both conveyed their views to Smith in private, neither was prepared to challenge him in open debate – for example, in the more open arena of the Shadow Cabinet. For Brown it was especially difficult; the victim of his own success as a shadow minister, he was already under pressure because he was increasingly seen by Smith and his allies as a potential rival for the succession to Kinnock. The result was an impasse. In 1998 Clarke claimed for the first time that Kinnock had at one point even considered sacking Smith – but had decided he was too strong.[18]

So, indeed, he was. The polls continued to find that Labour's position would be transformed if Smith became leader. Even loyalists like Mandelson, who were convinced that Kinnock would grow easily into the job of Prime Minister, now began to doubt whether he was capable of leading the party to the victory needed to put him in Downing Street. By January 1992 Mandelson, disillusioned and now largely cut off from contact with Kinnock and Clarke, was reluctantly coming to the 'tragic' conclusion – especially after Kinnock's poor speech in the pre-Maastricht debate in 1991 during which he called the MP Robert Adley a 'jerk' – that Kinnock should, in Labour's best interests, stand down. But there is no evidence that he communicated this private thought to any of his journalistic contacts or friends, or thought of plotting to replace him. It would probably not have made any difference if he had; but in any case he was still much closer to Kinnock than to the one man who could step into Kinnock's shoes: John Smith distrusted Mandelson and associated him with the polling and advertising techniques of Philip Gould, not to mention the eventual leadership aspirations of Gordon Brown.

In any case, Smith still made no move. In the autumn of 1991, according to one highly placed Labour source, some senior shadow cabinet colleagues had 'reached the rather collective view that we weren't going to win an election with Neil Kinnock as leader . . . a very tentative discussion took place with John Smith, over whether he might put himself forward.' Kinnock was made aware of the approach, but in 1998 he still refused to say who had been involved. But Smith was 'categoric' in rejecting the advance. A change of leadership could only have taken place if Kinnock had stood down voluntarily – in which case Smith would have replaced him by acclaim. But for all his deep lack of self-confidence at the time, Kinnock remained grimly defiant. There was a tense moment during a weekend trip to Paris with Alastair Campbell and his partner Fiona Millar when he picked up a newspaper with a poll showing that Labour would immediately improve its ratings if Smith became leader. 'If I wasn't leader we probably would do better,' he said, but, still believing Labour had a chance of victory, he was in no mood to give up.

Fortunately, Mandelson had a fair amount to occupy his mind, even though the job Stevenson had given him was designed to allow him time for politics – especially in the constituency. He now needed to make some money. Over the next two or three years, for the first and last time in his life, he managed to save money. SRU was a blue-chip consultancy, run jointly by Stevenson with Colin Fisher, who had given extensive research advice to the Labour Party, and Peter York, credited with inventing the term 'Sloane Ranger'. Mandelson went in at the bottom: 'It was quite a menial job he did, it wasn't a great job.'[19] He told Andrew Grice that he was particularly interested in the 'greening' of industry, that the job would not involve political lobbying, and – rather prematurely – that it reflected Labour's growing success in wooing business and the City.[20] He saw something of boardroom life at close quarters. Stevenson remembers taking Mandelson to see Colin Southgate, then chairman of Thorn-EMI; Mandelson's name was known and industrialists like Southgate were interested to see him working at SRU. According to Stevenson, through the SRU work Mandelson saw 'real business, international competitiveness, cost structures, strategic decisions'.[21]

He also took on another modest part-time job – thanks to meeting up again with his old friend and sometime political opponent Roger Liddle, then running a successful consultancy called Prima. Liddle had healed the breach, first by defending him during the Hartlepool selection campaign against charges of having flirted with the SDP, and then by writing to congratulate him after his selection. Michael Young, director of City and Corporate Counsel, to which Prima Europe had been sold in 1989, knew Mandelson socially and suggested that they hire him. He was paid £500 per month to help with presentations to firms like Abbey National and Boots demonstrating what a Labour government would mean for business; he would act as a 'kind of expert witness'.

As a third part-time consultancy he advised the BBC on its defence of the licence fee and its role as a public service broadcaster against the financial squeeze being exerted by the Home Office. Both John Birt and Howell James, the man who in 1987 had been chosen over Mandelson for Director of Corporate Affairs, had a hand in this. James's impeccably Tory past protected the corporation from charges of pro-Labour bias in hiring Mandelson. James and Mandelson became good friends – and continued to be throughout the 1997 campaign, when James was working in Downing Street as John Major's political secretary.

Finally, and most lucratively, he had his £400 per week *People* column. Richard Stott, the editor, asked Alastair Campbell, his friend and Mirror Group Newspapers colleague, to suggest the idea to him before he left Walworth Road in October 1990. Campbell 'was a bit surprised when Richard suggested it. He wasn't known for his writing skills, but Richard thought he was a character and that it would give the *People* something.' Mandelson would frequently go round to Campbell's house in Gospel Oak on a Wednesday evening with a pen and notebook, seeking ideas and suggestions for the column. As a result it frequently contained references to footballers and film stars 'that he had absolutely no knowledge of.[22] David Bradshaw observed that it was a column which had 'more writers than readers'.

But it gave Mandelson a platform and he used it to beat the Labour drum, fulsomely praising Kinnock (and, after the election, John Smith), handing out bouquets to modernisers in the Labour Party like Gordon Brown, relentlessly advancing causes in Hartlepool; and occasionally for shameless self-advertisement. In the column of 26 June 1991, for example, he told his readers that Prince Charles had enquired about him to Lesley Smith, a Labour press officer, when he met her at a polo match. 'He could come to my would-be constituency of Hartlepool and find out direct. There would always be a warm welcome.' And occasionally the prince of Labour glitz even indulged in a little old Labour populism: in December he questioned the party's £500-a-plate fundraising dinners: 'I wonder what sort of image it projects for a party committed to feeding the hungry and helping the poor.' In September he had consulted readers on whether he should shave off his moustache which, unlike his hair, he confided, had been growing grey – provoking an excruciating poem on why he should keep it. In the end he shaved it off the following year while on holiday in Majorca – on the unanimous advice of Philip Gould's and Alastair Campbell's children.

But his work also allowed him plenty of time to make a mark as a candidate in Hartlepool. He conducted a high-profile campaign against the Allied Lyons takeover of the town's brewery, Cameron's, and supporting a management buy-out. He became a governor of two schools – drawing a protest from the Tory candidate Graham Robb in the process – and of the Community Health Council. He annoyed the Rotarians by giving a speech on unemployment which they deemed too political. 'I don't know what they wanted me to talk about,' he told his *People* readers; 'the weather?' Some eighteen months before Tony Blair's 'Tough on Crime, Tough on the Causes of Crime' campaign, in the wake of the riots on neighbouring Tyneside he made headlines in the *Hartlepool Mail* by declaring, 'I am going to look very closely at my own party's policies to see if we have the right response to deal with the hard core of juvenile offenders . . . They should lose their liberty and be taught a lesson away from other criminal elements.'[23] He sent a well-publicised letter of protest to the *Wall Street Journal*, which had chosen the town to highlight Britain's social and economic problems, complaining, a little portentously, that the 'author failed to acknowledge Hartlepool's fortitude and the efforts of the townspeople to strive for improvement'. He was certainly assiduous in promoting his own candidacy. Alastair Campbell, on a visit to Hartlepool, found himself chatting to a young reporter from the local paper who had 'dropped round' to see Mandelson. 'The next thing I know I am quoted all over the *Hartlepool Mail* praising Peter to the skies and how the Tories have targeted him because he's so good.'

There was something in the 'targeting' claim. In an (ultimately needless) effort to keep Mandelson tied down to his local constituency and prevent him from playing too active a part in the national campaign, the Conservatives installed a full-time agent and started a monthly magazine. This would have made more sense had Mandelson, as some have subsequently claimed, been actively involved in the interstices of the national campaign. According to Anderson and Mann, 'In reality Mandelson played a key part in the campaign that even today he has never publicly acknowledged (though if Labour had won, perhaps he would have done).' Moreover, they assert, he was a member of the highly secret Campaign Advisory Team throughout 1990 and 1991.[24]

But the Mann-Anderson claim contrasts sharply both with Philip Gould's assertion that he tried to involve Mandelson in the CAT but that 'he had become a kind of non-person, banished, never to darken the campaign's doors again', and with the account of Tony Blair's biographer John Rentoul, who says that with Mandelson occupied in Hartlepool 'Brown and Blair were not on television as much during the campaign as they thought they ought to be'.[25] Gould, of course, is a close friend of Mandelson's, but his account is confirmed by a more hostile witness, Charles Clarke. Mandelson certainly attended at least one meeting in a London hotel with Gould and Hewitt to discuss the election grid, and he spoke regularly to Gould on the telephone. But Clarke was clear that senior members of the Shadow Cabinet would not 'touch him with a bargepole'. Clarke also says that in '92 the party had no one as good to handle the media and that this 'was a key weakness, maybe even a decisive weakness', while adding that he did not believe that Mandelson could – for example – have reversed the *Sun*'s hostility to Kinnock had he been both Director of Communications and the candidate in Hartlepool. Kinnock himself is more cautious, pointing out that 'in terms of policy . . . and expertise' 1992 was anyway a much more professional campaign: 'Maybe he could have made an additional contribution in terms of logistics and organisation. It is impossible to say, really. It would have been more of a help than a hindrance, let's put it like that.'

This is put rather more strongly by a contemporary observer with no particular link to Mandelson or vested interest of his own, but with uniquely privileged access to the campaign: the playwright David Hare. Hare, who was allowed to sit in on the key election planning meetings and interview all the central players as part of his preparations for writing *Absence of War*, wrote that 'In all the conversations I had had, both with politicians and with party workers, Mandelson had been spoken of as the missing element in the 1992 election effort. At some point, almost everyone I interviewed paused to regret his absence from this particular campaign and to attribute to him a strategic acumen which might just have made that vital difference.'[26]

That may have been too extravagant a claim, not least in the light of the substantial 7 per cent margin by which the Tories won. But whatever his absence cost Labour, Mandelson showed little evidence of *schadenfreude* when the defeat finally came. As the results began to pour in on election night, 9 April, he rang Gould from Hartlepool and told him that he did not deserve the defeat, that the campaign was better than 1987. Gould records this in his book, remarking that Mandelson was being kind. What he does not say is that the new MP for Hartlepool was in tears.

# CHAPTER FOURTEEN

## *The Wilderness Years*

After only two or three hours' sleep on the morning of 10 April 1992 James Purnell blundered blearily down to Tony Blair's kitchen at Trimdon to find some coffee. Assuming he was the first in the household to wake, he turned the television on and was first startled, and then distinctly impressed, to see, staring out from a studio in Newcastle, the man he had taken three weeks leave from his job in broadcasting to work for during the campaign. In the grey dawn of Labour's election defeat Blair had lost no time in explaining the modernising analysis of its meaning; that it had happened not because the party had changed too much, but because it had changed too little.

The weekend after an election defeat is a period of maximum instability in any party; and given that Kinnock had now lost twice, Blair knew that this weekend could be crucial to the future of the party. He did not need the polling experts to tell him a fact that in countless conversations over the next two years he would impress on anyone who would listen: that Labour, for all its gains in all parts of the country, had still secured a lower percentage share of the national vote – 34.5 per cent – than its 37.8 per cent in the epoch-changing defeat of James Callaghan by Margaret Thatcher in 1979. All sorts of explanations and solutions would be advanced by Labour apologists over the next forty-eight hours: that the party had fatally abandoned its socialist principles and needed to recover them, that it should espouse Proportional Representation as a means of mobilising the 'anti-Thatcher majority' in the country; that it was harder for people to vote Labour when they feared recession because they regarded redistribution as a luxury; and that given the gap was closing all that was needed was 'one more heave' next time. All these Blair now rejected, believing quite the opposite – that on the unions, on the party's constitution, and above all on tax, Labour needed to change much, much more if it was to appeal to the middle ground – an essential requirement for future victory.

He was not, of course, alone in this. He had discussed these questions endlessly with the newly elected Mandelson and with Gordon Brown, still identifiably the senior partner in the trio. That weekend, in a series of meetings, both bilateral and 'plenary', the three men, along with Gordon Brown's close ally Nick Brown, discussed the future. The first task, urged strongly by Gordon Brown, was to pump out the message that modernisation of party policy, and not recourse to a change in the electoral system, was the answer for Labour. The second issue, of course, as the four modernisers talked endlessly at Blair's house at Trimdon, at Brown's in Newcastle, and at a room in the County Hall, Durham, was who should succeed Neil Kinnock. There was no question of Blair himself standing. True, he would shortly be the subject of a lengthy profile by Barbara Amiel in the *Sunday Times* magazine, which appeared the day after the result of the leadership contest and opened: 'Yesterday Labour elected a new leader. Some feel the party should have skipped a generation and gone for Tony Blair.'[1] But Blair did not yet have the purchase on the party that he had on Ms Amiel. A *Sunday Times* poll of 138 Labour MPs showed that Blair did not even figure in the PLP's calculations. The results are worth rehearsing in full, with percentages attached: John Smith 64, Gordon Brown 16, Bryan Gould 7, John Prescott 4, Margaret Beckett 2, Tony Benn 2, Roy Hattersley 2, Ken Livingstone 2, Dennis Skinner 2.

Gordon Brown was another matter. Brown had indeed been seen as a possible successor by Kinnock – and as a rival by Smith – especially after he had stood in for Smith with spectacular success after the Shadow Chancellor's first heart attack in October 1988. Another colleague who thought of him as Kinnock's potential successor was his close friend Tony Blair. In March 1992 Blair had a highly significant conversation over lunch with a friend, who left with the clear impression that he expected Labour to lose, that

Brown would stand for the leadership, that Blair would act as his deputy and that Mandelson – naturally – would run the media campaign for both of them.[2]

Before the weekend had even begun, moreover, Mandelson had already deployed his famous black arts with the aim of keeping just such a possibility open. By chance Derek Draper, the young Labour activist who had been offered, but not yet installed in, a job as Mandelson's assistant, had given his new boss a highly exploitable piece of intelligence. Before the election Draper had attended a meeting of the right-wing Labour First group, convened by John Spellar (now the MP for Warley West and later a Defence minister). Draper had been struck by the group's decision to invite John Smith as the guest of honour to its annual meeting, apparently on the assumption that he would be the next leader. The incident may not have been quite as sinister as it sounded: Spellar – who admittedly would very much have liked Smith to replace Kinnock but found him absolutely resistant to any thought of a coup – had merely suggested that he was the obvious star speaker to invite to a meeting which would probably follow the general election. By that time, after all, he would almost certainly be Chancellor of the Exchequer or Leader of the Opposition. Nevertheless there was enough to make a story suggesting that right-wing elements had been plotting before the election to make John Smith leader. Which Mandelson now did, leaking the information to the *Sunday Times*; he was careful enough not to do it himself, but used his friend and former deputy Colin Byrne as the messenger. The purpose, by casting doubts on the loyalty of Smith supporters *before* the general election, was to raise a later question mark about his suitability as leader. It was, as Mandelson would later admit privately, to 'slow down' the Smith bandwagon, to allow time at least to consider the alternative possibility that Brown might replace Kinnock. Smith, of course, was furious and lost no time in upbraiding Spellar – although he knew nothing of the leak. But Smith need not have worried. The Mandelson-inspired story about pro-Smith plots was soon eclipsed by the polls and a series of Sunday newspaper stories confidently predicting that Smith would become leader. And Brown himself was dismissive of the idea that he might challenge Smith – so much so that Mandelson did not even, by his own account, try to persuade him otherwise.

According to one version of history, this was a missed opportunity. Philip Gould was told firmly by a 'close aide of Blair's' that Blair felt that Brown could have beaten Smith in 1992, and should have stood, with him as his deputy: 'Tony's view was that the party wanted to be led, it didn't just want to keep sleepwalking and if you sold it an out and out modernising message it would take it.'[3] According to another close Blair associate, 'Tony thought that Brown would have won. You could have presented the argument: "Smith's a nice guy but part of the old order"; you could have won the New Labour argument two years earlier [than in 1994].'[4] In the agonies over the leadership which followed John Smith's death two years later all this would assume a fresh importance, even though the idea of Brown running had not lasted long: deep within the inner Blair circle it was said in defence of Blair's steely decision not to yield the leadership to Brown in 1994 that Blair felt that Brown had had his chance in 1992 and had baulked at it. In the words of yet another ally, Blair felt that Brown had 'bottled out' of challenging Smith for the leadership in 1992. Although a Brown challenge would have looked unpromising at the start of a leadership campaign, it could have been very different at the end. Smith's Shadow Budget would have been squarely blamed for the defeat, and with Brown, backed by Blair, leading the charge against him, he might have been stopped in his tracks.

So the theory went. However, it is hard not to sympathise with Brown over his decision not to stand in 1992. A challenge by Brown would have meant a bloody contest – far bloodier than the one in 1994. For all their differences about the direction of the party, there was a close bond between Smith and Brown, and they had many close friends, such as Donald Dewar, in common; Scot would have been divided against Scot, right-winger against right-winger. The reasons for thinking that a modernising candidate might fail were vastly stronger than they were in 1994, as the *Sunday Times* poll figures indicated. Indeed, the process of further change might even have been arrested, rather than advanced, if Brown had been defeated. Moreover, by not entering the contest, Brown was honourably fulfilling an undertaking he had made, under some pressure, less than a year earlier – not to stand against Smith.

Around August of 1991 there had been signs of increasing irritation among close allies of John Smith (including Jack Cunningham and Mo Mowlam in the PLP, and John Edmonds, leader of Smith's – and, for that matter, Mandelson's – union) at suggestions that Gordon Brown was the 'crown prince' who would succeed Kinnock. Some of this, inevitably, surfaced in the press: a memorable cartoon in the *Daily Express* depicted Blair and Mandelson as tailor's assistants measuring up Brown for the leadership. One Friday night in the early autumn of 1991 Edmonds telephoned Mandelson at his home in Hartlepool, saying a little menacingly, that there was 'unhappiness' at the idea that Brown might be plotting to wrest the leadership from Smith in the event of an election defeat, and suggesting that it would be a mistake for Mandelson to enter parliament with the suspicion that he might be involved in such a plot; it would better for him to 'keep his nose clean' with regard to the leadership. Brown was sufficiently rattled to authorise Mandelson to let it be known through the press – the *Independent on Sunday* – that he would not compete against Smith for the Labour leadership. The pressure and the counter-briefing eased perceptibly.

The idea of a leadership challenge was discarded: Brown refused to countenance it, and it was becoming clear that the Smith bandwagon was well-nigh unstoppable. The discussion therefore turned to the deputy leadership. Much of this debate has been documented elsewhere. John Smith wanted Margaret Beckett to run on the grounds that being a woman and on the left of the party she would create a more balanced leadership ticket. She, however, hesitated to put herself forward, and Smith indicated that if she ultimately refused to stand he would prefer Blair to Brown – presumably because of the 'two-Scot' problem, and perhaps because he appeared the less dominant of the two.[5] Several people advised Blair not to run: Neil Kinnock wanted Bryan Gould; Roy Hattersley thought that Blair would and should be the next leader of the party and that being deputy was a graveyard job; and Nick Brown, an even closer ally of Gordon Brown's than he was of Tony Blair's, thought that he could not win. But in any case, as Blair was hesitating, Margaret Beckett made up her mind to run.

Most accounts assume that Brown's candidacy was a non-starter. But the possibility of Brown, Scot though he was, standing for the deputy leadership had been quite seriously considered, at least by

Mandelson. Indeed, at one point he propounded the case for Brown as deputy leader. It was, characteristically, written out in his clear, fluent handwriting, on a single side of A4 paper, under neat headings:

1. The candidate of the younger generation; 2. Tough, able and eloquent; 3. Knows the party inside out; 4. A unique blend of party manager, strategist and communicator; and 5. Smith and Brown together offer a combination of experienced authority and a lively imagination to carry Labour forward. Labour cannot take risks. They are the party's best brains, leading a team of front bench talent who will be in step with the party and in tune with the country.

According to Mandelson, he was confided in by both the Browns and by Blair throughout this period, but 'there was a presumption, I think, that I would put Gordon first . . . and that I saw Gordon as the stronger of the two.' Certainly up until the 1992 election Brown was more dominant. It was only in the aftermath that, as Robert Harris would put it, 'the iron entered [Blair's] soul'.[6]

But that weekend, when Mandelson finally came round to the idea that Blair, if Brown could not do it, might promote the modernisers' cause by standing for the deputy leadership, neither of the Browns appeared to agree. In the months and years ahead some in Blair's inner circle came to believe that Gordon Brown, while relying on the argument that Blair might be defeated, had actually been fearful that a Blair deputy leadership victory would immediately place him ahead of Brown as a potential future leader.

That week Robin Cook phoned Mandelson at home – itself a rare event – and asked him for advice on the media handling of John Smith's campaign. Mandelson met him for a lunch of sausage, beans and chips in the unglamorous surroundings of the upstairs dining room of the Red Lion pub in Whitehall. With the modernisers out of the race, Mandelson was glad to help. Smith was a 'grown-up' former cabinet minister, from the right, and distinctively pro-European. Typically, he again prepared a note for the meeting in which he listed Smith's 'image attributes' as: 'Cabinet experience, authority, knowledge, electoral appeal, stabilising, unifying, most feared by Tories'; and his 'image problems' as: 'Right man for last election, not next, no ideas, undynamic, uncomfortable in role'. Smith had made a faltering start in the campaign against Bryan Gould, who had now announced his determination to challenge Smith from the left. Indeed, this was the main reason why Cook had called Mandelson in. Mandelson suggested that, among other things, the campaign needed to demonstrate that Smith had sufficient energy: a national tour would 'neutralise Neil Kinnock's office' – which was still showing worrying hankerings after Gould – and identify 'the key contrasts with Gould', including the two candidates' sharply differing views on Europe.

Mandelson also proposed that Brown and Blair should be actively involved in the campaign; they went on to write large parts of Smith's 8,000-word manifesto. Cook was understandably irritated to read in the Sunday papers – news relayed, of course, by Mandelson – that Brown and Blair had 'ridden to the rescue' of the Smith campaign. But suggestions that Mandelson himself did not directly help in the Smith campaign are wide of the mark. He prepared a detailed paper for Cook's briefing to Sunday newspaper correspondents the following weekend, admitting frankly that the campaign had got off to a confused start and promising that the campaign would begin in earnest after Easter; he left the modernisers some room by insisting that Smith envisaged the leadership debate as 'kicking off, not concluding' the post-mortem into the party's defeat, and looking forward to a further reduction in the trade union block vote. He also collated some unashamedly knocking copy for use against Gould. Bryan Gould was indeed a 'man of ideas', journalists were told; 'he's an idea a day man.' Not once had Gould ever objected to the pre-election tax plans of Smith's which he now criticised; indeed, his supporters had been among the most vociferous agitators for the spending policies which the tax plans had been obliged to fund. He had also frightened potential investors in water and electricity before the election by saying that dividends would not be paid on shares. Gould's policies – in a phrase emanating from Gordon Brown – were a mix of 'old-style anti-European Peter Shore economics and Michael Meacher sociology'.

Mandelson dutifully used his column in the *People* – from which he would finally be sacked in November 1992 by the new editor, Bridget Rowe – to support Smith as the candidate with 'the strength of character to unite the party around its policies and put them across to the voters'. He praised Beckett, with more tact than sincerity, as 'pleasant, diligent and open to reason',[7] conveniently omitting any mention of her ferocious attack on Neil Kinnock for betraying the hard left in 1981 – though the following week, in the midst of a messy row over how the unions would wield their block votes in the contest, he went so far as to question whether the job of deputy leader 'justifies the acrimony and expense'. He pointed out that the modern post had only been invented as a means of keeping his own grandfather, Herbert Morrison, on the National Executive. Staying, along with the Blairs, at Derry Irvine's house in Argyllshire at Easter, Mandelson was teased by his host for constantly making telephone calls to the Smith campaign team. 'What's it got to do with you?' Irvine asked. 'Get off the phone, Mandelson.' Blair rose to his defence, saying, 'Now, Derry, just let Peter get on with what he's got to do.' The Smith campaign, efficiently organised by Cook, and the Beckett campaign, run by Cook's old adversary Gordon Brown, were both highly successful after the slow start. Smith annihilated Gould by winning 91 per cent of the electoral college, while Beckett secured 57 per cent and Prescott, the runner-up, 28 per cent. But the modernisers got less out of it than they had hoped, as subsequent events would prove. It was also the last time for almost two years that Mandelson would play anything approaching a central role in the party.

By now Derek Draper was working full time for Mandelson. One of Mandelson's first acts after his election at Hartlepool was to hire him as a new assistant. Over the next four years, from about a month after the election, Draper would get to know Mandelson as well as anyone ever has. By his own account a 'mad Labour boy' at Manchester University, Draper already had a history as something of a young Turk on the party's right wing when he first met Mandelson at a day school for Labour activists in Gateshead. He had been brought to London by Robin Cook to help on Roy Hattersley's deputy leadership campaign against John Prescott in 1988; he had become secretary of the Young Fabians, and was soon bored with his job as Nick Brown's assistant doing constituency casework in Newcastle, a city he strongly disliked. At the time 'I was thinking, "What am I going to do about this? This is a sort of pathetic job. I was a great star at Manchester University, now I'm wasting my time in Newcastle."' At Gateshead

I was introduced to [Mandelson] and was my normal chirpy self which he quite liked, having had to come to Gateshead and Newcastle and . . . there was this bright bloke and I was exactly like I am now . . . I believed in the Labour Party but thought they were shit. And then I read these stories about this bloke who had tried to turn it around, and improve it and make it good. At university I'd been entertainments officer as well as the Labour fixer so I had this dual thing where I was looking for glamour as well, and he seemed to combine this; it was quite natural to gravitate towards him. When you met him you realised he was sort of firm and weird.[8]

Mandelson had also been impressed by what he had heard about Draper. When Sally Morgan, now Tony Blair's political secretary, warned Mandelson that Draper was 'really tough, right wing and ruthless', she thought she might be putting him off. She clearly did not know Mandelson very well.

Draper had volunteered to organise some canvassing for Mandelson in Hartlepool before the general election, persuading five Newcastle University students 'to go over in a minibus to stand in a shopping centre for the day. He was deliriously happy about this. It was the most interesting thing that had happened to him and he made kedgeree for us in his kitchen.' The following incident shows Mandelson playing a part wholly in character. When Draper said something in his broad Lancashire accent Mandelson turned to him and said:

'Where exactly are you from?' And I said, 'I'm from Chorley.' And of course I was very nervous about it because I thought I was going to make an idiot of myself; he wouldn't then deliver me from my horrible life in Newcastle. And I said: 'Well, it's halfway between Preston and Bolton.' And Peter turned to me and turned to the whole table, and said: 'Oh, imagine coming from somewhere whose only claim to fame is that it's halfway between Preston and Bolton.' Now, in all sorts of ways that was absolutely outrageous ... I was a twenty-three-year-old lad who'd delivered for him and brought all these people round and he was basically humiliating me in front of them. But of course everyone laughed and I didn't care – so long as you understand that about him. The more cutting and sarcastic he is, with a little glint in his eye, the more friendly he is. And of course he uses precisely that tone, and precisely that level of horribleness with the Prime Minister now. You know: 'Oh, Tony, do you really think you should have said that? What did you look like?' It's a very gayish thing, but it can be massively misinterpreted. It's all very well to think ill of him and you can mount a legitimate prosecution of Peter Mandelson over certain things, but people just get it wrong.

On another occasion, after the election, Draper recalled, they were walking down a Commons corridor and passed Martin Redmond, the MP for Don Valley, 'and you could see him think, "Oh, Peter Mandelson." He'd heard of him, read about him, realised he was so powerful and you could see him thinking, "What do I do?" Redmond merely said, as they passed, "Hello." '

And Peter said, 'Hello.' And he took two steps and then turned to me and said, 'Who on earth was that?' Loud enough for this person to hear. Now, the fact is that Martin Redmond could legitimately hate Peter Mandelson for the rest of his life. But he didn't mean anything and once Martin Redmond got to know Peter Mandelson he would know that he didn't really mean it. And if I'd said, 'Well, you know who it is,' he'd have said, 'Yes, it's Martin Redmond' ... just mischievous.

Not everyone – even among those who became his friends – was as relaxed about the Mandelson style of mockery. Not long after Tim Allan started working full time for Blair, Mandelson paid a visit. Seeing Allan as he emerged into Blair's busy outer office, he said: 'Ah yes, so it's you. You're the one who's got a down on our brilliant leader. You're the one who's criticising him.' Allan was petrified; his mouth opened in shock. He had indeed made a not wholly complimentary remark about John Smith's leadership to Blair, who had clearly repeated it to Mandelson. So menacing was Mandelson's harangue that Blair had to step in and, laughing, tell him to stop it. 'He does like people to be frightened of him,' admitted one witness to this encounter. This was certainly true. Would he not rather proudly tell Oliver James some five years later, admittedly of the Tories, 'that the reason people like to discredit me is that they fear me'?[9]

Soon Allan, who would subsequently become one of his closest friends, also saw at first hand Mandelson's darker media skills at work – and learnt valuable lessons for the future. In January 1993 opinion polls showed Labour almost fifteen points ahead of the Conservatives. Meanwhile, however, the Shadow Cabinet were being presented with yet more research showing that most floating voters still regarded Labour as a party of the past, and that they had little idea of what it stood for. The research was a closely guarded secret; the shadow ministers who were given it – including Brown and Blair – were told that it must not be leaked. The modernisers were nevertheless determined to make it public, to underline their argument that the party had to undergo more far-reaching change than Smith appeared to want. Blair, in particular, was frustrated by his experience on the committee, chaired by Margaret Beckett, drawing up plans for One Member One Vote democracy in the party. No one seemed clear about what direction Smith wanted the party to take. Release of the research might give the arguments for change fresh momentum. But Mandelson bided his time, waiting until a specially convened meeting of shadow cabinet researchers was given the same findings, with the same exhortation to keep them secret. The following morning Mandelson, who, of course, had had a copy for several days thanks to Blair and Brown, immediately leaked the results to Patrick Wintour of the *Guardian*. It was a classic Mandelson operation, to which certainly Blair – and probably Brown – would have been a party. All suspicion would naturally fall on the researchers rather than on the Shadow Cabinet itself; sure enough, Nick Pecorelli, working for Margaret Beckett at the time, convenor of the researchers' group, launched an immediate – and inevitably abortive – leak enquiry.

Then, in a final touch, courting danger like an arsonist revisiting the scene of his crime, Mandelson chose to ram home the message in a lengthy letter to the *Guardian* after the story was published.[10] Claiming – of course – that 'like any other party member, I have only the *Guardian* reports [on the findings] to go on', he urged the party to 'change and widen its appeal even further in order to win . . . to identify with changing attitudes among voters, to think about and openly discuss new policy ideas and speak in a language which grabs rather than grates'. In a modernising flourish he concluded: 'Labour must develop popular policies which tackle the vested interests of power and privilege which hold Britain's economy and people back. By reasserting the importance of a strong community and supporting individual endeavour, Labour can develop a convincing message which offers something new and modern to all voters.'

This was cheek on a grand scale. But it also illustrated the relative ideological isolation of the modernisers in this period. The annoyance caused by Brown and Blair's January 1993 trip to Bill Clinton's Washington rebounded directly on Mandelson. A week before their departure Prescott launched an attack on the modernisers, claiming that some in the party were 'obsessed with image' and that they 'would draw exactly the wrong conclusions from the Clinton victory'. Clare Short also voiced suspicions that the 'secret, infiltrating, so-called modernisers of the Labour Party have been creating myths about why Clinton won, in order to try and reshape the Labour Party in the way they want it to go'. (After the US Democrat convention in July 1992 Mandelson had commented, 'I don't advocate that British political conferences introduce balloons, bands, fake snow, dancing girls, flags and unbearable noise . . . but the Democrat convention has been fun.') While Brown and Blair were in the US, Smith called in Mandelson and robustly expressed his irritation. He warned the junior partner of the trio that he did not need to be told what lessons were to be learned from Labour's recent defeat, or from Clinton's victory. Instead it would be helpful if he, the leader, could be allowed to get on with the business of winning the next election. 'All this Clintonisation business, it's just upsetting everyone. Stop boat-rocking with all this talk of change and modernisation. It will just divide the party. If we remain united we'll win. Do just shut up.'

Many witnesses attest to Smith's dislike, or at least distrust, of Mandelson. Colin Byrne claimed that, for those deemed to be 'Kinnockites', entering Smith's office – except for the ever-welcoming and universally liked Anne Barrett, Smith's faithful secretary – was 'literally like entering hostile territory'. According to Mandelson himself, Smith felt threatened, and even a little upstaged, by Brown and Blair: 'He didn't want to go along their course and thought they were globetrotters. There was only one quality he valued which was unity and they threatened unity by going on about modernising.' But according to David Hill, the hostility between Mandelson and Smith arose first and foremost because Smith, who personally dealt much more easily with the media than his predecessor, had an 'innate detestation of trickiness with the press'. As Smith himself put it bluntly in 1993, 'I don't like the black art of public relations that's taken over politics. We're talking about the government of the country – not the entertainment industry.'[11] It is a reasonable bet he had Mandelson in mind. The fact that Mandelson had a better relationship with Smith's wife, accompanying her on a fact-finding trip to Russia, did little to help his cause. 'I see he is playing with Elizabeth again,' Smith remarked to a colleague.

During much of this period Mandelson's isolation was mirrored by the frustration of Brown and Blair. The modernisers were paying a heavy price for pressing the case for One Member One Vote democracy in the party. It was becoming increasingly clear to them that, while Smith was prepared to force OMOV through the party conference, it might be a Pyrrhic victory for the modernisers, and involve concessions of other kinds – on economic policy and trade union law, for example – to their union opponents. At a real cost to his own popularity Brown had courageously extracted Labour from the tax and spending commitments contained in John Smith's pre-election Shadow Budget. But at one point, shortly before the summer recess in 1993, Blair gloomily confided in a journalist that the modernising cause looked doomed because of the price that would be paid for an OMOV victory. Sure enough, when it came to September and the TUC Congress, Smith went further than Brown had done by pledging to use 'all the instruments of macro-economic management' to ensure 'sustained growth and rising employment'. Brown, for one, would surely have also mentioned reducing inflation.

The modernisers were doubly despondent because the victory on OMOV at the October 1993 party conference – and it was a signal victory – in the end had very little to do with them. There is a danger of some modernisers rewriting the history of this important change. The proposals before delegates were for OMOV selections of parliamentary candidates and a three-part electoral college for the leadership election, in which both the union and membership decision would be by individual ballot. Philip Gould dwells at some length on the frustrations of Brown and Blair – including Blair's belief that the proposals were too 'timid'. In fact, as his biographer John Rentoul points out, Blair underestimated the momentousness of the change; it brought him his victory in all three sections of the electoral college in 1994. Philip Gould mentions only in passing that Smith was 'forced to threaten to resign' to get it through; and the conference's outstanding *coup de théâtre*, John Prescott's speech supporting OMOV, he mentions not at all.[12] But Smith had taken a stupendous gamble, warning his principal opponent John Edmonds that, unlike most members of the Shadow Cabinet, he could as a QC make a good living outside politics if he needed to. Prescott was aghast when he learned from Smith about the resignation threat, pointing out that not even Gaitskell, in his fight with the left over unilateralism, had gone as far. But Smith was adamant. If he was defeated he would make one last attempt, demanding NEC backing for a further appeal to the conference. If he failed again, he would certainly go.[13] No other Labour leader has ever taken such a risk.

Prescott's electrifying speech, urging the conference to back a leader who had 'put his head on the block', was of fundamental importance. Even if, as many claim, it did not actually change the outcome because the union votes had (just) been delivered, it transformed what would have been a sullen, and perhaps even reversible, vote in favour of OMOV into a tumultuous endorsement both of the leadership and of change in the party. As Prescott himself put it, 'I had to turn it into something which was about emotion, that they would feel safe about going back to their constituencies.'

But it also meant that the position of Prescott, as conference hero, was enhanced at the expense of Brown, Blair and, by extension,

Mandelson. For Mandelson especially, a new backbencher, not a shadow minister like Blair or Brown, and lacking even the authority he had once had as Director of Communications, the sense of alienation was considerable. Michael Portillo recalled meeting Mandelson at a party in early 1994: 'he poured his heart out to me as though we were soulmates,' he claimed. 'He had no access to the inner citadel, his talents and ideas were derided.'[14] Mandelson later dismissed this as a gross exaggeration. Nevertheless, according to Tom Sawyer, his own relationship with Mandelson remained good precisely because he made the effort to have a 'cup of tea and a chat' with him occasionally at a time when most people – including almost all his old adversaries on the Shadow Cabinet – 'wrote him off and distanced themselves'.

Another old colleague, Charles Clarke, engineered a rapprochement with Mandelson at this time because of fears that the modernisers were losing ground. From his junior position in the party Mandelson continued to push the modernisers' line in public. He used a letter to the *Guardian*, ostensibly defending the party against an attack by Norman Fowler, to comment that a 'new tactic is to contrast John Smith's style of leadership with the commitment to change and modernisation under Mr Kinnock. This tactic is more insidious but there is no reason why it should be any more successful.'[15] Perceptively Jeff Rooker replied three days later, 'It was difficult to detect to whom Peter Mandelson was sending his new year warning. Was it to shadow ministers? Certainly it was not to the Tories.' A month later Mandelson was at it again, defending Brown and claiming that those who wanted a 'multi-million increase in borrowing and taxes . . . are not doing the party any service'. Rooker had spotted the modernisers' doubts about Smith's leadership. Three years later Mandelson declared:

John Smith was a great believer in party unity, almost at any cost, even if it meant not facing up to one or two awkward choices and ticklish issues that we needed to address, which of course Tony Blair has done subsequently. People in the party, and young people in particular, felt that there was a sort of 'one last heave' . . . mentality creeping into the party and that however well we seemed to be doing in the middle of the parliament, that would not serve us successfully and decisively when the next election came along.[16]

This infuriated Roy Hattersley, who took it to mean that Smith would not have won the forthcoming election had he lived, and thought it both wrong and insulting to the memory of a dead man. But there is every reason to suppose it reflected the gloomy views of Brown and Blair at the time – and very few others. 'Journalists used to write of the modernisers as Brown, Blair, Mandelson *et al.*,' said Derek Draper, 'but in fact there was no *et al.*' Instead, the three of them enjoyed an unusual comradeship. Alex Stevenson, working cheek by jowl with Mandelson at the time, remembers the incessant calls from Blair and Brown – they spoke several times a day – but claims that Brown's calls were if anything more frequent. The three of them could hardly have been closer: Brown would help Blair; Blair, Brown. And Mandelson helped them both. When Draper complained he didn't have enough to do Mandelson suggested he help Brown and Blair with their NEC election campaigns; Draper chose Brown 'because I thought what he was doing in the economy was incredibly brave in the context of the Labour Party', and 'I'm more like Gordon. I'm about fixing things, shouting at people . . . Tony used to be in the Fettes play and so that's his political style.' The tensions of the weekend after the '92 election showed no scars in this period. When there was a late vote Blair, Brown and Mandelson would occasionally stay up in one or other of their offices drinking whisky, bitching amiably about some of their colleagues, and enjoying a 'a really jokey, rugby room, bar atmosphere'.[17] Normally, however, Blair, at least, would return home to bed as early as he could.

Mandelson, who had frequently been derided, particularly by Tories, as 'Gordon Brown's bag carrier', took a number of steps to help the Shadow Chancellor, currently facing a good deal of unfair and surreptitious criticism for extracting Labour from the tax and spending commitments embodied in John Smith's pre-election Shadow Budget. Mandelson engaged the services of his old friend Roger Liddle – still, remarkably, a Liberal Democrat but strongly committed to closer links with Labour – to help advise Brown. Liddle argued that the criticisms of Brown's economic policy –

including his determined opposition to devaluation in the previous summer of 1992 – were misplaced and stemmed from a failure to appreciate that there were no longer any 'quick fixes' in macroeconomic policy. He urged Brown to pursue an unexceptional list of goals: reduction of the Public Sector Borrowing Requirement, a 'comprehensive solution' to unemployment, greater competitiveness and labour market flexibility in Europe, and an attack on the short termism of the City. 'We all want and need Gordon to succeed,' Liddle concluded in the first of several lengthy notes.

Mandelson now successfully persuaded Sue Nye, who had worked for Neil Kinnock and was one of his closest friends, to run Brown's office and bring some order to it. He was also closely involved in Brown's decision to recruit the fiercely clever economist Ed Balls from the *Financial Times*. And, in what would turn out to be the most momentous step of all, he made the first move in recruiting Charlie Whelan as a bright, belligerent and streetwise press officer for Brown. Whelan, an ex-communist, boarding school educated but with a common touch, had worked for the AEEU, had been close to the far-sighted and courageous left-wing official Jimmy Airlie, and had proved himself a stalwart in the fight for OMOV at the 1993 conference. Mandelson arranged to meet him in the Pugin Room in the Commons for a drink, and was uncharacteristically late. Whelan made his irritation known. But Mandelson had no reason for now to regret the approach, as he would come to do, and profoundly, within a year. According to Whelan, when he was asked by Mandelson whether he would be interested in leaving the union for the Labour Party he said that he would only do so if it involved working for either Blair or Brown. Mandelson proposed Brown. The immediate effect was a dramatic improvement in Brown's press relations. Whelan persuaded Brown to slow down the frenzied schedule of speeches, press releases and weekend television interviews, and to be more selective in his appearances.

A more pressing question worrying Draper at the time was Mandelson's own future. He told the young Alex Stevenson that 'the concern . . . was that he was spending too much time helping Blair and Brown, particularly Brown, to do anything for himself, the career thing'. A similar fear was voiced by Mandelson himself, with a frankness which could not fail to irritate some fellow members of the '92 intake: 'most people come into the Commons to make a name for themselves,' he said. 'I had a name already and was swapping it for the relative obscurity of the backbenches.'[18] Nevertheless his friends tended to paint a rather grimmer picture of Mandelson the backbencher than was merited. According to Philip Gould (depending on a story subsequently aired by Derek Draper), 'Peter spent the two years of John's leadership kicking his heels in London and Hartlepool. On one occasion he recalls saving a visit to the supermarket so that he would have something to do on a Sunday.' This makes the 'wilderness years', as Draper would subsequently describe them, sound more pathetic than they were. Andy McSmith notes that in this period 'Mandelson was less personally unpopular than he had been before or has been since', and that, unsurprisingly, he adapted more quickly to the Commons than the two other 'celebrities' of the 1992 intake, the actress Glenda Jackson and the Olympic athlete Seb Coe.[19] Whatever Mandelson said to Gould, he was intelligent enough to know that he now needed to make his way as a backbencher and constituency MP.

Which he did with some energy, if at times idiosyncratically. He spent more time in Hartlepool than any other time in his career. Describing in the *House Magazine* his relief at returning to Hartlepool each weekend, he wrote: 'In London I need ear plugs to ward off the low din of the city – at Hartlepool I sleep like a log ready for any amount of surgery work the next day.'[20] He was – and has continued to be – dutiful about constituency surgeries; a rather imposing figure, he would sit straightbacked behind his desk, fountain pen in hand in the little office in the civic hall. Indeed, it was for Hartlepool's sake that he staged the only serious parliamentary revolt of his career. In his maiden speech he had promised to support its passionate desire to be a unitary authority, as it had been before local government reorganisation in 1974 had grafted the town, against its will, into the new county of Cleveland. The 1992 manifesto had been in favour of single-tier authorities, but a hugely effective lobby by Labour-run county councils, including Cleveland, fought to protect themselves from abolition by the Conservative government. Despite a whips' instruction to vote for Cleveland's preservation, the course being urged by two of the other four Cleveland MPs, Mo Mowlam and Frank Cook, Mandelson and Stuart Bell both abstained. This would not have been exceptional if Mandelson had not himself been a whip by this time, appointed by the new leader Tony Blair. He would certainly have run into serious trouble with his own Labour-controlled council had he toed the government line. Indeed, he faced considerable local criticism for merely abstaining rather than voting in the 'No' lobby. Although there were grumblings that he had got away with his defiance because of Blair's patronage, there is a long tradition of licence on narrowly local issues.

The Cleveland issue had also exposed Mandelson's tendency to go, theatrically, over the top. Mo Mowlam, using a thirty-minute Commons adjournment debate in June 1993 to press the case for Cleveland, found herself under attack from supposedly friendly fire. Mandelson interrupted her ten times in the space of a couple of minutes. Hansard conveys the flavour of the exchanges, described caustically by Roy Hattersley as 'unique in modern parliamentary history'. In fact, Mandelson regarded Mowlam as having ignored an understanding that the Teeside MPs would not expose their divisions in public.

MANDELSON: Will my Hon. Friend give way?

MOWLAM: They would be –

MANDELSON: Will my Hon. Friend give way?

MOWLAM: They would be accountable to the people –

MANDELSON: Will my Hon. Friend give way?

MOWLAM: They will be unaccountable to the people of Cleveland.

MANDELSON: Will my Hon. Friend give way?

MOWLAM: It is very clear I am not giving way.

MANDELSON: On a point of order, Mr Deputy Speaker.

DEPUTY SPEAKER: There is no point of order. Ms Mowlam.

MANDELSON: You do not know what the point of order is, Mr Deputy Speaker.

DEPUTY SPEAKER. Order. Ms Mowlam.

Nor would this be the only occasion on which he flouted parliamentary convention. He caused a fuss when he was rebuked by the

Speaker Betty Boothroyd in July 1994 for announcing, on the basis of a conversation that he had had – along with other north-eastern dignitaries – with the Queen aboard HMS *Britannia*, that Her Majesty would be quite content for the royal yacht to be laid up in Hartlepool docks. Reminded by Ms Boothroyd that he 'should not be divulging conversations' with the Queen, he replied 'in tones of withering command', as Matthew Parris put it, that 'Queen Peter the First' had the 'gracious permission of Her Majesty's private secretary' to disclose the conversation.[21] But the infuriated Speaker had the last word: 'It's actually the chair of the House,' she declared, 'not Her Majesty's private secretary who rules here.'

Yet on both occasions his showmanship made favourable head-lines, particularly where they mattered most to him at the time, settling in as a new MP, in Hartlepool. All his old flair for publicity was brought to bear when he 'played a key part in stoking up the row' over the government's planned D-Day celebrations by siding with the British Legion and veterans' organisations against the 'trivialisation' of the planned D-Day commemoration.[22] Mandelson deftly encouraged journalists to treat a guarded comment by Dame Vera Lynn, who said that she would support 'whatever the boys wanted', as a threat to boycott the jamboree. The *Daily Telegraph* noted with baffled and cautious approval that Mandelson seemed to have 'appointed himself spokesman for the old comrades'.[23]

But much of his backbench activity was of the more earnest kind. From early on he was in the forefront of the pro-European tendency among Labour MPs in the debates over the Maastricht Bill: he pressed Smith to offer John Major help in ratifying the bill in return for Major's acceptance of the Social Chapter – in effect conditionally subordinating the goal of defeating the government to that of demonstrating its pro-European credentials. Indeed, he seems to have been more sure of himself on this at the time than Blair. He risked attack from more mainstream Labour colleagues by being openly enthusiastic, in alliance with Gordon Brown, about the contentious Article 3a of the Maastricht Treaty, requiring member states to have 'stable prices, sound public finances, monetary conditions and a sustainable balance of payments'.[24] 'Why should we be in favour of unsound public finances and an unsustainable balance of payments?' he asked.[25] Because of the fissure in the Conservative Party little attention was paid by the press to the sometimes nightly slanging matches on the Labour benches. But Mandelson was repeatedly involved in heckling, and being heckled by, Labour's leading Eurosceptics – appropriately for an MP who would join Edwina Currie and Sir Edward Heath as a vice-chairman of the European Movement. He submitted a long paper – much of it drafted by Roger Liddle – to the party's Policy Commission on Foreign Affairs, which was broadly pro-EMU and proposed closer EU defence co-ordination. There was an added edge to the conflict. Some of his opponents on the Eurosceptic left over the Maastricht Bill, like Roger Berry and Peter Hain, were also his rivals for – albeit limited – backbench influence over economic policy. Securing his re-election in 1994 as secretary of the backbench Treasury Committee, he beat off an attempted coup by the PLP left to take over the committee and replace him with the neo-Keynsian Roger Berry – winning a 39–30 victory which Berry attributed to 'much of the front bench' turning out to support him. This minor triumph was widely seen as a victory for Gordon Brown over Robin Cook's attempts to promote an alternative, more reflationary economic policy.

Smith gave him one by-election to run, but Newbury, in May 1993, was a hopeless cause. In 1992 Labour had had only 6 per cent of the vote and not even Mandelson's supposedly magical powers could increase that. His principal contributions were to construct a plausible 'story' about the defeat – that 'Labour had shaken the tree but the fruit had fallen into the hands of the Liberal Democrats' and to insist (despite some pressure from members of the Shadow Cabinet) on treating Labour's Liberal Democrat opponents in a significantly more measured way than he would in Littleborough and Saddleworth a year later: he recognised that some tactical voting would at least help to guarantee a Tory defeat. This was indeed an election in which many Labour supporters – and even members – defected to the Tories' main challenger, the Liberal Democrats' David Rendel. The Labour candidate Steve Bilcliffe lost his deposit with just 1,151 votes and a nugatory 2 per cent of the vote – compared with Rendel's 65 per cent. On one level it was a humiliation on a scale which can hardly have been in Mandelson's script; on another it made the beginnings of a case for anti-Tory cooperation.

Mandelson dominated the daily press conferences, goading and teasing the reporters each morning and earning the sobriquet 'Mandeldrone', even from his friend Alastair Campbell, now political editor of *Today*. Otherwise he took the three weeks of Newbury just a little less seriously than he would have done a winnable by-election. Indeed, for the second fortnight he stayed in a cottage owned by 'Pip' Poole, a friend of Dennis Stevenson, on the Astors' grand estate. He loved it; he went for country walks each weekend and slept well.

It was an enjoyable campaign. Bilcliffe was known to the campaign team as 'Sergeant Bilko' – a testament to Mandelson's lifelong enthusiasm for nicknames. There were some rather juvenile jokes at the other candidates' expense. David Rendel, an old Etonian and now the Liberal Democrats' Social Security spokesman, had, on one occasion, been introduced by his agent as 'Dave' in one of the less well-heeled wards of the constituency, 'and Peter absolutely leapt on this and I remember when Rendel was doing a walkabout in a playground and I don't think we hijacked it but we were nearby – and Peter ran around saying, "Dave, hi, Dave, how are you?" as if this was someone he really liked.' Rendel retaliated by calling him 'Pete'. 'That was the sort of thing that Peter absolutely loved.'[26] Tim Allan, who also came down to help, was in the passenger seat of Mandelson's car when, seeing the Natural Law Party vehicle, complete with loudspeaker, Mandelson leant across him, wound down the nearside window and kept yelling through it, 'Levitate the car, levitate the car!'

How would Mandelson's career have developed had Smith not had his fatal heart attack in May 1994? Much less spectacularly for one thing. Smith's mistrust of him would have ensured that. Yet would this perhaps have been better for him? He was, after all, albeit in his own fashion, developing the kind of conventional parliamentary career enjoyed by the large majority of MPs. For all Smith's doubts, he would surely in time have had a junior front bench post. He would certainly have had the valuable support of Brown and Blair. If he had then risen quite fast through a series of ministerial or shadow ministerial portfolios (as there is plenty of reason to suppose he would have done) he would, by the time he had access to real power, have done much more to establish an identity as a politician in his own right. He would not have enjoyed the exhilaration and influence of his role at the leader's right hand – which Tony Blair would soon routinely describe as 'being Peter'. But he would not have been exposed to its dangers and frustrations either.

# CHAPTER FIFTEEN

## *I've Made an Enemy for Life*

The first news of John Smith's second heart attack reached Peter Mandelson via Tony Blair at 9.10 a.m. on the morning of 12 May 1994. Blair, deeply shocked, was telephoning from Dyce Airport in Aberdeen, where he had gone to campaign in the Euro-elections. Mandelson, who was at his flat in Wilmington Square, already knew that something had happened because he had been called by a puzzled Fiona Millar asking if he knew the whereabouts of Alastair Campbell, who had been reviewing the papers on early morning BBC TV, as the *Today* news desk was trying to get hold of him; a big political story had broken. Reflecting on the subject much later, Mandelson suspected that Blair already knew Smith was dead but had been told to keep it a secret; he had said merely that it was extremely serious. He went on to ask Mandelson what he thought he should do. Mandelson replied that he should get on the first available aircraft and return to London and that they should meet later in the day. He rang Anji Hunter, Blair's assistant, in Blair's office and recounted the conversation to her. She rang back a few minutes later to confirm that Blair would indeed be getting a plane soon, and would be back at 2 p.m. As Mandelson left to drive to Westminster through torrential rain and gridlocked traffic, there was still no clear news of Smith's condition. The news that he had been pronounced dead at St Bartholomew's Hospital was not broadcast until about 10.30 a.m. The announcement had been delayed until all the family could be told.

It would be hard to overestimate the sudden sense of loss inflicted by Smith's death, not only on the Labour Party but beyond. Acknowledging the outpouring of grief which followed it, Philip Gould says of the electorate at large that 'not really connecting with him when he was leader, they missed him greatly when he was gone', and goes on to suggest that 'through the extraordinary national response to his death, he gave back to Labour the confidence and pride it had lost for so long'.[1] This is the standard modernising analysis. Certainly, the qualitative research available to Philip Gould – whose latest campaign strategy had been presented to Mandelson two days (and to Blair the very day) before Smith's death – continued to imply that the party had much more to do in order to gain a campaigning cutting edge and make voters 'feel better off under Labour'. The unexpectedly heartfelt mourning among supporters of every political party did reconnect Labour to the heart of national life in a way that only an election victory could otherwise have done. But the national opinion polls also tell a slightly different story about Smith in life as well as in death. Through 1993 and the first four months of 1994 – admittedly still early in the parliament – Labour was consistently scoring well above 45 per cent. On the one hand Smith took risks with the electorate by accommodating the trade unions and, to some extent, the parliamentary left. On the other he was a witty, incisive, heavyweight and, at times, frightening opponent for John Major. He had, despite all the modernisers' impatience, laid his job on the line to democratise the party's constitution. He was also, with a record of Atlanticism and Europeanism much longer than his predecessor's, immune to charges of inconsistency.

It is certain that Blair and Brown represented the next generation of Labour leaders, but much harder to say what and under what circumstances they would have inherited had Smith lived. It is possible that Smith was a leader for 1992 but not for 1997. Maybe, as the modernisers, including Mandelson, feared, Labour's fortunes would have slid back as they had done after a similarly good year under Kinnock in 1990, and the party would have risked a fifth defeat – possibly one too many for a recovery. It is more likely that Smith would have narrowly won the next election against an exhausted and fractured Tory Party but that, without the wholesale transformation wrought by Blair, a Labour government would have once again been removed at the end of its first term; that it was going out with the end of the twentieth century, as it had come in at the beginning. It is possible, finally, that Smith would have run a successful government, possibly entering the single currency in his first parliament, and gone on to win a second term. But none of these propositions can be tested; Labour, as distinct from New Labour, did not get its chance to fight another election. What is clear is that Smith left a party more unified and more respected than it had been since the 1960s.

Mandelson now telephoned Brown in his flat in Church Street, Westminster, and arranged to meet him shortly after 11 a.m. In the meantime, in response to a series of calls, he went to the Millbank studios to broadcast some TV and radio tributes to the deceased leader in the interval before more senior Labour figures could be found. When he arrived at Brown's flat, Sheena Macdonald, the TV and radio journalist, an old friend and sometime girlfriend of Brown's, was in the flat tidying up; after a few minutes she went off to get some sandwiches. The two men discussed, with barely a pause, the question of the future leadership. It was clear to Mandelson, though this was not explicitly stated on either side, that Brown, simultaneously thoughtful and agitated as he was, anticipated being the modernising candidate. The unspoken bond of mutual loyalty was sustained during the conversation, though Mandelson said more than once that Brown, Blair and he would all need to discuss what happened next when Blair returned to London. Since 1989 this inseparable triangular team had taken no big decision or judgement on strategy without a three-way discussion and Mandelson was implying that this was no different. Neither man seriously considered the possibility of another candidate. It was clear to both that either one of Brown or Blair, the Shadow Cabinet's publicly acknowledged stars, would be the leader, and Mandelson's impression was that Brown had no doubt which it should be. Nor, he would insist later, had Mandelson. On the other hand, remembering a conversation with Blair some months earlier, he realised that it might not be so cut and dried.

One Sunday morning around the turn of 1993–4 he and Blair had taken a walk in a park near their homes; their conversation would, within months, take on a significance that neither man had envisaged at that time. One of the subjects under discussion was Gordon Brown, and the persistent – and frequently wholly unfair – criticisms levelled at him. Blair dwelt at some length on his all-consuming appetite for politics, his relative lack of family life, and the sometimes rebarbative impression he gave to close colleagues. Blair's remarks were shot through with his deep affection for and loyalty to Brown. He repeated what he had already said on many occasions – that he would be proud and happy to serve under him if Brown, in time, got the job of party leader. But his unspoken question was whether that was what the party wanted. For the first time Mandelson was left with the impression that Blair was hinting that the trio's unwritten assumption of Brown's primacy could not be taken for granted. It was almost as if he was putting down a marker with the man who, it was still widely assumed, would be Brown's principal campaign strategist if and when the moment came. As Mandelson drove home, leaving Blair to his family Sunday lunch, he speculated that perhaps Blair's mind had been stirring, that he did not intend to be written out of the script, and that he had probably discussed this issue with a handful of his other closest friends, including his wife. It was likely, for example, that, shortly before Smith's death, his old mentor Derry Irvine had told him of Smith's own preference for Blair as his successor – also recalled by at least three members of Smith's staff. Nobody, least of all Mandelson and Blair, knew that the day of decision would be so near at hand.

Mandelson's conversation with Brown on 12 May was curtailed by the arrival of Nick Brown, the MP for Newcastle and a close lieutenant of his namesake. The Shadow Chancellor wanted to talk privately with Nick Brown, and Mandelson left, the two men agreeing to speak later. That afternoon Mandelson went down to the members' lobby in the House of Commons, the routine meeting place for MPs and political journalists. For once the arch-manipulator had come to listen rather than to spin. Indeed, as journalists asked incessantly about Brown's and Blair's plans, he was unhelpful. What could not fail to strike him, however, was the even-handedness of the questions: not 'When is Gordon going to declare?' but 'What are *they* going to do?' That was understandable. Anyone who had been in that same members' lobby that morning, indecently soon after the news of Smith's death, could not fail to be struck by the extent of the interest in a Blair candidacy amid the mourning. Talking to a journalist and another MP, Chris Mullin, a member of the left-wing Campaign Group remarked that he could see no alternative to Blair. I noted the following exchange: MP: 'But he's a social democrat, Chris.' MULLIN: 'Yes, but social democracy is a lot better than what we've got [under the Tories].'

Part of the forcible impression made by this conversation turned out to be exaggerated; in voting for Blair, Mullin was relatively isolated among the Campaign Group left, most of whom eventually opted for John Prescott or Margaret Beckett. But it was far from untypical in the wider party or, even more strikingly, among Tories, who were tangibly apprehensive that Blair would be the candidate. Damien Green, then working in the Number Ten Policy Unit, recalled, 'Our first thought after John Smith's death was, "How awful, a man only in his mid-fifties." Another second later the next thought followed: "Well, that's stuffed Hezza then" – a moment of satisfaction. But then a new idea struck. "Oh my god, it'll let Tony Blair in. He'll be even more difficult." It's what we all thought.'[2] Without a single supporter of any putative candidate lifting a finger, the odds were already shortening on Blair.

This was hardly a surprise. Gradually between 1992 and 1994 Blair's popularity had overtaken that of Brown in a number of respects, several of them wholly beyond Brown's control. Brown had suffered collateral damage from the collapse in September 1992 of British membership of the European Exchange Rate mechanism, a policy which he had adhered to (incidentally with the strong support of Mandelson) despite the complaints of other members of the Shadow Cabinet, including Robin Cook. He had bravely delivered an unpalatable message to the party, again fully endorsed by his fellow modernisers, that the days of tax and spend were over. Both stances had cost him support; to the very extent that he had been serving the interests of his party, he had not been serving his own. The same conflict of interest was not inherent in the outstanding success Blair had made of the home affairs portfolio. Ever since January 1993, when Blair had used the phrase – coined by Gordon Brown – 'tough on crime, tough on the causes of crime' about Labour's stance on law and order, he had both increased the party's standing on a hitherto difficult issue, and advanced his own position in it.

After his visit to the members' lobby Mandelson returned to his office in Millbank. On the way he met Lord Irvine, probably the one man who was as close to Blair as he had been to John Smith. Calm despite his grief, Irvine asked Mandelson about his views on the succession. Uncharacteristically, Mandelson mumbled an inconclusive reply. 'It has to be Tony,' the eminent lawyer insisted. 'I am not persuaded of that,' Mandelson replied, suggesting that Irvine should discuss the matter with Brown before making that assumption. Irvine was surprised that Mandelson had not agreed with him. He swiftly passed on to the Blair camp his view that Mandelson was a Brown man.

Both his conversations in the lobby and his chance encounter with Irvine imply that Mandelson's mind was divided. On the one hand he had certainly begun to wonder whether Blair might indeed be the next leader. On the other his thoughts returned to Brown's strength as a potential candidate. Taking a handful of calls from journalists in his office, Mandelson contented himself with pointing out that Brown had a powerful claim and that he should not be written out of the script. In the midst of this Blair telephoned: he wanted to have a word but suggested – apparently wary of appearing to be plotting with Mandelson or anyone else – a meeting on neutral ground. In the heightened urgency of the moment the minds of both men went blank. Where could they safely meet? Eventually they settled on one of the division lobbies beside the Commons Chamber, certain to be empty in the late afternoon after the adjournment of the House as a mark of respect to Smith. They met shortly before 6 p.m., Blair still in the unsuitably pale suit which he had been wearing at Dyce Airport – and which, according to one ally, he vowed never to be caught wearing again in public. Blair told Mandelson that there was evidence of hostility to Brown's candidacy and that members of the Shadow Cabinet had already come to him offering their support – as indeed they had. When he had returned to his Westminster office four shadow ministers – Jack Straw, Mo Mowlam, Adam Ingram and Peter Kilfoyle – had already turned up pledging their backing. What was Mandelson's view? By his own subsequent account, Mandelson was distinctly cautious: of course,

Blair was entitled to consider himself a possible candidate. Blair had evidently hoped for more wholehearted backing but, faced with a noncommittal answer, merely asked Mandelson to do what he could to ensure that there was no bad blood between himself and Brown in the press. Once again they agreed to talk later.

Brown and Blair met that night at the house of Blair's brother. What passed between them remains a secret, though Brown, like Blair, appears to have made no secret of his leadership ambitions. The same evening, after having a drink with a handful of some unashamedly excited young Labour Party researchers at the Cork and Bottle in Leicester Square, Draper went to Mandelson's flat, where they talked until the small hours. He pressed Mandelson, still vainly, to accept Blair as the candidate. In the morning he drove him to Westminster in Mandelson's green Rover. Stopped at traffic lights in Charing Cross Road as they approached Trafalgar Square, he turned to Mandelson and said again: 'You can't really stop the front runner, can you?' Mandelson replied noncommittally: 'Hmm . . . perhaps,' but he seemed abstracted. Draper was not alone in pressing Mandelson to go for Blair.

By this time Brown had good reason to be alarmed by the press. According to the standard legend, this was skilfully orchestrated by the omnipotent Mandelson, starting with a favourable *Evening Standard* profile of Blair by Sarah Baxter. However, Ms Baxter, no friend of Mandelson, says emphatically that she had no contact with him on the day in question.[3] Most of the national newspaper political editors also predicted a Blair leadership, including – and perhaps especially – those who had had no contact with Mandelson at all. Moreover, on the previous night Alastair Campbell, then the journalist closest to the Labour modernisers, had tipped Blair on BBC TV's *Newsnight*. According to Campbell, '*Newsnight* was a complete accident. I went on to do a tribute and right at the end Mark Mardell asked: "Who do you think is going to be the next leader?" and I said, "Tony Blair, no doubt about it." Peter rang me straight away and said: "That was completely out of order, you can't rule Gordon out like that."'[4]

Mandelson now sought to reassure Brown. He agreed to ask Campbell to keep his head down – an invitation which Campbell ignored, writing a piece in *Today* implying that Brown would have to step down[5] – and proceeded to inform selected journalists that Brown, as well as Blair, was still in contention, but that they would not run against each other and that one modernising candidate would 'emerge'. This strategy had been agreed with Brown. Mandelson now set about – rather ostentatiously – 'evening things up'. He made no effort to conceal his appearance in the press gallery – at one point picking an unnecessary and trivial argument with the *Daily Express* journalist Jon Craig when he accidentally bumped into him on the stairs. He set about the task with his usual efficiency. The result was that the political editors of *The Times* and the *Independent* both wrote stories – clearly (to anyone in the know) sourced from Mandelson – for Saturday's papers claiming that the two stars would not both stand, but that Brown might still be the one who did. The standard explanation among Brown supporters has since been that Mandelson was playing a double game. If so, he was almost recklessly thorough in his briefings, giving a list of Brown's indisputable strengths as an exceptional politician – much like the one he had drawn up two years earlier after Kinnock stood down: Brown, he said, was the intellectual driving force in the partnership; he might well make a better Prime Minister; he had a 'robustness' that appealed to voters – including those in the South; and he had the perfect combination of deep roots in the party and a modernising outlook.

That afternoon Mandelson also spoke by telephone to Blair (as he often would during the next few days, though they would not meet face to face for a week) reporting his intention to 'even things up' by promoting Brown in the press, and securing Blair's assent to the line he had agreed with Brown. Blair only asked that Mandelson should not do anything in his conversations with journalists to harm *him*. The following day Mandelson relayed what was basically the same story – albeit in a more colourful form – to Andrew Grice of the *Sunday Times*; thus was born the 'secret pact' between Brown and Blair not to run against each other – which led Grice's paper the following morning.[6]

The problem now, however, was that polls in the Sunday papers – including the *Sunday Times* – showed Blair well ahead among the voting public, who had been, for the first time in a party leadership election, a crucial factor in the elevation of John Major to the premiership in 1990 and would now affect the fortunes of Tony

Blair. Moreover, in the only section of the electoral college surveyed that weekend, the *Sunday Express* even found Blair leading among 150 Labour-supporting trade unionists, with Prescott second on 22 per cent.[7] Not surprisingly, Brown complained bitterly to Mandelson about the *Sunday Times* story. But the problem with the 'secret pact' strategy – which Brown had approved – was that it had blown up in Brown's face; even if the intention had originally been to ensure that Brown would be the candidate because Blair would step down, it now looked, if only one of the two modernising candidates was going to run, as if it would be Blair.

Mandelson then fuelled suspicion among Brown's closest allies, at least retrospectively, that he had subliminally plumped for Blair in an interview on the Saturday evening on *The Week in Politics*. In the green room, again somewhat ostentatiously, Mandelson said he needed to speak to Charlie Whelan 'about how we're going to deal with the Sunday papers' – leaving the clear impression that he was cheer-leading for Brown. But when it came to the interview itself, listing the contenders, 'Tony Blair, for example, or Gordon Brown or Robin Cook or John Prescott' (in that order), he went on to say. 'Who would maximise support for the party in the country? Who will play best at the box office, who will not simply appeal to the traditional supporters and customers of the Labour Party, but who will bring in those extra, additional voters that we need in order to win convincingly at the next election?' This was hardly conclusive. The last two years of Brown's career, if not more, had been devoted to ensuring that the party appealed 'to those extra, additional voters'. To at least one Brown supporter, however, this was a clear invitation to the party to vote for Blair.

By Monday the press was, if anything, rather worse from Brown's point of view. The BBC's lunchtime news detected signs of a Blair bandwagon, which was perhaps unstoppable. It was at this point, on the afternoon of 16 May, that Mandelson wrote his famous letter to Brown:

Monday

Gordon,

I thought I should give you my best view of the situation from the media standpoint.

You are attracting sympathy from the Lobby for your position. You are seen as the biggest intellectual force and strategic thinker the party has. Most people say there is no-one to rival your political 'capacity'. I have thought a lot about your fear that you are being written down (out) by the press and I have read everything very carefully. I don't believe your fears are justified. Nobody is saying you are not capable/appropriate as leader, merely that the timing is bad for you or that you have vocal enemies or that you have presentational difficulties.

You have a problem in not appearing to be the front runner. It's not that people question whether you could catch up – people accept that your support is currently being understated – but that it would be very difficult for Tony to withdraw in your favour (how would it be explained in view of the polls, etc.) and that by standing you would trigger Cook and possibly others and this would surely not be in the interests of the party.

If Tony felt he had to stand and you did too, what would be the consequences? I think you both, and our cause, and the party, would be hugely damaged. It would be a gift to our enemies. Because you would be appearing to come in as the second runner, you would be blamed for creating the split. I think the media would attack you and that your standing in the party would suffer.

The only way to overcome this media resistance to you is to mount a massive and sustained briefing which concentrated on your political skills, ability to unite and manage all sides of the party, dominance in the House, blend of party transition and modernising agenda. I have not encountered much difficulty selling this so far but to be effective it would have to be greatly escalated, begun immediately, and I am afraid, only done by explicitly weakening Tony's position.

Even then, I could not guarantee success. Ultimately the card the media are playing for Tony is his 'southern appeal'. He doesn't need to point it out or build it up: it is there firmly in their minds and it is linked to their (and our) overriding question, is Labour serious about conquering the South?

My fear is that drift is harming you (cf. BBC lunchtime news). You have either to escalate rapidly (and to be effective I think I would need to become clearly partisan with the press in your favour) or you need to implement a strategy to exit with enhanced position, strength and respect.

Will you let me know your wishes?

Peter 16, v, 94.

Mandelson, in other words, warned Brown directly four days after John Smith's death that the odds were stacking up against him and that he would have to choose between bowing out and triggering a damaging – perhaps, for the modernising agenda, terminally damaging – split with Blair. It was a painful choice and there was already no doubt which way Mandelson's mind was going. But the myth that gained currency among the more zealous Brown supporters – that this reflected treacherous backstabbing on Mandelson's part – is baffling to say the least. Not for the first or the last time in his career Mandelson was laying out unpalatable truths – not to mention offering, by implication, to stand by Brown rather than desert to Blair if that was what Brown was determined to do. The truths, moreover, were not of Mandelson's making. Not even he, with all his dark arts, could have reversed the tide of opinion, both inside and outside the Labour Party, in favour of Blair.

Over the next few days the alternatives laid out in Mandelson's letter figured in a series of discussions between Brown and Mandelson – who, unlike Blair, located some way away in Parliament Street, had neighbouring offices in Millbank. This geographical accident played a much more important part in the early days of the campaign than it has been given credit for. It meant that those around Blair like Straw, Mowlam, Kilfoyle and even Neil Kinnock, another Blair supporter, could meet discreetly without ever setting foot outside the Parliament Street building because they all had offices there. A visit to Mandelson would have been as obtrusive as it would have been unwelcome to several Blair supporters at this stage. As a result Brown and Mandelson met each other more frequently than either did Blair. The two men had even discussed the fearsome probability that challenging Blair's early lead would mean summoning up 'forces of darkness' in the party – the left in the unions and the PLP – in order to eclipse him. It was not impossible that Brown might have succeeded in building a powerful base of support in the unions; the Transport and General Workers' Union might, in these circumstance, have opted for Brown rather than for Margaret Beckett. And the GMB, then in merger talks with the TGWU, might well have sought to ingratiate themselves by following suit. But it would have meant attacking Blair from the left as 'SDP Mark II' or 'Hugh Gaitskell or worse', with three possible consequences – none of them enticing. One was that Blair, a media favourite, would be politically destroyed and with him much of the Labour Party's electoral appeal. The second was that he would actually bring in Robin Cook and John Prescott, one a permanent enemy of Brown's, the other an enemy of the moment, in a coalition of interests which might fatally undermine Brown himself. The third was that, supposing Brown could still win against such a coalition, there would be a legacy of permanent instability. That Brown resisted these outcomes, particularly the use of the 'dark forces', is wholly to his credit. It is not necessary to assume that Mandelson was a treacherous and covert champion of Blair's to recognise that when Brown stood down he was making a painful and honourable sacrifice of his own interests to his political principles.

For the moment, however, Brown, having a possibly exaggerated view of what Mandelson could achieve in the media, pressed him to secure more favourable coverage without, as yet, a final resolution of this painful dilemma. Mandelson, for his part, kept offering a choice – basically that laid out in his letter – between Option A and Option B, which (clearly by now Mandelson's preference) was for Brown to 'exit with enhanced position, strength and respect'. But Mandelson did not discard Option A. The day after sending his letter he asked Philip Gould to draw up a Brown campaign strategy and emphatically rebuked Harriet Harman in his office for assuming that Blair would be the candidate.

Which made it all the more annoying when, on the following day (18 May) Nigel Griffiths, a close Brown ally, told the London *Evening Standard* about 'dismay' among Labour MPs that Mandelson was running a covert press campaign for Blair. Mandelson, by his own account, went 'ballistic' and shouted down the telephone to Whelan that he had fifteen minutes to have the story denied, or he, Mandelson, would make 'an on the record statement' about the tortured discussions under way about who should be the candidate. In five minutes Brown returned Mandelson's call: the matter should not be allowed to harm relations between them, he said; Griffiths had not meant it. Griffiths did indeed make an immediate public apology, though Mandelson subsequently became convinced that the intervention had been part of a strategy agreed among Brown allies the night before.

In fact, during this period Mandelson frequently spoke to Blair on the phone, and he certainly reported Brown's disinclination to stand down – but he also became increasingly aware that Blair was determined not to do so either. However, the idea that he was already helping to run the Blair campaign team is wide of the mark, for several reasons. For one thing there were suspicions in the Blair camp, fuelled by the chance conversation with Irvine, that Mandelson was indeed a Brown man; for another, any association with Mandelson was judged by others, including Mo Mowlam, to be positively harmful to the Blair cause. In addition, there was the sheer physical separation between the two men. Moreover Mandelson, unlike them, had still to declare his hand. Indeed, Roger Liddle, who spoke to him at some length during this period, believes that at one point he tried to talk Blair out of running: 'I think he was taken aback by Tony's determination to run . . . He said to me: "I said to Tony, does he realise the damage he's going to cause his family, to a young family, by pushing himself forward at this point?" But then he said: "But you know, he's adamant he's going to run."'[6]

In the middle of the week, after the Griffiths episode, Mandelson had, in the light of Blair's determination – and the continued polling evidence that he was the front runner – one of his most important conversations with Brown. By this time, he had firmly decided that, as he would later put it, Gordon had to be 'airlifted out of this situation before his people did him and us any more damage'. After the encounter Mandelson telephoned Liddle and told him in some agitation: 'I think I've made an enemy for life. I feel this is a disaster, I've made an enemy for life.' Moreover it had not worked: Brown would not stand down for another twelve tense and difficult days. And in the meantime he would increasingly turn to others like Charlie Whelan, Ed Balls and Nick Brown for advice.

*     *     *

298

So what had Mandelson been up to over the past few days? And, for that matter, the past two years or more? At one end of the spectrum John Rentoul, Blair's biographer, claims that Mandelson, although he had championed both Blair and Brown, 'was promoting Blair behind the scenes from the start' and had 'favoured Blair as a future leader since at least the 1992 election, and now [immediately after John Smith's death] became Blair's principal adviser straight away' – while pretending, for various underhand reasons, to some MPs and journalists that he was a Brown supporter.[9] One explanation, attributed to Labour MPs, is that he was making a deliberate – and deliciously devious – effort to exploit his own deep unpopularity in the Labour Party by damaging Brown's chances through association. Rentoul's main evidence for Mandelson's long-term support for Blair is his involvement in the Barbara Amiel profile of Blair back in the summer of 1992. (In fact the prominence, though not the content, of the profile caused some concern in Blair's office, given that it was published the day after Smith became leader. Anji Hunter made at least one – unsuccessful – attempt to keep it off the cover.) Against this is Mandelson's claim that if, after John Smith's death, 'Gordon had emerged there and then and Tony had signalled his support, I would not have thought twice. My loyalty to Gordon was intense. He had always seemed to be the leader of the pack, the man whose brainpower, political judgement and personality were dominant.' And it is supported by several of Mandelson's close friends: Alastair Campbell bears him out on the basis of his own knowledge of Mandelson and of several fierce arguments they had about the relative leadership merits of Blair and Brown – both before and immediately after John Smith's death. 'He can be very difficult. He can be very changeable, but he will stand by people. That's why he found the leadership crisis such a nightmare because he was faced with a choice between two people he wanted to stand.'

Some friends also attest to an easier personal chemistry between Mandelson and Blair than between Mandelson and Brown – but also to Mandelson's belief between 1992 and 1994 that Brown rather than Blair should succeed Smith. Draper found it very difficult being with Brown and Mandelson together: 'It's like the dinner party from hell, isn't it? Peter Mandelson, who's totally self-obsessed and into social climbing, and Gordon Brown, who's totally taciturn and brooding, sitting on a table with me in the middle and being intimidated by both of them. Whereas of course when I had dinner at Sedgefield once, Tony and Peter got on like a house on fire.'[10] This probably underestimates the genuine warmth that had existed between Brown and Mandelson – of which there have been occasional flashes even since the crisis of 1994. But anyway, according to Roger Liddle, while 'I think in a way the emotional relationship with Tony has always seemed to me a lot closer, they got on better, it was easier ... the great figure, the leadership figure was Gordon. It was as though there was a triangle with Gordon at the top and both of them working for Gordon, with Tony being slightly higher up one side of the triangle, as it were.'

These are friends, of course, broadly endorsing Mandelson's own version. Nevertheless the evidence against the claim that Mandelson had promoted Blair's interests over those of Brown between 1992 and 1994 is persuasive. He had consistently tried to help Brown offset the (unfair) hostilities he was incurring for constructing an economic policy that would make Labour electable (see previous chapter). Far from 'busily promoting Blair on the metropolitan dinner party circuit',[11] he frequently, and sometimes to their considerable irritation, pressed Brown's case as the future – and next – leader with Alastair Campbell, his partner Fiona Millar, and Philip Gould, all of whom were Blair supporters. There was even said to be a holiday video, made in Majorca in 1993, of Campbell and Gould ribbing Mandelson about his fixation with Brown as a future leader; some months before Smith's death, and well after Blair had started, as Rentoul correctly puts it, to 'overtake' Brown, he discussed the succession with his agent Steve Wallace. Wallace, now the chairman of Hartlepool's Education Committee as well as Mandelson's agent, had been a civil servant, ran a taxi firm for a while and had been a Liberal Democrat council candidate. But after defecting to the Labour Party he worked as a keen volunteer during the 1992 election and was taken on as full-time agent by Mandelson shortly afterwards. Mandelson assured him that Brown was the 'stronger' of the duo.[12] He took Brown round to Campbell and Millar's house in a vain effort to persuade them of his claim to the succession. As for the profile, Mandelson was interviewed for it, advised Blair about it, and encouraged it. But he appears to have had virtually nothing to do with the way in which it was presented. Even Mandelson does not design magazine front covers and write the stand-firsts. According to contemporary *Sunday Times* sources, the projection of the profile as that of a future leader was entirely down to the editor, Andrew Neil.

That Blair had ambitions for the leadership, even before the 1992 election, is not in doubt, any more than that Mandelson was aware of them. One strong Brown supporter recalls Mandelson musing before the 1992 general election that it might be time for the Labour Party to be led by someone other than a 'Celt'. Mandelson categorically denied this claim – and there is no evidence he thought Blair a plausible successor to Kinnock, or indeed that Blair would have been. On the other hand he certainly knew well before the 1992 election that Blair had long-term leadership aspirations. From 1992–94 it is likely that Mandelson never wholly ruled out the prospect that Blair might be the next leader. However the evidence supports his claim to Philip Gould that 'anybody who had any contact with me in the years preceding John Smith's death knows how committed I was to Gordon Brown', and that 'I also made sure that the machine served Tony Blair as well, because they were both leaders of the modernisers, manifestly the most competent and able, and they were both superb performers.'[13] Derek Draper, who worked for him throughout that period, said:

You don't have to choose in politics until you have to choose and Peter gets on with the sort of practicalities . . . His problem is that he isn't very long term, thinking things through. So I'm not saying that he'd have ever thought at any point, 'Am I a Gordon or Tony man this morning?' Now, when John Smith died, he had to think, 'Am I a Gordon man or a Tony man?' You would assume that Smith was probably going to survive and become Prime Minister and then we'd see how Tony and Gordon did as cabinet ministers and then I suppose one of them would be the obvious successor. But there wouldn't be a lot you could do about that because it would depend on what jobs Smith gave them and how they handled them.

What happened in the days after John Smith's death is a more complex matter. It appears that, from the first day, or at least after his discussions in the lobby and with Derry Irvine, Mandelson entertained the possibility that Blair might become leader. And the more he listened to Draper and other friends, including Campbell, the more his mind was prised open. But his remarks on *The Week in Politics* were not as conclusively pro-Blair as they were later made out to be. What was Brown's strength as a moderniser, as well as Blair's, if it were not also to appeal beyond Labour's core support to the floating voters beyond? Moreover Mandelson had been suggesting to journalists on the Friday that Brown would have appeal in the South. As one Blair supporter would put it sardonically in 1995: 'if in their [Brown's allies'] view the cap did not fit Gordon, then that was a fairly revealing admission'. Roger Liddle, whose wife Caroline was having a fortieth birthday party at their Kennington home, had an agonised conversation with Mandelson on the Saturday night after Smith's death. At least one guest at the party claimed to recall him saying that Brown was inevitably paying the price for his loss of popularity as Shadow Chancellor. On the other hand, while Liddle urged him candidly to play on the winning side, he still seemed to be entertaining notions of persuading Blair not to run. Further evidence of his indecision was produced in January 1999, when the political journalist Peter Oborne recounted the interesting testimony of Richard Medley, a visiting US political consultant, who had first met Mandelson at a conference in the Aspen Institute in Berlin, and now had a cup of tea with him in London on the afternoon of John Smith's death. According to Oborne, Medley saw a man 'tortured' about what he would do if both Brown and Blair entered the leadership race. 'He went on and on about how painful it would be if he had to make that choice.' Medley had a 'very strong sense that Gordon was hesitating about whether to run or not, whereas there was an instant determination in the Tony Blair camp.' Medley detected 'a general sense of relief in Peter that in this way the conflict was being perhaps resolved for him.'[14]

If Mandelson did have such a 'sense of relief' it was premature. But even if he *did* have Blair's appeal to southern England in mind when he spoke on television three evenings later, he was going with the flow created not by him, but by the polls, the press and an increasing number of named Labour figures. Within a week of John Smith's death Mandelson did indeed become utterly convinced both that Blair would stand and that he was the candidate with easily the best chance of winning. But so had almost everyone else in the Labour Party, including some of Brown's closest allies.

One further question remains. What if Brown had responded to the letter of May 16 by saying: 'yes, I realise I have been slipping behind Blair, but I intend to run *whether Blair goes ahead or not*. And I want you to promote my candidacy in the press even at the risk of damaging Tony Blair'? The question is impossible to answer because Mandelson's implicit, if very reluctant, offer to campaign in such a way was never tested. Mandelson's letter could certainly be interpreted as at once straightforwardly warning Brown of what was undoubtedly true – that a Blair bandwagon was rolling – while taking out an insurance policy against the possiblity that Brown would still decide to run. Equally, some close observers of the Blair camp at the time continue to think that, from the first, Mandelson knew that Blair was going to be the candidate, and was attempting, by tacit agreement with Blair, to promote Brown's cause simply in order to help him retreat with dignity and strength when the inevitable moment came. It still seems likelier that up to the first weekend after John Smith's death he was genuinely torn by his loyalties to both men. But in any case, the suggestion that Mandelson began to campaign, covertly or otherwise, for Blair in the forty-eight hours after John Smith's death is not supported by the evidence. Even if he was 'showing his hand' in the *Week in Politics* interview, it could only be to those intimately involved. It was too subliminal to have any influence on a course of events which had in any case already been set, and without any help from Mandelson. The polling evidence of Blair's success was relentlessly impressive, culminating in a BBC *On the Record* survey showing that he enjoyed the support of 47 per cent of the party, compared to 11 per cent commanded by Brown. Moreover it appears that only a minority of Shadow Cabinet members – including Donald Dewar, Ron Davies, Tom Clarke – firmly supported Brown. It is therefore hard to fault the analysis in Mandelson's letter to Brown. He was describing the circumstances accurately and he had played no part in creating them.

Of Brown's shadow cabinet supporters Dewar was easily the most important. Publicly Mandelson had not yet expressed any preference for either candidate. But within a week of Smith's death he was energetically trying to sell the idea of Brown's withdrawal to those most in a position to influence him; he bluntly told Dewar, during a lengthy conversation in the cafeteria in the MPs' office block at 7 Millbank, that if he were truly loyal to Brown he would save him from a terribly destructive knock-down fight with Blair. He subsequently said privately that he thought Dewar knew that, in the end, Brown would not run but was, out of loyalty, refusing to admit as much. It is also true that Dewar played an influential, if not a pivotal role in dissuading Brown from standing. But even without Dewar's influence there were doubts about Brown's support in his own heartland, which would later be reinforced by a straw poll of Scottish MPs published in the *Scotsman* on 27 May: this showed that while fifteen, the biggest single group, were firm Brown supporters and only six equally firm for Blair, another six, although loyal to Brown, said they hoped he would stand aside for Blair. The poll was also later attributed to Mandelson's black arts – rather annoyingly for Ewan MacAskill and Joy Copley, the two diligent *Scotsman* correspondents who had rung round forty-two of Scotland's forty-eight Labour MPs.

Mandelson did not engineer the *Scotsman* poll. But he had certainly by now set himself the task of helping to ensure Brown withdrew, albeit from a position of strength. Some thought this had been his secret intention from the moment of John Smith's death, and the letter on 16 May had been a way of persuading Brown to release him from his personal obligation to the Shadow Chancellor. Mandelson insisted that it was several days after it that he had finally attached himself to Blair. Either way it seems to have been a fairly traumatic event for him. According to Jon Snow, the *Channel Four News* presenter who knew him well, 'People say Bill Clinton is compartmentalized. Well perhaps Peter Mandelson is as well. He knew what had to be done which was to ensure Tony Blair became leader. But I think he grieved for Gordon as well.'[15] By Friday 20 May, when John Smith's funeral took place in Edinburgh, Brown was already beginning to plan his speech to the Welsh Labour conference on the following Sunday. That night his team of advisers was installed at his house in Inverkeithing drafting the speech. (There was nothing untoward about this; Blair campaigners were working every bit as hard.) Both Brown and Blair had been offered a platform in Cardiff, but it had been agreed that the Shadow Chancellor alone should speak to the conference. Widely billed in the press as the opening shot of the leadership campaign – and as a pitch to the left, with its appeal for unity and its hints of higher public spending – the speech worried and irritated Blair, who asked Mandelson to let it be known that he, for one, would not be bending the knee to old-time Labour religion. Sure enough, the next day, Monday 23 May, *The Times* carried a story indicating as much.

The pressures were now closing in on Brown. Some political dramas are fuelled by lunch; others by dinner. Following the Sunday's bleak poll findings, and a conversation between the two candidates in which the Shadow Chancellor gave the strongest hint yet that he planned to withdraw, Brown, despite his natural austerity, had three secret dinners, two of them on the same night. The first, on Monday night at Joe Allen's, was with Nick Brown and Charlie Whelan; here it was agreed that Brown should bow out – but on the best terms that could be secured. The view was that he could still win, despite the polls – but only by summoning up those very dark forces which Brown had agreed with Mandelson might sabotage the whole cause of modernisation. The second dinner was the now legendary encounter at Islington's fashionable Granita, at which he personally relayed this decision to Blair. And the third and final one, that same evening, was at the Rodin restaurant at Millbank, where he met his own close supporters and planned the tactics for retreat.

Which was no simple matter. On the Monday, at Blair's request, Mandelson had played a prominent part in persuading more gullible journalists to accept that Brown's support in the PLP and in the trade unions was almost, or actually, level-pegging with Blair's. This was patently untrue but the idea was that it would allow Brown to withdraw from what looked like a position of strength. Mandelson then took the train to Hartlepool and, as Brown and Blair talked in Granita, sat in Hutton Avenue drafting one of his famous 'line to take' briefings for the media. All through Wednesday morning the briefing note went through draft after draft, with Mandelson holding the ring from Hartlepool as Blair and Brown each objected to different words and phrases in the other's formulation. The principal argument was over Brown's insistence that he should be 'guaranteed' not only the Chancellorship in a future Labour government but also autonomous control over the whole range of economic policy. Blair, with Mandelson's help, sought to limit the scope of such a guarantee. At one point, as the drafts and redrafts spewed out of Mandelson's fax in Hutton Avenue, the machine broke down, threatening the whole delicate negotiation, and Steve Wallace had to be dispatched into town to buy another one. In the end, however, there was a compromise: in a careful *Times* column the following day Peter Riddell summarised it by saying that it had 'guaranteed Mr Brown that [his] fairness agenda, broadening employment opportunities and improving training and skills, will be the centrepiece of Labour's economic and social programme'.

The announcement itself was not free of hitches. Riding roughshod over the reservations of both the Brown and Blair offices, Mandelson insisted on bringing the discussions to a conclusion by tipping off the BBC, ITN, Sky and Channel Four to the pending news. The London *Evening Standard* shares a cramped office with ITN and Channel Four News: Charles Reiss, the paper's political editor, got wind of the story and filed a version ahead of the appointed time. A furious Charlie Whelan protested about Mandelson's behaviour to the Blair office, but the announcement went ahead at 3 p.m. as scheduled. Although neither Brown nor Blair was keen, both agreed to David Hill's suggestion, endorsed by Mandelson, that they should be filmed walking together round New Palace Yard. Brown joined the Blair campaign, providing (along with Ed Balls) regular advice, especially on economic policy. For all the tensions of the preceding negotiations, and the corrosive bitterness which was to follow over the next three years or more, Brown's decision guaranteed that the campaign would be won by the modernising tendency. He had subordinated his *amour propre* to the interests of the party.

While Brown sealed Blair's victory by standing down, election outcomes never seem quite such a foregone conclusion, at least to the participants. Blair did not feel confident enough about the effect either on the party or on his immediate lieutenants – among whom Peter Kilfoyle was at the time the most vociferous Mandelson opponent – to engage Mandelson openly as his senior adviser. However, Mandelson supervised every speech summary, every press release, and was part of the inner circle of Blair advisers on the speeches themselves. Above all, he was tireless in giving covert briefings to a wide range of selected broadcast and newspaper journalists on Blair's behalf. Media relations did not always go smoothly. Following a televised debate on *Panorama* which went much better for John Prescott than it had done for Blair, Mandelson sought to postpone Blair's appearance on *On the Record* so that his leadership interview would come third and last. This resulted in a screaming match with the programme's editor David Jordan, who warned him, reasonably enough, that he had already booked Margaret Beckett for the later date and might not be able to change her. When Mandelson threatened, as he often did, to invoke higher authority in the BBC, Jordan, with commendable resilience, suggested that Mandelson 'could go to the Pope' if he wanted; it would make no difference. Relations were strained enough for Anji Hunter to send a worried note to Blair saying that questions about Mandelson 'running the campaign' were becoming more prevalent than about anything else; David Jordan, she reported, had thanked Tim Allan for being 'absolutely straight, unlike PM' and added, 'PM's pissed a lot of people off in the BBC over the last couple of weeks.'

In the event Mandelson ensured that Blair telephoned Jordan personally to apologise for changing the date; Beckett agreed to shift her slot; and the Blair interview went ahead. Whatever the upsets, Blair regarded Mandelson's semi-clandestine media-handling – he headed a small unit comprising Tim Allan, Tom Restrick and Peter Hyman – as crucial. On one occasion the BBC correspondent Nick Jones, who had emphasised the number of Blair supporters, including Brown, backing Margaret Beckett as deputy leader, was bleeped five times by Mandelson on a single day; as a result of Mandelson's (correct) advice that several equally prominent Blair supporters – including, though Mandelson did not vouchsafe this fact at the time, Blair himself – were backing John Prescott, he accordingly amended his report for the bulletins. Yet reporters were persistently told by Mandelson, in the masonic manner of old-fashioned lobby journalism, that the conversations 'had not taken place'. When Jones tried to press him on his role in the campaign, he replied: 'I have no formal or official role in this. You know the relationship I have. I do talk to Tony. I do speak to him before interviews. Our relationship is governed by our friendship. I only exist to serve.'

When Andy McSmith wrote accurately about his role in the *Observer*, Mandelson tried desperately to prevent the story going ahead, even allegedly suggesting at one point that if he wanted to write an alternative damaging story about him, he should report on the breakdown in his relationship with Gordon Brown since Brown's decision to stand down. According to McSmith, 'What shone through all this deviousness was his loyalty to Tony Blair.' Mandelson's easiest defence would have been to explain that Blair had secretly engaged his services behind the backs of others in his team; and that the story would therefore backfire badly on Blair. 'Instead he took the whole responsibility upon himself and pleaded his cause on the grounds that he was the one who would be landed in trouble.'[16] But, as Nick Jones readily admits, the secrecy largely held, because journalists knew that, if they broke it, their contact with Mandelson would cease. Indeed, Jones did not break his cover until after the campaign, when he wrote an article for the *Guardian* describing in detail Mandelson's activities in the Blair campaign under the codename 'Bobby'.[17]

The codename, 'blown' by Jones after Blair first used it semi-publicly in his celebratory speech to his campaign team after he was elected on 21 July (though still without explaining to whom it referred), neatly underlines Mandelson's difficulties during the campaign. (Contrary to reports at the time, it was nothing to do with the Kennedys. It was hastily plucked at random by Kate Garvey, a member of Blair's staff, as a means of keeping Mandelson's extensive involvement in the campaign clandestine; it was very nearly 'Terry'.) The secrecy was thought necessary for the Blair campaign to ensure its appeal beyond the ranks of modernisers, to avoid putting off those who were personally hostile to the Hartlepool MP, and (ironically) to allay the fears of those who thought he was still a 'spy' for Gordon Brown. Mo Mowlam, initially hostile and part of the original Blair campaign, began consulting Mandelson regularly, while carefully maintaining the fiction to others that he had no role in it.

Even though he had agreed to it, Mandelson was frustrated, even hurt, by Blair's insistence on keeping his role in the dark. It was a kind of denial. His vexation surfaced early in the campaign proper – that is, after the Euro-elections on 9 June. Andy Grice, briefed by Mandelson, had led the *Sunday Times* with a comprehensive account of Blair's campaign themes, headlined (to Blair's extreme annoyance) BLAIR REVEALS SDP MARK II. Mandelson had remonstrated with Grice – as was his wont – but when a copy of the front page was faxed up to him in Islington Blair uncharacteristically went into what Mandelson later described to a friend as 'meltdown', partly because of its potential impact on trade union support and partly, perhaps, because the headline was a little too close to the truth for comfort. Mandelson was correspondingly upset, protesting that he did not write the *Sunday Times*'s headlines for them.

The incident prompted a melodramatic 'resignation' from Blair's inner circle. Telling Blair that he was 'just fed up because everything I do is wrong', Mandelson walked out of Blair's house in Richmond Crescent, slamming the door behind him, and into the night. His mood was now black. He could not take the credit for successes in the campaign because of his necessarily clandestine *modus operandi*. But he could all too easily be blamed for failures – and by the one person whom by now he could hardly bear to disappoint. The following morning Blair came round to Mandelson's flat in Wilmington Square in a much cheerier mood. He sought to reassure him: apparently 'everyone' was saying that the *Sunday Times* account of his campaign themes was 'very good'. A tearful Mandelson, sitting on his sofa in his white dressing gown, appeared inconsolable; while Blair valiantly sought to reassure him, he protested that he would not carry on 'doing these things, in a box, behind the scenes and then you complaining because you don't like the headlines'. Blair went further, promising that, once the campaign was over, he would 'legitimise' Mandelson and give him his own 'identity'.

Mandelson finally calmed down. The strains of 'being Peter' had already started to show, and Blair had not even become leader.

There would be more 'resignations' over the next four years. But Blair would invariably win his friend round – at whatever emotional cost. He knew how to make the best use of him – and it would be another four years before he wholly fulfilled the promise he had made to him that Sunday morning at Wilmington Square.

# CHAPTER SIXTEEN

## *Scorpions in a Bottle*

The 'inviting haven' of Chewton Glen, as the brochure puts it, is an eighteenth-century Hampshire house with a Palladian frontage, set in seventy acres of gardens, parkland and woods. Since the 1960s it has been a five-star hotel and country club, complete with a nine-hole golf course, four tennis courts and two swimming pools, much favoured for the classier kind of corporate conferences and executive brainstorming sessions. It was here, early in September 1994, less than two months after Blair became party leader, that some of New Labour's keenest minds had assembled in total secrecy to discuss the challenges ahead. The hotel's bedrooms started at £220 a night and the Marryat restaurant boasted a 400-item wine list, so rank-and-file Labour members would have been relieved to learn, if they had had the remotest inkling of it, that the meeting was not being paid for by the party. Instead the conference was paid for by SRU – for which Mandelson had worked after he left Walworth Road – and organised by one of its directors, Colin Fisher, a long-time public opinion adviser to the Labour Party.

On the agenda was essentially a single item: how to win. The participants were sent, in advance, polling data, some material from the Henley Centre for Forecasting on social and economic trends, and two further papers. One was a very short one from Fisher, lucidly setting out the four main themes of Margaret Thatcher's victory in 1979; blaming national decline on Labour's nanny state and union misbehaviour; giving a vision of a property-owning democracy; proposing a programme of privatisation and breaking

311

of 'counter-institutions' like the unions, the local authorities, the BBC and so on; and putting forward symbolic policies like selling council houses. Fisher argued that Labour needed a similarly simple framework, which capitalised on the national mood of anxiety and cynicism about the government. The other paper was a very long one (too long for Blair's taste) from Philip Gould entitled: 'Destroying the Conservatives, Rebuilding Labour'; it opened with the US Democrat pollster Stan Greenberg's comments on the 1992 Clinton campaign, suggesting that, before Clinton, both Democrats and Republicans had failed because they had the 'middle class'. The Johnson and Dukakis Democrats, it argued, 'began to represent minorities (black) not the middle-class majority (white)', took 'extreme positions on social issues' and supported 'excessive levels of taxation'. Meanwhile, the 'clear beneficiaries' of the Reagan Republicans had been the rich, and the 'middle classes' had felt betrayed. Clinton, by contrast, had targeted middle-class voters from aspirational, working families, by adopting 'mainstream (conservative) positions on key issues of social policy: crime, welfare', stressing 'values of work . . . responsibility and restraint' and aiming for 'tax hikes for the rich, tax cuts for the middle class'.*

The original plan for the conference – an all-moderniser event – was subjected to several last-minute revisions. It coincided with the last day of the TUC Congress at Blackpool, which Blair had visited three days earlier for the first time as leader, putting down an important marker by refusing to declare his support for striking railway signalmen. Alastair Campbell, whose appointment as Blair's press secretary had been announced the day before the conference, but who was still working for *Today*, had argued in vain for John Prescott to be included. Among those who did go, however, besides Blair, Brown and Mandelson, Gould, Fisher and Campbell, were Michael Wills (then a television producer and once a colleague of Mandelson's at LWT, but now an MP) and Roger Liddle. Moreover, all the participants had originally been scheduled to convene on the Thursday evening, 8 September, for dinner and formal discussion,

---

* By no means an exact equivalent of the British middle class as it includes skilled manual workers.

and then to proceed to more formal talks the next day. In the end, however, it was agreed that only Blair, Brown and Mandelson, the old triumvirate, should travel down together for dinner, to be joined by the others the following day.

Mandelson drove the future Prime Minister and Chancellor in his own Rover. As they chatted in the car on the way down, Blair disclosed to Mandelson for the first time that he had been thinking of putting him in the whips' office. Mandelson, fearing yet more backstage service to the leader, replied robustly, 'I should koko.' But Blair strongly defended the practice, started by the Tories, of putting all upwardly mobile front benchers through the whips' office. (He got his way: Mandelson became a whip, to the considerable dismay of several old guard members of the whips' office.) That night the three of them dined together with the express intention of deciding how the party would now be organised. Brown had arrived with a sheaf of plans and proposed personnel changes – including the installation of Michael Wills as deputy general secretary at Walworth Road. Blair was not keen on the idea, and Brown, expecting Mandelson to show the kind of support which would have been automatic a year or two earlier, was disappointed instead to find that he was on his own; Mandelson argued with his characteristic caution that more time for thought was needed. After Blair went to bed, Brown and Mandelson stayed up for a nightcap. According to an account subsequently given by Mandelson in confidence to a third party, Brown asked him why he hadn't backed him. He replied that he was not opposing Brown but that 'we had to think things through carefully'; Brown had argued that if *they* were both in agreement, Blair would always take their advice. Mandelson then said that his loyalty to Brown was not in question, but that he was not going 'to get into some sort of alliance to outmanoeuvre Tony', at which point, he insisted Brown replied: 'Choose for yourself' – or words to that effect.

Mandelson dated the breach in his close bond with Brown, not from the leadership contest in the early summer, but from that conversation in September. This can not, at most, have been more than partially correct. Relations had already been under severe strain at least once in the summer: while Mandelson was staying with friends on holiday in Cape Cod, he and Brown had had a furious and highly emotional transatlantic telephone conversation in the aftermath of a *Sunday Times* story on August 7 speculating that Tony Blair might be considering a long-term cut in income tax to 15p. In the first of what would be an endless series of briefing wars over the next four years, Charlie Whelan informed two journalists that Mandelson had been responsible for the story, and that Brown was deeply unsympathetic to such a proposal. In fact the paper had taken a punt, relying on several sources, Mandelson among them, who had refused to rule out Blair's support for a proposal by Frank Field for such an income tax reduction. It was true that Blair wanted to be the first tax cutting Labour leader; to attack Field's proposal might well have been to suggest otherwise. But it was not a planted story. Nevertheless one of the journalists, Patrick Wintour, thought Whelan's attribution to Mandelson interesting enough to mention it in a column for the *Guardian* a week later[1]; it was after all the first sign of a fissure within the modernisers' ranks, indicating the beginnings of a Brown-Mandelson, or even more sensationally, a Brown-Blair split. If that gained currency it would dwarf the impact of a speculative Sunday newspaper piece about Labour's, as yet unformed, tax plans. For all the traumas of the leadership crisis, there had been little, if any, public evidence at this stage that the modernising trio – men who had discussed every aspect of politics together for six years, could fall out on an important issue of policy. Mandelson was horrified and enraged at what he saw as Whelan's treacherous troublemaking. He complained bitterly to Brown and warned that if Whelan kept this up he would drive the two men apart. There was a row, at times poisonous; it was indeed becoming clear that it would be all too easy to drive a wedge between Brown and Mandelson, as Mandelson had been convinced Whelan had been trying to do.

Nevertheless it had seemed to Mandelson, until the Chewton Glen conference in September, that the relationship was reparable; it was severely threatened but not yet fully ruptured. But Mandelson now interpreted Brown as demanding a degree of personal loyalty which would outweigh, in relatively rare moments of dispute, his loyalty to the leader. One explanation may be that Brown, having made the supreme sacrifice of yielding the leadership to Blair was genuinely shocked, at a human level, at how complete Mandelson's switch of fealty had been; but to Mandelson it seemed that if Brown had simply not adjusted to the reality, however painful: there could only be one leader. Mandelson may well have been correct to reserve the right to disagree with Brown in tripartite discussion with the leader. But the great Machiavellian had behaved in rather an un-Machiavellian way. Had Mandelson simply agreed at this point to back Brown then the next two and a half years might have gone more smoothly than they did. Indeed, when Mandelson told Blair about the conversation about a year later, Blair suggested that this is what he should have done.

In the meantime there was work to do. It was at Chewton Glen that, as Philip Gould recalls, Blair told him 'that the party conference must rebuild New Labour. It is time we gave the party some electric shock treatment.'[2] And this meant replacing Clause Four of Labour's ancient constitution. Arthur Henderson, the Labour Party Secretary when the commitment to 'common ownership of the means of production, distribution and exchange' had been drafted by the Webbs in 1917, was already regretting it eight years later.[3] But it had long been a numinous symbol of Labour's socialism; to Blair this made its removal all the more attractive since it would be a correspondingly symbolic break with Labour's socialist past.

To those more embedded in Labour culture, however, this still seemed a dangerous move. Legend had it that, shortly after Mandelson took over at Walworth Road in 1985, he had deliberately tried to remove the famous wording from the back of membership cards; the cards had been pulped and replaced when the 'amendment' was discovered. In fact it had been a printing error, though Mandelson was happy to leave the cards as they were. It was Larry Whitty who insisted on reprinting them. With more Labour Party history flowing through his veins than Blair, Mandelson had a more potent sense of how the struggle to remove Clause Four had derailed and distracted Gaitskell's leadership after the 1959 election. The same was true of Roger Liddle, whom Mandelson rang to consult while Liddle, by now in effect a Labour 'sleeper' whose heart was no longer in Paddy Ashdown's party, was attending the Liberal Democrat conference. Mandelson nevertheless quickly became a convert in precisely the same manner as Alastair Campbell – best summed up in a speech by the MP Brian Wilson:

'My first reaction was why? My second reaction was why not?' Like Campbell, Mandelson soon saw that this would be the ultimate 'story' of Labour's modernisation. As it proved to be.

He became firmly in favour of the change while Blair himself, as the conference approached, was ostensibly still undecided on whether to go ahead. According to Campbell,

> Peter Hyman and I were working on the speech and Tony still hadn't decided whether to include it. Peter and Philip [Gould] certainly came round at one point. [Tony] was saying things like: 'I'm really going to have to take a decision on this.' It was a big problem writing a speech without knowing. On the one hand it had to be a very very good speech in other ways if you weren't going to carry the Clause Four point. On the other hand if you included Clause Four that took care of the news for you. I think actually that tension made it a better speech; it was a very modernising speech.[4]

Campbell and Blair were still having 'circular conversations' about the risks and merits of ditching Clause Four as they drove from Manchester Airport to Blackpool on the Saturday before the conference.

Although he was by now an enthusiast, and for all the wild rumours that he had written the speech, Mandelson had little, if any, hand in the final text of the momentous announcement. He was certainly not a great speechwriter – a point made by Campbell in one of his last *Today* columns.[5] He did not have Campbell's tabloid-honed brilliance with words or soundbites and, Campbell thought, was better as an amender of existing texts than an author of original ones: 'Peter is always good about not getting in the way. He didn't thrust himself into the writing process, unless he was making a bigger political point.'

This is just what happened in March 1995 when there was a draft of the new Clause Four. Mandelson became much more interventionist, regarding it as vital that the text should be right. His scribbles, made for Blair's benefit, on a draft of the text are revealing; they are all distinctively *New* Labour. 'Solidarity, liberty, and equality' was dismissed as an 'old-fashioned mantra'; he suggested instead 'rights and responsibilities' or 'duty to others'. The final text itself was a compromise, but one which removed, as he had suggested, the word 'equality'. The relevant section would read: '. . . where the rights we enjoy reflect the duties we owe and where we live together, freely, in a spirit of solidarity, tolerance and respect.' This change was highly significant: part of Roy Hattersley's charge would be precisely that New Labour had finally abandoned the Croslandite adherence to equality. Coincidentally, and without knowing about Mandelson's hand in the Clause Four text earlier in the year, in late August Hattersley badgered him on the very subject of equality over lunch in Robert Harris's garden in Berkshire, saying, 'I'm not talking about equality of opportunity. I'm talking about equality of outcome.' It was, by all accounts, quite an uncomfortable conversation.[6]

Mandelson went on to suggest – also successfully – excluding a disparaging reference to 'private profit' from the paragraph on the economy. A reference to the fight against crime in the paragraph on a 'just society' which, he argued, would 'make it meaningful to voters', was vetoed, however. He also tried – and failed – to prevent the new clause singling out 'trade unions' as allies with whom the party would work, preferring the more general 'to co-operate with others, at home and abroad, who share our values'. But he succeeded in rewriting the international section, which in a late draft spoke of the 'peaceful resolution' of conflict. Scrawling in the margin: 'Won't a Blair government ever go to war?' he proposed: 'We are committed to the defence and security of the British people and to co-operating in European and international (UN and Commonwealth?) institutions to secure peace, freedom, democracy, economic security and environmental protection for all the peoples of the world' – an amendment which was incorporated almost verbatim. At the end he added a characteristically no-nonsense note, by implication reminding Blair that the new clause was not, ultimately, for party members: 'Remember, this Constitution – suitably poetic and Jerusalem-like – is meant to get ordinary people to understand easily what we're about and to vote for us.'

The replacement of Clause Four was an unalloyed triumph – not least because Blair's campaigning zeal up and down the country persuaded the party not only to change it but, in the end, to *want* to change it. Thoughts could now turn to election planning, for which Blair could count on his two leading strategists, Gordon Brown and Peter Mandelson.

The problem was to get them to work together. By the beginning of 1995 relations between Mandelson and Brown were already at a low ebb. Brown had once again proved, in the first few months of Blair's leadership, what a commanding figure he was. He was the architect of a traumatic defeat for the Major government on December 6, when it lost by 319–311 the vote on a Labour amendment on VAT on fuel, ensuring it would not be increased to 17.5 per cent. It was a triumph. The Opposition could justly claim to have saved money for millions of voters, not least pensioners. Even those who had subscribed to the notion that Robin Cook might somehow become Shadow Chancellor (which was always fanciful since Blair had never doubted for a moment Brown's indispensability in his present role) were silenced for good. But below the surface, Brown was also troubled and restless. Just how painful his sacrifice had been in 1994 did not fully become public until 1997 and the publication of a biography written by Paul Routledge with Brown's 'full co-operation,' as the dust-jacket boasted. The book blamed Mandelson for inspiring favourable press coverage for Blair almost from the moment of John Smith's death, while Brown mourned (a claim examined in the previous chapter). It also cited Blair's 'closest advisers' as asserting that by running for the leadership at all Blair had breached a 'secret pact' stipulating that of the two of them, Brown would be the leadership candidate when the moment came.[7]

The *assumption*, in 1992, that Brown was the natural leader of the two men, was certainly not overtly revisited between Brown and Mandelson, or Brown and Blair, during the 1992–4 period. Mandelson denied the existence of such a pact; and how much force it would have had, given the constantly shifting political circumstances, is doubtful anyway. But that mattered less than what Brown thought. Brown continued to discuss everything freely and frequently with Blair; but he was much less willing to do so in the presence of others close to Blair, or to consult them himself. This did not only apply to Mandelson, but it did apply to him more than to anyone else. The three-way relationship which had sustained the Labour modernisers since 1988 was over. One side of one of the most remarkable relationships in British political history – a fraternal 'love triangle' as one close observer had once described it – had been smashed. Or if not smashed, it had been turned into a triangle of an entirely different, though more familiar kind, in which comradeship had been wholly eclipsed by rivalry. Brown in particular resented Mandelson as an alternative source of influence and advice to Blair. Equally, Mandelson felt angry and pained by what he saw as Brown's unreasonable rejection of his own role.

According to one of his closest members of staff, Blair himself would repeatedly, 'sometimes several times a day', ask, 'Why, oh why, can't my two best people get on with each other?' Although the troubles between Brown and Mandelson did not fully surface publicly until May 1996, they had certainly worried Blair since the turn of the year in 1994–5. The first real clash came over the structure of the campaign. While Mandelson willingly ceded overall strategic command to Brown, Blair was determined that he should nevertheless have a key role. Jonathan Powell, Blair's chief of staff, used all his considerable tact and diplomatic skill to bring about an agreement, but he could not prevent a prolonged power struggle between Mandelson and Brown over just how key this role would be. Blair, with commendable lack of regard for the bureaucratic niceties, had simply made it clear that he wanted one committee, probably meeting weekly, to consider the long-term strategy for the general election; and a second variant on this, meeting on a daily basis, considering day-to-day media tactics for attacking the government – much like the so-called 'Number Twelve Committee' which had already been set up by John Major's ministers. Mandelson, along with Campbell, Jonathan Powell, a senior whip to direct tactics in parliament, and the as yet unappointed Communications Director, would sit on both committees, but Brown would chair them. But the leader reckoned without a byzantine, though probably inevitable, argument between Brown and Mandelson over the chains of command.

Fighting his corner on 31 January in a memorandum to Blair, Mandelson made one undoubtedly powerful point. After agreeing with an earlier warning from Powell 'that we are dangerously late in commencing the detailed planning of our general election campaign', he added that plans had been further advanced in both the previous parliaments. He then continued: 'It is very important that immediate political pressures and strategy consideration do not squeeze out longer-term election planning. In 1987 the surprising strength of our three-week election campaign following the awful buffeting of the preceding six months was due to the separation of long-term planning from short-run handling.' He proposed a separate 'election planning group' preparing 'technical papers for the election itself' comprising 'around half a dozen individuals with expertise from your office and Walworth Road and outsiders whom it would otherwise be difficult to use. If I were to chair this group it would help to legitimise my role and membership of the strategy committee and presentation to the Leader's Committee.'[8]

The argument raged on throughout the spring and summer, so much so that at one point Mandelson wrote to Blair suggesting that he gracefully withdraw. Saying that he had been 'thinking hard' about 'my position in our weird and wonderful firmament', he added:

> Whatever the long-term prospect of Gordon reconciling himself to my role in relation to you, I do not believe this is going to happen now. Forcing it is going to aggravate the situation. I fear it will produce further confrontations between the two of you, which are very destructive to your future relationship with him, which is the pivotal one for the success of your government.

On the struggle over his own election planning role Mandelson indicated he was ready to concede to Brown.

> Whatever the practical difficulties of having him in both the Shadow Chancellor and Campaign Manager roles, I accept your judgement that there is no obvious alternative in the Shadow Cabinet. [Mandelson was not in the Shadow Cabinet.] It is therefore absolutely essential to make it work. We will have his team doing this and the reality is that they will have to work together with your team. Gordon knows this and I am sure will make it happen . . .

Mandelson also touched on a problem which went further than his relations with Brown: that of being part of the inner leadership circle while holding down a relatively junior front bench job.

> From your point of view, it is difficult and embarrassing to cast the 'leader's little helper' in way that is acceptable to everybody else. But I think neither of us has confronted the barrier to this of my being an MP, a new one, with all the sensitivities and hierarchical implications of this . . . There is no question of me ceasing to act as your friend and adviser. I am always thinking of you. I will do anything you ask of me. You are the most important thing to have happened for our party and the country. But we have to face up to the fact that we cannot go on like this.

It would now, Mandelson suggested, be better for him to pursue his career in a 'more normal way'. Not for the first or last time, Blair patiently talked through Mandelson's concerns, persuaded him to stay in the team, and continued the daunting search for a way round the problem.

What the episode had illustrated was Blair's determination to retain a central role, in both his and the party's interests, for both men, whatever the differences between them. As in the leadership contest, so in the larger one ahead. But he could not thaw a personal relationship which remained, at best, icy for much of the two years leading up to the election campaign itself. And this was far from academic: throughout this period there were frequent meetings between Brown, Mandelson, Campbell and Blair, usually along with Jonathan Powell. There would be issues of substance on which Blair's two moderniser colleagues differed: whether to impose a top rate of tax; whether to end child benefit for the parents of sixteen- to eighteen-year-olds; whether – as Mandelson constantly urged, reinforced, and to some extent prompted, by Philip Gould – to present a clearer 'economic message' to the electorate. But all these could have been resolved much more amicably if the once extraordinarily close bond between the two men had not been shattered by the series of events in 1994. This was not business, as Robert Harris would put it in an *Evening Standard* article three years later; it was personal.

321

At least some of these tensions were at work over the unhappy eleven-month saga of Joy Johnson's appointment, in February 1995, to the job of Director of Communications. A legendarily energetic and tough political producer (by now political news editor at the BBC), Johnson had been a constant – and engaging – presence at every big event since the late eighties. With cropped blonde hair, her face slightly weatherbeaten by hours spent with TV crews on doorsteps in every kind of climate, she was well known for her fearless technique, adopted from her American journalistic hero Sam Donaldson of ABC News; the shouted question, often from behind a security barrier, as a politician arrived or left a meeting, designed to turn a mere photo opportunity into a soundbite which would make a story. She had also transformed the BBC's live coverage of party conferences, interspersing it with lively interviews with senior politicians, transcribed and released to journalists within minutes, and frequently providing them with a fresh story line. She was also a committed Labour supporter and a particular fan of Gordon Brown, whom she would have liked to see as leader after John Smith's death. She was well to the left of the New Labour leadership, but eager to see the party win.

Although she was proposed by Brown and Charlie Whelan, Blair decreed that she should, as she put it, be 'vetted' by Mandelson. The conversation – wary, but quite candid on both sides – took place in Mandelson's parliamentary office at 7 Millbank. Mandelson said that he was a bit 'nervous' of her; she replied that this was ridiculous, since he knew where she was 'coming from'. They chatted about personalities rather than policy – 'which', said Johnson, 'is very Peter'. Mandelson made no effort to block the appointment which, with Blair's approval, sailed through the NEC. Looking back much later, Johnson felt that she had encountered difficulties from the beginning. She had a 'stale honeymoon' – disagreeing quite early on with Mandelson over whether she should be responsible, as he had been, for briefing newspaper correspondents as well as the broadcasters. He thought she should; she thought she should leave the newspapers to David Hill, a much more familiar figure in the lobby. By her own account, she also tended to ignore repeated requests, sometimes from Blair, to consult Mandelson, except when it was absolutely necessary to get his backing; she wanted to do the job, as she had done every other job, in her own way.[9]

The moment which infuriated her most, however, came on 4 July 1995, the day that John Major won the leadership contest called to face down his Eurosceptic critics. She was left to fume in the outer office while Blair, Campbell, Mandelson and Brown discussed what line to take on an event they had had ample time to plan for. She objected to being excluded from the inner sanctum, of course. But she had a strong point for, as they deliberated, Major's cohorts were taking to the airwaves to proclaim that he was out of danger – even though the majority he got was much narrower than that previously deemed 'safe' by many Tories. However short-lived, the Tories had a public relations triumph over the supposed masters of soundbites and spin. Although Brown could brief her on what had taken place at meetings she had not attended, Johnson regarded this incident not only as a needless failure of communications, but as a telling sign that she did not enjoy the full confidence of the leader. According to Alastair Campbell, Johnson 'was outside storming around and Anji [Hunter] was saying, "This is how it works." Tony quite liked her but she didn't understand that we would make the decision and then she would get her instructions to put it out. She just felt it was Peter and me keeping her out.'[10]

Mandelson was certainly pivotal in her eventual departure, deciding, according to one insider at the time, 'that she was impossible and had to be got rid of, [and] Gordon [was] resisting that, and that was a tremendous source of bitterness and dispute ... The Joy Johnson thing figured very large in that period because Peter's position was that he would not ... have anything to do with the campaign as long as Joy Johnson was involved.' But Mandelson was not alone in wanting her out. Some of her staff were openly hostile; and Blair eventually sanctioned her departure with a pay-off of a year's salary – close to £60,000.

Meanwhile the ten-month wrangle over Brown's and Mandelson's role in election planning was finally resolved in October 1995. Brown initially declined to confirm a draft plan giving Mandelson his election planning group and membership of the strategy committee on the grounds that he had not been given prior notice. It was the day of Mandelson's first ever appearance at the dispatch box in the Commons in his new role as junior civil service spokesman and he left the meeting early to prepare his speech, in a rage and fuming that if the new structure could not be agreed 'they can't agree anything.' But by the evening Brown had agreed. The structural dispute had been, at least formally, settled, though not as precisely as Mandelson had wanted, since it would now report directly to Brown's strategy committee. But Mandelson had finally got his general election Planning Group. And the representative on it from Gordon Brown's office was not Charlie Whelan, with whom relations had become impossible during the leadership campaign, but his oldest and closest friend from the mid-1980s, Sue Nye.

But while the practical conflict was settled, this did nothing to resolve what was an outstandingly dysfunctional relationship between the two men, given that they shared a common purpose. At meetings, Mandelson would complain, Brown frequently behaved as if he wasn't there. If, indeed, he responded at all to points made by Mandelson, he addressed his remarks solely to Blair, or, more time-consumingly, intimated that he would discuss a particular issue with him later, when Mandelson and Campbell were not present. Brown, for his part, was apparently worried that, if he had persuaded Blair on a particular course of action, Mandelson might then perversely take a contrary view just for the sake of it. Valiant attempts were made at various times to heal the rift – by Donald Dewar, Michael Wills and Sue Nye – though to little avail. This was a source of continual frustration to Blair and Campbell. Nor was it all one-sided. One occasional observer of Mandelson's behaviour at larger meetings, chaired by Brown, said he had 'got away with murder in his acid and contemptuous asides'.[11] Mandelson, for his part, remained convinced that Brown could or would not accept his own independent advisory role. At one point in the spring of 1995 Mandelson had offered Brown a remarkable pact: before important strategy meetings with Blair, he suggested, they should meet to agree a line in advance. On the rare occasions when they disagreed, they would both inform Blair that this was the case. But Mandelson would undertake not to sit through a meeting, let Brown persuade Blair of a particular course of action, and then go behind his back to persuade Blair of the opposite course. Draper, and others close to Mandelson, even attempted to draw up written parameters for the Brown-Mandelson relationship, rather like a set of school rules. Mandelson, they proposed, should be fully involved in the 'formulation and implementation' of strategy, should supervise general election planning, and should be an 'open' member – no more 'Bobby', in other words – of relevant committees and working groups. Brown would have the 'final say' on putting recommendations to Tony Blair on strategy; Mandelson, for his part, would not contradict him provided he was fully consulted. He would have the final say on (nuts and bolts) election planning, provided Brown was kept fully informed. Mandelson would be given a senior ministerial post below cabinet rank and then, after '12–18 months', be brought into the Cabinet on the model of Tony Crosland and Roy Jenkins. Finally, the back-of-the-envelope 'treaty' predicted, in passing, that the Blair-Mandelson relationship would become, at least on day-to-day matters, more distant once Labour was in power, concluding: 'Gordon acknowledges that Tony is bound to want Peter's advice as a trusted friend. But Tony will never act on that advice without first consulting Gordon on matters that are clearly within his responsibilities. Peter acknowledges the centrality of the Blair-Brown relationship to the success of government and that it must flourish.'

These tentative proposals were more significant for what they showed about the problem than in establishing a solution. The demarcation between election planning and strategy, and Mandelson's role in both, had been agreed in October. But Brown was not prepared to agree to the further formula on strategic advice to Blair put to him by Mandelson. Perhaps he was right; human feelings of rivalry, jealousy and betrayal cannot easily be regulated in such a schematic way. Nevertheless the failure of this initiative meant that the – to outsiders seemingly unstoppable – modernisation project continued, at least until the eve of the election, to drag behind it 'this great boulder' (as Mandelson put it at the time) of his ruptured relations with the Shadow Chancellor.

The issues of substance which divided Brown and Mandelson were real but by no means as many as the chronic tensions between them might have suggested. On the most serious shadow cabinet split of 1996, for example – Robin Cook's widely publicised objections to Brown's 'welfare to work' scheme, and the stipulation that young people refusing a place in it would be denied benefit – Mandelson was steadfast in his backing of Brown. One difference was over Brown's plans to end child benefit for the parents of sixteen- to eighteen-year–olds, and to tax it for those on higher incomes (a level which he finally proposed should be fixed at £100,000). Brown considered this a 'tough choice' which would lend credibility to Labour's election programme. He may have been right; it would certainly have given the future Chancellor much more fiscal leeway after the election. But Mandelson, among others, was extremely wary about launching it before the election, because it might have helped the Tories, being a potentially unpopular policy. Just how unpopular was demonstrated in research commissioned by Mandelson during the summer of 1996 from the pollster Deborah Mattinson; he had the unpalatable job of outlining these findings to Brown, then on holiday in Cape Cod. The policy was not, finally, included in the manifesto as a firm proposal. Another source of conflict was the question of what Labour's 'economic message' to the voters should be. Brown's intellectual talents as a policy-maker were unrivalled; but Mandelson, armed with findings from Philip Gould, regularly complained that his failure to distil a simple 'story' about the economy was confusing voters.

A third issue was the question of a new top rate of tax. From 1995 on Brown was certainly in favour of this, and Blair instinctively against it. Mandelson, with the strong backing of Philip Gould, opposed it because he was convinced, like Blair, that it would send to the voters a subliminal signal that Labour was still essentially a tax-raising party, as well as alienating potential business supporters. The argument was nevertheless a finely balanced one. A new top rate would have symbolically underpinned, as perhaps no other policy did, Labour's claim, to be the party of 'the many and not the few'. It would have made it easy to pay for the agreed goal of a new 10p starting rate to help those on the lowest incomes. And it would have gone some way to blunting the edge of the liberal left's unease about whether Labour was abandoning its redistributive principles. Moreover, public opinion was perhaps more divided than Philip Gould would later admit. The conventional opinion polling – which regularly showed as many as 90 per cent in favour of a new higher-rate tax band at £100,000 – was not reliable since it was matched by one showing that around 60 per cent also thought that if Labour increased taxes for the highest paid it would increase them for everybody else as well. But Gould also said that 'throughout 1995 and 1996 I conducted regular focus groups on this issue and the findings were always the same: people were wary of an increase in the top rate.'[12] Yet in October 1995 he was reporting privately that the 'focus groups were ambivalent: two groups thought a higher rate tax at £100,000 would penalise the rich, and they felt this strongly. However the other two groups were equally confident that it was fair.'

But on tax – and indeed on other policy issues – Mandelson was only one of the influences weighing in the scales against Brown. Another was Paul Keating, who told Blair during his 1995 trip to Australia at Rupert Murdoch's invitation that 'no party in the English-speaking world' in modern times had won an election promising to put up taxes.[13] And, Blair inferred, the British Labour Party, because of its tax-raising past, was particularly unlikely to win an election in such circumstances.

These were important issues, some of which went to the heart of how far Labour was prepared, as Brown wanted, to promote a redistributionist future. Moreover much of Brown's irritation that Mandelson might be influencing tax policy was hardly irrational. He was, after all, the Shadow Chancellor. But it was impossible to escape the conclusion that they could have been resolved with much less bitterness, if there had not been more emotional factors, rooted in the traumatic events of 1994. Brown's feelings of betrayal by Mandelson were strong enough for him to resist several concerted efforts by Blair to get him to work normally with Mandelson. In Mandelson's view Brown could not accept that 'Being Peter' meant that Mandelson's duty was to provide Blair with independent advice. Yet Mandelson appears to have been unable on occasions to contain his feelings of frustration and anger at what he saw as his rejection by Brown. He even subsequently explained his decision to approve Joy Johnson's appointment, which he subsequently regretted and helped to reverse, as an attempt to earn Brown's favour, like a child seeking endorsement from a parent. According to one insider at the time, 'If Gordon was nice to him Peter would come round and it would all be fine for a time.' But at a meeting on Thursday 9 May 1996, when he felt slighted yet again by Brown, something snapped.

The tensions which now came to a head were wholly personal. So little did the crisis have to do with policy that, three years later, few could remember whether the row had been about child benefit or some other issue of the moment. Feeling slighted yet again by Brown, and then even more so by Blair's backing for Brown – which Mandelson believed owed more to Brown's seniority than to the strength of his argument – Mandelson, by his own subsequent account, 'went nuclear, lost all grace'.

What happened next became a matter of dispute. There were at least half a dozen people in the meeting, Jonathan Powell as usual sitting behind the desk taking notes and the others, including Blair, ranged on sofas and chairs round the leader's office. Those in the room, including Blair, thought that Mandelson had stormed out, slamming the door behind him. He was later adamant that he had actually been bleeped by someone at Millbank, and had gone out to return the call, inadvertently allowing the door to slam behind him. In a sense it hardly mattered, because he did not return, leaving his colleagues temporarily silent and nonplussed. Still furious, though outwardly betraying little sign of it, he kept a lunch appointment with *The Times* journalist Mary-Ann Sieghart, and then flew off to Prague to an international conference organised by the North Atlantic Initiative, attended by, among others, Lady Thatcher and her former foreign affairs private secretary Sir Charles Powell, the *Telegraph* proprietor Conrad Black, and Henry Kissinger's speechwriter Peter Rodman.

This somewhat right-wing and distinctly Atlanticist conference was a curious gathering for a senior member of the Labour front bench to be attending. But Mandelson's presence had been sanctioned by Blair as part of his relentless consensus-building across the political spectrum. Also present was Sir Charles's highly extrovert wife Carla, by now already a good friend but, as another Mandelson friend noted at the time, 'perhaps not the most sedative of influences', given the circumstances. In fact, he gave only the barest details of the row to Carla Powell, who, along with her husband and Mandelson, was staying with the French ambassador (a friend of the Powells), though she would later remember him saying gloomily, when she asked him about it, that the problem could probably only be solved if Brown became Prime Minister.

*En route* to Prague, however, Mandelson had written a letter, dated 9 May, resigning as election manager at Millbank and, in effect, as a member of Blair's inner circle:

> I am very sorry that your meeting ended as it did, but I think we have to recognise that you and I have reached the end of the road. I am more than willing to carry on the general election planning if you wish – although we'll reach the same brick wall on that too, eventually – and I will be very sorry not to play my day to day role here in Millbank. All I can say is that Margaret [McDonagh] is excellent, the systems are broadly in place and the whole operation is in a very different state from the one I started with. I hope you don't think that *amour propre* is the root of my problem. I have long gone beyond that. But I felt greatly let down by you this morning and embarrassed. I do not want to be in that position again. Needless to say, I will always be available to you in any circumstance to help and advise. Operationally though, I think we have reached the glass ceiling. I wish your life and situation were simpler and I wish things could have worked out differently with our arrangements, Love as ever, Peter.

At the weekend Mandelson appeared, to those in Prague, to be his normal self. At the British ambassador's residence he had his first and only encounter with Margaret Thatcher. It was a brief and slightly stiff meeting. Mandelson said afterwards that he found her 'rather forbidding and unapproachable' and thought she was rather nervous about his presence – though he told Robert Harris later that month that the baroness, excited as usual to be in a rapidly changing eastern Europe, had impressed him with the power of her belief: 'Why can't we believe like that?' he asked. On the Saturday evening the Powells, Rodman and the journalist Anne McElvoy left the official mayor's reception early and wandered, at Mandelson's suggestion, into a disco, where the Prince of Darkness so thrilled McElvoy with his dancing prowess that she wrote about it in the *Spectator*: 'Before long we were the John Travolta and Olivia

Newton-John of the gathering. The member for Hartlepool's taut thigh muscles were locked behind mine as we flung this way and that . . .' Not every member of Labour's leadership team was anti-fun, she concluded.[14]

Back in London, however, his colleagues were not having so much fun. Blair would have been angry about Mandelson's walkout even if he had not faced difficulties on other fronts. But the press the previous weekend had made Blair even more sensitive than usual to stories about Labour splits. Mandelson had been staying with the Harrises and they had driven over to film producer David Puttnam's house in Wiltshire, where Blair was celebrating his forty-third birthday, to discover that the *Mail on Sunday* had what promised to be a big story: Chris Smith, the Social Security spokesman, it claimed, was deeply opposed to Brown's plans for radical changes to child benefit.[15] Since Blair and Mandelson were harbouring doubts of their own about the plan the topic could hardly have been more combustible. It was time for some Mandelson spin. Before Mandelson got out his mobile telephone, however, Blair told him that it was crucial that not even a shadow of division should appear between himself and the Shadow Chancellor. He then continued chatting to Puttnam's guests as they sipped champagne in the garden – but with half an ear open to Mandelson's attempt to smooth over the split in a conversation with the *Mail on Sunday*. Oddly, the story might have provided a respite in the difficult relationship between Mandelson and Brown. Brown telephoned Mandelson at Harris's house the following day – one of the few occasions he had spoken to him voluntarily in the past eighteen months – and the two men agreed that the problem over child benefit needed a speedy resolution.

But it was not to be. Not only did Mandelson cause serious consternation through his departure from the meeting on Thursday but the tensions between Brown and Mandelson had finally – and coincidentally – become public. On 11 May, the Saturday morning of Mandelson's trip to Prague, Philip Webster, *The Times*'s political editor, led his paper with a report, clearly well sourced, saying that Blair was making considerable efforts to resolve the chronic split between Brown and Mandelson. This was a sensational development since, while the friction had been evident to insiders for many months, the modernisers had still widely been assumed by outsiders – including many senior figures in the party – to be a wholly cohesive force. More serious still, from Mandelson's point of view, he was understandably, given his conduct two days earlier, the prime suspect as the source of Webster's story.

Blair subsequently pinpointed this as his worst moment yet since taking over as leader. Nor would he accept that Brown was exclusively to blame, telling Mandelson later that it was 'six of one and half a dozen of the other'. In any case, Blair had already made it clear to Mandelson on several occasions that he had to suppress his emotions in response to what he saw as Brown's persistent refusal to accept him as a colleague; he would be risking a place in the sun if he did not 'make it work'. Blair now wrote Mandelson a sombre letter: this was 'indeed a serious situation', he said; much as Mandelson had been his 'rock and comforter', the team was now in a 'dangerous' plight and 'simply cannot continue in this way'. While he freely acknowledged that it could be very difficult to work with Brown, he had come to a 'settled view' that there was 'culpability' on both sides. Both Brown and Mandelson were 'more desirous of victory over each other than of trying to make it work', and that he could not tolerate walkouts, or 'irresponsible' stories like that in the *Times*. He told Mandelson: 'We are not players in some Greek tragedy', and pointed out, 'We have one overriding responsibility to deliver an election victory, and though it may seem pious, it is just not fair to all those people who really want such a victory and are working for it, to be casualties of some Titanic but ultimately irrelevant personality feud'. He added: 'Have you any conception of how despairing it is for me when the two people that have been closest to me for more than a decade, and who in their different ways are the most brilliant political minds of their generation will not lay aside personal animosity and help me win?' He had no wish to lose one of his closest friends, but if the situation could not change then it would have to end. The subliminal sub-text was stark: unless Mandelson could reach an accommodation with Brown, Blair would indeed have to accept his 'resignation'.

Having received Blair's letter on his return from Prague on the Sunday, Mandelson immediately wrote back a second letter which, while fluent, was scarcely less emotional than the first. Despite a 'fascinating' time in Prague, he had been 'troubled and unhappy as you would expect'. He felt wronged – by Blair as well as by Brown – but he was still 'desperate to put things right'. Nobody in Brown's circle had been able to suggest to him how he could repair relations between them.

> Sue [Nye] describes it as a war of attrition and Michael [Wills] says Gordon is 'determined to kill me before I destroy him.' Destroy him for what, to be replaced by whom? As long as I enjoy *your* confidence and patronage why should I be bothered by what happens to him? Am I going to prosper from the rise of Robin Cook? It's simply ludicrous. All that is happening is, as a result of the situation with Gordon, I am losing your support, my career is being hampered, I am getting harmful publicity and I am creating further enemies for myself ... Nobody, you included, I suspect, thinks Gordon is going to change and therefore, as the number two, I have to go. You are too nice and too considerate towards me to say this, I know, so I had better say it for you. You have to do whatever you think is right for the party to win and, in everything you decide, I shall make it as easy for you as I possibly can ... Peter.

Wills, who has continued to be close to Brown, while remaining on good terms with Mandelson, had indeed taken that view of the Brown–Mandelson relationship at the time. He suggested to one friend in the period before the election that the two politicians were 'like scorpions in a bottle'. Only one of them would crawl out alive.

Of all the flare-ups that occurred between John Smith's death in May 1994 and the general election three years later, this was the one which came closest to fracturing the leadership cadre at the top of New Labour. But once again Blair used all his skill and forbearance to solve the problem. As Mandelson, Derek Draper and Benjamin Wegg-Prosser (his quiet spoken, bespectacled twenty-one-year-old researcher) sat gloomily down to dinner at Roger Liddle's house in Kennington, Blair telephoned Mandelson. It was the leader of the Labour Party, reinforcing the message of the letter that Mandelson had received earlier in the day. At the dinner table the crisis was almost the sole topic of conversation. The conclusion was that 'Peter would have to keep agreeing with Gordon; that was what Tony wanted him to do.' If this could be made to work, the crisis would pass.

Blair summoned Brown and Mandelson to a meeting in his office the day after Mandelson's return from Prague. By now the Webster story in *The Times* had created a flurry of speculation about the Brown–Mandelson relationship which was a good deal more solidly based than even those doing the speculating could possibly realise. On one point Mandelson protested: he had not been primarily responsible for Webster's story. Webster had been unaware of the crisis the previous Thursday, when he wrote it. Mandelson insisted to Blair that his only exchange with Webster had been about ten days earlier, when Webster had put it to him in typical 'lobby conversation' that he had heard things were pretty 'dire' between Brown and him, and he had not demurred. But he had no reason to expect a front-page story in *The Times*. Conscientiously Webster had sourced his account with all sides, including Alastair Campbell.

But Mandelson's walkout, and even more the blaze of publicity which followed Webster's story, had at least helped to bring matters to a head. After a series of well-publicised meetings Brown and Mandelson agreed to try and prevent such crises occurring again. In an interview with the *New Statesman* the following week Mandelson was lavish in his praise of Brown: 'He is the most creative and original mind in British politics today, which is why he will make a very great Chancellor. I do not mean to compare him to Nigel Lawson in all things but he would have the same intellectual dominance over his colleagues as Lawson enjoyed at the height of his powers.'

Neither Brown's deep suspicions of Mandelson, nor Mandelson's complex feelings towards Brown, abated in the months to come. But Blair's team remained intact. The leader's prodigious efforts to keep Mandelson in his service had paid off. They were a testament to Blair's determination to ensure that Mandelson continued 'being Peter', at once faithfully protecting his interests, and giving his own unique brand of independent advice, on public opinion, on the press, and on what the party would and wouldn't accept. But the incident had also demonstrated something else. Despite the huge value Blair put on his political antennae, Mandelson was clearly still the junior partner of the trio. To Mandelson, it seemed that the more he provided what Blair truly valued – independent advice in the leader's own interests – the more he alienated Brown. But while Blair had made heroic, and unsuccessful attempts to persuade Brown to work more closely with Mandelson, it was the Shadow Chancellor who would be truly indispensable in Government as well as in opposition. Blair had demonstrated, subtly but decisively, that if he was ever forced to choose between his two closest lieutenants, Mandelson would have to be the one to go.

# CHAPTER SEVENTEEN

## *The Joys of Carla*

It was during this period that Mandelson's range and network of contacts, and with it his social, or quasi-social, life, had gradually begun to change. One or two of his oldest friends, particularly those who had known him in the seventies or early eighties, would ruefully contrast his fortieth birthday party with his forty-third as symbolising the new social milieu Mandelson had entered during the years in between. Mandelson had always celebrated birthdays – and not only his own – in some style. He frequently gave parties – either in his flat in Kennington or, for occasional, more formal dinners, at Bigwood Road – in the late seventies. In February 1991 he, Julie Hall and Colin Byrne had thrown a fortieth birthday party for Gordon Brown at Doughty Mews, attended by the Blairs; here, too, the Kinnocks had been chief guests at Mandelson's thirty-eighth birthday. Colin Byrne's rather glamorous girlfriend of the time, an actress called Samantha, dressed up in Marilyn Monroe-style sequins and boa and sang for Mandelson, now happily selected in Hartlepool, 'Happy Birthday, Mr Candidate.' Byrne recalled that Kinnock's eyes had 'nearly popped out'.[1]

To be fair, Mandelson's fortieth birthday party in October 1993 was a much larger affair than the forty-third. Nor was it exactly spartan. It took place at Lloyd Square, just round the corner from his flat in Wilmington Square, in the home of Gavyn Davies, leading City economist and long-time adviser to Labour's front bench, and his wife Sue Nye. Neil and Glenys Kinnock came and stayed for the evening, the enthusiastic Kinnock being outshone on the dance floor only by an apparently indefatigable Mandelson. Women queued up to partner the birthday boy, who seemingly never stopped whirling around, patches of sweat showing through his shirt. And there was a sprinkling of favoured journalists, including Polly Toynbee, who later described how he had danced 'with inspired grace, lithe and mercurial, delighting all with his infectious pleasure'.[2] His family were invited: his mother came, while his brother and his sister-in-law would have done had their son, also called Peter, not been very ill in hospital with the cancer from which he died about three weeks later. Many of the other guests were either close Labour Party colleagues or old friends of long standing, like Sue Robertson, Jenny Jeger or David Jordan. He was deeply disappointed when Alastair Campbell had to turn down the invitation because his beloved Burnley were playing at home; but most of his closest friends from the eighties, and several from the seventies, were there. It was a happy, boisterous and distinctly Labourish occasion.

The same could not be said unreservedly for the forty-third. This was a dinner party given for Mandelson by Lady (Carla) Powell and her husband Sir Charles, who had been the longest-serving, most trusted, and conspicuously the most powerful civil servant in Margaret Thatcher's private office during her time in Downing Street. Some of the guests had also attended Mandelson's fortieth – among the cast (mainly Labour Party sympathisers or members) were John Birt and his wife Jane; Tony Blair and Cherie came for drinks but did not stay for dinner. Robert Harris and Gill Hornby were there. Mandelson had known and liked Harris since the 1980s, when he had been Director of Communications and Harris had been political editor of the *Observer*. He would say years later, after Harris had become a famous novelist, that he had always impressed him because of his resistance to 'spin'. At Mandelson's briefings other Sunday journalists, he recalled, would scribble furiously while Harris merely gazed out of the window. But they had become much closer friends when Mandelson went to stay with him and his wife in 1995 to work on his book. The Harris home would be a weekend refuge for the next three and a half years including after his entry to the Cabinet. The Harris's small son, Charlie, caused much amusement after the 1998 reshuffle by greeting him as 'the secretary in a state'. Among the other guests were Gavyn Davies and Sue Nye, a slightly uncomfortable Alastair Campbell and Fiona Millar, Madeleine and Jon Snow, Waheed Alli, not yet a Labour peer, Sir Charles's younger brother Jonathan, by now a key member of Blair's team, and John and Penny Mortimer. But Roger Liddle and Derek Draper, who had organised a surprise party for Mandelson the previous year, were not invited. Sir Charles made a joke of the company in a few welcoming remarks, first addressing Blair as 'Prime Minister' and jocularly correcting himself, and then remarking cheekily that many Tories had gathered round his dining table in the past but on this occasion there were only two – Blair and Sir Charles himself. Nevertheless, when news of the party filtered into the outside world, as it inevitably did, it publicly marked Mandelson's embrace into the hearth and home of one of Margaret Thatcher's most trusted lieutenants. He appeared to be, if not sleeping, at least dining with the enemy.

According to one of many myths, the MP for Hartlepool met Carla Powell on the aeroplane to Prague, fell into the clutches of that exuberant, well-connected and hospitable lady, developed an almost instant taste for high living and rich friends, forgot all his old ones, and was persuaded by her to buy the famous house in Notting Hill which led to his downfall. This was indeed myth; the truth was different and more complex. First, his connection with the Powells was more long-standing than it was given credit for. Mandelson had first met them in the early nineties at the New Forest home of a third Powell brother, Chris, an active Labour Party member and, as the senior figure in Boase Massimi Pollitt, the key advertising man in Labour's 1987 campaign. But Mandelson had cemented his relationship with Carla in particular at the Birts' fiftieth birthday party in December 1994, where they had, as she would put it later, 'flirted like mad' and got on famously. The empathy was not difficult to understand: both loved high-grade gossip and were fixated on the personalities of politics; both had a well-developed sense of fun; both had charm, style and, when necessary, discretion. But from Mandelson's point of view there was also another attraction: now a director of Jardine Mathieson, Sir Charles, as a hard-working and super-intelligent veteran of the Thatcher establishment, had more recent experience of the upper reaches of government than almost anyone easily accessible to the new Labour leadership, and had no objection to sharing it. He also had the strongest connections to members of the previously pro-Tory business constituency, not least those who were as disillusioned with John Major as they had been enchanted with Margaret Thatcher. Through Sir Charles, Mandelson was able to meet business people who, while they might not be willing to give funds to Labour, might at least be persuaded to withhold them from the Tories. Moreover, Sir Charles provided an entrée – though by no means the only one – to those Thatcherites who were prepared to suspend their distrust of Labour's European policy far enough to consider that Blair might make a stronger and more acceptable leader than the incumbent. Blair, of course, was no more immune to such attractions than Mandelson, which was one reason why he was willing to engage with high Thatcherite commentators like Paul Johnson and Simon Heffer or, more importantly, to court the empires of Rupert Murdoch and Conrad Black. In this context, it was not quite so baffling that the pro-European Mandelson should be consorting with one of Sir James Goldsmith's best-loved friends and admirers.

Many of these figures now sought out Peter Mandelson. He was funny, irreverent, socially poised – and, of course, good company. But he also found quite suddenly that he was now of interest in a way that he had not been in the Smith era. Previously a backbench MP and, while not obscure, hardly in favour with the leadership either, Mandelson was now known to have the closest relations with the new leader, someone already exciting attention well beyond the political classes. And while Blair teased him on one occasion by saying that every time Mandelson telephoned he seemed to hear 'the tinkle of glasses in the background', he hardly minded some socialising in the Labour cause. Mandelson may have been protesting too much when he defensively told a friend that he had not become a socialite but merely a 'Labour ambassador' to the rich, powerful and well-connected.[3] But it was not, at least initially, an entirely empty boast.

Nevertheless he also enjoyed the company of the Powells – and, by extension, some of the people he met through them – for its own sake. Their children, unlike the Harrises, were grown up and they did not have a large house in the country where he could retreat at weekends, but round their supper table, particularly on Sunday evenings, he could relax, say what he liked without fear of being reported, and enjoy Carla Powell's effortless north Italian cooking. Moreover Carla, in particular, not only found him wonderful company, but also felt increasingly protective towards him, keeping him supplied with Tupperware boxes of her homemade pasta sauce to put in his refrigerator. By mid-1996 he was, as another friend noted at the time, 'full of the joys of Carla'; they were speaking on the telephone almost daily – with Mandelson invariably calling her by his pet name 'granny' or, like his other women friends, 'darling'. When she was ill and confined to hospital in 1998, he managed to visit her quite frequently. And there were also less homely pleasures. The famous remark, attributed to Rupert Murdoch, that Mandelson was 'easy, he's a starfucker' may have been an oversimplification. But he certainly loved meeting, through Carla Powell, a range of celebrities, including Sean Connery whom Mandelson brought into the Scottish devolution campaign, Camilla Parker Bowles, and the lingerie millionaire Linda Wachner, in whose private jet, it would emerge after his resignation, he had notoriously enjoyed several transatlantic flights, even as Trade Secretary. Mandelson also stayed in Wachner's Long Island summer home in August 1998.

But Carla Powell did not, as legend had it, play a direct part in his most reckless act of all, the purchase of his Notting Hill house with a £373,000 loan from Geoffrey Robinson in 1996. Indeed, when he finally acquired it, Lady Powell, who had for many years led a glamorous social life on the salary of a far from wealthy public servant, sensibly advised him to leave the interior of the house as it was – rather than strip out its original features and entirely refurbish it, as he chose to do under the supervision of the fashionable architect Seth Stein, at a cost of around £50,000. She and her husband, like Robert Harris – and indeed all Mandelson's closest friends – knew nothing of the loan. She happened to live within ten minutes or so of the new house and so would be a conveniently close neighbour. But Mandelson had anyway fixed on the area when Robert Harris had been toying with the idea of buying a London house to share with him. They had looked at one in Holland Park, and Harris, before the arrival of his third child, Matilda, one of Mandelson's half-dozen godchildren, had considered making an offer on the house next door to No. 9 Northumberland Place – which Mandelson eventually bought. The street itself is one of the most elegant and quiet in central London. But Mandelson also fell in love with the neighbourhood; he revelled in the amiable street life of Westbourne Grove, its fashionable and expensive shopping, and the restaurants at the scruffier eastern end: Brazilian, Chinese and Indian, but also Iranian, Lebanese, Iraqi – a combination which reminded him, he told a friend, of Beirut.

The trouble was money. While looking for a mortgage he happened to lunch with Sir Ewan Ferguson, the chairman of his rather exclusive bank, Coutts, and previously known to him as British ambassador to Paris. Oddly, Mandelson's reasons for banking with Coutts were politically highly correct. As an undergraduate he had dutifully transferred his account – to the Midland – from Barclay's at the height of the row over its South African interests. But then there was fresh controversy over the Midland's investments, and a post-graduate Canadian student at St Catherine's College sent off, partly as a joke, on Mandelson's behalf an application to bank with Coutts. At this time, Mandelson would claim in later life, he had no idea about the bank's social cachet, and he duly signed up. At their lunch in 1996 Ferguson, who had some knowledge of London property prices, not to mention MPs' salaries, tactfully tried to steer him away from one of the more expensive square miles of London real estate. His own son had a girlfriend who had recently acquired a pleasant flat in Shepherd's Bush. Would that not perhaps be more suitable? But Mandelson was entranced by the area within a mile and a half radius of Notting Hill Gate.

It was during the summer that he went, at Geoffrey Robinson's invitation, for dinner *à deux* in the annexe of the Grosvenor House Hotel, where the MP, now a multi-millionaire, occupied a flat with a wide balcony looking across Park Lane and Hyde Park beyond. Unsurprisingly, the principal topic over the sole was Gordon Brown, and Mandelson's painfully fractured relationship with him. They had already spoken on this subject several times, often when they met by chance in the members' lobby in the Commons, since the traumas of 1994, when Robinson, unlike Mandelson, had remained steadfastly a Brown man until the Shadow Chancellor finally decided not to contest the leadership. Robinson always made it clear to Mandelson that one of his prime responsibilities was to ensure that the bond between Blair and Brown was never 'rent asunder'. Mandelson had always regarded Robinson, rather like his former LWT colleague Michael Wills, as 'family Brown but friendly Blair'. Mandelson told a colleague that

> Geoffrey would regularly say: 'Peter, you've got to make things work with Gordon.' And Peter would invariably reply: 'Geoffrey, I want nothing more than to make things work with Gordon. But he will not stop prosecuting this war.' Then Geoffrey would say, 'Oh Peter, there's wrong on both sides, all you've got to show to Gordon is that you like him and that you're committed to him and you're loyal to him' ... 'I have shown that but it makes not a halfpenny's difference ...' 'No you haven't tried hard enough.' And so on.

Geoffrey Robinson would say later, when both men had resigned from the government, that Mandelson had 'asked' for a loan. The Mandelson version was rather different: he had decided he wanted to 'get settled' soon; once he was a minister he wouldn't want to be bothered with selling his 'poky little flat in Clerkenwell'. According to Mandelson's friends, it was Robinson, a famously generous man, who said something like: 'Look, Peter, you'll be in the government and eventually you'll be in the Cabinet, you shouldn't have to worry about these things, you should have somewhere in London where you can be settled, where you can have a good home, where you can relax, where you can bring people round, and have a proper base.' Which, as Mandelson cheerfully acknowledged, was just what he was looking for. Robinson apparently suggested that he would need 'something substantial' – in other words, something rather more substantial (and expensive) than the Clerkenwell flat. Then, it seems, the two MPs went on to talk money. Mandelson said that he did not have the 'resources', and Robinson said, 'Well, you'll get the resources one day ... you'll write your memoirs.' Mandelson demurred and then told him that 'eventually I will inherit a substantial legacy that has been passed to my mother by my father.' When Robinson asked how substantial, Mandelson replied that it would be 'in the region of half a million pounds'. Then, as Mandelson would later confide in his friends, Robinson said: 'Fine . . . I could tide you over.' Mandelson was pursuing the option of a gift from his mother, but Robinson replied that he should forget it; helping out his friend would be 'as easy as falling off a log'.

The conversation was left hanging with the loan from Robinson not finalised until early October, when it became clear that Mandelson's mother could not help. In hoping for a gift from her, Mandelson was making a somewhat cavalier assumption. The total assets left by Tony Mandelson when he died in 1988 were indeed, if the house in Bigwood Road was included, estimated to have been getting on for £1 million. If the total was to be eventually split two ways between Miles and Peter Mandelson, then the figure was about right – or possibly even modest, given the likely appreciation in value of the house. But as Miles explained in an interview five months before his brother's resignation,

> What happened was that [Tony Mandelson] left the money in trust. If I remember rightly he left nothing to my brother and myself. He left the money in trust but [provided] that throughout my mother's lifetime she would have the income. And when she died what was left should be divided between my brother and myself. We actually executed a deed of family arrangement, which was something that the lawyers suggested, by way of actually giving the money to my mother so it became hers.[4]

Miles and Peter Mandelson inherited the maximum amount not subject to inheritance tax, which at the time of Tony Mandelson's death in 1988 were shares in a total of £110,000 – in other words £55,000 each – 'and my mother got the rest which seemed fair enough. And now it's up to her to do what she wants with it. And my mother has actually been very generous to Peter and myself over the years.' Particularly since, like many widows of her age, Mary Mandelson had an understandable and, according to Miles, deep anxiety 'about money and running out of it', 'she has been,' he repeated, 'very generous'. While Mary Mandelson – hardly, to put it mildly, a big spender – had been living on the income rather than the capital no one could exactly foretell the future. She was seventy-five at the time of Peter Mandelson's conversation with

Robinson, and was – and still is – a fit and vital woman. Neither the size nor (given Mary Mandelson's relative youth in an era of longevity, particularly for healthy women) the timing of the inheritance could be taken for granted. Equally, it was clear from Robinson's tone, and his suggestion that his forty-three-year-old dinner guest would eventually write some memoirs, that he would be in no hurry for the money to be repaid. Robinson was in a protective mood towards Mandelson that summer – in public as well as private. On 21 August he wrote to the *Guardian* defending his friend from a snidely critical piece suggesting he should work for the Royal Family. 'The Labour Party needs Peter Mandelson too much to spare him for the Royal Family', wrote Robinson.

Mandelson now accepted some immediate help from Robinson. As someone who knew about property, perhaps he should inspect 'some of these places you're looking for'. Robinson was taking a distinctly avuncular interest in Mandelson's affairs, rather as, sixteen years earlier, he had helped to sort out the trade union funds to pay Mandelson's salary as Albert Booth's researcher. It was the parliamentary recess. The weather was fine. It was a rather enjoyable prospect. Together, two of the Labour Party's more unusual MPs, driven by Robinson's amiable chauffeur John, set out house-hunting in W2 and W11. For all his preference for the anonymity of a London hotel as his own base, Robinson exhibited shrewdness and exacting standards. They visited two or three flats which Robinson pronounced unsuitable for the future cabinet minister. This one's bedroom was too minute; this one was too near what would undoubtedly be a noisy pub; this one was right next to a bus stop. Why not abandon the search for a flat and find a small house instead? It would not cost that much more than the – in Robinson's view, overpriced – flats they had been looking at.

This appealed strongly to Mandelson. To someone who set very great store by privacy, a property without common parts, which was entirely his own, was alluring. The first house which attracted him – and appeared to meet with Robinson's approval – was in Ladbroke Road, just behind Notting Hill Gate. It had been gutted throughout; it also had an expensive asking price – £500,000. Mandelson made an offer on it and would have gone ahead had he not swiftly been gazumped. But then they found the narrow, four-storey Georgian house in Northumberland Place, a significantly quieter street than Ladbroke Road and, though considerably further from the tube station, scarcely less fashionable. It also had the added advantage of being £35,000 cheaper. Mandelson had found a London home he wholeheartedly liked. It only remained for Stephen Wegg-Prosser (father of Mandelson's adviser Benjamin) and a solicitor to draw up an agreement. This provided for a loan of £373,000; Mandelson later explained that Robinson had lent it at the Midland Bank base rate.

The purchase of the house was part of a general change in lifestyle. The £1,800 leather armchair and the 1936 Wolfgang Succhitsky photograph of a Lyons corner house were two of his most highly publicised local purchases. An excellent Mandelson myth, around the time he resigned in December 1998, was that he bought his suits – for around £2,000 a throw – from Ozwald Boateng. This merely arose from a chance remark during London Fashion Week that he would 'love' to own a Boateng suit. However, by 1996 he was already buying – for between £600 and £700 – the odd suit from the discreet City tailors Couch and Hoskin: his interest in his appearance had come a long way from the V-neck sweaters and (admittedly invariably clean and well-pressed) jeans of the late seventies. Invited onto the *Today* programme to discuss the October 1996 party conference with Peter Mandelson, Tony Banks was startled when his fellow MP started to take off his trousers during the interview. Off air, Mandelson confided that he was due to go into a television studio, and needed to put on a freshly-pressed pair. When Banks protested that the average viewer was most unlikely to notice the difference, Mandelson replied: 'I have to be perfect.'* Indeed, in February 1998 Nick Foulkes, writing in the London *Standard*, breathlessly – and entertainingly – identifying Mandelson

---

* The obsessive media attention paid to Mandelson's perceived interest in his personal appearance would also give rise after his resignation in December 1998 to another truly first-class Mandelson myth: that having hairy arms he shaved the hair on the back of his hands. Not only that, but, it was claimed, he advised fellow MPs to do the same in the interest of voter appeal. Not true: he does have hair on the back of his hands and he never has shaved it.

as a 'style god', subjected the famous John Voos *Independent* picture of the then Director of Communications leaning against a pillar during his last party conference in 1990 to minute analysis, and concluded that the 'key anchors' of the Mandelson style were 'already in place'. Foulkes pointed to 'The neutral shirt, the bold yet unfussy tie; the choice of belt rather than braces, even with a suit (braces would speak too loudly of City greed or public-school chinlessness); the conspicuous absence of a pocket handkerchief.'

The PE slouch of Hendon County days had long been something of a fitness fanatic. He had always been an energetic long-distance walker, whether with the Birts in northern Italy or in the Black Mountains with friends like Jon Snow. Now he would join the fashionable Lambton gym off Westbourne Grove, swimming, working out and engaging in a kind of punishing exercise in the pool known as aqua-aerobics. He bought a Ridgeback cycle from E. J. Barnes in Westbourne Grove, which he used locally whenever he could. He also became more fussy about the comfort and privacy of his holidays, though it was not until he was a minister that he took a winter holiday in the French Caribbean island of St Barths or spent a few days at the Gritti Palace in Venice after two weeks in the US. He paid for himself, and at prices he could ill afford.

As, with his new lifestyle, he made new and more powerful friends, did he also forget his old ones? Some of his older friends felt that he did. As a close friend of the 1990s said: 'The closer you get to the top, you meet more interesting, entertaining, amusing people, who've done more in their lives, have got more to say, and you're not necessarily disloyal to your old friends. I think that's what happened, possibly – that he's not so much dropped them but rather found pashes which are more beguiling.' Yet there was a paradox. On the one hand Mandelson was often fiercely loyal, maintaining close bonds – however infrequently revisited – with some of his oldest friends like Steve Howell, whose absence from London, in South Wales, he would often lament. He defended people who worked with him against criticism – for example, Steve Wallace and Bernard Carr in Hartlepool. On the other, sudden exclusion from his circle could provoke strong feelings. He had always been volatile in his friendships, allowing disagreements to simmer in long, antagonistic silences. Someone who understood this better than most was his old friend from BYC days Trevor Phillips, to whom Mandelson had been best man in the early 1980s: 'The day we got married, Peter was great, he was there all the time . . . He was absolutely totally attentive and I think it's part of the problem people have when they fall out with him. I think his capacity to be completely there for you is huge.' Picking up the flowers for the wedding in Phillips's fiancée's little Citroën Dyane, they parked on a yellow line and Mandelson used all his charm to persuade a traffic warden not to give them a ticket. 'On the day . . . he made a great speech, he was very funny. I can't remember a word of it but all I remember is that people laughed a lot more at his speech than at mine because I was completely flustered, but he was very smooth and charmed my in-laws to pieces.'[5]

Yet at a dinner party after Mandelson went to work for the Labour Party in 1985 they had what in normal circumstances would have been a minor argument about the political rock movement Red Wedge – Phillips had argued quite playfully that the musicians were not 'serious' and could not be relied on to support Neil Kinnock when the going got rough: 'We got into a terrible row, and I can never remember which of us left the party early. I think it was him. There was a bit of stomping and we didn't speak for some time'; yet the relationship – they are still friendly – was robust enough to withstand the break. But as Phillips points out:

> He's one of those people . . . before people are afraid of him, people want to be in his good books and I don't know what the right romantic metaphor is here, not quite jilted lover, but people who would love to be in the sun, basking in the rays of Peter's approval, but somehow it's withheld and people absolutely hate him . . . everyone wants to be his best friend and the problem is that not everyone can be his best friend by definition, and if they're not his best friend people feel very resentful.

It is tempting to wonder whether this process did not play some part in the antagonism which Mandelson aroused in former political allies, as well as among friends who felt excluded as his social life began – at least partially – to change. In fact his new social network, enhanced by the cachet of being at the right hand of a man almost universally expected to be the next Prime Minister, may have encouraged him to expect a standard of living which, disastrously as it turned out, he could not afford. But, as most would acknowledge, it did not make him forget older friends altogether. Many of those who had felt resentful would then swiftly admit that Mandelson was always the first to visit them if they were ill or in trouble.

# CHAPTER EIGHTEEN

## *Being Peter*

It did not take long for Mandelson to re-establish his role after the upset of the Prague weekend. On 21 May, returning from a party visit to Oxford, he had called in on his friend Robert Harris in Berkshire, and they lunched in a local hotel. As they sped back to Harris's home in his open-top Jaguar XJS, the Labour leader rang him on his mobile telephone. John Major had suddenly announced a policy of non-cooperation with the EU in protest on the BSE ban on British beef. Prime Minister's Question Time was looming: what should he do? Mandelson, caught unawares, put his hand over the mouthpiece and asked Harris the same question. 'Be cautious,' replied Harris. 'Be cautious,' repeated Mandelson down the phone.

In other words, Mandelson continued in his old advisory role. Indeed, around this period Roy Hattersley was struck by how many members of the Shadow Cabinet mentioned that Mandelson was present when they met Blair. To Hattersley he was 'quite literally the man hovering in the outer office', more influential than any adviser to a party leader he had ever known.[1] At the same time, however, he was still only an MP of the newest intake, 1992. Not surprisingly, it grated with quite a number of his fellow MPs that he now enjoyed such a privileged position. And also not surprisingly, Mandelson realised that this was a potentially uncomfortable, and perhaps dangerous, position to be in.

In February 1995, seeking Blair's permission to go ahead with his plans to write a book with Roger Liddle, Mandelson had privately acknowledged to the leader that 'I am less use to you as a result of the fear of me, my strange, menacing unaccountable power, my media manipulation, my awesome ability to triumph over and rubbish those who get in the way of our project. I have got to do something about this situation before it does me and you further harm.' In his note he proposed taking a number of steps, including making more speeches in the House, paying ('if you give me a job planning the General Election Campaign') visits to the local party in every key seat, demonstrating his campaigning skills and, most ambitiously of all, making it a 'top priority ... to make no more enemies: charm, friendliness, approachability, finding ways I can use my skills to help people are all essential. And remember the Blair maxim: kill your enemies with cream.' This would prove harder to achieve than to promise. But if he was to continue 'being Peter', he would have to try to temper the irritation he provoked in some of his colleagues.

The reference to his 'unaccountable power' was meant to be ironic, but it tallied with his image within the party. Blair's leadership had marked Mandelson's return from exile. 'Ominously for the Tories,' Gavyn Davies, friend and economic adviser to both Brown and Blair, wrote in his *Independent* column in early November, 'Mandelson is back at command centre in the party, after being ostracised by the complacent John Smith regime.'[2]

It was not only the Tories who found this ominous. Now that his closeness to Blair was out in the open, it inevitably grated in the party's more traditionalist quarters. The week before he wrote his note to Blair, the *Guardian* had carried a profile by Seamus Milne. It suggested that Mandelson 'has become the focus for an unrivalled loathing that often verges on the unhinged', and quoted the man himself as saying that 'since they can't strike out at the leader they strike out at the next best thing. I don't enjoy it, but I'm not cowed by it.' Milne's piece also quoted a 'senior front bencher'* who suggested that Mandelson was the 'real deputy leader'.[3] There is no doubt some truth in Roy Hattersley's charge that, if Mandelson really disliked the repeated accusations about his excessive power, 'he would work to dispel the notion that the

---

* Some attributed the quotation to Gordon Brown.

party Leader relies on him'.[4] Nevertheless, following his letter to Blair back in February, he was making some effort to reconnect himself to the party faithful.

The Littleborough and Saddleworth by-election in July 1995, caused by the death of the popular Tory MP Geoffrey Dickens, provided him with an opportunity. Put by Blair in day-to-day charge of the by-election, Mandelson found himself working, for once, in comparative harmony with John Prescott, deputy leader and the shadow cabinet member responsible for targeting key seats. The campaign in the seat, held by the Tories in the 1992 election, became the most controversial Mandelson had conducted. With the enthusiastic assistance of Alan Barnard, the party's Targeting and Key Seats Officer, Mandelson set about reinventing Phil Woolas – who, like any former left-wing student, had had a healthily colourful past – as a churchgoing family man of impeccably bourgeois values, and conducting a ruthless attack on his Liberal Democrat rival Chris Davies. Even Mandelson drew the line at Barnard's inspired suggestion of flooding the constituency with posters depicting Chris Davies as 'Soft on Drugs, High on Taxes'. But he allowed the campaign to draw attention repeatedly to Davies's – perfectly respectable – view that there should be a Royal Commission on Drugs and his support for limited rises in income tax. The campaign was vigorously criticised; raising the issue of tax increases was, as Chris Davies himself put it, like holding up 'a crucifix to a vampire'. It was a rough, but not illegitimate line of Labour attack. The proposal for a drugs Royal Commission had been approved by the Liberal Democrats against the leadership's wishes. And Chris Davies had made no secret of his enthusiasm for increased taxation at the previous party conference. But the critics included not only Paddy Ashdown and the *New Statesman*, which urged Labour supporters to vote for Davies, but, on the Labour left, the MP Richard Burden, who used the campaign to trigger the first tentative but widely publicised summer mini-revolt against Blair. The LibDems won by 16,231 to Labour's 14,238; Mandelson adeptly treated the result like that of the 1987 general election: coming second had itself been a victory. Labour had demonstrated that it was a force in hitherto hostile Tory territory; that there were, as Mandelson put it, 'no no-go areas' for the party. At the same time, as Mandelson was one of the first to realise, it had now become clear that the Liberal Democrats were not going to be extinguished merely because Labour now had a centrist and charismatic young leader. In that sense the by-election had been a turning point; from now on, with Mandelson closely involved, Labour would seek some form of accommodation with Paddy Ashdown's party.

He himself was laconic in defending a rough campaign, telling Roy Hattersley: 'By-elections are about candidates. The Liberals have escaped scrutiny for too long.'[5] Woolas, the candidate, and now an MP, was awestruck by Mandelson's professionalism and single-mindedness on the party's behalf. Not hitherto close allies – the two men had been on different sides in the OMOV argument two years earlier – they bonded famously. Woolas recalled various vignettes of Mandelson's conduct of the campaign: tapping away endlessly on his word processor in the office he had looked up just as the campaign press officer Julie Crowley was about to send a press release to the local weekly paper. What time was the paper's deadline? 1.30. Well, send it at 1.15 then. That way it was sure to be on the front page. After a radio phone-in with all the candidates, Mandelson, who had listened to it on his little transistor radio, took Woolas briefly aside. 'You must make sure you're nearer the microphone,' he told him. 'He was right but I was gobsmacked. How on earth could he tell?' asked Woolas later. Then a *coup de grâce*: the BBC *Newsnight* correspondent Michael Crick, a by-election veteran, swooped at a press conference in response to a call by Woolas for a TV debate between all the candidates. Wasn't it always the loser who asked for a TV debate? Crick asked. Woolas hesitated fatally for a moment. Mandelson coolly stood up, waved his hand across the camera and said to Crick: 'Sorry, Michael, the camera isn't working. The red light isn't on. You'll have to ask the question again.' Woolas did not have time to work out whether the camera really had been working, because almost simultaneously Mandelson scrawled a note and passed it to Woolas with just two words, 'Lancashire accent' on it. Crick asked the question again. Woolas, who had been criticised for not being the local candidate, smoothly answered: 'Well if we have a TV debate, at least they'll be able to hear my good Lancashire accent.'

Finally Woolas noticed how, when Robin Cook came up for a

day's campaigning, he asked Mandelson whether he was required to weigh in on the drugs issue. As Woolas recalls, 'Peter said "No Robin, you're Shadow Foreign Secretary, you shouldn't get involved in that. Leave it to us." Peter didn't have to do that.'[6] Cook, naturally, was pleased to be absolved from having to strike below the belt. No doubt Mandelson also conveniently drew the fire for a campaign which Blair could easily have toned down had he wanted to. Prescott was straightforward in defending Mandelson's conduct of the by-election, declaring: 'It is a campaign I have been very much involved with, and we made these strategic decisions.' Ian McCartney, a high-flying Prescott ally who had been brought in as an additional front bench 'minder' for the candidate, made a warm speech at the campaign party after the count: he hadn't known Mandelson well before, he said, but he had been impressed by his leadership, and 'when his reputation was on the line he never buckled'. An appreciative Woolas was even more forthright in his thanks at the Littleborough and Saddleworth rally: 'He may be a bastard,' he told the activists to applause. 'But he's our bastard.' The by-election had been a low point in political discourse and had thrust Mandelson back into a less than flattering spotlight. But paradoxically, for many rank-and-file activists, if not for the Liberal Democrats, left-wing MPs or the metropolitan commentators he was frequently suspected of courting, this had been Mandelson at his tribal best.

The by-election helped to fulfil one part of the personal manifesto Mandelson had outlined to Blair in February. Another element was the book which Blair had now agreed to let him write with Roger Liddle, and which, he had told the leader, would 'show I can sustain the work and intellectual endeavour that writing a book demands'. The reason for his visit to the Harrises in August was to begin work on *The Blair Revolution*. He had been down to Kintbury the previous month to consult Harris on the project and Harris had not only given him expert advice but hospitably offered him the use of a room, overlooking the Kennet and Avon Canal, complete with word processor and its own bathroom.

As he invariably did with friends who had young children, Mandelson fitted in easily. In a sometimes sharply critical study of

Mandelson, Andy McSmith would remark, partly from personal experience:

> The falsified sincerity which has been the making of so many successful politicians does not work with children, who respond only to what they detect is genuine ... yet the Labour MP who other politicians regard as the reincarnation of Machiavelli has a wonderful rapport with the very young. There are numerous parents who can attest to his ability to talk to children without a trace of condescension, entering into their mental world as if he were their own age.[7]

Robert Harris's family, like Philip Gould's, Alastair Campbell's and Gavyn Davies's, among many others, was no exception and it was why he became a serial godfather. After his first, ten-day stay he inscribed in the Harrises' visitors' book: 'A very suitable resting place for the Prince of Darkness.' So it was – intelligent and sociable company, and plentiful supplies of those two precious commodities: sleep and well cooked food. The Harrises, who thought he was a 'bit lonely', were glad to envelop him in family life. They were also indulgent of his tendency to tie up telephones and faxes for hours on end. He rapidly became known at Kintbury as 'the Lodger' – and his favourite dish, lemon custard soufflé, lovingly made by Gill Hornby, as 'Lodger's Pudding'.

As Mandelson had implied to Blair, the book was part of his persistent effort to effect the transition from spin doctor to politician in his own right. Since before John Smith's death, he had often spoken with Roger Liddle about the need to establish himself as someone who was serious about policy, overcoming widespread scepticism within the party about his interest in ideas. His most serious attempt so far had been wholly abortive *because* of his umbilical connection to Blair – 'being Peter', in other words. With ample help from Liddle, he had written a substantial pamphlet broadly in favour of British EMU entry. But Blair had intervened to stop him publishing it: he feared that people would assume that Mandelson was speaking for his leader – a leader who was nowhere near as ready to commit himself to the single currency as Mandelson or Liddle were.

Mandelson took the book seriously enough for Blair to complain about the time he was spending on it during the autumn and winter of 1995. Both men had research help from Derek Draper, and while both authors rewrote one another's contributions Mandelson himself was mainly responsible for the chapters on 'Blair the Man', Europe, and the final chapter on Labour in government. At times Liddle had to restrain Mandelson's enthusiasm; when Mandelson wrote that Blair would not 'let anything get in the way of a Labour victory', Liddle remarked drily: 'In favour of hanging, are we?' Mandelson took the sentence out. Both the authors were keen to serialise the book in the *Guardian* to reach a Labour audience; Blair himself would have preferred *The Times* to interest more swing voters. The *Guardian* led its coverage with the most attention-seeking proposal, for a £5,000 state 'dowry' for young married couples.[8] Although he had proposed it, Liddle was sceptical, to say the least, about the workability of such a plan, but Mandelson was eager to include a 'story'. When the book was published in February 1996, the 'dowry' proposal was widely criticised inside and outside the party. Patricia Morgan of the Institute of Directors denounced it as an election bribe borrowed from Hitler – but 'Hitler was more generous' – while Ken Livingstone remarked that at least it was 'the first time I've heard Peter Mandelson talking about spending commitments so we can welcome him to the true path of socialism'. As Labour policy, the idea sank without trace. But Mandelson was right that it would make news – Liddle even found himself defending the idea on *The Richard and Judy Show*.

Indeed, the book – for which Faber had paid a £12,500 advance – would attract extravagant publicity, and sell 13,000 copies within a month of publication. As a means of establishing Mandelson as an independent political thinker its success was less easy to define. Writing it, he said, had been like 'emerging from a chrysalis', but the final version was so closely vetted by the New Labour high command that it was bound to be seen as largely reflecting Blairite thinking. On Christmas Eve 1995 the *Observer* led with an early synopsis – to the fury of Mandelson, who spent much of Christmas Day telephoning long-suffering journalists to repudiate it. Its proposals were indeed dramatic – coalition with the Liberal Democrats even if Labour won an overall majority, an end to universal child benefit, no-strike deals in the public services, an end to all local authority control of schools, and reductions of Scottish and Welsh seats at Westminster after devolution. Several of these, including the first and the last, were certainly under consideration by Blair, but no decisions had been taken. The leak probably dated, the authors thought, from the summer, when they were hawking an earlier version – with a much longer historical section – round three or four publishers.

The book was shown to Blair, though it was read most thoroughly by David Miliband, head of his Policy Unit. Nevertheless Blair himself proposed that the introduction should say – as it duly did – that New Labour's strategy was 'to move forward from where Margaret Thatcher left off, rather than to dismantle every single thing she did'.[9] Mandelson also discussed with him in great detail the section on Labour and the Liberal Democrats; there was 'no barrier' to cooperation 'in terms of principle and policy' between the two parties, it said, but then immediately qualified this for internal Labour Party consumption by adding, that 'does not imply or require a pre-election pact or post-election coalition'. Blair also approved the passage recommending a change to the Alternative Vote electoral system – which implies that he had already started to make the mental leap to this halfway stage towards a more proportional system. Mandelson would subsequently say that electoral reform was one of the few points of difference between Blair and himself, but the idea had been Liddle's; Mandelson's ignorance of electoral systems when he started the book was near total. Charlie Whelan gleefully told the BBC journalist Nick Jones that Brown had 'filleted' the book: 'Gordon put his foot down and said to Mandelson: "Take it all out or the game's off."'[10] This seems to have indicated simply that Mandelson and Liddle were careful to ensure that Brown vetted the sections on economic policy before the book went to the publishers. Brown made three or four drafting suggestions which were easily accommodated. Overall, the book was widely and carefully read by civil servants; it remains the most accurate route map of what subsequently became the course of the Blair government.

A third part of the programme outlined to Blair in his letter in February 1995, 'Killing your enemies with cream', came a good deal less naturally to Mandelson than to his leader. But true to his declared intentions, Mandelson made an extensive tour of local parties. Following him to Wellingborough and Tamworth at the beginning of 1996, the journalist Andy Beckett noted how successfully he worked the meetings. Beckett left Mandelson at Birmingham, 'Macintosh turned up against the wind, phone clamped to his ear, walking fast out of earshot across the car park,' deep in conversation with Alastair Campbell about the latest – and worst – crisis to engulf the party: Harriet Harman's decision to send her son to St Olave's grammar school in Bromley.

According to Campbell – who was inhibited in his own support for Harman by his own deep distaste for selective schools – the Harman affair was a good example of Mandelson's mettle under fire: 'He does like a fight. He was good when Tony had clearly decided to tough it out over Harriet. He was taking on all comers.'[11] All comers included large numbers of furious backbench Labour MPs, journalists understandably delighted to be able to redress the political balance with a story which was at least as embarrassing to Blair as the chronic internal troubles of the Tory Party had been to John Major, and several prominent members of the Shadow Cabinet, most notably John Prescott. He harangued the BBC almost hourly about its 'unhealthy' interest in the affair, advising Harman to give her first interview on the subject to Channel Four as a 'punishment'. Not for the first time, Mandelson found himself a lonely defender of an unpopular cause. Mandelson appears to have stiffened Blair's resolve to ride out the row. He was quick to realise that any retreat by Harman would provide the Tories with valuable evidence of the fragility of New Labour. One person who appreciated his position was the shadow cabinet member who had most reason to be infuriated by Harman's decision, the Education spokesman David Blunkett: 'Your job was to look after her, mine to look after the party,' he said to Mandelson after the crisis had passed.

The crucial decision on advertising for the election had already been taken in July 1995: this demonstrated both Mandelson's loyalty and his ruthlessness. The loyalty was to Chris Powell, the third brother in the dynasty which had furnished both Margaret Thatcher and Tony Blair with their chief fixers, the chief executive of BMP, and the long-term Labour supporter who had been largely responsible for the advertising in the 1987 campaign. The ruthlessness was directed at Leslie Butterfield, who had been engaged by the Smith regime to handle advertising, and who was now eased out to the sidelines: Mandelson, acting partly on the advice of Philip Gould, wanted BMP to be the sole agency responsible for Labour Party advertising. Given the change in Labour's fortunes, BMP was now prepared, as it had not been in 1987, to be publicly associated with the party. This would now help them commercially just as much as it would have damaged them in 1987. Moreover, Butterfield's agency, BDDH, was, by his own admission, probably too small to handle the account on its own. A joint proposal from Butterfield and Powell had originally envisaged the two agencies, BMP and BDDH, working in tandem, but Mandelson saw inherent dangers in a fudge. The ruthlessness was moderated by tact; in April 1995 Mandelson suggested to Blair that the imaginative and talented Butterfield might be retained in an advisory capacity if he was willing – which in the end he was not – and that 'we let his agency down gently so as not to damage' BDDH commercially.

This could all be dismissed as a secondary issue if it were not for the obsessive interest shown by modern party leaders in election advertising. Margaret Thatcher had had her own 'Wobbly Thursday' during the 1987 election, and throughout 1986 had taken a close interest in the work of Young and Rubicam as a potential alternative to Saatchi's; Blair would become similarly disenchanted with BMP over the winter of 1996–7. Some of his own staff, notably Peter Hyman, wanted a newer agency with 'more political nastiness and killer instinct'.[12] Blair, on the other hand, was concerned that their advertising was too negative and did not do enough to present Labour's positive appeal. (It was this last objection which was to inspire one of Campbell's notable 'stings' in February 1997. He proposed that BMP should run up some 'Mr Men' ads depicting John Major as 'Mr Weak', 'Mr Dither', 'Mr Spineless' and 'Mr Panic'. There was never any chance that the ads would go out since they were a gross infringement of copyright owned by the estate of the late Roger Hargreaves, creator of the Mr Men. But Campbell then 'leaked' the ads to the *Sunday Express* and the *Independent on Sunday*, and manufactured an almost entirely synthetic 'row' in which Blair was said to have overruled Mandelson and himself by rejecting the advertisements. The *Sun* followed up the story, ensuring massive free publicity for a highly negative advertising campaign which would have never otherwise seen the light of day. There is a 'Mr Weak' poster in Campbell's office in Number Ten Downing Street today. If Mandelson was ruthless at times, Campbell was hardly less so.

Throughout this period Mandelson defended BMP, sometimes to the exasperation of the young turks in Blair's office. He did take a second opinion, in deepest secrecy, from Saatchi and Saatchi, which Charles and Maurice Saatchi, the Tories' advertising men, had now left; armed with their critique Blair attended a meeting in November at which he would express some of his discontent. But Mandelson warned him in advance 'to be careful'. Remembering the destabilising effect Kinnock's depression had had on Powell and his colleagues in the run-up to the 1987 election, he told Blair: 'there's no point in demoralising or demotivating them if we're not going to get rid of them . . . I do not share your negative and gloomy view of BMP's efforts to date.'

One of the reasons for anxiety towards the end of 1996 was that things were not all going Labour's way. The trouble had started – for the party and for Mandelson personally – with Clare Short's outburst in August 1996 in an interview with the *New Statesman*: she denounced the 'people in the dark', adding, in a telling and unmistakable reference to Mandelson, that 'obsession with media and focus groups is making us look as if we want power at any price'. Those around Blair, she asserted, were trying to pass off the Labour Party as something which it was not: 'One, it's a lie. And two, it's dangerous.'[13] Mandelson and Brown, after hours of negotiation with Short during which she told Mandelson that she still 'loved' Tony Blair but would not rescind her remarks about spin doctors, drafted the statement for Blair to issue from Geoffrey Robinson's villa in San Gimignano; it blithely asserted that there was no difference between himself and his Transport spokesman. Mandelson deferred to Prescott's insistence that the deputy leader and not Mandelson should defend the government on the issue – which Prescott did with some relish, having been infuriated that Short had opposed him over the re-nationalisation of British Rail.

Short's intervention, and in particular her use of the term 'dangerous', prompted the Tories – already using their 'New Labour, New Danger' slogan and believing that further Mephistophelean imagery would serve them well – to unveil their controversial 'Demon Eyes' poster of Tony Blair. Mandelson immediately went onto a counter-offensive, taking every conceivable radio, television and press opportunity to denounce the advertisement as a 'crass and clumsy' attempt to represent Blair as the devil when he was in fact a 'practising Christian'. He spoke to Blair and Campbell, both abroad on holiday, but the decision to counter-attack was largely his own. In the *Sunday Express* he complained that a forerunner of the Tories' campaigning techniques had been 'evident in pre-war Germany' and lodged a formal complaint to the Advertising Standards Authority.

The counter-initiative was a high-risk strategy. It ensured that the 'Demon Eyes' campaign had saturation coverage and penetrated public consciousness far more deeply than it would otherwise have done. Moreover, the public reaction was mixed, to say the least. While Philip Gould claimed that the first twelve focus groups he conducted after the episode showed a 'strong and probably strengthening resistance to the government', an *Observer* focus group found the Tory advertisement effective and the Labour 'Same Old Lies' response ineffective. On the other hand Mandelson had withstood the attack and probably managed to seize the campaigning initiative from his Tory opponents. The ASA did rule against the advertisement; by the time the Saatchis were explaining that the red eyes in the picture of Blair were supposed to be those of Mandelson, it was too late.

The counter-attack was also hokum. As Peter Riddell would wisely write in *The Times* in November, after Mandelson deplored 'negative and spurious stories' at a meeting of the Westminster Media Forum: 'That would be more defensible if Labour, and Mr Mandelson, did not demean public debate by repeatedly accusing the Tories of "lying" . . . Politicians and spin doctors should spare us such sanctimonious and self-interested advice.'[14] And Riddell did not yet know the half of it. He might have added that the advice was coming from a party general whose campaign against a Tory fifth term, once the election got under way, would include the wholly unsubstantiated charge that the Tories planned to put VAT on food, and to abolish the state pension (the latter was theoretically true, in the very long term, but it was framed in such a way as to inflame needless fears among pensioners). The high mindedness was also a little less evident inside Millbank Tower. The intervention of the Bishop of Oxford, Richard Harris, who roundly denounced the satanic imagery of the 'Demon Eyes' advertisement, was itself a Mandelson coup. 'Get me a fucking bishop!' he had yelled frantically across the open-plan office at Peter Hyman.

But while Mandelson had successfully withstood the Tory attack, hairline cracks were nevertheless beginning to appear in Blair's supposedly impregnable public image. In early September Mandelson was warning Blair that focus groups, set up at his request by Deborah Mattinson, showed that he was 'slipping in trust, sincerity, convictions, "say anything to win votes"', and that Major was gaining ground. It was clear that Mandelson did not find his formal job as the 'nuts and bolts' election planner too confining. Such was the crossover between message and medium that he could hardly ignore the bigger questions of strategy, any more than Brown could be expected not to take an interest in – say – advertising. Moreover, as he explained in late September, he had 'three roles' – 'MP, friend and adviser to Tony Blair, and front bench spokesperson responsible for election campaigning'.[15] It was largely in the second of these three functions that he now shared with Blair a list of worries which made quite anxious reading for the leader. Efforts would have to be made, he said, to 'sort out John Prescott and Robin', who were encouraging indiscipline 'from the top'. He complained that Prescott was being 'irresponsible', and that a 'strategy' was needed to deal with him to ensure the deputy leader's cooperation with two men of whom he was currently highly suspicious, Brown and Mandelson. The party conference, Mandelson insisted needed to be conducted like 'a military operation' to 'defuse, discount, and, eventually, dismiss' any votes against the leadership. (In the end, thanks to tireless arm-twisting by Margaret McDonagh and the leader's backroom fixers John Cruddas and Pat McFadden, there were none.) While emphasising that the Tories had got less out of their conference than Labour had from theirs, he warned: 'What they have got – which means something to the journos – is a story: about us, about you, about Major. It is just enough to keep their chances afloat.

They have created doubts about our strategy – too middle-class, too Southern, too trendy and metropolitan.' Major had indeed used this argument effectively in his conference speech. Some of Mandelson's prescriptions were hardly startling – keep stressing Labour as 'fresh, for the future and for the many', while the Tories were in the past and for the few. He continued to fret about the lack of an economic 'message' that wouldn't be crowded out by good news of a recovery. He correctly read the problems of Neil Hamilton, the Tatton MP accused of taking bribes from Mohammed al Fayed as 'media largely on our side over Hamilton and looking for blood which would put Major very much on the defensive'. He allowed himself one personal flourish: 'Glad your speech and trip [to South Africa] went well. There was a *lovely* photograph of you on the front of the *Standard*.'

But this paled by comparison with Mandelson's most publicly theatrical act during his time as the 1997 election planner – one which became part of campaign folklore, distilling as it did all his reputation for bullying journalists, both press and broadcasting, on the very day after his denouncement of 'media trivia' at the Westminster Media Forum. The *Daily Telegraph*'s political editor, George Jones, had that morning written a story correctly predicting that the Tories were about to launch an attack on Labour for concealing spending plans which would require tax increases of £1,200 per year.[16] The 'calculations', made by William Waldegrave, the Treasury Chief Secretary, were highly suspect, to say the least. But as a story, Jones's report was legitimate – and indeed arguably helpful to Labour, since it revealed a government line which the party would have to rebut. Nevertheless, as Jones arrived at Millbank for a press conference, Mandelson clapped ostentatiously and shouted out: 'Applause, applause for George Jones, straight from *Newsnight* and Conservative Central Office.' Taunted not once but twice in this way, Jones walked out.

So why did Mandelson do it? He came perilously close to making a fool of himself – and might have done so had George Jones not, however understandably, risen to the bait, rather than making a 'playful' response, as his brother Nick Jones later suggested he should have done. There *was* an element of teasing, though of a sort that was calculated to infuriate and perhaps humiliate, as Miles had found almost thirty years earlier. And finally, no doubt, he may have been sufficiently rattled by the Tories' (in fact rather empty) attempt to repeat their hugely successful 'double whammy' attack on Labour in January 1992 to believe that some old-fashioned scare tactics might 'blunt' the edge of a still predominantly Tory press. On the other hand, there was an important caveat. There was a strong element, once again, of the pantomime villain in all of this. Was his behaviour frightening, or merely ridiculous? His intimidatory reputation stemmed largely from the fact that the 'victims' were usually in the media – the very prism through which his image was created. Because journalists – and usually the secure and influential ones who had little or nothing in reality to fear from Mandelson – were at once most often on the receiving end, and in a position to report it, in print or in conversation, his profile as someone who sought to inspire fear became sharper than was justified by reality. For this, of course, he was himself to blame; he had no need to treat Jones in this way. But it led to a largely distorted picture, though one principally of his own making.

No other contact Mandelson had with the media in this period was as dramatic. In any case, he had plenty else to think about. His responsibility for the campaign allowed him to dispense exhortation, advice and occasional rebukes to middle-ranking members of the Shadow Cabinet. These did not always conform to the pro-moderniser, anti-traditionalist stereotype. He sent Clare Short a detailed and friendly note listing, point by point, ways of 'selling' the launch of the party's policy on railways, suggesting that this should be done 'in a way to get people nodding in the pub . . . "we will pay more and get less and then spend an enormous amount more trying to put it right." This is the sort of effective line you take in *Today*-type interviews, all very noddable.' In November he told the shadow Health spokesman Chris Smith, a little more pointedly, that he was 'worried' about the 'roll' – a favourite Mandelson word – being enjoyed by his opposite number Stephen Dorrell and anxious that Smith's message was too geared to NHS professionals: 'We need some killer facts on funding, NHS performance, patient care before he speaks on Monday. Is it possible to pre-empt him and get a good story lined up in the Sunday papers? Perhaps some trails of your speech on Tuesday – but these need to focus on people and patients rather than organisation and structures in order to get the stories we need.' But Smith and Short were lucky to escape with mere Mandelson advice. After Harriet Harman underperformed at a press conference, Mandelson was quickly and ominously on to Blair:

Her initiative today on pensions . . . had to be canned at the last minute because the work had not been done thoroughly and in time [a capital offence in Mandelson's catalogue of crimes]. A meeting the other week on campaign story development was hopeless because she arrived unprepared and, largely, without ideas . . . I think she needs the reality of her situation to be brought home to her and I can think of nobody better to do this than you.

In October he drew up, for Tony Blair and John Prescott, his first lengthy overview of the coming campaign. It dealt much more diplomatically with some concerns about disunity which he had voiced to Blair before the conference, showing, in contrast to the George Jones episode, how Mandelson could be tactful as well as firm if he chose. Contrasting the 'cohesion' of the party conference with the uneasy period before it, when there had been a 'significant loss of support', he skilfully underlined the importance of Prescott, his old adversary, while seeking to yoke it to the common election effort:

The main symbol of our unity – of 'old' and New Labour . . . is the both of you enjoying a close, supportive relationship. That does not mean it is a joint leadership. The public are voting for one Prime Minister and it is a worry to people that Tony might be hedged in or constrained once in office. But the 'odd couple' has caught the people's imagination. They like it, find it slightly intriguing and want it to work. It represents different strains which they find complementary rather than antagonistic . . . Our opponents will do everything possible to turn this against us. It must be among their top strategic aims – and amongst ours to defeat. During our campaign therefore, without making the issue a distraction, you should be seen enjoying each other's company and talking about each other when appropriate in warm, humorous terms, as at Blackpool . . . New Labour has to be a unifying factor between you ( JP: 'I didn't necessarily agree with him at first, but I see he is right . . .' TB: 'We had to change but remain proud of our roots . . .')

Finally, he used all his own – and Prescott's – sense of party history to sketch out a role for the deputy leader which would inevitably keep him on the road and away from the centre – while giving him, as indeed it did, continuous TV exposure. A model, also involving a talented but potentially troublesome front-rank Labour politician, was at hand: 'I have no doubt that John's activity should reflect his popularity. In 1966 and more so in 1970 George Brown generated a lot of media coverage and goodwill from his spontaneous, whistlestop campaigning in which a lot of "back of the lorry, town square, strong message, quick flesh-pressing and on to the next call" reached a lot of people and delighted the media. Perhaps we need to invent a modern equivalent.' Such was the genesis of the deputy leader's frenetic and highly successful whistlestop coach tour on the 'Prescott Express'.

Mandelson had in some ways had a difficult 1996. He had been upset by critical coverage of his Barclay's Bank-sponsored tour of the Far East at Easter, the main purpose of which had been to reassure Asian companies, potential as well as current, that their investments in Britain would be safe under Labour. He also ran into unfavourable – if more light-hearted – publicity when his friend James Palumbo, owner of the Ministry of Sound nightclub, lent Millbank Tower (in theory, but Mandelson himself in practice) a chauffeur-driven silver Rover, which Mandelson then commandeered more or less for his own use. 'Although Peter Mandelson is not quite a Rudolph Nureyev,' his colleague Peter Kilfoyle quipped sharply, 'he is a renowned disco dancer. Perhaps this is designed to help him conserve energy between raves.'[17] The constant friction with Brown had taken its toll. And finally he was apprehensive about the energy he would need to get through a protracted election campaign.

He was therefore glad to get away twice in December to the

Harrises' house at Kintbury for some rest before the battle ahead. On 30 December Neil and Glenys Kinnock came to visit. The encounter started a little stiffly, and Harris noted a 'touch of the exile's melancholy' about Mandelson's old boss, who had watched from afar the build-up to an election victory which had eluded him and the fruits of which would not be his. With what Harris regarded as 'exquisite tact' Mandelson began to consult him on various questions – including PR, which Kinnock supported but about which Blair remained ambivalent.[18] Gradually the old campaigner in Kinnock reasserted himself. He was, he told the company, confident of a Labour victory; with heroic frankness he added that the key factor was that he was not the leader. Harris said the trouble for Labour in the eighties and early nineties had been that the Tories had been right – about Europe, unions, privatisation, the economy – everything. Mandelson froze with horror – telling Harris afterwards that he had wanted to hide under his seat. He need not have worried. Kinnock nodded. 'Absolutely right,' he said quietly.

There was nothing unusual about the fact that Mandelson spoke twice on the telephone to Blair – staying in West Cork with David Puttnam – on New Year's Eve. He seldom visited Kintbury without doing so. But this time Harris was aware of an almost tangible sense of something momentous ahead. Whatever else, the next New Year's Eve would not be the same. Mandelson typed yet another of his faxes to Blair, urging him to include in the campaign document currently in preparation a 'strong direct personal appeal to all but the most partisan Tory voters to support a reforming crusade to modernise Britain and make it fit for the next century'. At any other time this would have seemed portentous. But the next day a historic year was starting. In his own handwriting Mandelson added: '1997 will be such a good year for you.'

# CHAPTER NINETEEN

## *The Making of the Prime Minister*

The headline on the *Daily Telegraph*'s lead story was awful – just about as bad as you could expect in a general election: MANDELSON AND BROWN STAGE SHOUTING MATCH IN MILLBANK AS LABOUR LEAD FALLS. Fortunately for the Labour Party, it never appeared. It was from a list drawn up for Mandelson by the ever-fertile David Bradshaw, seconded from the *Mirror* to Millbank Tower for a meeting of Labour spin doctors to discuss how they would tackle certain worst nightmare scenarios, several of them gruesomely plausible: RICHARD BRANSON TELLS *MAIL* I WANT TO GIVE MAJOR ANOTHER CHANCE; MORTGAGE RELIEF WILL BE SCRAPPED IN FIRST BUDGET, SAYS FORMER BROWN ADVISER; EUAN BLAIR SAYS MUM TOLD ME WE ARE GOING TO LIVE IN DOWNING STREET; KEY SEAT POLL SHOWS TORIES NOW NECK AND NECK – SHORT WARNS LABOUR NOT RADICAL ENOUGH; SENIOR BLAIR AIDE GETS TOP JOB WITH BT AS COMPANY SUGGESTS THEY WILL ESCAPE WINDFALL TAX; BLAIR WENT PRIVATE TO STRAIGHTEN TEETH AFTER HE BECAME LEADER, *MAIL* CLAIMS; AND MANDELSON WANTS COOK'S JOB, BLAIR INSIDER CLAIMS.

The list testified to the party's preparedness. Every possibility, however remote, had to be catered for. Just after John Major called the election, with Gallup showing Labour at 56.5 per cent and the Tories at 28.5 per cent, a slightly hubristic Mandelson unguardedly told a journalist that he might as well take a holiday; nothing would change between now and polling day. But this was uncharacteristic. Mandelson regarded complacency as the clear and present danger of the campaign. Campbell, the fourth (and only non-politician) member – with Blair, Brown and Mandelson – of the quadrivirate at the centre of the campaign, agreed. His friend, the Manchester United manager Alex Ferguson, memorably warned Campbell at the beginning of the election that it was all too easy to be distracted into thinking about life after victory, rather than about what you had to do to achieve it: 'You're in the position of a manager a month out from the end of championship when you're seven points ahead. What you have to develop is tunnel vision. If you see anything that doesn't need to be there, get rid of it.'[1]

Mandelson was especially outraged by any mention of a landslide, rebuking Robin Cook when he dared to predict one in public; Cook, who was not involved in central planning of the campaign, mischievously announced himself in the few telephone calls he made to Mandelson at the time: 'Hello Mandelson, Landslide Here.' In February Mandelson had attended a lunch at the English Garden given by Robert Harris for Blair to meet Mick Jagger, Jerry Hall and Tom Stoppard. Asked by Blair what he thought the election result would be, Harris said: 'After it's all happened you'll wonder why you ever doubted it would be a landslide.' Mandelson and Blair simultaneously slapped their hands down on the table in horror: the 'l' word had become like the superstitiously avoided 'Macbeth'. After the New Year, of course, Mandelson had less time for his social life; he was able to get away for the odd weekend at Kintbury, though he was never wholly off his pre-election guard. On a Sunday in January Jeremy Irons and Sinead Cusack were among Harris's guests. There was a good deal of pointed but good-humoured complaining about how right-wing Labour had become. Mandelson winkled out the fact that their children were at Bryanston. 'Ah, freedom and flexibility,' he purred. '*Very* New Labour.'

Since 1985 Mandelson had been accused of 'Americanizing' British politics. How much help did Labour's campaign get from those who had worked with Clinton in 1992 and 1996? For a start, Mandelson was not alone in his enthusiasm for Clinton's campaigning tactics. Ever since Blair and Brown had – to John Smith's irritation – visited Washington in 1993 the Labour modernisers had maintained close links with Clinton's people. Philip Gould, who had also worked at Little Rock in 1992, remained in regular touch with Clinton's pollsters, including Paul Begala and Stan Greenberg. Greenberg had been giving advice to Blair on and off since 1995, when he pregnantly advised the Labour leader that, among other things, he needed 'to reassure ... voters again and again by visibly restraining the influence of the unions'. It was a message that Blair appeared to have no trouble in taking to heart. Several other strands in Greenberg's 1995 advice were noticeable in Blair's subsequent strategy. He cautioned against an 'economic vision' which centred exclusively on education and job training; he suggested that Blair needed to be buttressed by 'wise and experienced people, including some from outside Parliament, such as businessmen', and he noted that voters 'respond very positively' to assertions that problems would not be solved overnight.

Greenberg, meanwhile, discreetly spent the last ten days of the campaign in London, advising Gould on polling questions and analysis. When three members of the Labour Party staff, John Braggins, Margaret McDonagh and Alan Barnard, wrote a report on the 1992 Clinton campaign it had been largely ignored. When Blair became leader, it suddenly became relevant again. Several of the 1992 Clinton messages were borrowed directly by Blair, including 'Time for a Change', 'the Failure of Bush/Major', 'Clinton/Blair is Young and Dynamic' and 'Partnership between Government and People'.

Finally Mandelson himself made two visits to the US, in October and in December 1996, during which he had ample opportunity to discuss the forthcoming British election with the Clinton team. And not just with his team. Attending the televised debate with Dole in San Diego, he boldly went up to the President himself. Apparently even the most powerful leader in the free world was susceptible to Mandelson's famously concentrated gaze. He broke off from his conversation, gripped Mandelson's hand and asked him: 'Who are you?' When Mandelson, visibly melting, explained, the President said: 'How is Tony? – he will win, won't he? He's so good. You must look after him, they'll do everything they can, I know, but he'll pull through. Make sure he does ...' The conversation may have been a little banal – but to Mandelson it was still a momentous first meeting with Clinton. He did not leave without thanking the President 'for everything you have achieved for us', and was awestruck by the 'unbelievable' Clinton operation he saw in action at San Diego – of which 'Spin Alley', the huge room where the briefers held forth, was only a part. 'By comparison, we are so thin on the ground,' he faxed back to Blair, 'so few people, and, I am afraid to admit, so loose and unthorough . . . We are scratching the surface – but winning none the less.'

Mandelson was converted by James Carville, Clinton's campaign manager, to the idea, now transplanted in its essentials from Little Rock to Millbank, of the open-plan 'war-room'. And there was also something more personal. In 1998, during his ministerial trip to the US, Mandelson said on *The Charlie Rose Show* that the best advice he had been given by Carville had concerned that most precious commodity – sleep: 'how to make it easy for myself to sleep during the campaign day in order to maintain my energy and my effectiveness . . . to make it honest and legitimate to sort of sleep during the day, to lie down in front of everyone and just close my eyes and say: "You get on with the campaign for half an hour because I'm taking, you know, a back seat."' Mandelson had always been able to sleep during the day, in trains, cars, aeroplanes and in his office. In 1987 he hadn't dared to do so during the campaign; as a result he had been, like most of his colleagues, exhausted by the final weekend. But now, although he complained to Philip Gould at one point that 'there is no pressure in this campaign', this may have been bravado. He was treated for 'cluster headaches' – an extremely unpleasant, relatively rare, and probably tension-related condition, in which the victim is woken in the night by migraine-type pain. And he followed Philip Gould's example by having several acupuncture sessions – though he rejected his mother's solicitous suggestion that he should try aromatherapy. On occasions he dined at Gran Paradiso in Pimlico on the way home to Notting Hill – at least twice with Robert Harris. But he resolved to abstain from alcohol until Blair was safely in Downing Street, falling back on the cups of hot water and lemon which he had drunk for many years in preference to tea and coffee.

Mandelson's trip to San Diego in October had been to see what lessons could be learned from the live head-to-head debate – and whether it could benefit Blair. He decided that such a debate could be made to work for Blair and, on his return, allowed a challenge to be issued to Major. So much has been written about the tortuous eleven days of negotiations, which collapsed on 27 March, between the parties and the broadcasting authorities that they do not need to be rehearsed here. Mandelson told the post-election seminar at Nuffield College, Oxford, that he had been genuinely 'excited' by the prospect of a debate – even though some negotiators in other parties found him 'ambivalent', and the Labour MP Austin Mitchell blamed him explicitly for allowing the talks to break down.

Mitchell was probably right. Like Campbell, Mandelson had never been enthusiastic about the idea. He had not expected Major to agree to a debate: no Prime Minister ever had, except for James Callaghan, who unsuccessfully challenged Margaret Thatcher to a debate in 1979 at a time when his party was lagging behind in the polls while his own personal ratings were higher than his opponent's. Indeed, Major had initially rejected the proposal, only agreeing to discuss it on 16 March. Had the Tories been able to agree cast-iron terms with the Liberal Democrats, then Labour would have had to take part, and would have been prepared. But these were probably the only circumstances in which the party leader, way ahead in the polls, and therefore with little to gain and a lot to lose, would have been forced to the studio.

The fact that the Mandelson and Brown 'shouting match' headline never appeared, and would not have been justified if it had, was largely a tribute to the self-restraint of both men. For all the territorial rows and walkouts of the past three years, the two men buried their differences for the election. For the five weeks of the campaign itself Brown was in charge: he took control of day-to-day political tactics; chaired an extraordinary forty-five press conferences; and, like Mandelson, he maintained contact with Blair throughout the day. Meanwhile Mandelson managed Millbank. Apart from the economic secretariat, it was agreed that Brown's team would not give orders to members of the Millbank staff. That the two former friends were generally able to overcome their mutual antagonism was all the more remarkable given the serious tensions which had persisted past the New Year. Brown, supported by Donald Dewar, had objected to the January campaign of advertisements suggesting that a fifth-term Tory government would put VAT on food. However, the advertisements, originating from an idea by Peter Hyman, were effective, and Mandelson wanted to run them, modified to tone down the wording, arguing that Brown had originally approved the idea. Relations were sufficiently frigid at this point for negotiations to be conducted mainly through Ed Miliband, a member of Brown's staff, with whom Mandelson had always been on good terms. In a concluding note to Brown, Mandelson delivered on 2 April what amounted to an ultimatum: unless Brown agreed to them the advertisements would have to be pulled that very day and a fresh decision taken on what to do with the £500,000, as the sites were already booked. For better or worse, the campaign went ahead, though it was not repeated after Major called the election.

Mandelson also had a row with Ed Balls – the fiercely clever former *Financial Times* journalist who now advised Gordon Brown – over a story which he suspected him of leaking to the *FT*. He demanded – by lobbying Blair – that Charlie Whelan be brought into the main war-room to work with the other briefers, like Tim Allan and David Hill, rather than running 'a separate media operation' from Brown's side office. This followed over-zealous briefing over the weekend of 6–7 April on Labour's willingness to privatise in response to Tory claims about a 'black hole' in their financial calculations (claims that would have bitten more deeply into the Labour campaign had they not been eclipsed by Major's refusal to part with Neil Hamilton, accused of taking bribes from Mohammed al Fayed, as a candidate in Tatton). Brown had been away in Manchester, and Tim Allan was more to blame than Whelan. But lack of coordination between Whelan and Allan had been part of the problem. Nevertheless, according to Margaret McDonagh, 'It is widely known that it was a difficult period for Peter and Gordon; but if you were a member of staff in here, you would never, ever have known that there was a difficult relationship with them – ever.'[2]

Despite their close and long-standing friendship, Mandelson had two points of contention with Campbell. One was over Campbell's insistence that Tim Allan remain in Blair's Millbank office, even though Allan felt he did not have enough to do there. Eventually Allan, more or less unilaterally, came down and joined the briefers in the war-room. The other was over Robert Harris: Mandelson wanted him to have privileged access to Blair throughout the campaign so that he could write a book, *The Making of the Prime Minister*. Since his early teens Mandelson had been thrilled by the vivid and gripping book of that title, written by Anthony Howard and Richard West, about Harold Wilson's 1964 election victory, and he wanted this equally great moment of history recorded with equal style. Campbell was strongly opposed to the idea. Whatever guarantees Harris gave about writing nothing until after the election, he argued, his presence would be invasive, inhibit open discussion during the tour, and annoy other journalists with less privileged access. There may also have been an element of the Blair court jealously safeguarding its territory and repelling an outsider, however congenial and trustworthy. On Sunday 6 April, however, Harris wrote a notable column for the *Sunday Times*, praising the Labour leader but musing on the dangers of his strategy of pleasing everybody. How long, for example, could he expect to keep the right-wing commentator Paul Johnson and himself happy? That day Blair decided that it was time to bring Harris on board, as he had always wanted. He came off the tennis court and telephoned Mandelson to say he now agreed that Harris should join the entourage. By this time it was too late for Harris to embark on a book. Instead he would write a long and illuminating account of the election campaign for the *Sunday Times*.

Despite his apparent nonchalance when the election was called, Mandelson never 'totally lost the fear of losing'. Unlike the Tories, he pointed out to the post-election seminar at Nuffield, Labour had never suffered from the illusion that it was 'born to rule'. Nor was Blair any exception to the law that successful party leaders, however good the polls, almost always have a healthy fear of losing. Some of the most important pre-election decisions made by a leader are influenced by this fear. Choices made to safeguard victory can have consequences, and make an imprint on public opinion, long after polling day. Thus, to cite a classic example, Margaret Thatcher would never contemplate privatisation of the Post Office because, under pressure, she had claimed, in an impromptu remark at a 1987 election press conference, that she would not tamper with the Royal Mail. Whatever her instincts, she was not going to let a privatisation too far spoil her chances of victory.

One such choice made by Blair in 1997 concerned Rupert Murdoch, whose biggest-selling British newspaper the *Sun* announced on 18 March, the day after Major had called the election, that it was backing Labour. Partly because of routine – and exaggerated – reports that he was a close friend of Murdoch's daughter, Elizabeth, Mandelson was often assumed to have been the chief architect of this amazing volte-face. Mandelson lunched at least once, in a private room of the Athenaeum Hotel, with Rupert Murdoch to discuss politics, and he certainly supported the moves to woo his papers. Indeed, Mandelson had been unfashionably relaxed as long ago as 1986 about News International's move to Wapping – maintaining regular contact with senior *Times* and *Sunday Times* journalists in contravention of the official party boycott.

But Campbell and Blair were more directly involved in dealings – with the *Sun* editor Stuart Higgins and with Murdoch himself respectively. And the genesis of the switch lay in that same August 1994 walk that Blair had taken with Campbell who, conscious of Kinnock's utter contempt for, and refusal to deal with, the tabloid press, had exhorted Blair to start wooing it. In particular he had pointed out the desirability of getting the *Sun* 'on board'. This chimed totally with Blair's own thinking; he made sure he was on friendly terms with the editors of both papers even before he became leader in 1994. Campbell had been strongly in favour of – and had played a large part in arranging – Blair's trip to Hayman Island for the annual conference of Murdoch senior executives in July 1995. During his long talk with the Australian premier Paul Keating, Blair had also been told 'that it was better to have Murdoch on your side than against it'. Finally, Blair had been genuinely shocked when Mandelson showed him a dossier, culled from the Colindale newspaper library by Peter Hyman, of the *Sun* and *Mail* coverage of Kinnock's 1992 campaign. He himself, he joked privately in October 1996, would have had trouble voting Labour if he had been exposed to such coverage.

The difficulties of making an electoral cost benefit analysis of the *Sun*'s switch (followed on 27 April by the endorsement of the *News of the World*) are further complicated by the obscurity surrounding the price, if any, which the party paid. Each of the figures involved – Blair, Campbell and Mandelson – have always stuck to Blair's own line in a *New Statesman* interview on 21 March that 'we've never traded policies with Rupert Murdoch in return for the support of his papers'; qualified by the assertion that while Murdoch's power should be exercised responsibly, 'I'd like to see a situation where that happens not by legislation.' Mandelson had subsequently said that 'absolutely nothing at all was offered to Murdoch', but that 'Tony told [Murdoch] that he would be treated fairly like everyone else, there would be no victimisation of Murdoch'. However, there remains suspicion in the industry that Labour's largely market-driven policy towards the concentration of media power might have been different had Murdoch's two popular papers not backed the party in 1997. Certainly one senior BBC executive with close know-ledge of politicians of both main parties considers it significant that, well before the election, Labour allowed through a right-wing Tory amendment torpedoing a key provision of Stephen Dorrell's bill restricting cross-media ownership. Although he was told that a new Labour government would take a much more robust attitude to cross-media ownership after the election, the broadcasting executive said:

> The last government knew what the [issues] are, about reducing the amount of holdings people can have in each media sector and ensuring that they don't develop strength across the sectors. Stephen Dorrell's Green Paper was very sensible, set out all the options, nobody could much improve on it, and are [the Labour government] going to do it? No. This isn't what I was told before the election, I have to tell you. But they're not going to do it, that's my judgement.

One important test of the government's willingness to cross Murdoch was the quasi-judicial decision which would have been in the hands of Mandelson, had he not resigned in December 1998: the bid, examined by the Monopolies and Mergers Commission in the spring of 1999, to buy Manchester United Football Club. In the end, Mandelson's successor, Stephen Byers, upheld the MMC's recommendation not to allow the bid.

The other question was how far Murdoch influenced Labour's election stance on Europe. Again, senior Labour figures emphatically deny that Blair promised Murdoch that Britain would not enter a single currency in the next parliament – and this is credible, given that it was Blair who later in the year insisted that Gordon Brown's statement on EMU to the Commons should hold out the possibility, however slim and theoretical, that the country might conceivably join the single currency before the election. Whether he reassured him that Britain would not be joining in 1999 can only be a matter of speculation, since their conversations were entirely private. But it seems most probable that it was Labour's pledge to hold a referendum if it decided on EMU entry which reassured Murdoch. Initially Mandelson, as a strong pro-European, had joined Gordon Brown in having severe doubts about such a pledge. But he was persuaded of the political case by Blair. Indeed, on the single currency, there was little to choose between the formal positions of both main parties, namely that single currency entry was unlikely in the next Parliament.

Murdoch also met Major on two occasions in the cabinet room – equally privately. According to one well-connected Tory, 'Murdoch basically needed two things if he was going to support Major. One that he had a good chance of winning and secondly that he was prepared to rule out a single currency.' Major, whom Murdoch had never much rated (having never, in the words of one intimate of both Prime Ministers, 'come to terms with the fall of Margaret Thatcher'), was not in a position to provide either. Blair could at least reassure him on the first.

Of course, it is this very point which raises the greatest doubts about how worthwhile the *Sun*'s endorsement was. For Campbell and Mandelson the greatest impact of its unremitting hostility to Kinnock had been in breeding instability in the Labour camp and putting personal pressure on Kinnock himself. It followed that, at least to some extent, Major would experience a similar effect. The *Sun*'s switch, moreover, in the term beloved by Blairite campaigners, was a first-class 'story' about Labour's transformation, up there with many of the other election 'stories', big and small, single-mindedly promoted by Campbell and others in the media during the campaign. Some, like the *Sun*'s switch or Brown's pledge not to raise income tax during the next parliament, were events of real importance. Others, like the section of the manifesto in Blair's own handwriting, pictured in every newspaper, or the front-page 'news' that education would be the first bill to be introduced by a Labour government after taking office, were simply the skilful repackaging of already well-known policies, or a defensive stroke – like Blair's decision to go 'off the cuff' in his speech at an Edinburgh rally – against complaints that the campaign had become boring.

These benefits of the *Sun* switch were clear. But it is much more doubtful whether it had any more than a negligible effect on voting behaviour, despite Blair's fulsome message to Stuart Higgins after the election that it had 'really made the difference'. Tim Collins, Director of Communications at Conservative Central Office after the 1992 election, had always been scornful of the argument that 'It was the *Sun* wot won it', pointing out that most voters had already made up their minds by the time the paper turned the heat on Labour with headlines like NIGHTMARE ON KINNOCK STREET. This is borne out by research carried out by John Curtice, a psephologist at Strathclyde University, showing that the *Sun*'s persistent and sometimes vitriolic attacks on John Major between 1992 and 1995 had only a 'marginal' effect on the party preferences of its readers.[3] Similarly the authoritative study of the 1997 general election pointed out that the paper lost some of its journalistic edge by supporting Labour – not least because of the difficulties of combining its own Euroscepticism with support for the more pro-European of the two main parties. And it concluded that 'even if the *Sun*'s switch did impinge on its readers to a small extent, this effect was trivial in the overall context of forces shaping Labour's election victory. The *Sun*'s endorsement of Tony Blair was certainly remarkable evidence of the success of his political project but, like the rest of the press, the *Sun* was following opinion more than creating it. In 1997, for sure, it was not "the *Sun* wot won it".'[4]

It was in the *Sun*, of course, that Blair, on 21 April, wrote his famously jingoistic column under the headline WE'LL SEE OFF EURO-DRAGONS, provoking a not unreasonable warning from the editor of the *Independent*, Andrew Marr: the Labour leader, he said, was backing himself into a treacherous corner and after an election victory he would either be 'betraying the whole emotional tone of his *Sun* piece or betraying our nation's better future'.[5]

Europe was the other element of the campaign which would have a significant impact beyond polling day. It would have been a relatively complex issue for Labour even if Blair had not been trailing the *Sun* in its wake, as the pro-European – and instinctively pro-EMU – Mandelson had been one of the first to recognise. He had encapsulated the dilemma in a note to Robin Cook at the end of January: apologising for not having had more time to think about Cook's 'important' forthcoming speech on Europe, he emphasised pointedly to the then Eurosceptic Shadow Foreign Secretary that Gordon Brown 'has a firm view on keeping our options open [on the single currency] and we have to ensure cohesion in this area . . . We have both to take the high ground on Europe – standing up for what we believe – and protect ourselves electorally from accusations of federalism and poodleism.' The best solution, Mandelson suggested, was 'to become hard nosed pro-European reformers – not afraid to offend vested interests and confident in our ability to win people to our point of view to secure change and improvement.'

This was all right as far as it went. But as polling day approached, Mandelson was deluged with evidence of a Eurosceptic turn in public opinion, particularly – though not exclusively – among 'switchers' (ex-Tory voters now contemplating support of Labour). Shortly after Mandelson wrote his note to Cook, Philip Gould was reporting *both* that Europe was becoming more important as an issue, *and* that there was a 'clear shift in opinion against Europe'. This was anecdotal as well as scientific: on Thursday 24 April, a week after Major's appeal to his party not to 'bind my hands' on the single currency, Nick Humphries, a campaign infantryman humbly situated on the front line in the Walworth Road telephone canvassing bank, sent in a 'Dear Mr Mandelson' fax: 'We are losing voters in droves,' it said. 'Whenever Europe and the question of sovereignty become centre stage, people instinctively lurch to the Tories. Otherwise strong Labour supporters are prepared to vote Tory solely over the issue of "defending the nation". Interpretation: Avoid Europe at all costs. Blair must go overboard on his nationalism/patriotism.' Mandelson immediately sent the message, marked 'TB to see', up to Blair's office, a storey above the first-floor warroom at Millbank Tower.

It looked very much as if the speech by Jacques Santer, President of the European Commission, three days earlier, had badly damaged

Labour. A blistering attack on Eurosceptics throughout Europe, but by implication especially the British Conservatives, it had widely been treated in the Europhobic press as an unwarranted intervention by a foreigner in domestic British politics. Moreover, the alert Humphries's judgement was about to be handsomely vindicated. The very day after Mandelson received his fax he was sent by Opinion Leader Research the latest findings from two focus groups in Leicester surveyed the previous evening. On Europe, the report noted, 'there appeared to have been something of a sea change. Whereas before the issue appeared to be the Tories' in-fighting, it now appears to be one of "us" (the English, not the British) versus "them" (Europe) . . . the past performance of Major on Europe appears to have been forgotten and Labour and Blair's credentials (experience, negotiating skills) are beginning to be questioned.'[6]

Humphries's point about 'avoiding Europe' was well taken. But it was easier said than done. Exactly a week earlier Mandelson's pressure on BBC coverage had reached a new crescendo with a letter to John Birt announcing that 'Tony is becoming increasingly angry about the BBC treatment of Labour's election campaign'. Europe was, again, the main issue. The problem, Mandelson complained to Birt, was that when, as it had that morning (18 April),

> the BBC announces that 'Europe is again dominating the election campaign with the Conservatives depicting Tony Blair as Chancellor Kohl's ventriloquist's dummy' without reference to Labour's issue of crime . . . Yet . . . what is more relevant and interesting to the public: a Tory advert or crime-busting 'district attorneys' appointed in every locality to shake up the way the CPS and police combat crime, as we announced today?

Letters to Birt, as opposed to Tony Hall, head of News and Current Affairs, were relatively rare. And this one contained an unmistakable hint of menace: 'I realise it is not for you to start getting involved in the detail of news output. But if relations between Tony Blair and the BBC are heading for a major breakdown, this needs to concern you.'

Meanwhile Mandelson pressed on with unveiling his secret weapon: his cherished party election broadcast with 'Fitz' the bulldog. He rejected advice to drop it when it was discovered that Sir James Goldsmith's Referendum Party was also using one in its cinema commercial. 'Bulldogism' was a necessary antidote, he judged, to charges of 'poodleism'. He even proudly paraded with the dog for the TV cameras. Mandelson wanted Prescott to take the dog before the cameras; but when the deputy leader proved unavailable he was delighted to step into the breach. 'It was his one public outing of the campaign and he loved it,' said a member of the Millbank staff. He was fastidious about it in only one respect. A note from BMP warned that the dog's testicles were just visible in the shadow; should they be airbrushed out? 'Yes please,' Mandelson wrote firmly in the margin. It would, he was to point out, be 'a completely New Labour dog'.

Not surprisingly, the increasingly defensive and chauvinistic note struck in the Labour campaign had already begun to worry some of the Tory pro-Europeans, heroically holding the line against the tide of Euroscepticism in their own party. Before Major called the election, Mandelson had separately bumped into Ken Clarke outside the Speaker's house in the Commons and had met John Gummer over breakfast. With both he had agreed on the importance of sticking to the line that a single currency was an option in the next parliament. But what if Labour were now preparing to desert the cause and rule it out until the next election – matching, or even outdoing, the Tories in Euroscepticism? That would leave Ken Clarke, whose threat of resignation had prevented John Major ruling out membership, hopelessly exposed. On 6 April Robin Cook showed worrying signs of heading in just that direction. In an interview with Jonathan Dimbleby he said he saw 'formidable obstacles' to joining the single currency in 1999. More ominously still, he went on to say that it was 'very difficult to see a government that has taken the decision that Britain wasn't in 1999, coming to the decision that it would be ready by the year after, or the year after that'. So if not in 1999, 'the probability is that it is looking towards the subsequent parliament'. This appeared significantly to harden Labour's line against the single currency. Worse still, from the point of view of the Tory pro-Europeans, Blair did not slap down Cook's phraseology the following night in a *Panorama* interview – one in which he appeared unusually flustered.

At this point there was a rare occurrence – rare, at least, during a general election: secret contact across enemy lines. There was sufficient anxiety in the Clarke camp for Anthony Teasdale, Clarke's special adviser at the Treasury, to seek clarification. Roger Liddle, soon to go to Downing Street to work for Blair, was already acting as an unpaid adviser to the Labour Party, and to Blair and Mandelson in particular. Teasdale, who knew Liddle to be a fellow pro-European, now telephoned him to find out what was going on in the Labour high command. After all, if Labour was about to harden its line against the single currency, it seriously affected Clarke's position. There was not much point in Clarke fighting to defend the 'wait and see' policy if Labour suddenly ruled out EMU entry in the next parliament and killed it off as an issue in British politics. 'Keeping the entry option open was a major priority for Ken', said Teasdale. 'He had, after all, signalled his willingness to resign over the question. After talking to the Chancellor, I rang Roger and asked him point-blank if Labour's policy was about to change. He said that he did not think it would or should but that he would find out and get back. He did phone back days later: the policy was staying the same.' After the initial call Liddle sat down the following morning and wrote an urgent and highly confidential memo to Mandelson pointing out the facts of life. Cook had gone significantly further than the Tory government, which had stipulated that British entry on 1 January 1999 was 'very unlikely' but was officially neutral on entry at any time after that, and might even consider going in at the start if the launch date was delayed beyond 1999. Liddle put his finger on the problem: 'Is it really in our interests for Major to shift the Government's position to ruling out effectively a single currency in the next Parliament? If in Clarke's judgement, it is Labour that has sold the pass, I would not bank on a Clarke rebuttal or resignation. Rather I would expect Clarke to retreat in disgust as the Tories try to save themselves from oblivion by out-flanking us in Euroscepticism.'

This outcome would have been perilously close to the very first item on the list of 'nightmare scenario' headlines which David Bradshaw had produced for Mandelson a fortnight earlier: MAJOR AND CLARKE ANNOUNCE AT AFTERNOON PRESS CONFERENCE THAT TORIES WILL NOT JOIN SINGLE CURRENCY IN THE NEXT PARLIA-

MENT. Had Major unilaterally decided to defy his Chancellor and rule out the single currency, Labour would not have followed suit. Such would have been the disarray within the Tory Party – the loss of a Chancellor in mid-election making recovery inconceivable – that Labour could have capitalised on it while sticking to its own, broadly positive, pro-European line. But if, for whatever reason and however reluctantly, Clarke was forced by Major to assent to a policy of hardening his party's position against the single currency, then Labour might be facing catastrophe. It would mean either leaving the Tories to exploit the growing mood of Euroscepticism, or being humiliatingly obliged to follow suit, abandoning any pretence to fighting a principled campaign and closing its options for government – always supposing it got there.

Mandelson now swiftly sent the Liddle memo on to Jonathan Powell in Blair's office. And though some pro-Europeans, inside as well as outside Labour, continued to be alarmed by the campaign's nationalistic tone, the loose language used by Cook and, to a lesser extent Blair, about the single currency was not repeated. And Clarke did not abandon his stand against ruling out the single currency in the next parliament. Labour's campaign on Europe was less than heroic; the party did all it could to avoid turning the election into the kind of pro-European crusade which might have swayed some public opinion back towards the EU and perhaps made it easier to win an EMU referendum in the first parliament, but which would also have risked a serious loss of support on polling day. But it did not 'sell the pass', tempting though on occasions it would have been to do so. According to one senior Labour campaign insider: 'If you read all the articles and the speeches it was very skilful mood music. There was nothing actually that you could say changed the declared policy or was likely to be a commitment or a statement that would prevent you doing what you wanted to do in government. And I think Peter was very, very conscious of the need to avoid that.' This was borne out by a number of conversations Mandelson had during the campaign with Roger Liddle, who, as an ardent pro-European, was chronically agitated that Labour was taking too nationalist a line. 'Read every sentence,' Mandelson would say to him, '. . . and ask yourself: "Is there anything here which contradicts our policy, as we've said it is, and would prove a serious embarrassment to us in government?"' And it was true that on Europe, at least, Blair did fulfil the criterion which he unguardedly laid bare in an interview with the *Observer*: 'If we win this election, we will have done so without ceding any ground that cannot be recovered.'[7]

Butler and Kavanagh conclude their retrospective chapter on the campaign by claiming, correctly, that 'Peter Mandelson was credited with many things for which he was not responsible'; but they add that the tributes paid by the Conservatives to the operations of Labour's Millbank centre and their determination to learn lessons from it 'make it possible that 1997 will be seen as a landmark for Mandelsonisation'.[8] One of the things for which Mandelson could reasonably take credit was the level of practical readiness achieved since early 1995, when he had agreed with Jonathan Powell that general election planning was 'dangerously' behind schedule. Many other people – not least the clear-sighted Powell himself – deserved to share that credit. It was a huge team effort. But, as Kavanagh and Butler point out, it was Mandelson who had 'planned the details; a grid of "who does what" in the campaign; lists of themes and "messages"; research and rebuttal routines; key seats targeting and central control mechanisms'. This is not what Dick Crossman had in mind when he made his famous remark about elections not being decided by the short campaign, but many years before it. He was talking about politics, not practicalities; and the political message in 1997 had overwhelmingly been the responsibility of the leader, advised, admittedly, by Brown, Mandelson and Alastair Campbell. The physical preparations were designed to ensure that nothing – not indiscipline, nor confusion, nor imperfect communications, nor incompetence – got in their way. And if this meant, as Andrew Marr aptly put it, that the 'overall impression of a Labour press conference is of a roomful of zipped lips, buttoned imaginations and clenched buttocks – a party trapped by its opinion poll lead',[9] so be it. Victory was all that mattered.

On polling night Mandelson and Wegg-Prosser were joined at Teesside Airport by Robert Harris, who had been at the Sedgefield count with Blair and had persuaded the *Sunday Times* to charter a light aircraft to take him back to Stansted with his friend. It was a clear, still night, with the lights of Middlesbrough twinkling below them as they took off. Mandelson lolled back in his seat listening to his little portable radio, a black wire trailing from each ear, and 'like an oracle', as Harris put it, gave a sporadic commentary on the electoral wipeout which had taken place 30,000 feet below. 'No Tory seats left in Scotland ... None in Wales ... Portillo out ... Rifkind gone ... Bell defeats Hamilton in Tatton ...' At 6.30 a.m. on Friday, having been driven back to Millbank from the Festival Hall party in the now-famous Palumbo-owned silver Rover, Mandelson presided over a meeting of some of the key players in his team: Margaret McDonagh, Matthew Taylor, Tim Allan, David Hill, Wegg-Prosser. It was agreed that he should give some television interviews. Partly this gave him a chance to spray around congratulations for all those who had worked at Millbank – including Gordon Brown. Partly, no doubt, it was a pre-emptive strike in any potential battle of the airwaves over the question of who, Brown or Mandelson or both, deserved the credit for the campaign. In the end there was no such battle: the sheer size of the majority made the question somehow redundant. For a landslide of this size only the leader could be held responsible. Then, with a steely sense of party discipline that would have done credit to his old comrades in the YCL, Mandelson proposed that McDonagh and Faz Hakim should get on to the regional press officers and find out who the hell some of these unknown new MPs, washed so unexpectedly ashore on the tidal wave of Labour's massive election victory, actually were. Were they, er, sentient? Were they Blairite? Were they, in short, *trouble*?

Then, at mid-morning, almost everybody in the war-room at Millbank began to collect the green cards which would admit them to Downing Street for the 'spontaneous' demonstration of party workers awaiting the Blairs as they arrived triumphantly at Number Ten. Mandelson, back in his big blue chair at the central desk, did not stir. Where could he go? He could hardly, while the new Cabinet were busy round Whitehall installing themselves in their new departments, show his well-known face among the celebratory crowd in Downing Street. He did not yet have a department to go to. He watched the extraordinary moments as they unfolded on television in an empty, silent room strewn with paper and used coffee cups, deflated, solitary – and suddenly wiped out with exhaustion.[10]

# CHAPTER TWENTY

## *The Minister Without*

Polling day, at least in the North-East, had been brilliantly sunny. At the wheel of Steve Wallace's blue-grey Alfa Romeo, Benjamin Wegg-Prosser drove Mandelson along the A19, through the lush Durham countryside. When they finally juddered down the dirt track to Myrobella, Mandelson crouched low in his seat to avoid being seen by the waiting journalists outside – in stark contrast to John Prescott who, on a secret visit from Hull earlier in the day, had taken advantage of the fact that only Campbell could see him by cheerfully making vigorous V-signs at the backs of the listening reporters as he arrived to see Blair.

Their arrival was anti-climactic. Blair himself was asleep in the garden. His wife was resting upstairs in bed, as conscious as her husband that they wouldn't sleep that night. Leo Blair, the Labour leader's father, was just stirring upstairs. Wegg-Prosser sat reading the *Guardian* in the study, barely furnished with a sofa and a small desk with fax and photocopier, while Mandelson chatted desultorily with Jonathan Powell, who was clutching a list of cabinet ministers handwritten by Blair earlier in the day. When Blair was woken by some local children asking if Euan, Kathryn and Nicholas could come out to play, Mandelson and Powell saw their opportunity and went out through the back door into the garden.

There was a lot to talk about. Blair had telephoned Mandelson at Hutton Avenue that morning at 7.30 to warn him that he had already discussed with Brown the possibility of making the Bank of England independent in the days after the election and would want to know Mandelson's view. This did not of course mean that Mandelson had a say in the matter that was anything like Brown's. But it was typical of Blair to seek as much advice as possible before any big decision. Mandelson had immediately asked Liddle – up in Hartlepool for the last day of the campaign – to put his thoughts on paper. Within an hour Liddle, unfazed by the momentousness of a policy proposal of which he, like the British electorate, had had negligible prior warning – had produced a handwritten and characteristically clear-sighted analysis. He listed the advantages of the move: it would be a powerful sign that Labour meant what it said about economic stability; it would reassure the financial markets, bound to be nervous about Labour's determination to tighten fiscal policy in Brown's first July budget; it would shift responsibility to the Bank for an unwelcome rise in rates which it would certainly recommend and which an incoming Labour government could not afford to resist (ironically, in the event, Brown, Iron Chancellor from the first, actually wanted to raise rates by 0.5 per cent but the Bank, backed by the treasury permanent secretary Sir Terry Burns, insisted that a rise of more than 0.25 per cent would be destabilising if the Bank was also to be made independent); it would send a welcome signal to European capitals in that it was in line with the Maastricht Treaty and would therefore be seen as evidence that Britain was really serious about keeping its options open on a single currency; and it would get a tricky decision out of the way before 'old Labour' resistance could be mobilised against it. Liddle was also frank about the risks: a rise in rates would ramp up sterling, causing more pain among manufacturers; the Bank had got it wrong two years earlier, and might be exaggerating the inflationary risks once again; and finally the Eurosceptics might argue that Blair had been a closet EMU fanatic all along, and that this was merely a first move to British EMU entry (the answer to this was that it would also show that the government was determined to avoid devaluation if it stayed *outside* EMU, but that might be a difficult message to sell, given the national mood of Euroscepticism, a legacy of an election campaign in which Labour had been defensive on Europe).

Like all the best advisers, however, Liddle did not duck a firm recommendation: go in, while making it clear that the decision was quite independent of any considerations about EMU. At this stage, of course, no one knew that Labour was about to see its biggest landslide ever. The advice was crucial to Mandelson's view that Brown, whose own economic adviser Ed Balls had long been an advocate of an independent Bank, was right, and he now told Blair as much.

Mandelson did not presume to interfere with the carefully selected names on Powell's ministerial list beyond arguing firmly that if Frank Field and Harriet Harman were both to go to Social Security, it should be with Harman as boss. He, like Brown, had never believed that Field's signal intellectual gifts and imaginative radical-ism qualified him to be a cabinet minister. (In the end of course, both Harman and Field left the government in the first reshuffle.) The conversation turned, not for the first time, to Mandelson's own role in the government. Would he get a proper job – or would he go on 'being Peter'? Twice Mandelson now repeated that he wanted a job with definable content, outside Blair's immediate circle – and wouldn't Minister for Europe in the Foreign Office be ideal? The European job – which went in the end to Doug Henderson, a close Gordon Brown ally, though Giles Radice was at this stage pencilled in for it on Powell's list – was very much what the incumbent made it. Several politicians – including Henderson – were scarcely memorable in the role; others – like the Tory Tristan Garel Jones, a pivotal figure in the Maastricht negotiations – had made it perhaps the best job outside the Cabinet. Mandelson pressed his case. He knew his way round both the subject of Europe and the Foreign Office. He was, as he put it, 'a committed European without being a starry eyed federalist'. He understood better than most the domestic politics involved in the European brief. And he would like to do the job. Blair did not share this view: apart from anything else, Mandelson would simply find himself uneasily sandwiched between Cook and himself. Mandelson's chances of breaking what he later wryly described to a friend as his 'dog and whistle' relationship with his comrade and about-to-be Prime Minister looked slender. The one consolation, however, was that Blair, in Mandelson's pres-ence, and with Powell as witness, said that Mandelson would be brought into the Cabinet after six months (in fact the first reshuffle would not happen for over a year).

Later, Mandelson would look back and be relieved that he had been brought into the centre and saved from the inherent tensions of being Blair's man under Robin Cook in the Foreign Office. Later still, by the following summer, the old frustrations of not having a job in his own right would return with a new intensity. But for now, left with little alternative, he was slowly beginning to warm to the job for which Blair had clearly destined him. It would, he told Blair the following day after a few hours' sleep, enable him to focus on the broader strategy of the government, 'embedding' New Labour principles, acting as the Prime Minister's representative on 'non-departmental or cross departmental issues', to adapt the previous government's working methods to the party's methods in opposition and, on occasions, to be a 'frontman', explaining what the government was doing.

This was a reasonable, if ambitious, description of the job of Minister without Portfolio, 'being Peter' or, as Mandelson would put it nine days later in an *On the Record* interview, 'sort of the Minister for Looking Ahead', as originally intended by Blair.[1] But it underestimated both the problems of trying to coordinate a government from outside the Cabinet – something of which Mandelson would soon become painfully aware – and the amount of time he would still be devoting to media management. It also required some negotiating – and that only after a strange, dead Friday and Saturday morning spent at Northumberland Place, feeling a sense of anti-climax and anxious about his all-too-infrequent contact with the Blair machine being frantically assembled in Downing Street. It would be tempting to think that Blair was leafing cautiously through Mandelson's security file which, along with those of other potential ministers with youthful backgrounds on the left, like Jack Straw, had been handed to him by Stephen Lander, head of MI5.

The truth was more prosaic; there was a lot going on. Indeed, when Mandelson did get through to Downing Street, he found himself drawn into negotiating delicate issues which affected everything but his own future. He mediated between an anxious officialdom and the Blairs over whether they would in fact uproot from their home in Richmond Crescent to the much less child-friendly surroundings of Number Ten. And he had to weigh in to ensure that the faithful Anji Hunter would be allowed a role – and a desk – by the Whitehall hierarchs. Of his own position he was told tantalisingly little until, after making a congratulatory telephone call to Stephen Twigg, who had vanquished Michael Portillo in the defining constituency triumph of the election, and doing a little desultory Saturday shopping at Brompton Cross with Wegg-Prosser and Derek Draper – during which Draper bought him a kitchen blender – he was finally paged and asked to go and see Sir Robin Butler in the Cabinet Office.

Gradually he was to secure, as part of the tight 'terms and conditions' he had warned Blair he would want, unrivalled access to the paper travelling between the Policy Unit and the Prime Minister and between Downing Street and the departments. During his forty-five-minute meeting with the Cabinet Secretary the bones of his job began to fall into place. He was given the cabinet-level red Rover Sterling which had been used by his predecessor as Minister without Portfolio Brian Mawhinney, rather than the more modest Rover 416 or Vauxhall Cavalier normally reserved for ministers of state. He would chair, as Michael Heseltine had done, the 'presentation meeting' of advisers and key spokesmen at 8.30 or 9 a.m. each weekday. He would meet the Cabinet Secretary for an hour every week; likewise the senior officials in the Cabinet Office's Economic and Social Secretariat. He would, despite the fact that he was not even in the Cabinet, be on eleven out of nineteen cabinet committees. He would meet weekly for a political strategy meeting with Blair, Gordon Brown, Alastair Campbell and Jonathan Powell. Since officials – and the Policy Unit – knew that he was a trusted adviser to the Prime Minister, his scribbles on the sensitive policy papers would be taken seriously. It was assumed, not unreasonably, that he knew what he was talking about when, at meetings, he would say judiciously: 'my guess is that the Prime Minister's view is so and so . . .' He usually did know, either because he had asked the Prime Minister himself, or Jonathan Powell, or the Downing Street principal private secretary – until July Alex Allan and then John Holmes – or because he could simply guess on the basis of his long experience of working with Blair since 1994, and indeed for the six years before that. It was power all right, though almost entirely the refracted power of a new Prime Minister with an immense majority.

The substantive meeting with Butler took place on the Saturday afternoon; the presentational visit, when he was shown his office – the special advisers' room outside what had been Heseltine's own gilded and imposing Cabinet Office home – and said a few words for the cameras, was on Sunday morning. He was then spirited away in Dennis Stevenson's chauffeur-driven car to the Stevenson home in Suffolk, where he arrived 'absolutely shattered'.[2] After a long sleep and supper he revived sufficiently to cajole the family party into gathering round the piano and singing extracts from *West Side Story*, including a rather rowdy version of 'Tonight'. It was an isolated moment of relaxation on the eve of the real Day One of the first Labour government for eighteen years.

By the time he sped away to Suffolk, the Cabinet had been appointed. There were few real surprises. Above all, speculation that Blair might bring in a handful of Liberal Democrats in an unprecedented act of pluralism proved unfounded. Yet not only did he come much closer to doing so than was realised at the time, but relations with Paddy Ashdown remained, post-election, a Blair priority to an extraordinary extent for a leader of a party which had just secured a huge overall majority and had no parliamentary need whatever for the support of the minority party.

Mandelson had been in on negotiations with the Liberal Democrats from the start. This was in keeping with Blair's 'horses for courses' approach to the use of lieutenants. Just as Campbell had been the right man – say – to entice the Spurs chairman Alan Sugar to the Labour cause, so Mandelson was the right man to deal with the Liberal Democrats. For a start Mandelson, after close discussion with Blair, had committed himself to electoral reform. True, he was by now famous for indulging his deeply tribalist instincts with an unbridled attack on the third party in the Littleborough and Saddleworth by-election, not to mention a couple of shamelessly populist – and fairly vicious – attacks on Ashdown and 'his beard and sandals brigade' in his *People* column three years earlier. It was understandable that Ashdown initially regarded Mandelson with a certain suspicion. At one meeting with Blair, at which Mandelson was present, Ashdown made his familiar point that Liberal Democrats could not make their minds up whether Tony Blair was a 'pluralist' or a 'control freak'. Mandelson, his palms pressed together and fingertips stretching upwards in praying motion, asked: 'And which are we, Paddy? Which are we?' Ashdown, to his credit, laughed off the taunt, but his fear was that it was Mandelson who was the control freak and Blair the pluralist.

But while Mandelson may not originally have been as inspired as Tony Blair or Roy Jenkins by the grand vision of reuniting the Liberal and Labour traditions, he knew the cold facts: that since as long ago as 1992 the similarities between Liberal Democrat and Labour policies were vastly more pronounced than the differences; that New Labour had more in common with Paddy Ashdown than it did with – say – Ken Livingstone; and that coalition with, perhaps even absorption of, the most important Liberal Democrats offered a route to prolonged power. Years earlier Mandelson had discussed with Blair the possibility that a social democratic Labour Party might somehow simply 'hoover up' the leading Liberal Democrats – but that hadn't happened, not least because Ashdown had succeeded in preserving the party's identity and increasing its electoral strength. And Mandelson's original synopsis for *The Blair Revolution* had proposed a post-election pact with the Liberal Democrats even if Labour won an overall majority – though this had been excised on the grounds that it would inflame too many Labour sensibilities. Moreover, Mandelson actually *liked* senior Liberal Democrats like Jenkins, Lord Holme and Menzies Campbell. Ashdown did not have the extraordinarily warm rapport with Mandelson that he had with Blair; he had started talking to Blair about the possibilities of Lib–Lab cooperation even before Blair became leader in 1994. But in the end Ashdown found that he could work with Mandelson; he paid him warm tributes – privately as well as publicly – when he resigned from the Cabinet at the end of 1998.

At the turn of the year 1995–6 Mandelson had been among those who attended a seminal and wholly secret meeting at Lord Irvine's handsome house in West Hampstead. The future Lord Chancellor was a hospitable host; and his paintings, from the Scottish contemporary colourists to the Sickerts, one of the best private collections in the country. But the ten men now assembled were not there to see the pictures. The Liberal Democrats were Ashdown, Lord

Holme, Bob Maclennan and Archie Kirkwood. On the Labour side, besides Dewar, Mandelson and Irvine himself, were Blair and Cook. This was an interesting selection: the gathering was heavy with Scots; even more important, all the Labour participants were by now either open to, or like Cook and Dewar, actual enthusiasts for, electoral reform. Gordon Brown and John Prescott, the former deeply sceptical and the latter an outright opponent, were not of the party.

The lengthy and amicable encounter, lubricated by some of Lord Irvine's excellent claret, reached three important conclusions. The first was that a committee jointly chaired by Cook and McLennan would establish an agreement on constitutional reform including a possible alternative electoral system for the House of Commons. The second was to work towards a Lib–Lab coalition in the Scottish parliament in the event of Labour getting no overall majority, or an unworkably small one. And the third was that the two parties would strive not to damage each other more than was necessary in the coming general election.

This delicate but incalculably important pledge was intended to draw a line under the savagery of Littleborough and Saddleworth – to ensure that nothing of the kind happened again, least of all in the general election. It would be policed by Lord Holme and Mandelson in the run-up to polling day. Indeed, Holme and Mandelson spoke at least once a week during the ten weeks before polling day. Dozens of parliamentary candidates in each party, fighting the election in Tory seats, were concerned that their leaders were not doing more to encourage tactical anti-Conservative voting. They might have been less worried if they had known of the elaborate efforts being made behind the scenes to ensure that the two parties kept attacks on each other to a minimum. Some of these were listed in an eight-point document drawn up by Holme and sent to Mandelson, and by Mandelson to Blair, in late February 1997, proposing among other things that 'where Liberal Democrat representatives express differences from Labour they should do so without using the standpoint or language of Conservative propaganda that New Labour has not changed, that it poses "new danger", that it is shielding a "hidden left", that it remains a trade union dominated party, and that the party is split and divided.'

Labour, for its part, would campaign 'without arguing that Liberal Democrats are a "high tax" party with spending commitments which are uncosted and unfunded and that a Liberal Democrat vote is a wasted vote because of their small representation in Parliament'. The main point of difference between the parties – the Liberal Democrats' policy of a 1p increase in income tax for education – 'should be acknowledged but emphasis should be placed on attacking the Tory tax record . . . and John Major's dishonesty on the subject'. Broadly, this joint strategy yielded handsome dividends in both parties as the anti-Tory vote coalesced to the advantage of each. Holme and Mandelson had worked on the accord, with the blessing of Ashdown and Blair, after alarming signs that Labour was actually becoming too popular for its own good. On 9 February Colin Rallings and Michael Thrasher had argued that Labour was overperforming in Tory–LibDem marginals and that the Tories might hold otherwise vulnerable seats because of the split in the anti-Conservative vote.[3]

This secret coordination was itself unprecedented. But even further below the surface another agenda, more radical still, was taking shape. The word coalition, other than in the Scottish context, had not been mentioned at the original talks at Irvine's house. But it hung heavily in the air; and it was explicitly discussed in the privacy of the frequent meetings that would now take place both between Blair and Ashdown, and in the discussions between Holme and Mandelson which invariably followed them. Blair and Ashdown would often get carried away with the limitless possibilities of reuniting Labour and Liberalism, but agree at the end of their meetings that Mandelson and Holme would be left to examine, enthusiastically but sometimes a little more hard-headedly, the practicalities. On several occasions all four, sometimes with Jonathan Powell present, would convene together. Late in 1996 these clandestine discussions focused on the possibility of a public pre-election agreement that, post-election, the Liberal Democrats would be invited into a coalition – or, as it would have been called, 'a Partnership of Principle'. This need not have required a formal electoral pact – though there might well have been local agreements, with, to take a random example, Labour standing down in Oxford West and the Liberal Democrats standing down in Oxford East. What it *would* require, at the very least, would be an undertaking from Tony Blair to back electoral reform in the referendum to which Labour was already committed.

There were many attractions to such a commitment. Mandelson himself was privy to excellent intelligence that change in the electoral system would encourage pro-Europeans like Ken Clarke and Michael Heseltine eventually to form a separate breakaway party, suddenly made viable by PR, if they could not persuade the Conservative leadership to embrace a more positive policy on Europe, EMU included. But in the end there was no such public pre-election arrangement. Such a deal might have indicated a lack of self-confidence on Labour's part, and a self-serving marriage of convenience to guarantee victory would be all too vulnerable to attack from the Tories. Blair, Brown and Mandelson had all broadly taken the view, rightly or wrongly, that the hints about PR given by Neil Kinnock in the last week of the 1992 campaign had hindered rather than helped the party.

Instead, the accord was limited to two important elements – neither of them public. One was the 'non-aggression pact' described above. The other, and potentially more explosive, was a private understanding that Blair would indeed invite the Liberal Democrats into a coalition, not only in the case of a hung parliament but also if he secured what was officially described as a 'small overall majority' (in practice accepted by the Liberal Democrats to mean a majority of anything up to around fifty seats). This was more than just a matter of a ministerial seat or two in the Cabinet. The Liberal Democrats argued that there should be a written coalition agreement on the European model, including, but not limited to, Commons electoral reform, to which Blair would now become personally committed – at the very least by promising to campaign for the conclusions of what was to become the Jenkins commission. The LibDems would also require a commitment on education spending and the dropping of the second question in the Scottish devolution referendum on whether the new Edinburgh parliament should have tax-raising powers. The Liberal Democrats would have minority representation at every level of government: cabinet, minister of state and parliamentary under-secretary. Not all the details were agreed: the Labour team were talking in terms of 'two-plus' cabinet seats; the Liberal Democrats of 'three plus'. Ashdown and Menzies Campbell were the obvious candidates for cabinet entry; but the Liberal Democrats argued that a place should be found for a third – probably the respected Alan Beith. The participation of Beith, a sceptic about agreements with Labour, who had not taken part in the clandestine discussions about coalition, would also help to reassure dissidents in his own party.

Although none of these details had been finalised, there was telephone contact between the two leaders' offices on the Sunday afternoon before polling day; they agreed both that their plans were still on track and that they would speak later in the week. During the course of the week Ashdown sent a message warning Blair against summoning him to Downing Street unless they had already agreed a deal – because the speculation generated by such a meeting would be dangerously counter-productive. At the same time he sent a highly confidential letter to LibDem parliamentary candidates in winnable seats advising them to stand by for a possible meeting of the new parliamentary party on the Saturday after the election – and to keep it secret in the meantime.

The Labour landslide of 1 May, and the Liberal Democrats' own wholly unexpected tally of 46 seats, was an outcome neither Blair nor Ashdown had bargained for. Indeed, the eve of polling day prediction of 'Mystic Greg' Cook, Labour's in-house polling expert, was an overall majority of nearer 50–60. Nevertheless as late as polling day, when it began to look as though the majority might be much bigger than anticipated, the prospects for coalition were still alive. Lord [Tom] McNally came down to Yeovil on the Wednesday evening to report as much to Ashdown. With Holme and Mandelson both fully occupied in their parties' respective election campaigns, McNally had been entrusted with maintaining regular contact with Jonathan Powell over the weeks immediately leading up to polling day. Shortly before noon on polling day Ashdown was at the Richard Huish sixth-form college at Taunton, talking to students alongside the candidate Jackie Ballard, when he was told that Tony Blair wanted to speak to him. He took the call in the head teacher's office, while an intrigued David Cracknell of the Press Association waited outside. At this point Blair's view – supported by Ashdown – was that a larger than expected majority would increase rather than reduce the possibility of 'doing things' with the Liberal Democrats. In other words, it might actually be easier to bring them into a coalition. Nevertheless for the first time Ashdown raised the possibility that if coalition could not be made to work, a joint cabinet committee might be a possible substitute and first stage towards a wider agreement. Once again the two men agreed to speak again. When Ashdown emerged from the head's office he said nothing about Blair; he 'explained' that he had just been briefed by Lord Holme on the state of the campaign.

When Blair and Ashdown spoke again the following morning (Friday), however, Blair's mood appeared to have changed. He was not yet constitutionally Prime Minister; he was about to go to Buckingham Palace to see the Queen when he spoke to Ashdown. He was still warm and friendly, still keen to emphasise his determination to move towards ever closer cooperation with the Liberal Democrats. But he was much less positive about the idea of coalition, at least in his first Cabinet. This was neither such a surprise nor such a disappointment to Ashdown as it might have been. The scale of not only Labour's but the LibDems' electoral success – his party was now at its largest in parliament since 1929 – had taken him aback. Indeed, the Labour landslide, having exceeded all expectations, had given rise to some worrying thoughts in Ashdown's mind in the early hours of Friday morning. Was a coalition what the British people had voted for? Did the scale of Blair's victory not really point to an exclusively Labour government? Would it not be almost a violation of democracy to surprise the voters now with a two-party administration?

Assembled in Ashdown's office at the Commons when he took the call from Blair were two of the Liberal Democrats' wisest heads, Lord Jenkins and Lord Holme. Holme, by temperament a long-time enthusiast for coalition and almost certain to be a minister of state in the Lords if it took place, was nevertheless particularly hard-headed. Given the Liberal Democrats' success, he pointed out, the party would certainly not agree to coalition with Labour unless Blair gave an unequivocal personal commitment to the cause of electoral reform; given the size of his overall majority, and the fact that it had been delivered by the very electoral system such a reform would seek to replace, it would be well-nigh impossible for Blair to do so.

How, for example, would he explain such a move to the anti-electoral reform majority in his own Cabinet? In such circumstances, Holme had reluctantly concluded, this was hardly the time for the two parties to come together in government. Ashdown was inclined to agree. When Lord Jenkins asked Ashdown whether he was 'relieved or disappointed' by Blair's apparently cooling on coalition, Ashdown paused for a moment before replying: 'A little relieved, I suppose.'[4]

Mandelson, winding down from the election campaign, would lay some of the blame on the Liberal Democrats. Amid all the confusion of Labour's first hours in power, he had picked up the idea that Blair had indeed offered Ashdown ministerial posts, but that the Liberal Democrats had turned him down. A fortnight later, encountering Menzies Campbell in a TV studio after the Queen's Speech, Mandelson asked him: 'So what happened to you then?' Campbell shrugged. It was true that, by the Friday morning, Ashdown had become hesitant. Moreover his refusal to walk into Downing Street unless a deal had already been done made negotiations more difficult than if he had been prepared to meet Blair to discuss terms on the Friday. But it is still likely that he would have been unable to resist the temptation, had Blair made a firm offer, and on acceptable terms, with a formal coalition agreement of the sort that had been envisaged well before polling day. In reality, in the extraordinary circumstances they confronted on 2 May, neither leader was eager to take the risk. The proposal was effectively shelved by both parties.

Shelved but not extinct. On 12 June 1997 Ashdown, Jenkins, Blair and Mandelson gathered for dinner at Number Ten to discuss how to keep cooperation alive. Having listened to Ashdown's plan for 'constructive opposition',[5] Blair let his guests know how little he had been deflected from his desire for a reunion of the centre and centre-left by Labour's landslide, agreeing to PR for the European elections, seats on a new constitutional cabinet committee, and an early commission on electoral reform. Henceforth, Mandelson would remain a principal conduit for Blair's relations with the Liberal Democrats – sometimes giving them the bad news as well as (usually in private) the good. On the first day of the Liberal Democrats' conference in September an article would appear under his name excoriating another attack by Ashdown, playing to the Lib-Dem gallery, on the government's economic policy. Blair personally ordered the article to be written after hearing Ashdown on the *Today* programme, and it was actually written by Tim Allan in Downing Street; Mandelson had barely had time to read it, let alone write it – an interesting, if harmless, illustration of Blair getting his message out but allowing Mandelson to take the blame. But Mandelson was also a key figure at a further dinner at Number Ten, on 21 October 1997 – recorded in a lengthy leaked extract of Paddy Ashdown's personal diary – during which Blair discussed with Ashdown and Jenkins the idea of bringing two Liberal Democrats into the Cabinet. Pregnant with the possibilities of coalition though this meeting was, there were residual worries among the leadership of both parties that the moment might have already passed, at least as far as Blair's first term was concerned. According to Ashdown's diary entry, Blair said that while his instincts were to move quickly, he thought it might not be possible before May 1998, and that he would have to 'prepare the ground a bit' with his own party. Ashdown proposed that there should be two waves of Liberal Democrat entry into the government: the first, he suggested, would involve Beith and Campbell, whilst he would enter at a later stage. The diary entry recorded that: 'PM [Peter Mandelson] made clear his very considerable irritation about Malcolm [Bruce, LibDem Treasury spokesman], "He never seems to be off the airwaves and he is always attacking us in the most unbridled language. Can't you send him back to his family or to look after his children or something?" PM said he was half-joking and we all laughed . . .' The participants, who included Jonathan Powell, left the dinner apparently agreed, at least in principle, to the desirability of a Lib-Lab coalition.[6] It was not to happen, mainly because of growing opposition, not least within the Cabinet.

But had Ashdown and Blair missed their opportunity on 2 May 1997? Perhaps. On the one hand the obstacles were daunting. Conferring cabinet seats on an alien party after eighteen years in opposition, when the electoral arithmetic did not remotely require it, might have seemed dangerously eccentric. And yet this was a revolutionary moment: having secured a vastly more convincing mandate than he had ever dared to claim, the new leader could have done almost anything he wanted. He might never be so powerful again. He could not, of course, foresee back in May 1997 that he would lose Mandelson, and that his departure would unleash a new outbreak of hostility to further cooperation with the Liberal Democrats among those cabinet members who had seen the Trade and Industry Secretary as among its main proponents. But there are some grounds for thinking that, even before that, Blair and Ashdown had wondered, with the benefit of hindsight, whether they had not 'missed a moment' on 2 May 1997.

After the election Blair had nevertheless remained determined to keep the Liberal Democrats in play. If nothing else the Downing Street dinner – and several such occasions which followed it – demonstrated that Blair had not lost sight of his desire to reunite the centre-left and centre in all its nineteenth-century glory. The common gibe on the left was that he wanted to make Labour more like the US Democrats. But the Blair-Jenkins vision was closer to Gladstonian Liberalism; they saw a return to an era in which the divisions between two parties, each with its own business supporters, was deep rather than wide, in which both shared considerable common ground, not least on economic policy, and in which the radicals had as much chance of dominating the century as the reactionaries. Indeed, the previous September Blair had articulated this vision in an *Observer* article devoted to making the twenty-first century 'not a Tory century'.[7] He took a liberty with history, claiming that the TUC had only been founded because some trade unions disliked the idea of unions forming the Labour Party (the TUC was in fact founded in 1868, thirty-two years before the Labour Party), but his point was persuasive as well as taboo-breaking on the grand scale. It had been Labour's split from the Liberal Party of Lloyd George, Keynes and Beveridge that had helped to deliver the twentieth-century into the hands of the Tories. Blair's *'consigliere'* might not have originally seen the landscape in such visionary terms; but for all his Labourist pedigree he had been eager, perhaps more eager than any other senior figure in the party, to help the leader realise this vision.

A second seminal event in Mandelson's opening weeks was the decision to press ahead with the Millennium Dome. Under considerable pressure from Michael Heseltine, who was arguing that Labour hostility to the project was deterring potential investors, Blair had cautiously agreed to support the project while still in opposition. But before a June meeting of the Cabinet to discuss the Dome the Prime Minister, fretful about the costs (Jennie Page, chief executive of the Millennium Experience, had drawn up a budget of £758 million), sent for Mandelson. Mandelson had intervened to prevent a ministerial subcommittee from ditching the project after Chris Smith had submitted a paper recommending that, at the very least, it should be drastically scaled down. But a hefty cabinet majority, including Gordon Brown, was against what looked like the wrong priority and a very risky project for a supposedly prudent government – £399 million of lottery money had been earmarked. The *Sun*, despite its still *Pravda*esque support for the government, was violently opposed. So was much of the London intelligentsia outside the immediate circle of Lord Rogers, friend of New Labour and the architect with the main contract to design the Dome itself.

But, as they discussed it with Powell and Alastair Campbell, they were joined by John Prescott, who suggested that if a Tory government had had the guts to risk the Dome, a Labour government could hardly do less: 'If we can't make this work, we're not much of a government.' This weighed heavily with Blair, as did a letter from Dome arch-enthusiast Simon Jenkins, the *Times* and *Standard* columnist, which, at Mandelson's suggestion, highlighted those aspects which would appeal to Blair's children. Blair was swung round; though he left Prescott, with impressive determination, to force the decision through a highly sceptical Cabinet. And Mandelson, partly at the instigation of two of the young turks in the Number Ten Policy Unit, James Purnell and Peter Hyman, was given the job of seeing the project through – 'Inevitably', as John Lloyd put it in the *New Statesman* later that year, 'because of his swathe of connections and acquaintances in the worlds of media and showbiz; his appetite for work and organisation; his flair for histrionics and the grand gesture; and his mastiff like grip on the job in hand.' The 'high wire nerviness' of the project also appealed, Lloyd thought, to the 'impresario side of the man'. Besides, 'he was born to it'.[8]

There was also another reason. Mandelson had imagined that he would join PX, the public expenditure committee chaired by Gordon Brown. It might have given the Cabinet Office a greater say in the allocation of funding priorities between departments and Mandelson had already commissioned a paper from Sir Robin Butler on how this could be done. But Brown, apparently perceiving this as a threat to the Treasury's control over domestic policy, blocked the move. The idea had been partly to make the Cabinet Office responsible for monitoring the performance and use of funds in individual spending departments – a role finally publicly granted to the Chancellor at the time of the 1998 budget.

In fact, the PX committee – in stark contrast to the Chancellor himself – played little part in the early life of the government. Nevertheless the failure to get on PX was a symbolic moment for Mandelson. On the one hand he was scarcely ever absent from the Prime Minister's inner counsels when a big decision was taken or a crisis confronted. He also saw a huge volume of the most sensitive papers and usually spoke daily to Blair, either on the telephone or by using his swipe card to slip through the famous wooden door between the Cabinet Office and Number Ten. The summonses were frequent: on 14 May, for example, on the day of the Queen's Speech, he departed early from a star-studded dinner party given by George Weidenfeld for the *Washington Post* proprietor Katherine Graham and attended by – among others – Robin Cook, Sir Isaiah Berlin and Giovanni Agnelli, to go to Downing Street. The distinguished former diplomat Sir Nico Henderson remarked drily to a fellow guest that not even Henry Kissinger or Charles de Gaulle had dared to leave one of Weidenfeld's grand dinners before the end. But on the other hand his powers of intervention were not quite as great as some of his rival ministers feared they would be – or thought they were.

Nor, as he was clear-sighted enough to recognise, did his presence at Cabinet Committee meetings have as much impact on the outcome as was popularly imagined. True, he would be able to report their progress to the Prime Minister whenever he wished and, sometimes, to express his own, or the Blair view of the politics of this option or that. But it was often, as he would retrospectively describe it to his DTI ministers, largely 'a spectator sport' (he was referring to his membership of the committee on the New Deal, chaired by

Above: Campaigning in Hartlepool, general election 1992.

Below: With Ben and Rosie Nye Davies.

Below: At Leo Gillen's house, Hartlepool.

Above: Arthur Scargill speaks, Peter Mandelson listens. Bernard Carr chairs Clause IV meeting, 1995.

Below: Peter Mandelson speaks, Princess Diana listens. English National Ballet reception on the day of the royal divorce, summer 1996.

Above: Gordon Brown and Peter Mandelson before the launch of the Youth Employment Initiative, Institute of Civil Engineers, 18 September 1996.

Below: Gordon Brown, Peter Mandelson and Ed Balls at a press conference pre-briefing by Tony Blair, ICE, 18 September 1996.

Above: At Millbank Tower, September 1996.    Below: At Hutton Avenue, Hartlepool.

Geoffrey Robinson, the Labour MP who lent Mandelson £373,000 in October 1996…

… and the single-fronted house in Northumberland Place, Notting Hill, which he bought with it.

Left: With Charlie Whelan at Millbank, general election 1997 …

… and with Alastair Campbell.

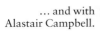

Above: Robin Cook, John Prescott, Peter Mandelson and Neil Kinnock, election night, 1/2 May 1997.

Below: On the stump in Rutherglen, Scottish devolution referendum, 21 August 1997.

Left: Coming up from Kellingley Colliery in the Yorkshire coalfield with Jon Trickett, Mandelson's Parliamentary Private Secretary and MP for Hemsworth (*right*) and John Grogan, MP for Selby, 9 January 1998.

Above: With supermodel Elle Macpherson, at the Serpentine Gallery summer party, 9 July 1998.

Left: Walking back from Downing Street after being appointed to the Cabinet as Secretary of State for Trade and Industry, 27 July 1998.

With Mo Mowlam after she was given a standing ovation at the party conference in response to Tony Blair's tribute to her, 29 September 1998.

Peter Mandelson and Benjamin Wegg-Prosser.

Brown). His influence in any case stemmed from being part of the Number Ten loop in which candid and confidential advice passed between the Policy Unit, the Downing Street private office and the Prime Minister himself. This meant that, as Blair had intended, he was able to give Number Ten his views on virtually any subject. In general, he confessed to a journalist at the time, he was 'not a big wheel' so much as an 'oiler of the wheels' in the field of domestic policy. The Dome at least gave him something concrete to do; it allowed him to take decisions in his own right.

Moreover, Lloyd was right when he said that Mandelson was 'born to it'. As Max Nicholson, formerly Herbert Morrison's private secretary, wrote to remind Mandelson, it had been his grandfather who had ushered into being the Festival of Britain in 1951. Before Mandelson went on a trip to France (to visit the high-tech entertainment complex at Poitiers to see what lessons could be learned for the Dome) the Foreign Office dug out from their archive as bedside reading a copy of *A Tonic to the Nation, The Festival of Britain 1951*,[9] which described how Morrison faced down opposition within the Cabinet, in Whitehall and, led by Churchill, among the Tories to see the ultimately successful project through. Some of the parallels, as in other aspects of Morrison's life, were almost eerie. Once entrusted with the task, Morrison refused to let it go, even after he became Foreign Secretary in March 1951; having guided it through a barrage of criticism he wanted to be there if – or, in his view, when – it triumphed.[10] Similarly, as the reshuffle approached in the summer of 1998, Mandelson stubbornly let it be known that he had no intention of parting with the Dome whatever job he got – and for reasons which were similar to Morrison's half a century earlier. He was also as capable as Morrison had been of seeing that, if his pet project were a success it would be good for the party as well as the country. Had Disraeli not remarked of the Great Exhibition in 1851, 'this exhibition will be a boon for the government, for it will make the public forget its misdeeds'?

At present, however, it was in the eyes of many critics itself a 'misdeed' – possibly New Labour's greatest. Even Blair was reported to have joked drily that he had decided in favour of the Dome because he was sick of all his popularity. Simon Jenkins remained bullishly optimistic, remarking that 'For some curious reason the

British hate large projects. They always assume they're going to be a disaster. Until it happens and then they miraculously turn round and say thank goodness we've got it. It's costed and on schedule: on target and on budget.'[11] The sceptics pointed out that the purpose of the Dome was nowhere near as clear as that of either the Festival of Britain, which had been designed to cheer the country up after more than a decade of wartime – and peacetime – austerity, or the 1851 Great Exhibition which, as Roy Hattersley would put it, was, at the dawn of an era of free trade, 'a great celebration of what Britain could make and what Britain could sell abroad and what Britain could import'. In contrast, Hattersley pointed out, the Greenwich Theatre, in the shadow of the Dome, was having to close 'and schoolkids in the borough won't be able to see their set text plays performed any longer because a great theatre lacks £190,000 while £800m is being spent on the Dome'.[12] One of the environmental activists in the Time Bomb direct action group, Dave Grumpus, was more savage still: 'The government and private industry have conspired to capture the Millennium celebrations for themselves and are intent on creating a pompous monument to the throw away consumer society in which we live.' The attack expressed what a lot of more conventionally minded people thought.

Undeterred by all these doubts, Mandelson, as the sole ministerial shareholder of the Millennium Experience Co., set about his task with relish. He did not make the Dome any less controversial, of course. But he imposed a new order and discipline on the project from the first. Heseltine had already formed a core of corporate supporters: British Airways, British Aerospace, British Telecom and GEC among them. Mandelson brought in, as new board members, Sam Chisholm, who had been the boss of BSkyB until he fell out with Rupert Murdoch, and Michael Grade, the former chief executive of Channel Four and new boss of First Leisure, a leading company at the most populist end of the entertainment market, running everything from bingo halls to Blackpool Tower. There would be a series of mind-bending problems and setbacks to come; but Mandelson would never lose his determination to see the Dome through. It was an irony that, when he left the DTI, he was still the Cabinet's greatest Dome supporter. 'What will happen to my Dome?' he asked plaintively on the day he resigned. But by May 2000, with criticism heaped upon the Dome because of its failure to meet the attendances predicted for it – not least by Mandelson – he had reason to be glad that he was no longer directly associated with it.

One task which coloured the whole of what would prove to be a damaging summer for Mandelson was trying to get elected to the Labour Party National Executive. In retrospect Blair would regret that Mandelson had ever stood; a less controversial figure like Glenda Jackson would have had a better chance of beating off Ken Livingstone.[13] But at the time the views of Downing Street, expressed through Blair's political secretary Sally Morgan, were strongly in favour. It would have been a largely symbolic victory, since after 1998 a rule change would mean that ministerial representatives on the NEC would anyway be appointed by the Prime Minister rather than elected – though it would also make it much easier for Mandelson to be among those appointees, should Blair so choose, if he had been elected the previous year under the old system. Mandelson certainly had a personal agenda. He was keen to stand; his election would give the lie to the idea that he was hated in large sections of the party; but, more importantly, it would indicate that he had a base which was not dependent on the Prime Minister's patronage. From the Prime Minister's point of view, it would also go a long way to realising Blair's famous dictum that the Labour Party would have truly changed when it learned to love Peter Mandelson. The vacancy arose because Gordon Brown was standing down, but the proposal from Downing Street came only at the eleventh hour. Mandelson instructed Benjamin Wegg-Prosser to check with Ed Owen, his counterpart in Jack Straw's office, that the Home Secretary did not want to stand as an alternative modernising candidate to Brown. The message came back that Straw was not interested and was perfectly happy for Mandelson to stand. In a single morning, before nominations closed, Mandelson had to write his personal manifesto and secure, by telephoning the constituency officers in Hartlepool, the necessary permission of his local party. It was also a risk. Mandelson thought that, thanks to his role in the election campaign, he would probably win. But he was also realistic enough to know that he might not. Not for the first time, he was prepared to take a gamble.

Almost immediately, however, he was caught up in more dramatic events. On Friday 1 August Robin Cook's marital problems exploded on the administration. Mandelson was dutifully carrying out a surgery in Hartlepool, having just dealt with a slightly deranged constituent who thought that there was poison in the local flour and potatoes, when he took a call on his mobile phone from the Prime Minister, about to leave for Geoffrey Robinson's handsome villa in San Gimignano. It was, Blair told him, 'about Robin'. Blair, still reeling from the first incident of private turmoil to engulf one of his ministers, could scarcely express himself. Instead he put Alastair Campbell on the line, who bluntly told Mandelson the facts: the *News of the World* was about to expose the Foreign Secretary's affair with his diary secretary Gaynor Regan just as he was about to leave for a holiday in America with his wife Margaret. By now Campbell, contacted by the newspaper, had confronted Cook with the argument that only 'clarity in news management' would ensure that the story was not protracted. Cook, correctly interpreting this as thinly coded warning not to postpone embarrassing and painful decisions, told his wife in the VIP lounge at Heathrow's Terminal Four that he was cancelling the holiday and leaving her. Mandelson returned from Hartlepool the following day and went to Downing Street, where Tim Allan – his boss Alastair Campbell having finally got away to France on holiday – was waiting for the Sunday papers. A diversionary tactic was already at hand. While the *News of the World* screamed the facts of Cook's affair, the broadsheet market leader, the *Sunday Times*, led with a very different story which, on the face of it, might be of greater interest to the more fastidious of Monday's daily papers: the Foreign Office was examining claims that Chris Patten might have been in breach of the Official Secrets Act for passing classified information to Jonathan Dimbleby in the course of Dimbleby's researches for a book on Patten's governorship of Hong Kong. As it happened the story did not come, as everyone assumed, from Mandelson but independently from another senior figure in the government who has subsequently admitted being the source.[14] Moreover, it was passed to the *Sunday Times* on the Thursday, the day *before* the *News of the World* contacted Alastair Campbell. In other words, the purpose of the original leak was not to distract attention from Cook's problems but the scarcely worthier one of discrediting a prominent Tory. Nevertheless on Sunday Mandelson ensured that it had the maximum play by standing it up in an interview on BBC Radio's *World This Weekend*. Initially, Benjamin Wegg-Prosser had flatly turned down the invitation to Mandelson to discuss Cook's troubles. However, seeing his opportunity, Mandelson had swiftly told him to ring back and accept. After uttering some cautious banalities in defence of Cook, prompted by an advance call from Tim Allan, the presenter asked Mandelson about both the Patten story, and one (originally emanating from Charlie Whelan at the Treasury) about the possible reprieve of the royal yacht. Mandelson indicated that both were accurate – incurring in a telephone call that evening the full wrath of the Defence Secretary George Robertson, who knew nothing about any rethink on *Britannia* and was struggling with the delicate and potentially unpopular task of finding her a retirement home. It was decided in December to take no action against Patten, and the reprieve for the royal yacht never took place.

The only explanation for this high-risk and somewhat unsavoury media strategy, agreed in a series of long conversations between Mandelson, Campbell and Tim Allan on the Friday night, was a sense of panic that the Cook revelations threatened to bring the new government's extraordinary honeymoon with the press and electorate to a premature end. It didn't. But it succeeded only too well, with the suborning of the unsuspecting Patten becoming more of a story over the next few days than the Cook affair itself. On the Monday, during *The World at One*, the BBC correspondent John Sopel took the lid off the government operation to stimulate interest in the Patten affair as means of diverting attention away from Cook – this time prompting a furious reaction from Mandelson, who went so far as to claim publicly that Sopel's disclosures were motivated by an ambition to replace Robin Oakley, the BBC's political editor.[15] It also caused a lengthy *froideur* (now at an end) between Sopel and his old friend and golfing partner Tim Allan.

Behind the scenes Mandelson would now be involved in trying to prevent Margaret Cook from taking her revenge in public. She was annoyed with a letter from Blair, in which he seemed to be commiserating with her about the media attention rather than about the separation itself. She contacted Mandelson out of the blue, who immediately called her back in the middle of his train journey, stressing that Blair was very upset for the Cooks and that he had in no way intended to sound cold. Within a couple of days, during the Scottish referendum campaign, he travelled to Edinburgh and visited her at home, allowing her to make him hot water and lemon – and, according to Mrs Cook, 'laying on the charm'. There were danger signals in the conversation; she poured out some of the stories of their marriage she would later put in her book. In fact Mandelson took to her, finding her, as he told a friend at the time, 'an intelligent and vulnerable person', and they now had a series of telephone calls on a matter of some delicacy: the divorce settlement. Robin Cook's friends have emphatically denied that Mandelson acted as a go-between. But when he met her again to assure her that Cook was eager to be generous but that he regarded it as important that, in return, she would not go public on the collapse of their marriage, Mrs Cook reacted in some anger – saying it was disgraceful that she should be 'gagged' but also that she would not dream of damaging him professionally. Mandelson now returned to Cook, saying that while he would not 'get it in blood' she had indicated that she was not going to 'kiss and tell'. She herself confirmed this to Cook when she told him, in a more important conversation the following month, that she had given an interview to the television journalist Linda McDougall, wife of the MP Austin Mitchell, for a book about parliamentary spouses, but that it should not be damaging. However, Ms McDougall incorporated into her text some off-the-cuff remarks made over a dinner, and then ignored Mrs Cook's pleas to tone them down; when they were reproduced several months later in *The Times*[16] Mandelson was again brought in, urging her to 'clarify' her remarks. Which she did, claiming that she had been referring to their life before marriage.

It was this conversation which gave rise to another fine example of the 'Mandelson myth' genre – that the Minister without Portfolio effectively gave her the 'green light' to write her astonishingly candid book about her marriage. That was the burden of the lead story with which the *Sunday Times* publicised the second episode of its serialisation of Margaret Cook's story in January 1999[17]; it was based on her observation that, when Mandelson rang up 'to find out how I was coping', she had 'picked up' that 'there would be considerable resistance to the media deciding which and when cabinet ministers would resign, and he did not seem to think Robin was in danger of losing his job'. Certainly Cook, the only victim of his ex-wife's book, was utterly dismissive to friends of the notion that Mandelson had given her any grounds for going ahead with a book. His tactful treatment of Mrs Cook had had quite the opposite intention.

If Mandelson created problems for himself in this period, they were of another sort. It became apparent during August that he was at times taking his 'frontman' role to excess. Although Blair was frequently in touch with him from abroad; it was not until he returned from holiday that he began to realise, as he himself put it, how much Mandelson, rather than merely managing the story, had *become* the story. Admittedly this was not entirely his fault. When John Prescott, on a visit to Greenwich, jokily named a crab 'Peter', he reasonably did not imagine that, even in a relatively news-starved silly season, it would be the lead story in the following day's *Telegraph*, suggesting a fresh rift between the old sparring partners. Prescott rang him to warn him that the press were taking an unhealthy interest in the remark; but it had still been a calculated warning shot.

Mandelson could not, of course, be blamed for any of the events which appeared to mark the end of labour's honeymoon: the Cook episode, the fourth interest-rate rise since Labour took office, and the disclosure on 6 August of the tragic suicide note left by the gentle and ailing Scottish MP Gordon McMaster, which lifted the lid of the cesspool of West of Scotland Labour politics. But he had, as someone may or may not have said to Ernie Bevin of his own grandfather, been 'his own worst enemy'. He gave a succession of high-profile newspaper, television and radio interviews – some of them in order to boost his campaign in the NEC election. To the *Observer*'s Patrick Wintour he countered Roy Hattersley's now openly dissident attacks on New Labour by citing the New Deal and pointing out – in somewhat old Labour language – 'that we have just raised £5bn worth of tax to stop poverty'.[18] And to the *Independent* he revealed details of the Social Exclusion Unit, whose existence he was to announce the following day in a Fabian Society lecture. In the short term this associated Mandelson with the fight against social inequality and the misery of life on sink estates – and he was excited by the initiative, which was partly intended to end the bewildering and counter-productive disharmony between the various departments concerned with urban regeneration. But his grabbing of the limelight seriously upset Geoff Mulgan of the Number Ten Policy Unit, who had been the brains behind the idea, and Mandelson's subsequent operational responsibility for the unit was heavily circumscribed as a result. Before this, at a long-prearranged press conference on 8 August with John Prescott to trumpet the achievements of the first 100 days, Mandelson had ostentatiously turned on the BBC reporter Nick Robinson for daring to ask him why he was making so many public appearances when he had no portfolio: he had 'never heard such a stream of vainglorious self-indulgent questions coming from the media', he said. He then went on gracelessly and angrily to refuse to answer questions from the BBC's Martha Kearney about why he had become the 'face of the government', saying that he would prefer questions on education, health and employment. No doubt he was entitled to steer the interview back to government policy; but by picking a distinctly ungallant fight with Kearney rather than answering the question politely before moving on, he ensured that the clash would be the big news of the day. Even he half-acknowledged the interview as a mistake when he spoke of 'losing my temper' while 'it made me feel much better . . . the next day's papers were not so generous'.[19]

On one level, no doubt, Mandelson could rationalise this attention-seeking behaviour on the grounds that his cause was Blair's cause; a defeat for him in the NEC election would be seen as a setback for modernisation of the party. On the other hand the profile he was adopting did not exactly help him in the campaign; moreover, there were clear signs that Blair himself, not to mention Campbell, was now increasingly uneasy about identifying himself too closely with Mandelson's NEC bid. After all, had Mandelson been giving disinterested advice to Blair on the subject, he would have told him to do precisely that; he might, after all, lose. When, after his return from holiday, Blair gave an interview to Andrew Grice of the *Sunday Times*, he was distinctly displeased to find his supportive reply to a question about Mandelson's candidacy the main story in the first edition.[20] In fact, it was wholly eclipsed as a story by the death of Princess Diana, and as a result its impact was negligible.

In the end Mandelson's forebodings were justified. By the Saturday before the party conference, as he drove down to Brighton with Wegg-Prosser at the wheel, he knew the bad news from the Prime Minister himself. He had lost to Ken Livingstone. When he and Blair chatted in the Prime Minister's suite in the Metropole on the Sunday, Mandelson agreed that the message from the NEC elections would have to be that it was a defeat for him and not for New Labour. Partly this was a matter of political necessity; partly, however, it reflected Blair's view that, if Mandelson was going to run at all, he should have conducted a much lower-profile, and less media-oriented campaign based on his general election record. Mandelson, inevitably, wrote a 'line to take' which was quite tough on himself – but not as tough as Campbell decided it should be. Mandelson was uncomplaining about Campbell's changes. Prescott rather generously tried to cheer him up by saying that the party would probably like him more now that he had been defeated.

It could be – and was – said in mitigation that by gaining 68,023 votes to Livingstone's 83,669 he had made a creditable first shot at the NEC; few candidates succeeded at the first attempt. Ken Livingstone had also benefited from the large concentration of party membership in London. But it was the most severe reverse of his career to date, and to those in his closest circle it was clear that he had taken it hard; more painful still, when Wegg-Prosser was taking champagne up to Mandelson's room for a consolatory drink on the Sunday evening, he was spotted by Charlie Whelan, who deduced that they were celebrating a victory and tipped off Piers Morgan, the *Mirror* editor – giving rise to rumours among journalists that he had won. But though it was a blow, he appeared unflinching to the outside world. Indeed, his big match temperament in the face of adversity was not in doubt. He did not hide away, any more than he would after his resignation from the Cabinet in 1998, when he went into the Commons every day after it was back in session at the New Year. He conducted a full programme of fringe meetings. Indeed, at one trade union meeting he caused considerable excitement when the industrial correspondents assumed that he was suggesting, in an off-the-cuff answer to a question, that there would be a lower minimum wage for younger workers. Was he merely stating government policy, which was to have a lower rate for trainees, or going further and proposing what was not yet government policy – a lower rate for *all* younger workers? As it happens the exact transcript is ambiguous, leaning towards the first interpretation:

> On the minimum wage we believe that the National Minimum Wage must take account of the needs of young trainees and it must not penalise occupational training activity. And that's why we have asked the Low Pay Commission to look at this area and to consider it very carefully indeed. We've got to ensure that the minimum wage does not provide a disincentive for young people to stay in education and training.

Ironically, moreover, if he *had* been hinting at a lower rate for all younger workers, he would only have been echoing the views of Gordon Brown who, when the Low Pay Commission reported, argued strongly – and successfully – for just such a lower rate for all workers under twenty-five. Brown won his case partly by pointing out that the inflationary consequences of not having a differential rate would encourage the Bank of England to keep interest rates higher than they would otherwise be.[21]

The whole episode – his conduct during August rather than the defeat itself – resulted in a real, though temporary, setback in Mandelson's relationship with Blair. What had irritated some of those closest to Blair was that he had made a concerted effort to establish his own identity independently of the Prime Minister and had then failed to pull it off. Why, he was asked by at least one close Blair aide, couldn't he be satisfied with the influence he wielded thanks to his closeness to his boss? Why did he have to have a power base of his own as well? It was a classic expression of the view that Mandelson was acceptable as long as he continued to 'be Peter'. He was far from frozen out of the inner circle, but for a while, perhaps, he was consulted rather less readily than before.

He was badly hit by the episode; but he was also able to treat it with a certain self-parodying humour. It was, he realised, time to display an un-Mandelsonian quality: humility. In a piece drafted for him by the (as usual) word-perfect David Bradshaw (now at Downing Street, but then with the *Daily Mirror*) the 'h'-word figured with just the right frequency. Bradshaw did not, of course, tell his editor Piers Morgan that he had written it; and was delighted to be told by him what an excellent article he had received from Mandelson. At least the ghosted article, which appeared under his name in the following day's *Mirror*,[22] provided Mandelson with a good joke which could only be fully appreciated by those fully immersed in the language of New Labour spin, in which nothing, including authorship, is ever quite what it seems. As he struggled manfully to come to terms with his new, humbled persona in his room at the Metropole, he carefully read the article to appear under his name: 'It's OK,' he remarked, 'as long as no one thinks I wrote it.' Bradshaw did not pause. 'I wouldn't worry,' he replied. 'No one will.'

# CHAPTER TWENTY-ONE

## *A Most Pro-European Minister*

The event which propelled Mandelson forcibly back into his familiar role of trusted Blair lieutenant was the worst for the government since it had taken office. Mandelson was in Hartlepool when, on Friday 17 October, he took a routine late-evening call from the Media Monitoring Unit at Millbank telling him that *The Times* had what by any standards was a scoop. An on-the-record interview with the Chancellor of the Exchequer was splashed across the front page under the headline: BROWN RULES OUT SINGLE CURRENCY IN THE LIFETIME OF THIS PARLIAMENT. The headline – although, as often with headlines, not wholly justified by the story beneath it – was particularly shocking to anyone who did not know of the convoluted steps which had most immediately led to it. Mandelson, precisely in that category, telephoned the Prime Minister, beginning his weekend in Chequers, to register his shock.

Europe, after all, had been one of his special concerns. His ministerial involvement in it had started on 11 May. He had spent a pleasant day with Robert Harris's family in Berkshire, arriving for the first time with the ancient red box he had inherited from Brian Mawhinney. It was so difficult to open that he had to jump up and down on it – on one weekend with the help of his private secretary Rupert Huxter, summoned from his home in Shepherd's Bush – to force open the lock. The Harrises allowed him complete relaxation and a steady supply of his favourite lemon custard soufflé. He would occasionally baby-sit, the Harrises leaving their daughter Holly in the living room reading Enid Blyton while Mandelson struggled

412

through his red box. Two weeks later he would become godfather at the christening of their youngest daughter Matilda – the Prince of Darkness solemnly promising to help her 'renounce the devil and all his works'. This Sunday he much amused the Harrises with a highly coloured story that, following reports that Cherie Blair disliked Humphrey, the Downing Street cat, Alastair Campbell had arrived for work and said, 'Forget about the economy, forget about Europe, today is cat day,' and had then drugged the animal and locked it in a cupboard so that it could be produced for a photo call with the Prime Minister's wife. That evening, however, he was summoned to Downing Street for more serious business.

Blair had been thinking hard, in his first full week as Prime Minister, about European policy. On the one hand he felt the need – the rather urgent need, given the defensive and at times sceptical tone of the Labour campaign, and the fact that, formally at least, there was no practical difference between the two main parties on EMU – to reassure Britain's European partners that Labour's election victory had indeed been a positive and decisive turning point in its relations with the EU. On the other hand he had been alarmed to be shown the list of regulatory measures coming up under the heading of the Social Chapter, which the new government had signed, in its first act of foreign policy. Mandelson was now entrusted with carrying out a delicate mission over the next few months: key members of the European governments had to be reassured about Blair's strongly pro-European views and, at the same time, reminded that these were laced with a certain Anglo-Saxon distaste for over-regulation, particularly on labour market issues. He might not be the Minister for Europe; but thanks to his stated qualification of being 'a committed European without being a starry eyed federalist' he would have the role of part-time prime ministerial emissary to the European chancelleries.

The immediate impact of both the *Times* headline (if not Philip Webster's more carefully calibrated story beneath it) and of the attendant briefing from both the Number Ten and the Treasury spin doctors was to suggest that Brown, the Cabinet's most ardent pro-European, had broken through the very barrier which, hardly more than six months earlier, even the instinctively anti-EMU John Major had shrunk from crossing. Mandelson was aghast at what he saw as the new and dangerously Eurosceptic tone of Brown's utterances. It would, as he would discover on Monday when he took calls in his office from – among others – Adair Turner, Director-General of the CBI, and Niall Fitzgerald, the chairman of Unilever, cause grave anxiety to those in the corporate sector who had welcomed Blair precisely because he had abandoned the Euroscepticism of the previous administration. On the basis of the headline/spin, businesses were being offered no guidance, whether they wanted Britain in EMU or not, on whether to plan and prepare for a single currency. It looked as if the supposedly pro-business New Labour government simply did not appreciate the real-world impact of this uncertainty. But Mandelson did not need to wait until Monday to be told this. The expert view in Downing Street was that there would be 'extreme turbulence' in the markets when they reopened. Other ministers, needless to say, had been equally left out of the loop: Frank Dobson, interviewed on *Breakfast with Frost* on Sunday, with the jubilant Tories by now demanding a recall of parliament, stuck doggedly to the line which the Cabinet had held before the Friday interview – we may not go in in 1999 but our options are open after that. Given the sudden fluidity of EMU policy, it was the only possible course.

Because almost all the accounts of this episode have concentrated on the immediate run-up to it, and in particular on the destructively colourful role played in it by the Chancellor's press spokesman, Charlie Whelan, it is important to understand the larger context. Almost from the start, the government had been preoccupied with the question of how to translate the Labour Party's version of a 'wait and see' policy towards EMU into practice; there had been several meetings at Downing Street before the summer break to discuss what to do as it became increasingly apparent that the Prime Minister did not intend to go in at the starting date of 1999. Even if that were not the inevitable price paid for the continuing support of the fearsomely Eurosceptic Rupert Murdoch, there were other reasons. First, while before the election Kenneth Clarke, heroically, and the Labour Party, rather less heroically, had held the line against ruling out EMU in the next parliament, the winning campaign did not exactly go out of its way to turn the tide of Euroscepticism. It would take much longer to do so, especially with the combined forces of the Black and Murdoch press ranged against EMU. Defeat in an EMU referendum would be disastrous, a much more damaging equivalent of the Tories' Black Wednesday, and Blair was not prepared, in Clarke's apt phrase, to 'bet the ranch' on a referendum he might lose, at the cost of his precious second term. (Clarke, and then Brown, had vainly tried to resist a referendum commitment by their parties in the first place, partly because they wanted to avoid precisely this situation.) Secondly, in the summer of 1997 it was still far from clear what kind of creature EMU would be. How many countries would eventually sign up? Would the criteria be fudged? These were both unresolved questions for much of 1997. And finally, in the words of the authoritative account of the European question in post-war British politics, 'Tony Blair ... never wholeheartedly believed in an EMU which included from the start, the pound sterling. He placed himself in the classic line of those British politicians who [in the period when the Common Market was being formed] were sceptical about the success of the weird integrationist scheme and argue that we must wait and see if the Common Market worked, which it probably wouldn't.'[1]

That was truer of Blair's instincts than it was of either Gordon Brown's or Peter Mandelson's. Indeed, it was Mandelson whom Blair had prevented from publishing a pro-EMU pamphlet for the Fabian Society before the election lest it be interpreted as reflecting the Labour leader's own views. The pamphlet had been simply passed, more or less complete, with considerable drafting help from Roger Liddle, to the MP Keith Hill for publication under his own name – another price Mandelson paid for 'being Peter'. Brown, in particular, made valiant efforts in the early summer of 1997 to make Blair's scepticism – in the true sense of the word – about EMU compatible with the pro-European message both he and Blair wanted to convey to Britain's EU partners. He proposed that the government should publicly demand a postponement of EMU, with a strong hint that it might join in the first wave if the first wave was delayed. For several weeks the idea was discussed in Whitehall. But the advice from Christopher Meyer and Michael Jay, Britain's ambassadors in Bonn and Paris, was emphatically negative. The idea of calling for postponement was rejected by Blair, very much in accordance with Meyer's strongly expressed advice, on the grounds that it would be regarded, chiefly by Helmut Kohl, as a British impertinence too far, would not work and would jeopardise British–EU relations with very little positive result. When Mandelson met an anxious Joachim Bitterlich, Kohl's foreign policy adviser, in Bonn in September he was able to assure him that Britain 'could and would not' advocate such a postponement. While speaking very frankly to Bitterlich he also put as pro-European a gloss as possible on government attitudes. The government's commitment to a referendum was valid only for the lifetime of this parliament; it had agreed only 'reluctantly' to a referendum. But while ministers could have 'ridden out' a defeat on Scottish devolution, a defeat in an EMU referendum would be 'catastrophic' and the government was reluctant to risk one until public opinion had moved to 'higher ground'. When Bitterlich said that Germany wanted Britain in the single currency as soon as possible, Mandelson replied that this was also the 'disposition' of the Prime Minister and Chancellor. Yet the Brown interview in *The Times*, just a month later, seemed to those in Bonn to be completely at variance with this assurance.[2]

The well-documented saga which led to Brown's decision to give his interview started with a market-moving story in the *Financial Times* of 26 September; its political editor, Robert Peston, suggested that the government was planning a more positive approach to EMU than hitherto, and quoted one unnamed minister as saying that 'It is now clear that we must indicate our willingness to be in there.' The result was a series of denials, most emphatically from the Treasury, which had widely been assumed to be the source, and an appreciable fall in the value of the pound as the markets adjusted to the prospect of early entry. The more immediate trigger, unsurprisingly in a government almost uniformly obsessive about the media, was yet another newspaper story, this time by Tony Bevins in the *Independent* of Tuesday 14 October, which said, in effect, that the Treasury was trying to bounce a resistant Tony Blair into early EMU entry. The Bevins story had no effect on sterling, but it infuriated Brown, who had by now resolved on an alternative strategy: to embrace a generally positive medium-term approach to EMU while both ruling out British entry in the first wave and promising a subsequent period of stability before entry was considered – a period long enough, it would be assumed, to last the lifetime of a parliament. Exactly when Brown so resolved was a matter of some controversy. It was before the Bevins story – but how long before? Pym and Kochan, with good access to sources close to Brown, insist that he had already decided on this strategy before the *Financial Times* report appeared.[3] On the other hand more than one journalist was left with the distinct impression by Whelan, after the Brown team's return from a trip to the Far East but before Peston's report appeared, that Brown had been taking a distinctly upbeat view of the prospects for British EMU entry.

Peston remains confident to this day that Brown had not determined his subsequent strategy by the time he wrote his story – which triggered a record rise in the FTSE index, a sharp slump in the value of the pound, and quite possibly the crucial change of heart among the Treasury team. But when Bevins's story appeared three weeks later, Brown was immediately determined to correct the impression it had created. The Chancellor was almost certainly close to indicating that there would be no EMU entry in the current parliament. But he may also have had exaggerated fears that the Bevins story had been inspired by Alastair Campbell. If so he might find himself dangerously – perhaps even fatally – at odds with Number Ten, with Campbell in a role akin to the one Sir Alan Walters had played in Nigel Lawson's terminal rupture with Margaret Thatcher in 1989.

Whatever his motives, the Peston and Bevins stories had both shown that policy on such a market-sensitive and politically fundamental topic could not be conveyed, much less run, on the basis of deniable hints and half-truths from middle-ranking ministers or of the unattributable messages of spin doctors, whether at Number Ten or at the Treasury. This, events rapidly proved, was a lesson only half-learnt. But by giving an on-the-record interview – and, indeed, faxing to Webster as part of it the sensitive passage on EMU – Brown would at least be putting the government's authoritative stamp on the policy, albeit in a highly unorthodox way. Moreover, there was a logic in the content of what Brown told *The Times*. The ambiguity of the Thatcher government's stance of entering ERM 'when the time is right' had mightily contributed to its downfall. If every ministerial pronouncement or newspaper story was going to be interpreted as an auspice of the imminence or otherwise of British EMU entry, there was a good deal to be said for a fixed interval, disappointing as it might be for the business cheerleaders of British membership of the single currency. Given that the Prime Minister was himself still an EMU agnostic, was it not in his interest for the Chancellor to relieve him of such pressure? On the Thursday evening Brown had telephoned Blair at Downing Street to discuss his proposal for a statement to *The Times*. Blair had some difficulty focusing on it as he was in the middle of a difficult meeting with another cabinet minister with a personal problem. But he suggested that Brown should consult (the, on EMU, sceptically inclined) Alastair Campbell, who went along with, and indeed participated in, the strategy. The transaction with Webster was completed, with Whelan adding to the high drama by being spotted telephoning confirmation of the *Times* scoop to ITN and BBC *Newsnight* from the Red Lion pub in Whitehall.

Whelan's woefully public carelessness came to symbolise the haphazard nature of the episode, and he was subjected to the full force of Mandelson's acid tongue at Monday's media presentation meeting at the Cabinet Office; Mandelson was able, in the process, to rebuild some bridges with Robin Cook and John Prescott, also in the dark about the sudden change of policy. Whelan was memorably immortalised in a Steve Bell cartoon in the *Guardian*, which portrayed Mandelson's old adversary as an unmistakable wide-boy inside Brown's open mouth, declaring, his thumb jerked backwards over his shoulder, ''E's talking bollocks, and I should know.'[4] For Mandelson and several members of Blair's staff at Downing Street the incident looked like an opportunity to get rid of Whelan, which Blair had intended to do after entering government. Brown had talked the Prime Minister out of it; but surely this time Whelan had gone too far. According to one dispassionate and senior Whitehall mandarin who observed these events at close quarters: 'it wasn't just Charlie who was putting stuff in the press. It was also suspected that Ed Balls was putting stuff, particularly into the *Financial Times*. And this was organised, it was a way of life of the Brown camp which Number Ten couldn't control adequately and didn't always work in their interests.' The official added that the EMU crisis 'became a *cause célèbre* when Charlie undoubtedly put his foot in it and went too far and caused a great deal of embarrassment for the government and for everybody. And that in my perception caused Peter and Alastair and the Prime Minister all to emerge and say: "Charlie has got to be got rid of or reined in." And it was impossible to get rid of Charlie.' So, thanks to Brown's loyalty to his lieutenant, it was not until January 1999 that he left in the wake of Mandelson's resignation.

It was also unfair to blame Whelan alone. The aim was more fundamental than one of mere spin. Whelan was only, however clumsily, following orders from Brown. Indeed, this was a point made by Blair in response to the renewed clamour for Whelan's head. The question of who was to blame was secondary; the real problem was that a hard announcement on an issue of fundamental importance – the central elements of which were still carrying force eighteen months later – was made without collective discussion, without the Prime Minister being fully informed of its contents, by means of a faxed statement to a Eurosceptic paper in response to a story about alleged splits between Brown and Blair which had not been followed up.

Blair and Brown had allowed policy on what was arguably the central issue confronting the government to be made, if not exactly from a crowded bar by a spin doctor with a mobile telephone and a cigarette in one hand and a spritzer in the other, at least in a laughably informal way. For one thing, on this occasion at least, Campbell had – an error he later acknowledged – approved the *Times* interview. Secondly, the whole episode illustrated a haphazard approach to government which went further than one out-of-control press officer. Only Brown, Campbell, Whelan and Ed Balls were fully privy to the operation. The only senior Treasury civil servant told of the interview in advance was Nigel Wicks, the second permanent secretary, and even he was not let in on the precise 'spin'. Indeed, to add to the confusion that Friday night, when BBC reporters contacted officials in the treasury press office, they were told that there had been no change in the policy of keeping all the EMU options open. Nor was the notorious tendency of the treasury quartet of Brown, Whelan, Balls and Geoffrey Robinson to play their cards close to their collective chest the only problem. The failure to engage the senior civil service experts, like the Cabinet Office's Brian Bender, the permanent UK representative in Brussels

Stephen Wall, and Wicks himself, was at this point a Downing Street deficiency as well. In the view of senior civil servants, Brown and Blair were all too often meeting without a single official, even a private secretary, present. As early as August the Cabinet Secretary, Sir Robin Butler, had gently suggested that the Prime Minister might like to have a note-taker sitting in on his discussions with the Chancellor – and on the occasions when he did not, to 'debrief' his private office as soon as the meetings were over.

Of course, it was essential that they should be able to meet without officials from time to time; as Lord Jenkins remarked to one official who expressed concern about this, he had always much preferred to meet Harold Wilson on his own when he was Chancellor because the discussions were franker. Brown and Blair, moreover, were much, much closer than Wilson and Jenkins – they had worked together, on every conceivable subject, for almost a decade. They had been used to picking up the telephone, or visiting each other's office many times a day, every day. But in government the continuance of this practice contributed to a sense of imprecision at the centre, because the conclusions were often not noted and mutually ratified in the normal way of Whitehall. As it was, there was a risk of the prime ministerial wants and intentions being inaccurately conveyed around Whitehall. Not enough was put down on paper by the Prime Minister himself, or drafted for him to approve and amend. And there were officials who suspected that both Campbell, to the press, and John Holmes (Blair's principal private secretary), to a Whitehall audience, tended to put a more Eurosceptic gloss on the Prime Minister's position than was always justified.

The *Times* interview marked the zenith of the informal government style. After the catharsis of the EMU episode some, at least, of these tendencies would be checked. The engagement of Jeremy Heywood, a high-flying treasury official, as Number Ten's economic private secretary, for example, would in the long run inject a new formality into some of the meetings between them. He would sit in on many – though not all – meetings between Prime Minister and Chancellor, and listen in on many of their telephone calls. More immediately, Wicks, one of a tiny handful of Europe's leading EMU experts, as well as Britain's acknowledged master of the subject, was finally brought into the crucial negotiations which followed the crisis.

So was Mandelson. Of course, it was highly fortunate for him that he had not previously been involved. He certainly felt a sense of *schadenfreude*, after the humiliation of the NEC defeat, as he enquired into the events of the past few days. At a meeting convened by Blair in Downing Street, Brown, Whelan, Balls, Campbell, Powell and Mandelson listened as the Prime Minister caustically summed up the shambles: it stemmed, he said, from a lack of coordination, implying that this was because Mandelson, among others, had not been consulted. According to Campbell, Blair 'took the line that when everyone consulted everyone else and the line was clear, it all worked. He basically said: "If this can't be restored then there are going to be a lot of changes around here."'[5] This was followed by a series of meetings between this group minus Whelan but plus Wicks and other civil servants, at which a draft House of Commons statement by the Chancellor was considered in minute detail. That weekend, however, Blair departed for the Edinburgh Commonwealth heads of government summit with many of the bigger questions still unresolved, and with much of the task of negotiating the text with Brown left to Mandelson and Lord Irvine.

Brown's view was that if Britain was not going to enter EMU in the first wave it should make it clear that it was not going to do so until 2002. Mandelson, fortified by his conversations with industrialists, with pro-European Labour MPs like Giles Radice, with Downing Street's European policy man Roger Liddle and above all, with Cabinet Office and Foreign Office officials, argued forcefully in a series of meetings and telephone calls with Brown that such a straitjacket would have a wholly adverse impact on some of Labour's most significant business supporters. Moreover, Blair, a man pathologically reluctant to close his options before it was necessary, saw no reason to do so in absolutist terms over EMU. One theory was that Brown, while eager to use warm language for the longer term about EMU, was determined to limit the retreat from the *Times* piece because it would look like a defeat for the Chancellor at the hands of the Prime Minister. But in any case Mandelson insisted on Blair's behalf that the statement should allow for the *possibility*, however remote, that Britain might still enter EMU in the current parliament. Especially at one point when Blair threatened to make the statement himself, so as to assert full Prime Ministerial authority over the policy. In the end the text was a compromise pronounced acceptable to Blair in Edinburgh: on Monday 27 October the Chancellor announced formally to a full House of Commons that Britain did not envisage EMU entry until after a further general election other than as a result of a 'fundamental or unforeseen change in economic circumstances'. But in what was widely read – and 'spun' in pro-European quarters of the government, including the Treasury itself – as acceptance of EMU in principle, Brown added that if the single currency worked, and the economic case was 'clear and unambiguous the government believes that Britain should be part of it'.

The outcome was a disappointment, if not a surprise, to the most ardent pro-Europeans in the Commons. Not only did it eschew entry in the first wave; it qualified even the government's eventual commitment to go in, ensuring that in 1999 Blair, by then warming visibly towards EMU, would come under heavy pressure to make a more unequivocal pledge. But it had a surprisingly good reception in the European capitals, British officials having hastened to reassure their counterparts that this was another turning point in Britain's reconversion to Europeanism. And a typically confident performance by Brown, coupled with a lamentable one by his shadow Peter Lilley, set the seal on the government's sense of relief. The crisis was over.

The episode *was* in some senses a turning point for both the administration and for Mandelson. It began a painfully slow and faltering process towards a more ordered and conventional style of government. For Mandelson it marked not only his rehabilitation as a central player but his emancipation as a definably pro-European minister. He had intervened at an opportune moment: he had exercised influence on policy. As a leftist eighteen-year-old he had in 1971 precociously condemned the Common Market in a school debate for enshrining 'free enterprise capitalism' as 'a fundamental law' and attacked the Treaty of Rome for seeking as its ultimate objective a 'United Federal States of Europe'; but he had come a long way since his conversion to the pro-European cause by his fellow students in YEL, at Oxford – a cause he was now able to pursue as the Prime Minister's envoy. He had already, in September, been on a mission to Bonn. In a curious lead story the *Sunday Telegraph*[6] had reported the visit under the headline MANDELSON IN SECRET BID TO TOPPLE KOHL, suggesting that his true purpose had been to give clandestine advice to SPD leaders on their forthcoming campaign in the federal elections the following year. Mandelson was sufficiently nervous about the story – because of the embarrassment it could cause him (and Blair) with his CDU hosts in Bonn – to spend a large part of his Saturday evening train journey from Teesside to London on a much-interrupted mobile telephone call, personally persuading Kim Fletcher, the paper's deputy editor, to tone down and demote the report. With all his old spin doctor's thoroughness he checked that the story had been amended in time to miss the home counties editions, by ringing his friend Robert Harris. Did his copy have the offending headline? he asked Harris. No it didn't. 'Well let's hope yours is the edition that goes to Chequers,' he replied cheerfully.

During his trip he had paid a short visit to the SPD headquarters to discuss political campaigning. But if anything the opposite criticism would have been more appropriate, in the light of Schröder's election victory a year later; that Mandelson spent too much time schmoozing with government figures in Bonn, and not enough with the Opposition. Indeed he could not but admire Kohl, the greatest European, not to mention the greatest election-winner of them all. On his next visit to Bonn in early March 1998 he described – in a private address at an Anglo-German seminar on 'European Integration and National Sovereignty' – how the German Chancellor, in London a fortnight earlier to receive the Freedom of the City of London, had 'tellingly and movingly' pointed to how European attitudes in the young, buying Eurorail tickets in their hundreds of thousands, had changed since he was a boy; he had needed an official pass to cross the Rhine from one occupied zone of Germany to another. Mandelson's was an important speech, the first to give voice to a growing Blairite worry about EMU: the so-called democratic deficit embedded in greater integration of the EU. But most notable was his observation that the 'era of pure representative democracy is coming slowly to an end'. What did this mean? Was the Labour Party's most consistent user of polls and focus groups saying that modern measurements of public opinion and mass psychology were rendering parliaments obsolete? The initial draft of the passage had been written by a rising and clever young Foreign Office official, Robert Cooper, then the minister in Bonn. It went on to argue that the era when 'important decisions' could be left entirely to élites – whether landowning, industrial, academic or, in the case of British Labour, 'trade union bureaucrats, city bosses and socialist intellectuals' – was being brought to an end in the age of the Internet; increasing attention was being paid, at least in Britain, to referendums and something which Mandelson described a little vaguely as 'citizens' movements'.

The remark, when it was reported – along with a sharp retort by his co-panellist at the seminar, the senior CDU politician Wolfgang Schauble, that it was the job of elected politicians to govern and not to put every choice to referendums – caused an immediate stir. One of the most prominent to protest privately was former Prime Minister Lord Callaghan. Mandelson wrote back enclosing a copy of the whole speech and Callaghan, mollified, accepted that this put 'a different slant' on the remarks. Recognising that the present-day public was better informed than ever before, he quoted Disraeli's exhortation that 'we must educate our masters'. But he added, going to the heart of the concern aroused by Mandelson's remark:

> Schauble is right in emphasising that politicians should not slavishly follow public opinion and make their decisions subject to focus groups, referenda and all sorts of things ... To take an example ... I would never allow as Prime Minister focus groups to have a major influence in determining the Government's attitude to ... nuclear weapons. Presentation yes, substance no. If when Prime Minister, I could not have settled the policy to my satisfaction on a matter I regarded as vital to Britain's security, then I would have had no hesitation in resigning ... I guess under similar circumstances you would have done the same.

Yet the most interesting aspect of the publicity given to Mandelson's comments was that it drew the sting from an idea that was indeed an element of Blairite 'permanent revisionism' – that, as Blair said in his own 'Third Way' pamphlet sixth months later, 'for too long a false antithesis has been claimed between representative and direct democracy. The truth is that in a mature society representatives will make better decisions if they take fuller account of public opinion' – in other words, you might infer, referendums, focus groups, instant polling and, within parties, membership ballots rather than total reliance on elected representatives. When Mandelson mentioned it in March it was greeted as sinister and unconstitutional. When Blair said something very similar in September, no one reacted at all. It was, after all, old news by then.

The attention paid to this remark, when it leaked out, over-shadowed the main point Mandelson was seeking to make, which was of increasing concern to Blair as decisions about EMU grew nearer: that there was a growing 'crisis of legitimacy' in the EU and that it lacked the democratic institutions to make it accountable. Indeed, his complaint about the European Parliament – with its members each representing up to one million people – was that it was not representative *enough*. The European Parliament was not strong enough to provide the answer; and he totally rejected the right-wing panacea of abandoning the collective institutions of the EU altogether. Mandelson instead turned tentatively to what had come to be called 'subsidiarity'. It was not, Mandelson told his audience of diplomats, intellectuals and politicians, 'anti-European to question what should be a matter for Brussels, what a matter for the Member States . . .'

This was the authentic voice of Mandelson in the role which Blair had allotted him back in May the previous year – that of ministerial envoy conveying at once the Prime Minister's pro-Europeanism *and* his nagging doubts about how Europe was run. It was a theme to which he returned as the government's unofficial delegate to the 'Club of Three', a rather exclusive, little-publicised organisation backed by the publisher George Weidenfeld, for advancing Anglo-Franco-German cooperation. He went so far as to declare that 'there had not been since Edward Heath as pro-European a Prime Minister as Tony Blair' – thus laying to rest the ghosts not only of a hostile Major and Thatcher but of a hesitant Wilson and Callaghan as well. The British government 'hoped in the course of the next ten years to play a role in Europe as significant as that of France or

Germany. There were still swathes of people to be converted to the idea of a positive role in Europe, not to mention a few newspaper proprietors. This more positive role could not happen fully with Britain outside the single currency.' But he again returned to the question of 'democratic legitimacy': there was need for 'greater subsidiarity, perhaps . . . direct link between Europe ministers and heads of government . . . a second chamber of national parliamentarians'.

The importance of the Club of Three speech was that it followed, and was based on, a prime ministerial seminar at Number Ten, attended by senior Whitehall officials including Sir John Kerr, the permanent secretary at the Foreign Office and an old Europe hand, at which Mandelson had been the only other minister present. The seminar commissioned further work for Robert Cooper on ways of injecting greater democratic legitimacy into the institutions of the EU, and drawing up initiatives on greater coordination between EU governments on defence and home affairs. But it also broadly confirmed Mandelson's formulation of a 'leapfrog' strategy – that the UK should 'leap over' its integrationist partners by projecting themselves as the new Europeans, setting out the case for EU political and economic reform and seeking to confer on the EU a greater popular legitimacy for the more integrationist steps the UK's EU partners wanted to take. Political reform of the sort outlined in Mandelson's Club of Three speech was a central theme of the Cardiff EU summit under the British presidency in December 1997; and British ideas, particularly on defence, were taken up. Conversely, however, the government's reform agenda was always going to be constrained by its failure to take a definite decision on EMU.

Mandelson's role in Europe was not, on the whole, headline-grabbing. But along with management of the Dome, it was probably the most fulfilling of his period as Minister without Portfolio. For one thing, he found that he was good at it. He got on well with the able, high-flying EU officials in the Cabinet Office led by Brian Bender, head of the EU Secretariat. According to one Whitehall official who sat in on many of his meetings with EU ministers: 'Mandelson is better than any other minister I've ever seen at doing the business with European counterparts in a way that was both friendly and effective.' He had more time to play this role than the Chancellor, who was too busy, and was better qualified to play it than the Foreign Secretary, who was at this stage at once instinctively less of a Europhile, particularly on EMU, than he subsequently became, and less alienated by excessive social regulation. Robin Cook's interests in Europe, partly flowing from the former anti-Atlanticist's unexpectedly close and warm relationship with Madeleine Albright, the US Secretary of State, lay at this stage more in its foreign policy, from the Balkans to the Gulf. It was not until towards the end of 1998 that he became much more fully engaged in internal EU questions.

Unlike Blair, Campbell or, since he had started zealously taking French lessons, Jack Straw, Mandelson suffered from the notorious British inability to speak a foreign language. But he liked, as he had since his time at Oxford, to travel. He enjoying the flattering welcome which European governments extended to him as the politician most identified with Blair himself; he relished receiving ministers who arrived in London but found the Prime Minister himself too busy to see them. But he also felt that he was engaging in something of more lasting value than the endless scraps and tensions of a domestic policy agenda over which his influence was more marginal than his enemies imagined. The points he made at meeting after meeting, both when he was at the Cabinet Office and at the DTI, about the need for a stronger democratic structure of the EU, came better from him because he was identified abroad as perhaps the most pro-European senior minister in the British government. Indeed, the commentator John Lloyd, after Mandelson's resignation from the Cabinet, went so far as to suggest that the best strategy for dealing with the relentless drive towards political union in the EU – for the EU to 'pay more attention to its people' – was likely to 'suffer because of [Mandelson's] exclusion from the government'.[7] (Nor was Blair backward in keeping Mandelson informed. After returning from the Luxembourg summit, for example, one of his first calls was to Mandelson, who was being driven by Steve Wallace to Teesside Airport from Hartlepool, to give him a full account, including a blow-by-blow description of how he had successfully led Kohl to recognise that the measure of political control sought by the French over the European Central Bank would threaten the Bank's market credibility as a guarantor of low inflation.)

427

Once he was at the DTI, where he was shadowed by the arch Eurosceptic John Redwood, his Europeanism had an outlet that was more distinctively his own, not least because he was quickly and extravagantly identified by his more Europhobic critics on the right as a 'doctrinaire federalist' and architect of the sell-out of the nation state. It was useful to Blair; by being that much more aggressively pro-European, Mandelson, fortified by his regular contacts with the most pro-single currency industrialists and by the firmly pro-EMU and Jenkinsite Liddle, who was helping to draft his speeches, could test public opinion to the limits without anyone assuming that he was exactly reflecting Blair's own views. At times he might even seem to be trying to push the Prime Minister towards more publicly decisive support for EMU. In late 1998 the former Tory MEP Michael Welsh, acting on behalf of pro-EMU Tories urging Blair to use the first half of 1999 (and therefore the first six months of EMU's existence) to stimulate business preparations for EMU by making a clearer declaration of intent to join, judged Mandelson the most suitable intermediary.

When he spoke to the North West Chamber of Commerce on 26 October Mandelson went his furthest yet on the single currency. Apart from an arch joke about how much he had enjoyed his trip to the Classic Couverture chocolate factory ('I'll let you into a secret. You know what they say about hard exteriors and soft centres. Despite my fearsome reputation I have something of a sweet tooth') the speech was notable mainly for the staunchly pro-EMU note which it struck – albeit coupled with a renewed warning against over-regulation and anti-competitive domestic policies by EU member states. 'No one should doubt our policy. We support the principle. We will work to ensure the Euro's success.' It was, he said, 'a barmy idea, a red herring if ever there was one', to suggest 'actually withdrawing from Europe and applying to join a transatlantic free trade area instead'; to 'imagine that Britain can pull up anchor and set sail to become the fifty-first American state is dangerous naiveté'. This was a calculated barb directed principally at the *Telegraph*'s owner Conrad Black, who had suggested that Britain would fare better in NAFTA than in the EU. He had considered a public swipe at 'foreign newspaper proprietors' who sought to break Britain's links with Europe, but decided that this was a provocation too far – not only to Black but to Rupert Murdoch. Nevertheless the speech, which delighted DTI officials, belied suggestions that Mandelson would do nothing to alienate the Murdoch press. His approach to the Euro could hardly endear him to the *Sun*, even though it was reasonable for him to calculate that, as they waited for him to rule on BSkyB's bid for Manchester United, the Murdoch empire would be reluctant to attack him head on. On the single issue on which Murdoch's papers most regularly expressed their fears about Blair, Mandelson was at least prepared to show that he was not on their side of the argument. Finally, at the CBI conference both he and Brown made speeches which were warm in tone about EMU. In contrast to an anti-single currency, Eurosceptic speech by the Shadow Trade and Industry Secretary John Redwood, which was heard in almost eerie silence, both ministers were as well received as any speaker is by the routinely unexpressive CBI audience. Mandelson went a little further than Brown – though by accident – referring to 'when' we join the single currency rather than 'if and when'. He did not, however, rush to apologise.

The Federal German elections in October injected a new element of instability into European politics. Helmut Kohl, Europe's dominant figure, and the motor of integration, left the stage to be replaced as Chancellor by Gerhard Schröder, a figure light on ideological baggage but with a party much less dramatically transformed than Labour. In Oskar Lafontaine in particular, Schröder had a powerful neo-Keynesian, expansionist Finance Minister whose differences in outlook from his leader made those between Brown and Blair look utterly trivial by comparison. Partly in order to strengthen Schröder's hand against the 'old Labour' elements of the SPD, Blair appointed Mandelson, at his first meeting with Schröder after he became Chancellor, to join with Bodo Hombach (the German Chancery minister, a Third Way enthusiast, and – to some extent – the German Peter Mandelson) in drawing up a modernising agenda for Europe – to spread, in other words, the Anglo-Saxon model of liberalisation and flexible labour markets to Europe, including Germany and France. Hombach, an enthusiast for welfare reform, had written his own tract after Mandelson's and Liddle's: *The Breakthrough – the Politics of the New Centre*. Letting slip to the *Observer* that the ministers were seeking to draw up a 'New Clause

IV for Europe', Mandelson sat down on 22 November 1998 with Liddle and David Miliband, across the table at Terence Conran's Pont de la Tour restaurant from Hombach and Klaus Gletschmann, another key Schröder ally and the 'sherpa' for the G7 meeting to be convened under German presidency in the following year, to begin work. Mandelson had been hesitant about the role; having inherited a department with a full agenda only four months earlier, he was preoccupied by his forthcoming competitiveness White Paper and the highly sensitive negotiations on union legislation which would follow his predecessor's 'Fairness at Work' White Paper. But it was an opportunity to make his mark as a fully fledged European politician, and it was the one task which Blair insisted he keep after his fall in 1998. It was also a role in which, apparently, the Germans had already cast him. A fortnight earlier a black-tie dinner had been given in his honour in the grand, gilded, dining room of the palatial Belgravia residence of German ambassadors since the Adenauer period. In front of a distinguished if varied audience, including Lord Jenkins, Lord Dahrendorf, Michael Portillo, Baroness Jay, Nick Serota, Paul Johnson, the writers Robert Harris and Alain de Botton, the Cabinet Office's senior Europe man Brian Bender, and some leading German businessmen, the ambassador paid him a handsome compliment. He was happy to welcome to his home, he said, 'the most pro-European member of the Cabinet'.

# CHAPTER TWENTY-TWO

## *The Seventeen People Who Count*

If EMU had been the new government's most dangerous hour yet, the Bernie Ecclestone affair was the most wretched. Under any circumstances, the policy of seeking an exemption for Formula One, of which Mr Ecclestone was the boss, from the imminent European ban on tobacco advertising would have been highly dubious. Given that Ecclestone had made a £1 million donation to Labour Party funds in January 1997 and was in discussion about a further donation, it now also looked venal. On 5 November several papers reported that Tessa Jowell, Minister of State at the Department of Health, was seeking an exemption for Formula One from the EU ban. Ms Jowell, an able and personable minister, made an unconvincing job on the *Today* programme of defending what by any standards was a spectacular U-turn by a government which had hitherto been militantly in favour of a wholesale advertising ban. This was unsurprising, since neither she nor her boss Frank Dobson had supported the decision to seek an exemption. The press immediately smelt a rat – but it was the wrong rat. Ms Jowell's husband David Mills, it turned out, had an indirect commercial connection with the Benetton racing team. But this was largely irrelevant beside the real reason for the U-turn: for a fortnight earlier, after a meeting with Ecclestone, his associate Max Mosley and his public affairs consultant David Ward (who had been a long-time adviser to John Smith), Blair had asked Frank Dobson to seek a compromise which fell well short of a total ban on advertising and sponsorship. And it was a good deal less interesting than the fact, which remained undisclosed as controversy over the decision

431

mounted through the week, that Ecclestone had given the party £1 million less than a year earlier.

Mandelson, privy to the thick file of correspondence on the issue which had accumulated in Whitehall throughout the year, had been an early advocate of exempting Formula One from the tobacco advertising ban. Like Blair he became convinced by the argument – highly suspect, but persuasively disseminated by Ecclestone and his colleagues – that if Formula One was driven out of Europe, (a) it would not protect television viewers since motor racing, complete with tobacco advertising, would simply be beamed in from Asia or elsewhere, and (b) the ancillary design and production industries might be lost to Britain, with many thousands of jobs. This latter argument was hotly contested, not least by Martin Jacques, who besides being a political moderniser and, for a long time in opposition, a Blair enthusiast, was also an expert on motor racing – which the former editor of *Marxism Today* often described as his own 'first love'. Blair, Jacques asserted, had been 'gullible, poorly briefed, and badly served by his own instincts'.[1]

But Jacques did not know the half of it when he wrote that. Late on Thursday afternoon the *Sunday Telegraph*'s Tom Baldwin had approached Downing Street, having been told that Ecclestone had been a party donor. This was well known to Blair, as was the fact that party fund-raisers were in discussion with Ecclestone about a further donation. The question was whether, given the controversy which was already raging, to disclose it at this stage. Alastair Campbell wrote a note for internal consumption proposing that he should tell the press (a) that Frank Dobson and Tessa Jowell had been quite unaware of the donation, (b) that there had been a donation of £1 million, and (c) that the party saw no reason to give the donation back. The next day being Friday there was no presentation meeting for Mandelson to chair; but he expressed his support for the Campbell strategy. Nevertheless, since only the *Sunday Telegraph* appeared to be aware of the donation, a final decision, while pressing, could wait twenty-four hours.

The following day Blair discussed the problem with Gordon Brown in the car on the way back from the Canary Wharf Anglo-French summit; when he arrived at Downing Street he now said that he was not so sure of the need for an immediate briefing.

Instead, the whole issue should be referred to Lord Neill's Committee on Standards in Public Life. In this way, if and when the donation became public, there was a good chance that the government would either have secured an independent guarantee that there was nothing improper about it, or have paid it back. At the very least it could say that it had referred the donation to Lord Neill. A letter was duly drafted by Jonathan Powell and sent, under general secretary Tom Sawyer's name, to Lord Neill. The existence of the letter was not disclosed until 10 November, when Lord Neill disobligingly proposed that the donation should be sent back. In retrospect this proved to have been a mistake. The tactic required a holding operation which was unable to prevent Blair experiencing his worst week since becoming leader. Faithful to the agreed strategy, Mandelson, in Hartlepool, directed Benjamin Wegg-Prosser, a regular contact of Baldwin's, not to confirm the donation but to try and ease the story gently into the direction of 'Tory-land' – by pointing out that Ecclestone had also been a donor to the Conservative Party and had been proposed by it for an honour, which was true, and implying that the government's Tory critics might also have an embarrassing past with the Formula One boss. This failed to halt either the *Sunday Telegraph*, which ran the story, including a remarkable but quite false denial by Ecclestone's solicitors Herbert Smith, or the media feeding-frenzy over the following few days. By the end of the week it was notable that the task of defending the government was left to Mandelson, who appeared on BBC *Newsnight* to be booed and jeered by a rowdy studio audience in London. (The latest, and lavishly reported, spat involving Mandelson personally had been with the comedian Harry Enfield: the previous week, in a self-confessed drunken moment at a party of the Prime Minister's, Enfield had demanded that Mandelson should be sacked, telling him, 'No one likes you,' before being dragged away by his girlfriend.) Mandelson had been extracted from a meeting of the annual Anglo-Spanish colloquy in Cambridge by a Downing Street summons to appear on the programme. The judgment back in London appeared to be that Mandelson, as one of the few politicians who was both well informed about the Ecclestone affair, could, as usual, be relied upon not to crack under the pressure of a hostile interview.

Nevertheless Mandelson himself, as well as Blair and Campbell, watching the broadcast in London, became convinced that the Prime Minister would have to do an interview to answer his critics. Plans were drawn up for his appearance on *On the Record*, with Mandelson doing LWT's *Dimbleby*. In his own interview Mandelson was somewhat cavalier when describing the sequence of events. Both Dimbleby and the *On the Record* presenter John Humphries asked an interesting question: had the government only taken action on the donation *after* press enquiries about it? Mandelson replied, not strictly accurately, that by the time the *Sunday Telegraph* made its first enquiry, 'the Prime Minister had decided that the original donation should be returned and that the further donation should not be accepted.' In fact a decision (of sorts, given that the letter to Sir Patrick, Lord Neill written the day after the press enquiries began, asked whether a further donation would be acceptable) had already been taken by Blair only in respect of a *future* donation. The question of what should be done with the previous donation was still an open question on the Friday, the day after Baldwin's first enquiry. The kindest explanation, though an unsatisfactory one, in view of Mandelson's intimate knowledge of the affair, was that he had misinterpreted, as others watching the Prime Minister's interview had done, what Blair himself was saying. In *his* interview Blair also robustly rebutted John Humphries's suggestion that he had only taken action on the donation as a result of press interest. But he was more careful about the detail. As soon as the final decision had been taken to seek an exemption, Blair explained, at the beginning 'of last week' (i.e. some ten days earlier), he had made it clear that he would not allow the party to accept a further donation. The day after the decision to seek an exemption, Blair said, 'we start to discuss what we are going to do about the original donation. Again before any press enquiry had begun we discuss what the options are, we then – intervening in that period is the French/British summit – I say finally – "Look, I think we should consult Patrick Neill . . ."' This skated lightly over the Baldwin enquiry by omitting it altogether. Blair's broadcast was judged to be an immediate success in defusing the crisis; and Mandelson's was lost in the attention paid to the Prime Minister's. In reality it was not the finest hour for either man – even allowing for the fact that they alone of ministers were exposed to the full heat of public questioning on the subject.

Blair's immediate circle of advisers, who had been in favour of full disclosure but also robustly determined to hold on to the first donation, were inclined to blame Gordon Brown's advice to rely on Neill. Certainly that strategy unravelled. But in reality the failing was, at least in part, similar to that shown over EMU. First, as Campbell himself admitted subsequently, 'alarm bells should have rung earlier than they did'. Certainly all those involved in discussion of the issue in the run-up to the crisis should have considered the relationship between the donation and the policy decision. 'Just imagine what all this would have been like if we had a Special Prosecutor here,' as another Downing Street insider wonderingly commented after the affair had died down. It would have been better if Blair had summoned a single meeting of all those he trusted, and reached an agreed line. But the lessons went rather further than these merely tactical ones. Blair was, of course, quite right gently to remind Humphries in his BBC interview that up until the crisis, 'I'd spent maybe forty-five minutes, an hour, on Formula One in the first six months of government.' Nevertheless the affair cannot merely be dismissed as an irrelevant distraction. First, there had been a blithely inadequate assumption within the government, not entirely cancelled out by Blair's interview, that New Labour could rely on public trust simply because they were New Labour and *therefore* incapable of Tory 'sleaze'. Secondly, from Blair down the government was guilty, not of doing favours for party cash, but of a naiveté – born perhaps of the novelty of belonging to a party suddenly capable of attracting funds from the corporate sector – about the altruistic intentions of businessmen with large cheque books.

In the end, the episode was a staging-post on the Labour Party's bumpy transition from opposition to government. It was Mandelson, as one of those most exposed during the crisis, who went public with the first lessons to be learned from it. In a speech three days later to a Post Office and Civil Service College conference on 'Effective Communication by the Public Sector' he defended both the government and, as the minister in charge of presentation, himself. 'My verdict on the week is very simple,' he asserted. 'The government behaved out of character. We acted against our own principles – that honesty is the first principle of good communications; that quick communications are essential to good government; and that the purpose of communicating is not to stall or to hide but to put in context and to explain.' It had also forgotten, Mandelson might have added, the distinctly New Labour view that policy and presentation were inextricably linked; if a policy wasn't saleable it probably wasn't worth pursuing. Privately, his advice to Blair was that public opinion indicated the affair had cast doubts not on the government's integrity, but on its competence. He suggested an urgent 'crusade' on Lords reform and on combating social exclusion.

If Mandelson was not the protagonist of the Ecclestone affair, he rapidly became one in what came to be known as 'Drapergate'. By June, the reshuffle twice postponed, Blair was losing patience with Margaret Beckett's stewardship of the DTI, not least because he had had to become more and more directly involved in the drafting of the 'Fairness at Work' White Paper. It was at this comparatively late stage that he began increasingly to envisage Mandelson in the job – from Mandelson's point of view a highly desirable promotion to a more senior cabinet role than he had been led to expect. Then on 5 July came an event which, at least to the outside world, appeared to threaten Mandelson's chance of being promoted at all, let alone to a post running a key economic ministry with a substantial policy agenda and close links with business.

The full impact of the *Observer* front-page lead was remarkably slow in making itself felt in Mandelson's immediate circle, given its sensational character. For one thing, Roger Liddle, the only government official to be confronted during its preparation, did not contact Downing Street, as the spin doctors would frequently lament as the week wore on. Essentially the story was this: Gregory Palast, an American journalist/business consultant, had, by posing as a potential client, insinuated himself into Derek Draper's confidence and had made public a full and highly embarrassing account of conversations conducted over a drink with the unsuspecting Draper and – much more fleetingly – with Liddle, now a member of the Number Ten Policy Unit, at a reception given by GPC-Market Access, the lobbying and consultancy firm which had bought Prima from Liddle and for which Draper now worked.

According to Palast, Liddle, pointed out by Draper at the GPC reception, had said in endorsement of Draper's credentials: 'There is a circle and Draper is part of the circle. And anyone who says he isn't is an enemy. Derek knows all the right people.' Asked if Draper could introduce him to helpful policymakers, Liddle was reported to have replied: 'Whenever you are ready, just tell me what you want, who you want to meet and Derek and I will make the call for you.' Liddle had later told the *Observer*, 'I had had several glasses of champagne. I did say "give me a call" but I can't remember any more than that.' Among the choicer quotes from Draper himself were remarks – none of them, of course, knowingly for quotation – like 'I just want to stuff my bank account at £250 an hour'; 'What I really am is a commentator-fixer. Your Mayor Daley has nothing on me.' He described his successful prediction of Gordon Brown's spending growth target as 2.75 per cent instead of 2.5 per cent as 'inside information'. He had given the figure to a GPC client, Salomon Smith Barney, and 'if they had acted on it they'd have made a fortune'. He apparently promised that if Palast, purportedly representing a US energy company, hired him, he would go 'straight to Number Ten, one of my best friends Liz Lloyd' (handling environmental issues in the Downing Street Policy Unit); and, perhaps most memorably of all he was supposed to have said: 'There are seventeen people who count. And to say I am intimate with every one of them is the understatement of the century.'

By nine the following morning the potential dangers were beginning to become clear. Mandelson phoned Wegg-Prosser, asleep after returning from a party in the small hours. Why had he just seen Alan Clark on BBC TV's *Breakfast with Frost*, denouncing Derek Draper as a 'dodgy bloke'? Wegg-Prosser, physically trembling as he did so, began to read out selected passages from the *Observer* to his boss over the phone. They agreed a 'line to take' – namely that this was a piece of 'typical Derek Draper swaggering', that Draper risked doing himself great harm, and that he should learn some lessons from the episode. All this was duly relayed to enquiring political correspondents, most of whom seemed at this point more interested in the alleged leak of Gordon Brown's Mansion House speech. But then, at around 1 p.m., Trevor Kavanagh, political editor of the *Sun*, warned Wegg-Prosser that his paper was going to call for Liddle's resignation. This was perturbing news for

Mandelson, already infuriated that, without checking with his office, the *Observer* had reported Draper as saying that he regularly faxed Mandelson – by implication, for vetting – his *Daily Express* column.[2] He lost little time in writing to the paper's editor Will Hutton rejecting the charge. The reality was that Draper did quite often fax his column to his friend and successor Wegg-Prosser; he showed it to a number of people, including colleagues and friends, for their comments and advice. Mandelson, however, frequently out of town on Fridays, had scarcely ever bothered to read it himself. Wegg-Prosser repeatedly asked Mandelson whether he should try and contact Draper, currently staying with his friend Jane Bonham-Carter at her family's villa in Campania. Eventually he did so, reaching him mid-afternoon, and breaking the news of the *Observer* scoop. He reported to Mandelson that Draper had seemed 'taken aback but not that concerned'. That evening Mandelson, at the very moment when, according to the following weekend's *Observer*, he was holding crisis talks at home, went to a private pre-release screening of *Saving Private Ryan*, which had been arranged for him and a few friends by the London office of Steven Spielberg's production company. 'His attitude at this point was basically "shit happens" . . .' said one of those present.

Mandelson's initial attitude, as he surveyed the press on Monday morning, was that Draper's bragging had been indefensible but that Liddle had been quite unfairly caught up in the story. In fact it was initially Blair himself who, in the course of routine meetings at Number Ten, had taken the view that Draper, as a long-time Labour activist who had worked tirelessly for modernisation of the party, should also be defended. It might be much too cavalier to say, as his ex-girlfriend Charlotte Raven would tell Draper later in the week, that the story really only amounted to boastful boy drinks champagne. Nevertheless the *Observer* sting, as the more hard-bitten Fleet Street professionals now began to point out, was oddly incomplete. Given the paper's entrapment of Draper, why had it not gone a stage further, waiting at least another week to see if Draper – and perhaps Liddle – was genuinely prepared to peddle influence on behalf of their pseudo-client? Alastair Campbell now embarked on a tough but high-risk strategy: since the evidence against Draper and his government friends depended on what the paper indicated were taped conversations, let the paper produce the tapes. That night Palast did indeed play selected pieces of tape to Mark Mardell on BBC *Newsnight*, and hinted strongly that next weekend's story would be that Lawson Lucas Mendelsohn had persuaded Tesco to sink £12 million into the Millennium Dome in return for the government dropping a plan for an environmental tax on supermarket car parks. (As a result the *Observer* lost their story; the *Daily Express* ran it instead.) But by the following morning, by the arbitrary deadline set by Downing Street at 11 a.m., the paper had still failed to produce the tapes, a decisive moment at which the government began, though very slowly, to roll back the engulfing tide of adverse publicity.

Monday's 5.40 p.m. ITN news bulletin, meanwhile, had made unremittingly gloomy viewing for Mandelson. Draper had been summarily sacked by Rosie Boycott, editor of the *Daily Express*, and suspended from GPC – at least one of whose senior directors shared the view expressed to Mandelson by Adair Turner, the Director-General of the CBI, at a long-prearranged lunch that day at the Halkin Hotel: when he met Draper, he told him, he had thought he was a 'bit disreputable'. Liddle was under mounting pressure to resign. Draper, having cut his holiday short and flown into Gatwick during the afternoon from Naples, spoke to Mandelson at around 7 p.m. When he asked his former boss if he really believed he had said all the things quoted in the *Observer*, Mandelson was overheard saying, 'Unfortunately I can imagine you saying most of it all too easily.' Correctly, as usual, reading where the story would go next, Mandelson saw that the heat would turn on him.

Although Liddle had denied the remarks attributed to him by the *Observer*, and the paper had failed to confront him with taped evidence, he was still under pressure. Mandelson argued that he himself should now do what no minister had yet done – for all the valiant challenges made by Peter Kilfoyle and Ann Taylor on BBC Radio to the *Observer* to produce its evidence – and explicitly exculpate Liddle. This was a courageous, perhaps even foolhardy course, and Campbell, also seeing that Mandelson was vulnerable, given that Draper and Liddle were both among 'Peter's friends', was distinctly unenthusiastic about the idea. Nevertheless Mandelson was determined to go on the offensive. Wegg-Prosser and Lance Price, Campbell's deputy, duly set about telephoning the lunchtime news programmes. Mandelson's judgement might have been at fault much earlier – for example, in agreeing to speak at a GPC seminar, and in having continued to be on cordial terms with Draper, despite being warned against this by other friends, like Colin Byrne. But he could not be accused from running away from a fight.

The government was beginning to regain partial control of the agenda. Blair, whose main preoccupation at the time was the now-blocked march of Orangemen down the Garvaghy Road in Porta-down, said judiciously at the launch of an initiative on homelessness that 'we have to be very careful with people fluttering round the new government, trying to make all sorts of claims of influence, that we are purer than pure, that people understand we will not have any truck with anything that is improper in any shape or form'. The Prime Minister also instructed Sir Richard Wilson, the Cabinet Secretary, to draw up some belated guidelines for govern-ment dealings with lobbyists. Liddle was interviewed exhaustively – for a total of some eight hours – by Sir Richard and Cabinet Office official David Wilkinson, chiefly about the disclosure that he had entrusted an old SDP friend, neighbour and successful invest-ment manager, Matthew Oakeshott, to be the blind trustee of his shareholding in Prima while he was in government service. He would subsequently be cleared of any irregularities, news conveyed in a letter from Wilson to the Shadow Cabinet member Francis Maude. Nevertheless Mandelson was at a low point by Wednesday. He had had the worst press coverage since his defeat in the NEC elections almost a year previously. Even though present and past advisers of other cabinet ministers were also implicated in the origi-nal *Observer* story, it was Mandelson's association with Draper which had excited his enemies inside and outside the party. They had not worked together for two years, and Mandelson had recently rebuked his ex-researcher for describing himself as Mandelson's 'former chief political adviser' under a *Spectator* article (predicting that Rupert Murdoch would change his mind about EMU). But they were still friends. As one unnamed 'senior' Labour MP told the *Observer* a week later: 'It's mainly Draper people are after because they think that's the best way of getting at Mr M. That's the general view.'

On the Friday evening Mandelson, Wegg-Prosser, Alastair Campbell and Fiona Millar gathered at the Hampstead house of Philip Gould and Gail Rebuck to take stock over dinner. There was a certain amount of black humour, with Campbell unnervingly taunting 'Farmer Pete' Mandelson with the notion that the Ministry of Agriculture was the best he could hope for in the now imminent reshuffle. Gould fulminated against Draper, and was particularly put out that he had agreed to go on *Newsnight*, in yet another TV appearance, that very evening. Nevertheless the whole group solemnly watched Draper's – rather uneventful – appearance, Wegg-Prosser remarking that the only six people in Britain still interested in the story were all gathered round the same television set. 'Five', insisted Campbell. Certainly by Sunday the *Observer* was reduced to leading with a story claiming that Draper received faxed information – though the paper admitted there was 'no suggestion' that any of it was confidential – from Mandelson's office. Not even the headline, in a typesize appropriate to announce the Normandy landings, could disguise the fact that the story was running out of steam. However, the whole episode had a significance which went wider than the immediate, week-long excitement.

So what was left as the smoke began to clear? The lasting damage, finally, did not stem so much from the more specific allegations about cash for favours, most of which were, with admittedly varying degrees of persuasiveness, rebutted. It was true that Draper had been involved at GPC-Market Access in arranging a meeting between the House Builders' Federation and Geoffrey Norris on the Number Ten Policy Unit. To suggest, however, that Norris would have refused to meet an important business associate of that sort without the good offices of Draper strains credulity. The treasury spokesmen robustly denied that Draper – who the *Observer* trumpeted, had entertained Ed Balls to a £100 lunch at the Savoy[3] – had access to 'inside information' or that any lobbyist had any advance preview of the Mansion House speech. And the New Millennium Experience Company rejected outright the most damaging claim that Tesco's donation to the Dome in January was linked to the subsequent decision not to tax supermarket car parks. The *Observer* itself was careful to cover itself against possible legal action by saying that 'there is no suggestion that Tesco sought to influence improperly government policy or that it solicited inside information'. Regrettably, this damaging charge was virtually unprovable either way.

Nor was Liddle's role as an arch-villain sustainable. A convivial and kindly man, with a loud and infectious laugh, Liddle may well have been, in a party mood, over-loyal to his old friend and protégé. But those who had known him longest united in dismissing the idea that he was anything but honest and proper in his professional – and, for that matter, personal – life. Peter Riddell of *The Times*, one of the country's most respected political columnists, wrote that if he had to choose between the world of Liddle or Palast, he would certainly opt for Liddle, a man he had known for twenty years.[4] On a private visit to the *Independent* in the week following the *Observer* story Paddy Ashdown, the leader of the Liberal Democrats, who had no pressing reason to be loyal to Liddle, given Liddle's well-publicised defection to Labour, was adamant in telling senior journalists that Liddle was 'totally straight' and should definitely not be made a casualty of the affair. Liddle also had a signal merit in Downing Street, which had occasionally provoked irritation among some of his hyper-pragmatic young colleagues: he possessed beliefs as well as a superior intelligence. You knew what his politics were. He was an admirably old-fashioned Jenkinsite, ardently pro-European, mildly redistributive, pluralist, certain that the state had a role in protecting the least fortunate.

Nor, finally, had he been shown to have done anything wrong. The Prime Minister himself, under heavy pressure from William Hague at Prime Minister's Questions the Wednesday after the story broke, defended his staffer:

A freelance journalist claiming to be an American businessman said he wanted to invest in Britain. He asked Mr Liddle to help and he perfectly properly agreed to do so. It is emphatically denied that, in doing so, he in any way offered to act on behalf of a lobbying company. The journalist claimed to have words suggesting that on tape but it is now admitted that the claim was false and that no such tape exists ... The Rt. Hon. Gentleman alleges that if Mr Liddle had been a civil servant he would have been suspended immediately. I have checked that with the head of the civil service and it is not correct – he would not have been suspended.

What left an inescapably sour taste, however, was the widespread belief among the young Blairite lobbyists that there was nothing even remotely suspect in the way they translated their close connections and knowledge into commercial gain. Draper's incautious remarks were easily the most spectacular, but by no means the only, expression of that view. It was Ben Lucas who was caught trumpeting, in connection with Tesco, that this was a government that 'likes to do deals'. The charge of cronyism stuck. It was all very well to say, as some close to Blair did, that, having worked night and day for little pay for Labour's victory, and having not tasted the fruits as members of the administration, these bright young people were now entitled to their due reward. Even if this doubtful proposition were true, many of the interests which they now represented did not share, and often directly conflicted with, the goals of the party, the government and the electorate which had propelled them to power. At the same time the lobbyists' lives were inextricably intertwined with those of the government's own young turks. They went to the same parties, they played in the same football games, they drank at Soho House together; at a summer reception given at Dell'Ugo by LLM around this time there were as many Downing Street staff members as there were – say – journalists. In a free country men and women had an inalienable right to choose their friends. But a government that had made trust a unique selling point also had a solemn duty of vigilance which, as the Draper exposures had usefully demonstrated, it had not yet begun to appreciate.

More resonant still, at least within the party, was Draper's claim about the 'seventeen people who count in Britain'. The list, which appeared that weekend in the *Observer*, was the paper's.* But it

* Tony Blair, Gordon Brown, Peter Mandelson, Alastair Campbell, Ed Balls, David Miliband, Charlie Whelan, John Prescott, Anji Hunter, Jonathan Powell, Philip Gould, Jack Straw, Geoff Norris, Sally Morgan, Roger Liddle, Lord Irvine, Alistair Darling.

was a reasonable stab at what might have been Draper's own. It was not lost on activists across the country that it included no more than a quarter of the Cabinet and that well over half had been elected by no one. This caused deep resentment – and not only on the left. Tom Sawyer, the party's outgoing general secretary, was to conclude that it played a part, three months later, in the protest vote for left-wing candidates to the National Executive. He himself, while defending Draper against moves to expel him from the party, ensured that he was removed from the board of *Progress*, the Sainsbury-financed Blairite magazine which Draper had founded and in which the party hierarchy had taken an increasingly friendly interest.

On Friday evening, returning from a trip to South Wales, Mandelson granted the *Observer*'s Patrick Wintour an interview. Suffering from a heavy cold and pouring Lemsip into a GWR plastic cup of hot water, he looked 'tired and sepulchral-white'. The spectacle of competing lobbyists making ever more 'ridiculously inflated claims', he said, was pretty nauseating. He insisted that as a minister he had never once been entertained by lobbyists. And he admitted that many of the new lobbyists were 'of the same generation as the people working inside government, and many of them have been friends. As a result there has been some blurring of the line between personal and professional.' Almost as an afterthought he added that Draper had been a 'fool' to be caught out as he had by Palast. Using words that might have been uttered in an earlier generation – that may indeed have been pure Tony Mandelson – he could not resist a final flourish: 'Derek should not have trusted an American who wears a trilby hat indoors.'[5]

# CHAPTER TWENTY-THREE

## *The Leader's Little Helper*

Back in 1995 Blair had neatly encapsulated Mandelson's role as a *consigliere* – recalling Robert Duvall's role as counsellor to Al Pacino's Corleone in *The Godfather* – and said that his peculiar talent was in being able to see several moves ahead. The image survived the general election. 'OK, Mr so-called *Consigliere*, what are we going to do about this?' Blair asked him cheerfully when a cabinet row loomed over Gordon Brown's proposal to freeze ministerial pay. Mandelson was one of the three, along with Campbell and Brown, most consistent participants in the 'circular conversations' which Blair regularly had before making crucial decisions. That way he knew he was getting the genuine personal judgements of those he talked to, rather than a 'pre-cooked' line. On 'big picture' political decisions Blair continued to consult Mandelson as closely as ever: before the election Mandelson had advised in favour of a referendum on Scottish devolution – or rather had been the only senior Labour figure, apart from Lord Irvine, to react wholly enthusiastically when Blair tentatively floated the idea. Mandelson's view was that it was an each way bet. If the referendum was lost the government would pay a short-term price, but save itself long-term heartache over the future of Scotland. If it was won, devolution would be entrenched and the Tories would no longer be able to make political capital out of a continuing issue. Equally, after the election, he would advise in the summer of 1998 that Blair should proceed cautiously on the subject of a referendum on Commons electoral reform in the current parliament. Mandelson was enthusiastic about cooperation, and even coalition, with the Liberal Democrats. But he was nervous, on Blair's behalf, about the dangers of losing a referendum. After all, the Welsh devolution referendum – also on a subject which interested few voters and on which Blair had campaigned actively – had just voted 'Yes' by the narrowest of margins.

Blair could be confident on such occasions that Mandelson was protecting the Prime Minister's own interests, and he continued to fulfil this role throughout his time as Minister without Portfolio. On more day-to-day matters, as the transition was completed by the beginning of 1998, the role played by the Cabinet Secretary Sir Richard Wilson and the private office, led by John Holmes, became more important. And while Mandelson did little outwardly to disabuse colleagues who regarded him as omnipotent, he was privately clear-sighted enough to be struck not only by Blair's growing confidence in his own superlative political antennae and judgement, but also by the fact that he himself was often reinforcing the view that Blair had already arrived at.

The grand plan for a Prime Minister's department which Mandelson had presaged in *The Blair Revolution* did not come to fruition, and indeed Mandelson himself was persuaded, partly by Sir Robin Butler, that the Cabinet Office would coordinate government departments more effectively if it retained some of its role as neutral broker between all of them. Moreover, the Treasury moved more quickly to consolidate its pre-eminence among domestic departments than Downing Street did to strengthen the centre by enhancing the power of the Cabinet Office. Brown's refusal to accept Mandelson as a member of the PX committee (which was nominally in charge of overseeing public expenditure negotiations) was only one – and not necessarily the most important – example of this. In the first weeks after 1 May there was endless discussion with papers flying around Whitehall, about the age-old question of how the Prime Minister's institutional, as opposed to exclusively political, grip on government could be tightened. And although some at Downing Street tended to blame Sir Robin Butler, reaching the end of his career, his proposals for a stronger centre, worked up in the weeks before the election, were not pursued with as much political vigour, by Blair or even Mandelson himself, as they might have been. Partly the Prime Minister had a great deal more to think about than the machinery of government. It may also have been a matter of ignoring Butler's more modest proposals in favour of a grander, but illusory, goal of a Prime Minister's department in fact if not in name. According to a senior Whitehall official, Butler proposed a formal machinery whereby the Cabinet Office

> should ask the departments specifically to state what their priorities were ... in a way that could be followed up by Peter Mandelson initially and then if satisfaction wasn't given by the Prime Minister himself with the Secretary of State.... The key was that it was getting the departments to say 'We mean by such and such a date to have done such and such,' so that you could say to them: 'Well, are you actually doing it and if you haven't done it, why haven't you done it?'

But Butler's ideas, which had been agreed with the permanent secretaries, were not pursued to the limit and the Treasury maintained its unchallenged primacy among Whitehall departments. 'Number Ten moved rather slowly on it,' said the official, 'and the Treasury saw it and grabbed it.'

However, Mandelson did connect almost instantly, and successfully, with the mandarinate. He met weekly with Butler on his own; it was enjoyable for both men, Mandelson giving the Cabinet Secretary a no doubt colourful and gossipy account of New Labour's personalities and alliances; Butler reciprocating with an elegant verbal cutaway diagram of the government machine. The Cabinet Secretary showed his appreciation at the beginning of August 1997 by giving Mandelson, like his immediate staff, a bottle of Corney and Barrow *Pêche* – a peach champagne which, as Butler put it to his own private office, was ideal 'for drinking somewhere under a tree'. Mandelson held out – eventually enlisting Butler's support – for easily the outstanding candidate among possible private secretaries: Rupert Huxter, a tough, irreverent, young high-flier, originally from the Foreign Office, who had been the number two in Heseltine's private office and who told Mandelson bluntly at his interview that he had had enough of traditional private office life, working all the hours the minister wanted. He had two young children, he was going to see something of them, and if Mandelson could not put up with him arriving in his cycling gear at 9.30, there were plenty of other civil service jobs he could go to. He told a colleague afterwards that he knew, from the first interview, that he was going to like Mandelson. The minister clearly regarded hiring him as a challenge; he had asked him, 'Why don't you want to work for me?' and then, after granting these – for private offices – unconventional hours, had said, in a very 'Peterish' way, 'Do look in and see me sometime,' as if Huxter was hardly going to be there at all. Huxter was invaluable in maximising Mandelson's clout in Whitehall because, having worked for Heseltine, he was respected by other private secretaries there. On the one hand Mandelson made precious little effort, which he might have done, to maintain friendly contact with David Clark, Chancellor of the Duchy of Lancaster, his ministerial colleague in the Cabinet Office, but nowhere near as influential – which made life difficult for the few civil servants who served both men. On the other he was much liked by the Cabinet Office officials, particularly Brian Bender, and as early as July was given glowing marks for his 'responsible, considerate and decisive chairmanship' of a referendum campaigns ministerial committee, in an internal civil service report which was far from flattering about some other ministerial chairmen. One official said, only half-joking, that he 'was a bit like Heseltine only more right wing'. But according to another: 'He'd occasionally piss me off when he'd suddenly get up and go and ring people for ten minutes [invariably at Number Ten] in the middle of a meeting and we'd all hang around. But essentially the man was a serious minister and he goes beyond party politics. They found there was a national interest, British interest sort of person there whom they appreciated.'

However, another constraint on Mandelson's supposed omnipotence as Minister without Portfolio – as opposed to his informal role as a behind-the-scenes adviser to Blair, which was as great as ever – was that for all his membership of all the important cabinet committees, his widely touted 'mission to meddle' and his undoubtedly privileged access to Number Ten papers, committee membership was not all it was cracked up to be. Being a secretary of state, and a member of the Cabinet, which Mandelson was not, counted for something. That did not mean that he did not exercise influence on a bewildering variety of subjects. Far from it. Several of the leaks against Mandelson concerned his attempt to stop the resurgence of the old Labour, or anti-business, tendencies – for example, in querying whether the Food Standards Agency should concern itself with food which was not nutritious as well as food which was unsafe, and in mid-November pressing for ministerial powers to vary and create exemptions from the minimum wage. In both cases he was effectively acting as Blair's agent while Number Ten kept a low profile. And this did reflect much of his role as commissar, watching for all things un-Blairite, including vestiges of what the modernisers saw as nanny-statism. In one short and fairly typical period during November, to take a random example, he backed the Culture Secretary Chris Smith against the idea of applying restrictive national insurance contributions to actors and musicians to avoid vocal opposition from the arts lobby; laid the blame squarely on the Department of Social Security after being asked by Blair to find out why an announcement on cold weather payments had been mishandled; was consulted on how to deal with public concern about high-profile murders committed by mentally ill people; cautioned Jack Straw against ordering a full-scale government review of law relating to transsexuals; and issued advice to the Prime Minister on how to minimise William Hague's impact, and his own defensiveness, in Prime Minister's Questions. To take two further utterly random interventions, he urged Downing Street, after a meeting with Tam Dalyell, to explore his case for 'taking a more flexible approach' than the previous administration to the Lockerbie bombing, and urged Jonathan Powell to ask Blair to raise in Cabinet the distressing tendency of ministers to cancel official speaking and dinner engagements at short notice.

This all mattered, and it was often time-consuming because it sometimes required detailed examination of large volumes of paperwork; but it was hardly grand strategy. He also intervened – on the illiberal side – over the Freedom of Information Bill, though he did briefly step in on the other, liberal side of the argument, backing Clark and Lord Irvine when it looked as if the White Paper was in danger of publishing proposals on the disclosure of official policy advice that were more restrictive than those of the previous administration. Nevertheless he remained, as Blair became, a conservative on the issue, regarding the bill as a low priority. On coal, however, even his critics in the PLP admitted that, after his visit down Kellingley Colliery, he played an influential role in extending the life of the industry in the discussions between the Treasury and the DTI. It was his most old-Labour intervention as Minister without Portfolio.

What was also clear, however, was that a decade after he became the party's Director of Communications he could not escape the party's preoccupation with a role from which – ironically – only the John Smith leadership had fully released him: media management. True, he was no longer, though he continued to speak to some journalists, a front-line spin doctor. He had meant it when he told Peter Hyman, after Campbell's appointment back in 1994, how glad he was that Blair had at last got someone who was even better at 'spinning' than he had been. But his chairmanship of the early morning presentation meetings still remained the most consistent, if sometimes fractious, element of his life. Underlying this was a belief which he, Alastair Campbell, Blair and, to a large extent, Brown, all shared – in Mandelson's case ever since the 1987 election and the policy review which had followed it: that policy and presentation were inseparable. In theory at least, if the mantra that 'we won as New Labour, we will govern as new Labour' meant anything, it was that everything should be done to preserve for as long as possible the mystical coalition of interests which Blair had assembled to ensure his election victory.

This meant, first, not letting up in selling New Labour to the electorate just because the election was over. The obsession with presentation surprised, and disturbed, many in the government machine. Oppositions have no other weapons at their disposal save the media – 'hand-to-hand fighting for the day's headlines', as Blair had once described the business of an electorally ambitious opposition to a group of MPs. Surely government – where there were many other things to do besides keeping the press happy – was different. There was a culture clash, especially in those early weeks; the young turks of the Downing Street Policy Unit simply could not believe, for example, that a permanent secretary on his way home on a Surrey commuter train might not be equipped with a mobile telephone or even a pager. They had a building, Millbank Tower, equipped for electoral war, which had monitored every new news bulletin, every paragraph, however obscure, of political news; they had found a government machine whose culture still seemed to them to be working to nineteenth-century time – and, worse still, to regard the publicity operation as defensive rather than offensive. The Millbank media monitoring unit was quickly rescued from extinction. How could a government function without knowing what the press or television and radio were saying at any given minute? Some of this impatience, which resulted in the departure of a series of experienced and senior government press officers in the space of a few months, was unfair. For their part, some of the mandarins wondered that a government with a parliamentary majority as big as Blair's was not more easily weaned from its chronic preoccupation with the next day's headlines. In some important respects the critics had already been vindicated; some of the worst headlines would be produced by straining too much to manage the news in the first place; nor should Mandelson – though he largely did – escape some of the criticisms for that. Blair would also come to realise that even a press unprecedentedly sympathetic to a Labour government would not act as ideological banner-carriers, connected by some sixth sense to the national leader, as it had for Margaret Thatcher. But he would not stop trying to influence them.

In this Campbell and Mandelson continued to be Blair's two principal instruments. On the one hand Mandelson was more sympathetic to the civil servants on press issues than many of his colleagues. He listened to their concerns about the haemorrhage of senior Government Information Service officers, and made a point of writing to Jill Rutter, the efficient and clever Treasury civil servant, when she was dispensed with as Head of Information by Gordon Brown – a task made all the more piquant, no doubt, by the fact that she was replaced by his old enemy Charlie Whelan. On the other hand he had almost certainly been handling the media for too long by the time he came into government. The barrage of complaints he kept up with the press and the broadcasters were sometimes on his own behalf, sometimes on others – as, for example, when he launched a characteristically ferocious attack, including a letter to John Birt, on a *Panorama* team for walking off (accidentally, as they insisted) with some papers of John Prescott's, and then using the material in them. But he also complained to Birt about John Sopel's exposure of his and Downing Street's dubious diversionary tactics during the Cook affair. Birt sensibly passed the complaint to Richard Ayre, the deputy chief executive, News, who wrote back courteously but firmly inviting Mandelson to 'accept that there is a public interest in audiences having an understanding of the mechanisms by which, on occasion, parties may seek to influence the news agenda'. Some of these protests to the broadcasters, to national newspaper editors and, on occasion, to night editors later in the evening, were sometimes more appropriate to an opposition fighting to wrest the news agenda from its political enemies, than to Her Majesty's Government. They demonstrated his liking for a fight. But they would not help his case when the crisis came late in December 1998. It was time to leave the handling of the press to others. It was also time he got a proper job. But what?

Long before the 1997 general election Peter Mandelson dreamt that Gordon Brown had become Prime Minister. In the dream, he told a friend, he had already been put in a significant job in the Cabinet by the now departed Tony Blair. Brown sent for him and told him the good news, which was that he could stay in the Cabinet, and the bad news, which was that he would henceforth be Secretary of State for Wales. Like a lot of dreams, there was a certain plausibility about it. On the cold January evening in 1998, when Gordon Brown did send for Mandelson, however, Brown himself was still Chancellor of the Exchequer and Mandelson was not yet in the Cabinet.

Mandelson's arrival at Number Eleven Downing Street – the first of his life – could have been a scene from Harold Pinter or, at the very least, Gogol. There was nobody to be seen except a solitary and rather elderly woman sitting on a chair – 'like a granny who had wandered in off the street', as he would tell a colleague later. Had she seen the Chancellor? 'I don't know about that,' she said, pointing to one of the big wooden doors off the hall, 'but there is a man who went in there.' It was a surreal start to what promised to be a momentous encounter, one of only very few face-to-face meetings since 1994. Mandelson was there at Brown's request, in the wake of another calamity of clashing personalities within the modernising faction of the party, triggered by a biography of Brown which had dwelt at length, and with professed first-hand knowledge, on the Chancellor's continuing and smouldering feelings of betrayal by both Mandelson and Blair over the leadership in the period after John Smith's death.[1] Extracts from a bootleg copy obtained by the *Guardian* and splashed across the front page,[2] complete with a few hostile comments from a 'senior Labour source' (correctly assumed by Brown to be Mandelson), had appeared even before the book had been published. But the saga had moved on a long way since then. There had been endless speculation about the relationship not only between Mandelson and Brown, which was already assumed to be dysfunctional, but, much more damagingly, between Blair and Brown. Blair was known to be irritated with the Chancellor for cooperating with such a venture. Sensationally, the *Observer* columnist Andrew Rawnsley had reported the view of 'someone who has a claim to know the mind of the Prime Minister' that it was time for the Chancellor to get a grip on his 'psychological flaws'.[3] For once Mandelson was not under suspicion. The phrase had emanated from within Downing Street itself – with the result that Blair rebuked his official spokesman Alastair Campbell, as the head of the department responsible for press relations, though not, some thought, with quite enough menace to suggest he was really angry. Against this unpromising background Brown had sent for Mandelson for a talk.

Lloyd George's famous dictum that there is no 'friendship at the top' has become a cliché in modern politics. Yet relations between close ministerial colleagues are more subtle and many-layered than they seem. On the most superficial level they are eternally loyal, defending each other at every opportunity. Indeed, that is the face of collegiate government the public normally sees when a politician is interviewed. So unusual is it for a minister or shadow minister – save only in periods of licensed dissent like leadership contests – publicly to criticise, or even refrain from praising, another in the same party that it is invariably news if he – or she – does so. By contrast in the supposedly sophisticated world of those 'in the know', like political journalists, this picture is a subject of ridicule. There are close alliances, of course, but otherwise within the narrow, village world of Westminster 'everyone knows' that politicians are at each other's throats, competing for attention, undermining rivals and imagined enemies – usually more at odds with each other than they are with their supposed opponents in another party. And yet the sophisticated model, for all the truth it undoubtedly contains, is not quite perfect either. At the very moment when the mutual hatreds are being publicly highlighted, rapprochement of a sort may be taking place. Certainly candour, even occasional warmth, is possible between supposed adversaries and, though much more rarely, between their lieutenants to a larger degree than the caricature allows.

Thus it was, to some extent, with what is one of the most notorious personal enmities in contemporary British politics, that between Gordon Brown and Peter Mandelson. For a start there was pitifully little Brown and Mandelson disagreed about. They shared the same perspective, honed in six unusually close years of daily contact and cooperation, on Europe. The ideas of Brown, as the dominant modernising figure in the party from before the 1992 election, on the need for Labour to turn away from its 'tax and spend' past, and the importance of work in rehabilitating those dependent on welfare, were by now second nature to Mandelson. They even agreed, and only partly for different reasons, about Mandelson's own future – that it was time for him to emerge from the shadows and have a proper job, with his own department. And finally, the intimacy which they had enjoyed up to 1994 was still surprisingly easy to pick up again, on the rare occasion the opportunity arose in a climate of otherwise unremitting hostility. There had even been odd little moments in the 1995–6 period: for example, when Mandelson had arranged to pick up Sue Nye from Brown's flat and the three of them had an entirely friendly drink – Mandelson noticing aloud a belt which he had bought the Shadow Chancellor several years earlier; or when Mandelson had turned to Brown for help and advice – which he freely gave – because he was having difficulties with John Prescott over whether he could continue in his frontbench team while preparing for the election. There was no discussion, at this or any other meeting between Brown and Mandelson, until after he had resigned, about the explosive fact of Geoffrey Robinson's home loan to Mandelson.

While not exactly cordial, the reunion at Number Eleven was therefore rather less stilted and frigid than an outsider might have imagined. Brown had been damaged by the Routledge book which had backfired on him; but the main reason for the meeting was that Blair was determined once again to stop the feuding between his two closest lieutenants, and had wanted a reconciliation. Mandelson, having passed through an empty room to the Chancellor's study, found 'the man' standing there waiting for him, and began, in an implicit reference to the 'psychological flaws' episode, by saying as tenderly as he could: 'I suppose you're pretty mad and angry.' Brown was magisterially dismissive. He was 'beyond caring' about such things; instead he was briskly business-like. All he knew was that the government had a 'hell of a lot to do if we're going to bring about the changes we want'. The only way the changes were going to be carried through was if Blair, he and Mandelson started working in something approaching harmony again. Brown did not want to discuss the past – though Mandelson did. There were, he thought, 'an awful lot of misconceptions, an awful lot of stupid things which have been said'; these ought to be resolved. No, Brown indicated, that was impossible. He had his version, Mandelson had his, others would have theirs. It was time to look to the future. In a sense Brown was offering a pact: he would back Mandelson as a promotee to the Cabinet, indicating his strong preference for Mandelson to go to the Department of Culture, Media and Sport (DCMS). The almost unspoken *quid pro quo* was that Mandelson should use his influence to stop the briefing against him. Mandelson said that he needed a conduit through which he could communicate with Brown when he couldn't speak directly to him. Brown said, 'Charlie Whelan?'; no, said Mandelson, it could be neither Whelan nor Ed Balls because he felt 'very threatened by them'. That was 'ridiculous', said Brown. But Mandelson persisted. He suggested that a better 'conduit' would be Sue Nye – just about to leave to have another baby – or Ed Miliband, the quiet-spoken, cerebral younger brother of David Miliband, head of the Policy Unit, and on Brown's political staff at the Treasury.

The conversation lasted forty-five minutes – and towards the end Mandelson volunteered that, when the time came – and both men agreed it could be a long time, perhaps even fifteen years – he would support Brown as Blair's successor. This was an unsolicited promise; in a conversation before the meeting Mandelson had indicated to Blair that he would make it. It was Mandelson, and not Brown, who raised the subject. There was no reason to suppose that he did not mean what he said: Brown, after all, was the only other senior figure in the party whom Mandelson had ever supported for the leadership before. On the other hand Brown could be forgiven for wondering how bankable a promise this would prove if the modernising forces gathered around an alternative candidate – say Jack Straw – as they had seemed to gather around Tony Blair after John Smith's death in 1994. Nevertheless the two men parted fairly amicably and agreed to continue meeting. When Mandelson told the Prime Minister about the outcome, Blair said, 'For God's sake make it work,' or words to that effect.

And so, after a fashion, it did. They would meet again at least twice before Easter, this time at Mandelson's request, to discuss his own future. At one meeting they were talking intently enough in the Chancellor's Commons room to miss a 10 p.m. vote because the television monitor giving minute-by-minute progress of a debate was switched off. They resumed the following morning at the Treasury. Brown would continue to urge Blair to give Mandelson a department. Partly, no doubt, this was to reduce Mandelson's influence as an alternative source of advice to Blair. Certainly he did not want him as a cabinet minister at the centre, vested with the power he was denied in his present job as a minister of state, acting as a counterweight to the Treasury. Equally, however, he believed – rightly – that it would be in Mandelson's interests as well as the government's for him to step out of Blair's shadow. One of Brown's most consistent suggestions, in conversation with Mandelson and others, was that he should go to – as he invariably described it – Culture. Brown, not an ally of Chris Smith, knew that John Prescott was seeking a more effective Transport Minister than Gavin Strang and thought that Smith might be suitable. Moreover, it was hardly unreasonable for Brown to propose the job for Mandelson; in an interview before the general election with the *New Statesman*, Mandelson had unashamedly punted himself for the job, and his unrivalled network of contacts in the worlds of media, arts and entertainment made him a natural, though it would have given him an opportunity to indulge his own showmanship to a positively dangerous extent. Mandelson, for whom at this stage the DTI was not yet a serious prospect, was well aware, as reshuffle speculation began to grip the political classes in the early spring, that DCMS was not a central post. Nevertheless that drawback might be nothing compared with his present frustrations of not having, for all his celebrity, a true ministerial identity. Of electors asked in a *Daily Telegraph* poll whether Mandelson 'was doing a good job' 34 per cent said yes, 36 per cent said no, but an exceptionally high 30 per cent said they didn't know.[4] Why should they? He might enjoy a notoriety greater than any other colleague. He might figure in the newspaper diary columns almost every day. His sinister and robotic figure might well be a highlight of *Rory Bremner* each week. But how could even the most intelligent voter define what he actually did? All this spoke for getting out of the centre and into a department.

Certainly, in the first quarter of 1998, he wavered from time to time. He would, after all, miss the unlimited access not only to all important papers, but to Blair himself. There was, as he put it to one friend, 'a bit of me which says: don't be an ass. Do you really think you're going to have the same satisfaction, stimulus and sense of being at the centre by being at DCMS dealing with cricket?' Blair rather reinforced this view, telling him, a little mischievously perhaps, that if he thought he could flourish by somehow distancing himself from him, he was being 'ridiculous'. Had the peace talks in Northern Ireland not reached their climax in Holy Week, and the reshuffle taken place at Easter, as originally planned, he would almost certainly have been given David Clark's job; indeed, had Blair carried out his original promise to put him in the Cabinet 'within six months' it might have consisted of only that move – perhaps with the addition of replacing Strang at Transport. Instead, Clark and Strang were left, hardly defensibly, to do their jobs, with speculation about their demise hanging over them for the best part of a year. And in March Mandelson was half-reconciled to the idea of becoming a cabinet minister without portfolio. He liked the Cabinet Office, and to run it *de jure* rather than merely *de facto* was certainly an attractive prospect. And there was some discussion of the possibility that the Cabinet Office job might be substantially enhanced by transferring a new responsibility from one of the two biggest departments of state. One possibility was political reform – including electoral systems and the implementation of the Neill recommendations for party funding – from the Home Office; the other, more sensational, was to transfer responsibility for Europe from the Foreign Office. The latter would no doubt have caused a full-scale Whitehall row: the mandarinate within the Foreign Office, not to mention Robin Cook, would also have risen up against this stripping of one of its most high-profile functions. On the other hand there was also a logic in the putative move. From the Social Chapter at the DTI to farm subsidies at the Ministry of Agriculture there was no department unaffected by European policy and law. A single central office close to a Prime Minister continually preoccupied with European policy might be more effective in coordinating relations of each department with the rest of Europe than a Foreign Office which, for all its glamour and prestige, was only another single department – and not one fully engaged by the workaday economic matters which were the bread and butter of European policy. All this was considered – but did not happen, though it might conceivably have done so had Mandelson been kept at the centre.

In late March Mandelson again expressed his doubts about a job at the centre in a discussion with Blair. Such discussions were actually rarer with Blair than with Brown. For all their intimacy, they did not usually discuss Mandelson's own future. Indeed, one of Mandelson's frustrations was that because of his own involvement in the forthcoming reshuffle – 'pivotal', as commentators would routinely describe it – he was excluded from giving Blair his normal rounded political advice on a subject of clear importance. For Blair, however, Mandelson's own interests were by no means necessarily identical with his own. This time Blair merely said that if he was going to be removed from the centre, he would have to 'find a replacement'. Mandelson proposed one of his most long-standing colleagues – Patricia Hewitt – who, he now told the Prime Minister, would bring political skill as well, having been elected an MP for the first time in 1997, as a fresh eye.* The discussion was otherwise inconclusive, and in the end Blair opted in the July 1998 reshuffle for his own long-standing friend Charles Falconer.

By May, however, Mandelson's frustration with 'being Peter' had substantially hardened. The main reason was that in another dis-

---

* She was made Economic Secretary to the Treasury in the July 1998 reshuffle.

cussion with Gordon Brown around Easter, the Chancellor had made clear, in the strongest terms, his determined opposition to any strengthened ministerial role at the Cabinet Office, and to Mandelson's candidacy in particular. Partly, it was weariness with being the government's lightning conductor. A perceptive, and only slightly tongue-in-cheek, piece in April by Robert Shrimsley in the *Daily Telegraph* pointed to the dangers for Mandelson of continuing in a position, whether elevated to the Cabinet or not, in which 'his popularity remains low – not least because he is routinely wheeled out to fight the corner of ministers in difficulties'.[5] Shrimsley correctly pointed out that Mandelson's 'influence was enormous but his power is negligible' and that he 'had been thrown ever more starkly on the patronage of Mr Blair' who, Shrimsley asserted, had 'treated him shabbily' by not giving him a conventional departmental job. Shrimsley concluded with a cautionary tale from Machiavelli's *The Prince* – 'a text with which [Mandelson] can hardly be unfamiliar' – in which Cesare Borgia pacified Romagna by putting it under the control of Remirro de Orco, 'a cruel efficient man to whom he entrusted the fullest powers'. Borgia, wanting to secure the people's affection, was then able to argue that the cruelties were not his, but 'prompted by the harsh nature of his minister . . . One morning Remirro's body was found cut in two pieces on the piazza at Cesena, with a block of wood and a bloody knife beside it. The brutality of this spectacle kept the people of Romagna for a time appeased and stupefied.' It was a melodramatic way of making an effective point: that the longer Mandelson was at the centre to take the blame for everything wrong while Blair took the credit for everything that went right, the more vulnerable his position would be in the longer term. It was also a reminder that, for all the routine accusations directed against Mandelson for being 'Machiavellian', it was really Blair, rather than his lieutenant, who was playing the role of the Prince.

In any case Mandelson longed to be a politician in his own right, with programmes to deliver and decisions to make; taking credit as well as blame for his own performance, and with a chance to build a reputation not solely dependent on prime ministerial patronage. He now dismissed the notion that a job at the centre, even at cabinet level, would be anything more than an extension of what, as he put it at the time, 'I have been doing since 1985'. So strongly did he now agree with Brown that he should have a department that he started to form the notion of refusing promotion at the centre. This would have been a bold move, to say the least, though there was a precedent. Roy Jenkins, offered by Harold Wilson, as his first cabinet job, the Department of Education in January 1965, turned it down and remained outside the Cabinet as Minister of Aviation. This gamble showed considerable nerve, not least because it allowed his friend and rival Tony Crosland to enter the Cabinet before he did, but it paid off. Jenkins was propelled into the Home Office less than a year later. On the other hand Jenkins's relationship with Wilson was crucially different from that between Mandelson and Blair. Paradoxically, Jenkins benefited from the fact that he was a Gaitskellite and Wilson had credentials as a Bevanite. Jenkins was a force to be reckoned with by Wilson – a potentially dangerous opponent if his career was left to languish. Had Gaitskell lived to be Prime Minister he might have been more inclined to take his friend's loyalty for granted. So it might be with Mandelson, as Jenkins himself remarked at one point to their mutual friend Robert Harris. Precisely because Blair could count on Mandelson's support, he might think it less necessary to promote him, especially if Mandelson had the temerity to reject the first cabinet post offered to him.

Nevertheless by the early summer Mandelson appeared to have come to a settled view that, rash as this seemed, it might be a risk worth taking. As the reshuffle approached he let it be known that he would refuse the job of Cabinet Office Enforcer. Indeed, when for a period he feared that Blair would seek to keep him at the Cabinet Office whatever his own wishes he even toyed, however fleetingly, with the idea of leaving politics altogether for business. He himself took the notion seriously enough to have several discussions on the subject with his old friend Dennis Stevenson, the ideal person to advise him if he was going to transfer his career to the private sector. According to one colleague, he conveyed to Blair through Lord Irvine the notion that he would refuse a post at the centre. According to Stevenson, 'I think to some extent he was using me, as he does, as a kind of safety valve . . . to some extent he was letting off steam and emotion, of which he has a great deal, but I also think at another level . . . it was real, and rationally real.'[6] After all, Stevenson said, Mandelson was now approaching forty-five and a

> person of huge talent and ability . . . one of the few politicians, on either front bench, who really could do extraordinarily well at other things. And I think that's a rational calculation. If he had still been doing a version of the same job . . . whether in the Cabinet or out of it, in three or four years' time, it would be a lot more difficult for him to change career . . . I think there was letting off steam but I think there's a real thing. I don't think at that point he would have seriously left politics . . . I said: 'Look, do you or do you not really believe in and support Blair?' . . . And the answer was Peter admires him and likes him enormously and rates him very highly as a human being and everything else . . . 'And do you not think he's got a very difficult job?' 'Yes.' 'Well, for Christ's sake, you've got to back him.'

Stevenson nevertheless assured Mandelson that '"if by this time next year you're still thinking this way I will sit down with you and discuss what your real choices are . . . and I'll help you transfer," but I was encouraging him to stick in and back Blair. But no, I think it was serious.'

It is hardly credible that Mandelson would have carried out his threat. His behaviour after his fall from the Cabinet in December 1998, when he was famously in debt to the tune of over £300,000, and could, according to the estimate of a not particularly friendly cabinet minister, have easily picked up a £500,000-a-year job outside Westminster, yet still showed every sign of staying in politics, certainly suggested otherwise. Nevertheless the frustrations were real. He did not yet know how richly Blair would reward him for all his loyal service.

# CHAPTER TWENTY-FOUR

# Congratulations, You've Got One of the Top Jobs

Peter Mandelson was at Carla Powell's, about to sit down to home-made *tortellini*, when the pager message came at 8.42 p.m. on Sunday 26 July: 'Please phone 930 4433 to speak to TB.' It had been a strange weekend. For the first time since Tony Blair had become Labour leader in 1994, great events were unfolding and Mandelson was out of the loop. As a pivotal figure in the Prime Minister's reshuffle plans he had not even been consulted about them. He had no idea what they would mean for him. Uncharacteristically at a loose end, he had taken the opportunity to drive up to his mother's house in Hampstead Garden Suburb for lunch before returning home to Notting Hill and bicycling over to the Lambton Club off Westbourne Grove where he regularly went for a 'wet workout' – aqua-aerobics in the club swimming pool. He often went to the Powells' Bayswater home for dinner on Sunday evenings, but at the moment he was actually staying there, having lent Northumberland Place to the visiting family of his Brazilian friend, Reinaldo Avila.

That Sunday evening Sir Charles, now a director of Jardine Mathieson, was away on a business trip to Paris. Lady Powell had returned that day from her house in her home village high in the Apennines; over a glass of champagne and salami bought that very morning in Domodossola market, she and Mandelson chatted about the reshuffle. The big question, she mused, would be whether Blair had 'the balls' to give her close friend the big job he wanted. This was not an academic issue. The main problem, it scarcely needed to be acknowledged as the late evening sunshine flooded in through the french windows of the Powells' drawing room, was Gordon Brown. Brown had definite preferences about which job Mandelson should get in the reshuffle, and these had not included the DTI; as head of an economic department, Mandelson would be working in close professional contact with Brown himself. Was Blair prepared to face down opposition by giving him the big departmental job he wanted?

Lady Powell's question was left unanswered by the call Mandelson now made to Number Ten from an upstairs sitting room. When he was connected to the Prime Minister, they greeted each other, as they had hundreds of times before, without using names, in the intimate manner of people who continually speak on the telephone. But Mandelson was confronted with a wholly unexpected – and not especially welcome – request: to go and see the Chancellor. He should, Blair told him, present himself at 10 p.m. at the small flat in Great Peter Street, Westminster, which Brown had kept on despite the fact that he now enjoyed the use of an official residence in Downing Street. It was important, Blair emphasised, to establish that Brown and Mandelson could enjoy a good working relationship in the Cabinet. The meeting with Brown should be kept secret. Nor was Blair going to tell him at this stage what job he had in mind for Mandelson to conduct this relationship from. Mandelson sat down to eat his pasta in some agitation.

Blair had originally intended to give Mandelson the one cabinet post which would have guaranteed him a place at the centre of power: running a strengthened Cabinet Office as Blair's 'enforcer'. Both Brown and Mandelson himself were against the idea, but if they were agreed on the undesirability of the Cabinet Office role, they had by no means settled on an alternative. There had been rumours that Blair might be lining him up for another junior department, Agriculture. Although Mandelson had contemplated refusing that too, if it was offered, Roger Liddle had urged him to accept on the grounds that because of the European dimension he might actually like it. As he sat at the dinner table with Lady Powell and Benjamin Wegg-Prosser, he paged Anji Hunter in the hope of learning more. When she rang back she did not tell him any more than Blair had. But she speculated cryptically that he would hardly be having a nocturnal meeting with Brown unless it was to discuss something big – like the DTI.

Mandelson's apprehension, however, went deeper than that. Suppose he *was* going to the DTI (as the well-informed Trevor Kavanagh, political editor of the *Sun*, had predicted to him in another pager message that afternoon). What price was Brown planning to exact for his support? The Chancellor was famous for requiring 100 per cent loyalty from his allies. Mandelson was eager, he had insisted in his telephone conversation with Blair, to work as closely with Brown as he had for the six years until their rupture in 1994. But he was not going to undertake in advance to agree with him on every occasion. The Prime Minister was sympathetic but appeared to believe that Mandelson was making heavier weather of all this than the circumstances required. Surely he was enough of a politician to devise a way of working with the Chancellor?

Driven in his own green Rover by Wegg-Prosser, Mandelson, in jeans and sweater, arrived early at Great Peter Street. It was a measure of his estrangement from Brown that he had been there only once – and then fleetingly – since the shocking morning of John Smith's death on 12 May 1994, when they had met there as the closest of friends and colleagues to discuss the leadership. As a result, when he pressed the bell, as Wegg-Prosser drove off in search of a parking place, and got no answer, he wondered if he had the address right. He went back to the car and started to telephone Sue Nye, Brown's political secretary. Nye was an old friend but the strains of Mandelson's relationship with Brown meant that they had barely spoken for months. He dialled a number and handed the mobile phone to Wegg-Prosser, who found himself speaking to the switchboard of the *Guardian*. In a rare outward sign of nervousness, Mandelson had dialled the wrong 278 number. Having found Sue Nye, and established that he had the correct address, Mandelson rang the bell again. This time Brown came to the door.

Brown greeted him with much more warmth than he expected. He produced a cold bottle of champagne and appeared genuinely surprised that Blair had not told him what job he would be getting. 'Congratulations', he told Mandelson gracefully. 'You've got one of the top jobs. It's a promotion you deserved and I've always wanted you to be in the Cabinet. I want you to know that.' 'Even if not actually in this job,' Mandelson could not resist replying. Waving this aside, Brown got down to business. He did not demand unswerving loyalty in quite the terms Mandelson had feared. Instead he pointed out with incontestable logic that harmony between Chancellor and Trade and Industry Secretary was of vital importance. A minor difference on monetary policy, for example, could easily be magnified into a huge one. They would be working closely on the forthcoming Competitiveness White Paper, and on the subject currently preoccupying Brown – and the theme of his Green Budget in November – productivity. Anything which suggested friction between them – or that one department was more pro-business than the other – would inflict huge damage on the government's credibility. What Brown was saying could hardly have been clearer: the dozens of petty frictions which had marred their relationship since what Brown had seen as Mandelson's betrayal of him in favour of Blair were a luxury they could no longer afford. The stakes were now too high. Mandelson agreed. The two men parted, after about forty-five minutes, on more cordial terms than at any time in the last four years.

Mandelson was elated as Wegg-Prosser drove him back through light Sunday-night traffic. He telephoned his mother with the momentous news that he would be a secretary of state by tomorrow afternoon. He mechanically ticked off Wegg-Prosser for taking the wrong route through Pimlico, but he also confided in him how 'genuinely nice' Brown had been. And when he got back to the Powell home in Caroline Place, just off the Bayswater Road, he flicked through the untouched Sunday newspaper business sections, joking that he had better read them before he went to bed, given his new responsibilities. In his excitement he slept badly, and for only about four hours. Since he was a child Mandelson, a pathologically early riser, had continually complained that he never got enough sleep. But the following day the adrenalin would carry him through.

There was an almost surreal, end-of-term atmosphere at the Cabinet Office the following morning. Mandelson walked through the connecting door between his office and the meeting room for this last session of the media strategy group which had met under his chairmanship every day since the general election. The 'presentation meeting' began five minutes late, just after 9 a.m., and moved quickly to routine matters: in a slick – perhaps a little too slick –

piece of media management, it had been agreed to bring two mildly embarrassing pieces of news out on a day when they would be bound to be dwarfed by the reshuffle. The Legg report on the Sandline affair – the arms-to-Africa scandal, in media shorthand – would give Foreign Office ministers no specific problems, the meeting was told; but there might be criticism that the government was also taking the opportunity to issue new rules drawn up by the Cabinet Secretary, Sir Richard Wilson, in the aftermath of 'Drapergate'. Mandelson expressed disappointment that the government's important announcement on new immigration and asylum rules was also coming out that day – because of the pressure of the parliamentary timetable. On any other day it would have been a big moment for the junior Home Office minister Mike O'Brien, who was a Mandelson favourite. The meeting was told that Jack Straw was still discussing with MPs and peers what to do about the Lords' reversal on the gay age of consent; and there was a murmur of satisfaction when it was pointed out that a big speech by William Hague that day would get little coverage thanks to the reshuffle.

By now the drama of Blair's reshuffle was beginning to unfold; through much of Whitehall televisions were tuned to Sky TV, carrying continual live coverage of the comings and goings at Downing Street. With one eye on the set in the corner of the room, Mandelson looked a little abstractedly through the departmental briefing papers on the parliamentary questions on the Dome that he would be taking that afternoon. Barring accident, this would be his last day in this office on the third floor of the Cabinet Office. He would no longer enjoy its one huge advantage – the swipe card which came with the territory and opened the thick wooden door connecting the ground floor with Number Ten. Otherwise it was light and pleasant, but unremarkable. The most interesting pictures were the series of Chris Orr etchings of John Ruskin, recording the young artist's sexual agonies, which Mandelson had dug out of the government art collection – more risqué, but part of the same series as the etching which had been bought by his father and which had hung, and still hangs, over his desk at home in Hampstead Garden Suburb when he was doing his 'A' levels. Above the mantelpiece was a framed text from Abraham Lincoln, given to him by an American friend of Philip Gould: 'I do the very best I know how – the very best I can, and I mean to keep doing so until the end. If the end brings me out all right, what is said against me won't amount to anything. If the end brings me out wrong, then angels swearing I was right would make no difference.'

Robbed of the element of surprise, at the meeting with Blair in Downing Street, Blair gave him some sensible advice, including an exhortation that he should consult Ian McCartney, the Minister of State for trade union matters, on the bill that would arise out of the Fairness at Work White Paper. Indeed, Mandelson was extremely lucky in his team of junior ministers. Apart from anything else, although very different from Mandelson himself, two of them were very able ministers who had shown they could work harmoniously with him before – McCartney, who had been part of the team at Littleborough and Saddleworth, and Brian Wilson, who had been in charge of rebuttal at Millbank Tower during the election. Both were coincidentally also on warm terms with John Prescott. John Battle was experienced and a safe pair of hands in the energy portfolio, and Kim Howells, an ultra-moderniser and anti-interventionist, was ideologically on Mandelson's wavelength. Barbara Roche and Lord Simon, the ardently pro-EMU chairman of BP completed the team.

Mandelson now walked back from Downing Street, received a briefing for his Questions in the Commons, and went through them as if in a dream. He would say afterwards that he had never felt so relaxed at the dispatch box. He could not have been more exhilarated. There is no reason to suppose that it even occurred to him, having failed to bring the matter up with Sir Robin Butler the weekend after the election, to mention the Robinson home loan at his first introductory meeting with Sir Michael Scholar, the DTI permanent secretary. If he had done so, on either occasion, he might have escaped the catastrophe that was to engulf him six months later; that was certainly the retrospective view of Sir Robin. Instead, he could not but savour his promotion. Not only was he in the Cabinet at the age of forty-four, but he at last had the chance to escape the stigma of his shadowy previous existence as the Prince of Darkness. By now he had become the man to revile in the Labour government, a prime target for satirists; few other politicians, apart from Margaret Thatcher, had been subjected to such relentless abuse. He had been depicted as a snake by *Spitting Image*, as a swivel-eyed animatron by Rory Bremner, vilified to his face at a Downing Street drinks party by Harry Enfield, and immortalised as the sinister church warden in the *Private Eye* strip 'the Vicar of St Albion's'. It was hard not to imagine that every quibble with the still stubbornly popular Blair government was being visited on him personally; he had certainly become lightning-conductor-in-chief. So much so that there had been something of a counter-reaction. The *Guardian*'s Hugo Young described him as a 'grotesquely maligned politician'[1], and writing in the *New Statesman* the writer Jo Glanville posed the interesting question of whether, as with Svengali, to whom he was routinely compared, latent anti-semitism might not be the 'disturbing, prevalent sub-text' of his depiction as a 'devilish, vengeful, omnipotent fiend'.'' Would that depiction have been quite as strident if his name had been Roberts? If nothing else, it would make a change for the word Mandelson to figure in sober headlines about merger policy in the *Financial Times*. It was also a proper, and potentially hugely fulfilling, job.

The initial reaction of most civil servants in the DTI was surprise. They had not expected Mandelson; their only knowledge of him had been as the Prime Minister's outrider in one or two bloody quarrels in which Margaret Beckett, the previous Secretary of State, had been involved – including one memorable occasion when she had refused to accept Downing Street's amendments to the Fairness at Work White Paper unless they were in the Prime Minister's own handwriting. Mandelson, as Minister without Portfolio, had been charged by the private office with explaining that if wording came from Downing Street it could safely be assumed to have prime ministerial authority. For the last three years the department, first under the Tory Ian Lang and then under Beckett, his Labour successor, had become a rather introverted backwater; both these ministers had been a 'safe pair of hands', competent, and not prone to serious mistakes. But neither had had notable clout within the Cabinet and Beckett had not been perceived as a particularly dynamic secretary of state.

Mandelson was clearly going to be different. He even dropped the title of 'President of the Board' of Trade, resurrected by Heseltine and continued by Beckett, in favour of the less grandiose 'Secretary of State'. Moreover, he arrived at Victoria Street considerably earlier each day than she had done (at about 8.15), completed his boxes on time, took decisions – including quite complex merger decisions – quickly, and showed every sign of wanting to enjoy his job. The enjoyment was infectious, at least among officials. Business reacted warmly and that transmitted itself back to the department. Morale, particularly in those directorates in which he quickly started to focus interest, like Europe and Information Technology, rose sharply and almost immediately. At a meeting with some of his senior civil servants he declared he intended to 'live dangerously'. It was unfortunate that this observation finally surfaced publicly in *DTI News* on the day he resigned because of doing just that. But it was a sign that Mandelson's term in office was going to be an exciting ride, and that he would deal with the big beasts of government, whether at Downing Street or at the Treasury, with more authority than Beckett had done. Suddenly DTI civil servants felt that they had started to matter again.

That did not mean there were no anxieties. If they had not expected Mandelson, they had certainly not expected Mandelson *plus* Millennium Dome. Several of his advisers were uneasy about him keeping the Dome – among them Lord Hollick and Dan Corry, whom he inherited from Margaret Beckett. Blair wanted Mandelson to continue with the Dome because he regarded him as the minister likeliest to ensure its completion on time; but even if he had not, Mandelson had been determined to keep his beloved project wherever he went in the reshuffle. Having weathered all the problems it had caused over the past fourteen months – with the sacking of the volatile and flamboyant design guru Stephen Bayley and the cancellation, much to Cameron Macintosh's disappointment, of ambitious plans for a twice-daily live show on the theme of Time – he was not going to miss out on the credit for what he never seemed to doubt would be its success. But whether the DTI was the right department to take responsibility for the Dome was, to put it mildly, doubtful. There was unease from the start among some officials about the potential conflict of interests, given the prominence of leading businessmen and the scale of their companies' donations to the Greenwich project. The unease first surfaced when senior officials formally expressed concern about Mandelson's responsibility for adjudicating over the sale of British Airways/American Airlines slots at Heathrow, because of the BA chairman Bob Ayling's prominence in the Dome, not to mention his close acquaintance with the Secretary of State. Mandelson rejected the clear implication of their protest, which was that he should stand aside from decisions relating to British Airways. He was able to do so because the officials had stopped short of issuing unequivocal advice; indeed, some junior civil servants felt privately that their seniors had let the department down by not pressing the point harder; particularly since it meant that when, in turn, there were strong internal concerns, on the same grounds, to his adjudicating on BSkyB's bid to buy Manchester United (BSkyB had agreed to divert a £6 million donation, originally intended for school computers, to the Dome), a line had already been crossed.[3] If he could take quasi-judicial decisions on British Airways, he could hardly, his office argued, be stopped from doing so on BSkyB. As it happened, the BA/American decision was deferred in the absence of an 'Open Skies' agreement and Mandelson referred the BSkyB bid to the Monopolies and Mergers Commission. Nevertheless a politically smooth ride on these issues could hardly have been assured had he stayed. It was a recipe for controversy, and it might not have been indefinitely sustainable. There were, or should have been, limits to living dangerously.

As it happened, when Mandelson held his first meeting with Gordon Brown after his appointment, the Chancellor had raised with him an idea he had been floating for some time – that just as interest rates had been handed over to an independent Bank of England, so these quasi-judicial decisions should be handed over to an independent competition agency, possibly a beefed-up Office of Fair Trading. Not for the first time, Mandelson found it easier to agree with the Chancellor than to get on with him. There was strong resistance to losing this heavy responsibility within the DTI. Partly this was territorial; partly it was a fear that decisions which might look sensible on very finely balanced competition grounds might be indefensible on others, like the need to preserve strategic industries: a competition agency would not be able to take such grounds into account. There was also a nakedly political argument against hiving them off; it would mean that, in the run-up to an election, for example, governments would not have the power to prevent a merger which might lead to factory closures in marginal constituencies. But, as with interest rates, that might be a reason against retaining the adjudication powers; despite official hostility within the DTI Mandelson was inclined to agree with Brown that, for the sake of healthy competition, hiving off the decisions was the radical, and correct, option. He had been on the point of publishing a Green Paper on the subject when he resigned in December 1998.

But whatever the strains in the department over competition policy, general and specific, civil servants were by and large delighted that the DTI was at last going to enjoy a higher profile. Indeed, one of Mandelson's first challenges was, in the largest sense, presentational. Just after 2.30 p.m. on Friday 4 September a large blue chauffeur-driven Mercedes pulled up outside his house in Hutton Avenue, Hartlepool. The short, beige-suited Japanese passenger who stepped out of the back was one of the most powerful and innovative business executives in the Far East. He had just brought grim news to the North-East of England from Tokyo, telling 600 workers at a microchip plant a few miles away in Tony Blair's neighbouring constituency of Sedgefield that their jobs had fallen victim to the Asian economic crisis and the global collapse in semi-conductor prices it had brought in its wake. The Fujitsu factory, opened only seven years earlier after being underwritten by £50 million of government grants, was closing and now Mr Takamitsu Tsuchimoto, chief executive of the company's Electronic Devices division, had come to explain the reasons to the Secretary of State for Trade and Industry. Mr Tsuchimoto, three colleagues and an interpreter crowded into Mandelson's living room and appeared a little embarrassed, contrite even, over tea and fruit biscuits from the local corner shop. Japan experts in the DTI had advised Mandelson that a visit to his home would be considered an honour by Mr Tsuchimoto and they were right. He lingered for an hour, insisting to Mandelson that the two other British plants, at Maidenhead and Manchester, were safe, that the company would do its best to help find a buyer for the closing factory, and that the decision was caused solely by a market collapse which had seen D-ram prices crash from £45 to £1.20 and not because of the high value of sterling.

The Fujitsu closure, which followed hard on the heels of another in the North East by Siemens, had overshadowed a busy constituency Friday for the Industry Secretary. In his ministerial Rover on the way to Heathrow to catch the 9.30 British Midland flight to Teesside airport he grumbled about inaccuracies in that morning's front-page *Guardian* report on the closure, ringing what he insisted were errors as he listened to the BBC *Today* programme. He fulminated against Roger Lyons, general secretary of the white-collar union MSF, as he declared on the programme that he would be asking Tony Blair at a meeting on Monday to make the 'so-called independent' Bank of England bring down interest rates. Nor could he resist, out of sheer force of habit, drawing another circle around the hair cascading over the prime ministerial ear in a photograph of Blair and murmuring: 'He always comes back from holiday needing a hair cut.' (Blair once joked to him that only 'you and Anji [Hunter] could be relied on to bother with such things'.) And as *Today* returned to the Fujitsu story, he shook his head in silent and patronising rebuke when the Shadow Chancellor Francis Maude echoed Lyons's remarks, blaming government management of the economy for the closure: 'He shouldn't have gone on; it's the wrong issue and he's got nothing to say.' Gordon Brown, he asserted, would never have made a similar professional error when he was shadowing Kenneth Clarke.

As he toured his constituency Mandelson again spoke to the Prime Minister on his mobile telephone. He sounded assured:

This has got nothing to do with the economy and we have to be very firm with these people. It's not our economy which has caused this, it's a world market which has collapsed. The thing to bear in mind is that more than 10,000 jobs have been created or safeguarded by inward investment. But the other thing which is very irritating and is catching on here started at 6.30 this morning, pushed in that ridiculous Roger Lyons interview – did you hear it? He kept saying he was seeing you on Monday to argue against foreign investment. What kind of economy is he living in? . . . No, I don't think you should cancel the meeting. I think you should tell them the facts of life.

But the local MP, from his office at Number Ten Downing Street, had had a good tip. Fujitsu, he happened to know, had written to William Hague saying that the closure had nothing to do with interest rates or the level of sterling. Hague was due on *The World at One* just before Mandelson himself was scheduled to give an interview. Mandelson had no hesitation about the next step: Wegg-Prosser was instructed to ring the programme and alert them to the letter. Sure enough, a few minutes later the presenter, Charlie Lee Potter, let Hague use the closure to attack government economic policy before pressing him – twice – on the letter. Result: Hague discomfited; Mandelson given a relatively smooth ride. After Mr Tsuchimoto's visit, five more radio and television interviews, a constituents' surgery and a chatty visit to the enthusiastic but modestly attended pub quiz night of the newly formed Young Labour Group in the town, he finally sat down in the rambling kitchen at Hutton Avenue to a glass of wine and a meat stew cooked by his full-time agent Steve Wallace.

All in a day's work, of course. But it raised an ominous point. At a time of economic slowdown, if not recession, had Mandelson simply been handed the poisoned chalice of the Ministry for Closing Things Down? He had little problem defending the government and the Chancellor against the charge that the handing over of interest rates to the Bank of England had caused the closure. But what of the more telling point that Fujitsu reflected Britain's status as 'a branch line economy', as a local businessman in his own constituency had put it that very day, over-dependent for its strength on inward investment vulnerable to the vagaries of the Asian economic crisis. Back in the early nineties a Treasury official, asked what Britain now excelled at, had answered dryly: 'Some forms of banking and assembling Japanese cars.' This was a gross underestimate, of course: in home-grown sectors like – say – pharmaceuticals Britain was a worldbeater. But it still made a point. There were two distinct dangers in being Trade and Industry Secretary in the current economic climate. One was that, however defensible the government's monetary policy, it was inevitably putting manufacturing industry, especially exporting manufacturing industry, under pressure; the other was that this could hardly, given the economic collapse in Asia, be a worse time to be over-dependent on inward investment from Japan or Korea.

The second point, as Roger Liddle had been one of the first to point out to Mandelson, was important: foreign investment could not be regarded as the sole answer to the problems of the British economy. It was a theme which Mandelson pursued enthusiastically in his speech to the North West Chamber of Commerce on 26 October – the same speech in which he was notably bullish about the prospects for EMU. 'Inward investment continues to be important in creating jobs, introducing new ideas and techniques,' he said. 'But my message to you tonight is that inward investment cannot be our only or indeed our main source of new jobs. It must be matched by the creation of indigenous, home-grown companies and jobs. A new enterprise sector of the British and regional economy.' This was one, though only one, strand of thinking which would bear fruit in the Competitiveness White Paper two months later: this drive for what he saw as a 'knowledge-based economy', in which British science and technology would be better exploited by more creative entrepreneurship, and actively encouraged by government, would also incidentally involve less dependence on external investment. He prided himself on being the 'most science conscious minister since William Waldegrave'. And in all this the state, without trying 'to second-guess boardroom decisions', as he put it when he launched the White Paper, had a defensible role.

But before he could define it there were a number of urgent issues to settle. In his energy review, Mandelson proved himself to be something of a closet Peter Shore man, fostering 'security and diversity of supply' and prolonging the life of the coal industry. It was true that he had deep reservations about the moratorium on Advanced Gas Cooled Reactors as a market intervention too far. But he went ahead with it, nevertheless, and had certainly been impressed, ever since his visit down Kellingley Colliery, by the argument that over-dependence on gas, which would in the long term have to come from such volatile producing countries as Russia and Algeria, might be dangerous.

So too with the Post Office, over which Mandelson eventually, after much heartache and a good deal of grandstanding, also found a third way. Following his statement on the Post Office there was a murderous briefing by Gordon Brown's Treasury press secretary Charlie Whelan (or, as its recipient, Paul Eastham of the *Daily Mail*, would later delicately put it, 'someone so close to ... Whelan it could have been him'[4]) describing the announcement as a 'dog's breakfast' and claiming that Mandelson had 'bottled out' of privatising the Post Office. According to some journalists, Whelan had given two alternative briefings – one to right-leaning papers claiming that Mandelson had funked a desirable privatisation of the Post Office, and another to left-leaning papers, and the trade unions, that Brown had 'saved' the Post Office from privatisation.

As frequently with Mandelson, and with Brown as well, the truth was more complicated, and more interesting, than either of these caricatures. But it once again demonstrated that the dysfunctional nature of the Brown-Mandelson relationship had not ended with Labour's election victory or their subsequent attempts at reconciliation. When Mandelson had his first substantive meeting with Brown after the reshuffle he raised the issue of privatising the Post Office, to establish where the Chancellor stood. Mandelson understood the Chancellor to take the viewpoint that the politics were not right for privatisation; it was best to leave it alone. Given that the Major government had shrunk from privatisation for fear of a Commons defeat, and given the manifesto commitment to retaining it in the public sector, this was surely sound advice. Indeed, both Brown and Mandelson separately dissuaded Blair from his own chosen preference for selling off at least a minority stake in the Post Office. Instead Mandelson decided in favour of maintaining it in the public sector but with much more commercial freedom both to reinvest its own profits and to borrow for expansion on the commercial money markets. As the plans were worked up in the DTI it became clear that the Treasury was worried about the potential loss of revenue. In the period when the losses of unprofitable state industries had to be met by the taxpayer, those losses were offset by a rule that those few industries in the public sector which were making profits would have to return most of them to the Treasury. This rule still applied, even though most of the rest of the nationalised industries had long been privatised. The Post Office was therefore a useful source of revenue to the Exchequer; the more it was allowed to keep its profits for reinvestment, the less useful a source it would be. Indeed, the Treasury case was that if it was not going to be sold off, it should continue to make money for the Exchequer.

The DTI's counter case was that without investment the business would decline and shrink, becoming no use to anyone, including the Treasury. It faced a changing market with increasing competition for postal services. There was also a related problem. If the Post Office was to have more freedom to borrow, this would add, because of the way in which the rules were drawn up, to the Public Sector Borrowing Requirement – though admittedly without breaking Brown's 'Golden Rule' that borrowing was permissible for investment.

It was on the second of these points that Brown launched a démarche. Well before the scheduled announcement – for which both the Post Office and its unions were clamouring – Mandelson wrote to Brown outlining his plans in some detail and inviting him to comment. There was then a long delay during which the Chancellor failed to respond. Eventually, the week before the scheduled announcement, Mandelson's private secretary Anthony Phillipson telephoned Tom Scholar, Brown's principal private secretary, to protest that the Treasury's failure to respond was holding up progress on the Industry Secretary's urgent plans. The very next day a letter arrived from Brown, enclosing a detailed paper containing the Treasury's analysis of Mandelson's proposals. The 'Dear Peter . . . Yrs Gordon' letter from the Chancellor was courteous and friendly. But when DTI officials studied the paper which accompanied it they found that while Brown was no longer objecting to the threatened loss of revenue from the Post Office's profits, he was putting severe restrictions on its borrowing powers – severe enough to extinguish any government claim that it was giving the Post Office the commercial freedom it wanted. At issue was the amount the Post Office would be able to borrow and its freedom to invent and form 'strategic alliances' with other international postal operations. The Treasury was proposing that all this would require the approval of a committee chaired by the Prime Minister – a suggestion regarded by Mandelson as a deliberately obstructive tactic. The DTI wanted an overall borrowing limit of £750 million over five years, within which it would be able to borrow up to £100 million per year without consulting ministers. Above that it would have to seek approval, but on the assumption it would get it – within the overall parameters – provided the proposal was 'commercially robust'. The Treasury view was that the limit on unapproved borrowing should be £50 million – and that there should be no assumptions about any amount above that.

At this point Mandelson considerably upped the ante by personally ringing Tom Scholar (the son, by coincidence, of his own permanent secretary) and throwing a (more or less) controlled tantrum. If Brown was going to stick to this position, he indicated, he would pull the announcement altogether, no doubt detonating a public row with the Post Office and with the Opposition, in which case the reasons for the announcement's cancellation would rapidly become clear. This was a clear breach of Whitehall protocol in which minister speaks to minister, private secretary to private secretary. Indeed, Phillipson felt obliged to telephone Scholar and apologise for his minister's solecism. But the tactic worked. A meeting was set up: on the Thursday before the announcement Mandelson, his Minister of State Ian McCartney, his special adviser Dan Corry, Phillipson and Martin Baker, the lead DTI official on the Post Office, trooped over to the Chancellor's office at the Treasury. At Brown's suggestion the meeting took place not across the huge wooden conference table in the middle of the room, but crowded into the sofas and chairs at one end, where Brown preferred to hold most of his meetings.

This appearance of informality, however, did nothing to make the confrontation any less tense. To Mandelson's fury, while the Treasury case was put partly by a senior official Harry Bush, and partly by the Chancellor himself, much of the interrogation of the DTI team was conducted by Brown's economic adviser, Ed Balls, who was sitting in a chair behind Brown's right shoulder, his face betraying frequent signs of contempt at the answers he elicited. Mandelson snapped. Raising his voice, he complained that Balls's 'behaviour' was inhibiting the progress of the meeting. Brown retorted that he had no idea what Mandelson was talking about. Mandelson said that the Chancellor, unlike him, could not see Balls's face; Balls should either 'behave' or leave the room altogether. According to one mortified official, the exchanges were like an 'awful family quarrel'. It was finally agreed, to the intense relief of the officials present, that the meeting should adjourn and that the two departments should seek, without ministers, to negotiate a formula acceptable to both sides.

The negotiations between the Treasury, the DTI and Jeremy Heywood at Number Ten, continued throughout the weekend and well into Monday, by which point the difference had become deep but very narrow. Phillipson and Scholar had agreed a compromise – that the discretionary borrowing limit should be £75 million a year. But the Treasury was continuing to insist that no assumption should be written into the statement saying that the limits would be exceeded, even with the proviso that it was for 'commercially robust' purposes. In other words, there was no indication that the Post Office would normally get more than £75 million a year.

At this point Mandelson decided to appeal directly to Blair. It was not a step to take lightly. As a secretary of state, particularly one engaged in his first serious interdepartmental conflict, he could not go running to the Prime Minister every time there was a dispute with a colleague, let alone with the Chancellor. But there were only a few hours to go until his statement; as the Treasury position stood it meant that either the statement would have to be pulled or, Mandelson insisted, it would invite damaging protests from the Post Office that it was unworkable. Less than ninety minutes before the statement Blair ruled broadly in favour of Mandelson and the logjam was broken. One view among Whitehall officials was that Mandelson would not have won his victory had Gordon Brown not been told during the morning the sad news that his father had died, and thus been taken out of the final negotiations. Conversely, others thought that in Brown's absence and with Balls in charge, the Treasury was more intransigent than it would have been if the Chancellor had been present. Under normal circumstances, it was thought, the row would have been resolved by some form of fudge. There was also a view, at least at the DTI, that had Brown's father not died Whelan might have been sacked for his unremittingly hostile briefing after the statement. Finally, the statement contained a clause rather under-reported at the time, and which Blair was keen to see inserted, making it clear that future privatisation, or part-privatisation, would not be ruled out.

The second big issue of Mandelson's term of office at the DTI was trade union legislation. He was determined to make his speech to the TUC in Blackpool in September a distinctively modernising one, and though he was delighted to be reported by the *Evening*

*Standard* immediately after it, as giving the Congress a tough 'modernise or die' message, he had taken great trouble with his speech. It was a big occasion, not only because he was revisiting his employers of twenty years earlier as a Cabinet minister, but also because he had never before spoken at either a TUC or a Labour Party conference. He was nervous about the speech, and took the trouble to show the draft to John Monks, the general secretary of the TUC, the night before. Monks suggested one or two minor drafting changes, including making it clear that no decisions had yet been taken on the Post Office, to allay fears of privatisation (though he was unable to persuade Mandelson to dwell at length on the virtues of a 'social partnership' a consistent TUC theme).

The speech on 17 September was nevertheless the most coherent account yet of how New Labour saw the trade unions. Mandelson accepted that there were reasons of 'sentiment' for a Labour politician to value the unions, 'not just because I will always remember how the trade unions helped Neil Kinnock save the party in the 1980s and put it back onto the long road to electoral credibility, just as in my grandfather's time, the trade unions saw Labour through the upheavals of the 1930s'. But he went on to deliver an uncompromising message to the unions that they would be increasingly irrelevant unless they, too, changed. He reminded the Congress that only 6 per cent of young employees were now trade union members, and only 18 per cent of employees under the age of thirty. Worse still, the density of the trade union membership was the lowest in the fastest growing sectors of the economy. He added that

of course I accept that there are rogue employers who actively discourage trade union membership. But for many ordinary working people, trade unions appear only marginally relevant. Many companies have built honest and credible partnerships with their employees with no involvement of trade unions at all. And if employers and employees are content with that, it is not the job of government to order them otherwise.

The unions, he insisted, needed to deliver 'quality services to their members', to be focused on employers' success, and to be 'seen to be responsible by the general public.' This meant showing 'flexibility and adaptability in the face of change. And let me be honest, flexibility, not just in terms of hours and skills, but in terms of employee numbers and pay levels as well'. He added, 'We will never again contract out the governance of Britain to anyone, not to the TUC or its member unions any more than to big corporate interests. But we would much prefer modernised trade unions to be our active and committed partners along the way. The choice is yours – opposition or legitimate influence?'

Mandelson succeeded in making a favourable impression on the less Neanderthal of the union leaders with his re-statement of belief in the value of strong, outward-looking unions. In a warm private note after his visit, Monks congratulated him on a 'triumph' adding, 'As you say it was a risk, but it was a risk which came off handsomely.'

Relations with Monks (once a senior colleague at Congress House in the seventies), did not go so smoothly once the negotiations on the bill following the White Paper on trade union law, 'Fairness at Work', had started. Mandelson rather prided himself on taking a tough line with the unions, and he was certainly determined to recover some of the ground which Blair thought had been conceded to them in Margaret Beckett's White Paper. Despite Blair's original exhortation to work closely with Ian McCartney, McCartney at times felt left out of some of the key discussions within the department. This was partly a case of ministerial trade craft. Under Beckett, McCartney, a shrewd minister with a comprehensive knowledge of trade union law who fought his corner and was more supportive of the TUC case than Mandelson, managed to ensure that he saw papers from officials before they went up to the Secretary of State. He would put his own comments on submissions, thus ensuring that it was much more difficult for Beckett to go against them without being seen to be overruling the Departmental ministerial expert. Mandelson rightly respected McCartney, but he managed to evade this problem by reducing the number of written submissions and inviting officials to come into his office and put their points orally. It was not until the closing stages that McCartney came back into his own, negotiating some of the important line-by-line detail with Number Ten.

Nevertheless, the final outcome was not quite the union-bashers' charter the unions had feared. Mandelson reimposed a cap on the amounts of compensation to be paid in unfair dismissal cases. But since this had been what the TUC had been expecting, and since Mandelson had specifically exempted 'whistle blowers' who had been sacked for exposing malpractice by their employers, this was hardly a catastrophe for the unions. More controversial was Mandelson's determination to limit the scope for automatic union recognition, i.e. recognition without a ballot, in cases in which the unions could claim sufficiently high membership. The TUC believed that this would avoid damaging and divisive campaigns between employers and unions. The employers believed that it would provide a ramp for securing bargaining rights where the size of the membership did not necessarily represent a majority desire for recognition. Mandelson had privately been against any automatic recognition at all. But he believed that to abandon it would be too much of a retreat from Margaret Beckett's White Paper. Instead he insisted that the Central Arbitration Committee should consider such cases and take into account the amount of time that employees had been members and the circumstances in which they had signed up before approving recognition.

Although the overall package succeeded, as Mandelson had promised it would to the Labour Party conference, in correcting the 'basic imbalance' against employees left by the Tory legislation, the negotiations caused serious tensions in Mandelson's long relationship with John Monks. The TUC general secretary fought him every inch of the way, the row culminating in a difficult tête-à-tête between Monks and the Prime Minister of Downing Street. But while he solved the most pressing problems (the Post Office and the trade union legislation), in his relatively short tenure at the Department his main achievement was probably to give the DTI a coherent sense of how it might turn the business-friendly rhetoric Labour had used before the general election into something which the business community could accept as having real meaning. He was a highly proactive trade minister, almost invariably agreeing to see relatively obscure visiting ministers from abroad if he thought it might help job-creating trade links. Officials travelling with the Prime Minister to South Africa in January were forcibly struck by what a favourable impression Mandelson had made on the business community during his own visit there as Trade and Industry Secretary. But it was in industrial policy that he was most innovative. In this he found the enviable track record of the US economy in the Clinton years instructive. Sharing both the Chancellor's and the Prime Minister's American interests, he had expected to be impressed by his visit to the United States – and he was. He met luminaries of the exponentially growing information technology industries based in Silicon Valley, like Jack Welch, the head of General Electric, and the top venture capitalist and lawyer, Larry Sonsini. Several aspects of the trip had been planned by Charlie Leadbeater, Mandelson's old LWT colleague – a leading exponent of the 'knowledge-driven economy' and the man hand-picked by Mandelson to be responsible for much of the thinking behind the Competitiveness White Paper, which crowned his term of office. In particular, Mandelson was struck by the skill and determination of the American entrepreneurs to harness the best scientific research, the much greater availability of capital for such entrepreneurs, and the willingness of some of the best brains in American universities to share in their success.

In a speech to the British American Chamber of Commerce in New York on 13 October, he described how he had sat on a Long Island beach in the summer and read *The Road Ahead* by Microsoft's Bill Gates, before going on to say:

> Britain is great at inventing things, but less good at turning them into business ideas and ventures. Too often, products are invented in the UK but manufactured elsewhere ... We need more entrepreneurs in the British economy – they are the real agents of economic change, because enterprise is the bedrock of a modern economy ... to make money the entrepreneur needs to take an idea, see it as an opportunity, find a means of financing it, make it, market it, move it and sell it. In the process he or she is creating employment and creating wealth.

In seeking to put this mission into practice he became, during his brief tenure, the living embodiment of how far industrial policy had changed since the previous Labour government eighteen years earlier. The Labour right, of which Mandelson had been part since leaving Oxford, had been devoted to a mixed economy of state industry coupled with a heavily planned and directed private sector. The New Labour approach was wholly different. Ownership, of course, was no longer an issue. It was now accepted that the private sector, subject to the disciplines of capital markets and with a management motivated by profit, was now more likely to be efficient (and so to grow and provide jobs) than had been the state-run industries subjected only to the variable discipline of sponsoring ministers. Indeed, Mandelson was more dubious than Gordon Brown about the use of company law to curb the salaries of the top executives on the grounds that ample managerial rewards were an essential element of a dynamic business sector. Secondly it was now assumed that small and medium-sized enterprises would be the main motors for growth. This made old-style interventionism not only undesirable but impossible. It was no longer feasible, as it had been in the heyday of the large enterprise, for a minister to summon the leaders of the biggest companies and biggest unions and feel reasonably confident that he had assembled in one room those who controlled the British economy. And anyway, as Mandelson's White Paper would unequivocally put it, 'the present government will not resort to the interventionist policies of the past. In the industrial policy-making of the 1960s and 1970s to be modern meant believing in planning. Now, meeting the demands of the knowledge-driven economy means making markets work better'.

It was now accepted that government policy had to encourage rather than hamper entrepreneurship. This was why Mandelson's predecessor, Margaret Beckett, to her credit, had produced a Competition bill which went a long way towards encouraging competition and protecting small firms from their larger predators. This was why it was no longer a Labour assumption that capital gains taxes should be set at the highest feasible level. And it was why, in the December Competitiveness White Paper, Mandelson, fortified by his experience in the United States, foreshadowed, amongst many other measures, once unthinkable changes to the bankruptcy laws to make it easier for those businesses that had failed to pick themselves up and try again. As he said in his New York speech

Rather than discouraging anyone from risking failure, we need to encourage entrepreneurs to take further risks in the future.

Here in the US I am told that some investors prefer to back businessmen with one or more failures under their belts because they appreciate the spirit of enterprise and recognise the experience that has been gained. In Britain, rather than sharing the risk with entrepreneurs in this way, most creditors are much more wary of supporting those who have experienced business failure.

Most of these lessons, of course, either already had or might well have been learned by the Tory government. It was easy to see how dramatically far the Labour Party of Blair, Brown and Mandelson had changed from the days when Mandelson's grandfather had been the eponymous architect and overseer of the great 'Morrisonian' post-war industries. And this posed a different question: was Mandelson, as Trade and Industry Secretary, any different from his *Tory* predecessors? In his first-ever speech to the Labour Party conference, he declared that in the new information age, 'economic growth will depend both on how well we invent new industries and how we can reinvent and smarten old ones', before going on to say, 'we must be crystal clear about what governments can and can not do. Neither centrally to plan nor control the economy. Not the Tory idea of *laissez faire*, letting individuals sink or swim. Neither old left nor new right, but a third way for government action.'

Could this familiar mantra of the third way mean anything to his own department apart from hacking out a workable and intelligent compromise on the Post Office, balancing the interests of working in trade union legislation, or a modest degree of protection for the coal industry? The first answer was that New Labour's conversion to capitalism still meant a continuing, if transformed, role for the state. This was obvious in the Blair-Brown-Blunkett commitment to investment in education and the skilling of the workforce. But it could also apply to the responsibilities of the DTI. Here, the Competitiveness White Paper proved instructive. It was withering in its dismissal of old-style state aids whilst punctuated with a £150 million public/private venture capital Enterprise Fund here, £15 million for fostering links between business and education there, £20 million to put small businesses on the Internet, an extra £100 million for the Regional Development Agencies (the bodies which Mandelson actively encouraged more than his predecessor, who had been fearful that the RDAs were a Prescottian ramp to extend the domain of the Deputy Prime Minister over most of non-metropolitan England). Much more of this and it would be adding up to real money.

Of these initiatives, the Enterprise Fund was perhaps the most illustrative of the new approach. What Mandelson had done was to identify a market failure; venture capital was nothing like as evident as in the US where it was much more freely available to entrepreneurs. As the White Paper pointed out: 'Many entrepreneurs are . . . reluctant to raise equity finance either through ignorance of the products available or because it involves ceding a degree of control over their business'. The department would be discussing the new fund with six of the leading banks in order to support 'very early-stage, high technology businesses'.[5] This was not some old-fashioned recipe for subsidising key strategic industries however. It is true that when Rover's parent company BMW threatened to close its biggest plant, Longbridge in Birmingham, Mandelson entered talks as determined as any of his Labour predecessors would have been to prevent that outcome. While the essential component of the rescue plan was a cost-cutting deal with the unions (involving the loss of at least 2,500 jobs), Mandelson also indicated that public money would be available for the development of the new Mini and a middle-range model. But it was difficult to imagine an Industry Secretary of any party allowing Longbridge, in the heart of the electorally volatile West Midlands, to go down. The Enterprise Fund was, rather, a modest state-funded attempt to change the culture of the financial services industry so that in future it would take the risks – and reap the potential rewards – of funding entrepreneurs in one of the fastest growing sectors of the economy. If it worked, then the state funding could be run down. Of course, many measures contemplated in the White Paper did not cost money, for example, those to make it easier for entrepreneurial or 'skilled professional' immigrants to enter Britain. There were also proposals to reduce planning restrictions to stimulate 'clusters' of high-tech industries, including the biotechnology industry (which was at the centre of fierce controversy over the use of genetically-modified crops in February 1998, and which Mandelson had strongly supported because of the dominant competitive position of British companies).

Mandelson had scandalized some of the left because of the enthusiasm with which he pronounced the last rites on the corporatism of the 1970s; but the White Paper still underlined that there was a continuing role for targeted public investment, including some regional investment to pump-prime the growth of the most modern industries. You could imagine Michael Heseltine producing something similar; it was much more difficult to imagine those in the neo-Thatcherite tendency who dominated Hague's Conservative Party after the 1997 election doing so.

The public impact of the White Paper on 16 December 1998 was overshadowed by the mounting crisis over Iraq. Mandelson had, in any case, proved his single-minded championship of industrial growth, especially in the information technology sector, by a notable one-man, behind-the-scenes battle to promote electronic commerce on the Internet against some of the most powerful interests in Whitehall – those of the intelligence services. Having secured a place for his bill in the 1998–9 legislative programme to promote 'E-commerce' – which in the US is already forecast to grow from a $12 billion industry to a $350–$500 billion one by 2002 – he then came up against stiff opposition from the Home Office (acting on behalf of MI5 and MI6) to the liberal encryption regime which business was seeking. Business transactions require codes to prevent fraud, and the information technology companies argued that the supervision envisaged by the security services would stifle the growth of British generated E-commerce without achieving the goal of halting coded communications by terrorists and organised crime that the services were pursuing. Mandelson argued ferociously – and successfully – for the intelligence services to be overruled. Although the final decision was not taken until early 1999, after Mandelson had resigned, it was widely acknowledged in Whitehall that the victory had been his.

Mandelson had achieved quite a lot in his first six months at the DTI, and was well on the way to establishing himself as a front rank departmental Secretary of State. In particular he was liked by, and liked, the civil servants under him. If he was bored he would wander round the department and introduce himself to officials, which they appreciated. They liked the fact that he had good access to Number Ten and could deal with other departments like the Treasury, with some clout at his disposal. According to one official 'he enjoyed big meetings with meaty submissions to chew over'. Above all, in a department which had been racked with self-doubt about its purpose under Ian Lang and Margaret Beckett, the officials now felt it mattered. There may have been muffled cheers in the Parliamentary Labour Party when he resigned but there was deep gloom among civil servants at Victoria Street.

# CHAPTER TWENTY-FIVE

## *Secretary in a State*

The first torrent of personal publicity which looked as if it would engulf Mandelson as 1998 drew to a close was not, of course, about money but sex. Unlike many of those who would speak, write and read hundreds of thousands of words about it over the next few weeks, Peter Mandelson actually saw himself being outed on *Newsnight* on the evening of 27 October. He was reclining on his bed at Northumberland Place, going through a red box with the television on, as Matthew Parris, the *Times* sketchwriter, ex-MP and openly gay, was interviewed by Jeremy Paxman about the personal crisis which had caused Ron Davies to resign as Welsh Secretary that very day. Davies had admitted wandering on Clapham Common, a well-known gay pick-up location, before he was robbed. Mandelson paused and looked up as Matthew Parris told Paxman: 'There are at least two gay members of the Cabinet.' Paxman, appearing to search his memory for whom Parris might mean, asked: '*Are* there two gay members of the Cabinet?' Parris replied: 'Well, Chris Smith is openly gay and I think Peter Mandelson is certainly gay.' At which point Paxman, looking a touch flustered, said: 'I think we will just move on from there. I'm not quite sure where he is on that.'

Remarkably, Mandelson would say later that at first he simply returned to his box and carried on working. This had happened several times before, after all. That year there had already been several newspaper articles referring to his sexuality, including two in the *Independent* (one by the psychologist Oliver James and one by John Lyttle)[1] and one in the *Evening Standard* by Peter Kellner, a largely sympathetic profile which contained the words: 'Mandelson is gay'.[2] Finally, as Lyttle, himself a gay activist, had claimed, not only had the minister's sexuality frequently been referred to in *Gay Times*, but if you typed 'gay' and 'Mandelson' into a data base, you came up with 111 newspaper stories – 'all hints, nudges', as Lyttle put it, and 'dull, dull, innuendo'.

But while Mandelson had not complained about the *Gay Times*, and according to Lyttle, had 'very cordially' turned down the paper's request for an interview before the election, he had been vigilant in the past about references to his sexuality in the mainstream press: he had asked for references to the 1987 episode to be kept out of the authoritative book about the 1987 election; he had succeeded in having a reference to his sexuality excised from the October 1995 profile of him in the *Sunday Times* magazine; he had protested vigorously to Oliver James over his article; and, once he realised how much coverage the *Newsnight* interview would detonate, he became passionately exercised about containing it. And even if Mandelson did not at first see the newsworthiness of Parris's gratuitous remark – he didn't take long to do so. When Wegg-Prosser arrived twenty minutes later from the nearby Good Restaurant, where he had been eating with friends, having been unable to reach Mandelson on the telephone, his pager was filling up with messages from the newsdesks of every national newspaper. It was an old story, but Mandelson was now a cabinet minister, and the man doing the outing was famous in his own right.

Someone less single-mindedly determined to protect his privacy might have given up at this point. It was widely known in Hartlepool, as well as throughout the Westminster village, that he was gay. Indeed, he had never made any attempt to conceal it from those known to him. Would it not be a relief to let the tidal wave of publicity roll over him? It was, after all, the 1990s and not the 1950s. But that was not how Mandelson saw it. Indeed, the episode became a classic of Mandelsonian muscle-flexing against the media in general and the BBC in particular, maximising the publicity and transforming Mandelson from a genuine victim into a much criticised aggressor. After Wegg-Prosser, his pager by now bleeping non-stop, arrived at Northumberland Place, he went into overdrive.

When he was called by Alastair Campbell, who told him that the *Sun* were planning to lead with the story, Mandelson telephoned the editor, David Yelland. In what Yelland would describe as a 'heated' conversation Mandelson failed to persuade him not to run the story. However, it was relegated from page one to page two. At 12.40 a.m. a *Sun* reporter turned up on Mandelson's doorstep and rang the bell. Wegg-Prosser told him that Mandelson had nothing to say.

When Mandelson left home at 7 the following morning for a workout at the Lambton gym, there were several photographers outside the door. He nevertheless went as normal into the DTI. At around 10 a.m. Wegg-Prosser took the first of what would be many calls from a senior BBC executive, Richard Clemmow. Could he speak to Mandelson? No he couldn't. Well, said Clemmow, please pass on to Peter that Paxman was very upset about what had happened and would shortly be biking round a letter of apology. In fact Paxman delivered the letter himself, making a short detour on his way to work at BBC Television Centre to drop it off at Northumberland Place – where he was spotted doing so by Philip Knightley, an observant neighbour and former *Sunday Times* journalist, who subsequently mentioned Paxman's visit to the *Daily Express* diarist Christopher Sylvester at a party, thus ensuring that the fact, though not the content, of Paxman's apology would quickly become public.

Dear Peter [the letter read],

I'm sorry that Matthew Parris mentioned your name on *Newsnight* last night. In the heat of the moment, he rather caught me out, and I tried to brush over things as soon as possible afterwards.

I fully respect – and share – your view that your private life is your own affair. I am sorry if I have been the cause of your embarrassment.

With kind regards,

Jeremy Paxman

This fairly unequivocal apology did little to mollify Mandelson. For one thing, he believed that Paxman – a friend, if not a close one –

knew not only that he was gay but who he had been going out with. Indeed, whether fairly or not, he had suspected Paxman of having gossiped to friends back in the summer about having met Reinaldo Avila at Robert Harris's house in Berkshire, with the result that his existence was reasonably well known in London social circles. But in any case, before he had even returned home to read it, Mandelson had already gone straight to the top. He telephoned Sir Christopher Bland, the chairman of the BBC governors, and suggested that he acquaint himself with the facts. He also – contrary to subsequent denials – telephoned Birt, also to protest. That evening, having returned home and read Paxman's letter, he hand-wrote a reply, unforgiving even by the standard of many similar letters he had sent to journalists over the years.

Dear Jeremy,

Thank you for your letter, which frankly I found perfunctory considering what you did to my night and day, with help from Matthew. Journalists at my door, until the early hours, photographers in the garden, and chasing me all day.

If you were not looking for a cheap angle for your interview you behaved very unprofessionally. Anyone could see where Matthew was going in his remarks. You had more than one chance to stop him and head him off, you egged him on until his remarks became indefensible. If I didn't know better, I would think it was all accidental. But I know how thoroughly *Newsnight* thinks about its output and interviews, and I know what licence it gives itself in traducing and demonising its pet hates. I have been one of these for too long.

Yours

Peter

P.S. I do not want a correspondence, so please do not bother to reply.

At this point Paxman, feeling that Mandelson's hint about a *Newsnight* witch-hunt was out of order, wrote back a robust but amiable 'come off it' sort of letter to tell him so. Paxman's bosses, however, were more respectful. By this time the Labour MP Diane Abbott, an old sparring partner of Mandelson's, had referred at some length to Mandelson's homosexuality on *Question Time*. Sir Christopher, writing to Mandelson the following morning, was contrition itself:

Thank you for your telephone call on Wednesday, arising from the previous night's edition of *Newsnight*. I have now looked into the matter. It was clearly inappropriate for a studio guest to have taken the opportunity to comment on your private life. I can assure you that neither the programme nor Jeremy Paxman intended this to happen and we very much regret that it did. The fact that a contributor to *Question Time* repeated the allegation last night compounds our error. I can only apologise sincerely on behalf of the BBC both for the original mistake and for the widespread press coverage that has resulted.

Yours sincerely,

Christopher

With the BBC now obviously on the defensive, Wegg-Prosser, on Mandelson's behalf, was already taking steps to prevent any repeats of the Abbott intervention. He telephoned the BBC News and Current Affairs executive Richard Ayre, and suggested that he ensure that nothing similar happened on the following evening's *Any Questions*, pointing out as he did so that the BBC's own guidelines precluded discussion of the private life of a public figure unless there were clear public interest grounds for allowing it. It was as a result of this overture that Anne Sloman, a highly experienced senior producer and now chief political adviser on Editorial Policy, sent out a succinct memorandum throughout the corporation: 'Please will all programmes note that under no circumstances whatsoever should allegations about the private life of Peter Mandelson be repeated on any broadcast.'

From Mandelson's point of view this was a public relations disaster. It was easy to draw the inference – as the member of the corporation staff who leaked it to Saturday's *Daily Telegraph* clearly realised – that Mandelson, friend of John Birt, powerful ally of Tony Blair, and the minister responsible for at least some important matters affecting the corporation itself (like whether BSkyB would be allowed to buy Manchester United), was now getting special treatment. On *Any Questions* that night, before the programme went out, an embarrassed Jonathan Dimbleby explained the directive to his panel. Although Mandelson's name was not mentioned during the programme, the ban was; Mandelson's cabinet colleague Mo Mowlam described it as 'insulting' and declared that 'if there are guidelines by the BBC they should apply to all politicians'. Suddenly the BBC 'gag' on Mandelson's private life was becoming a bigger story than the original 'outing'. Mandelson's office blamed Sloman's 'clumsiness' in sending out a memo which mentioned the Industry Secretary by name. But in fact Sloman had a strong defence if she was going to react to such pressure at all. For one thing, a repeat of the blanket guidance could well be open to misinterpretation. It had already been judged, for example, that the case of Ron Davies was very different: a minister had resigned, and a crime been committed (of which he was admittedly the alleged victim rather than the perpetrator). Glyn Mathias, the BBC's Welsh political editor, had been judged to be within his rights in asking Mr Davies, 'Are you gay?' For all the frustration expressed by liberal social commentators – such as Suzanne Moore in the *Independent*[3] – at Mandelson's failure publicly to declare that he was gay, he had a persuasive argument in favour of his right to remain silent, underpinned by the steadily mounting evidence in the US that the voting public did not regard the private lives of leading politicians as relevant to their performance in government. As when, just over a year earlier, he had harried Martha Kearney, Mandelson's bullying of the BBC was letting a good case go by default. Nevertheless his determination to keep his private life private was becoming heroic.

That weekend, moreover, the coverage of Mandelson's private life threatened to take on a new dimension. He had received sympathy from some unexpected quarters. OutRage, the gay rights organisation which had lived up to its bad name by sporadically 'outing' prominent but undeclared homosexuals, condemned Parris on the grounds that Mandelson had never acted hypocritically or against the interests of other gays. And after an instant poll of 100 constituents the *Hartlepool Mail*, under a headline which screamed: WHO CARES IF OUR MP IS GAY?, reported that 94 had decided that it didn't matter. But the national newspapers were not going to be put off. The *Sunday Express* was on the track of Reinaldo Avila, as Mandelson had learned in a telephone call from his friend in Tokyo. Avila had been in a steady relationship with Mandelson, frequently staying at Northumberland Place from March until he went to Tokyo to study Japanese in the autumn.

The *Sunday Express* did not know this. But they knew enough to consider it worthwhile sending the reporter John Chapman – by coincidence the very same journalist who had 'exposed' Mandelson's relationship with Peter Ashby eleven years earlier – to Tokyo to talk to him. Mandelson telephoned Lord Hollick, claiming to have been tipped off by the *Mail on Sunday*, to report that the *Sunday Express* had flown a journalist halfway round the world to talk to Avila in Tokyo. Mandelson's relations with Hollick, a Labour peer as well as Chairman of Express Newspapers, were cordial, but not without their tensions. When Mandelson had arrived at the DTI, he was far from sure that he wanted to keep him on as a one-day-a-week unpaid special adviser in the department. He believed that, with much better business connections than his predecessor Margaret Beckett, he had correspondingly less need of Hollick's advice. Secondly, he took the view – showing a fastidiousness, perhaps, that he would be accused of failing to show over his own loan from Geoffrey Robinson – that it might cause a conflict of interest, given Hollick's wide media and other business interests. He had diplomatically suggested to Hollick that the work he was doing on the 'knowledge-based' economy would be the last he would be required to perform for the department, a message which had been rather more bluntly reinforced, at Mandelson's instigation, by their mutual friend Philip Gould. Hollick had gracefully resigned, pleading pressure of time, and had departed amicably enough for Mandelson to turn to him now, on the Saturday morning of 31 October. Did the *Sunday Express* really want to be delving gratuitously into the private life of a politician?[4] Hollick thought not, but insisted that it was a matter not for him but for the editor of the *Daily Express* and the editor in chief of the two *Express* papers, Rosie Boycott. When Mandelson telephoned Boycott she told Mandelson that she too felt uncomfortable about it but that she could not be seen to interfere with an accurate story in the sister paper of the *Daily Express*. Mandelson also telephoned Guy Black, a senior official of the Press Complaints Commission, who in turn telephoned the paper to be told that the story had been obtained legitimately. Finally, a negotiation ensued in which it was agreed that the story would be carried on an inside page, and with a 'spokesman' for Mr Mandelson denying that he and Avila were an 'item'. Indeed, the report on page seven – under the headline BRAZILIAN STUDENT WHO IS MANDELSON'S CLOSE FRIEND – was so archly written that anyone unable to read between the lines, which included the vast majority of the paper's readers, would have found it hard to grasp what it was doing there. It was not followed up elsewhere.

What followed was much disputed, with the *Spectator*'s media commentator Stephen Glover claiming over the next fortnight that Mandelson was seeking vengeance by demanding Amanda Platell's sacking – a claim *Express* executives have continued to dismiss, both before and after January 1999 when Platell was indeed moved from the editorship of the paper. A senior editorial executive on the paper vehemently denied that Mandelson had made any request for her sacking, and is adamant that Platell had anyway been moved because the *Sunday Express* had failed to fulfil management hopes. It was true that her case was not helped when an internal investigation following the publication of the story established, according to *Express* executives, that Chapman had entered Tokyo University saying he was a friend of Avila's father; and that when he had subsequently revealed himself as a British reporter – and, it is agreed, Avila continued to chat to him over a glass of wine – the pictures of the Brazilian were taken against his will. Indeed, his hand, raised to block the lens, had been airbrushed out of the photograph used in the paper. Certainly, Hollick at one point asked Boycott whether she was sure Platell was the 'right editor' for the Sunday paper, and on the Thursday after the story appeared expressed his displeasure in terms which in hindsight are not without irony. He pointed out that the *Daily Express* had been relentless in trying to disentangle Geoffrey Robinson's financial interests, but he was nevertheless confident that he could 'look Robinson in the eye'. There was a clear public interest in these investigations, and all their stories had been properly documented. In contrast, he couldn't, as the proprietor of a paper which had intruded into the Industry Secretary's privacy without any pretension to be defending the public interest, 'look Mandelson in the eye'. This was a reasonable point. But the idea that Amanda Platell's head was delivered up to Mandelson on a platter – after he had resigned – appears to have been another Mandelson myth.

But the press frenzy over ministers' sexuality was only just beginning. For a start the criticism of his heavy-handed approach to the BBC continued unabated. Then, after the 'outing' of Nick Brown by its sister paper the *News of the World*, the *Sun*, in a remarkable display of split personality, first complained that there was a 'gay mafia' running Britain, then indefensibly mocked Brown for carrying out his duties as Agriculture Minister with considerable dignity, and then sacked Matthew Parris as a columnist because he had 'outed' Mandelson. All in the space of three dizzying days.

Then on 17 November *Punch*, a magazine now specialising in the scurrilous, published a highly coloured and baseless report that Mandelson had, on his ministerial trip to Latin America back in the summer, plunged into the gay nightlife of Rio in the company of the director of the British Council in Brazil, Martin Dowle. That night Mandelson, leaving instructions that he would sue any paper that reprinted the allegations, briefly attended a party given by the *New York Times*'s London correspondent Warren Hoge. He nodded momentarily to his old friend Howell James. There was still a slight frostiness between them: James was Avila's previous partner, and had introduced him to Mandelson. But he did not stay long enough to chat to another of Hoge's guests, Peter Stothard, editor of *The Times*, who had heard that the rival *Daily Telegraph* was intending to refer in print the following morning to Punch's Rio article. As a result Mandelson was not told until much later in the evening. He telephoned the *Telegraph*'s editor Charles Moore at home and gave him his 'word of honour' that there was nothing in the *Punch* story. Moore ordered the report, which said that Mandelson would be 'under pressure' to sue *Punch* over the allegations, to be taken out of subsequent editions. Then, on 23 November, the day of the Queen's Speech, William Hague, in an otherwise witty and well-crafted speech, surprised MPs by referring to 'Lord Mandelson of Rio'. Many – though by no means all – MPs inhabiting the most gossipy workplace in London, understood this gratuitous and unpleasant gibe. But, rather like the *Sunday Express* story, it was incomprehensible to the vast majority of the wider public – until, that is, both the *Mail on Sunday* and the *Sunday Telegraph* trawled over the Rio allegations and found they could not make them stand up. Finally in an almost farcical dénouement on 30 November, the (gay) actor Nigel Hawthorne was interrupted and eventually silenced by the BBC news presenter Edward Stourton when he referred to the consuming press interest in Mandelson's sexuality in an interview to mark the unveiling of a new statue of Oscar Wilde – occasioning more 'BBC gag' stories in the press.

Between 27 October, when Matthew Parris had appeared on *Newsnight*, and 30 November, the day of the Hawthorne incident, there had been perhaps two days at most on which the press had not referred to Peter Mandelson's sexual identity – much of the coverage, admittedly, arising out of the BBC ban. Some commentators defended Mandelson as the victim of a witch-hunt; others became maddened by his refusal simply, as Suzanne Moore put it, to say the three words 'I am gay'. Others, like Richard Littlejohn, the populist columnist on the *Sun*, pruriently – and ludicrously – suggested that the 'virtual freemasonry' of homosexuals 'operating at the highest levels in politics' had been helpfully exposed by Mandelson's outing; given the 'top priority' accorded by the government 'to reducing the age at which schoolboys can be buggered legally to sixteen ... If MPs and cabinet ministers have a vested interest in furthering this agenda, we should be told.'[5] This might have been a shade more convincing if the three gay members of the Cabinet had not all been markedly distant from one another as colleagues, for reasons that had nothing to do with their sexuality – and if any one of them had had even the remotest departmental responsibility for reducing the gay age of consent.

It was after the Nigel Hawthorne incident that some of those closest to Mandelson, both inside and outside Downing Street, nevertheless decided that the open acknowledgement of his homosexuality which he had denied the press for eleven years might finally end the media obsession with it. Nobody, after all, any longer wrote about Chris Smith, who had long ago 'come out', lived with a long-term male partner, and had no special celebrity as a result. Indeed, after a few days, Nick Brown had speedily returned to living a normal ministerial life. On the afternoon of 30 November Anji Hunter, Lance Price, Alastair Campbell's deputy in the Downing

Street press office, and Benjamin Wegg-Prosser agreed in principle that Mandelson should give an interview to the *Independent* acknowledging at long last that he was gay. At 5.10 a correspondent at the paper was alerted. At 5.45 the interview was called off. What had happened in the intervening period was that the three aides had been summoned to see the Prime Minister. Wegg-Prosser put the case for going public. Blair took the view that 'it was a bit late in the day to take a decision' and that anyway a simple statement for general issue would be better than an interview with a single newspaper. It was as close as Mandelson would come as a cabinet minister to saying anything about his sexuality. Several of his closest allies thought that a public declaration could also, because of Hague's comment in the Commons, be turned effectively on the Tories. But with Blair's casual intervention, the moment passed, and those (notably including Mandelson himself) who had been in favour of 'riding out' the frenzy would henceforth prevail.

The whole saga nevertheless raised a puzzling question. Why was Mandelson quite so determined not to acknowledge what had by now become public property from Hartlepool to New York? There was no doubt an element of cussed pride about it. He saw no reason why his private life should become public property, even though by not declaring his sexuality he was probably triggering even more coverage. In retrospect, he was more justified in this view than he seemed to many people at the time. Was he not entitled to maintain his privacy? He insisted angrily to one journalist pressing him to come out publicly that it was a 'metropolitan, liberal middle-class obsession' which didn't 'matter a damn to people in Hartlepool'. In this he was almost certainly right. It is odd how irrelevant in retrospect the subject which had become a press obsession in early December now seems.

He was also certainly anxious to protect Reinaldo Avila from intrusive publicity. It was the most serious relationship he had had since Peter Ashby. Some of his closest friends thought that the aftermath of his resignation was all the more difficult for him because Avila had had to return to Tokyo for the academic term. Avila, from a middle-class home in the suburbs of Rio, is highly intelligent, charming, and a strong personality with a drive for academic qualifications. His studies in Tokyo followed a year at the School of Oriental and African Studies in London. Whether the relationship proves permanent or not, Mandelson has never spoken about it and may never do so. He had previously admitted to the fear that if he discussed his private life in public, the next line of defence would be against persistent enquiries about whom he was sleeping with. But was he, at least subconsciously, also attempting to reinforce a protective shell around the deeper and more dangerous secret that he was harbouring? Did he fear that, like those Russian dolls that fit inside one another, each layer that was removed would bring his enemies that much closer to the truth that could actually destroy him? With hindsight, Mandelson made a different, and opposite, connection. He believed that when on 27 October he was 'outed' as a homosexual for the fourth or fifth time, on this occasion by the journalist and ex-MP Matthew Parris, it was like a breach in the dam which had hitherto protected him from a torrent of interest in his personal or 'non-political' life. Because the baying media had not been placated by any admission about his sexuality, it had become ravenous for another confession on which to impale him. Thus he became vulnerable to the exposure of what would otherwise have been a forgivable lapse. That was surely an underestimation of the controversy the loan would have caused whatever the circumstances. One friend of Mandelson's suggested at the time that many gay men, from the moment they first struggle in late childhood with their sexual identity, tend to be, if not secretive, at least compartmentalised in their behaviour, having learned the habit of concealment from an often hostile, intolerant and oppressively conventional world. But it would be baffling in hindsight, even to some of Mandelson's greatest sympathisers in Downing Street, that so much energy had been deployed on the much less dangerous question of his sexuality – of commendably little concern to the Prime Minister – while all along an infinitely more destructive nemesis was on the point of overtaking him.

Mandelson's own explanation for the secrecy about his home loan was that, back in 1996, he was honouring Robinson's request to keep it confidential; however, he would not have been able to withhold what would have been a prize item of gossip had Blair asked him how he had paid for his house. But Blair had not asked him; and to have told Blair once he was in government would have unacceptably complicated every judgement Blair made which had the remotest bearing on Mr Robinson or his future. But did this really explain why Mandelson did not tell anybody about the loan, apart from Wegg-Prosser, whose father, a solicitor, had carried out the conveyancing for the house purchase and had processed the loan agreement? True, he was bidden by Robinson to keep it confidential – quite possibly for the honourable reason that Robinson did not want to confer burdensome obligations on the borrower's master. But why, when a series of journalists were repeatedly asking him how he had paid for his house, did Mandelson not at the very least seek to be released from the pact of secrecy?

After the meeting between Mandelson and Sir Michael Scholar on Thursday 18 December, Wegg-Prosser telephoned Alastair Campbell to break the bad news, first about the loan, and secondly that it would shortly be made public. The timing was unfortunate. In two hours' time the Prime Minister was due in the House of Commons to make a statement about the bombing of Iraq which had begun the previous night. Indeed, when Campbell, recognising immediately that the loan was what he would later call a 'big bad story', went to pass the unwelcome information on to Blair, the Prime Minister looked with understandable irritation at his watch, as if to say: 'Why is he bothering me with this now?' Nevertheless Blair paused long enough to ask Sir Richard Wilson, the Cabinet Secretary, to look immediately into the question of whether the loan had placed Mandelson in a situation where there was a conflict of interest because of the DTI investigation into Robinson's affairs.

At this point the prognoses of some in Downing Street and Mandelson himself appeared to be somewhat at variance. At Downing Street there was almost straight away a strong sense that this might be serious enough to lead to Mandelson's resignation; Mandelson himself believed that, provided it could be established that there was no conflict over the investigation, he would be able to ride it out. Indeed, at the meeting with Scholar in the morning he had asked the permanent secretary whether, in relation to the Robinson investigation, he had 'done anything wrong. Have I infringed any rule or broken any rule?' No, said Scholar, but you would have been wiser to tell me in order to protect yourself; you should have taken the precaution of mentioning it, so that in the event of it becoming public you would be safeguarded. He was not alone in taking this view. At least one other senior civil servant confided to Mandelson after the crisis was over that if he had told the Cabinet Secretary when he first became a minister the problem could have been sorted out.

How was it that it was now going to become public? The responsibility for taking the loan was Mandelson's and his alone. He was not the victim of some elaborate honeytrap. He had acted of his own free will. The question of who had exposed him was therefore secondary. But according to all the evidence, exclusively circumstantial as it was, he would not have been exposed had it not been for the fratricidal conflict between himself and the politician he had once idolised above any other. The loan was very secret, as it was very inadvisable to Mandelson to take it. But its existence had long been known to a handful of Gordon Brown's closest allies, of whom Robinson was one, at least since the turn of the year 1996–7. Paul Routledge, the author of a 1997 biography of Brown, which announced that it had been written with the Chancellor's 'full cooperation', had been one of Charlie Whelan's closest friends. Whelan and Routledge categorically denied that Whelan had been the source, Routledge being, by his own account, so fastidious in exculpating Whelan that he had tried at the eleventh hour to excise the story of the loan from his book about Mandelson in order to protect his friend even though he was not responsible for it. But even if that is true, Whelan was not alone in Brown's circle in knowing about it. There is no reason to suppose that Brown himself was responsible for its disclosure; the secret was much more likely to have leaked out from among his most zealous supporters, who knew what deep feelings of betrayal and mistrust he had harboured against Mandelson since 1994. It now seems probable that the informant was someone who had believed, as one Brown ally would express it six months before the loan was transacted, that if Mandelson was not first destroyed, *he* would destroy Brown; someone who therefore, like Henry I's knights, set out to rid him of this troublesome priest. If Brown did not kill, however, he did not strive officiously to keep alive. During the period of the loan one of his lieutenants had described Brown and Mandelson as being like 'a pair of scorpions in a bottle: only one of them will crawl out alive'.

The cardinal fault was Mandelson's, for incurring the debt and then not telling Blair, or anyone else, about it. A lesser one, arguably, was Brown's. Despite the fact that he had known about it, according to one of his closest allies, since the end of 1996, he had neither intervened nor told the party leader. The reality, however, is that once Robinson's links with Robert Maxwell were being investigated, Mandelson, Brown and Blair should have ideally come together and pooled the details of their links with Robinson.

Mandelson nevertheless showed little outward sign of anxiety at this stage; on Thursday he went about his office duties as normal and in the evening went to three separate parties. At one, given at Duke's Hotel by the *Independent*'s editor Simon Kelner, he stayed for an hour or more, chatting amiably to a number of journalists on several topics, including, remarkably, the future of the *New Statesman* and whether his friend Robert Harris would succeed in buying it from Geoffrey Robinson. He suggested that anyone who had 'looked at the figures' would be wary of making the purchase. He went on briefly to a party given by Max Hastings, editor of the *Standard*, before returning to the DTI, where the Christmas party held by all the ministerial private offices was in full swing. Never one to pass up an opportunity to dance, Mandelson enthusiastically led the assembled company in a boisterous conga. The following day he travelled to Hartlepool and held his own annual Christmas party for his constituency activists at Hutton Avenue. There were delicious vol au vents prepared by a local party member, and copious amounts of drink of every kind. The general view among the great and the good of Hartlepool CLP was that it was one of the best parties Mandelson had given since he had first become the candidate almost exactly nine years earlier.

Should Mandelson now take the initiative in releasing the information? Wegg-Prosser, when he first spoke to Campbell, mentioned the possibility of a *Sunday Telegraph* story on the loan the following weekend. He and Mandelson had conceived the idea of giving it to the *Sunday Telegraph* as a means of pre-empting Routledge's book, which Wegg-Prosser now knew would refer to the loan. The rationale behind this was that if it appeared in a newspaper broadly of the Tory right, some of the ill effects would be neutralised. Because the *Guardian* and the *Independent* had carried the most damaging stories about the disgraced Conservative minister Jonathan Aitken, for example, it was felt that the Tory Party had been more inclined to rally round Aitken than they would have done if Conservative newspapers had broken the news. But it also appeared that Wegg-Prosser had mentioned the radioactive possibility of a Sunday newspaper story simply in order to concentrate minds in Downing Street, already mightily preoccupied with the Gulf. The prospect of exposure would ensure that the issue would not be put off amid other more important ones.

Campbell, however, was firmly against the idea of cooperating with the *Sunday Telegraph*, or indeed any other newspaper, and remained so over the weekend. This was partly because of the extent to which minds were being focused on the Gulf, and specifically, at least by Saturday, because Blair had an important press conference to give about the end of the operation there, from which Campbell did not want attention distracted. But he also thought, not unreasonably, that to try and 'smuggle out' the story in the midst of the Gulf crisis would be to increase rather than reduce the obloquy which would greet it. But this did not mean that he did not recognise the dangers now facing Mandelson. It was a problem because it was 'yet another Robinson story'; because it provoked hostile questions about Mandelson's relatively high living; and because he was presiding over a department investigating Robinson. Each of these aspects made it combustible from a press point of view. Indeed, it was when Campbell spoke to Mandelson on the telephone from Downing Street – where he spent most of the weekend because of the Iraq bombing – on Saturday, that Mandelson began to realise just how serious his problem was. He would have to reschedule the loan. And this was precisely what Blair, in two separate telephone conversations with Mandelson that weekend, firmly advised. The loan, he was clear, would have to be paid off. By Sunday Mandelson was able to reassure him that he had spoken both to his mother and to his brother Miles and that they had agreed 'in principle' that his mother would take an 'equity stake' in the house so that he could repay Robinson. But he also acknowledged to Blair that his mother's funds were not so accessible that this could be done 'immediately'.

Or in time to stave off mounting crisis. Exposure was now imminent; by Monday the *Guardian*, quite independently of the forthcoming book, had assembled enough information formally to put to both the principals the explosive story that Robinson had lent between £300,000 and £400,000 to Mandelson to buy his house. By this time the wise lawyers of the Blair political family, Lord Irvine, the Lord Chancellor, and Lord Falconer, Mandelson's emollient successor as Minister without Portfolio, had gathered with Campbell, Lance Price and Benjamin Wegg-Prosser at Downing Street (while Mandelson paid what would be his last ministerial visit to the Dome) to discuss both when to release what would now inevitably become public, and what line of defence, if any, would be credible. In the end, despite Campbell's lingering reservations about the timing, Mandelson and Wegg-Prosser confirmed the *Guardian* story, adding the detail of the exact amount. So began Mandelson's twenty-four-hour fight for his political life.*

* The *Guardian* disclosure triggered an immediate sub-plot, a 'whodunit' of consuming interest to journalists and politicians, though much less so to the reading public. Had Mandelson himself been responsible for a pre-emptive strike against later, more hostile, exposure? It was true that someone had briefly looked at a proof copy of the Routledge book after it went in error to his previous *Independent on Sunday* office in the House of Commons on 2 December and before it was redirected, the packaging torn open, to his present one in the *Mirror* office. This informant had given Wegg-Prosser an extremely sketchy but adequate account of its contents. It was true, too, that in the closing stages of the *Guardian* investigation Wegg-Prosser and Mandelson had assisted the newspaper in reaching its conclusions. Seamus Milne, the paper's labour editor who was close to Mandelson, was told about the loan on 18 December. But Wegg-Prosser was not told about the book until 15 December. And on 8 December the *Guardian*'s David Hencke, who had been assiduously but so far vainly investigating the financing of Mandelson's house for several months, had met a source who told him about the loan, subsequently confirming it in a second conversation on 14 December with a *Guardian* colleague present. But Hencke had had woefully bad relations with Mandelson for many years. His correct perception was that Mandelson, even by the standards of his bitter and long-standing feuds with some journalists, deeply disliked him. Hencke therefore has no reason to protect Mandelson as a source; yet he is '100 per cent' adamant that his story did not come from Mandelson or from any source that could have been informed by him. The likeliest, but of course wholly unprovable, explanation, therefore, is that the story came, if not from the same source as Routledge's, at least from the same group of sources, closer to the lender than the borrower.

The line of defence concentrated on the narrow conflict of interest in relation to the Robinson investigation. Given that Sir Richard Wilson had accepted the DTI view that Mandelson had been 'insulated' from such a conflict, Mandelson at least had a story of sorts to tell, which he now proceeded to do, from the evening of Monday 21 December onwards, in a series of radio and television interviews on all the major networks. All the next day he went from studio to studio to make his case, saying as he did so, in the words of his official statement – stretching the circumstances to the limit – that 'the loan was always intended to be a short-term arrangement and I am in the process of repaying the remainder of the loan [apart, that was, from the £40,000 that had already been repaid] in full with the help of my mother'. As the day wore on, however, two further questions posed themselves. Had Mandelson been in breach of the Ministerial Code on Private Interests or of the Register of Members' Interests? Both, in fact, were maddeningly silent on the specific case of an MP who borrows a large sum of money. The ministerial Code, which Mandelson was adamant he had not violated, does, in paragraph 123, place a burden on ministers to consult the permanent secretary about 'any action which they are considering to avoid any actual or potential conflict of interest' and to inform the Prime Minister 'in cases of doubt'. Equally, the Members' Interest Register requires registration of 'Any gift or material advantage received by the Member . . . from a UK source, which in any way relates to membership of the House'. In January, Elizabeth Filkin, the incoming Registrar of Members' Interests, accepted that there was 'considerable doubt' about how the rules applied to transactions between members, but advised him to register the loan, which he then did (subsequently repaying the loan when he sold the house).

There was, however, a third question, quickly spotted by the Tories. Had he mentioned any loan when he filled in his application form for a Britannia Building Society mortgage? He had not, though he said that he was sure he would have filled the form in properly, and later that the loan had not been agreed when the form had been filled in. In January the Britannia announced the information at the time of the application had been accurate and there had been no undue risk to the Society.

This would not be the view taken by the Registrar, Elizabeth Filkin, in May. After formal complaints about the loan from, among others, John Redwood, the Shadow Trade and Industry Secretary, she produced a fierce – and from Mandelson's point of view – politically dangerous report. It upheld two of the complaints saying that Mandelson should indeed have registered the loan, that the mortgage had been obtained 'outside normal commercial practice', and that his 'mortgage application was incomplete and inaccurate and he therefore breached the Code of Conduct for Members of Parliament'. However the Commons Select Committee on Standards and Privileges reached a more emollient conclusion in June 1999, after a lengthy investigation in the wake of Filkin's report. The committee stated that Mandelson should have 'given full and accurate information to Britannia', but that he had 'acted without any dishonest intention' and recommended no further action. Six months after his resignation Mandelson would be able, at long last, to draw a line under the affair.

On Tuesday morning, as he continued his fightback, Mandelson was still surprisingly confident. The commentator Hugo Young, coincidentally visiting him for a prearranged discussion about Europe, vividly captured his mood, and the circumstances, at the time:

Mr Mandelson seemed genuinely unperturbed by what he'd done ... [Robinson] being a generous fellow with a vast amount of money, [had] offered to help at no cost to himself that he would notice. He was indifferent to the repayment date, knowing that one day, the Mandelson memoirs, if not the family inheritance, would take care of that. At this point the problem of the Britannia mortgage hadn't arisen. I can believe Mandelson signed the fatal form without thinking the £373,000 personal loan counted as a lien of the property though he did say he'd woken up that morning thinking to himself that the purchase had perhaps been more trouble-free than it should have been. But the larger innocence concerned how this would all be seen. If ever there was a story waiting to come out it was Geoffrey's loan to Peter. The lender, through the ongoing investigations of his past business, was in total thrall to the borrower, whose department was conducting them. Yet here was the great merchant of appearance, the doctoral graduate *summa cum laude* of spin, who had blinded himself for months, still doing so yesterday, to the impression he'd created, however carefully he'd built the Chinese wall to insulate his ministerial self from his private debt.[6]

As the day progressed, however, his vision, perhaps, became a little clearer. In between his visits to the studios, with the experience of mounting a public defence becoming more and more, as he would put it later, 'wretched', he telephoned two of his closest friends, Robert Harris and Dennis Stevenson, to review the struggle. Stevenson, in particular, advised him not to rule out the 'option' of resignation as the cleanest way to defuse the crisis. When he telephoned Roger Liddle at 8 p.m. he was in tears. At 10 p.m. he had his first direct conversation with the Prime Minister, by now at Chequers, since the weekend. Blair, worried, tired by the Iraq crisis, and concerned for his friend, asked him for his assessment, as he had done in the past on countless issues in which Mandelson had not personally been involved. Mandelson's reply was that the press were 'completely hysterical, out of control, and out for my blood'. He was prepared to say that he had made a mistake but not that he had done anything 'fundamentally wrong'. The press, however, was unwilling to view either the mistake, or his acknowledgement of it, sympathetically. He was therefore faced with a choice: either he could continue to defend himself and hope – probably vainly – that the tide would turn; or he could go on to say that when politicians made a mistake, they should pay a price – this would almost certainly mean resignation, which would be 'very painful'. It was at this point that Mandelson appears to have mentioned the dangers of seeming to be, as Blair would later recall it in writing, 'like the last lot'. Blair listened and suggested that the two of them should sleep on it.

Which Mandelson did. At 7 a.m. he telephoned Wegg-Prosser and proposed that he should telephone Downing Street and ask Campbell, his deputy Lance Price and Jonathan Powell to go over to the DTI later in the morning. The purpose was to discuss the next stage of any fightback. But Mandelson now acknowledged to Wegg-Prosser for the first time that he might have to resign. At around 8.30, not yet having read what was certainly the most uniformly hostile press coverage he had ever received, he telephoned Gordon Brown. The very fact that he did so illuminated the complexity of his relationship with that complex man. On the one hand Mandelson firmly believed that the story now threatening his destruction had been leaked by one of Brown's closest allies. On the other he was reverting at a moment of maximum crisis to the one trusted friend and colleague he would have consulted unhesitatingly at any point in the period between 1988 and 1994. Brown, moreover, sounded traumatised by the unfolding events. Nor did he think, at this stage, that Mandelson should resign, believing instead that he should face out the embarrassment, make an admittedly quite fulsome apology, but live on to fight another day. Not long after 10 a.m. just as Mandelson was perched on his desk reading his papers, Powell, Price and Campbell arrived; after a short period Price and Powell, though not Campbell, left the room so that Mandelson could telephone Blair. Campbell had been at his side at each of the two most traumatic points of his life: his 'outing' by the *News of the World* in 1987 and the immediate aftermath of his father's death in 1988. Now he was about to witness at first hand his traumatic resignation from the government they had both lived for.

Before his second and most substantive conversation with Blair, Mandelson now faxed Brown (in Scotland and permanently engaged on the telephone) a handwritten note asking him to call him immediately. This time Brown, having spoken to Blair, was less sure that Mandelson could survive. His second conversation with Mandelson illustrated the fact that Blair was coming rapidly to accept that Mandelson would have to go, more than his own mood, which still appeared to be sombre and shocked. When Mandelson, tears in his eyes, spoke to Blair again at Chequers it was already becoming apparent that resignation was the only option. There was little doubt that this was Blair's view: there was one moment of light-headed humour, when he said: 'I just hope I'm giving you the right advice, I would normally take your advice on whether I should give somebody this advice, but unfortunately it's you that I'm giving the advice to.' They both laughed at this; otherwise the conversation was, as Mandelson would later describe it, 'sober and rational'. Blair's view, which he clearly expressed to Mandelson, was that his long-term prospects would be best served by resigning. If he stayed, he would be damaged; if he left he could yet return to the front rank. Mandelson asked him more than once if that was his view. Blair replied that it was. Tears were shed by Mandelson, and briefly by Campbell, who hugged his old friend. The official letters exchanged between Blair and Mandelson were, in a distinctly New Labour touch, *both* drafted by Campbell: Blair changed his to make it more personal; Mandelson changed his scarcely at all, pausing only to write a separate, private, handwritten note congratulating Blair for being such a decisive and strong leader.

In retrospect this all seems embarrassingly maudlin. At the time it seemed like a family bereavement, which in a sense it was. Indeed, Cherie Booth indicated as much when she telephoned Mandelson from Chequers at around noon and told him warmly that he would 'always be part of the family'. Where was he going to be later? At home. No, that wouldn't do. He must come down to Chequers in the evening; her children would be there, along with her mother Gale. It would, in other words, be a family occasion. Blair came onto the line and reinforced the invitation: 'We want you to be with us.' And of course he should bring with him Reinaldo Avila da Silva, due to return to his studies in Tokyo early the following week; which that evening, driving in a borrowed car up to Buckingham-shire, Mandelson did. They had a drink, a family supper – with Mandelson, but not Blair, breaking off to watch his resignation interviews on the television news – stayed the night, and returned to London around noon. Blair had gone out of his way to say in the exchange of letters that he expected Mandelson to do 'much, much more with us'; he has always believed that politicians can rebuild themselves. He took the trouble to write out, for Mandelson's arrival at Chequers, some advice on how he might do just that: rebuild a base in the party; sell the house; be open about his relationship.

The invitation to Chequers was a warm gesture from Blair, a kind man – but also a steely one. Did Mandelson jump or was he pushed? The answer appears to be twofold; Mandelson acted with propriety in raising spontaneously and directly with Blair the possibility of resignation as early as his telephone call of Tuesday evening. By Wednesday morning, Blair had come to his own clear view that

Mandelson should go. In a *Times* article Lord Rees-Mogg suggested that Blair was not 'loyal enough' to his Trade and Industry Secretary and magisterially warned that 'No Prime Minister can afford to butcher his friends in order to appease his enemies'.[7] Moreover, Michael Scholar (now Sir Michael), who was deeply dismayed by Mandelson's departure, had cleared him of a conflict of interest over Robinson's affairs. Lord Jenkins, a former Home Secretary and Chancellor of the Exchequer, subsequently told a friend of Mandelson's that in view of that he did not need to resign. On the other hand the political price paid by the party and the government, not to mention Mandelson himself, had he remained in office would have been too heavy to contemplate. In the event Blair appears to have taken the view that it was in Mandelson's interests as well as those of the government that he should resign now. The advice Blair wrote out for his friend at Chequers was full of common sense. Having faced the knocks, he should accept them and get on with life. He should demonstrate that he was a conviction politician 'freed to do and say what you believe in.' He should spend time 'reconnecting with the public' and getting round the party 'talking to and learning from party members.' Having bought a flat in place of his house in London, he should also spend more time in Hartlepool. He should 'mix more in Parliament and be a team player'. By taking such advice, it was becoming clear that Mandelson would have a better chance of rehabilitating himself in the long term than if he chose to stay and fight as a damaged politician. In the end, staying in office had not been a realistic option. Mandelson was prepared to resign; but if he hoped – and it would have been unnatural if a part of him had not – that Blair would try and talk him out of it, he was disappointed.

# CHAPTER TWENTY-SIX

## *Rebuild Your Political Life*

After the hubris and the nemesis, the catharsis, or at least the chance of one. One of the most unexpected events in the aftermath of Mandelson's resignation was a meeting on a sunny January morning at the home of Sue Nye in Clerkenwell, between Gordon Brown and Mandelson. Brown had been asked by Blair to have the talk but he put the whole of himself into it. Cold and angry, Brown can be fearsome; when he is warm and friendly it is hard to imagine anyone more solicitous or empathetic. It was precisely in the latter mood that he now met, alone, his old friend and enemy, comrade and rival. It was a remarkable reconciliation. Whelan was now on his way out, another casualty, like Robinson, of the loan. Brown, soft spoken, did not pretend for a second that the government, and its modernising fraction, had not suffered huge damage; now was the time to mend and 'get back on track'. He told Mandelson that he was absolutely confident that he could and would return to government. Then he gave him some interesting and undoubtedly sound advice. Mandelson, he said, should go back to his political roots, to what had interested him as a young man: Africa, the developing world, youth employment, all the things that had pre-occupied him as a young councillor in Lambeth. 'What brought you into politics,' he said, 'you should now rediscover and on that foundation you should rebuild your political life.'

They talked also, and quite intimately, about the rupture in their own relationship. The 'three of us', Blair, Brown, and Mandelson, had had a very special relationship which had been brought to the brink of destruction by the collapse of the Mandelson-Brown side of the triangle. The two of them had always, since 1994, thought badly of each other but now they had to rediscover the good. At one point Brown commented – something that was undoubtedly true – that some of the people 'around us', having known them only since the breach, did not understand the empathy and fondness which had existed between them before it happened, and was rooted in those six years of working together. And he said that he himself had discovered that it was important to be happy in your personal life in order to be happy in your political life – advice he now passed on.

What did this all mean? Was Brown, now that Mandelson had finally been brought down, wanting to make a fresh start? Was it realistic to expect that this, initially one of the most creative relationships in British politics, and then one of the most destructive, was now actually reparable? And above all, was Brown's confident assertion that Mandelson could return to high office well founded?

Of these questions, as it turned out, only the last could be answered with an unqualified 'yes'. Mandelson's return to the Cabinet as Secretary of State for Northern Ireland within a mere ten months of his fall, on 11 October 1999, was earlier than many of his friends – and enemies – had expected. The process of rehabilitation which Blair had proposed for his friend the previous December was underway rather than complete. He had sold his house in June for an estimated £777,000 – paying off Geoffrey Robinson's loan and the Britannia mortgage. He bought a modestly-sized two-bedroom flat near Notting Hill Gate, living in a two-room, rented flat in Holland Park while it was renovated. He had – eventually – survived a lengthy and, for Mandelson, painfully anxiety-arousing Commons Select Committee enquiry which had acquitted him at the end of June of 'dishonest intent' in failing to disclose the Robinson loan. And he had managed to keep himself as far out of the limelight as was possible given these inevitably high-profile events.

In particular, he had kept his ongoing work for the Prime Minister – and his regular contacts with him, often in early morning telephone calls – concealed from the public eye. There was an initial burst of embarrassing publicity when it became known in early January that he was continuing the talks with his German counterpart Bodo Hombach,[1] on a new economic model for Europe. But the subsequent meetings for the drafting of the Blair-Schröder paper on economic reform, finally published on 8 June, with far-reaching consequences for German politics, were kept entirely secret. He went to Cologne, for example, with Lord Falconer and Roger Liddle for an official meeting with both the Hombach team and the Dutch government. In late June he and Liddle visited Paris to reassure ministers that the Anglo-German exercise was not intended to disrupt Anglo-French relations. They met not only Pierre Moskovici, the French European minister, who welcomed Mandelson as warmly as ever as Blair's representative, but also Dominic Strauss-Kahn, the French finance minister. The French expressed surprise that Schröder had signed up to a document which so clearly sought to spread the Blairite and distinctively Anglo-Saxon message of economic liberalisation, welfare reform, and more flexible labour markets to a hitherto much more regulated German economy. But they were worried less by its contents than by the threat that London and Bonn might be seeking to bypass Paris, and by the unfortunate timing of the paper's publication, in the immediate run-up to the European elections.

The paper – which sparked off serious controversy within the German SPD – seemed in tone to cut across the more conventionally social democratic tenor of the joint manifesto of the European socialist parties, to which the British Labour Party had signed up. One fruit of the Paris meeting was Tony Blair's subsequent visit to the Socialist International, also in Paris, at which he made a warmly-received speech emphasising in terms which could only appeal to the French Prime Minister, Lionel Jospin, that the Third Way was really 'modernised social democracy'. The main failing of the paper was that on the two themes of the Third Way (enterprise and economic efficiency on the one hand, and social justice on the other), it was much stronger on the former than on the latter, largely because Schröder had wanted social policy relegated to an annexe. But its main achievement was that as well as provoking controversy within the SPD it provided Schröder with at least an ideological basis for pushing through necessary economic reform.

But while Mandelson kept this work for Blair unpublicised –

sensibly since it would have infuriated many in the party given how recently he had resigned – he was much more open about his stance on Europe itself. An option for his rehabilitation, at least with powerful elements of the press, might have been to either keep quiet on the single currency or even to be seen to cool on it. This would have pleased both the *Daily Telegraph* and the *Sun* and would have made it likelier for them to call for his return if the government ran into trouble. After all, Gordon Brown had become something of a hero to the *Sun* because of his allegedly growing scepticism about early EMU entry.[2]

Mandelson used two speeches, one in Brussels at an event on 28 June convened by *Prospect*, and another at the Amalgamated Electrical and Engineering Union annual conference in Jersey two days later, to emphasise his support for British EMU entry. He told the Brussels conference, during a speech largely devoted to the much wider issue of European reform: 'The single market and the Euro are the right responses to today's world.' In private he became, along with Robin Cook, identified with the argument that the government needed to start preparing public opinion for Euro entry before the general election if it was to be confident of winning a referendum on the subject in the next parliament.[3]

At that same AEEU conference he showed some humility in the wake of his fall: 'My true friends always have been and always will be in this party and this movement. If I did not realise it once, I certainly know it now.' He did, as Blair had advised, start tangibly to reconnect with the party. While he had always been fanatical about New Labour – as a football supporter is fanatical – this fanaticism had, before he resigned, begun to take on something of the quality of the Millwall crowd about it: 'Nobody likes us, we don't care.' Outside the party he had as a minister been more reassuring than demonic; reassuring to those outside Labour ranks who knew that his sheer presence was a guarantee against the return of the left, or even old Labour. But within the party he had almost ceased to bring people with him. Believing, whether because of his leader's patronage, or his professed lack of interest in leading his party, that he did not need to build a base, he had become less a persuader than an enforcer, for New Labour.

During his backbench exile, all this began to undergo a subtle change. Even had he wanted to, and he did not, he would not have been able to reinvent himself. He did not, for example, suddenly become a clubbable and humble regular in the Commons tearoom, and there were some in the party who would never become reconciled to him. Nevertheless by crisscrossing the country to address annual constituency dinners and by speaking at informal meetings of party members, he found much more warmth than he expected – and he responded accordingly. This replicated the reaction in Hartlepool shortly after his resignation from the Cabinet, where he had also been gratified that the party officers who gathered at Hutton Avenue had expressed such strong support for their MP. They, like others in the party, started to see him as less omnipotent and more vulnerable.

It helped that he had resigned so swiftly after the exposure of his loan; and it helped, too, that he had never altogether lost his reputation as a magician who made election victories possible. At York in July, when Blair was conducting a question and answer session with party members, one, commenting on the poverty of Labour's election performance in the recent European elections, added as an afterthought 'perhaps you need Peter Mandelson back'. When Blair said tentative words to the effect that this might indeed be right, he was surprised to be greeted with applause. The incident made a forcible impression on Blair and may have influenced his decision to bring Mandelson back so soon.

As with the wider party, so with many Labour MPs. Mandelson was pleased and surprised by the welcome of many of his colleagues. Despite his initial nervousness about doing so, he went daily to the Commons, voting and attending debates with regularity. One of the more symbolic images of the first parliamentary session in 1999 was the sight of the MP for Hartlepool speaking in the second reading debate on the Lords Reform bill, to a chamber almost deserted by the dozens of MPs in both parties who had gone to the glitzy Brit Awards in London's Docklands.

Mandelson also began to show several signs of taking Brown's advice to return to his roots – as well as Blair's to rebuild his base. At the instigation of John Prescott and his ministerial lieutenant, Richard Caborn, Mandelson went in February to Capetown and Johannesburg to talk to ANC officials preparing for the coming presidential election, and to make a promotional film for the Voluntary Service Overseas on its links with South African business. He arrived back in London declaring himself, with every sign of being sincere, thrilled by the visit.

For the first time since the 1997 election, he attended regular meetings at Millbank Tower on subjects ranging from the forthcoming local council and Scottish parliamentary elections to membership recruitment. Early in March he slipped into the neo-Gothic town hall in the old Labour stronghold of Sheffield to advise the local Labour group on their forthcoming electoral struggle with the resurgent Liberal Democrats. In the event, Labour lost control of the city.

He was probably helped too by going through the October party conference as a backbencher. He addressed a large number of fringe meetings, avoiding controversy and excessive publicity. Again he was struck by the relative warmth with which he was received. After a reception given jointly by the GMB and TGWU after their conference, he told the *Guardian*'s Ewan MacAskill: 'The nicest thing for me is rediscovering the party. I have been on the fringe, not at the centre of events and it has been rather rejuvenating. It is nice to be received with warmth. People have been kind.'[4]

There may have been in this an element of Labour's tribal tendency to close ranks, and of Phil Woolas's comment, expressed after the Littleborough and Saddleworth by-election in 1995: 'He may be a bastard but he's our bastard.' It may have been too that the party liked Mandelson more when he was down than it had when he was up. But either way the sentiments were reciprocated. The party no doubt owed a lot to Mandelson, and Mandelson now appreciated rather more clearly than before the debt he owed to the party.

Mandelson appears to have had no inkling, when he received the summons to Downing Street at around noon on that day at his Holland Park flat, that he was to be appointed to the Northern Ireland Office. If he was going to take part in the reshuffle at all, the Ministry of Defence seemed a likelier destination, especially as Sir Charles Guthrie, the Chief of the Defence Staff, would have approved. He had commended himself to Sir Charles when, as Minister Without Portfolio, he had championed the Forces' cause in the fierce battle over Whitehall spending which had followed the Strategic Defence Review of 1998. He had also indicated his preparedness to come back below cabinet rank, as a minister of state. Blair had toyed with this idea during the summer but had decided that it was impractical, not least because it would have created tensions with whichever cabinet minister would have become Mandelson's boss.

The surprise value of the Northern Ireland appointment was enhanced by the fact that unlike Blair's much messier reshuffle in July, the October one was preceded by almost no press speculation. Blair had considered replacing the then Northern Ireland Secretary, Mo Mowlam, with Mandelson in July, proposing to her that as a politician still at the peak of her popularity she would be wonderfully well placed to become London's first directly-elected mayor. She was probably the one politician who could be guaranteed to defeat Ken Livingstone in a straight fight for the Labour nomination; and she would surely have won the election itself. But Mowlam insisted she wanted to remain in the Cabinet, underpinning her resistance by publicly declaring during the Eddisbury by-election her desire to stay in Northern Ireland.[5]

This may well have deterred Blair from moving Mowlam at this point. But after the Eddisbury episode Mandelson himself wrote to Blair stating firmly that he did not want to be considered for the job at that time, explaining that both he and Blair might face adverse reaction in the party if it appeared that Mowlam had been forced out of office to make way for his return after only six months. She was probably the most personally popular Secretary of State since direct rule, not least, perhaps, because she was a woman in an identifiably man's job, and was seen, at least in the first eighteen months, to be succeeding in an intensely masculine world. Her bravery in going into the Maze to confront loyalist prisoners threatening the cease-fire was justly admired. And her courage in overcoming serious illness became in the minds of much of the public, a kind of symbol of hope that the obstacles to peace could be overcome.

Mandelson started at the Northern Ireland Office with a number of advantages, one of which was that the Ulster Unionists had wanted him appointed. At an off-the-record briefing in London in

July 1999, Trimble had given an unmistakable hint that he regarded Mandelson as the ideal replacement for Mowlam. The near break-down of Trimble's relationship with her was already a matter of public knowledge. Partly, no doubt it was a matter of style. Her breezy hard-swearing informality did not easily mesh with the rather puritanical and patriarchal unionist culture. More pertinently she had come to be seen by the Unionists as finding nationalists instinctively more personally sympathetic. Some of the reasons for this, of course, were understandable. For one thing, part of her job, from the moment she took office on 2 May 1997, had precisely been to draw the republicans back into serious negotiations. But while Trimble was himself blamed for causing some of the tension between the NIO and Downing Street by frequently insisting on meeting the Prime Minister directly, he was not responsible for all of it.

The choice of Mandelson as Mowlam's successor came as a con-siderable relief to the NIO. This was helped by the fact that the NIO Political Director, the key official responsible for negotiations with the Northern Ireland parties, was the shrewd and widely-respected Scot Bill Jeffrey; Jeffrey had formed a high opinion of Mandelson's abilities when working for him at the Cabinet Office. And the appointment of someone who so evidently enjoyed Blair's confidence meant that the NIO could be once again at the centre of the peace process, rather than face the prospect, as tiresome to Number Ten as it was to the NIO, of continual Downing Street crisis management.

And Downing Street, with many other issues on its collective mind, was becoming irritated with the regularity of those visits. Trimble was therefore eager to see in the post a Secretary of State who both enjoyed the Prime Minister's full confidence in a way that would make visits to Number Ten less necessary, and who was tough enough to stand up to those NIO officials who, as he saw it – not always fairly – were too susceptible to the influence of the Irish government. As a man in his first job after a fall from grace, Mandelson would surely be determined to make a success of it. Such a high-profile appointment would also signal that Blair had not abandoned Northern Ireland, despite the long and frustrating eighteen months spent trying to implement the Agreement. The latter point weighed heavily. David Trimble had remarked to a colleague shortly before the reshuffle that if Blair appointed one of the other two possible candidates – Jack Cunningham or John Reid – it would mean that he had more or less given up on political progress and merely needed a 'safe pair of hands' in Belfast to manage direct rule.[6]

In October Trimble would brutally encapsulate these points by telling the Prime Minister that what he wanted was 'a Secretary of State'. At the same time Mandelson was free of some of the unfortunate baggage which, from a Unionist point of view, both Mowlam, and to some extent by now, even the Prime Minister carried. Though he would be bound to defend it, Mandelson had not been a party to the large-scale releases of paramilitary prisoners which Mowlam had urged on an initially rather reluctant Blair.

The reports in the early summer that Trimble would like to see Mandelson replacing Mowlam did not come as a complete surprise to Number Ten. He had already mentioned his preference to Sir Richard Wilson, the Cabinet Secretary, when Sir Richard paid a courtesy visit to him on a trip to Belfast. But while Blair seemed relieved when Trimble told him he had not intended the off-the-cuff remark to be front page news, the Prime Minister warned him it would not make it any easier for Blair to do as Trimble wanted. He did not need to explain that nationalist anger would be easily provoked by being seen to make an appointment at Trimble's behest.

When that summer the first speculation surfaced in the press that Mowlam might be moved, Martin Mansergh, the Oxford-educated adviser on Northern affairs to three successive Fianna Fail Taoiseachs, Charles Haughey, Albert Reynolds and now Bertie Ahern, had remarked in conversation with a British official that the Irish government would not be able to understand if Mowlam, with whom it had excellent relations, was moved.

Yet the appointment was not, perhaps, as inflammatory to the republican leadership as it might have seemed earlier in the year. As the *New Statesman*'s John Lloyd noted, Mandelson was indeed 'harsher on Sinn Fein [than his predecessor], more respectful of the unionist community's household gods.'[7] On the other hand, as highly-skilled negotiators, Adams and McGuinness were intelligent enough to see possible advantages in Mandelson's arrival. Sinn Fein leaders had also begun to doubt her value in negotiations. They tended, as 1999 wore on, to treat her as a mail box for their demands. And, to match Trimble, they now increasingly sought to deal directly with Number Ten. Put brutally the republicans might calculate that they had got as much out of Mowlam as they could, and that she was no longer in a position to deliver their support on devolution, or the more unpalatable changes – from a Unionist point of view – for example, police reform. A successor just might be.

There was a little family history which may have played a part, though a minor one, in the Unionist welcome for Mandelson. As Home Secretary in the wartime coalition government, Mandelson's grandfather, Herbert Morrison, had been responsible for Northern Ireland. Having started with traditional Labour prejudices against the Unionists, he changed his view during the course of the war, becoming 'impressed by the passionate loyalty of the Ulster Protestants and deeply angered by the neutralism of some of the Catholic Irish . . .'[8] Not only was the Province of strong strategic importance, made all the greater by De Valera's declaration of the Republic's neutrality, but it also suffered the devastating impact of war at first hand: on a single night in April 1941, for example, Luftwaffe bombing claimed over 750 lives in Belfast, almost 200 more than in the bombing of Coventry.

After the war, Morrison maintained, as Lord President and Deputy Prime Minister, fairly regular contact with the Unionist government at Stormont, and personally ensured that five parliamentary private secretaries were sacked for joining a sixty-six-strong Labour rebellion against the Attlee government's 1949 Ireland Act, which established that Northern Ireland would remain British unless Stormont decided otherwise. According to a nationalist commentator, James Kelly, 'A cocky individual, Morrison was wined and dined by the local Unionists who found his right-wing ultra-Brit attitude to their liking . . .' The Province's Prime Minister, Sir Basil Brooke (later Lord Brookeborough), told a lunch that 'he could imagine Mr Morrison one day heading the twelfth of July Orange procession along the Royal Avenue. Instead of being affronted by such a dubious honour for a socialist, Morrison was delighted.'[9]

In fact Morrison was probably not as sectarian as this caricature suggested. Arriving at Hillsborough Castle for a family Christmas in December 1999, Mandelson's mother, Mary, recalled making a visit there with her father more than fifty years earlier, during the war, for a lunch hosted by the then Governor, the Duke of Abercorn. When one of the other guests, Sir Basil Brooke, made a disparaging remark about Catholics, Morrison was extremely chilly in response.

Mandelson arrived at the Northern Ireland Office with a lively interest, some background understanding, but not much detailed up-to-date expertise on the subject. He had known the Troubles at first hand, travelling frequently to Belfast and Dublin in the early 1980s as a television journalist with LWT.[10] He had been one of those who had urged Blair to make his famous revision of 1994, in which the new Labour leader had used a radio interview[11] to end the party's broadly nationalist policy (in favour of 'Irish unity by consent') for one leaving the future status of Northern Ireland in the hands of its majority.[12] He had followed the subject since then as an intelligent layman. He had helped with Blair's big post-election speech relaunching the peace process in May 1997. And he had been, by coincidence, in Downing Street for a private talk with Blair on the very afternoon the Prime Minister had been preparing to leave for Belfast, at the urgent behest of David Trimble, for the momentous talks in 1998 which led to the Good Friday Agreement.[13] Otherwise Mandelson had been little involved in the issue; Downing Street policy on Northern Ireland being kept to a tight circle, comprising Jonathan Powell, John Holmes (Blair's Private Secretary) and Alastair Campbell.

Physically he settled in quickly, an event made considerably easier by Mo Mowlam generously accompanying him to show him round Hillsborough Castle (the elegant Georgian house which served as the Secretary of State's official residence, and which had been the viceregal home of the Governors of Northern Ireland until the office was abolished in 1973). He exercised often at the army gym close to Hillsborough. He bought an appealing, if demanding, golden retriever puppy whom he called Bobby in honour of his own code-name during the 1994 leadership campaign. Not surprisingly Mandelson's arrival in Belfast triggered immediate interest, not least among the city's middle class. Attending a concert in the Waterfront Hall soon after his appointment, many in the audience, as they listened to Messiaen's *Turangalila* symphony, 'craned to catch a glimpse of the Secretary of State ... who is still, in Belfast terms, very much a new boy'.[14]

One of Mandelson's first acts on the weekend of his arrival in Belfast was to repair to Hillsborough to read into the job. The paper prepared for him by Bill Jeffrey and other NIO officials made for sober reading. The prospects for settlement by October 1999 were beset with difficulties and it seemed all too possible that he would find himself quickly thrown into mere crisis management. In September Mitchell had been recalled to try and break the impasse, leaving his wife and six-month-old son at home in New York once again. But the review, which Tony Blair and Bertie Ahern had asked Senator George Mitchell to undertake, was in the words of one NIO official, 'in the doldrums'. When Mandelson arrived in Belfast, Mitchell told him bluntly that he expected it to fail.

The issue at the heart of the Mitchell review was, of course, decommissioning of paramilitary, and specifically IRA, arms. The Ulster Unionist position remained one of 'no guns, no government'. While insisting they would seek the completion of decommissioning by May 2000, Sinn Fein were adamant that the Agreement required the new Executive to assume its powers before the process of disarmament could begin. For his part, Trimble needed something positive from the republicans if he was going to recommend the new political arrangements to his party – at the very least more unequivocal language from Sinn Fein making it clear that it was henceforth committed to peaceful means – in other words that the war was over; a statement from the IRA itself indicating it would decommission; and/or some action – such as the IRA appointing a representative to deal directly with John de Chastelain, the Canadian general entrusted with supervision of decommissioning.

The first few weeks of the review, during which the two sides stated, restated, and rebutted their family grievances, could hardly have been more dispiriting for the new Secretary of State. Mitchell would later recall that hours were wasted 'every morning on going over what was in the papers and having people accusing each other of planting things'. 'It was confrontational and acrimonious,' Mitchell reflected. 'There was nothing but harsh words and recriminations.'[15] Outside the talks there was growing pessimism; inside, they were dominated by 'taunts and rebukes'.[16]

During a flight back to London with Tom Kelly – the Director of Information at the NIO, and a former BBC Political Editor in Northern Ireland – Kelly told Mandelson: 'You do realise that your honeymoon could be over in about ten days. George might come back to you and say it's not going to work. And the next question is what next? And the answer is: you are.'[17]

Mandelson gave the Prime Minister a bleak assessment of the hopes for the Mitchell review. Behind the scenes Blair approved plans for a 'soft landing' if the talks failed. Mitchell could not stay in Northern Ireland indefinitely. But if the talks ran out of road because Mitchell was returning to the US, and enough progress had been made, then Mandelson and David Andrews, the Irish Minister for Foreign Affairs, had been earmarked to take his place. Failure to make progress would mean the resumption of direct rule, followed by a diplomatic pause and a further attempt to resuscitate negotiations. Mandelson therefore constantly reiterated to the parties that Mitchell was the only chance they all had.

However, one aspect of the timing of Mandelson's appointment was fortuitous. This was not only a matter of the decision to award the George Cross to the Royal Ulster Constabulary, which delighted Unionists. Although Mandelson gave the final approval, and was responsible for ensuring that his presentation of it was a well-planned event with a substantial public impact, the work on the award was already under way when he arrived. Paradoxically, he was helped even more significantly by the highly controversial – but certainly from the point of view of the peace process, correct, decision taken by Mowlam the previous August that the cease-fire had not been breached either by the arrests of republicans in Florida on 27 July for alleged gunrunning, or the murder by republicans of taxi driver Charles Bennett, three days later. Both had placed huge strains on the peace process, provoking outraged calls from Unionists that the cease-fire be declared null and void. If Mowlam had given in to this pressure there would have been no peace process for Mandelson to preside over. Equally, his credibility with Unionists was helped by the fact that he had not actually had to take the decision.

One of Mandelson's assets would be his tendency – wholly at odds with his image – to maintain a fairly consistent line whoever he speaks to. This paradox did not go unnoticed at the NIO. The commentator John Lloyd noted that a senior NIO official had asked him to his face how he thought 'the straight-talking Ulster folk would take to the country's Machiavelli?[18] In fact, according to one senior Whitehall official who has worked closely with him, 'on a one-to-ten scale of straight talking, Mandelson is fairly high up as politicians go'. In Northern Ireland, where accusations of bad faith were routine, the quality of not promising one thing to one party and the opposite to another would be at a high premium in dealing with both sides over the coming months.

Being in the words of one NIO civil servant 'a people person', Mandelson was eager to meet the main Northern Ireland politicians as quickly as possible, not least Adams, about whom he had a strong – and by all accounts fully-reciprocated – curiosity. Both men, albeit for wholly different reasons, had enjoyed at once notoriety and a reputation for bringing change about in their respective organisations. Both were tough, skilful and manipulative negotiators. Mandelson was determined not be 'spooked', as he put it to a colleague, by the republican leaders, whom he knew to be formidably clever and intimidating politicians. He was wary enough to ensure that he was fully prepared for his meetings with them by a thorough discussion beforehand with Bill Jeffrey and the associate Political Director Jonathan Stephens, another high flier. He realised that both Adams and McGuinness were much more focused in their shopping lists of demands than the Unionists. But he also thought that at times their skill ran away with them, accusing them at one point of 'over-negotiating' and not leaving Trimble with enough room to bring his own people with him. And while accepting that their desire for peace was genuine, and that they had difficulties in persuading some of their own supporters of the need to disarm, he was not starry-eyed about their intentions. The mood of their encounters varied between the coldly businesslike to the more informal. At his first meeting with McGuinness he took some pleasure in recalling to him that when he was at LWT some seventeen years earlier McGuinness had kept him waiting several hours for an interview.

In his early talks with Adams and McGuinness, Mandelson was straightforward. He valued the Union, he said, and ending it was not what the majority in Northern Ireland wanted. But he was not a passionate Unionist and he saw his role as neither to impede, if and when a majority of Northern Ireland citizens wanted it, a united Ireland, nor to promote it. He was in favour of co-operation by the Irish people as a whole, which was the only way for them to flourish. He would try to bring the Unionists on board with the idea that devolution should begin before decommissioning. But that did not mean, he made clear from the start, that he was not ready to reinstate direct rule if decommissioning did not take place within the terms of the Agreement. He would have no compunction in laying the blame squarely at the republicans' door if they reneged on this.

With the talks still in what Mitchell called their 'in-the-psychiatrist's-chair phase', there was no question of Mandelson's taking charge of the negotiations. But while in 1998 Mitchell had had a largely American staff of his own, this time he didn't, being provided with a secretary by the NIO. His office was on the same floor of the drab Castle Buildings office as Mandelson's and Bill Jeffrey's. Mitchell promised the parties that he would not divulge anything to the governments they did not want divulged and forbade statements to the press. This time there would be no media circus, as there had been in July. The geography of Castle Buildings meant that Mitchell and the local negotiators could discuss progress, if they wanted, with the NIO people, or with Jeffrey's counterpart from the Irish Ministry of Foreign Affairs, Dermot Gallagher. Mandelson could not influence the talks directly, but he could complement them.

Gradually, the atmosphere of the Mitchell talks improved. This was helped by a marked change during October in the attitude of the republicans. Adams, they had complained, had set out to be as hectoring and unpleasant in the negotiations as was possible. And this was a matter of substance as well as style; it was clear that they were not offering anything like enough to allow Trimble to recommend a deal to his party. Then, to the surprise of the Unionists, Alex Maskey, a Sinn Fein councillor, bumped into Michael McGimpsey, an equally middle-ranking Ulster Unionist in the talks, and said – in terms most unusual within the normally close-knit republican movement – that he disapproved of the way Adams had been handling the talks so far and planned to tell him so.[19]

The talks were also significantly helped by a change of venue. Mitchell was keen to get the talks away from the hothouse of Belfast, and the grim strip-lit conference room at Castle Buildings, which Adams, in a reference to the notorious RUC interrogation centre where he had himself been often questioned in the 1970s, had called 'Castlereagh with coffee'. But Mitchell had initially intended they should take a suite of hotel rooms. It was Trimble who proposed the choice of Winfield House, the rambling neo-Georgian official London residence of the US ambassador Philip Lader, set in twelve acres of Regents Park. First, even if the press found out about it, it would be impossible for them to gain access. Secondly, it was a pleasant and relaxing house to have the run of. And finally, one Unionist suggested only half-jokingly, if the meetings were bugged at least they would be bugged by the CIA and the republicans might behave better for a US intelligence audience than for a British one.

Mitchell began as he meant to go on, trying to improve the chemistry between the parties, particularly when they were not actually negotiating. At one of their first dinners, in the ornate, gilded and chandelier-lit Winfield House dining room, dominated by a self-portrait of the eighteenth-century American painter and London resident, Benjamin West, Mitchell told the negotiators that he wanted to talk about anything but Northern Ireland politics. When someone mentioned opera, Mitchell said: 'You know why I love opera? When I go home and put on *La Boheme* I know Rodolfo's going to sing the same words every time, and it gets me prepared to come to Belfast because the one thing I know is that I'm going to have sit here and listen to you guys saying the same thing over and over again . . .'[20] Everyone joined in the laughter, and the mood, almost imperceptibly at first, began to relax. As one negotiator from the SDLP put it: very gradually 'trust crept in'.

It took another three weeks to get a result. Although the outlines of what was needed were clear to all the parties, the wording took endless negotiation. Unionist suspicion – that the IRA would do anything to avoid beginning the process of decommissioning – was clear. They were deeply worried – as they frequently reminded Mandelson – about what would happen if the IRA failed to decommission. How could it be fair that the Executive and Assembly would be stood down, punishing all the parties for the delinquency of only one, Sinn Fein? But there were also grave, and less publicised, suspicions on the republican side.

Sinn Fein had of course long accepted that Trimble would be First Minister of the devolved government. They needed reassurance, however, that the Executive would be genuinely power-sharing and that the Unionist parties would not, despite their divisions, use their majority to caucus and then simply impose their will on the nationalist minority – making it effectively like the Stormont governments of the past. In the first week of November, with the prospects of agreement still alarmingly uncertain, there was a pause. Trimble flew to America to fulfil speaking engagements there. The NIO were not unhappy about this, judging that the Ulster Unionist leader, having been negotiating endlessly, might be refreshed by a break, and it allowed George Mitchell to report on the state of play to Blair, Ahern and Clinton, over the next few days.

On the day Trimble left for the US, Mandelson, characterising the pause as neither a breakdown or a breakthrough, said he was still 'hopeful' and that he was 'satisfied with the very serious way people are talking to each other'.[21] He was probably sounding a shade more optimistic than he felt. It was true that an outline of the deal had by now been agreed, but the exact wording had not, and as so often in Northern Ireland, the devil would no doubt be in the detail. Indeed Mitchell was slightly alarmed at Mandelson's tendency to make mildly upbeat statements when the outcome was still in the balance. But Mandelson judged, probably correctly, that his task was to contain public expectations without demoralising the parties themselves. For example, addressing the SDLP in his first speech to a Northern Ireland party conference, five days later, the Secretary of State declared: 'These talks might, just might, bring the compromise that secures a peaceful, democratic future for generations to come.' In a nod to the image he had acquired over fourteen years of Labour Party politicking, however, he warned the SDLP delegates: 'Contrary to what you might read in the newspapers, I have no smoke and mirrors at my disposal. If I ever had them, I'm afraid I have left them behind.'[22]

The talks now resumed in Belfast, and over the next two days the party leaders drifted with increasing regularity into the ministerial and officials' offices, allowing Mandelson and the officials, both NIO and Irish government, to help, from the sidelines, to clear roadblocks and coax the parties to a conclusion. By Wednesday 10 November it at last seemed to the parties, and to Mitchell himself, that they had gone as far as they were going to go. In a carefully 'sequenced' series of statements, the Ulster Unionists would make a statement which recognised the legitimacy of nationalists to pursue their cause of a united Ireland by peaceful means and by pledging their commitment to a genuinely inclusive Executive. Sinn Fein would publicly recognise the importance of the political process in making conflict a thing of the past, they would accept that decommissioning was an essential part of the Agreement, and state their opposition to violence, including the paramilitary punishment beatings which had continued to scar the cease-fire. And for the first time 'P. O'Neill' – the notional spokesman in whose name IRA statements were always issued – would acknowledge the political leadership of Sinn Fein, and therefore by implication, its stipulations about decommissioning and violence, while promising the appointment of an 'interlocutor' to the de Chastelain Commission once the Executive was in force.

But while Trimble realised that he was not going to get more, he still had to secure the agreement of his party. By the following day, Thursday, Mandelson was already active. Despite a warning from officials that it might upset more fragile nationalist sensibilities, he had already agreed to attend – as Mo Mowlam had not been in the habit of doing – the traditional Remembrance Day ceremony at the parliament buildings. He attended such ceremonies in Hartlepool, he said, and he saw no reason not to do so in Belfast. Mingling with Unionist politicians at the ceremony, he was picked up by the television cameras urging them to back the deal. 'Put these people [Sinn Fein/IRA] on the spot,' he was overheard saying. 'They say they are going to deliver. See if they do.'[23]

At 2 o'clock that afternoon, after a series of meetings with small groups of colleagues, the Ulster Unionist leader met the twenty-seven UUP members of the Assembly. There was clear, if unenthusiastic, support from a numerical majority of this group. The problem, Trimble now judged, was that the opposing minority included some of the more influential figures in the party – notably John Taylor, the MP for Strangford and Trimble's deputy. After a short discussion, the First Minister-designate ended the meeting fairly abruptly saying, 'Look we have been consulting all morning. And I know I don't have a united group and in that case there is no point in trying, so I am going and of course that means we are at the end of the road.'[24]

Trimble returned to Castle Buildings with two of his closest allies in the party, Sir Reg Empey and Michael McGimpsey. When he arrived in Bill Jeffrey's office he was as downcast as any of those present could remember seeing him. He had taken huge risks to achieve the political settlement and the devolved Executive. He had a deal which he personally thought could justify the creation of the new Assembly. He desperately wanted the Agreement to work. But he did not believe he could persuade the wider party, and in particular its sovereign body the Ulster Unionist Party Council. At best it would split the party irrevocably. He could not therefore go ahead. All of which he now conveyed to Mitchell, Adams, McGuinness, Mandelson, Jeffrey and the other officials assembled together at Castle Buildings. There had not been a vote, he explained, but he could tell that the opposition was too strong. To some in the room – probably including the infinitely-patient George Mitchell, who had come to know every nuance of opinion within every party – this had the ring of inevitability about it. But Mandelson, much fresher to the tortuous business of Northern Ireland negotiations, was by his own later account to a colleague, 'gobsmacked'. The Secretary of State paused before saying that he was 'very disappointed' and that he believed his decision would have 'calamitous consequences' both for the party and for Trimble personally. At this point Gerry Adams intervened: 'Can I ask you a question, David?' he said to Trimble, 'Did you actually try and persuade your people and make the case for the Agreement?'' Trimble reacted to this question with considerable irritation, saying that how he dealt with his party was his own business. Adams persisted, saying: 'I think we are entitled to know whether you tried to persuade them.'

Trimble, visibly annoyed, said he had said as much as he was going to say on the subject. Adams had hit a raw nerve; up to this point it had not occurred to Mandelson that Trimble might have merely reported, rather than actively 'sold', the Agreement to the UUP assembly members, but it was becoming more and more evident that this was the case. Increasingly anxious that they would not actually hear the arguments for the deal, Mandelson now revived a previous suggestion that he had made, and to which Trimble had been initially receptive, that he should address Trimble's assembly members himself. Intervening in support of Adams's point, he said: 'Well, I think we are entitled to know whether you tried to persuade the assembly members to accept the settlement. I think at least that I am entitled to speak to the assembly members as I believed you agreed earlier I could.' Trimble replied: 'Well, we can discuss that separately.' Which they now did, alone. This time, Mandelson was much blunter. Without any effort being made to persuade the assembly members, Trimble would come out of the episode very badly, looking weak. He now insisted, moreover, on being allowed to make a direct appeal to the twenty-seven Unionists gathered at the parliament building. Saying he would see what he could do, Trimble returned to meet his colleagues.

Mandelson did not hear from him for another ninety minutes, when he got the message that he could address the meeting – in fifteen minutes time. After some hasty preparation with Jeffrey and Jonathan Stephens, he was driven with the two officials on the short trip from Castle Buildings, through Stormont park, past the majestic, larger-than-life statue of the Unionist leader Sir Edward Carson – who helped sabotage the Asquith government's attempt to introduce Home Rule ninety years earlier – and up to that imposing symbol of Protestant hegemony, the parliament building.

The NIO visitors were then taken into the meeting room where the assembly members were waiting. Their faces, ranging from the stony to the openly hostile, betrayed little of what had gone on, but even before Trimble had returned from Castle Buildings there had been quite a bitter argument between pro- and anti-Agreement assembly members after Trimble's abrupt departure. 'I found that in my absence that there had been blood shed and there were some people who were of the same view as myself who were saying, well who is letting us down?'[25]

Mandelson now spoke for about twenty minutes. Speaking calmly, but with great emphasis, he said there was no fallback; this was the best position that could be negotiated. He was not, he stressed, going to threaten the Unionists by saying that if the Mitchell review failed, the two governments would impose some settlement which might be less favourable to them. He believed in 'local politicians deciding their own future together'. But he added: 'I am saying to you this is the best opportunity for a generation.' Insisting that another chance as good would not come again in the foreseeable future, he added: 'You have nothing to lose. If the IRA don't follow by decommissioning, I'll stand by you. I won't allow you to bear the burden of being blamed for the failure.'

Mandelson, by all accounts, gave an impressive performance both in his speech and in the hour of questions which followed it. One Unionist opposed to the settlement remarked grudgingly afterwards that Mandelson had at least been 'better than Blair'.[26] It was all the more impressive since there were some complaints that he could not meet. He could not, for example, yield to demands from some members for decommissioning to be completed by January when May had long been the agreed deadline. He could not say what some of members would have most liked to hear – that if the IRA failed to decommission he would expel Sinn Fein from the Executive and let devolution continue without them. In the closing stages of the Mitchell process he had privately met Seamus Mallon, the deputy leader of the SDLP, to find out if his party would give their backing – a minimum requirement for a power-sharing Executive without Sinn Fein – for such a course. Mallon, had once, many months earlier, hinted that that might be his own preference if the IRA failed to start disarming. But that was not the view of John Hume, the party leader and Mallon had not repeated his earlier hint. Mandelson was hardly surprised when Mallon now made it plain that the support of the SDLP – and therefore of the Irish government – for continued devolution without Sinn Fein was unlikely.

The best therefore that Mandelson could say was that if the IRA failed to start decommissioning the 'default' mechanism would mean a return to direct rule in Northern Ireland. He would then try to involve local politicians in the running of Northern Ireland, but how and whether this could be done would depend very much on the attitude of the SDLP at the time. As Mandelson knew, it would be an uphill struggle at best to persuade the SDLP to accept devolution without Sinn Fein even if the IRA had defaulted. But implicit in his remarks was an undeniably strong point. There was no chance at all of devolution – a goal long cherished by the Unionists – if they rejected the settlement now.

Mandelson and the officials now returned to Castle Buildings to await the result of the UUP assembly members' deliberations. It was at this point that Trimble took what he called a 'straw poll', which was in fact a secret ballot on the settlement. As Trimble looked at the voting slips he noted that support for it had increased somewhat but that the party was still split on broadly similar lines to before. When he returned to Jeffrey's office, he was in a slightly better mood. But he repeated to Mandelson and Jeffrey that he still had a problem. He had, as he put it, the 'numbers but not the weight', even though he thought that two members had now been swung over to backing the Agreement since the original meeting which Mandelson had addressed. Mandelson quickly seized on this point, asking Trimble how he knew, since he had understood there had been no vote at the earlier meeting. Trimble said that he had been able to 'sense' the balance of forces at the first meeting. Nevertheless he still did not have Taylor on his side. At this point Mandelson became more emphatic. Was Trimble now saying that he had had a clear majority in the morning, and it had now been bolstered by two more, but that he was still not going ahead? With such a vote, he had a 'duty' to take the settlement to the ruling council for its approval. 'David,' he added, 'how are you going to explain to the world that the assembly party have voted in favour of doing this, but you haven't done it?'

It was the turning point. Trimble did not commit himself to calling a council meeting. But seeming suddenly energised, he walked briskly down the corridor from Bill Jeffrey's office to Mandelson's to begin ringing his closest allies: Ken Maginnis, the party's security spokesman, Sir Reg Empey, Michael McGimpsey, and others, and convened a 'council of war' of around seven or eight for that night at the house of a senior party officer.[27]

Nor was Mandelson inactive. After Trimble had left he too began ringing some of those who he rightly guessed would be at the meeting that night. And true to his lifelong reputation as a correspondent, he now sat down to compose a letter to be hand-delivered to the

Ulster Unionist leader. Expanding his earlier arguments, he emphasised that he understood – and indeed shared – many of the Ulster Unionist concerns about whether the IRA were going to decommission. But if the UUP did not enter the Executive, Trimble would never know whether Sinn Fein would have delivered on decommissioning or not. His opponents within the party, moreover, would turn on him anyway, saying that as the Unionist politician most closely associated with the peace process, he had led them down the garden path. If he fought and lost he would no doubt have to go. But if he didn't fight, he would probably have to go anyway. It was better to go down fighting, if at all.

The following morning Trimble had good news for Mandelson. He had secured the support of his allies for pushing the settlement through the council. Whatever his earlier hesitations, he had now shown considerable leadership, telling his colleagues the previous night: '"Right we are going to push this through," because I had a feeling that if I really pushed hard, I could actually get the assembly group to come round with me.'[28]

The carefully planned sequence of statements by the UUP, Sinn Fein and the IRA could go ahead from Monday. But in the meantime, Trimble emphasised, there would have to be a news blackout while he sought to build a coalition of support – because, as he put it later, 'if they knew what we are running the press would start hunting down the dissidents and creating explicit groups'. When Mandelson and Trimble went to see Mitchell he was understandably reluctant to grant a news blackout. He would have to say something to the world's waiting press, now wholly confused about whether the deal was on or off. In the event, Mitchell made a skilful holding statement, saying he was asking everyone to reflect over the weekend and return on Monday. Privately Mitchell told Mandelson: 'I don't know how you've turned Trimble round, but now you'll have to do the same with the whole party. It'll be some campaign but good luck to you, Mr Secretary.'

Most notably there was still the problem of John Taylor. Deep down, Mandelson shared Trimble's view that Taylor's continued opposition could yet be terminal to hopes of the settlement being ratified by the party's council. Indeed, he had made an effort to contact Taylor after Trimble had left his office on Thursday. When he had arrived back from Belfast at his home in Armagh on Thursday evening there was a message to ring Mandelson, though the Secretary of State had left his office by the time he rang back. Thinking it could wait until the morning, Taylor was then surprised to be telephoned by Geoff Hoon, the Secretary of State for Defence, whom he had known well in Strasbourg when they had been fellow MEPs. Hoon, enlisted in a telephone call from Mandelson, proposed a meeting on Friday, as he was visiting military units in the Province. In the course of a friendly conversation the next morning Hoon gently reminded Taylor of the importance of the settlement going through. Meanwhile Mandelson cancelled a trip to Strabane, where he had been due to lunch with civic leaders and switch on the Christmas lights, and spent ninety minutes talking to Taylor, stressing how influential he was. 'He kept saying "the thing is everyone I talk to says what does JT think?" '[29] Taylor was courteous, and he did not reject Mandelson's arguments outright, while still remaining – for now – uncommitted to the deal. Characteristically, Mandelson now wrote to Taylor, twice, urging on him the arguments in favour of testing Sinn Fein's sincerity.

Taylor was central to Mandelson's strategy of winning round the Unionists, but he was not the only target. In the run-up to the Ulster Unionist Council, now fixed for Saturday 27 November, he discreetly saw small groups of UUP constituency representatives who might be influential at the council meeting. But he also made two more public interventions, the first of which, a visit with David Trimble to the Edenderry branch of the UUP in Portadown on the evening of 23 November, was a hair-raising exposure to the forbidding face of 'no surrender' loyalism. 'Scores of police in riot gear pushed [the demonstrators] back, and the road was sealed with a dozen RUC vehicles,' wrote one correspondent. 'It was just like old times.'[30] In an audience of around 150, the fourteen members of the branch who would actually be at the council were swamped by hectoring members of Ian Paisley's Democratic Unionist Party and other non-aligned opponents of the Agreement.

Outside the hall an ugly crowd, held back by police with riot shields, bayed at the two politicians as they arrived, some, according to the *Guardian*, screaming at Mandelson 'Homo, homo'.[31] Recognising Tom Kelly, now Mandelson's Director of Information, and a familiar face on television from his time at the BBC, others yelled 'Kelly, bastard.' Inside, though, Mandelson spoke and answered mainly hostile questions without much interruption. When one anti-Agreement Unionist challenged his pledge that he would not allow devolution to continue with Sinn Fein on the Executive by asking pointedly: 'So it depends on you holding the line, does it?' Mandelson replied: 'I don't easily roll over for anyone. I am not a natural appeaser and I do have my own reputation to think about.'[32] But the atmosphere was tense and volatile, particularly after another dissident provoked an angry wrangle with the chairman, Ken Twyble, when he tried to make a speech laying out the opposing case. Trimble, the local MP, did not speak at all so as not to infuriate his enemies in the audience, dozens of whom left before the end to join the chanting, menacing crowd in the freezing cold outside. While a police escort ushered Trimble and Mandelson safely to their cars, other members of the branch, known to be pro-Agreement, had to be driven away in RUC armoured vehicles for their own protection. Mandelson remarked to an official the following day that by giving him an insight into the local pressures on Trimble, the visit had markedly increased his respect for the Ulster Unionist leader.

His other significant public attempt at persuasion, two days later, was a much more peaceful event. In a speech at Belfast's Victoria College, Mandelson went as far as he could on the question of what would happen if he had to suspend the institutions and return Northern Ireland to direct rule, because the IRA had failed to decommission. He appeared to hint obliquely that he would at least attempt during the 'interregnum' to secure the support of the SDLP for devolved institutions which no longer included Sinn Fein because it would now be in breach of the Good Friday Agreement. 'In the entirely new political context that would apply,' he said, 'the attitudes of some players cannot be predicted at this stage. But I think the desire to keep the deal on track would be great ... I would do my best to keep alight the flame and the spirit of devolution, maintaining political continuity as best I could.'[33]

But as he continually emphasised in his dealings with Unionists in the days running up to the council meeting, even if this did not happen, they would simply be living once again – as now – with

British direct rule. As he put it at Victoria College, the council should back the deal in the knowledge that 'there is a lot to gain but that if the process fails they will be no worse off'.

But he also sought at Victoria College to outline a more far-reaching, if optimistic, vision in which the two traditions in Northern Ireland did not seek to blur, much less eliminate, the distinctions between each other, but in which, as he put it, 'Orange and green can live side by side in mutual respect, as keen to protect each other's rights as their own.' He had been quickly struck, after his arrival in October, not only by the divisions within unionism, but also by its underlying lack of self-confidence, its siege mentality. The new settlement, in which republicans would continue to pursue their goal of a united Ireland, but only through peaceful means, offered a new opportunity to the unionist cause. 'Put aside the fear of failure,' he appealed to Unionists at Victoria College. 'Present the face of progressive, tolerant, confident, unionism. A unionism that reaches beyond the politics of "not an inch". A unionism that is justifiably proud of its traditions, including its Orange ones, and knows they can flourish alongside the expression of Gaelic ones. A unionism that is on the front foot and comfortable with those who hold a democratic nationalist aspiration.'[34]

Admirable an ambition as that might be, it was not the spirit in which many members of the council would be approaching their meeting the following Saturday. The *Daily Telegraph*, by now the cheerleader of the party's anti-Agreement dissidents, was reporting that the party was evenly split on whether to allow devolution to go ahead. Its editorial line caused considerable anxiety at Downing Street, which urged the *Telegraph*'s proprietor Conrad Black to try and restrain the 'no surrender' instincts of its editor Charles Moore. This was at best only partially successful; the leading article on the morning before the council meeting was less ferocious than it might have been; but its message was nevertheless fairly unequivocal. Headlined 'If in doubt, don't deal,' it concluded: 'At present the situation remains "no guns". In these circumstances the logic is the same – no government.'[35]

The leading Protestant newspaper in Belfast, the *Newsletter*, however made rather cheerier reading for the government that morning. For it reported, on the basis of a leak from members of the Strangford constituency that their local MP John Taylor, would after all back the Agreement.[36] When Taylor was asked by reporters about this as he arrived at the meeting he mentioned the two letters he had received from Mandelson, and said that the 'private and confidential assurances' they contained had now satisfied him 'that Unionists will not be trapped into a system of government with Sinn Fein without IRA decommissioning'.

But while Mandelson's letters were certainly influential, they contained no new policy and were probably not the decisive factor. When Taylor had left at the beginning of the week for a meeting of the Council of Europe in Bulgaria, Trimble knew from speaking to him that he had still not made up his mind. Then on the Tuesday evening he had received a call on his mobile phone in his Sofia hotel room from the Ulster Unionist leader's office, disclosing the tactic that Trimble had now decided, in considerable secrecy, to adopt at the council meeting. If the IRA did not begin decommissioning by the beginning of February, he would resign as First Minister. And he would announce at the meeting on Saturday that he was submitting to the party officers a post-dated letter to that effect. What did Taylor think?' Taylor had paused for a moment. 'I'll run with that,' he said.[37]

Mandelson did not know about that conversation but he did know that Taylor had now agreed to back the Agreement. He therefore flew out of Belfast on his ministerial jet on the day of the meeting (27 November) uncertain of the outcome, but more hopeful than he would have been without Taylor's change of heart. He was determined to be at the wedding in Norfolk of his old friend Tim Allan – who had left Downing Street in May 1998 to work for BSkyB – and Carey Scott, the deputy news editor of the *Sunday Times*. But he had resolved to turn back if Trimble was defeated. He did not have to.

The decision itself, reported to Mandelson at Norwich airport, was a huge relief. Although the vote, by 480 to 389, meant a relatively narrow majority of only 58 per cent, it fell – just – within the best of three different scenarios for which the government had prepared in advance. The NIO had drawn up three different statements: one expressing sadness at a defeat; one acknowledging the narrowness of the margin; but a vote of over 55 per cent would be promoted as a clear success for Trimble. The Executive could now be formed on Monday.

What Mandelson, let alone Gerry Adams, had been wholly unprepared for, however, was the announcement of Trimble's post-dated February resignation. For Trimble it seemed to be the only way of getting the decision through; some of his hardliners wanted clear evidence of decommissioning even earlier, in January. But the ploy caused immediate alarm in the republican leadership who saw – and said they saw – the Trimble move as confronting them with a deadline and one, moreover, which was four months earlier than that in the Good Friday Agreement, and had not been discussed in the Mitchell review.

By the time Mandelson had arrived for the wedding at the Priory Church of St Mary and the Holy Cross at Binham in his bullet proof NIO Jaguar, at around 2.50 p.m., with Bobby on the back seat, Adams's angry reaction had already been played back to him, and a three-way conference call with the Sinn Fein President and the British Prime Minister had been arranged. Mandelson took the call from his mobile phone in his car. Both he and Blair emphasised that they understood that any act of decommissioning would have to be voluntary, but they urged Adams not to overreact and destabilise the creation of the Executive. It already looked probable – and this judgement was convincingly vindicated in the coming weeks – that Trimble had been obliged to make his resignation promise in order to secure a majority.

The Allan wedding was a pleasant interlude in a hectic weekend. The two men had built up a close rapport since Allan's first intimidating meeting with Mandelson when he was working for Blair during John Smith's leadership nearly seven years earlier. Allan was one of the few people capable of teasing Mandelson effectively, remarking in his speech at his Downing Street leaving party: 'I like to think of myself as a close friend of Peter's and I'm not even a member of the Royal Family.' (Entering Mandelson's room at the Cabinet Office, well into 1998, Allan had noticed a solitary Christmas card still on Mandelson's mantelpiece, the signature clear for any visitors to see, and he made, to Mandelson's horror, as if to throw it in the wastepaper basket. It was from Prince Charles.) But it was a mark of that close friendship that he had been invited to the wedding. While Alastair Campbell and Fiona Millar were also there, Mandelson was the only elected politician. He introduced Bobby to the Campbell children. He flitted in and out of the drinks reception at the Morston Hall Hotel between calls to Belfast and taking the dog for a walk, and sat down with the other guests for dinner, taking his place between Emma Hardcastle, a publishing friend of the couple, and Steve Hilton who had worked for Maurice Saatchi on the 1992 and 1997 Tory election campaigns. He left at around 8 p.m.

The following morning in a live BBC interview with Sir David Frost, he struck a delicate balance between paying what he himself called a 'fulsome tribute' to Trimble for his courage in facing down his Unionist opponents, and mollifying the republicans. On the resignation pledge, he advised against a 'judgemental' attitude 'about what David needed to do in order to manage his party'. But expressing optimism that Adams and McGuinness – 'two forward-looking politicians who have worked very hard to put in place this political strategy' – would deliver on decommissioning, he emphasised, twice, that decommissioning was a 'voluntary act' for the IRA. When Frost asked Mandelson about the looming problem of the SDLP's Seamus Mallon, who had resigned as Deputy First Minister after the collapse of the talks in July, Mandelson replied that 'the architecture . . . requires . . . his stepping back into the shoes of the Deputy First Minister . . . a very, very wise, sage man'.

This was an understatement. The presence of a nationalist figure of Mallon's stature as Deputy First Minister was essential to underpin the cross-community institutions of the Executive and the Assembly. But there was a big problem. Under the standing orders of the Assembly, Mallon required not only a clear majority of assembly members, of which, thanks to a coalition of nationalists and pro-Agreement Unionists, he could be confident, but also a vote by 40 per cent of Unionists. This would be impossible because of a combination of Paisley's DUP, the little UK Unionist Party, and hardline anti-Agreement Ulster Unionists. It is not too fanciful to think that Mandelson drew on his long years of experience in Labour party management in devising a way of overcoming this obstacle.

His solution was what David McKittrick, the *Independent*'s

Ireland correspondent, called 'some nifty procedural footwork'.[38] He proposed to Lord Alderdice, the Assembly's presiding officer, a change in the standing orders to allow Mallon to be reinstated by a simple majority of assembly members. Since the change could itself be made by a simple majority, this was a way of ensuring that Mr Mallon could be reinstated by what the DUP's William Macrea angrily but vainly protested was 'the back door'. Alderdice, with the backing of Trimble as well as the nationalists, firmly overruled the objections. Mallon was reinstated. The new cabinet was formed, with Trimble presiding as First Minister, and including two Sinn Fein members: Martin McGuinness at Education and the Dublin-born Bairbre de Brun at Health. What had for so long seemed impossible, had happened, a devolved, inclusive government in Northern Ireland and new cross border and British-Irish bodies to go with it. Twenty-four hours later Mandelson travelled to Dublin to set the seal on the new political order and to sign a formal exchange of letters with the Irish Foreign Minister, David Andrews.

How far had Mandelson himself played a decisive part in bringing all this to pass? He was lucky, of course, in the able officials assisting him: Jeffrey and Stephens at the NIO, Ivor Roberts, the British ambassador in Dublin, and at Downing Street, John Sawers, the Foreign Affairs Private Secretary, and Jonathan Powell. Huge credit, moreover, accrued to George Mitchell. The senator, who had told his wife it would take three weeks at most to complete his review, remained at it for three months.[39] Without his painstaking chairmanship of the talks, there would have been no agreement, any more that there would have been without the – eventual – determination of Adams and Trimble to make one. But from his arrival, Mandelson's personal skills and energy did have a notably positive impact on the outcome. Before the Mitchell process was completed, he played a significant role from the sidelines, partly by encouraging the Unionists to focus more coherently their demands of the republicans. As David McKittrick wrote: 'To the public he has seemed more of a cheerleader than a full participant. But the politicians know that he has been highly active behind the scenes.' Among the 'important messages' Mandelson had sent out to those involved, 'it was conveyed to both [Trimble and Adams] that they would be unwise to block progress in the Mitchell review in the hope of faring better in a later Mandelson initiative.'[40]

After the Mitchell deal was concluded, however, his role was even more influential, especially when it came to persuading them that he would stand firm against an inclusive executive if the IRA, in the end, failed to decommission. He was able to reassure wavering Unionists in a way that Mo Mowlam, however unfairly, would almost certainly not have done, that if the IRA failed to decommission he would not allow the Executive, complete with its Sinn Fein members, to remain in power. And while he might not have been the only, or even the principal, agent of John Taylor's change of heart, he certainly did much to stiffen the resolve of Trimble and his closest supporters in those uncertain hours after the first meeting of UUP assembly members on 11 November, not least by furnishing them with critical arguments to use against their own dissidents. Perhaps Trimble would have eventually reached the same conclusion without Mandelson's intervention. But he might not have done. At the very least, the period after the first assembly members' meeting would have been an even more dangerous one. It is impossible to know what would have happened if Mandelson had not been closely involved. But it is hardly fantasy to think that once the Mitchell deal had been concluded, Mandelson made the difference between its acceptance and its rejection.

Nominally, of course, his powers were now severely reduced by devolution. In reality, however, he was hardly going to be idle. Beside his continuing responsibility for law and order and security, he would, as McKittrick put it, 'be expected to act as the Executive's protector and, in effect, guardian angel, helping to guide it through the many difficulties that still lie ahead'.[41] If anything this was an understatement. Cause for celebration though the creation of the new Executive had been, the crucial piece of the jigsaw was not yet in place to ensure its permanence. This was the huge issue of decommissioning. There was no guarantee, and indeed as the New Year came and went, it had begun to look increasingly improbable, that the IRA would put any of its weapons beyond reach before the February meeting of the council, eventually scheduled for the twelfth. Every decision he took would be judged on whether it helped one side or the other – and whether it made the final implementation of the Good Friday Agreement more likely. Of these the most difficult, in the short term, was what to do about the report on the future of the RUC by an independent commission chaired by the former governor of Hong Kong, and now European Commissioner, Chris Patten.

The Patten Commission, which reported in September, was set up as a direct result of the Good Friday Agreement which called for a 'new beginning to policing in Northern Ireland with a police service capable of attracting and sustaining support from the community as a whole'. It proposed a radical series of measures on its 'composition, training, culture, ethos and symbols' of the force.[42] These were intended – among other things – to deal with an imbalance in the force which had meant that only 8 per cent of officers were Catholic compared with 40 per cent of the population as a whole, and more widely to counter what the Catholic Bishops had told the commission was 'the deep legacy of distrust' between the nationalist community and the police compared with the equally 'deep sense of possession of the police force by the Unionist community.'[43]

Part of the political problem for Mandelson was precisely that 'deep sense of possession' felt by Unionists for the RUC, which during the Troubles had seen 302 officers killed and many thousands maimed and injured. While most of the Patten recommendations were uncontroversial, some were not. In particular Unionist fury fastened on the Patten recommendation that the name of the force be changed to the Northern Ireland Police Service. Mandelson modified some proposals. He deferred a decision on councillor-dominated district boards being allowed to buy in outside security services – which had given rise to fears that they could engage ex-paramilitaries. He decided that a new oath emphasising human rights would be taken only by new officers, not by existing ones as Patten had also recommended. But the bulk of the recommendations, including the new name (apart from inverting it to the Police Service of Northern Ireland), he accepted, knowing that it would provoke inevitable, and far from synthetic, anger among Unionist politicians including Trimble, who had pleaded with him not to do so.

Part of his frustration with the republicans as the February crisis drew nearer without any sign of decommissioning, would stem from what he saw as their failure to appreciate just how difficult this had been, or how wounding it had been to mainstream unionist opinion. Both in the run-up to the announcement in the Commons, on 19 January, and on the day itself, Mandelson went to great lengths to indicate that he understood the pain the change of name caused to Unionists, not least to the families of those officers who had been killed or injured. It was true that he had visited scarcely a district of Northern Ireland without meeting local police, and that he had regularly been exposed to that pain. In an interview with Desmond McCartan of the *Belfast Telegraph* he was asked about the criticism of the Patten report, that it did not sufficiently acknowledge the sacrifices made by officers during the Troubles: 'Frankly, I agree with that criticism,' he said.[44] He told McCartan that after witnessing the continuing grief of the widow of an RUC officer, David Eade, killed many years ago, he could not work for the rest of the afternoon.

The Commons announcement on Patten was Mandelson's most testing appearance at the dispatch box yet. He allowed himself to be provoked, unwisely, into a brief but bitter exchange with Ken Maginnis, the party's security spokesman, and a moderate, pro-Agreement Unionist, who said the announcement 'degrades, demeans and denigrates an honourable force . . . you have changed the name of the RUC but one thing that has not changed is the name of the IRA'. Mandelson replied icily that Maginnis had 'many times in the past' complimented him on his statements about the RUC and added: 'I am therefore very surprised that he chooses to say different things in public to what he has said in private.' Maginnis, furious, shouted back: 'I'm not the betrayer.'[45]

But otherwise it was a pretty faultless performance. 'I understand exactly why serving and former officers, their families and indeed widows are proud of the RUC and its name,' he told the Commons in his statement. 'The issue is whether a change in name, underlining a new start, is a necessary and indispensable part of attracting balance in recruits. Of course it is not the only barrier to recruitment. There has been at times disgraceful intimidation of nationalists who wished to join the RUC. But a change of name was in [Chris Patten]'s view essential, and I agree.'

Despite a critical editorial line from the most staunchly pro-Unionist papers like *The Times* and the *Daily Telegraph*, he had a good press the next day for what was widely seen as a precondition of a long-term settlement in Northern Ireland. Even *The Times*'s Belfast correspondent said, 'Whatever the final outcome, no independent observer could fault Mr Mandelson for lack of energy or ingenuity.' The *Irish Times*, no ally of hardline republicanism, said that Mandelson was to be 'commended' for changes which signified a 'new beginning for a divided society'.

It would not end there. Unionist pain over Patten would return to threaten the peace process many months later. But for now, there was a more immediate crisis. Trimble's unexpected and post-dated resignation threat had lit a fuse which was now burning steadily. It may never be possible to know for certain whether the republicans would have produced a concession on arms during this period if Trimble had not written his post-dated resignation letter. But it was becoming increasingly clear that they were not going to do so now.

Much later there would be considerable debate over what, if any, indications about decommissioning Sinn Fein had given at the end of the Mitchell review back in November. What was certain was that Senator Mitchell himself had made it clear to the parties that he regarded the IRA as being under an obligation to make a significant first gesture on arms once the devolved institutions were established, and that he expected them to do so. This was not an irrational supposition. Geoffrey Martin, the editor of the Belfast *Newsletter*, would recall that at a Labour Party conference fringe meeting in early October, Martin McGuinness had referred 'positively' to an article by the Unionist writer Stephen King, a week earlier, which had suggested that the Executive could be established and then collapsed within four to six weeks if decommissioning had not taken place by then. In subsequent conversation, the editor went on to report that McGuinness had said that unionism would be 'surprised' by the IRA's response if he set up the Executive, despite the absence of guns on the table. Trimble would discover that 'if he noses things forward, that would have more influence with the IRA than anything he or Gerry Adams could say to them'.[46]

These were significant hints; but there were no guarantees. When Mandelson was appointed, he checked that no private pledges on decommissioning had so far been made to the Irish government by the republicans, subsequently remarking to a prominent Belfast journalist that Unionists would have to make a 'leap of faith'.

Mandelson was certainly encouraged by Irish government hints that some movement on arms would take place by 31 January, and was deeply dismayed when that date came and went without anything happening.[47] But while there was a widespread expectation among the other parties that IRA decommissioning would follow swiftly, there was no explicit promise during the Mitchell review that arms would be decommissioned. Indeed Adams, reinforcing his refusal to give Mitchell such a promise, told Mandelson at the beginning of January that no decommissioning would start by the end of that month and that the parties would be lucky if it happened by 22 May. The only question was whether he was bluffing, as some signals from Dublin seemed to imply.

Ultimately it hardly mattered whether Trimble's post-dated letter of resignation stopped the IRA making a concession on arms which they had planned to make, or merely gave them the excuse for not doing what they never had the intention of doing in the first place. Either way it was becoming dauntingly clear that there was no movement within the IRA. De Chastelain's report of 31 January, though in the unpromising circumstances it was as upbeat as possible on the prospects for decommissioning, made for bleak reading; so much so that the two governments delayed publication, at Dublin's insistence, in the hope that he would soon have something more positive to say. Despite the shock inflicted on the Protestant majority by the sight of two prominent republicans driving round in ministerial limousines, devolution was seen as a success by much of the population. But it was living on borrowed time.

It was becoming gradually clearer that the republican leadership had done little to prepare the IRA for decommissioning and appeared to believe that decommissioning would be 'forgotten' once the Executive was in operation. Indeed one analysis of the leadership's opaque deliberations with the republican base was that the rank and file had explicitly been told much earlier that, having made the two historic concessions of a cease-fire and an acceptance of the principle of consent embodied in the Good Friday Agreement, they would never be expected to decommission their arms. But in any case the post-dated Trimble ultimatum served to reinforce their reluctance to offer any concession on arms in two ways.

The first, no doubt, was a perception that to act to a deadline – let alone a Unionist-imposed deadline – would serve only to increase the sense of surrender implied in the act. The second was what appears to have been quite a widespread and complacent belief among senior republicans that neither government would allow the devolved institutions to collapse, once they were established. Such a belief was made explicit when two senior Sinn Fein figures, Pat Doherty and Martin Ferris, addressed Irish-Americans on a trip to the US in November. Indeed those remarks had been cited by defenders of Trimble as one of the reasons for his tactics in setting a decommissioning deadline on 27 November.[48]

Overall, the republicans appear to have miscalculated what was required of them, namely a positive start on the arms issue that would satisfy de Chastelain to take place by the end of January. Equally they underestimated Trimble's determination to resign, and Mandelson's to suspend the institutions, if it proved necessary. (In part this misjudgement may have stemmed from the more relaxed attitude of the Irish government.) At the British ambassador's dinner at Glencairn on the eve of devolution, the Progressive Democrat ministers present, had according to one participant, been insouciant about the looming problems. Their import appeared to be that either General de Chastelain would find some formula which would satisfy the Unionists, or David Trimble would have to call the bluff of his backwoodsmen.[49] In public, Bertie Ahern had made it clear in the Dail the previous November that in the case of ' "difficulty" either in relation to devolution or decommissioning . . . where the Agreement was not being implemented in significant respects, the Governments would have to step in and assume their responsibilities, including through the appropriate suspension arrangements.' Such 'difficulty' appeared to be at hand; after all, the Good Friday Agreement specified the completion of decommissioning by 22 May 2000. General de Chastelain, moreover, had indicated privately to the governments that this process would have to start by the beginning of March at the latest if the completion date was to be met. At the absolute minimum, a firm declaration of intent would be necessary before Trimble's February meeting with the Ulster Unionist Council

– and even that might not be enough given that many in Trimble's party were demanding 'product' – in other words the decommissioning of some actual weaponry.

But in practice Irish ministers appeared to underestimate the seriousness of the deadline, even though they and republican contacts were emphatically warned by the British ambassador of the fragility of Trimble's position. As Frank Millar, the *Irish Times*'s London editor, would subsequently put it: 'Incredibly, it has seemed the Irish government either didn't believe Mr Trimble's bottom line was as stated, or somehow imagined the British could find some way round it.'[50]

But this was not at all how Trimble saw it. Back in November, he had handed his letter of resignation as First Minister to the UUP's president Sir Josias Cunningham. It was post dated to 4 February, five days after the 31 January deadline for de Chastelain's report on decommissioning progress. If the General had nothing new to say by then, the resignation would be implemented, with the automatic consequence that the Executive would be aborted. It might well follow, too, that, his strategy having been shown to fail, he would be ousted as leader as well, extinguishing just about the last chance of keeping the peace process on track. Finally there would have to be fresh assembly elections. The legislation stipulated that if the First Minister went, so, automatically, would the Deputy First Minister. If the parties could not agree alternatives – as they certainly would not have done – then elections would follow in six weeks. In the recriminatory atmosphere which would follow a Trimble resignation, such elections could only be good for hardliners on both sides of the sectarian divide.

As the deadline grew nearer, however, the urgency of coaxing at least some movement from the IRA began to dawn on the Irish government. Mandelson had by now come to a settled view that if the attempt failed, he – preferably with the support of the Irish government – would have to suspend the institutions himself to pre-empt the catastrophic consequences of Trimble's resignation. This was the course that Mandelson had pledged, in the event of default, in his Commons statement of 22 November, which had been ratified in the frequent discussions with Tony Blair throughout January. It was what Blair had also promised to Trimble. In order to maximise the chances of avoiding this unpalatable decision, however, Mandelson first persuaded Trimble to postpone his threatened resignation until 11 February, the eve of the planned meeting of the UUP Council. This would at least allow Irish government officials a little more time to persuade Sinn Fein/IRA to move on decommissioning, and they set about intensively trying to do so.

Nevertheless, by the first week of February time was running out. If suspension was to take place it would require primary legislation. Moreover a formal statement that Mandelson intended to introduce such legislation might help to concentrate republican minds over the few remaining days. Shortly after 7 p.m. on 3 February, therefore, Mandelson made a sober statement in the Commons. He paid tribute to all those who had helped to make the Assembly work in the previous two months, and to the paramilitaries for maintaining their cease-fires. But he made it clear a bill would be introduced and enacted by the end of the following week – the day before Trimble's scheduled Council meeting – if there was no further progress on decommissioning. 'In the case of the IRA,' he said, 'it has to [make] clear that decommissioning is going to happen.'

The statement was, perhaps surprisingly, well received. Seamus Mallon registered, albeit in measured tones, his fairly unequivocal opposition to the suspension threat, but repeated the two questions on which, famously, he had said the IRA had to satisfy General de Chastelain: 'One: "Will you decommission?" Two: "If yes, when will you decommission?"' Tony Benn commented that if suspension proved necessary then 'direct rule by London and Dublin working together' would be preferable to a mere return to British direct rule. But he thanked Mandelson for his 'cautious, confident and moderate' statement. Meeting him outside the chamber, Benn astonished Mandelson by telling him that it was the best Commons statement he had heard from a minister for several years. This was all the more surprising since the two old enemies had not exchanged a word since Mandelson had stopped working for the Labour Party in 1990.

Inevitably, the talks – the most important of which were between Irish officials and leading republicans – ran up to the wire. Dublin shared Mallon's pessimistic assessment that suspension, if it happened, would make it much more difficult to wring concessions out

of the IRA. Moreover, it had, somewhat surprisingly, secured advice
from its government law officers that such a suspension would be
unconstitutional. But realising by now that Mandelson was serious,
Dublin became, even if belatedly, all the more determined to persuade the IRA to move before Trimble's deadline. An earlier IRA
formulation, code-named ANGEL, was judged to fall well short of
what Trimble would require to survive his meeting; it talked only
of the IRA considering 'how' it might put its arms beyond use. And
in any case two days after Mandelson's Commons statement, the
IRA man charged with liaising with General de Chastelain had
mysteriously told the general that this earlier text was no longer
'authorised'. Eventually, in the small hours of Friday 10 February
– the very day suspension was due to take effect – a breakthrough
appeared to have been made. At 10.15 a.m. Downing Street received
a message from the Taioseach's Office in Dublin that a new form
of words from the IRA was on its way. At 10.45 a fax, marked
SECRET, described as a 'draft statement' of an IRA leadership
position, and with a heading which made clear that its circulation
was to be limited to the two Prime Ministers, Mandelson, and the
new Irish Foreign Minister, Brian Cowen, arrived at Downing Street.
It said:

> The peace process contains the potential to remove the causes
> of conflict and to deliver a durable peace if the political will
> exists. This can be advanced by full implementation of the Good
> Friday Agreement.
>
> In the context of a process that will progressively and irreversi-
> bly remove the causes of conflict, the leadership of Óglaigh na
> hÉireann will initiate an internal process subject to our consti-
> tution that will finally and completely put IRA arms beyond use.
>
> This process will be designed to avoid risk to the public and
> misappropriation by others. The leadership of Óglaigh na hÉire-
> ann will facilitate verification of this.
>
> This will be done in such a way to ensure public confidence and
> to resolve the issue of arms in a complete and acceptable way.

This text, which has not been published before, clearly represented
a highly significant advance. It was the first that could be construed

as containing an answer to Seamus Mallon's first question. As such it was clearly a hugely important development. There were, however, several problems. The first was that it did not answer the second Mallon question – when? Indeed by linking decommissioning to the removal of 'the causes of conflict' (hitherto republican code for the British presence in Northern Ireland), it could, on the most sceptical interpretation, be read as implying that decommissioning would not happen until there was a united Ireland. The second problem, as Ahern would make clear in a telephone call to Blair some thirty-five minutes later, was that Gerry Adams was not prepared to make the new formulation public – and indeed it would be withdrawn if it was disclosed. The IRA leaders who had drafted the text had not yet 'briefed' their rank and file and it might well provoke an uncontainable backlash from grassroots republicans if it was made public first. Which meant that it would be all the more difficult to convince ultra-sceptical Unionists that it was substantial, even supposing it would be shown to them. Indeed, as Mandelson would explain to journalists in Dublin the following week, the document lacked formal status; it was 'just a form of words on a piece of paper'. It was a 'leadership position', not shown to or agreed by anyone other than a limited group of republican leaders.[51] The third problem was that beside a complete absence of timetable, there was no hint of a gesture to show good faith, much less the actual 'product' Unionists had been seeking before their council meeting the following day.

As if to underline these deficiencies, Mandelson, who had telephoned Trimble at the UUP's Glengall Street headquarters to tell him that a new IRA formulation was in the making, was himself rung by Sir Josias Cunningham – who, having charge of Trimble's resignation letter, now had virtual life or death control over the peace process. Saying he thought it sensible to 'touch base' with Mandelson, Cunningham was emphatic that words alone would not get Trimble safely through the UUC meeting, all the more so, Mandelson might reflect, if the words were ambiguous and undisclosable. Pointedly Cunningham said he did not think there was any point in his meeting Mandelson 'until there was some progress to meet about'.

At around 11.20 a.m., in the first of half a dozen telephone calls the two Prime Ministers would have with each other that day, Blair, having discussed the IRA 'statement' paragraph by paragraph with Mandelson in Belfast, spoke to Ahern. He acknowledged that the draft went significantly further than any of its predecessors. Could it be given to de Chastelain, on whose assessment of the prospects for decommissioning, the Ulster Unionist decision would now hang, and its contents conveyed to Trimble? No. However, Ahern pointed out that it was a definitive, if conditional, commitment to decommission, and added that the IRA had indicated that it might be prepared, under pressure from Dublin, to take part in an 'Act of Reconciliation'. (This idea, originally floated at the abortive Hillsborough talks the previous Easter, might even have involved a small, symbolic handover of arms. But since it would almost certainly have to be matched by a similar handover by the British Army it would probably be unworkable; senior Army officers had already made clear their deep distaste for such an idea.) Ahern went on to warn that if suspension took place the IRA would withdraw posthaste from any contact with de Chastelain and would not take part in a formal review – a mechanism to revive the Agreement after a breakdown – until there had been fresh elections for a new Assembly. Blair pointed out that elections of any kind would be disastrous for moderates on all sides because they would undoubtedly polarise opinion. He also indicated that if there was to be any chance of the new development impressing Unionists, Adams and McGuinness would have to, at the very least, publicly present the advance as a breakthrough and make it clear that decommissioning would now happen.

At 11.30, with the scheduled time for suspension only half-an-hour away, Blair then spoke directly to Adams. By this time Adams had already spoken to Mandelson, who had told him first that a text had to be given to de Chastelain and to Trimble. The Sinn Fein president now conceded that the text could be given to de Chastelain, though not actually quoted in his report. For the text to become the IRA's formal position, Trimble would have to withdraw his resignation and Mandelson would have to repeal the suspension legislation. (Mandelson would brief Irish journalists in Dublin the following week that Adams had also insisted that Trimble would have to call off the following day's Council meeting.)[52] Adams was willing to talk to Trimble and to say publicly that there was a commitment to putting 'arms beyond use'. But before taking matters further, Adams would need to know for certain how the British government was going to proceed – a demand which contained the obvious risk that the government might be wrong-footed into, say, cancelling suspension, only to find the republicans still dragging their feet, and Trimble as exposed as ever.

Against this uncertain background, in which it was only too possible to imagine the somewhat unpredictable Sir Josias Cunningham purposefully fingering the envelope containing Trimble's resignation letter, Mandelson decided to postpone suspension for three hours. Both before and after doing so he spoke at some length to Trimble. Although initially Trimble seemed to acknowledge the IRA had made a significant shift and that it now appeared to be doing what it had earlier refused to do, he was hesitant. For one thing, his pro-Agreement Unionist ally Sir Reg Empey, who was present in the office with him, appeared to take a negative view of the latest development. Indeed Mandelson reported at one point that Trimble was 'sniffing' but that Empey was holding him back. Trimble stressed that time was rapidly running out and argued that suspension should go ahead while the IRA position was further explored and clarified. Mandelson pointed out that in that event the IRA might well simply disengage from the process; instead, he proposed, perhaps suspension should be post dated by two weeks – an offer which both Trimble, and when it was put to him later, Adams, rejected. Mandelson pointed out that the IRA might at last be 'blinking'. If that was so, replied Trimble, they could be pushed to move further. At the moment the Unionists had been offered the vague possibility of, at best, no more than half of what they wanted – a commitment but no timetable. If de Chastelain was going to be able to do no more than report that the IRA was going to discuss 'modalities' – the burden of the ANGEL position, on which it now looked as if de Chastelain was now going to have to depend – then he, Trimble, would either have to resign or face destruction. Mandelson stressed that the government was not about to let the Unionists down after their brave and honourable risk in agreeing to devolution in November, and again proposed the post-dating idea. Trimble again, though after a moment's hesitation, said no. With just a hint of irritation, Mandelson confided to Downing Street his view that Trimble now seemed more interested in 'survival than solutions'.

Having heard a summary of Trimble's position from Mandelson, and having himself spoken to de Chastelain who said he had told Dublin that he needed to know what the IRA were actually prepared to say on the record about their position, Blair spoke again to Ahern, at about 12.30. The only approach that would work with Trimble, he told the Taoiseach, would be for de Chastelain to be put in such a position by the IRA that he could report an unambiguous commitment to decommissioning and then call for a few weeks to work out how and when it would take place.

At this point events moved rapidly – and confusingly. Shortly after 1 p.m., with British and Irish officials now mutually resolved to try and stretch the extent to which de Chastelain could report a clear commitment by the IRA, the Canadian general received a call from the IRA representative, Brian Keenan, widely seen as the leading hardliner on the IRA Army Council, asking him to a meeting – which only took place after de Chastelain had had to take a complicated cloak-and-dagger journey, involving a switch of cars and his eventual arrival at a safe house on the outskirts of Belfast. As these contacts were under way, Mandelson spoke to Adams by telephone at around 1.50 p.m. and reported on his conversation with Trimble. Mandelson made it clear he had put as positive a gloss as possible on the latest developments, but also warned that Trimble was under considerable pressure, not made easier by Cunningham 'hovering in the background'. Adams, seeming tired, and at times almost detached, urged Mandelson to be restrained in any interviews he gave, and said that he was at present fully preoccupied with 'internal management' – presumably of dissident IRA figures uneasy at the idea of looming concessions. He was adamant that this proposal was the republicans' final effort and that Trimble should be told that the suspension legislation would be withdrawn on the basis of a positive report by de Chastelain. In the meantime Martin McGuinness would be seeing Trimble personally. Mandelson replied pregnantly that McGuinness had better be persuasive.

In the event, he was not. As Trimble would later claim to Mandelson, McGuinness was at his most charmless when the two men met at Stormont at around 2 p.m. Instead of giving Trimble a detailed account of the new IRA position, McGuinness merely insisted that Trimble should withdraw his resignation, cancel the party council meeting scheduled for the following day and agree to the repeal of the suspension legislation; unspecified proposals had been made by the IRA which could lead to a solution within the next couple of weeks. Trimble retorted that he had no more than a couple of hours. Trimble would later complain that, while not overtly threatening, McGuinness had come close to being so. On this basis he could not possibly survive the council meeting. If anything, Trimble's position had hardened as a result of the abortive meeting with McGuinness. Mandelson replied that he would safeguard Trimble's position but that time must be allowed for de Chastelain to make his report, even if at present it did not look as if it would be enough to save the situation. Trimble, understandably conscious of the ever-hovering Cunningham, said he hoped this would happen as quickly as possible. The UUP leader then spoke directly to Blair, saying he recognised that the IRA's – still secret – position was an advance, but would not be enough to sustain a deal as currently presented.

Once again Mandelson, despite Trimble's now much more vehement warnings that time was running out, deferred signing the commencement order for suspension, in the hope that de Chastelain could secure further concessions from the republicans which might just save Trimble. Trimble protested that a decision would have to be taken within the next hour, while the office of the Assembly Speaker, Lord Alderdice, was still open – a stipulation about which Mandelson expressed some scepticism, saying he thought Alderdice was available to receive notification of suspension whenever it took place. In fact, Mandelson had deliberately urged Alderdice, a doctor by profession, to make himself scarce and 'do a clinic or play a round of golf', in case Trimble's resignation should be prematurely enacted. And certainly, de Chastelain, who had by now returned from his excursion to his office in the Upper Newtonards Road, was not inactive. At 4.25 p.m., he reported to the NIO. The IRA were still refusing to allow the inclusion of a harder commitment to decommissioning in Paragraph Five of his report, along the lines of its secret text. Instead the paragraph would have merely to refer to the IRA considering 'how to put arms and explosives beyond use in the context of full implementation of the Good Friday Agreement and in the context of the removal of the causes of conflict'. There would be no reference to verification; though the words 'in a manner to ensure to public confidence' could be added to the somewhat hedged reference to putting arms 'beyond use' in Paragraph Seven. And the word 'commitment' in Paragraph Eight would have to be heavily qualified and undergo a change of meaning by being followed by '. . . to further discussions'.

The upshot of all this tortuously-negotiated wording was that de Chastelain's report would not go as far as an IRA text, which even in its unvarnished form was highly unlikely to be enough to sway the UUP council meeting. The IRA text had been gnomic enough in the first place; the summary in the general's report was necessarily more so. At 4.35 p.m. Blair spoke to Adams and said – what was indisputably true – that the report would not be enough to satisfy Trimble. He understood that the discussion between McGuinness and Trimble had been – using something of a euphemism – 'unfruitful'. Adams said that suspension would itself be a breach of the Good Friday Agreement. Blair replied that suspension was the only way to save the peace process and urged Adams not to make it impossible for Sinn Fein to take part in a review of the Agreement by setting preconditions. At least one official listening to the conversation thought that Adams was 'tellingly' keen to finish the conversation; it was almost as if he was keen to make his next move. Rightly or wrongly the British view was that Adams was as much seeking to shift the blame for suspension as trying to avoid it altogether.

The die was now cast. With Cunningham increasingly restive, and Trimble increasingly agitated, Mandelson's options had now run out. Just before 5 p.m. his private office took a call from the First Minister's Office at Stormont saying that Trimble feared Cunningham would leave to deliver the resignation letter 'at any moment' – with all the dire consequences that would inevitably follow. Although the public announcement was delayed in order to allow Blair and Mandelson to work on the text together, Mandelson signed the commencement order at 5.03 p.m. At 5.15 Gerry Adams issued a statement that there had been a 'new and significant' breakthrough by the IRA – though without specifying it in detail – and he called on Mandelson to rescind the suspension legislation. At virtually the same moment Martin McGuinness, having spoken to Adams, and apparently now taking over the negotiations from Brian Keenan, told de Chastelain that the IRA were ready to agree to one further amendment in the wording of the general's report: the words 'to further discussions' could now be omitted from the reference to 'the commitment' in Paragraph Eight. At 5.20, determined to make sure he had not been duped into withholding the resignation letter, Cunningham telephoned Mandelson's office to make sure that the suspension order had indeed been signed. And at 5.25 de Chastelain was telephoned by his IRA contact with confirmation of the agreed change.

The change was another modest advance; it removed one hedging phrase from what nevertheless remained a pretty hedged report. De Chastelain and his colleagues, moreover, would tell Mandelson early the following week that they had had the impression after the afternoon's hectic negotiations that the move was not merely 'tactical', and that they were making a genuine effort to grapple with the decommissioning issue. But it was almost certainly too little as well as too late. Even if it had come earlier in the day, it would hardly have been enough to change Trimble's mind. As Mandelson now pointed out to Blair, Adams had seemingly not produced the final amendment until he knew that suspension had gone through.

The Irish government, appalled at the idea of the still-so-far-unannounced suspension going ahead, pressed for a further delay on the strength of the new developments. In another call to Blair, Ahern admitted that Adams's statement had fallen well short of making the new IRA position public in a way that might – just – have convinced Trimble's Unionist opponents, and which Paddy Teahon, the senior official in Ahern's office dealing with Northern Ireland, had been led to expect. By making such a statement – and agreeing to his final position after the suspension order had been signed – he had acted, Ahern said, in a way which was 'dubious but enough to delay suspension'. Blair replied both that it was not clear that there was anything really new in the statement, and in any case the order had been signed.

Anglo-Irish relations were now about to go through their most strained period since Blair had taken office in May 1997. But Ahern had one trump card still to play: the President of the United States. Bill Clinton, apparently at the urging of Ahern, now called Blair to urge him to defer suspension. According to one official, when the Prime Minister started briefly to sketch in the background of the day's events, Clinton cut him off, seeming 'keen to cut to the chase'. Surely, the President said, Trimble understood that this was a break-through? Blair was firm in reply. First Adams had held off making his best offer until the suspension order had been signed. Secondly Trimble had been so 'dicked around' by Sinn Fein that the republi-cans' latest ploy would hardly be helpful. Bluntly Clinton asked whether the suspension order could be reversed. Equally bluntly Blair said it could not. Showing that he now accepted this, Clinton said at least Trimble should welcome de Chastelain's new report. Blair said he would indeed try to persuade Trimble to do just that. But in return he would like Clinton to persuade Sinn Fein not to disengage from the process.

Mandelson announced suspension of the institutions of Northern Ireland at 5.55 p.m., and about half an hour later published de Chastelain's initial report of 31 January. He acknowledged in a statement that: 'We ... are much closer than two weeks ago, to resolving the issue of decommissioning.' But he added: 'Until com-mitments are clear they simply cannot command confidence.' He urged all participants to 'do everything to ensure that we achieve an agreed outcome as soon as possible'. But Clinton's failure to persuade Blair to cancel suspension had left the Irish government deeply unhappy. As expected, there would be nothing in de Chastelain's report – when it finally arrived at Downing Street nearly an hour after it reached Dublin after delays caused by what de Chastelain would later explain were faxing difficulties, at 6.45 p.m. – to make them change their minds. But this would not stop them from trying to reverse the decision as quickly as possible. The best part of two hours was spent by British officials on seeking to dis-suade their counterparts in Dublin and Washington from suggesting that the institutions could somehow be miraculously revived on the basis of de Chastelain's second report. Then at around 8.30 p.m. Ahern came on the line yet again to try and persuade Blair to agree to London and Dublin issuing a joint statement welcoming de Chastelain's report. The statement proposed by Ahern, which one British official described as 'hopelessly over-positive', would have said that Blair now intended to go back to Parliament to rescind suspension. Blair stood firm. Realising he was getting nowhere, Ahern took the unusual step of putting an incandescent Paddy Teahon on the line. According to British sources, Teahon went to the outer limits of normal protocol for an official speaking to another country's prime minister in urging the joint statement. He also roundly condemned Mandelson. He said the Secretary of State had acted in a precipitate and disgraceful way, unaware that – as during all the calls between Dublin and London that day – Mandelson had been plugged into the conversation by the Downing Street switchboard. In the end, however, he recognised a joint statement was not going to happen, and dropped the matter. When de Chastelain's second report was finally published after 9 p.m., Downing Street welcomed it along the lines of Mandelson's earlier statement.

In hindsight, the decision to suspend the institutions was handsomely vindicated by the much clearer breakthrough achieved in May. But at the time it plunged Mandelson into immediate controversy. The republicans were far from the first politicians to find Mandelson an easy figure to demonise and they set about doing so with some efficiency, blaming him personally for putting the peace process in its worst danger yet. There was a robust defence to be mounted. Sinn Fein knew that back in November both Senator Mitchell, and more importantly David Trimble, had expected decommissioning to start by the beginning of January. But nothing had happened. Mandelson had been crucial in persuading Trimble to jump first in November; but he had no chance of averting his resignation on the basis of what had been produced. And for Trimble to resign instead of having his position frozen by suspension would have had far more serious consequences. Had the advance made at the beginning of the day been outlined perhaps two weeks earlier, as Mandelson indicated to Dublin journalists the following week, they might have been able to extract something acceptable to the Unionists. But it came too late. Nor could Mandelson be accused of not maximising the republican leadership's opportunity to persuade its own rank and file to move on decommissioning. He had held off publication of de Chastelain's 31 January report for fear of inflaming anti-republican opinion. He had faced down Unionist wrath by pressing ahead with the Patten reforms to the RUC. He had persuaded Trimble to postpone his council meeting for a week. On the day he had postponed suspension three times. All this was true; but it did not alter the hostility with which republicans, and indeed moderate nationalists, greeted the decision. Sinn Fein immediately ended its liaison with de Chastelain. The Irish government made no effort to disguise its displeasure. To most observers the prospects appeared bleaker than at any time since before Good Friday 1998. Nor did it look to most observers as if the British government had a Plan B. As one prominent Northern Ireland public figure put it to a British official: 'Once the communication chord was pulled no one seemed to know how to start the train again.'

But Mandelson had meant what he said on that Friday evening: there was 'no rational basis' for letting suspension undermine the process permanently. Indeed it was – just – possible that suspension could even be turned to advantage. The answer to the communication chord problem might be to transfer to another, parallel, train.

# CHAPTER 27

## Start Wrapping the Clock

On the evening of 11 February, a few hours after he had signed the order suspending the devolved institutions, Peter Mandelson took his final call of the day from Gerry Adams. If anything, the Sinn Fein president was calmer than the Northern Ireland Secretary, who said forcefully that Adams had let the government down by failing to come up with a viable new position which could rescue Trimble, or even to make a public statement heralding an IRA 'breakthrough' until half an hour after suspension had taken place. Adams remarked that there seemed little point in talking further since the Secretary of State was obviously in a bad mood. 'For God's sake, Gerry,' Mandelson exclaimed. 'What do you expect?' Ominously, however, Adams added that he should not take 'personally' the attacks the republicans would now launch on Mandelson's decision to suspend.

Mandelson would soon find out what Adams had meant. A combination of public statements and selected off-the-record briefings by the republicans would pin blame for the collapse firmly on Mandelson – despite Tony Blair's full involvement in the events of 11 February – accusing him of acting to a 'Unionist agenda'. Sinn Fein posters would soon appear in nationalist areas depicting Mandelson, Paisley and Trimble as the men who had, as McGuinness and Adams put it in a meeting with Mandelson, 'put back the cause of peace by thirty years'. Indeed in some of his encounters with the Sinn Fein leadership over the next few weeks, Mandelson would reflect ruefully that the historic roles of the British state and republicans had been reversed and that it was as if he was under the bright lights at Castlereagh facing his interrogators. At one meeting, during which they had warned him that 'he would never be able to show his face in a nationalist area again', he had suggested the Sinn Fein leaders stop treating him 'like a specimen in a psychiatrist's chair'. Hardly a stranger to the difficult meeting and a politician capable of being fairly intimidating himself, Mandelson stood up to the abuse much better than other ministers in his place might have done. But it could not fail to take a toll.

Nor was the atmosphere helped by the bad blood which now existed between the Irish government and – in particular – Mandelson and the Northern Ireland Office. The Irish continued to press for the institutions to be restored within days, arguing, on the basis of the advice of the Irish Attorney General Michael McDowell, that they should not cooperate with the UK in suspension and that both Dublin and London were vulnerable if Sinn Fein should resort to the courts to have the decision overturned. Both governments had explicitly warned of suspension: in the case of London, repeatedly before it took place; in the case of Ahern, in the Dail back in November. Moreover, Irish ministers had little answer to the question of what alternatives there might be, given the paramount importance to the Good Friday Agreement of preserving Trimble. Dublin argued that the Agreement had provided only for a review in the case of default by one of the parties, not suspension. But the British were adamant that a judicial review would not succeed; more tellingly, they argued that Sinn Fein would be taking a big risk by going to court since the weakness of their pledge to decommission would be exposed; de Chastelain would be called to testify and would hardly be able to say with any confidence that he now expected them to disarm.

When Mandelson met the Irish Minister for Foreign Affairs, Brian Cowen on Tuesday 15 February, however, he was careful not to inflame the Irish further. Cowen, who had succeeded David Andrews in January, was a much more belligerent figure than his predecessor. From County Offaly in the Irish midlands, and almost universally nicknamed BIFFO[1], Cowen is in his own way as obtrusive a figure in the politics of Ireland as Mandelson is in that of Britain. But they were not, to put it mildly, natural soulmates.

According to a profile of him in the Irish magazine *Magill*, Cowen 'is as republican as they come in Fianna Fail, though it is tempered by a deep antipathy towards the IRA'. As the article perceptively concluded: 'His relationship with Northern Ireland Secretary Peter Mandelson will be an interesting one to watch ... one displaying an iron fist in a velvet glove, the other displaying only an iron fist – sure, what need would he [Cowen] have of a glove at all?'[2]

But while Cowen had already made clear his opposition to suspension, their relationship was not yet as abrasive as it would become. Mandelson readily acknowledged the importance of restoring the institutions. While implying that the early prospects for a positive outcome on 11 February had 'melted away', especially after the 'disastrous' meeting between Trimble and McGuinness, he agreed that the new IRA move had been 'promising'. (He would repeat this point to Irish journalists three days later, suggesting that if it had come two weeks earlier it could have been clarified enough to persuade Trimble to defer his resignation threat.)[3] But while the situation was now 'different' it had not been 'transformed'. The Irish government's reluctance to accept this analysis was underlined when Dermot Gallagher, the senior Irish Foreign Ministry official on Northern questions, suggested that Trimble should now go back to his party and say that on the basis of further meetings he was now convinced that the IRA would disarm. Jonathan Stephens spoke for the British when he said that this would put Trimble back in exactly the same situation as November of having to make a blind act of faith.

In reality there was no question of Trimble doing any such thing without further movement by the IRA. Nor was de Chastelain going to be coerced into persuading him to do so. The day after the Cowen-Mandelson meeting the General came under pressure from the Irish government to confirm suggestions that he had received 'confidential information' in his talks on 11 February which had reassured him that the IRA would disarm. This de Chastelain resisted, apparently on the grounds that the leadership text from the IRA on that day did not constitute such an assurance. Equally, there seemed little or no chance that the IRA, who on the very day of Mandelson's meeting with Cowen formally broke off all contact with de Chastelain, would begin to produce a new formulation which could satisfy Trimble while the institutions were in abeyance. Indeed it looked increasingly as if, so far from completing decommissioning by 22 May, it might be years before they did so – leaving an impasse which would require some lateral thinking to overcome.

Initially, however, Mandelson was most anxious to restore the momentum which suspension had taken out of the peace process. In the last week of February he flew to Washington and New York to brief the White House and defend suspension publicly. Reporting back to London on a day of meetings with the Irish-American press (including the pro-republican *Irish Voice*, the editorial board of the *New York Times* and some leading political figures in the Irish-American community), Paul Johnston, the British consul in New York, reported a 'very good day's work in which the Secretary of State mixed persuasion with forthright rebuttal and a few home truths'.

After his return, on 25 February, Mandelson wrote to Blair with a bleak, though not hopeless, account of the post-suspension landscape. He was able to report a 'better understanding here, in Dublin and the US' of why suspension was 'inevitable and preferable to an uncontrolled collapse'. But he warned against complacency in the face of 'continued heavy briefing by Sinn Fein, aided by Irish government activity', to the effect that 'we looked an IRA gift-horse in the mouth and gave up a chance of the IRA permanently ending the war'. He had, he went on, sought to settle nationalist opinion by stressing the British government's commitment on those parts of the Agreement for which it was directly responsible: the Patten report, criminal justice reform and equal rights, while appearing open on 'demilitarisation' (the issue, also known as 'normalisation', of reducing the visible British army presence in Northern Ireland).

But he had also detected the 'worrying' view in Dublin and Washington that suspension had so boosted Trimble as to have given him strength within his own party to yield further to the republicans. This Mandelson had tried to counter because his own assessment was that a feeling within Unionism that Trimble had been 'duped' by Sinn Fein 'runs deep' and that the UUP leader's position was in fact weaker than it seemed, adding: 'He is certainly only secure as long as he hangs tough.' (This judgement would be graphically vindicated exactly a month later when Trimble only narrowly survived a leadership challenge from his fellow MP, the Revd. Martin Smyth.)

Mandelson's view, now relayed to Blair, was that the two governments were now facing a 'fierce Catch 22'. Trimble needed some move on decommissioning that could be deployed publicly before the institutions were restored; but that appeared to be the one thing that was not on offer. The White House view, he told Blair, was that Trimble would have to 'rely on something less than publishable assurances [from Sinn Fein]'. But, he warned, that did not 'get round the basic problem', of it being 'extremely unlikely' that after taking 'a leap in the dark' once, the UUP would be ready to do so again.

Mandelson went on to report that the Irish government and Sinn Fein had now convinced themselves that the real issue for the IRA was 'about disbandment rather than the giving up of arms'. Dublin was arguing that the ultimate prize might not be so much disarmament but the actual disillusion of the organisation – and that the governments should not be deflected from that goal by the 'short-term considerations' of insisting on an early gesture on decommissioning. On one level, Mandelson acknowledged, the Irish were right: total decommissioning would anyway be tantamount to disbandment since it was impossible to imagine an army without guns. But there was no intelligence or other evidence, he added, that the IRA were even contemplating disbandment.

If he was right that Trimble would need an early gesture on decommissioning to be able to return to government, then it made sense to focus on how one could be secured – and presented, as the IRA would certainly require it to be, as entirely voluntary. It was clear, however, that the idea of an 'Act of Reconciliation' in which both the IRA and the British engaged in some symbolic laying down of a quantity of arms was no longer an option – 'if it was ever realistic' as Mandelson now put it. The idea was in fact, not his; it had first surfaced at the Hillsborough talks between Ahern, Blair and the parties at Easter 1999, before Mandelson arrived in Belfast. But there had recently been a spate of adverse publicity after a leak of the Service Chiefs' extreme dislike for such an approach, which Mandelson calculated, with some relief, had now 'done for' the proposal. Instead, he suggested it might be better to consider how to allow some (justified) security normalisation which could give the IRA cover for a subsequent gesture of their own. Above all, Mandelson argued, the governments should not allow the Good Friday Agreement's deadline of 22 May to drift by without some concrete progress being made. Although as a date for the completion of decommissioning it had become meaningless, it might, he reasoned – just – spur Trimble to sell the idea of an early restoration of the institutions to his party on the grounds that since the IRA had still not acted, then even the Irish government and the SDLP would support the UUP in blaming them.

The biggest problem, however, was that for the time being both sides seemed 'relatively comfortable in their intransigence'. While Trimble was firmly of the view that the onus was now on the republicans, Mandelson believed that Sinn Fein was 'milking the genuine disappointment of nationalists by demonising the British government and me in particular' – attempting to drive a wedge between himself and the Prime Minister in a way which he warned Blair would not be in his long-term interests to tolerate. Overall, the republicans were in no hurry and would probably be happy to see the 22 May come and go without further steps being taken. Finally, Mandelson advised, the Irish should be encouraged in their efforts to re-engage with Sinn Fein, and the British government should also do so. The principal objective should be as it was before suspension – a clear commitment by the IRA to decommission and a timeframe in which to do it, thereby building on the IRA leadership position of 11 February. Prophetically, Mandelson added: 'We should keep in mind that even if that objective can be achieved, it is likely to be deliverable only after the institutions have been restored.'

In fact, the Irish government needed little encouragement to re-engage with Sinn Fein. As Mandelson was giving his views to Blair, they were already actively seeking the best information they could on the Provisionals' bottom line. Meanwhile Mandelson determined to take his own advice – and meet privately with Adams in the hope of finding a way to release the 'fierce Catch 22' at the centre of the impasse.

With the prospects of decommissioning being completed within the Good Friday Agreement timetable now virtually extinguished, Mandelson began to turn over, with Bill Jeffrey and Jonathan

Stephens, ways of persuading the Unionists that the inexorable link between disarmament and devolution was no longer serving the interests of any of the parties. By saying that one could not take place without the other, they had given the paramilitaries, he reflected, a stranglehold on democracy in Northern Ireland. In a Commons statement on 3 February Mandelson acknowledged that the republicans believed the 22 May deadline for decommissioning had lost its force, since the Agreement had first envisaged a period of eighteen months or so of continuous devolution. But whether justified in this way or not, the IRA's refusal to decommission within the Agreement timetable had given them what amounted to a veto over the devolved institutions and a leverage over the peace process which eclipsed the role of the parties. There were real dangers in continuing to insist on decommissioning by a fixed date, as a precondition to restoring devolution. The government might be gradually forced into conceding too much to the IRA – not least in respect of normalisation – to have any chance of securing IRA agreement. And even supposing it were possible, the price of persuading the republican leadership to comply might be an IRA split creating a far more destabilising threat from dissident paramilitaries. Decommissioning remained as important as ever; but treating it as a precondition of devolution might not be the best way of achieving either. That was what Mandelson was already hinting at, on the evening of 11 February, when he stated in broadcast interviews that the decommissioning issue had to be settled 'one way or the other'.

All these arguments might in time be deployed to persuade Trimble to this new line of reasoning. But first Mandelson would need substantive help from the republicans. Mandelson decided to share some of his new thinking at an informal private talk with Gerry Adams at Hillsborough Castle on the afternoon of Saturday 4 March.

The meeting was significantly more relaxed than many which had preceded or would follow it – partly thanks to the ubiquitous presence of the adolescent Bobby, who accompanied the Sinn Fein president and the Northern Ireland Secretary on a walk round the Hillsborough gardens. For all the volatile chemistry between the two men, they shared, however improbably, a love of dogs. Indeed it had been Adams who had first suggested to Mandelson, shortly after he arrived in Belfast, that he got a dog. In response to a casual enquiry of Mandelson's, Adams said he had spent the weekend 'doing the garden and walking the dog'. Mandelson said he had always regretted not having a dog and Adams said he should buy one, even suggesting that he himself would get him a puppy. In the end Mandelson was given a dog by friends in England. But Adams played amiably with Bobby on his visit to Hillsborough. At one point, the dog bounded into the small ground floor drawing room as Mandelson and Adams were talking, with something clenched between its teeth. Adams teasingly tried to extract the object from the animal's mouth, just as Mandelson realised with mounting alarm what it was: a plastic baton round of the sort that had been standard use in the security forces during the Troubles, and given to Bobby to play with by one of the RUC men on guard at Hillsborough. 'Is this what I think it is?' demanded Adams. 'I'm afraid so,' said Mandelson weakly, recovering enough to add: 'It's my contribution to decommissioning.'

Amid this relative jollity, Mandelson began to spell out his new thinking. Decommissioning by all paramilitaries remained an essential goal. But instead of being a condition of devolution – most brutally expressed by the Unionist doctrine of 'no guns, no government' – it could now be seen instead as being linked to the full implementation of the Agreement including the Patten report, criminal justice reform, equal rights and normalisation. It was desirable that once re-established, the institutions should not be suspended again. But the IRA would have to respond to that shift in ways which were much clearer than had been declared in the 11 February text which could have been interpreted as meaning that disarmament would only be completed when the end of British rule had been achieved. It would now have to pledge, in whatever terms, an end to war 'in the context of full implementation' of the Agreement. There should, moreover, be an 'early gesture' to show the IRA's good faith. But in return for a more specific pledge by the IRA, the British government might be able to shift from an emphasis on decommissioning in the short term to one which linked it to the implementation – some of it inevitably long term – of the rest of the Agreement. In this way the institutions would be able to run, as the republicans had always wanted, for a lengthy period before arms were finally – and verifiably – put 'beyond use'.

It was in the nature of the private discussion at Hillsborough that Mandelson did not commit himself to any course; nor, naturally, did he expect Adams to. The talks were, as lawyers say, 'without prejudice'. But Adams was interested; he expressed disappointment some days later when Mandelson was forced to decline his request to put his proposals in writing, having been advised by Downing Street that to do so would risk aggravating the Irish on the grounds that they needed to be brought into any governmental initiative as equal partners. In fact, many of the most important and detailed discussions that followed would be between the NIO officials – led by Bill Jeffrey – along with Jonathan Powell from Downing Street, and Irish government officials, and between the two prime ministers.

There would, moreover, be many twists and turns, mutual recriminations, setbacks, near breakdowns and moments of total despair in the weeks that lay ahead. When Mandelson next met Adams it was in the company of Brian Cowen and Adams's tone was completely different – and much more aggressive. So much so that Mandelson responded to Adams's denunciations of his action in suspending the Executive by resorting to the high-risk tactic he had deployed with Ken Maginnis in the Commons after the Patten announcement, remarking that 'You don't have to berate me just because you're with other people. You don't do it when we're on our own.' That exchange was also a harbinger of the tense and difficult relationship he would continue to have with Cowen. He was irritated that the Irish Foreign Minister gave him no support, moral or otherwise, as Adams harangued him, especially as Mandelson on another, parallel, occasion, had intervened to ease the atmosphere when David Trimble had similarly lambasted Cowen. None of this, however, altered the significance of that first Hillsborough meeting. For in essence the ideas exchanged between Mandelson and Adams that Saturday afternoon – of which Mandelson had scribbled a note as the two men spoke – would form a basis of the often deeply fraught negotiations over the next two months.

In Dublin four days later, Mandelson cautiously allowed a little of his new thinking to surface in public. By this time the Irish government – to the discomfort of the Unionists – had softened its public line in the face of the increasingly plain fact that the IRA would not have decommissioned by 22 May, by saying that they would no longer be required to do so. Mandelson did not publicly endorse this view; but his approach was, if anything, more interesting. In a speech to the Irish Management Institute on 8 March, he summed up the 'familiar conundrum' thus: 'Unionists say there must be certainty about decommissioning before they will participate in the institutions. Republicans say that certainty about decommissioning can only be achieved when the political institutions have been functioning for some time.' Whatever the merits of the two positions, Mandelson added, the trouble was that they were 'mutually exclusive. The end result ... is not guns and government but no guns and no government. It is reasonable to ask ... whether we risk the one becoming an obstacle, rather than a stepping stone, to the other. The integrity of positions on both sides is easy to preserve. They can just maintain some sort of Mexican stand-off. But the inevitable consequence of the decommissioning stalemate is political instability, thus threatening the very peace which everyone wants to preserve.'

The Dublin speech received the minimum of press coverage the following day. Mandelson predictably attracted far bigger headlines that week for a gaffe in an RTE radio interview in which, during a description of his visit as an eleven-year-old to the Trooping the Colour parade he unwisely referred to his impressions at the time of it featuring 'you know, chinless wonders with bright scarlet uniforms ... playing and marching around'. He expressed his regrets in the Commons and wrote to Major General Evelyn Webb-Carter, the CO of the Household Division to apologise. By contrast, the change of tactics on decommissioning caused, initially, hardly any stir at all. Which was probably just as well, since it would soon be apparent that a very substantial body of Unionist opinion was far from ready to confront the true import of Mandelson's remarks – that it might now be time to bury the rigid doctrine of 'no guns, no government'. Nevertheless it was an important first public sign that that the government was prepared to switch their approach on decommissioning to 'another track'. It also went some way to meet Cowen's insistence, expressed on the very same day, that the talks needed to break out of the 'narrow context' of decommissioning.

In the meantime, the pace and variety of contacts between the two governments and the republicans was increasing. The view of senior Irish officials was now that the IRA remained committed to 'politicisation', but that, while it would disarm 'in time' it would certainly not do so now. Intelligence received through intermediaries with paramilitaries had punctured ideas that the IRA would disband in the foreseeable future, indicating that if it did so, it would allow the dissident groups, like the Real or Continuity IRA, to take on new legitimacy by claiming to be the true heirs of the IRA's founding fathers. Their public position was likely to be that there was no question of any gesture which could be seen as decommissioning and that there would be no surrender of any arms at all to the British Army; but that after – and only after – the institutions had been operating for an – unspecified – period and the 'Unionist veto' had been therefore removed, their arms could be put verifiably 'beyond use'.

There was one further sign that it could be fruitful to explore a solution to the arms question which, in at least the short to medium term, did not rely on decommissioning in the conventional sense. Ivor Roberts, the British ambassador in Dublin, reported to Mandelson that on 9 March, at very short notice, he had been contacted by an Ulster Unionist councillor Harvey Bicker, who suggested a meeting in a Drogheda hotel. Bicker, who was born in Dublin, had been put in touch with Roberts by a mutual contact. Bicker was a former British army colonel and unusually as a prominent Unionist had helped on the Belfast-born Mary McAleeses's successful campaign to succeed Mary Robinson as President of Ireland. He had also built up a friendship with Father Alex Reid, a Belfast priest and a champion of the peace process known to have close contacts with the IRA. Although Bicker was sanguine, if not downright gloomy, about immediate prospects for a breakthrough, he revealed to Roberts that he had been discussing with Father Reid – and was pressing UUP party leaders to consider – the possibility that IRA arms might not be handed over but placed in 'two or three deep hides' which could then be inspected regularly, possibly by some independent agency outside the de Chastelain commission, which the republicans said they now regarded as discredited because of de Chastelain's refusal to produce a more positive report on 11 February. This chimed with reliable intelligence separately received by the British government, indicating that the IRA had discussed the possibility of opening armed dumps to inspection as an alternative to decommissioning.

All these developments, including Mandelson's own now semi-public switch of strategy, were as yet tentative. In particular there was little indication – let alone guarantee – that the IRA would countenance opening dumps up as 'confidence building measure' (what became known as a CBM), to help David Trimble keep the Executive and Assembly going, always assuming that they could be first started up again. But they were enough, as most of Northern Ireland's leading political figures – including Mandelson – gathered in Washington for the annual St Patrick's Day celebrations, to start crystallising thinking, not only within the British government but also, as it would more significantly emerge, in the mind of Trimble himself.

Before setting out for Washington, Mandelson wrote a second note to Blair on how he now saw the process, including emerging prospects of a carefully ordered 'sequence' of steps by which devolution might be revived and which had already been discussed, without commitment, in crucial talks between Dermot Gallagher and Mandelson's political director at the NIO, the trusted official Bill Jeffrey. The 'basic thinking', he now told Blair, was that 'we will have to redefine the decommissioning issue' to the extent of accepting that the IRA would not decommission under duress or until they had seen the institutions working for some time, along with the implementation of other aspects of the Agreement; recognising in other words that the 22 May deadline was no longer sustainable. In return they would need to give the Unionists confidence that arms would be put verifiably 'beyond use'. This would require agreement between the two governments on a plan to implement the non-devolution aspects of the Agreement and a 'much clearer IRA statement than the one which appeared to be on offer on 11 February', which would tie the IRA – not just its leaders – to putting arms beyond use 'in the context of the Agreement's implementation'. In addition, Mandelson reported, his own officials were pressing the Irish on two further points about which Dublin was far from agreed: an early confidence building measure from the IRA and acceptance that if the IRA returned to violence, the SDLP, and by implication the Irish government, would accept the exclusion of Sinn Fein from the Executive.

Mandelson warned that securing agreement from either the Unionists – still seeking 'product' i.e. the handover of actual arms – or Sinn Fein, likely to resist an early gesture, would be difficult. Secondly he feared – rightly as it turned out – that the Irish would be overambitious in their expectations of how far the British could 'normalise' security. He had already written to Cowen to express concern about the Irish Foreign Minister's 'increasingly unhelpful public statements' on demilitarisation, and he suspected that Blair would need to 'inject a bit of realism into the Irish' in his personal discussions with Ahern. Finally the 'high pressure deployment' of both prime ministers in the talks themselves should take place at the optimum time. In Mandelson's view, this would be towards the end of the period of talks.

The strategy was now broadly in place. Executing it would be a traumatic and perilous process – starting with an imminent crisis in the Ulster Unionist Party. The problem arose not because David Trimble reacted with outrage to the new thinking but because he went an unexpectedly long way towards embracing it – and in public. At a press conference in Washington on 17 March Trimble suddenly, and without giving details of what he had in mind, announced that 'we are prepared to be involved in a fresh sequence which probably will not involve arms up front'. He added that to be involved in such a sequence, 'I've got to be able to persuade the party to do it.'[4] That was a masterly understatement. His most resolute anti-Agreement opponent within the UUP, the MP Jeffrey Donaldson, lost no time in declaring that he would be 'absolutely astonished' if the party agreed to let Sinn Fein back into government without decommissioning.[5]

The remarks were not accidental. It seems almost certain that Trimble had intended to fire a warning shot across the opposition within his own party, by making clear that he was not going to be bullied into permanent refusal to take part in devolved government. The stance Trimble was setting out was in fact identical to that which he had adopted back in November and December, that the Unionists were prepared to share power first and expect decommissioning second, instead of the other way round. But given how let down his party felt over what they saw as the IRA's total failure to respond the last time, Trimble was showing real courage, and taking a real risk, by confronting the 'no guns, no government' tendency in his party now. And indeed he had over-reached himself, as he would later candidly admit to Tony Blair. Not only had he apparently signed up to the search for an 'alternative context' in which to discuss decommissioning, but he had done so 'while 4000 miles from home, in the context of a distinctly Green event [the St Patrick's Day celebrations] without prior notice to many of those presumed close to him'.[6] Worse, he was facing, a mere eight days later, what already promised to be a difficult meeting of his party's ruling council. David Burnside, a former colleague of Trimble's from Vanguard who now had his own public affairs consultancy in London, and who was until quite recently a close adviser of Trimble's, was ambitious for a parliamentary seat and tabled a motion seeking to tie Trimble's hands by making return to the Executive conditional on 'Royal' still being in the title of the post-Patten police service. The further threat of a challenge to Trimble's leadership had appeared to have receded by the time he left for Washington. His remarks now rekindled it.[7] The Revd. Martin Smyth, the anti-Agreement UUP MP and former Grand Master of the Orange Order decided to challenge Trimble, citing at a press conference on the eve of the critical council meeting Trimble's Washington remarks as the factor which had persuaded him to do it.

Trimble survived the meeting on 25 March. But with the 120 Orange Order members of the council backing Trimble's opponents as a block, it was a close run thing: 57 to 43 per cent among the 805 delegates present. Worse still, the Burnside motion was – albeit fairly narrowly – carried. This was a serious reverse. Not for the first time it looked to many as if this could be the beginning of the end for Trimble's leadership and his steadfast vision of a return to something approaching a normal civil society in Northern Ireland.

When British and Irish officials met the following Tuesday, 28 March, the circumstances were therefore not exactly auspicious. The NIO officials were now joined by Jonathan Powell, from Number Ten. The advantages of Powell's presence – beside the considerable experience of Northern Ireland he had built up during Mo Mowlam's term of office – were that he would match the presence in the negotiating process of Paddy Teahon from the Taioseach's Office. Secondly – in dealings directly with the Irish or, later, with Sinn Fein – Powell combined his added status as Blair's chief of staff with the fact that he was not actually a plenipotentiary minister. Just as Jeffrey and Stephens could always refrain from making a hard and fast commitment without referring back to Mandelson, so Powell could always draw a line under discussions by saying that he would have to refer back to Blair. This allowed the talks to explore all the possibilities without final commitments. Thirdly Powell was able, to some extent, to play the converse role to that he had played under Mo Mowlam. Just as he had then been at hand to allay fears of the Unionists that she leant too closely towards the republicans, so he could now present a more republican-friendly face to the Irish and Sinn Fein than they believed Mandelson had been doing.

Despite the apparent fragility of Trimble's position, Mandelson had continued to press on him the desirability of getting the institutions up and running again – not least because if they were it would be the republicans who would get the blame if decommissioning did not take place. But the Burnside motion was a big setback; the name change of the RUC, as Blair personally confirmed to Trimble a few days after the council meeting, was not up for negotiation. But it also became apparent that opposition to the Burnside motion had been mishandled at the council meeting – with one speech counterproductively personal in its attack on Burnside. This suggested that Trimble might, if the right IRA terms were ever forthcoming, be able to get it rescinded. Some relatively minor internal elections at the same meeting had resulted in victories for pro-Agreement party figures.

There was something, therefore, to play for. But time was short. Firstly there was the symbolically important decommissioning deadline of 22 May; if no progress had been made by then it would suggest that the Good Friday Agreement had failed. Secondly there was the precariousness of Trimble's position. One Unionist analysis was that the IRA were unlikely to move on arms for a year or more. Informal indications from republicans suggested that while there was a possibility that the IRA would eventually agree to dump arms, it was too soon after suspension. But Trimble told Mandelson firmly that he did not think there was more than a 'month or two' in which a deal could be done before his leadership was threatened again.

The meeting of Anglo-Irish officials therefore agreed to work for a fresh IRA statement and for a joint communiqué from the two governments which would set out how – principally – the British intended to fulfil their side of the Good Friday Agreement. Beyond this, however, it as clear that the two governments were some distance apart. The Irish, whose team now included Tim Dalton, the Permanent Secretary in the Department of Justice, appeared to accept that the IRA would have to set a date for arms disposal, and they did not rule out the possibility of a symbolic gesture on arms which could be taken by Unionists as a token of republican good faith. But they pressed hard for 'normalisation' – in other words a drastic reduction of the visible military presence, particularly in the border country of South Armagh, including the watchtowers particularly disliked by the largely nationalist population. For their part the British team referred specifically to the idea of IRA arms being put in 'verifiably secure' dumps and said that a clear statement – much clearer in other words than that on 11 February – along with a confidence building measure, would be the minimum Trimble would need to seek his party's backing for a return to devolved government. They were adamant that any normalisation would have to take account of the serious and growing threat from republican dissidents in the breakaway Continuity and Real IRA. They were adamant that there was not going to be any trade off between normalisation and the disposal of illegal arms. And they were, to put it mildly, dissatisfied by the Irish argument, derived from Martin McGuinness, that if the watchtowers were removed and the Real IRA then carried out an act of violence, public opinion would turn against the dissidents.

These issues would be batted to and fro in talks at official level over the next five weeks. The broad pattern was that the Irish were responsible for negotiations with the republicans, and the British with the Unionists, bringing their respective positions back to the inter-governmental talks. At least once, however, in mid-April, the two governments met jointly with the Sinn Fein president Gerry Adams. Although the talks were intensive and workmanlike, they were far from easy, frequently looking as though they would end in stalemate. The Irish continually sought to maximise the detail and timings with which the British would implement the Agreement, including reform of the police, criminal justice, the release of remaining prisoners, normalisation – from the dismantling of watchtowers to the return of troops to barracks going further than the Agreement itself, an amnesty on 'public interest' grounds for at least some of those still wanted for terrorist offences committed before Easter 1998. The British continually sought to minimise this agenda. But the governments quickly agreed between them the kind of formulation they would like to see from the IRA itself. In early April they anticipated that they would publish dates for British implementation of their obligations to nationalists under the Agreement and that the IRA would state publicly that their arms would be 'finally and completely put beyond use within the timeframe set out in the two governments' plans'. While the IRA statement would not say so explicitly, the British assumption was that the arms would be located in sealed dumps, on a model which had been applied as part of the settlement of the Kosovo conflict in 1999. By the third week of April Jonathan Powell had proposed that the dumps should be subject to regular inspection by 'people of international status'.

The problem was twofold, however. First, it looked increasingly as though the envisaged IRA statement would not be enough to satisfy Trimble in its present form. Trimble also wanted to see an early confidence-building measure of some kind; and secondly, at least in early April, he was seeking a joint commitment that the institutions would be suspended if the IRA failed to live up to their undertakings. But the other, converse, problem was that it would be hugely difficult to persuade the IRA even to deliver such a statement; let alone to agree to Trimble's additional demands. In theory each side had good reasons for settling; the Unionists would be back at Stormont leading the power-sharing Executive, with the republicans committed to pursue their goals by peaceful means. For their part, Sinn Fein's principal hopes of making electoral gains, in the South as well as the North, lay with recommitting themselves to exclusively political methods. The Irish government had made it clear they would not, for example, form a coalition government which included Sinn Fein unless the IRA had agreed to decommission. This was indeed one reason why the Sinn Fein leadership were so keen to see the Assembly and Executive restored – and had been so upset by its suspension. But the main leverage brought to bear by one side on the other had more to do with sticks than carrots. The British could argue that unless the republicans settled, Trimble's already fragile position would be untenable. He would be elbowed aside by some alternative leader, like Jeffrey Donaldson, who was against the Agreement. But the Irish could – and frequently did – argue that without more flexibility from the Unionists there was a real danger of a return to violence. It was a source of concern to the Irish that Mandelson tended to affect a lack of interest in such warnings; in fact he invariably checked their threat announcements against his own intelligence reports, which he always read with great care. The Irish warned the British in early April of signs of possible moves by republican critics of the Adams-McGuinness strategy to call an extraordinary meeting of the Provisionals' General Army Council with a view to changing the leadership. That might not lead to an immediate return to violence; but it might damage the prospects of a settlement every bit as seriously as Trimble's demise. Nor, it seems, was this an empty threat. The British had received separate intelligence that Brian Keenan had held a meeting with critical senior republicans shortly after suspension, which appeared to testify to a growing restiveness about the Sinn Fein political strategy. The Irish urged the British to accept that they might have to persuade the Ulster Unionists to accept terms well short of ideal, from their point of view. Trimble would have to be warned that the rest of the Agreement – including Patten and normalisation – would be implemented whether or not the Unionists agreed to a return to devolution.

There were further setbacks. Mandelson reacted angrily when in early April a senior Irish official showed documents, including the IRA draft text, and the Irish-drafted joint statements by the two governments – which had not been endorsed by the British – to Sinn Fein. This had been done in good faith, in an attempt to hasten the pace of negotiations, but Downing Street backed Mandelson, complaining forcefully that it compromised the inter-governmental talks and that they would be forced to disown the texts. Mandelson, however, considered, whether justifiably or not, that part of the

reason for the negotiating failure two weeks before suspension had
been that the Irish had closeted themselves with the republicans in
order to thrash out a new IRA text without sufficient reference to
the British on the subject of what the Unionists might take. He
feared they might be about to do the same. He also resented what
he saw – despite Bertie Ahern's crucially cordial and productive
relationship with Tony Blair – as a tendency of the Irish to be less
arms length in their negotiations with Sinn Fein than the British
government were in their equivalent relationship with the Unionists.

But gradually, as April wore on, the differences, while still deep,
began to narrow. The idea of the IRA committing themselves to a
date for decommissioning remained elusive; when Adams met
officials of the two governments he raised a significant objection
to the idea of it happening within the 'timeframe set out in the
government's plans'. After all, London might commit itself to completing the Patten legislation by the year 2000, and setting up the
new recruitment process, designed to attract more Catholics, by the
year 2001. But the composition of the police would not have begun
truly to reflect that of the wider community for another ten years.
The implication was that if the British were so keen on the IRA
naming a date for decommissioning, ten years would be as logical as
any. And while Adams did hold out just a possibility of a confidence
building measure, he gave no encouragement to the governments
that an advance promise of it could be included in the IRA statement. By contrast, Mandelson continued to insist that Trimble
would not be able to return to his council without such a confidence
building measure being clearly in prospect.

By the end of April, the time for what Mandelson had called back
in March 'the high pressure deployment' of the two prime ministers
had clearly arrived. After Adams and McGuinness met Blair, first
at Chequers on the May Day weekend, and then at Downing Street
the following Tuesday, to reassure themselves that the Prime Minister backed the terms set out by Mandelson and his officials, the
bones of a deal began to fall into place. By the time Blair,
Mandelson, Powell and Jeffrey met the four leading pro-Agreement
Unionists, Trimble, John Taylor, Sir Reg Empey, and Ken Maginnis,
for dinner at Downing Street on the Tuesday evening, it was clear
that the IRA were ready to produce a clear public statement which

went much further than the draft 'leadership position' of 11 February. There would be no specific date for decommissioning. But there would be a confidence building measure, and even more crucially, the IRA's commitment to put arms 'verifiably beyond use' would be no longer linked to removing 'the causes of conflict' (which might mean the end of partition), but to the full implementation of the Good Friday Agreement. Nevertheless, although the mood of the meeting was good-humoured, the UUP members raised a number of concerns. Trimble made the point that while there might not be a set date for decommissioning, it would need to become apparent over time when decommissioning was going to be completed. Sir Reg Empey raised a sharp question; in relation to the confidence building measure, what guarantees would there be that the weapons could not be taken out by the IRA and simply put back for the inspections? (That question would not be answered in the public statements; it was understood between the parties that the dumps would be sealed. The task of ensuring that they were would be entrusted to the two international figures by now earmarked for the job of inspection, Cyril Ramaphosa, the former Secretary-General of the ANC, and Martti Ahtisaari, the former Finnish president.) The Unionists were also insistent that the confidence building measure must be explicitly pledged in the IRA statement, and that the weapons dumped must include significant amounts of explosive, including Semtex and detonators. The UUP team also argued that the British must retain the right to suspend the Executive again in the event of the IRA failing to fulfil its pledges on arms. In fact it was already becoming clear that in the event of default, the first step would be a review provided for in the Agreement. But Mandelson pointed out that the legislation which allowed suspension would not be repealed. The government, he added, had at hand implicit leverage on the IRA to fulfil its side of the bargain. At present it was the release of prisoners; in the future, he suggested, it would be normalisation which the IRA would have to earn by their actions.

The Unionists left Downing Street reasonably reassured. But it would still be far from plain sailing. On 4 May, as Bertie Ahern and Tony Blair prepared to fly to Belfast to close the deal, the Ulster Unionist politician Chris McGimpsey announced that he had taken receipt of a leaked document which was bound to alarm Unionists and cast an unwelcome light on the lack of rapport between Mandelson and Cowen. Part of an account by a civil servant of a dinner meeting on 14 April at which the two ministers had discussed the neuralgic issue of the RUC name and cap badge, the document recorded Cowen as saying that 'beyond the constitutional acceptance that Northern Ireland remained part of the United Kingdom, there should be no further evidence of Britishness in the governance of Northern Ireland. It was an argument presented with all the subtlety and open-mindedness that one expect from a member of Sinn Fein . . . It underlined the view which I know the Secretary of State holds, that Cowen has no feeling for, or understanding of, Unionist concerns and can usually be reliably counted on to tack to the green at every opportunity'.

But while the leak was widely reported as 'overshadowing' the talks in Belfast the following day, the issues of substance were rather more central. When at the end of a long day's intensive negotiations between Blair, Ahern and the parties at Hillsborough, the final IRA text was produced, Mandelson handed it to Trimble whose immediate reaction was one of sharp disappointment. After reading it quickly, Trimble, who was with his negotiating team, turned to Mandelson and said: 'You've been conned'. At this point, in an effort to prevent a clearly edgy Trimble from prevaricating in the hope that he could secure more still from the IRA, he reacted as harshly as he had in any encounter with the UUP leader. 'Don't accuse me of selling you out,' he retorted. 'I've done my best. It's difficult to know what Secretary of State could do more. This is the best IRA statement you are ever likely to get, and if you don't like it you can throw it in the waste basket.' He then suggested they ponder on this and exited the room with Bill Jeffrey and his private secretary Nick Perry, leaving Trimble with his delegation, but saying he would return.

By the time Mandelson returned twenty-five minutes later, Trimble's mood was much more reflective. For one thing, he had been listening to John Taylor. Taylor had long played a pivotal role. It had been his November statement on arms which had forced Trimble to make his ill-fated resignation threat at the Ulster Unionist Council meeting which had then agreed to devolution. And he would soon be causing considerable trouble over this one. But it had been Taylor's nod which had famously given Trimble the confidence to accept the Good Friday Agreement two years earlier. And on this evening at Hillsborough he did much to persuade Trimble how important an advance the IRA had made. For the ten paragraph statement did indeed break new ground. It did not name a date for decommissioning. It did not proclaim 'that the war is over'. Nor was it at all free of ambiguous Provo-speak. But it said that the cease-fire was the IRA's contribution 'to the creation of a future in which the causes of conflict are resolved by peaceful means'. It envisaged that in the context of 'the full implementation by the two governments, especially the British government, of what they have agreed . . . the IRA will initiate a process that will completely and verifiably put arms beyond use'. It promised that its arms remained silent and secure 'to facilitate the speedy and full implementation of the Good Friday Agreement'. And for the first time it explicitly promised a 'confidence building measure' in which 'a number of our arms dumps' could be inspected regularly to ensure that the weapons remained secure.

Creative ambiguity had been a watchword of the peace process since its outset. And while the new IRA statement might be more creative and less ambiguous than previous ones, it clearly retained both elements. But this was surely a genuine turning point. As the unionist academic Arthur Aughey would write the following day: 'There is a sense that movement is at last taking place . . . If there is a hidden agenda to the Agreement it may not be the conspiracy many Unionists fear. It may be the one which Martin McGuinness allegedly told the British government at the beginning of the peace process. The IRA's war is over. How can it most effectively be brought to an end?'[8]

Trimble was not yet quite ready finally to gamble on that interpretation. He now started to press for amendments to the IRA statement – something which Mandelson told him firmly but calmly was a non-starter. This Trimble accepted. But he turned to the issue of the Patten report. In another three hours of talks he pressed vainly for a hard and fast concession on the name of the new police force, the most that he could secure was further talks – including between the Irish and British governments – on how to resolve the policing issue in a way that could get Trimble round the Burnside motion passed at the last council meeting. The British promised to help him – but without saying how.

Almost universally, the headlines proclaimed the press' view the following day, in London as in Dublin, that this was indeed the big, and long awaited, breakthrough. The two governments followed up with a joint letter to the Northern Ireland parties promising the release of all paramilitary prisoners by 28 July, the legislative enactment of the Patten report by November 2000 and the operation of a new policing board by 2001. And the British promised 'as early a return as possible to normal security arrangements in Northern Ireland consistent with the level of threat'.

The question, however, was whether it would be equally be accepted as a breakthrough by the Ulster Unionist Council. On Monday 8 May, Mandelson told the Commons that he now felt 'hopeful and confident that the ultimate prize – stable, inclusive government in Northern Ireland and an unbreakable peace – will at long last be within our grasp'.[9] But while Trimble welcomed the 'positive elements' of the IRA's statement he made it clear he would not sell the deal to his party without clarification of its ambiguities. As a tactic, this no doubt had the advantage of not dangerously isolating the UUP leadership from the many sceptics in its own ranks. But it had the disadvantage of checking the momentum towards the resumption of devolution which the two governments had hoped would follow the IRA statement.

Although they were by no means Trimble's only problems, the most high profile were, as ever, symbolic. The first was the question of flags. During the brief period of devolution the two Sinn Fein ministers had refused to fly the Union flag over their departments on days when it had been traditional for the United Kingdom government to do so. Baffling though the issue might be in mainland Britain, it went to the heart of a conflict between the principles enshrined in the Good Friday Agreement. For Unionists, the flying of the British flag was a symbol of consent, the principle that Northern Ireland was part of the United Kingdom until a majority of its people decided otherwise. But for republicans the right not to fly it, or as a minimum to fly both flags at the same time, was a symbol of the 'parity of esteem' supposed to apply to both communities. In a modest concession to the Unionists, Mandelson now proposed to issue an order which would allow him to give a ruling on flags if the Executive could not agree a solution among themselves.

The policing issue, and in particular Unionist demands that the name of the RUC be preserved, was more complex still. Mandelson's initial instinct, relayed privately to Blair back in December, had been firmly in favour of implementing the Patten recommendations on policing in full, with the sole exception of a stipulation that the new oath – which replaced the old one to the Crown and included a commitment to equal rights – should apply only to new officers. Mandelson had originally intended to face down Unionist hostility and enact almost all its most contentious aspects. And in January, although he indicated that he was reserving judgement on some other sensitive issues, his statement provoked fury from Unionists. By the time the bill came to be published on 16 May it included several detailed qualifications which were not in Patten's original report, thus provoking fierce nationalist charges that the Patten report was being watered down, or tempered, by allowing many more discretionary powers to the Secretary of State or Chief Constable than had been expected. Taken separately each of the alterations could no doubt be justified, for example: to allow district police partnership boards to levy 3p in the pound for extra policing services had given rise to widespread fears that they might engage 'paramilitaries on the rates'; the unitary, partly-elected police board envisaged by Patten might, if given unfettered power to conduct enquiries into the force, do so for nakedly partisan reasons; and to allow former convicted terrorists to be co-opted as non-elected members of the police boards could cause real anguish in both communities. But taken together they amounted to a critical mass bound to upset nationalists.

This had been only partly a matter of Mandelsonian tactics and timing. His main motive was a policing one; he was determined not to shackle the new service, as he saw it, by going too far in the changes he was announcing. But in a climate in which one community's pain is all too often seen as the other community's gain, every protest from republicans would also act as a reassurance to the Unionists that Patten would not be as bad for them as they thought. When on 21 May, Gerry Adams told a commemoration for a volunteer killed by a plastic bullet that there was 'no way' he could recommend to nationalists or republicans joining a police service 'as described in that legislation',[10] it was not unhelpful to Trimble in his attempts to win over doubters in his own ranks the following weekend. It was all too the easy to imagine the effect on the wavering Unionists if he had said the bill made the police service fit for ex-IRA men to join. That did not mean that police reform could be treated merely as a lever with which to influence the various parties. Creating a police service which could appeal to Catholic recruits as strongly as to Protestant ones was integral to the peace process. But a bill was a bill. With an Ulster Unionist decision out of the way, it could be amended to meet at least some of the nationalist complaints as it passed through the Commons – including by the government itself.

Not that the Unionists were yet satisfied. Trimble continued to press hard for a further concession on the name. Indeed he continued for more than a week after the talks at Hillsborough to call for concessions of various kinds when the two governments would have preferred to see him using every public platform to 'sell' the new breakthrough to Unionist opinion. Originally a meeting of the Ulster Unionist Council had been pencilled in for 20 May. But that was deferred amid hints that if the Unionists could not be satisfied on their worries over Patten, and their desire for further clarification on the IRA's intentions on decommissioning, they might not call a council meeting at all.

When Mandelson met Trimble and his closest advisers in Belfast on 16 May, the prospects looked bleak. In the absence of a clear lead from Trimble, Unionist opposition to restarting the Assembly was mounting. It was far from certain that he would be able to win over his party, even with the concessions he wanted. Trimble himself was in a pessimistic and complaining mood. The policing bill had been published, and the government had deferred the issue of the name by not including one in the bill. That, Trimble grumbled, would annoy nationalists without helping Unionists. It was no good Mandelson simply giving reassurances about his intentions to find a way round the problem; such assurances were 'devalued currency'. Some way of incorporating the RUC into the statute was what was needed. On decommissioning, he had had a far from reassuring meeting with Ahtisaari and Ramaphosa; they too were unclear about the precise meaning of the IRA statement. What proportion of arms would be located in the dumps as part of the confidence building measure? The widely drawn inference had been all of them; but actually it could be as little as 20 per cent. Trimble had expected that the IRA statement would have had a much bigger impact on public opinion than it had done. There were too many ambiguities. If the confidence building measures were not enacted by October it could lead to another crisis in his party, with its annual conference due, not to mention the looming South Antrim by-election where the UUP was facing a strong challenge from the anti-Agreement DUP.

Although Mandelson treated the meeting as largely a listening exercise, he intervened sharply when Trimble complained that there was 'growing suspicion' that the government had promised Sinn Fein and the Irish that they would never suspend the institutions again. Had McGuinness and Adams not spent over eight hours at Chequers the weekend before the Hillsborough talks? Trimble asked. Did this not mean that the deal had been done before Blair had taken the Unionists through his negotiating objectives? Mandelson said this was nonsense. Neither Sinn Fein nor the Irish had even asked for such an assurance, let alone been given one. And Blair's meeting with the Sinn Fein leaders had been much shorter than Trimble suggested. Nor had it been decisive.

Trimble had now – at last – persuaded his executive to call a council meeting for 27 May. But he had only been able to do this by appealing to the personal loyalty of his colleagues. As it was, the decision had been carried by the unusually narrow majority of 8 to 5. While the anti-Agreement forces in the party were intensifying their campaign, Trimble told Mandelson, he himself had 'nothing to campaign with'. The previously supportive mood in the golf clubs, a reliable indicator of the feelings of middle-class Unionists, was now turning negative. John Taylor, who had by now been expressing grave doubts about what was on offer was again setting out for foreign parts – this time Taiwan and Japan. He would be able to sabotage the whole project with one parting shot if he chose – and he would be particularly influential on David Burnside, the author of the RUC motion at the last council meeting. Most ominously of all, Trimble added that while not recommending the deal to the Ulster Unionist Council would be a bad outcome, it might not be as bad as recommending it and losing the vote.

Mandelson and Trimble had been here before, of course. The whole situation, complete with Taylor's central role, had resonances from November. But even though the new IRA statement put Trimble on altogether firmer ground, Mandelson moved to shore up Trimble's resolve. He undertook to meet Taylor in the Commons that evening to urge him to revert to his original backing for a deal. He handed Trimble a letter seeking to reassure him on a number of points – including a promise that the final releases of prisoners by 28 July would only proceed if the cease-fires were maintained. (When in early June the murder of Edmund McCoy in Dunmurry was suspected to be the work of the IRA, Mandelson warned that if this proved to be the case it could have a direct impact on prisoner releases.) He pointed out that the decommissioning process would have to have the approval of General de Chastelain. And on the extremely fraught issue of the police cap badge he also confirmed a concession. Patten had proposed that the force's badge, hitherto composed of a harp, a crown and shamrocks, should be 'entirely free from any association with either the British or Irish states'. Mandelson said that he would now allow the new cross-community police board to design a new badge, again reserving the right to intervene if its members could not agree. And on the name, he repeated that in view of the 'strong case' made by Trimble over the need to demonstrate that – as Patten had himself insisted – the RUC was not being disbanded, he would seek to 'find ways of retaining an honourable and permanent place for the RUC name, consistent with implementing the reform proposals of the Patten report'.[11]

Over the next few days, Trimble, to the intense relief of both governments, determined at last to campaign vigorously for a yes vote. Meanwhile Mandelson argued in favour of government backing for an amendment to the bill, to be announced before the Ulster Unionist Council meeting, which would both lay down that the new name for the force would be the Police Service of Northern Ireland and that 'Royal Ulster Constabulary' should be incorporated into the 'title deeds' of the new force to show that the RUC was not being disbanded. (There was a familiar commercial parallel for such a compromise: the *Daily Telegraph* 'incorporated' the *Morning*

*Post*, for example but no one used the old title in common parlance.) Mandelson went as far as he could in hinting at such a change in the Commons on 24 May.[12] Downing Street were reluctant to make an announcement before the council meeting. The issue was a matter of intensive argument between London and Dublin in the three weeks between the Hillsborough talks and the Ulster Unionist Council meeting, and was discussed directly between Bill Clinton and Tony Blair in a telephone call. Although the President was initially very sympathetic to Irish resistance to the 'title deeds' idea, the British would later insist that his stance had softened after Blair explained it to him. He would not support it publicly, but he would not oppose it either. And this was more or less the stance adopted by Chris Patten himself, when Mandelson consulted him on the proposal. The government gave the continually-pivotal John Taylor its assurances that it would back such an amendment after the council meeting, and he reciprocated by guaranteeing his support for a yes vote.[13]

Mandelson took one more step before the council meeting. In a lengthy article for the *Belfast Telegraph* he used all the arguments he could marshal to persuade Unionists to take another leap forward. Seeking to expose the poverty of the anti-Agreement case he recalled how, listening to the radio the previous weekend, he had been 'jolted' by Ian Paisley's remark that if the IRA did not surrender their arms, they must be 'taken from them'. He asked: 'In what way would we go in pursuit of arms, most of which are not in our jurisdiction, with what sort of force and with what consequence for a return to the conflict? The IRA has not surrendered. I believe it will, in the right conditions, fade and wither away.' The principle of consent had been won; so, now, had a commitment to non-violence and the complete and verifiable putting of weapons beyond use. He added that while the legitimacy of 'nationalist culture and traditions' had to be recognised 'there is only one sovereignty, British sovereignty, while a majority wishes this . . . the Union flag flies here, alone, not with the Irish tricolour'. With a nod to the exploitation by anti-Agreement Unionists of the Cowen leak, Mandelson said: 'I reject utterly . . . the conclusion that bit by bit, Britishness is being dismantled.' He pointed out that there were no plans in the criminal justice review to take the word royal out of the Royal Courts of Justice, and added the royal family's close connection and interest in Northern Ireland 'will be not only sustained but enhanced in line with what I know to be the Queen's wishes'.

Finally, inside this glove of royal velvet, there was just a hint of the iron fist noted by the *Magill* writers back in February. He was careful not to threaten joint-sovereignty between London and Dublin, or some other government-imposed settlement in the event of a no vote. But he did say that while, if the answer was 'no', he would 'try and defend to the hilt' all the principles and safeguards won by Unionists in the Agreement adding 'my task will be made infinitely harder if the anti-Agreement forces prevail. Those of us who believe the union has great strengths . . . will be made weaker'. By contrast, if there was a yes vote, 'Unionists . . . would be able to control their own destiny because they will be in power.'[14] It did not take much imagination to read this as a stark warning that the alternative to a yes vote was the relentless progress of the least palatable parts of the Agreement for Unionists, and their loss of influence over implementation because they would not be in office.

In the end, the need to confront such an alternative did not arise. With Taylor's backing, Trimble won the day at Belfast's Waterfront Hall on 27 May, outmanoeuvring his chief opponent Jeffrey Donaldson, and, speaking both first and last, saving his most persuasive arguments for the last three minutes before the vote was taken.[15] The vote – by 53 to 47 per cent – was once again worryingly close, prompting the *Independent*'s David McKittrick to reflect that the 'the position of Mr Trimble and thus of the peace process is going to be a permanently edgy one, with the UUP leader forced to take one day at a time, forever on the look out for menace'. Nevertheless, he added, a win was still a win, and the fact remained that while none of the 459 Unionists who voted yes could have any sense of warmth for Martin McGuinness, 'that flinty icon of armed republican insurrection', they had all voted – without the promise of immediate IRA arms decommissioning – for his return to government. However numerous the diehards, there had still been a majority to put 'their doubts to the side and put the past behind them'.[16]

Mandelson scarcely needed reminding just how edgy the process was going to be. Within hours of the Ulster Unionist Council vote, and after he had signed the order to restore the devolved institutions from midnight the following night, he took a call at Hillsborough from the 'flinty icon' himself who was in a far from celebratory mood. McGuinness was furious at the pledges which Taylor had apparently secured on the name of the RUC and shouted down the telephone at Mandelson that he had 'destroyed any chance' of an early gesture on arms. When Mandelson protested that Taylor had been promised nothing that had not already been foreshadowed, McGuinness retorted: 'I tell you, if you do what you've already said you're doing there won't be any confidence building measure.' Vainly, Mandelson urged him to 'reflect a little on what you're saying'. The conversation ended with Mandelson indicating there was little point in talking further with McGuinness in this mood, that he was going out to walk his dog.

McGuinness's call was indeed an indicator of the formidable problems that lay ahead. The arguments over the Patten report – not only with Sinn Fein but with an equally upset Seamus Mallon – would last into the autumn. Nevertheless, while the Ulster Unionist vote was by no means a sufficient condition of permanent political normality in Northern Ireland it was an absolutely necessary one. A no vote might have extinguished the last hopes of devolution – and with it so many of the hopes vested in the Good Friday Agreement – for a generation. After all the heartaches of the past two years, the peace process was once again back on track. In public even McGuinness acknowledged this – saying tersely that the Ulster Unionists had made 'the right decision'. Mandelson was equally brief. It had, he said, been 'a good day for Northern Ireland'.

At the Hillsborough talks in early May, Gerry Adams had made a minor but unusual request of Mandelson. Could he have, as a memento of the talks, the modest clock on the wall of the ground floor conference room which had been used as a base by the Sinn Fein delegation? The clock, an English replica dating from around 1920 was from S. D. Neil, the well-known Belfast makers; but worth £150 at present prices, it was not especially valuable. Nevertheless Mandelson was uneasy. It was, as he pointed out to Adams, the property of the British state. Adams was pressing; if everything went according to plan surely Mandelson could see his way to transferring the clock? Still far from certain that everything *would* go to according to plan, since that meant Unionist assent and the IRA actually producing its confidence building measure, Mandelson promised somewhat reluctantly to consider it in that happy event, and thought little more about it.

Until that is, he got a message on the last weekend of June, when Bill Jeffrey telephoned him to say that Adams had asked him to pass on a message. It was, the Sinn Fein President had said, time to 'start wrapping the clock'. The import was clear, unexpected in its timing – and momentous. For the first time in its long and bloody history the IRA had agreed to expose arms to inspection. It would swiftly emerge that Ramaphosa and Ahtisaari had been allowed to see substantial dumps of weaponry and would now report that the Provisionals had kept to their side of the bargain. This was the 'gesture' which Trimble had been seeking before the general election; it was a concession, however symbolic, which many observers had thought would never happen. Above all it created some space in which the roots of the devolved institutions could be strengthened.

Devolution had itself naturally been a source of satisfaction to the Northern Ireland Secretary. But as long as the IRA failed to fulfil its side of the Hillsborough bargain, it remained dangerously fragile. Formidable problems still remained, starting with the continuing dispute over the policing bill and the spate of loyalist violence in protest at the banning of the Orange marchers at Drumcree from passing through the nationalist Garvaghy Road. But it significantly bolstered Trimble against his ubiquitous hard-line critics. It was hardly surprising that Mandelson could scarcely contain his jubilation – and he swiftly instructed his officials to find a means of seeing that Adams took delivery of the clock.

For the IRA gesture was also a symbol of another kind – marking a further staging post in what by any standards was one of the most remarkable political comebacks of modern times. Mandelson was never going to be loved in Northern Ireland as Mo Mowlam had been. Much of the Belfast press corps viewed him, especially after the suspension of the institutions, with deep suspicion. A lengthy and savage piece in the May issue of *Magill* by the *Economist*'s Northern Ireland correspondent Fionnuala O'Connor – strongly reminiscent of some of the coverage he had received in London through much of 1998 – dwelt on his reputation for 'knifing' colleagues, complained of the 'the thread of self-promotion which runs through his frequent off-the-record briefings of journalists' and suggested that in contrast to the 'whispering campaign' against Mo Mowlam, Downing Street would not blame Mandelson whether or not he 'he left Northern Ireland in a better state than he found it'. By contrast, other journalists such as Mary Holland, his old colleague from LWT days, now a highly-respected *Observer* correspondent and *Irish Times* columnist, remained a warm admirer of the professionalism with which he handled the complexities of the job. Certainly he had at one time or another upset politicians in almost every party. But that came with the territory. Even his fiercest critics were forced to respect his skill. Despite the many remaining difficulties, it was impossible to argue by July that Northern Ireland was not politically in a 'better state than he found it'. Blair himself believed strongly that devolution would not have happened without Mandelson and that his ability to handle not only Trimble but Adams had been exceptional. His old adversary Gordon Brown had even paid him a gracious compliment, saying that he admired the way he had, as the Chancellor put it, 'boxed in the IRA and made a statesman of Trimble'.

Indeed Mandelson's comeback had been mould-breaking in two ways: by happening so quickly and by being, as it looked in mid July, a tangible, if still fragile, success. An instructive comparison was with Cecil Parkinson, who had been almost as favoured a lieutenant of Margaret Thatcher's as Mandelson had been of Blair's, and who was also brought back to the Cabinet after disgrace and exile. Parkinson had had to wait longer because of Margaret Thatcher's view that only after having been endorsed by the voters in his own constituency in a general election would he be sufficiently rehabilitated to return to office. Even then, he never fully recovered.

The first explanation, at least for the speed of Mandelson's return, was luck. Blair did not see the interval imposed on Parkinson by Mrs Thatcher as a precedent. But Mandelson was lucky that Frank Dobson eventually decided to run for the London mayoralty, ensuring that there would have to be quite a wide-ranging reshuffle in October 1999. And he was lucky that after months of anxiety and a damaging and hostile report by the Registrar of Members' Interests, he had escaped so lightly from a parliamentary enquiry into his home loan. Partly under the influence of two of its more independent-minded members, Labour's Dale Campbell-Savours and the right-wing Conservative Eric Forth, who believed that Filkin had exceeded her remit by enquiring into the details of the Britannia mortgage application, Mandelson was let off with a reprimand.

But the second, and most important factor was the notable friendship shown him by the Prime Minister. Blair had, it became increasingly clear, actively encouraged Mandelson to resign. But that Blair brought him back so speedily was also a testament to the loyalty which the Prime Minister felt for his friend. To understand that loyalty, however, it is important to understand that Mandelson had also demonstrated, from 1994 onwards, that he gave him disinterested advice and that he shared, to an exceptional degree, Blair's ideological outlook.

After Mandelson's fall, Philip Stephens, political columnist for the *Financial Times* wrote, 'The Prime Minister has lost from his cabinet not just a close friend but the most remarkable political strategist of his generation. Plenty of others now march under the banner of Mr Blair's twin projects to modernise his party and remake the landscape of British politics. Most do so from a sense of duty or self-interest. But like Mr Blair (and only a few others) Mr Mandelson has New Labour in his soul.'[17]

This is surely correct. He did not, whatever the myth, invent Labour's modernisation. When he went to Walworth Road in 1985 Neil Kinnock had already started to make the intellectual leap that so many of his colleagues had failed to make in realising that Labour was losing elections because of failures by the party and not the voters. But Mandelson had an honoured place on Labour's long march to electability, as one of the three big figures who founded New Labour. He was the junior partner in this trio, but he also represented the continuity from the dark days of the mid 1980s to the moment when he helped, as campaign manager, to deliver an election victory greater than his grandfather had helped to produce for Attlee in 1945, and for which he had worked pretty well unceasingly for twelve years. And he continued to be Blair's most unflinching outrider in government, on Europe, on electoral reform, on relations with the Liberal Democrats, and on relations with business.

Peter Mandelson was of course ambitious. What politician is not? In Mandelson's case this trait was admittedly unusual, nurtured as it was by his upbringing in the shadow of that same grandfather, with whom he shared some uncannily similar characteristics. As his grandson went through the Young Communist League, so Herbert Morrison had his youthful fling with Marxism-Leninism in the Social Democratic Federation. Herbert Morrison was also an assiduous cultivator of journalists, a moderniser who recognised that the Labour Party could not always depend on class solidarity, a scourge of the left, the proud progenitor of the Dome of his day, the 1951 Festival of Britain, and even, like his grandson, an accomplished dancer. There is a dispute over whether it was about Morrison, as Patrick Gordon Walker said in the seventies, that someone commented to Ernie Bevin that 'he's his own worst enemy', and Bevin memorably replied, 'Not while I'm alive, he ain't.' But it could be said as much of the grandson as of the grandfather. Peter Mandelson can be funny, self-deprecating, kind, unaffectedly courteous, affectionate, and steadfastly loyal. He can also be reckless, arrogant, volatile, manipulative and a bearer of grudges, if not permanently, at least for long periods.

But the ambition, fierce as it is, is of a particular kind. In politics anything is possible; nothing, even a Mandelson premiership, could be ruled out absolutely. But despite the legend woven by some of his most ardent detractors there is no evidence that Peter Mandelson's career was built from the beginning, as it is for many politicians, on the burning desire to reach the very top. The evidence that he did not expect to be prime minister goes wider than his frequent protestations to that effect. Despite his reconnection with the party during the first nine months of 1999, he had not spent a lifetime courting it in a way that laid reliable foundations for a leadership campaign. His legendary electoral skills had given him a constituency in the wider party. His firmly pro-European stance gave him appreciable support in the unions. But the process needed to fulfil Tim Allan's remark, made in 1995, that Blair believed the Labour Party would have really changed when it learned to love Peter Mandelson, was not, and perhaps never would be, complete. Moreover, he had attached himself to other leaders, first Kinnock, then Brown, then Brown and Blair, and finally Blair with more single-minded loyalty than would be natural in a man who saw himself as a future leader. He became, in the words of his friend Robert Harris, 'the most superb, efficient and capable staff officer you'll ever come across ... If he says he'll meet you at a certain time he will. If he promises you that something will be done, it is. His usefulness to a party leader is his political intelligence and his courage. He's cool under fire and he's willing to take risks.' In the case of Blair, moreover, his mission was to protect and advance the leader's interests. It was small wonder that Blair wanted him for himself to 'be Peter' for so long, or that the Prime Minister continued regularly to consult him in early morning telephone calls after he had resigned.

There is little evidence, moreover, for a more modest version of the myth, that he sought to replace Gordon Brown as chancellor, whether Brown's fretful allies and lieutenants had believed it or not. Mandelson appeared to think he would be no good at the job, and he was surely right. For all their long years of deep dysfunctionality, he could see that Brown's tireless intellect, his ability to marry fiscal and monetary prudence with his redistributive instincts, and his ability to read the economy right when others foresaw recession in 1998, made the Chancellor's an awesomely hard act to follow. Since Oxford, after all, his one declared ambition had been to succeed in the one job that his grandfather had demonstrably failed at – that of Foreign Secretary.

In that sense he had not been a classic 'greasy pole' politician. If he had been, he would surely not, from the time he was at Walworth Road, have made so many enemies or have become the lightning rod, at least in his first year as a minister, for discontent within his party and outside it. That had been extraordinarily useful not only to the party but to its leader. According to his close colleague Margaret McDonagh, now general secretary of the party, 'He would not, during the [1997] general election, fall into the trap of asking himself, "If I take this decision, where does this leave me? Am I vulnerable? Is someone going to stab me in the back? Aren't I going to get to X if I do that?" He accepted blame, he accepted responsibility.' This was one of the reasons why he had once again, in the autumn of 1999, been designated, with Gordon Brown, to manage the next general election campaign. Despite his duties in Belfast, he continued to attend all the key political meetings he could – apart from the daily 8 a.m. sessions at which Gordon Brown and Alastair Campbell planned day-to-day government presentation. In the strategic argument which rumbled through the early summer between keeping the 'big tent' of support for the government and identifying opponents – like Oxford and Cambridge, which Gordon Brown excoriated in May for discrimination against state school pupils, he reinforced Blair's preference for the former. He inspired the move of Lance Price, Campbell's deputy, and Pat McFadden, Jonathan Powell's deputy, from Downing Street to Millbank to strengthen the Labour HQ's campaigning edge. This was part of what he described in a message to Blair in May as helping to fulfil the need to 'move up a gear and to go onto a clearer election footing' (without unduly exciting premature election fever) in the wake of a series of policy initiatives by William Hague which, he lamented, had caught the government 'unawares'.

A secondary consequence of his resignation – itself a notable stroke of luck – was that in losing office he also lost responsibility for the Dome. He had bemoaned that loss when he stood down. But there is little doubt that all the steadfastly mounting criticism that was made of the project after its launch, would have been visited personally upon him had he stayed. The larger point was that he had preserved a much greater share of his political capital by a swift resignation than if he had allowed it to ebb away by fighting his nemesis.

But he had also replenished it through his ten months of exile. He had done as Blair had proposed. He had sold his house, he had devoted energy to rebuilding his relationship with the party. He had demonstrated, principally on Europe, that he could take Blair's advice to show he was a conviction politician 'freed to do and say what you believe in'. After returning to the Cabinet, he continued, in a growing alliance with Robin Cook and his successor at the DTI, Stephen Byers, to promote the cause of British entry into the single currency. In particular he believed strongly that the government could not go into the next election without seeking to make a virtue of its support 'in principle' of entry. This brought him, yet again, into conflict with Gordon Brown who was strongly of the opposite view, that to allow the Euro to become the dominant issue of the election could only damage Labour's fortunes among a still sceptical electorate – and undermine the government's capacity to campaign on its economic record. When Mandelson declared in Belfast that jobs were bound to be at risk from a volatile sterling exchange rate as long as it stayed out of the Euro, Brown angrily insisted that any future speeches on the subject by Mandelson would have to be cleared with him. But that would not stop Mandelson continuing to advise Blair that silence on the Euro would be more damaging to Labour than a willingness to challenge head-on William Hague's decision to rule out Euro entry for the next parliament.

Sticking to the opposite view, Brown had argued strongly during 1999 against Blair chairing the launch of the business-led 'Britain in Europe' campaign. That Blair did so, and then in the late spring of 2000 went further by allowing BiE's organisers to campaign openly in support of British entry into the Euro, was in a sense a victory for Mandelson, and the grandees – such as Lord Jenkins, Michael Heseltine, and Ken Clarke – whom he mobilised in support of Blair's engagement.

But the argument complicated the already complex relationship with Brown. On the one hand they were widely – and not inaccurately – depicted as having been in a state of chronic enmity over how to handle the Euro issue in the run-up to the election. Mandelson wanted the Prime Minister to give more expression to his own strong support for that principle, and for a date to be set – probably October 2002 – by which the necessary assessments of the economics of entry would be made. Brown was opposed to both suggestions. On the other hand Chancellor and Northern Ireland Secretary talked with some frequency, and by all accounts candidly, not only about the plans for the coming election but a wide range of subjects. Having first done so in January 1998, Mandelson again, not once, but twice, after coming back into the Cabinet, insisted to the Chancellor personally that he would support Brown in the leadership contest which would eventually follow Blair's standing down – whenever that should prove to be.

There was also a deep irony in the widespread belief that it had been one of Brown's allies – though certainly not the Chancellor himself – who had undone Mandelson by revealing his home loan in 1998. The leak was assumed to be malevolent, and at the time it seemed an unqualified catastrophe for Mandelson. Yet perhaps it had also been Mandelson's greatest stroke of luck. It could hardly have remained secret for ever. Mandelson might have continued to labour anxiously under the incubus of the home loan – perhaps for several years – only for it to be revealed at a time and in circumstances in which it was impossible for him to recover. Instead it allowed him to resume the backbench apprenticeship which had been prematurely brought to an end by John Smith's death and Blair's accession. Above all, his fall had happened under a leader who wanted to bring him back and was strong enough to do so.

That said, Mandelson's startling and unprecedented recovery was not only a function of luck. For this courageous, talented – and frequently infuriating – man had taken his rehabilitation with the same seriousness as he takes everything else in politics. There were signs that after months of exile and then grappling with Northern Ireland, he was more fulfilled than he had ever been. The job was the most professionally challenging of his career; and he had grown increasingly happy in his personal life. What his post-election future held was far from certain – and entirely up to Blair. While there was little doubt that the Foreign Office was the ultimate goal, it was equally probable that he would also relish a major domestic ministry like the Department of the Environment, Transport and the Regions. Whatever job he was given, it was clear that Europe, the issue on which Mandelson's personal convictions were strongest, would unavoidably dominate the next parliament. He could of course still implode, the victim of another misjudgement, political or personal. But provided he is able to treat his colleagues with restraint that now seems less likely.

As Mandelson surveyed the green, undulating landscape of County Down from Hillsborough Castle, his own future seemed brighter than would have been thinkable a year earlier. Having had his second chance, he showed every sign of seeking to make the most of it.

# Notes

PROLOGUE
1. Eoghan Harris, Irish *Sunday Times*, 16 April 2000.
2. Private information. But see Irish *Sunday Times*, 5 December 1999.
3. Hugo Young, *Guardian*, 24 December 1998.
4. *Evening Standard*, 4 January 1999.

CHAPTER ONE – *Osmold Smish*
1. Bernard Donoughue and G.W. Jones, *Herbert Morrison*, p. 521.
2. Beatrice Webb, *Diary*, 17 January 1932.
3. Donoughue and Jones, op. cit, p. 173.
4. Ibid., p. 520.
5. *Jewish Chronicle*, 23 May 1997.
6. Private information.
7. Interview, Dick Wrathall.
8. *Big Issue*, 8 December 1997.
9. Interview, Miles Mandelson.
10. Oliver James interview, *The Chair*, BBC2 1997.
11. Ibid.
12. Leo Abse, *The Man Behind the Smile*.
13. David Aaronovitch, *Independent on Sunday*, 2 March 1996.

CHAPTER TWO – *An Incredible Anorak*
1. Interview, Steve Howell.
2. Interview, Keren Abse.
3. Susan Crosland, *Tony Crosland*, p. 148.
4. *Independent on Sunday*, 4 December 1996.

CHAPTER THREE – *A Bourgeois At Heart*
1. Roy Hattersley, *Mail on Sunday*, 27 September 1995.
2. Interview, Dick Newby.
3. *Cherwell*, 8 November 1973.
4. *Cherwell*, 15 November 1973.
5. Interview, Venetia Porter.
6. Interview, David Aaronovitch.
7. Interview, Charles Clarke.
8. Bernard Levin, *The Times*, 16 May 1978.
9. Peter Mandelson's letter to *The Times*, 19 May 1978.
10. Interview, David Aaronovitch.
11. Interview, Trevor Phillips.
12. *The Times Higher Education Supplement*, 21 July 1978.
13. Interview, Trevor Phillips.
14. Interview, Nina Temple.

CHAPTER FOUR – *A Very Grown-Up Young Man*
1. Interview, Nina Temple.
2. Interview, Trevor Phillips.
3. *Observer*, 11 May 1980.
4. Interview, Paul Ormerod.
5. Lambeth Council Minutes, Councillor Sawdon.
6. Interview, Paul Ormerod.
7. Interview, Roy Hattersley.
8. Interview, David Hill.
9. Interview, Paul Ormerod.
10. *The Times*, 24 July 1981.
11. Tony Benn, *Diaries*, p. 155.
12. Interview, Roger Liddle.
13. *Guardian*, 2 October 1989.

CHAPTER FIVE – *The New Mood*
1. Interview, Samir Shah.
2. Interview, Trevor Phillips.
3. Michael Tracey, *In the Culture of the Eye*, pp. 30–31.
4. *You* magazine, *Mail on Sunday*, June 1983.
5. Broadcast, 15 October 1984.
6. *You* magazine, op. cit.
7. Broadcast, 15 October 1984.
8. *The Listener*, 10 January 1980.
9. Private information.
10. Tracey, op. cit, p. 149.
11. Interview, Samir Shah.
12. Interview, Michael Maclay.
13. Interview, David Aaronovitch.
14. *Irish Times*, 31 October 1998.

CHAPTER SIX – *Bonkers about Kinnock*
1. Colin Hughes and Patrick Wintour, *Labour Rebuilt: The New Model Party*, p. 13.
2. Interview, Charles Clarke.
3. Interview, Roy Hattersley.
4. Interview, Andy McSmith.
5. Roy Hattersley, *Who Goes Home?*, pp. 293ff.
6. Ibid., p. 294
7. Interview, Alastair Campbell.
8. *Guardian*, 23 September 1995.
9. *Guardian*, 25 September 1985.
10. Interview, Lord Sawyer.
11. Interview, Neil Kinnock.
12. Philip Gould, *The Unfinished Revolution*, p. 41.
13. *The Wilderness Years*, BBC2 1995.
14. Ibid.
15. *Campaign*, 11 October 1985.
16. *Guardian*, 15 October 1985.
17. Peter Mandelson interview with Philip Gould, November 1985.
18. Interview, Michael Ignatieff, *Three Minute Culture: Politics*, 29 January 1989.


CHAPTER SEVEN – *Roses and Thorns*
1. Interview, Trevor Phillips.
2. Interview, Dennis Stevenson.
3. *Guardian*, 5 September 1997.
4. *The Times*, 24 September 1985.
5. David Owen, *Time to Declare*, p. 604.
6. Gould, *The Unfinished Revolution*, p. 58.
7. *The Wilderness Years*.
8. *Guardian*, 23 April 1986.
9. *Economist*, 26 April 1986.
10. *Mail on Sunday*, 20 April 1986.
11. Interview, Neil Kinnock.
12. Gould, op. cit, p. 66.
13. *Elle* magazine, December 1986.
14. Hattersley, *Who Goes Home?*, p. 295.
15. Gould, op. cit, p. 65.
16. Interview, David Hill.


CHAPTER EIGHT – *Deirdre, Defence and Disarray*
1. Margaret Thatcher, *The Downing Street Years*, p. 566.
2. *The Times*, 23 December 1986.
3. Tony Benn, *Diaries*, p. 494.
4. Ibid., p. 495.

5. Private interview with Peter Mandelson conducted by Butler and Kavanagh.
6. Gould, *The Unfinished Revolution*, p. 76.
7. *Sun*, 6 March 1987.
8. Colin Brown, *John Prescott*, p. 168.
9. Hattersley, *Who Goes Home?*, p. 296.

CHAPTER NINE – *What to Say on the Night*
1. *Private Eye*, June 1987.
2. *News of the World*, 17 May 1987.
3. Interview, Colin Byrne.
4. Interview, Joy Johnson.
5. Interview, Colin Byrne.
6. Sebastian Faulks, *Independent*, 26 May 1985.
7. Nuffield General Election study papers, 1987.
8. Bryan Gould, *Goodbye to All That*, pp. 184–85.
9. Interview, Neil Kinnock.
10. *Daily Express*, 6 June 1987.
11. Hattersley, *Who Goes Home?*, p. 283.
12. Bryan Gould, op. cit, p. 189.
13. Interview, Charles Clarke.
14. Interview, Andy McSmith.
15. Interview, Alastair Campbell.
16. Hughes and Wintour, *Labour Rebuilt*, p. 27.
17. Interview, David Hill.
18. Interview, Neil Kinnock.
19. Interview, Charles Clarke.
20. Hattersley, op. cit, p. 294.

CHAPTER TEN – *Neil Feels...*
1. *Independent*, 23 January 1999.
2. *Independent*, 1 July 1989.
3. Interview, Colin Byrne.
4. Gould, *Goodbye to All That*, p. 206.
5. Private information.
6. Interview, Joy Johnson.
7. *Guardian*, 2 October 1987.
8. Nick Jones, *Spin and Spin Doctors*, p. 132.
9. Interview, Lord Sawyer.
10. Interview, Charles Clarke.
11. *The Times*, 27 July 1987.
12. *Independent*, 17 December 1987.

CHAPTER ELEVEN – *Aiming for the Stars, Fighting in the Gutter*
1. Colin Brown, *John Prescott*, p. 179.
2. *The Times*, 21 January 1988.
3. Interview, Roy Hattersley.
4. Interview, Alastair Campbell.
5. *Guardian*, 3 February 1989.
6. Hughes and Wintour, *Labour Rebuilt*, p. 113.
7. Philip Gould, *The Unfinished Revolution*, p. 92.
8. Interview, Neil Kinnock.
9. Interview, Colin Byrne.
10. *Guardian*, 2 October 1989.
11. Jones, *Spin and Spin Doctors*, p. 125.
12. Hattersley, *Who Goes Home?*, p. 284.
13. Gould, op. cit, p. 181.
14. Conversation with David Bradshaw.
15. Interview, Lord Sawyer.
16. Hughes and Wintour, op. cit, p. 148.
17. *Sunday Times*, 28 May 1989.
18. *Guardian*, 28 September 1989.
19. Bryan Gould, op. cit, p. 218.
20. John Sopel, *Tony Blair*, p. 93.
21. John Rentoul, *Tony Blair*, p. 172.
22. Nyta Mann and Paul Anderson, *Safety First*, p. 336.
23. *Sunday Express*, 25 June 1989.

CHAPTER TWELVE – *I Have This Friend Who Needs a Seat*
1. Interview, Dennis Stevenson.
2. Interview, Tom Burlison.
3. Interview, John Burton.
4. Interview, Olga Mean.
5. Interview, Jack Doyle.
6. *Daily Telegraph*, 31 August 1996.
7. Interview, Bernard Carr.
8. *Daily Express*, 4 November 1989.
9. Interview, Steve Wallace.
10. Interview, Charles Clarke.
11. Interview, Neil Kinnock.

CHAPTER THIRTEEN – *Why Don't You Have Peter Back?*
1. Interview, Charles Clarke.
2. *Guardian*, 13 June 1990.
3. Interview, David Hill.
4. Interview, Colin Byrne.
5. Jones, *Spin and Spin Doctors*, p. 131.
6. Interview, Joy Johnson.

7. Bryan Appleyard, *Sunday Times*, 19 May 1991.
8. Interview, Neil Kinnock.
9. *Guardian*, 5 October 1990.
10. Gould, *The Unfinished Revolution*, p. 105.
11. *People*, 9 June 1991.
12. McSmith, *Faces of Labour*, pp. 315–16.
13. *Observer*, 19 May 1991.
14. *Sunday Times*, 19 May 1991.
15. *McSmith*, op. cit, p. 317.
16. From Kinnock Archive, ibid, p. 319.
17. *Guardian*, 30 June 1992.
18. Gould, op. cit, p. 126.
19. Interview, Dennis Stevenson.
20. *Sunday Times*, 9 August 1990.
21. Interview, Lord Stevenson.
22. Interview, Alastair Campbell.
23. *Hartlepool Mail*, 26 September 1991.
24. Anderson and Mann, *Safety First*, p. 368.
25. Rentoul, *Tony Blair*, pp. 245–6.
26. David Hare, *Asking Around*, p. 246.

CHAPTER FOURTEEN – *The Wilderness Years*

1. *Sunday Times*, 19 July 1992.
2. Private information.
3. Gould, *The Unfinished Revolution*, p. 187.
4. Private interview.
5. Rentoul, *Tony Blair*, pp. 261–62.
6. Interview, Robert Harris.
7. Peter Mandelson, *People*, 19 April 1992.
8. Interview, Derek Draper.
9. Oliver James interview, *The Chair*, BBC2 1997.
10. *Guardian*, 6 January 1993.
11. *Woman's Own* magazine, 21 June 1993.
12. Gould, op. cit.
13. Interview with the author, *Independent*, June 1994.
14. *Spectator*, 7 August 1997.
15. *Guardian*, 1 January 1994.
16. *The Wilderness Years*.
17. Interview, Alex Stevenson.
18. Roy Hattersley, *Mail on Sunday*, 27 September 1995.
19. *House Magazine*, 15 February 1993.
20. Matthew Parris, *The Times*, 20 July 1994.
21. McSmith, *Faces of Labour*, p. 328.
22. *Sunday Express*, 24 April 1994.
23. *Daily Telegraph*, 19 April 1994.

24. See McSmith for an excellent account.
25. *Hansard*, 24 March 1993, col. 1041.
26. Interview, Alex Stevenson.

CHAPTER FIFTEEN – *I've Made an Enemy For Life*
1. Gould, *The Unfinished Revolution*, p. 182.
2. Anthony Seldon, *Major*, pp. 461–2.
3. To author and subsequently in *Sunday Times*, 17 January 1999.
4. Interview, Alastair Campbell.
5. Alastair Campbell, *Today*, 16 May 1994.
6. Sunday Times, 22 May 1994.
7. *Sunday Times*, 15 May 1994.
8. Interview, Roger Liddle.
9. Rentoul, *Tony Blair*, p. 365.
10. Interview, Derek Draper.
11. Paul Routledge, *Mandy*, p. 271.
12. Interview, Steve Wallace.
13. Gould, op. cit, p. 197.
14. *Sunday Express*, 17 January 1999.
15. Conversation with Jon Snow.
16. McSmith, *Faces of Labour*, pp. 331–2.
17. Jones, *Spin and Spin Doctors*, pp. 159–60.

CHAPTER SIXTEEN – *Scorpions in a Bottle*
1. *Guardian*, 16 August 1994.
2. Gould, *The Unfinished Revolution*, p. 218.
3. Ben Pimlott, *Hugh Dalton*, pp. 633–4.
4. Interview, Alastair Campbell.
5. *Today*, 6 October 1994.
6. Interview, Robert Harris.
7. Paul Routledge, *Gordon Brown*, pp.196–204.
8. Some of this correspondence first surfaced in Anderson and Mann, *Safety First*.
9. Interview, Joy Johnson.
10. Interview, Alastair Campbell.
11. Private source in interview with Butler and Kavanagh.
12. Gould, op. cit, p. 289.
13. Interview, Alastair Campbell.
14. *Spectator*, 25 May 1996.
15. *Mail on Sunday*, 5 May 1996.

CHAPTER SEVENTEEN – *The Joys of Carla*
1. Interview, Colin Byrne.
2. Polly Toynbee, *Guardian*, 8 July 1997.
3. Private information.

4. Interview, Miles Mandelson.
5. Interview, Trevor Phillips.

CHAPTER EIGHTEEN – *Being Peter*
1. Interview, Roy Hattersley.
2. *Independent*, 4 November 1994.
3. *Guardian*, 11 February 1995.
4. Hattersley, *Mail on Sunday*, 24 September 1995.
5. Ibid.
6. Interview, Phil Woolas.
7. McSmith, *Faces of Labour*, p. 347.
8. *Guardian*, 24 February 1996.
9. Peter Mandelson and Roger Liddle, *The Blair Revolution*, p. 1.
10. Jones, *Campaign*.
11. Interview, Alastair Campbell.
12. Gould, *The Unfinished Revolution*, p. 317.
13. *New Statesman*, 9 August 1996.
14. *The Times*, 20 November 1996.
15. *Guardian*, September 1996.
16. *Daily Telegraph*, 20 November 1996.
17. *Sunday Times*, 22 December 1996.
18. Interview, Robert Harris.

CHAPTER NINETEEN – *The Making of the Prime Minister*
1. Interview, Alastair Campbell.
2. Interview, Margaret McDonagh.
3. Harvard International Journal of Press/Politics, May 1997.
4. Scammell et al., in Butler and Kavanagh, *The British General Election of 1997*.
5. Andrew Marr, *Independent*, 23 April 1997.
6. Private information.
7. *Observer*, 27 April 1997.
8. Butler and Kavanagh, op. cit, p. 243.
9. *Independent*, 10 April 1997.
10. This version of events was initially contested by the commentator Sîon Simon in the *Spectator*, 1 May 1999. He has since kindly accepted that it was correct (*Times Literary Supplement*, 9 July 1999).

CHAPTER TWENTY – *The Minister Without*
1. *On the Record*, BBC, 11 May 1997.
2. Interview, Alex Stevenson.
3. *Sunday Times*, 9 February 1997.
4. Private information.
5. Derek Draper, *The First Hundred Days*, p. 114.
6. *Sunday Telegraph*, 28 November 1999.

7. *Observer*, 15 September 1996.
8. *New Statesman*, 12 December 1997.
9. Edited by Mary Benham and Bevis Hillier.
10. Donoughue and Jones, *Herbert Morrison*.
11. Interview, Simon Jenkins, BBC *World This Weekend*.
12. Interview, Roy Hattersley, ibid.
13. Private information.
14. Private interview.
15. *Independent*, 14 August 1997.
16. *The Times*, 10 January 1998.
17. *Sunday Times,* 17 January 1999.
18. *Observer*, 17 August 1997.
19. *Observer*, 26 April 1998.
20. *Sunday Times*, 31 August 1998.
21. Private information.
22. Peter Mandelson, *Mirror*, 30 September 1997.

CHAPTER TWENTY-ONE – *A Most Pro-European Minister*
1. Hugo Young, *This Blessed Plot*, p. 492.
2. *The Times*, 18 October 1997.
3. Gordon Brown, *The First Year*, pp. 136ff.
4. *Guardian*, 18 October 1997.
5. Interview, Alastair Campbell.
6. *Sunday Telegraph*, 21 September 1997.
7. John Lloyd, *New Statesman*, 22 January 1999.

CHAPTER TWENTY-TWO – *The Seventeen People Who Count*
1. *Observer*, 9 November 1997.
2. *Observer*, 27 July 1998.
3. *Observer*, 12 July 1998.
4. *The Times*, 8 July 1998.
5. *Guardian*, 12 July 1998.

CHAPTER TWENTY-THREE – *The Leader's Little Helper*
1. Paul Routledge, *Gordon Brown*.
2. *Guardian*, 6 January 1999.
3. *Observer*, 18 January 1998.
4. *Daily Telegraph*, 12 September 1998.
5. *Daily Telegraph*, 16 April 1998.
6. Interview, Dennis Stevenson.

CHAPTER TWENTY-FOUR – *Congratulations, You've Got One of the Top Jobs*
1. Hugo Young, *Guardian*, 27 July 1998.
2. Jo Glanville, *New Statesmen*, 17 July 1998.
3. Private information.
4. *Daily Mail*, 2 October 1997.
5. *Our Competitive Future, Building the Knowledge Driven Economy*, HMSO, December 1998, p. 19.


CHAPTER TWENTY-FIVE – *Secretary in a State*
1. *Independent*, 7 April 1998.
2. *Evening Standard*, 6 May 1998.
3. *Independent*, 30 October 1998.
4. Private information.
5. *Sunday Express*, 1 November 1998.
6. *Sun*, 30 October 1998.
7. *Guardian*, 22 December 1998.
8. *Guardian*, 24 December 1998.
9. *The Times*, 4 January 1999.


CHAPTER TWENTY-SIX – *Rebuild Your Political Life*
1. Hombach resigned on 27 June 1999 in superficially similar circumstances to Mandelson's, ostensibly over the refurbishment of his house. But his head was also demanded as a concession to the SPD by Schröder in the uproar which followed publication of the paper.
2. *Sun,* 23 January 2000.
3. Philip Stephens, *Financial Times* , 14 January 2000.
4. *Guardian,* 30 September 1999.
5. *Guardian,* 29 July 1999.
6. Interview, David Trimble.
7. *New Statesman*, 31 January 2000.
8. Donoughue and Jones, p. 308.
9. I am indebted to David McKittrick for this quotation.
10. See p. 84.
11. BBC Radio 4 *Today* programme, 1 September 1994.
12. This shift mirrored that of the Conservatives who had moved to the same position, but from the opposite direction, to a policy of prescriptive Unionism.
13. The Good Friday Agreement was signed after multi-party talks at Stormont on Friday 10 April 1998. It provided for a devolved assembly, the creation of new cross-border bodies, and the ratification by all parties, including Sinn Fein, of the principle that any change of the status in Northern Ireland required the consent of a majority of its citizens.
14. David McKittrick, *Independent*, 3 December 1999.
15. Warren Hoge, *New York Times,* 27 November 1999.

16. Ibid.
17. Private information.
18. John Lloyd, *New Statesman*, 31 January 2000.
19. Interview, David Trimble.
20. *New York Times,* op. cit.
21. David McKittrick *Independent*, 3 November 1999.
22. *Irish Times,* 8 November 1999.
23. *Daily Telegraph,* 25 November 1999.
24. Interview, David Trimble.
25. Ibid.
26. Ibid.
27. Interview, David Trimble.
28. Ibid.
29. Interview, John Taylor.
30. John Mullin, *Guardian,* 25 November 1999.
31. Ibid.
32. Peter Mandelson, speech at Victoria College, Belfast, 25 November 1999.
33. Ibid.
34. Ibid.
35. *Daily Telegraph,* 27 November 1999.
36. *Newsletter*, 27 November 1999.
37. Interview, John Taylor.
38. David McKittrick, *Independent*, 30 November 1999.
39. *New York Times*, 27 November 1999.
40. David McKittrick, *Independent*, 3 December 1999.
41. Ibid.
42. Peter Mandelson, Commons statement, 19 January 2000.
43. *Report of the Independent Commission on Policing for Northern Ireland*, p. 9.
44. Desmond McCartan, *Belfast Telegraph,* 17 January 2000.
45. *Hansard*, 19 January 2000.
46. *Newsletter*, 26 February 2000.
47. Frank Millar, *Irish Times*, 17 February 2000.
48. John A. Murphy, *Sunday Independent*, 13 February 2000.
49. Eoghan Harris, *Sunday Times*, 16 April 2000.
50. Frank Millar, *Irish Times*, 17 February 2000.
51. *Irish Times*, 19 February 2000.
52. Ibid.

CHAPTER TWENTY-SEVEN – *Start Wrapping the Clock*

1. Originally an acronym for 'Big fat fucker from Offaly', a name commonly, if unflatteringly, given to natives of that county by those outside it.
2. Harry McGee and Damian Corless, *Magill*, February 2000.
3. *Irish Times*, 19 February 2000.
4. *Irish Times*, 18 March 2000.

5. Ibid.
6. Frank Millar, *Irish Times*, 20 March 2000.
7. Ibid.
8. *Observer*, 7 May 2000.
9. *Hansard*, 8 May 2000.
10. *Sunday Times*, 28 May 2000.
11. *Irish Times*, 17 May 2000.
12. *Hansard*, 24 May 2000.
13. *Sunday Independent*, 28 May 2000.
14. *Belfast Telegraph*, 24 May 2000.
15. *Sunday Independent*, 28 May 2000.
16. *Independent on Sunday*, 28 May 2000.
17. Philip Stephens, *Financial Times*, 24 December 1998.
18. *Spectator*, 15 January 2000.

# Select Bibliography

Anderson, Paul, and Mann, Nyta, *Safety First: the Making of New Labour*, Granta, 1997.

Bayley, Stephen, *Labour Camp*, Batsford, 1998.

Benn, Tony, and Winstone, Ruth (ed.), *The End of an Era: Diaries 1980–90*, Hutchinson, 1992.

Brown, Colin, *Fighting Talk: The Biography of John Prescott*, Simon & Schuster, 1997.

Butler, David, and Butler, Gareth, *British Political Facts 1900–1994*, Macmillan, 1994.

Butler, David, and Kavanagh, Dennis, *The British General Election of 1987*, Macmillan, 1988.

Butler, David, and Kavanagh, Dennis, *The British General Election of 1992*, Macmillan, 1992.

Butler, David, and Kavanagh, Dennis, *The British General Election of 1997*, Macmillan, 1997.

Donoughue, Bernard and Jones, G. W., *Herbert Morrison: Portrait of a Politician*, Weidenfeld & Nicolson, 1973.

Draper, Derek, *Blair's 100 Days*, Faber & Faber, 1997.

Gould, Bryan, *Goodbye to All That*, Macmillan, 1995.

Gould, Philip, *The Unfinished Revolution: How the Modernisers Saved the Labour Party*, Little, Brown, 1998.

Hare, David, *Asking Around: Background to the David Hare Trilogy*, Faber & Faber, 1993.

Harris, Robert, *The Making of Neil Kinnock*, Faber & Faber, 1984.

Hattersley, Roy, *Who Goes Home? Scenes from a Political Life*, Warner Books, 1996.

Hughes, Colin, and Wintour, Patrick, *Labour Rebuilt: The New Model Party*, Fourth Estate, 1990.

Jones, Nicholas, *Soundbites and Spin Doctors: How Politicians Manipulate the Media and Vice Versa*, Cassell, 1995.

Jones, Nicholas, *Campaign 1997*, Indigo, 1997.

Kampfner, John, *Robin Cook*, Victor Gollancz, 1998.

Leapman, Michael, *Kinnock*, Unwin Hyman, 1987.

Mandelson, Peter, and Liddle, Roger, *The Blair Revolution: Can New Labour Deliver?*, Faber & Faber, 1996.

McSmith, Andy, *Faces of Labour: The Inside Story*, Verso, 1996.

Lord Morrison of Lambeth P.C, C.H, *Herbert Morrison: An Autobiography*, Odhams Press, 1960.

Pelling, Henry, *A Short History of the Labour Party*, St Martin's Press, 1993.

Pym, Hugh, and Kochan, Nick, *Gordon Brown: The First Year in Power*, Bloomsbury, 1998.

Rentoul, John, *Tony Blair*, Little, Brown, 1995.

Routledge, Paul, *Gordon Brown: The Biography*, Pocket Books, 1998.

Routledge, Paul, *Mandy: The Unauthorised Biography of Peter Mandelson*, Simon & Schuster, 1999.

Seldon, Anthony, *Major: A Political Life*, Weidenfeld & Nicolson, 1997.

Sopel, Jon, *Tony Blair: The Moderniser*, Michael Joseph, 1995.

Young, Hugo, *This Blessed Plot: Britain and Europe from Churchill to Blair*, Macmillan, 1998.

# Index